THE WORLD OF MISS READ

THE WORLD OF
MISS READ

An omnibus edition containing

FRESH FROM THE COUNTRY
THE MARKET SQUARE
THE HOWARDS OF CAXLEY
MRS PRINGLE

Miss Read

MICHAEL JOSEPH LTD

Published by the Penguin Group
27 Wrights Lane, London W8 5TZ
Viking Penguin Inc., 375 Hudson Street, New York, New York 10014, USA
Penguin Books Australia Ltd, Ringwood, Victoria, Australia
Penguin Books Canada Ltd, 10 Alcorn Avenue, Toronto, Ontario, Canada M4V 3B2
Penguin Books (NZ) Ltd, 182–190 Wairau Road, Auckland 10, New Zealand

Penguin Books Ltd, Registered Offices: Harmondsworth, Middlesex, England

This omnibus edition first published 1995

Fresh from the Country first published by Michael Joseph Ltd in 1960
© Miss Read 1960; illustrations © John S. Goodall 1960
The Market Square first published by Michael Joseph Ltd in 1966
©Miss Read 1960; illustrations © Harry Grimley 1966
The Howards of Caxley first published by Michael Joseph Ltd in 1967
© Miss Read 1967; illustrations © Harry Grimley 1967
Mrs Pringle first published by Michael Joseph Ltd in 1989
© Miss Read 1989; illustrations © John S. Goodall 1989

Copyright © *This omnibus* Miss Read 1995

Filmset by Datix International Limited, Bungay, Suffolk
Printed in England by Clays Ltd, St Ives plc
Set in $10\frac{1}{2}/12\frac{1}{2}$ pt Monophoto Garamond

A CIP catalogue record for this book is available from the British Library

ISBN 0718139984

The moral right of the author has been asserted

CONTENTS

FRESH FROM THE COUNTRY

To Lil with love

CONTENTS

Part One
TRANSPLANTED

Chapter One

COUNTRY BEGINNINGS

'And baths extra, of course,' said Mrs Flynn.

She crossed the diminutive landing in four steps and hurled herself against the bathroom door. It creaked, as if in protest, but remained closed.

'All our doors,' gasped Mrs Flynn, getting her shoulder to it, 'are well-fitting.' At the third shove the door groaned open and Anna Lacey peered over her prospective landlady's shoulder into a white-tiled cube of a room which reminded her of the small recess in the dairy at her farmhouse home where two milk churns habitually stood.

'It looks very nice,' said Anna politely. One of the frosted glass windows, studded with perpetual raindrops, was open, and through the chink she caught a glimpse of half-finished houses in another road on the new estate.

Mrs Flynn flicked a speck of dust from the green plastic towel rail and adjusted a mauve bath-mat, sprigged coyly with violets, which hung over the edge of the bath.

'And now I'll take you to the bedroom,' said Mrs Flynn, edging sideways past the girl and taking another four steps across the landing to an open door. She spoke, thought Anna, as though she were about to embark on a lengthy traversal of corridors and staircases rather than this shifting from one foot to the other in order to get from one room to the next in this doll-size house. Used as she was to the big shabby farmhouse on the Suffolk-Essex border, the toy-like dimensions of Mrs Flynn's establishment both fascinated and depressed her.

'This would be *all yours*,' Mrs Flynn announced, waving her hand, with a spacious gesture, at a strip of a room which was roughly the size of the broom-cupboard at Anna's home. The girl looked at it in wonder.

A narrow bed, covered with a fawn folk-weave bedspread, lay close against the wall behind the door. There was one small window placed high, directly below the eaves of the house, and under this stood a prim cane-bottomed chair. The only other piece of furniture was a small chest of drawers round which Mrs Flynn edged towards a cretonne curtain hanging across the corner of the room.

'And here's your wardrobe,' she said proudly. She twitched the curtain aside to show a rail containing three yellow wooden coat hangers. 'You've probably got hangers of your own,' added Mrs Flynn, looking suddenly anxious.

'Oh yes, indeed,' said Anna hastily. 'I could bring my own hangers.'

Despite the July sunshine the room seemed cold and dark, but the red patterned lino was well polished and the thin rug was clean. With a few of my own things about, thought Anna, it might not look so bleak.

She pressed back against the wall to allow Mrs Flynn to pass, and followed her downstairs. The sitting-room door was as stubborn as the bathroom one, the new wood protesting as Mrs Flynn forced it to give way.

She motioned Anna towards a small plump couch, which rested upon skittish surprised wooden legs, and seated herself in a chair which matched it. The room was sparsely furnished. Four pale pictures of pink and blue birds in flowery branches hung, one on each cream wall, very high up near the picture rail.

'From my *Woman's Monthly*,' said Mrs Flynn following the girl's gaze. 'And my nephew Ray passypartooed them.'

Anna switched her gaze to the tiled mantelpiece where a young man's photograph stood. He looked an unprepossessing youth in R.A.F. uniform, and glowered beneath a bar of black brows. His aunt's sharp little face had softened as she surveyed the boy, but now she turned abruptly to Anna and became her business-like self again.

'Three pounds a week is my charge,' said Mrs Flynn, 'and, as I said, baths extra.'

'I should be going home at the weekend –' began Anna shyly.

'I'm afraid I couldn't make any reduction for that,' Mrs Flynn said, with a wintry smile. 'Not with the overheads.'

'I suppose not,' murmured Anna, wondering just exactly what overheads might be.

'You'd have your main meal at school, I've no doubt,' went on Mrs Flynn, 'and we usually have high tea when Mr Flynn gets in at seven. You probably get a cup of tea at school during the afternoon?' Her voice held a query.

'I'm not sure about that –' Anna began.

'It's usual,' Mrs Flynn assured her swiftly. Anna, who was fond of her food and had the healthy appetite of one just twenty, wryly watched her meals being whittled away by Mrs Flynn's sharp business methods. She felt that she was no match for this woman, but knew that the headmistress's words to her an hour ago were true.

'Digs in this neighbourhood are few and far between. If Mrs Flynn can't take you you will have to face a bus journey each day. I'd try her for a bit,' she had said, and Anna had recognized the soundness of the case.

'I'll know more about that when I start next term,' said Anna. She was pleasantly surprised to hear how firmly this remark had come forth, and, much emboldened, she followed up her small advantage.

'I should need somewhere to work in the evenings. There will be books to mark and handwork to prepare, you know.'

'There's the bedroom,' Mrs Flynn pointed out. She sounded slightly affronted. Anna determined not to give way.

'But I shall need a table.'

'Then I suppose you might have the use of this room occasionally,' said Mrs Flynn somewhat grudgingly. 'It would be a little more of course. I hadn't bargained for letting two rooms. In fact, I think I shall have to speak to Mr Flynn before deciding about that.'

What a useful thing a husband must be, thought Anna! She looked at the clock on the mantelpiece. It was an impressive object made of black marble in the form of a Greek temple. It began a preliminary whirring before striking three o'clock.

The girl remembered her long journey back to north Essex, collected her gloves and bag, and rose to her feet.

'I'm sure we shall be able to come to some arrangement about using this room,' Mrs Flynn said hastily, in a slightly more conciliatory tone, as she saw her prey escaping. 'But, you see, I must have somewhere to bring friends, and when Ray's here he likes somewhere to play his guitar.'

'Perhaps just one or two evenings a week it might be possible for me to use it,' suggested Anna. 'In any case, I'll think it over and let you know before the end of the week.'

Mrs Flynn jerked open the door and led the way to the front door.

'Holiday times,' she said, as she opened it, 'there would be a retention fee of ten shillings.'

'Oh yes,' said Anna, a little bewildered. 'Ten shillings for each holiday?'

'Ten shillings a week!' Mrs Flynn answered, with a hint of triumph. 'It's quite usual.'

'I'll remember,' said Anna.

Mrs Flynn accompanied her down the tiny tiled path to the gate. Under the hot July sun six young golden privet bushes were struggling for existence in the dusty new front garden, and a forlorn stick of a lilac bush drooped by the gatepost, its tag still fluttering from one twig.

'We should have a really nice hedge this time next year,' observed Mrs Flynn looking fondly at the privet.

'I'm sure you will,' agreed Anna bravely. And on this note of hope they parted.

Anna's spirits rose as she approached her home. The journey took over two hours from the new raw suburb where she was to take up her teaching appointment next September. She had travelled across the vast sprawling mass of London which sweltered in the throbbing heat and had felt the oppression of spirits which row upon row of streets always produced in her.

As the streets gave way to leafy suburbs and then to the gentle flat country of her own neighbourhood, happiness returned. The wind blew refreshingly through the open window of the Green Line coach, fragrant with the smell of freshly-cut hay and the flowers of many a sunny meadow.

The coach breasted a slight incline and Anna looked with love at the familiar view spread before her. Clumps of elms, blue-green with dense masses of leaves, made dark pools of shade among the wide pale fields of rural Essex. Away to the east the gentle blue of a cloudless sky met the darker blue of the horizon, and beyond that the North Sea heaved and murmured, tossing a lacy froth of shallow waves along the broad sands.

Westward, where Anna's farm lay, little streams made their leisurely way to greater water courses seeking the sea. Willows lined their banks, their silvery leaves shimmering in ceaseless quivering. To Anna, now waiting at the coach door ready to descend at her cross-roads, they seemed to he fluttering in welcome.

The Land Rover was waiting in the shady lane, her mother at the wheel. Anna bounded towards her, eager to tell her of all that had befallen.

Margaret Lacey, Anna's mother, was now approaching fifty, but her energy and youthful looks were the envy of many younger women.

She had been born just before the outbreak of the First World War within a dozen miles of her present home. Her father had been a miller and had lived and worked all his life in the tall lovely building which stood by the waters of the river Low. The sound of the rushing mill race was the background music to her happy upbringing, so much so that when she went to stay elsewhere she would lie awake at night missing the voice of those tumbling waters which normally hushed her to sleep.

She was the youngest of four children. Her father, James North, a burly, red-faced giant of a man, had brought up his two boys and two girls to lead as energetic a life as his own. His wife bad been of gentler stuff, and although she baked and mended and ran her boisterous household with method and cheerfulness, there was a quality of secret reserve about her which her family recognized but, with the exception of Margaret, did not understand.

Poetry she loved and the wild flowers and animal life of the countryside. Limp-backed editions of Browning and Tennyson lay beside her bed and in her gleaming drawing-room. Bowls of primroses scented the air in spring, and the tang of autumn was carried into the house with the great sprays of tawny leaves which she bore home from her solitary walks. More often than not some small wounded creature, a bird with a broken wing or a nestful of baby field-mice orphaned by the hay-cutter, would be receiving care and hospitality in the great kitchen, and Margaret shared her mother's compassion, treating the rest of the family's good-natured teasing with the same unsentimental charity which characterized all her mother's actions.

Margaret had cycled with her brothers and sister into the market town six miles away for her schooling, and, that over, had worked at the council offices there overlooking the wide river which earlier in its course had splashed past her mill home.

She had entered into the life of the friendly little town, acting in the Dramatic Club's plays, playing tennis, and boating with other young people, but still in her dinner hours she would go into the library near by or the local bookshop and find her way to the shelves where the modern poets could be found, a secret joy which was to endure through her whole life.

She had known Patrick Lacey and his family from her school-days. He was a hefty, good-tempered young man, a stalwart forward in the local rugby team and a welcome addition to any party in the neighbourhood. His father farmed within a few miles of Margaret's home and he too worked there and would eventually take it over.

He and Margaret slipped into marriage naturally and happily, after a brief courtship notable for its complete lack of lovers' quarrels. They had set up house in a cottage on the farm, but within six months Patrick's father had died and the young couple moved into the farmhouse.

And it was here, one snowy morning during the following winter, that Margaret's first child, Anna, was born.

She had been a happy child, with her father's good-nature and fair good looks, and the births of her two younger brothers caused her no undue jealousy.

Her upbringing was as practical and sensible as her mother's and father's had been. She early learnt the simple virtues of truthfulness and neighbourliness, prized perhaps more keenly in a place where all one's past was an open book, and encouraged in the low church of St Jude's where the family worshipped regularly every Sunday morning.

She had grown into a straight-backed, long-legged girl with a mop of fair curly hair which defied any of Anna's attempts to wean it from its natural exuberance to more sleek and modish styles. She had cycled, as her mother had done, the few miles to the same school and had been taught by several of those teachers who had taught her mother too. Her academic ability was average, her disposition patient and cheerful, her health boisterous. Her pleasure in children's company extended even to that of her vociferous young brothers! It was no wonder that she was advised to take up teaching by her headmistress.

Margaret too was pleased when Anna decided to accept the advice and had filled in her forms for admission to a training college for teachers. Firstly, she wanted her to be happy and to be engaged in work which she was capable of doing with zest and efficiency. Secondly, she wanted the girl to do something useful in the world. Her own family and her husband's had been brought up in the tradition of useful service to those among whom they lived. 'Using one's talents' was the theme of many a sermon by their present vicar, and it chimed with their own feelings and experience.

Both these reasons she spoke of to Anna and to her husband. Patrick, as is the way with fathers, was very content to leave the arrangements to his women-folk, but was wholeheartedly in favour of Anna's choice and generous in his financial proposals to the girl.

'It's a good training,' was his verdict. 'Working with children will stand you in good stead if you have a family of your own, and if you don't – well, other people's children are the next best thing. What's more,' he added, with practical wisdom, 'you can earn a living wherever you choose to go in the world, and have a pension at the end of it! Which is more than I shall.' He had ruffled his daughter's yellow hair, and gone out, whistling, to feed the pigs. For him, the matter was comfortably settled.

To Margaret this prosaic assessment of the decision was only part of the matter.

There was another reason for her pleasure in Anna's choice which Margaret had not mentioned to her husband. It would mean that she would have a few more years at her studies and that the love of books and poetry which meant so much, and to which she could afford to give so little time, in her own busy everyday existence, would be fostered in Anna.

For Margaret believed that the love was there but not yet fully awakened. So far, in Anna's eighteen years, the healthy open-air life of the farm, riding with her brothers, playing games with her friends and relishing all the joys that the windy wide meadows and the glittering river offered, had filled the girl's time. But, as Margaret knew, there were things of the mind which could offer a more powerful refreshment of the spirit. As the years passed she had found the distillation of men's experience, the essence of their emotions and beliefs in prose or poetry, a source of inner strength and comfort.

The second commandment, 'To love thy neighbour as thyself,' was the everyday standard which the family had set itself and which, by dint of good fellowship, pleasant circumstances, an unhurried way of life and a genuine warm-hearted interest in those around them, it was comparatively easy to keep. It was a rule-of-thumb code of behaviour which could carry a man successfully through a lifetime. But Margaret knew that it was not enough.

She realized that 'the first and great commandment' held the key to essential happiness. To recognize absolute goodness and absolute truth translated in terms of fine music, painting, or poetry, was to feel that answering, powerful, thrilling rightness which one knew one shared with mankind the world over. It was this mercurial leap of the spirit to something above and beyond it which Margaret wanted her daughter to know, the incandescent flash caused by the fusion of two minds, albeit centuries apart.

Without it, Anna could live the useful, happy life her father envisaged. But with it, her mother knew, 'something rich and strange' would weave its unalloyed gold thread through the serviceable homespun of her working days.

During the early part of the evening, after Anna had told her mother of the afternoon's happenings, the girl wandered through the garden to a leafy lane near by.

The air was very still. Far away she could hear the sound of her father's baler clack-clacking in a distant hay-field. She leaned upon a gate and looked at the wheat spreading acre after acre before her. It was sturdy and green, and the girl realized, with a start, that by the time it had turned golden she would be teaching, and would not be there to see all the days of harvest.

For the first time, she had doubts. The great new primary school, flashing with glass, the rows and rows of little tables in each classroom for the infants and juniors, and the formidably long queues of children traversing the endless corridors had daunted her. It was unlike any of the schools she had met before, either during school practice at college or in the rural neighbourhood of her home county.

The building, she admitted, was magnificent. Never had she seen such lightness, such colour, such gleaming expanses of floor and such flashing rows of wash-basins. Around this palace had stretched ten acres of grass beyond the immaculate asphalt area which would have served many schools as their only playground.

And yet the place had depressed her. She remembered the string of new factories which she had passed on her way there that afternoon. The school was not unlike them at first sight, massive, immaculate, teeming with life, and yet impersonal. She remembered the square red-brick school which she herself had attended, its comfortable domestic outline shrouded in homely creeper. Here two hundred girls had worked and played and had thought themselves a large body of people. How would she fare with six hundred under one roof?

Ah well, thought Anna philosophically, plucking a sprig of honeysuckle and smelling it while she could, there were all the summer holidays before her. The great school, the ugly raw new estate and Mrs Flynn were a long way ahead.

Meanwhile all the joys of home and summer thronged about her. The whinny of her pony in the paddock lifted her spirits, and retracing her steps Anna made her way back to the home which, to her surprise, suddenly seemed doubly dear.

As she emerged from the leafy tunnel of the lane the sound of the hay-baler came more clearly, thumping out its cheerful noise across the golden evening fields.

'Make hay while the sun shines,' quoted Anna aloud. It seemed as encouraging a proverb as any under the circumstances, and much comforted, she ran up the flagged path and into the open door.

Chapter Two

MORNING AT ELM HILL

The golden days slipped by all too swiftly and on the second day of September Anna crossed the playground to start her first day's teaching.

She had spent a wakeful night in the narrow bed under Mrs Flynn's roof. The mattress had seemed uncommonly thin and hard after the engulfing softness of the feather-beds of home, but it was not only that which had kept sleep at bay. The thought of what the morrow might hold had kept her mind active. Would she be able to keep order? Would the children be ready to listen and willing to learn? For that matter, did she honestly know anything to teach them? And if so, could she impart it?

She had tried to remember her college lectures and the criticisms she had received during school practice in the ancient cathedral city in which the college had stood. But coherent thought eluded her. Her mind slipped about, turning and twisting like a fish in tumultuous waters. Jumbled images of the half-forgotten faces of fellow-students, the swinging clapper of the college bell above the great gate, and the musty half-light of the crowded college chapel swam before her, and that was all.

At last, as the first lorries began to drone their way along the main road near by, she had fallen into a deep sleep which was soon shattered by the alarm clock beside her.

She had eaten her first breakfast at Mrs Flynn's in a daze, had scrutinized her reflection in the little mirror in her bedroom and decided that the flowered cotton frock and white sandals were suitable for her first appearance in public, and had gone forth, inwardly quaking, to meet the day.

And now, as she crossed the playground, she was conscious of a dozen young eyes upon her. The first few children paused in their play, and followed her progress with silent curiosity. It was very early, barely half past eight, and the school bell would not summon the children until ten to nine, but Anna was anxious to get into her classroom and see to her preparations.

She made her way first to the headmistress's room upstairs, trying to remember, as she mounted the shallow stone steps, the geography of the school from her quick and bemused tour of it on that July afternoon.

This primary school had two floors, she knew, the infants, aged five to seven, being housed on the ground floor, and the junior children, of seven to eleven, on the first. The building was a hollow square round a quadrangle, which was attractive with mown grass and bright flower-beds. The east and south sides were given over to classrooms, five below for infants and five above for the older children. On the north side lay the cloakrooms and the cleaners' cupboards and store-rooms on the ground floor, and above them the staff rooms and capacious stock rooms holding books, stationery, and all the paraphernalia of school life; while the west side of the square was entirely taken up by a lofty hall, with a stage at one end, and a green room beyond it.

Anna reached the landing, tiptoed past a door marked STAFF CLOAKROOM and approached a distant one bearing a neat label encased in a brass frame. It said:

HEADMISTRESS
(MISS F. R. ENDERBY)

It was unnaturally quiet in the empty corridor. Anna was conscious of the clean smell of furniture polish and carbolic soap mingled together, an ineffable emanation from the woodwork and stone of the great building, which she was to recognize all through her life as the very essence of first-day-of-term in any school throughout the land.

She knocked timidly upon the pale polished wood of the door just below the brass frame and stood back to wait. Silence engulfed her again. She read the directions on a bright red fire extinguisher with an intentness born of extreme nervous tension and wiped her damp palms with a crumpled handkerchief.

A faint measured clicking sound reached her straining ears, and she realized that it was the ticking of the electric clocks each watching over a classroom with a bland indifferent face. Somewhere, far below, a door banged and a child squealed, breaking the spell of near-panic which bound the girl. She moved away from the cold corrugation of the radiator against which she had been pressing herself and approached the door again, swallowing painfully to relieve the constriction of her throat.

This time she knocked more loudly, and before the noise had died away into the implacable, waiting emptiness of the vast building, she had her answer.

'Come in!' echoed very faintly from within and, grasping the cold oval handle in her sweaty palm, Anna prepared to meet her headmistress.

Florence Rhoda Enderby was a handsome large woman in her late forties. Her white hair was cut short and waved becomingly above her square brown face. Dark eyes, under strongly-marked brows, added to her air of lively intelligence. She dressed with taste and care, and her attractive appearance did much to impress both pupils and their parents with her general capability.

A large square-cut sapphire on the ring finger of her left hand, about which she was mysteriously reticent, also added a touch of glamour and pathos. It was generally supposed, from the few clues which she had dropped and from the clouding of her fine eyes when she surveyed the ring, that her fiancé had been killed whilst flying during the last war. Anna was to learn more of this mystery later.

She had been appointed the first headmistress of Elm Hill School when it had opened three years earlier and had already received praise for work well done there. Before her present appointment she had taught, first as an assistant near Wolverhampton, the town of her birth, and later as the headmistress of a small infant and junior school in the same area. Her appointment to Elm Hill had caused some chagrin among local teachers who had hoped for this plum to be plucked by one of their number, but resentment towards the newcomer had soon died down and she was generally admitted to be making a good job of it.

The school had been built for three hundred and fifty children, but within eighteen months was housing over five hundred. Now, at the beginning of its fourth school year, almost six hundred children were crammed into the majestic building.

The ten classrooms which were to have held less than forty children apiece, were now a tight mass of desks, wedged so closely together that it was difficult to move up and down the meagre gangways left between the rows. The numbers were nearer fifty than forty in each class, and the spacious hall which had so delighted the new headmistress and her staff now housed two more classes.

Here, where Florence Enderby had had such high hopes of staging frequent plays, of daily dancing sessions, of physical training periods in wet weather, and of ample room for a dozen communal activities, stood tables and chairs for eighty infants. One class faced the stage, the other the back of the hall, and two much-tried teachers pitted their voices against each other and grew daily nearer dementia as they watched the back row of their own class twisting round to attend to the lesson going on at the other end of the hall.

The green room too had been commandeered. Here there was only room for a very small class and eighteen backward juniors lived amid a welter of tidy-boxes, educational apparatus, glove-puppets, half-finished models of farmyards, railway stations, and the like, as well as a large table map of the immediate vicinity of Elm Hill School complete with model lorries, tankers, and cars much too big for the crayoned roads.

And now this term, the last free space had gone. Two staff rooms flanked Miss Enderby's apartment, one labelled

STAFF

(MISTRESSES)

a large airy room, and the other, with

STAFF

(MASTERS)

on the door, a smaller establishment. It was this latter room which had been furnished as another classroom, and here that twenty children, just risen from the infant department downstairs to the dizzy height of first-year juniors upstairs, would have their lessons.

The masters were to share the same staff room as the women on the staff, but as there were only four males to add to the ten females normally using it there would be plenty of room.

There was no doubt about it, Florence Enderby had been telling herself just before Anna had knocked, the new building was already overdue. Work was to begin some time this term on an entirely separate school, but in the same grounds, which was to be solely for infants, while Elm Hill would remain as the junior department.

'And the sooner the better,' thought the headmistress, looking out of her window upon the playground which was growing uncomfortably full as ten to nine approached. Her thoughts turned, as they had so often done lately, to the headship of the new establishment and that of her present school. She had no doubt that a man would be appointed in her place in the fullness of time. The infant school headship might well be hers if she applied for it. Certainly a headship somewhere near by would be offered her, but at the moment Florence Enderby was not sure of her plans.

She was an ambitious woman and she intended to get on. Already she was known as the 'Manners-Maniac' among her critics, for she insisted on punctilious courtesy at all times in her school, sometimes carrying it to such excessive lengths that it bordered on the ridiculous. The Elm Hill children were known by their old-fashioned courtliness which could be both charming and exasperating.

She had certainly made her mark upon the place already. She was a born organizer and adept at creating order from chaos. Forms, statistics, and questionnaires were a joy to her and new theories and methods in education she found engrossing and challenging. Her capabilities seemed to match her competent and pleasing appearance. Here, people said, is surely the perfect headmistress!

Only in one respect did Florence Enderby fail. Although she hardly realized it herself and would have denied it strenuously if she had been told, the fact remained, Florence Enderby did not like children.

She recognized that they were essential to her job. They were the raw material upon which her skill could work and upon whom new methods could be tried and results noted.

She was proud to see them, hundreds of them, in neat rows in the hall at morning assembly, answering her greeting with their shrill light voices accompanied by those curtsies from the girls and bows from the boys which so many of her staff deprecated as 'olde-worlde' and distinctly bad for their head-mistress's ego which they felt was already too confidently established.

She liked too to see them at play on the wide green expanse of grass about the school, scampering and fluttering in their bright clothes, bringing colour and gaiety to the raw open neighbourhood as yet unbeautified with trees and mellowed gardens. They were her school, her children, the living evidence of her work and effort. Collectively she gloried in them. As individuals she found them tiresome.

This morning as she gazed down upon them arriving thick and fast in the playground, the feeling of pride was dominant A school of nearly six hundred! she told herself triumphantly. She had done well. She had never thought, when she had started on her career almost thirty years before, that such a head-ship would ever be hers! She had come a long way from the grimy Victorian building in Wolverhampton where she had faced her first class. She believed that she might find further glories before she finally retired from the field after forty years' service, and the vision of the new infants' school glowed brightly before her inward eye. It would be the culmination of a lifetime's teaching.

Anna's light knock at the door put an end to these dreams of the future and brought her abruptly back to the present.

'Come in,' she called in the sonorously flat Midland tones she had never quite lost.

The door opened and, for a brief moment, the headmistress felt herself thirty years back in time. Just so had she stood once, nervous and defenceless, on the threshold of her career, as young and as bewildered as the girl who hesitated in the doorway.

'Don't be afraid,' said Miss Enderby, suddenly compassionate. She advanced across the room, regaining her usual official poise as she came nearer the girl. Her warm smile thawed Anna's chill forebodings as much as the words which followed it.

'I'll take you to meet your class and, I promise you, you'll like each other. This way, my dear.'

Together the old teacher and the young made their way towards Anna's classroom whilst the clanging of a distant bell brought sudden peace to the hubbub in the playground.

'School's begun!' said Anna's headmistress.

Chapter Three

ANNA MEETS HER CLASS

While Anna prepared herself to meet her class of forty-six exuberant and inquisitive children her landlady was busy preparing the high tea for her husband and the new lodger.

She had screwed the ancient mincer to the kitchen table and now fed it with rather tough strips of beef, the remains of the Sunday joint. There was not very much, to be sure, but Mrs Flynn's pinch-penny spirit had been roused to meet this challenge and the heel of a brown loaf, a large onion, and a tomato on the table were ominous portents of the rest of the proposed cottage pie.

'If I open a tin of baked beans,' said Mrs Flynn aloud, 'there'll be no need for gravy. No call to waste gas unnecessarily!' She pursed her thin lips with satisfaction, remembering, with sudden pleasure, that she had purchased the beans at a reduced price as 'THIS WEEK'S AMAZING OFFER' at the local grocer's. She twirled the handle of the mincer with added zest.

Yesterday's stewed apple, she thought busily, could be eked out with a little evaporated milk, and arranged in three individual dishes. A cherry on top of each would make a nice festive touch, decided Mrs Flynn in a wild burst of extravagance. She straightened up from her mincing and opened the store cupboard where she kept her tinned and bottled food. In the front row a small jar of cherries gleamed rosily. For one long minute Mrs Flynn studied its charms, torn between the opposing forces of art and thrift. Victory was accomplished easily.

'Pity to open them,' said Mrs Flynn, slamming the cupboard door, and returned, spiritually purged, to her mincing.

*

Anna watched her class file in a ragged two-by-two column through the doorway of her classroom. Miss Enderby, large and imposing, a professionally bright smile curving her mouth, stood beside her and kept up a brisk flow of directions.

'Choose any desks, dears. Yes, you may sit by Bobby if you can behave yourself, Arnold. No, I don't want to see birthday cards now, dear. Nor dinner money. Nor your tortoise's egg. Put it on the window-sill, dear, in the cool.'

She clapped her hands with a sudden deafening report, making Anna, and several of the children, start nervously.

'All behind chairs! Quickly now! I want to introduce you to your new teacher.'

There was a noisy shuffling of chairs and an upheaval of those who had already taken their seats and now must struggle from them. Under cover of the confusion Miss Enderby inclined her well-corseted figure sideways towards Anna and whispered:

'This may seem a little formal to you after the advice you had at college for free movement in the classroom and so on, but we must have a little order with these large numbers.'

Anna nodded agreement. To her bewildered senses the scene presented chaos incarnate. Another thunderous clap from Miss Enderby brought some appreciable quietening of the uproar.

'RIGHT behind chairs!' boomed the headmistress. 'And standing on TWO feet! That's better.'

By now an unholy hush had fallen upon the classroom. Outside Anna could hear the whirring of a cement-mixer. It sounded uncomfortably close at hand, and later that morning she realized that it was just below her window and likely to keep up its merry din for most of the term.

The children fixed their eyes unwinkingly upon Anna. Anna gazed back warily, feeling as helpless as a jelly-fish exposed to the proddings of innumerable sharp sticks.

'Now, children,' began Miss Enderby firmly, 'you are very, very lucky this term to have Miss Lacey for your new teacher.'

Anna gave a watery smile. The children's faces were unmoved.

'Miss Lacey,' repeated Miss Enderby with emphasis. 'Can you say that?'

'Miss Lacey,' chorused the class obediently.

'Perhaps you could say "Good morning" to your new teacher?' suggested Miss Enderby with massive archness.

'Good morning, Miss Lacey,' came the polite chorus.

'Good morning, children,' responded Anna in a croak which bore no resemblance to her normal voice.

The civilities over Miss Enderby motioned to the children to take their seats which they accomplished with the same deafening uproar as before. Anna began to wonder if she would ever get used to it or if she would be compelled to stuff cotton-wool in her ears before these mass upheavals and jerk it out when the class had settled.

'I should give out paper and coloured pencils,' said Miss Enderby, 'as soon as you've called the register. Keep them busy, while you're finding your way about the cupboards and so on.'

She gave a swift look round the docile class. There was a straightening of backs and demureness of demeanour which spoke for an awareness of Miss Enderby's disciplinary powers.

'I expect you to help Miss Lacey in *every* way,' said the headmistress with a slight edge to her voice. 'D'you hear me, Arnold?'

The little boy addressed, who had been crossing and uncrossing his eyes in an unlovely manner for the delectation of his neighbours, looked suitably crest-fallen.

'Watch that boy,' murmured Miss Enderby, in an audible aside. 'Broken home – brother in Borstal – enlarged tonsils – and some rather dreadful habits which the school psychiatrist says are compensatory, but I think are nasty and nothing more!'

Anna looked with fresh interest at Arnold and thought he looked far too innocent and apple-cheeked to have such a record. But, even as she looked, she saw a fleeting grimace distort his pink face expressing, in no uncertain terms, his scorn of Miss Enderby who was giving her final messages to the new teacher.

'Break at ten-forty-five, dear,' said the headmistress. 'Come straight to the staff room and I will introduce you to those you didn't meet on your first visit, and we will have a cup of tea then.

If there's anything that puzzles you, I shall be in my room. Just send a message by one of the children.'

She made her way to the door and waited before it, eyebrows raised as she turned her affronted gaze upon the children. They gazed back in some bewilderment.

'Is *no one* going to remember his manners?' asked Miss Enderby, carefully grammatic.

With a nervous start Anna hastened forward to the door, but was waved back by an undulation of her headmistress's hand, the sapphire ring flashing in the light. Galvanized into action a dozen or more children leapt to their feet knocking over their chairs as they made an ugly rush to open the door. A freckled mite with two skinny red plaits was the first to hurl herself upon the handle and drag open the door. She was rewarded by a gracious smile.

'Thank you, dear, thank you,' said Miss Enderby and sailed majestically into the corridor. A faint sigh of relief rippled round the class as the door was closed behind her, chests deflated, backs slumped, and the forty-six tongues which had so far kept unnaturally silent began to wag cheerfully.

Anna watched this degeneration with some dismay. For all the notice the class was taking of her she might have been non-existent. She remembered, with sudden relief, some advice given her at college to use in just such a situation.

'Stand quite still, be quite calm, and gradually the children will become conscious that you are waiting. Never, never attempt to shout them down.'

With monumental dignity Anna stood her ground waiting for the chattering to subside. But, far from diminishing, the noise grew in volume as conversations became more animated and far-flung. One or two children scrambled from their chairs and crossed the room to see distant friends. Two little boys attacked each other in brisk amity, a group converged upon the tortoise egg on the window-sill while its owner spread-eagled herself over it protectively, squealing with apprehension. The child with the birthday cards was displaying their beauties to an admiring crowd round her desk and carrying on a high-pitched running commentary on the donors. Arnold, Anna noticed with some trepidation, had removed his blue pullover and was busy scrabbling at the back of his shirt, attempting to pull it over his head, in order, it seemed, to show his friends a minute scar on his shoulder-blade.

Amidst mounting chaos Anna remained silent and statuesque, clinging desperately, but with receding hope, to the dictum of her college mentor. So might a lone rock stand among tempestuous seas, thought Anna grimly, and with as much hope of quelling them. She looked at the electric clock which jerked spasmodically from one minute to the next and decided to let it leap once more before she abandoned hope.

One crumb of comfort, if comfort it could be called, remained with her. This was no outburst against her, but simply an ebullience of natural high spirits among themselves. Her presence, she noted wryly, meant nothing at all to them.

A chair fell over, someone yelped with pain, there was a burst of laughter, and Anna saw the clock jump to another minute. Abandoning her dignified immobility Anna advanced into action. She strode to the front desks and clapped her hands with a resonance which rivalled Miss Enderby's own.

'To your desks!' she roared. 'And quickly!'

With a pleasurable shock she saw her words obeyed. There was a scuffling and a scuttling and within a minute order had returned. Refreshed by their break the children turned attentive eyes upon her.

Anna's self-esteem crept back.

'And about time too!' she commented severely to her waiting class.

The morning dragged on. Anna felt as though she had been weeks in the classroom and felt unaccountably exhausted. The thought of break and tea at a quarter to eleven gleamed in the distance.

She had called the children's names and marked her register with care. Fearful lest uproar should break out again she had kept her voice stern and her face unsmiling. She had mispronounced one or two names and quelled the resulting sniggers with her most daunting glances. This was not how she had envisaged meeting her new charges. She had meant to advance with happiness and confidence, as she had been told to do at college, but she felt neither at the moment, and guilty into the bargain.

Two bustling, self-important little girls had given out paper and pencils to the rest and the class settled itself, with only a minor buzzing, to filling its empty sheets with horses, ballerinas, cowboys, and anything else which engaged its attention, leaving Anna free to roam up and down the aisles and to look from the windows upon the windy sunlit wastes of the new suburb which surrounded the school.

It had rained in the night and although the pavements and the old metalled roads had dried there were still long puddles lying in the ruts of the new muddy lanes which criss-crossed the area. From her high window Anna could see how flat the country was. The new houses were being built on what had once been waste marshland, and the glint of a sluggishly-moving stream and pools of standing water reflecting the pale sky, gave a hint of future fogs and floodings.

It could never have been very pretty, decided Anna, resting her arms on the window-sill. Only a few desiccated elms remained at the side of the distant main road, wearing flamboyant hoardings round the base of their trunks like tawdry shabby skirts. The few fields which remained stretched, flat and monotonous, towards the horizon, hedgeless and with tufts of coarse marsh weed sprouting through the rusty shabbiness of the dying grass. Only the sky was beautiful. It arched above the sad wasteland with bright iridescence, and Anna remembered with amusement a wonderful phrase from an old copy of *Suggestions for Teachers*. 'Direct the children's attention,' it had said, 'to the ever-changing panorama of the heavens.' The stilted primness of this sensible advice had never failed to please her, and now, tense and worried, the old charm still worked and had power to cheer and comfort her.

Smilingly obedient to the injunction she looked up at the sky. Great pillars of white cloud, billowing into fantastic shapes, moved majestically across the pale blue sky, dwarfing the insignificant countryside below into an untidy shabby toyland of houses, fact-ories, and hoardings spilt haphazard across the acres of dingy grass and mud. This glimpse of ever-changing but enduring beauty revived Anna's young spirits.

'Bell, miss!' chorused the class joyously, as a shrilling noise broke the uneasy peace of the classroom.

Pencils clattered into the grooves of the desks, papers were stuffed inside, and before Anna could give any orders her class streamed out through the door and were gone.

There seemed nothing for it but to follow their example. The corridors were full of hastening noisy children, clutching paper bags with their lunch inside, skipping ropes, balls, and other impedimenta.

Anna battled her way against the stream and found herself at last at the staff room.

There were only fourteen members of staff at Elm Hill School, but the staff room appeared crowded to Anna's timid eyes. Several of her colleagues she had met already, either during her July visit, or before school began that morning, but now Miss Enderby bore down upon her and took her to the large central table.

Two men scrambled clumsily to their feet and balanced cigarettes carefully across the edge of their saucers.

'This is Alan Foster,' said Miss Enderby, 'who takes the top class here.'

Anna found herself holding the soft podgy hand of a middle-aged man. He wore a dark, shabby suit, creased from the heavy folds of his pear-shaped body, and decorated with cigarette ash. His eyes were moist and kindly behind horn-rimmed spectacles.

'Hope you'll be happy with us,' he wheezed politely. 'I'll get you some tea.'

'And this is Andy Craig,' continued Miss Enderby, 'who is in the classroom next to yours.' Anna wondered if she could detect a faint coolness in her headmistress's tones as the introductions were made.

Andy Craig was a younger man than Alan Foster, a slight jaunty figure dressed in a jacket of rather large dog-tooth check and tightish cavalry twill trousers. His shoes were as glossy as horse-chestnuts and he sported a bloodstone ring on his little finger. A sandy moustache matched his sandy hair and his eyes were startlingly like bottled gooseberries in their soft opaque greenness. Anna felt that she would rather not be alone with Mr Craig for any length of time.

A large, well-corseted figure in a navy-blue costume whom Anna recognized as Miss Hobbs, the second-in-command, now approached Miss Enderby and said importantly:

'A traveller, dear, outside your door. I told him you were engaged and he'd have to wait –'

'I'd better see him,' said Miss Enderby, depositing her half-filled cup on the table. Miss Hobbs's eyes watched her departing figure with concern.

'*Quite* selfless!' she announced in a dramatic aside to Anna. 'The school *always* comes first!' She turned solemn dark eyes upon the girl.

'You just don't know how lucky you are to be serving under Florence Enderby,' she said earnestly. 'She's a really *wonderful* woman!'

At this point a plastic beaker full of steaming tea was thrust between them by the tall young woman Anna had seen standing at the side table busy pouring out.

'Remember me?' she asked. 'Joan Berry? Are you completely exhausted?'

Miss Hobbs, looking a little huffy, moved away to make room for the newcomer and Anna smiled at the elegant Miss Berry whose glamorous appearance had impressed her so much at their first meeting.

'Do you know everyone now?' continued Joan Berry. 'We're all here, I think, except Tom Drew and John Fraser who are on playground duty, and the two moles who've gone to earth again.'

She laughed at Anna's bewilderment, but rattled on.

'You'll have to bring a cup and saucer for yourself. We all do. That's why you had to wait for the beaker.'

'I'll bring one,' promised Anna, making a mental note to go shopping as soon as school was over. Mrs Flynn was not likely to offer such richness to her lodger, Anna thought to herself.

The electric bell shrilled again and Anna, copying her fellows, gulped down the remains of her tea.

'We go down to the playground to see our classes in,' said Miss Berry taking Anna's arm.

'Tell me about the moles –' began Anna as they descended the stone steps.

'Hush!' whispered her companion. 'Too many ears about now. But I warn you, my dear, we're a very rum lot at Elm Hill. Very rum indeed!'

Chapter Four

PAVEMENTS AND PARENTS

The new streets of Elm Hill, which spread daily further and further across the wasteland, enclosed the old village of that name. All that remained of it was a shabby towered church built of grey flints, a row of cottages of the same stone, a square white vicarage with a slated roof, and a dingy pub.

There had once been a village green, bordered on one side by a row of horse-chestnut trees; and a rough area of grass, bare in patches from many feet, was still to be seen near the pub. Half-a-dozen chestnut trees still stood, their lower branches broken off by the hands of hooligans, and gaps showed where their fellows had been cut down one here, one there, to be taken to the timber yard.

Three families lived in the vicarage, the vicar having only the ground floor for his domain. The garden, shared by all, had that neglected, 'someone-else-can-do-it' look so often found in communal property.

A rusty tricycle and a headless doll lay under the rhododendron bushes. Plantains and daisies starred the shabby lawns, and formal flower beds, which had once glowed with geraniums, lobelias, and roses to delight the eyes of former incumbents whose stipends allowed gardeners, had been grassed over, only their shape showing like pale ghosts against the older sward.

Only the massive cedar retained its dignity. Lofty, superb, its blue-black branches spreading horizontally like massive hands in constant and magnificent blessing, it surveyed both the fading gentility of its own house and the new ugliness which pressed around it. It stood inviolate, like a lone hero who, surrounded by a mob, fears none but pities all.

A mile away lay the railway station and here, almost a hundred years ago, another village had grown up. The square yellow houses, early grimed with smoke from the trains, still stood, mean and dejected, topped with grey slates. A row of small shops, The Railway Tavern, and two or three detached villas hidden behind grimy laurels were all that remained of the original second village, but over the years the streets had crept between the two, first over the flat fields that bordered the railway and then over the slight rise in the meadows, once crowned with a clump of elm trees, which had given its name to the village.

A gas-lit Post Office, a Working-Men's Institute, more public houses, a British Legion Hall, fish-and-chip shops, temporary churches, a new Broadway built in the mid thirties and flashing as garishly as false teeth in a faded face, were added to the mess which gradually covered the fields.

Anna had explored this sad hinterland, one sunny evening on a solitary walk, soon after her arrival. She had walked half a mile through the new half-made roads among which her lodgings lay and crossed the old turnpike road, busy with homeward-going traffic to the north-west.

She could not decide which was the more depressing, the arid near-slums on one side of the main road or the new chaotic rawness on the other. She had made her way towards the church knowing that the origins of the place would be near by and anxious to see what remained of the village it had once been.

Her spirits had fallen as she walked. There seemed nothing, absolutely nothing, to cheer the heart or delight the eye. Even the 'ever-changing panorama of the heavens' was unremarkable that evening.

She had stopped at the vicarage gate, arrested by the sight of the one splendid cedar tree. In her present mood it only seemed to emphasize the pitifulness of its surroundings. As she looked she became conscious of a gnarled old man in a cloth cap who had approached in carpet-slippers and now stood beside her.

'Fine tree that,' he had said, following her gaze. 'Been here all my lifetime, it has.'

Anna made a non-committal noise.

'I was born in one of them cottages,' he went on, nodding towards the flint row. 'But 'orrible damp they was, always. I'm round the corner now in a new place. Electric and that. Bit of garden too, but it don't grow flowers all that well.'

Anna remained silent, hoping that he would go away. She had enough depressing thoughts of her own without this garrulous old man, with his unpleasantly moist nose, adding to them. And then he said something which pricked into reality all the numb ache which Anna was enduring.

'Used to be lovely beds of white violets under all our street. Us kids picked 'em in handfuls. I can smell 'em now!'

He sniffed wetly and Anna's distaste was softened by the expression of rapt memory which wrinkled his old red-rimmed eyes.

She wished him good evening and walked on, the words echoing inside her head.

'Lovely beds of white violets under all our street,' she repeated wonderingly to herself, watching her feet tread the hard grey pavements. Beneath them, she thought with a pang, innumerable small beauties of flower, leaf, and convoluting root had smothered and died, remembered only by the very old, ready to die themselves.

It was soon after this that Anna experienced her first Parents' Association meeting.

It had been mentioned casually, in the staff room on the morning of the day in question, by the glamorous Joan Berry. She was sitting on the staff-room table surveying a ladder which was running the length of her elegant leg.

'That leaves one pair for the Parents' do tonight,' she said bitterly. 'Ruination!'

'Do we all have to come?' asked Anna, in some alarm. She had been looking forward to as cosy a domestic evening as Mrs Flynn's bleak premises could offer, intending to wash her hair, write to several friends, and sort out pictures for the walls of her new classroom. This innocent vision seemed about to disappear.

'Hasn't Miss Enderby said anything? She will, don't worry. Our Parent–Teacher Association is one of her hobby-horses.'

'What do we wear?' asked Anna, turning her back bravely upon the domestic evening and facing the new project with a natural womanly reaction.

'Oh, anything,' responded Joan Berry vaguely, hitching up her skirt to study the upper rungs of the ladder which now approached a froth of white underclothes. 'A frock, you know, or a suit. Not slacks, of course – but nothing too dazzling.'

Anna mentally checked over her wardrobe. She was weighing the merits of her tartan frock (loathsomely familiar to her, no shoes to go with it and decidedly spotted about the skirt) against her blue silk suit (too tight across the back, the blouse which looked best with it languishing at home in Essex, and probably much too conspicuous in any case for such an occasion), when the bell put a stop to her speculations.

Miss Enderby spoke of the meeting at prayers and later caught Anna as her class began to swarm up the stairs.

'I should have mentioned it before, dear, but really the beginning of term is so hectic –' She left the sentence in mid air, and passed a fine hand across her white hair with an air of harassed weariness.

'About half past seven in the hall. All the staff will be here, and the parents are a very friendly set. You'll find meeting them such a help with the children.'

A scuffle at the head of the stairs caused her weariness to vanish in a flash. With remarkable agility for a heavily-built woman she raced up the stairs past the children, who cowered nervously to one side, and plucked a small boy from the landing above.

'To my room!' thundered Miss Enderby in an awe-inspiring boom. She turned flashing eyes upon Anna who had toiled up after her.

'*Jumping*,' said Miss Enderby, outraged, '*jumping*, I say, on his neighbour's toes! The very idea! Perhaps you'd like *me* to jump on yours?'

The child, wide-eyed, surveyed the bulk of his headmistress with acute alarm, and shook his head, too apprehensive to speak.

'We'll see!' Miss Enderby said grimly. She raised a massive arm and pointed towards her door.

Meekly the little boy set off on his lone journey to await judgement, while his classmates, unusually subdued, went into the classroom and the blissful safety of their own desks.

'Be *very* firm, dear, when they are going from one place to another. That's when accidents happen,' said Miss Enderby, in a low aside.

She gave Anna a reassuring smile.

'Don't forget the meeting. You'll enjoy it immensely,' she said, in a voice that brooked no argument, and then set off along the corridor in pursuit of the malefactor.

The school hall was ablaze with lights when Anna arrived that evening. She had crept upstairs to leave her coat in the staff room, hoping that the blue silk suit would not look as tight as it felt, and very glad to postpone her entry into the throng which she had glimpsed through the glass of the hall doors.

The cheerful din of crockery being stacked on trays, the clattering of tea spoons, and the exchange of badinage between members of the refreshments committee as they bustled merrily about in the kitchen, receded as Anna climbed towards the merciful silence of the upper floor.

Only 'the moles' were in the cloakroom. These, it had transpired, were two young members of staff, who had been together at the same training college and who now were inseparable, drawn together by past ties and by an incredible likeness in personal appearance and outlook.

They were both small and swarthy, both wore glasses and faint moustaches, and dressed in the same dowdy colours – the curious musty greens and terracotta shades beloved by the Victorians. They were extraordinarily diligent and earnest. As soon as they had bolted down their school dinner they disappeared into their classrooms, there to make gargantuan preparations for the afternoon's hand work, or to concoct strange, up-to-the-minute apparatus for the infants in their charge as shown in the latest number of *Child Education*.

They rarely dallied in the staff room, and looked with some impatience at those who lolled at the table, stirring their after-dinner Nescafé, talking of football pools, clothes, and the current films. In return they were treated with affectionate tolerance by the rest of the staff, who recognized, but did not relish, their dedication to their work.

They were silent creatures and now, as Anna entered, contented themselves with smiling and shifting to let the girl see her reflection in the mirror above the wash-basin. They were busy patting their lank hair into place and dabbing their sallow complexions with tiny discs of powder-puffs about the size of a penny – and much the same colour, as far as Anna could see.

'What happens at these affairs?' she asked nervously. Miss Jones waited for Miss Smith to answer, but, after a full minute, was obliged to give tongue herself.

'People sing, and we dance a bit, and have sandwiches,' she said at last, with a heavy sigh. It certainly sounded the wildest orgy, thought Anna, applying lipstick carefully. She decided not to put too much on. After all, she would like to give the parents of her charges an impression of wholesome gentility, and respectability appeared to be the keynote of the evening. She hoped her skirt was not too short nor her heels too high. It would be dreadful to be thought frivolous. The moles, she noticed, wore their usual flat shoes and their ankles rose from them like sturdy pillars of rectitude.

'Better go down, I suppose,' said Miss Smith resignedly, leading the way. Anna was not sure whether she should accompany the two inseparables, but was so nervous of making her entrance alone that she risked their displeasure by following them closely down the stairs and into the hall.

The school radiogram had been fed with records and was emitting a high-pitched squealing noise which Anna recognized after a few excruciating minutes of concentration as a Scottish reel. Whether the bagpipes or the ancient radiogram's reproduction was to blame for the distressing racket was difficult to decide. About three hundred people, with voices raised above the background cacophony, added to the pandemonium.

Miss Enderby, magnificent in flowered silk, took Anna to meet the chairman of the managers who sat with his wife and a number of friends uncomfortably close to the radiogram. He was incredibly old and frail, his skin stretched like yellow parchment over the fragile bones of his skull. He was very deaf (which Anna could not help feeling was a blessing in his present circumstances) but nodded kindly to Anna and spoke welcomingly to her in an almost inaudible little speech, holding and patting her hand the while.

Dumb show introductions were made and Anna felt quite exhausted with smiling and nodding and mouthing polite nothings under the battery of noise. It was quite a shock when someone switched off the radiogram and only the hubbub of three hundred voices stirred the air.

Miss Enderby mounted the platform and made a brief speech of welcome. She then went on to outline the term's programme and Anna took advantage of the lull to look at the other members of staff who had scattered themselves among the throng. They were all unusually resplendent. Miss Hobbs, her eyes fixed, like some devoted spaniel's watching its master, upon Miss Enderby, wore a man-tailored grey suit and a small diamond brooch. Joan Berry was in a flame-coloured frock, and even the masters appeared comparatively elegant having changed from their usual depressing uniform of baggy grey suits or subfusc hacking jackets.

Her gaze wandered over the assembled parents. They were a cheerful-looking collection on the whole, she decided, but the sight of so many strange faces filled her with a sudden piercing longing for the small familiar world of her own home. There, at any gathering, she would have known them all. Even in the larger sphere of the market town where she had had her schooling almost all the people were known to her. She had felt that she belonged. But here, in this strange hall, set among the sad ravaged fields, where now no violets grew, she felt overcome with the hopelessness of ever getting to know, or even wanting to know, the host of strangers before her. A sudden vision of the Essex farmhouse appeared in her mind's eye. The lights would be shining out from its comfortable bulk, and from the clump of elms near by the old owl would be slipping down the wind on noiseless wings. A star or two would be studding the night sky. It was almost more than the homesick girl could bear, and it was lucky that at that moment Miss Enderby's little speech ended and Miss Hobbs caught her arm and led her to meet Mrs Crossley who was the mother of a chubby, placid boy in her class.

'He's such a *frail* child,' Mrs Crossley assured her earnestly, 'and terribly sensitive, you know. Just like me, I'm afraid.' She gave a self-conscious laugh and Anna tried to think of a suitable rejoinder.

'He seems very happy at school –' she began timidly.

'Oh he's wonderfully *plucky*!' asserted Mrs Crossley. From the way she spoke one might have thought that the child was called upon to face torture daily at Anna's hands. She did not add 'Just like me,' to this statement, but her tone implied that the boy's pluckiness aswell as his sensitivity was inherited from his mother.

She gave a quick look round, hitched her chair more closely to Anna's and spoke in a lowered voice.

'Of course, I think you should know something about the little chap which I don't usually broadcast.'

Her conspiratorial manner alarmed Anna considerably. She did so hope that she was not going to hear a number of obstetrical details which so many married ladies seemed to enjoy disclosing.

'Oh please don't –' began Anna hastily, hoping to spare them both embarrassment. But Mrs Crossley's face wore that disheartening look of one who knows where her duty lies however unpleasant, and Anna braced herself to hear the worst.

'He was a seven-months baby,' whispered Mrs Crossley darkly. Anna nodded and did her best to look suitably impressed.

'No one,' continued Mrs Crossley raising her voice a trifle, '*but no one*, can imagine what I went through with him. It's not surprising that he's still so highly strung.'

Anna wondered if it would be of any use to tell her that Andrew appeared to be the strongest, noisiest, greediest, and most irrepressible of all her class, but realized that it would simply be waste of breath. The image of an ethereal creature, almost too fragile for this coarse world, was firmly fixed in his mother's mind and it would take more than Anna's testimony to eradicate it.

The arrival of a dish of sausage rolls terminated the conversation and Anna turned thankfully towards Andy Craig who was bearing it round the room. Normally she evaded this particular member of staff. His habit of ruffling his sandy moustache and gazing speculatively at her did not endear him to her, but as a refuge from Mrs Crossley he was more than welcome. He looked surprised and pleased at her unusual warmth of greeting.

'Anything I can get you?' he asked preening himself.

'I ought to meet a few more parents,' said Anna hastily. His face fell, but he gazed round obediently.

'What about old Chapman?' he suggested, pointing to a purple-faced heavy-weight across the room. But old Chapman had to be left for another time, for at that moment the radiogram sprang into hideous life again, someone called 'Take your partners for a quick-step!' and Anna found herself jerking round the room with her face uncomfortably near Andy Craig's R.A.F. tie.

There was really no room to dance. Fathers and mothers, neighbours and friends jogged patiently about together and even the moles were on the floor clamped to the best suits of two perspiring fathers.

'Hell, my wrist!' said Andy Craig, removing a moist palm from Anna's and surveying a yellow leather wrist strap of impressive width.

'What have you done to it?' asked Anna. Andy Craig gave a light laugh.

'Nothing, nothing, my dear. Just a relic of the war days, you know. But there, you wouldn't know – way before your time.' He gave a wince, but bravely replaced his hand.

'Andy Craig, War Hero!' thought Anna mischievously, and then chided herself for being uncharitable. She must find out more about this mysterious war incident, she decided.

The dance over, two of the mothers settled themselves at the piano and gave a spirited, if inaccurate, duet which was warmly applauded. They were followed by an exuberant father who sang

'Take a Pair of Sparkling Eyes' ('What again?' had been Andy Craig's audible comment when this was announced), with a sprightly archness which Anna found hard to endure.

She spoke to more parents but felt that she would never remember them if she met them again in one of the muddy half-made streets of this strange new world. As the evening wore on she longed for quietness, for fresh air, and the peace of her country home.

She felt dazed but listened politely to the accounts of her pupils' home life, but the children that their parents spoke of seemed quite different from those same children whom she met in class. Beauty is indeed in the eye of the beholder, thought Anna. She had never before realized how precious, special, and fragile were those in her care, nor how privileged she was to have such riches in her charge.

At the end of the proceedings as she was about to leave the hall, her mind bent on bed and the dubious comforts of Mrs Flynn's establishment, a wispy little woman caught her arm and introduced herself as 'Julia's mummy.'

'Before you go,' she whispered nervously, 'do let me tell you one thing.' Anna smiled reassuringly, nothing much could be wrong with Julia, she felt sure. She was the bounciest, bonniest extrovert that ever bullied her classmates.

'She may look a big girl,' said her mother, as though divining Anna's thoughts, 'but she's a bundle of nerves really and terribly highly-strung!'

She paused for a moment and looked apprehensively about her at the departing crowd, and Anna had the doomed feeling that this had all happened before.

'It's probably,' she said, dropping her voice to a faint conspiratorial sibilance, 'because she's a seven-months child.'

'Believe me,' Anna heard herself replying earnestly, 'she's not the only one!'

Chapter Five

A RUM LOT

As the first weeks passed, Anna found her work a little less tiring. No longer did she totter home at four o'clock to her narrow little bed, carefully remove the folk-weave coverlet, and lie exhausted for half an hour before facing Mrs Flynn's dry slab cake and thin tea. Tired she still was at the end of the day, edgy with the constant noise of movement of hundreds of exuberant children, and over-anxious about her ability to keep order and to teach her carefully prepared lessons; but not so completely drained as at first.

Now she was able to take stock of her progress and was amused, and slightly alarmed, to hear herself lapsing into the imbecile speech and turns of phrase which she had so healthily despised in teachers of young children.

'I can see,' she had heard herself say sternly, 'several naughty little people, not a hundred miles from here, who will certainly not be chosen for the Christmas play. I'm looking for two really *trustworthy* rabbits and six sensible *clear-speaking* frogs!'

It wouldn't do at all, she told herself in panic, and yet the dreadful truth was that the children seemed to respond to this way of talking. It was contrary to all the text-books, to Anna's teaching notes taken down so laboriously at college, and to her own dislike of debasing her mother tongue. She decided that she must keep an ear cocked for the treacheries that escaped her lips.

She found herself called upon to teach Scripture, Physical Exercise, Arithmetic, Writing, Reading, English Composition Written and Oral, History, Geography, Nature Study, Art, Handicrafts, Music and Singing, Hygiene, and a mysterious subject called Rhythmic Work which had somehow eluded her during her studies.

'Don't worry,' Miss Enderby had said kindly, when Anna had confessed her ignorance. 'It is all part of our musical training here. Miss Hobbs is particularly competent. You must watch one or two of her lessons.'

And so Anna found herself one afternoon sitting nervously in the corner of the school hall, her notebook open on her lap, watching Miss Hobbs's Rhythmic Work lesson with forty-eight lively nine-year-olds.

'Find a space! Find a space!' Miss Hobbs's hearty voice boomed out as the children struggled through the doors. Little knots of friends charged boisterously about together, intoxicated with the space of the hall after the narrow confines of their desks and the decorous pace demanded by the stone corridors if plain murder were not to result from the passing of masses of children from one part of the building to the other.

Miss Hobbs gave a brusque nod to Anna as she strode towards the piano. A crashing chord caused the majority of the class to stand still. The glare of Miss Hobbs's eye, which swivelled over the top of the piano like a searchlight, stilled the rest within a minute. Anna was overcome with awe at such a demonstration of authority.

'Remember last week's lesson?' boomed Miss Hobbs. 'Butterflies? Off you go.'

Tinkling music in the highest two octaves of the school piano set the children running haphazardly about the hall, flapping their arms. Anna noticed that Miss Hobbs did not seat herself on the piano stool. Most of the class would have been hidden from her sight had she done so. She half-stood, therefore, with her knees bent in a most unbecoming way and kept a sharp look-out for malefactors over the top of the instrument, while her hands led an independent existence of their own scampering vivaciously along the upper keys.

'Up on your toes! On your toes!' exhorted Miss Hobbs above the uproar. 'You sound like a herd of stampeding elephants, Class Four. And don't flail you arms like that, Bobby Byng. You nearly hit your neighbour just now. You're a *butterfly*, not a mad bull.'

Anna noticed that even Miss Hobbs's discipline was strained by these conditions and felt quite sure that her own frail hold on her class would be snapped asunder as soon as she brought them into the hall, and bedlam would inevitably break out. Several naughty little boys were charging wildly about the hall catching their friends and enemies indiscriminately with blows from their butterfly wings which caused considerable pain and resulted in recrimination. A vicious little set-to was being conducted at the back of the piano, which was out of range of Miss Hobbs's piercing gaze. Only when one of the butterflies stumbled against the piano as the result of a flesh-wound, administered by a fellow-butterfly of powerful physique, did Miss Hobbs realize what was going on. Retribution was swift. Both butterflies were stood one at each side of the hall while the lesson continued.

The children became mettlesome horses, snowflakes, trees in the wind, and waves on the shore. They fell prettily asleep to lullaby music whose soothing whispers were shattered during the slumbrous arpeggios by Miss Hobbs shouting: 'That boy who's snoring can just stop it!' They woke up again to chords so resounding that the windows rattled.

At one stage they sat on the floor bending forward and back rhythmically while Miss Hobbs strode among them intoning: '*Row* the boat, *row* the boat!' and '*Pull* your oars and *pull* your oars!' like an overseer among the galley-slaves. Anna noticed the opportunities this exercise gave for shooting out the legs energetically and kicking one's immediate neighbour.

As she made ineffectual little notes in her book she wondered if she would ever manage to take a Rhythmic Work lesson without having to send for the First Aid box, which was kept, unfortunately, in the room of Miss Enderby herself.

The clock showed that only five minutes more remained of the lesson. The children were beginning to flag but Miss Hobbs, with the physique of an ox and determined to set Anna an inspired example, was as fresh as a daisy. She exhorted them to smell the delicious roses which they held in their hands. Her own weather-beaten face took on an expression of ecstasy as she inhaled the imaginary perfume, but this changed swiftly when forty-eight noses obediently sniffed forty-eight bouquets, and her tone, on demanding the production of handkerchiefs immediately, was peremptory.

As a final exercise the puffing children were told to skip freely about in a beautiful field.

'End the lesson on a note of carefree happiness,' said Miss Hobbs to Anna. It sounded remarkably like a quotation from somebody's Rhythmic Work manual, thought Anna, but she nodded dutifully and prepared to watch.

There was no doubt about it, Miss Hobbs knew her stuff. She had left the piano and now capered from one end of the hall to the other among her stumbling and perspiring companions. She pointed her toes, she bent gracefully to left and right, winning smile set upon her face As she skipped she chanted rhythmically: 'Skip about, skip about! Smell the flowers. Feel the sun! Hear the birds! A lovely day! Skip for joy! Skip for joy!'

The leaden-footed efforts of the children began to annoy her. Seizing some luckless child by the wrist she bounced it along with her, trying to instil into its lumpish frame some of the energy which drove her own. The rest of the children made a last valiant attempt to emulate their teacher's steps, except for Bobby Byng, a slow adenoidal child who had a mulishness which was at its worst in Rhythmic Work.

Out of the corner of her eyes, Miss Hobbs, still capering in the sprightliest manner, caught sight of the boy. He was standing absolutely still! It was too much. Dropping her bouncing partner, she flew to Bobby Byng's side and administered a resounding slap on the boy's leg.

'*Now* will you skip for joy?' she boomed wrathfully.

Anna averted her gaze hastily from Miss Hobbs's scarlet face and looked at her notebook.

'End the lesson,' it said blandly, 'on a note of carefree happiness.'

On many occasions Anna had cause to remember Joan Berry's remark about the staff being 'a rum lot – a very rum lot'.

Joan Berry herself was unique on the staff for her elegance of appearance and for her thinly disguised contempt and amusement at her colleagues' coiffures and costumes. From her spike-heeled shoes to the top of her outrageous hats she was a vision of delight to unsophisticated Anna, used as she was to country clothes of a more utilitarian design. Clothes were Joan Berry's overriding passion and with their help she expressed not only her flair for line and colour but also her disdain of those who lacked such interest. Anna was secretly appalled at the amount of money which she spent on her appearance. She had seen Joan Berry's dressing table with its rows and ranks of bottles and jars lined up like soldiers in battle array ready to keep the enemies, wrinkles, flabbiness, spots, and blemishes, at a distance. She compared it with her own modest lipstick, cold cream, and powder, and stood amazed. To spend so much time, thought, and money upon such things seemed out of all proportion to Anna.

It wasn't as though it made Joan any happier, Anna thought. The older girl's passionate interest drove her to gaze in shop windows at shoes and furs and jewels which it gave her real pain to eschew. It was as if some insatiable secret hunger could be alleviated by a stream of new adornments, of one sort or another, yet never really satisfied. It puzzled Anna very much.

The redoubtable Miss Hobbs's outstanding passion was for her headmistress which expressed itself in a fierce loyalty which Anna found embarrassing at times. When Miss Enderby expressed a wish to see Anna's record book in which she kept her notes for her week's work, it was maddening to have Miss Hobbs say brusquely: 'And mind it's handed in at once! Miss Enderby's overworked as it is, and doesn't want to have to run around after you!' Such devotion may have had its admirable side once, but taken to such irritating excess it simply made Miss Hobbs appear ridiculous in the sight of her younger and more ribald colleagues.

Miss Smith and Miss Jones, the two moles, were set apart by their earnest overwork. As far as Anna could judge they spent their evening solely in the continuance of school work, making apparatus, filling in records, filing pictures, and the like. She had never heard them mention a theatre, a cinema, a television programme, or any book not immediately connected with education. They were a daunting pair, but Anna found them pitiful too.

Andy Craig, of the gooseberry eyes and damaged wrist, she felt no pity for. He was lazy, vain, and boastful, and his jejune attempts at lady-killing irritated Anna. Occasionally the wide wrist-strap was exchanged for a sling made from a spotted silk scarf.

'What's the matter with Mr Craig's wrist?' asked Anna innocently of Joan Berry one day.

'Don't give him the satisfaction of asking,' said Joan shortly.

'But is it serious? I heard him say something about the war. Was he shot down?'

'That's what he'd like you to think,' said Joan grimly. 'But the nearest he ever got to an aeroplane was pulling the chocks away. As a matter of fact he got his arm caught in a swing door at his R.A.F. camp. I happen to know someone who was there with him – but dear Andy doesn't know that. I must say I get a lot of secret fun out of his antics. Still it's an innocent conceit, I suppose, and hurts no one. The old inferiority complex, my child. Put it down to the usual bogy!'

They certainly were a rum lot, Anna thought, and the more you got to know them the rummer they became. She had taken a liking to middle-aged Mr Foster because he seemed so pleasantly normal, a shabbier and more vague edition of her uncles. He had two children, much about her own age, she knew, and a wife who taught part-time to help make ends meet. She first became aware of Mr Foster's secret ambition when she had a free period one wet morning and they were alone in the staff room.

Anna was busy at one end of the table, correcting a pile of English exercises. At the other end Mr Foster scribbled industriously in an exercise book. Occasionally he sighed through the mists of blue cigarette smoke that wreathed around him. At last he set down his ball-point pen with a clatter, blew wetly at the cigarette ash which he had dribbled down his crumpled jacket, and spoke to his companion.

'Ever do any writing?' he asked.

'Only letters,' answered Anna, startled from her marking. It was obvious that Mr Foster was disposed to talk, and Anna put down her own marking pencil. 'Why? Do you?' she asked.

Mr Foster waved a pudgy hand deprecatingly at the exercise book before him.

'Oh, I'm always at it. Had a go at pretty well everything in the writing line.'

'Have you had anything published?' asked Anna with proper awe. She was glad to see that Mr Foster looked gratified and guessed, rightly, that he had.

'One or two little things,' he admitted with a very fair show of *insouciance*. He tapped his cigarette ash carefully into the empty carton he had put on the table, and watched his own operations through narrowed, world-weary eyelids.

'How lovely!' said Anna enthusiastically. 'What in?'

A shade of annoyance seemed to quirk Mr Foster's puffy countenance, but he answered readily enough.

'Well, I had a review on a woodwork manual in a teachers' paper last year, and a country magazine accepted a poem of mine some months ago.'

'A poem!' breathed Anna admiringly.

'Of course you don't get a lot of money from Poetry,' Mr Foster hastened to explain, with the air of one who tosses off half-a-dozen odes before shaving, 'but it's good training in the *Use of Words*.'

'Naturally,' agreed Anna.

'Where the *money* is,' went on Mr Foster, warming to his theme, 'is in books for the twelves to fifteens. That's what this is. He held up the exercise book. 'It's really a novel for young people. The publishers are falling over themselves for downright, realistic stories, with a working-class background, for teenagers. Aimed at the secondary moderns, you know – and showing the home background. This chap – my hero – has a drunken father and a mother out at work. He has to dress the younger children and give them breakfast before going off to school himself. Of course he's appeared in the juvenile court once or twice, and in the next chapter I'm having a pretty strong scene with the Probation Officer. Oh, I think it will be acceptable to schools and libraries too.'

'But surely,' protested Anna, 'that's not a true picture of an average secondary modern schoolboy? Why, lots of my friends at home went to our local school till they were fifteen, and I can't think of one of them who had a drunken father – except perhaps on Harvest Home night or Christmas Eve,' she added, as an honest afterthought.

'The country, my dear,' said Mr Foster, heavily avuncular, 'is a very different kettle of fish from our large towns!'

'But even so – all this talk of juvenile courts and Probation Officers –' expostulated Anna.

'Life in the raw!' Mr Foster assured her pontifically. He rummaged in a baggy pocket, produced a catapult, two pieces of chalk, and a grubby handkerchief before discovering the packet of cigarettes for which he was searching. Anna watched his fumblings indignantly, like a small ruffled owl. It was true she knew mighty little of life in large towns but she was positive that Mr Foster's picture was grossly overdrawn.

'The other thing that brings the money in,' went on Mr Foster, blissfully unaware of Anna's inward smoulderings, 'is a thoroughly good text-book. Say, a series in English. Four books, one for each year of the primary school. Why, some of those chaps who got in early must have made a fortune!'

His moist eyes brightened at the thought.

'Think of the numbers one school alone would have to order! Forty-eight in a class, say. That's four dozen for each year. Sixteen dozen!'

Mr Foster's normally flat tones grew quite sharp with enthusiasm. He turned his exercise book sideways and began to do excited little sums in the rather wide margins.

'Sixteen dozen a school – let's say five hundred schools –' he began busily, pencil flying. His voice dropped to incoherent whisperings as he worked out his multiplication sums.

Anna's indignation subsided as she watched him. There he sat, a great flabby, hulk of a man, living in the dream-world of Get-Rich-Quick. She thought suddenly of her father and the work that went into one of his fields of wheat which he would be harvesting now.

He too would be thinking of the rewards of his labours, but he would have done the major part of them before counting his gains. To see the man before her exciting himself, like a greedy child, at the thought of vast wealth for something which had not even been started and which, Anna suspected, never would be started, let alone completed, filled her with disgust tempered with pity.

Joan Berry was right, mused Anna. They certainly are a rum lot! She cast her mind over the other two male members of staff, of whom she had seen little. One of them, John Fraser, was newly married and lived in a particularly horrible house near the school, with windows containing panes of coloured glass in the form of tulips. He was the last member of staff to enter the school gates and the first to leave at night. Only his newly-married state had kept him so far from Miss Enderby's verbal disapproval. The rest of the staff, left to cope with his unruly class in the cloakrooms, sincerely hoped that retribution would come upon him before long. There must be an end some time to Miss Enderby's romantic tolerance.

The fourth and last male member was Tom Drew, a dark young man, entering upon his second year of teaching and saying very little to anyone. Anna had exchanged only half-a-dozen sentences with him since she arrived, but she liked him and guessed that he missed the countryside home from which he had come as much as she did her own.

It was he who came into the staff room just as Mr Foster looked up, flushed and happy, from his sums.

'At ten per cent, I make it almost a thousand pounds!' he said exuberantly.

'It'd be guineas in the literary world,' said Tom Drew, lighting a cigarette.

'So it would! So it would!' agreed Mr Foster, returning to his calculations with even greater fervour.

Tom's eyes met Anna's in a dark amused glance and Anna felt curiously happy. Could this possibly be an exception among such a very rum lot?

Chapter Six

GENUINE ARTICLES

Home at the weekends became doubly dear. The journey from Elm Hill across the sprawling mass of London seemed interminable, but once clear of the eastern suburbs Anna's heart rose higher with every mile that passed.

As summer changed to autumn the trees near her home deepened in colour from fading green to gold and then to bronze, and Anna looked out for these much-loved landmarks weekly and noted the change that each week wrought in them.

The joy of home-coming was ever fresh. The smell of the old farmhouse compounded of years of wood smoke, stone floors, and the linseed oil which was used to polish the ancient oak staircase, was like a benison to Anna, after the bleak gas-tainted air which greeted her as Mrs Flynn's front door yielded grudgingly to her pressure. The feel of the old flagstones in the farmhouse hall, worn and uneven from generations of sturdy boots, gave Anna a lift of the heart which Mrs Flynn's impersonal, even linoleum could never do: and the sight of the great fireplace, a cavern of glowing wood from her father's fields, flinging a wide welcome of cheerful warmth, made Anna realize how thoroughly she loathed Mrs Flynn's meagre gas fire, with row upon row of little white skulls looking like some tidy, ghastly, miniature Golgotha.

Anna had time to ponder over the differences one autumn evening when her parents had gone to visit a neighbouring farmer. The fire crackled and leaped. Little red-hot twigs snapped and fell into the glowing ash, sending up spurts of yellow flame which were reflected in the pieces of copper and the old polished furniture in the darkening room. It was a joyous living thing with movement, noise, and colour of its own. Mrs Flynn's carefully adjusted gas fire gave only a hint of its presence with its faint warmth and sibilant hissing. It was no gay company as the farmhouse fire was, thought Anna, watching the latter lazily through half-closed eyes.

It was the same with the food. At Mrs Flynn's Anna never saw an identifiable joint of meat. She supposed that such a thing might conceivably find its way into Mrs Flynn's kitchen at the weekend when she was not there. Certainly rissoles, cottage pies, and other meat concoctions appeared occasionally for supper and these might have been the residue of an earlier joint. But here, at home, Anna saw a leg of mutton or a loin of pork brought sizzling and savoury from the oven, and her appetite was whetted at once. The apples that she peeled were great golden beauties from the tree in the garden. She had lain in the shade in the hot July sunshine and looked up at them when they had been hard green pom-poms among the young leaves. But Mrs Flynn's apples were bruised from much travelling and their smell was as much of the blue tissue paper in which they had been wrapped for so long as of the fragrant apple itself.

Anna thought of the celery she had prepared for tea. It had been freshly dug that afternoon and was thick with moist black soil which she had watched swirl away in the sink under the onslaught of the tap water. The celery was left glistening and pearly. She had cut through its cold, crisp heart and a slim young worm, pink and agile, had made his escape when she parted the stalks. The celery which Anna had seen stacked in the Elm Hill shops had looked dull and flabby, patched with rusty brown. It would have made a poor home for any self-respecting worm, she thought.

She recalled too the conversation she had overheard between two old countrymen who had boarded the Green Line coach that evening on its last stage. Their voices were warm and burred and they talked slowly of everyday country matters. One had had a fine crop of runner beans. His wife had salted some down. Tomorrow he was going to shift his pig into that little copse at the end of his garden. The other said that last week's rain had 'come down a treat – been a real blessing, it had', and Anna thought wryly of the comments of the Elm Hill people on that same day's rain as they had queued miserably for buses or complained of splashed stockings. In the country the rain's blessing could be seen. Trees, flowers, and plants reached up refreshed and the birds splashed in puddles and noisily relished newly-found worms. In the town the rain was simply a nuisance, drumming on the hard pavements and forming pools for unwary and flimsily-shod feet to encounter, and dripping from shop blinds on to expensive hats. And to Mrs Flynn and her like, rain meant only one thing – an unnecessary mess trodden in.

One phrase in the old men's conversation stuck in Anna's mind. They had been talking of a neighbour's well, how deep it was, and how cold the water even on the hottest day.

'Ah!' said one meditatively and with deep appreciation, 'that's lovely – water is – straight from the spring!'

It was a simple statement of fact, but to Anna, repeating it to herself, it sounded like poetry, for she had her mother's ear for such things. It gave her great comfort to think that such a lovely phrase had come from the appreciation of something so elemental and so everyday. Where in Elm Hill, she wondered, would she meet anyone who praised, so splendidly, the water that flowed from his gleaming taps?

The next day she and her mother walked to the village to buy a loaf. They crossed one of their own fields, to take a short cut, and were watched by a herd of curious young bullocks who watched their passing with large, liquid, unblinking eyes. Anna wondered what went on beneath those curly polls – hope of food, apprehension, or simply a vague interest in another moving animal?

The hedges were full of colour and the two picked sprays of bright yellow hornbeam and rose hips to decorate the house. The autumn air was delicious to Anna, with a tang about it that reminded her of nuts and rustling leaves underfoot and other joys of the dying year.

She chattered animatedly to her mother about life at Elm Hill and tried to put into words not only the difference in outlook between the people she had met there and those in the village, which she had pondered the night before, but more particularly the foibles of the members of Elm Hill school's staff.

'They all seem to have something odd about them,' explained Anna, frowning with concentration. 'There's Andy Craig, being mysterious about a war wound and hoping we'll think him a hero. Then there's Joan Berry – whom I like, mind you,' she added hastily, 'but she's always in an absolute fever about clothes or her hair or some infinitesimal spot no one can see. And even Miss Enderby sighs over a sapphire ring as though she hopes you'll ask her about the Great Tragedy in her life!'

'They're no odder than the people here,' responded her mother. 'Look at Miss Chubb and Miss Bower and that wretched hedge of theirs they're always squabbling about.' The two maiden ladies in question kept up a pleasurable feud over the boundary of their adjoining gardens, and the rest of the village had to be on guard when meeting one or the other in case more fuel were added to the fire by a misplaced word either of sympathy or censure. Mrs Lacey had not lived in a village without meeting the dangers that spring from an unguarded tongue.

They reached the stile that bordered the lane leading to the village and the baker's. Mrs Lacey stood thoughtfully athwart it, one foot firmly planted on each side of the crossbar, and gazed reflectively into the distance. Anna looked up at her parent with merriment. There she stood, engrossed in her thoughts, clutching to her the wild lovely bouquet which would later give her so much pleasure in the farmhouse, so different, Anna commented again, from the faded artificial daffodils which Mrs Flynn dusted carefully each day. Ah, *that* was it! thought Anna triumphantly. *That* was the simple difference between her two abodes. One was genuine, wholesome and homely – the real thing. The other was false and artificial. The words of a pretty and plaintive song that she had heard her mother sing, flashed into her mind:

> It's a Barnum and Bailey world,
> Just as Phoney as it can be,

and she was about to share that moment of truth with her mother, but found that she was still mentally pursuing the oddities of her neighbours, on her high perch.

'Take the Charltons and that quite dreadful boy of theirs they're so horribly proud of. They talk of nothing else but the dreary examinations he's passed.' Mrs Lacey stepped briskly off the stile and into the lane.

'Or poor old Captain Lett,' went on Mrs Lacey, warming to her theme, 'with those interminable stories about life in the North West Passage, or Frontier, or wherever-it-was, in 1905. They drive us all mad, but they do him good, poor old dear.'

She stopped suddenly in the road and gazed at her daughter with intensity.

'That's it, of course,' she cried. 'They're odd – both your people and mine – because they are clinging to something to make them look more important than they really are. It makes them different, and more impressive, they hope, than the rest of us.'

'Well, I think it makes them look pathetic,' answered her daughter sturdily, one hand on the knob of the shop door.

'I don't agree,' said her mother slowly. 'I think it makes them more lovable.'

The village grocer was a large cheerful man who had known Anna all her life and took a great interest in her new job. He was also the village baker, and he led the way to the bakehouse at the rear of the shop across a narrow paved yard.

Anna had always loved the bakehouse. It smelt deliciously of Mr Crook's far-famed doughnuts and lardy cakes and was a warm fragrant haven on a cold winter's day. An enormous scrubbed wooden table stood in the centre and wooden racks near by held the crusty loaves as they aired.

Anna thought of Mrs Flynn's flabby wrapped slices of bread as she surveyed the beauties lined up before her. There were fat cottage loaves with a generous dimple in their crusty tops, long golden 'twists', oval-topped wholemeals, Coburgs with four perky ears, and double-length quarterns which would be taken, Anna knew, to a boarding school or two near by. A batch of small rolls on a separate wire tray meant that someone in the village was giving a party. Mr Crook made those specially, for there was no particular demand for such refinements every day in the village.

Propped against the whitewashed wall near the great oven were two long wooden shovels or peels, which were used to lift the hot loaves out; and in the corner an enormous mixer already held the flour and other dry ingredients ready for the next batch of loaves. On the red brick floor clean flour sacks were spread, and Mr Crook's smoke-grey cat lolled upon one of them, washing a paw indolently and enjoying the luxurious warmth around her.

It did one's heart good, thought Anna, remembering the flash of truth which had illumined the clouds in her mind during the walk, to see something so genuine. She looked with new affection at Mr Crook as he busily shrouded her mother's lovely loaf in generous swathes of tissue paper. He looked as cleanly comfortable and as warmly cheering as his own bakehouse, and with his lifelong knowledge of the community which he served he had his place as surely in village affairs as the parson, the schoolmaster, and the doctor.

And where else, thought Anna, as they made their farewells at the shop door, would you find a man willing to spend his Christmas morning cooking innumerable turkeys because his neighbours' ovens were too small, as she knew Mr Crook would be doing before long?

'Not in Elm Hill, I'll be bound!' said Anna aloud, and then laughed at her mother's astonished face.

Part Two

FINDING ROOTS

Chapter Seven

OCCUPATIONAL HAZARDS

Anna's affection for her class grew as the weeks passed. The children were at the stage she liked best – old enough to be able to work and read on their own and yet young enough to be unselfconscious and keen to learn. Their zest for every kind of activity was incredible, and Anna found that provided she could supply a variety of educational tasks for them to do, all was well; but should they ever come to the end of a piece of work and have to wait for attention, then trouble began. The old adage about Satan finding mischief for idle hands to do was certainly in line with the teaching of Anna's tutors and her own growing experience.

The one great, glaring, wicked problem to Anna was the size of her class. Fond of them as she was as individuals, collectively they constituted an unwieldy, noisy, and exhausting mass. The physical difficulty alone of taking a long, long line of forty-eight children about the corridors was tremendous, and Anna suffered much anxiety as she saw energetic leaders vanishing round one comer on the ground floor while the rest still straggled down dangerous stone stairs and along their own corridor above. It was impossible to watch them all, and one high-spirited push would do much damage. One small boy was lame, with his leg in irons, and though Anna let him follow last in the line and put him in the especial care of a sensible friend, he was an added hazard to all their many expeditions.

In the daily physical training sessions in the vast playground Anna found that her voice was often unheard – sometimes, she knew, wilfully – but quite often because the noise of passing traffic, aeroplanes, or the wind that swept the flat wastes, blew the sound away. The freedom of space and air went to the children's heads like wine and Anna always returned to the classroom with mixed feelings. She hated to leave the open air, but was relieved to get her charges back into conditions in which she could manage them more easily.

The classroom, of course, was far too full. Desks were crammed together and such close quarters meant jogged elbows (both by accident and design), kicked legs, and the general irritation engendered by neighbours breathing on each others' necks, overlooking each others' work, and playing with each others' property. To Anna, who had been trained to allow freedom of movement and a certain amount of talking in the classroom, the conditions were doubly frustrating. She found herself bound to quell quite legitimate noise for the simple reason that she was trying to deal with twice its normal volume, and the free traffic of children from their desks to the shelves and cupboards to fetch their own working materials had to be severely restricted. Monitors were chosen to give out the apparatus required, and Anna was amused to notice that, quite unconsciously, she seemed to have appointed the four smallest children for this task, those that could thread their way more nimbly in the meagre space left between the classroom furniture.

It perturbed her too to think how little time she could conscientiously give to each child. She liked to mark all written work with the child beside her, but soon found that this was impossible to do every time with over forty children. She set herself to hear each child read at least twice a week, and knew in her heart that it should be a daily exercise if conditions would allow. When an epidemic of influenza swept the school, towards the end of her first term, Anna was astonished to find how light and rewarding it was to teach thirty children and how much less strained the atmosphere of her classroom. More than once she thought of the village school at home where about fifty children were divided between three teachers. Despite the difference in the range of age, and the difficulties this raised, Anna envied those three heartily. No wonder they looked cheerful and motherly and had time and energy to chat in the lane as they wheeled their bicycles beside the mothers, thought Anna.

The question of the placing of desks had presented some problems to Anna who had been told that 'never, never, should they be in straight rows facing the blackboard', by an earnest lecturer at college.

'As informal as possible,' she had emphasized. 'Let friends put their desks together and get to know how to work with each other. Turn the desks this way and that as the lesson demands. Make a lovely big work-table for cutting-out activities by pushing four or six together. Or make a cosy half-circle ready for story time and the picture-drawing session after, it. Be imaginative with your space and your furniture!' she had exhorted her pupils.

Anna often thought of this good advice as she wryly surveyed her jammed classroom. There never seemed to be time, let alone space, to plan all these manoeuvres, and the sound of forty-six desks, forty-six chairs, and their forty-six owners would have been almost too much, even for Anna's healthy young nerves.

She had, after many experiments, evolved a system which seemed to combine a certain informality with ease of movement and yet allowed each child to see the blackboard which ran across the width of the wall behind her desk. She was rather proud of her arrangements, but criticism was soon to come – not from Miss Enderby, who approved the final pattern – but from a visiting inspector.

Anna was amazed at the consternation with which his advent was greeted by the staff of Elm Hill. She had always imagined that an inspector's primary purpose was to help and advise teachers. She had certainly known no reason why she should fear them, so that the trepidation felt by the older members of the staff, in the face of these necessary visitors, surprised her. It was probably a legacy from the bad old days of 'payment-by-results' of which she had heard.

The first she knew of Mr Andrews's approach was the dramatic entry of Miss Hobbs into her classroom.

'He's come!' she announced, eyes flashing.

For one dreadful moment Anna thought she must be referring to a dangerous lunatic who had escaped two days before from the local hospital and still remained at large. She was weighing up the merits of sending her class home immediately against those of barricading the door and submitting to a state of siege until the local fire brigade could be summoned to evacuate the children from the windows, when Miss Hobbs elucidated a few further details.

'An inspector, Mr Andrews. A fiend incarnate, dear. And has a phobia about lighting. He's with Miss Enderby now. Thought I'd warn you.'

'But what is there to do about it?' inquired Anna, bewildered but reasonable.

'Well, you might see your cupboards are tidy,' suggested Miss Hobbs, already retreating to fly to the next classroom with the dire tidings. 'He's the one that opens cupboard doors.'

'Then he'll have the lot falling out on him in here,' retorted Anna to Miss Hobbs's receding back. The skinny red-haired door monitor, who rejoiced in the name of Gabrielle Pugg, had barely time to close the door behind her before it opened again and Miss Enderby entered with Mr Andrews in tow.

Introductions were made and the children rose politely, if tardily, after a few menacing grimaces from their head teacher. Gabrielle attended to her duties and Miss Enderby left Mr Andrews in Anna's care.

He was a portly little man, with a pink, gleaming, bald head and bright blue eyes which Anna saw were fixed anxiously on the windows which ran down the side of the room. He looked, with growing agitation, at the row of children who sat with their backs to the window as a result of Anna's careful arrangement of the desks.

'Oh dear, dear, dear!' clucked Mr Andrews, hastening across the room. 'This will never do! Never do at all! We must alter this, my dear young lady, before their eyesight is quite ruined!'

Anna thought that he was uncommonly like the White Rabbit in his fussy anxiety.

'Jump up, children, jump up!' he exhorted the long row of

delighted boys and girls, waving his plump hands up and down energetically. In various parts of the classroom other children leapt joyously to their feet, only too glad of an excuse. The noise almost drowned Mr Andrews's running commentary, delivered rather breathlessly as he began to drag the desks into a line, one behind the other, facing the blackboard.

'Can't have them sitting in their own light,' puffed Mr Andrews, stepping heavily on to a child's foot. 'I can't think why you haven't been told of it before –'

'It's difficult to fit the numbers in,' began Anna. 'It seemed the best way –'

'Never mind the numbers,' said Mr Andrews grandly, as though a dozen or so excess children could easily be disposed of in the waste-paper basket. 'The first essential of any classroom is Correct Lighting!'

He paused for a minute in his labours, partly to regain his breath and partly to wag an admonitory finger at Anna. The hubbub, she noticed with alarm, was becoming tremendous as the children threw themselves into desk-shoving with joyful and aimless abandon.

'The light must *at all times*, and at *whatever cost*, come from the left-hand side. In that way the child works with the light on his paper, unshaded by his body or his working right hand.'

'What about the left-handed ones?' asked Anna, beginning to feel rebellious at the wagging finger.

Mr Andrews looked a trifle taken aback but recovered with commendable aplomb.

'They must be catered for separately,' he said firmly, bending to his task again. Anna wondered if this meant that one or two classrooms should be reversed in the architects' plans and labelled 'For Left-Handers Only'. There was no end to the complications if one really let oneself go.

The noise was now so great that Anna felt that the best thing was to settle Mr Andrews's desks as he wanted before trying to quieten her class again. In any case, he seemed oblivious to the chaos around him, tugging busily at the furniture and brushing aside any children who crossed his path. After ten minutes' furious work he had all the desks facing front in the style most deplored by Anna's college tutor. She waited, in secret amusement, for the next move.

'Now, children,' said Mr Andrews, wiping a glistening forehead with a neat white square of folded handkerchief. 'Put your chairs behind your desks and let us see how you look.'

As Anna knew, this simple request proved impossible to obey. About half the children – the quicker half – squeezed themselves into place by dint of shifting their desks forward a little. The slower twenty-odd did their valiant best to man-handle their chairs, with vigour and appalling noise, into the minute space available. Anger made their complaints more than usually vociferous, and the smug gaze of those already seated did nothing to alleviate the grievance of those unseated.

'No room miss!'

'They've pinched my place, miss!'

'We're all squashed up, miss. Can't get in here nowhere!'

So rang the despairing cries, and Anna began to feel quite sorry for Mr Andrews and wondered how he would cope with the situation. She need not have wasted her sympathy.

Mr Andrews, who must have faced this dilemma many times, appeared impervious to the complaints and turned a happy face to Anna.

'That's the way to have the desks, my dear. The only way! Don't let anyone try to get you to alter them. Light over the left shoulder, remember!'

He nodded cheerfully and made his way to the door. Gabrielle was not quick enough to keep pace with his brisk trot.

'I'll try and call in again before I leave,' he said to the flabbergasted Anna, left among the chaos of her class, and then vanished through the door.

Anna soon found that Mr Andrews was not unique in being a monomaniac. Visitors to her classroom were frequent. Some were inspectors, some were salaried advisers on a particular subject, some students on educational visits, and others were friends of the school.

The inspectors and advisers Anna had expected, for her first year of teaching was probationary and she knew that she would be under surveillance but she had not expected so much vigilance.

There was another reason for the spate of callers, she discovered. Elm Hill was only a small part of the great new suburb which sprawled further and further across the fields to the north-west of London. The education authority was hard-pressed to keep pace with the rapid growth of population. New schools, new teachers, and new methods abounded, and the inspectorate was kept busy as well as the builders.

Many young teachers like Anna had been appointed straight from college to keep pace with the growing mass of pupils and these needed particular supervision. When, as in Anna's case, the building was grossly overcrowded and a new school due to open near by, even more interested officials from headquarters came to pay visits, and Anna came to view these callers with dismay.

The advisers, she thought, were the most trying. Each, rather naturally, felt that his own particular subject was the most important on the time-table and gave so many suggestions, not only for classroom work but for out-of-school activities and involved apparatus to be constructed by Anna, that the poor girl felt quite overwhelmed. These zealous souls, each riding his own hobby-horse, did not seem to see that Anna faced daily two fearsome foes – too many children and not enough time. True, they were sympathetic, in a perfunctory way, about the difficulties which confronted her; but Anna suspected that overcrowded conditions and pressure of time were such commonplaces to them, and their own burning passion consumed them so remorselessly, that they lost all sense of proportion and, as specialists, expected from the hard pressed teachers they hoped to inspire far more than those bewildered general practitioners could possibly give, no matter how willing they might be.

Anna felt at her most helpless when the adviser for arithmetic had had her in her clutches. She had arrived on a morning of torrential rain and wind. One of the classroom windows had defied all efforts to close it, and the roaring wind played havoc with the papers on the children's desks. Rain had spattered in and Anna, much-tried and irritable, had moved some of the desks to the further side of the classroom.

Outside, the cement-mixer rattled merrily and the thudding of another machine told of the birth of the new infants' building, scheduled to be opened next September, in the same field as the present school.

The children were restless and worked uninterestedly at their sum books. The lowest group were having some difficulty in multiplying by five despite Anna's efforts, when the door opened and Miss Birch introduced herself. She looked, more in sorrow than in anger, upon the little band of children plying their pens and struggling with their fives.

'You've done plenty of *active* work about *five*, of course?' she queried.

'Of course,' echoed Anna. 'And in any case, the infant department copes with –'

'The infant department may do,' interrupted Miss Birch forcefully, 'but I hope you continue that good work.'

Anna began, with sinking heart, to submit herself to yet another homily.

'Are they ready to work in the abstract?' pursued Miss Birch. 'Do they *know* five? Do they *experience* five? Have they got a *real feeling* of *fiveness*?'

'I think so,' Anna faltered, 'and in any case they know they've got five fingers on each hand,' she added more bravely.

'Ah!' pounced Miss Birch. 'They may have – but in a row! Now, I do feel most strongly that they should see five in a *pattern*, in a *cluster*, in a *five-group*, which is automatically flashed into their mind's eye when they hear the number five!' She warmed to her theme and Anna's battered senses began to wander.

At the back of the room Arnold had his pen poised close to the cheek of his unsuspecting neighbour. Within a minute, Anna knew from bitter experience, he would call his friend and thus impale his victim's cheek on his nib. It was a simple trick which gave the innocent child much pleasure, and there were still a number of gullible classmates who had not yet had the wit to avoid the trap. Two more boys were having a tongue-stretching match, their eyes hideously crossed.

Children whispered, sniggered, fidgeted, copied each other's work, snatched each other's books, and tormented each other's persons in a dozen irritating ways, while Miss Birch's voice rolled remorselessly on. At last, Anna could bear it no longer.

'Excuse me,' she said, firmly, and advancing to the front desks gave a fair imitation of Miss Enderby's ear-splitting clapping. Hush fell.

'Get on with your work without a word!' said Anna sharply. 'There will be no play for those who talk!'

Meekly, with a martyred air, the children returned to their labours. Miss Birch watched with a reproving eye such heavily repressive methods. Anna could see that she was debating whether she should make some comment on these harsh dicta, so very much in contradiction to her own free activity, but evidently she decided against it, preferring, Anna had no doubt, to make a dignified note, couched in psychological terms, in the report which she would make later on this visit.

With the air of one wishing to change a painful subject for one of agreeable interest Miss Birch opened a leather case and emptied a large number of rings of assorted colour and size upon Anna's table.

'While they're busy,' she said, her eyes lighting up with enthusiasm, 'I'll explain this simply wonderful method of teaching mathematics. Have you met it?'

Anna confessed that she had not, and secretly viewed the project with the greatest misgiving. There was hardly enough room for a book and a pen on each desk, let alone a mountain of assorted rings, and the thought of the numbers that would fall by accident, be projected by design, and generally find their way floorwise accompanied by their own and their owner's noise, appalled her, but she did her best to look happily responsive as Miss Birch handled the rings affectionately and positively crooned to herself over them.

'You can *actually prove*,' said Miss Birch, looking at poor Anna with a fanatic light in her bright blue eyes, 'H.C.F. and L.C.M!'

'Really!' said Anna faintly, watching Miss Birch's nimble hands pounce here and there. In a trice she had taken a handful of rings and arranged them into a pattern.

'I'll show you,' said Miss Birch inexorably. And for the next ten minutes, to her uncomprehending but quiescent pupil, she did.

Later that day in the staff room, Anna was relieved to find that she was not the only one so bedevilled.

Miss Hobbs, bridling with outraged self-esteem, had met her match in a smooth-faced young man, known as the newly-appointed county musical adviser, who had watched one of Miss Hobbs's celebrated rhythmic lessons and had criticized it mercilessly.

'He said it was "*too martial*", if you ever heard such rot!' fumed Miss Hobbs, puffing explosively at a cigarette, 'and that they should *never* march in, or be directed to do things that I say. And the music he suggested!'

Miss Hobbs flung her eyes heavenwards.

'"Woodland Frolics" and "Sousa's Marches" which have been my standby for years have been just tossed aside! Look at this list!' She unrolled a paper on which several titles were written in a flowery italic hand in green ink.

'Prokoviev, Shostakovitch, Bartok – the lot!' said Miss Hobbs, dramatically, 'and not one in less than six flats, I'll be bound! If it weren't for backing up dear Florence I'd have told that young man what I thought of him!'

Chapter Eight

AN EVERYDAY YOUNG MAN

Christmas approached, and Anna began to count the days to her return home. The thought of the quiet countryside, with its bare sleeping trees and empty brown fields, was like a benison amidst the mounting excitement of the exuberant children and the fraying tempers of her fellow teachers.

The draggle-tail shops of Elm Hill began to deck themselves in tawdry finery. Fly-blown paper bells and balls hung in newsagents' windows, and blobs of cotton-wool, strung on thread, simulated snow in the little greengrocer's shop which Anna passed each morning. The piles of flaccid cabbages and sprouts were enlivened by boxes of dates and a silver-papered tangerine or two which appeared among them like some strange exotic blooms in a winter field.

Even Mrs Flynn had caught the infection and had made Christmas puddings from an 'Economical Wartime Recipe' which satisfied her frugal soul and involved a prodigious proportion of shredded carrots. She had been buying, for some time, only the soap powder which offered free Christmas wrapping papers: 'For,' as she remarked to Anna, 'it's just silly to spend money on something that will be thrown away; and yet one doesn't like to look mean.'

Mrs Flynn's economies, Anna realized after several weeks' experience, were the offspring of two strong urges. The first was her inborn love of a bargain and a burning ambition to make sixpence do where another woman would use a shilling, and the second and stronger urge was to appear a little more comfortably-off and genteel than her neighbours. Anna could forgive the first, but not the second, of these reasons for her landlady's cheese-paring efforts.

She had not met, in the country world she knew best, quite such petty ambition. Perhaps it was because people's affairs were more generally known, perhaps her own family minded less than most about outward show – Anna could not tell; but this vying with one's neighbours was a new thing to her. Absorbed interest in others' affairs she recognized only too well, as do all country dwellers, and the diverse pattern of lives influenced by thrift, industry, shiftlessness, and illness was as fascinating to her as her own life was to her neighbours; but it was an interest born of true neighbourliness and not a shallow and spiteful assessment of others for the purpose of self-glorification.

Anna had been shocked one day by Mrs Flynn's bitter contempt for the family next door. They had moved in soon after term began and Mrs Flynn's inspection from behind the top floor curtains, both back and front, had been prolonged and painstaking in the ensuing weeks.

'Put the whole of the garden down to vegetables, they have!' said Mrs Flynn censoriously.

'Why not?' answered Anna mildly. 'They've several children – they probably need lots of vegetables.'

'Letting the neighbourhood down,' snorted Mrs Flynn. 'We've all got a bit of lawn, and a bird bath, or a sundial or something nice. And she actually had washing out on a Sunday! It's so common!'

Anna made no reply.

'And despite that she takes a bag of washing to the launderette. You'd think with all those children she'd prefer to wash herself and save the money,' said Mrs Flynn spitefully.

'She probably has a very good reason,' said Anna firmly and Mrs Flynn subsided into self-righteous silence.

It was about this time that Tom Drew invited Anna to tea.

'I wish I could see the programme about wild animals tomorrow night,' she had said in the staff room one play-time, and was surprised to hear Tom's prompt reply.

'Come and see it at my digs. I've got a television set there. Come and have tea.'

'But what about your landlady –' Anna had faltered, thinking of Mrs Flynn's reaction if she had had such short notice of a visitor's arrival.

'She'll love it,' said Tom firmly; and thus it was settled.

Anna found his lodgings very much more comfortable than her own. The house was a solid Victorian structure, set in a garden thick with the evergreens so beloved by our great-grandparents, about four miles west of Elm Hill along the old turnpike road.

As well as a bedroom, Tom had a small sitting-room which had once, Anna suspected, been the smoking den of a Victorian pater-familias. She could imagine him sitting there, a century ago, at a great roll-top desk, a beaded smoking-cap upon his greying locks, going through the household accounts and wondering what on earth the housemaid did with all those candles and if she were really worth the five pounds per annum she was so fortunate in receiving.

Tom's landlady was a widow of majestic appearance who gave them tea in the drawing-room which ran the width of the house at the back. A verandah shadowed the room, but it was pleasant for Anna to see a matured garden in the dusk through its archways, after the bleak rawness of Mrs Flynn's surroundings.

She gave them hot buttered crumpets spread with 'Gentleman's Relish', wafer-thin bread and butter with home-made apple jelly, and generous slices of a fine dark plum cake which compared favourably with Anna's mother's prized recipe. Anna found herself enjoying it all immensely. To sit in a soft easy chair, with a log fire scorching one's legs, eating twice as much as usual, was extraordi-narily pleasant after a day's teaching, and the contrast with her usual meal of a cup of tea, four Osborne biscuits or a dank thin slice of slab-cake served on a pseudo-Chinese metal tray by Mrs Flynn's grudging hand, made this richness all the more heart-warming.

It was plain that Mrs Armstrong was devoted to Tom. She kept a solicitous eye on his tea-cup, pressed her excellent food upon him, and generally spoilt him. Anna guessed that she had been brought up in a household where the men's comfort came first, and suspected that Tom made a very good substitute for the two sons who had recently married and left home.

'I'll see if your fire needs making up,' she said, rising to her feet.

'I'll do it,' said Tom, forestalling her, and vanishing towards his sitting-room. Mrs Armstrong smiled indulgently.

'He's really such a dear,' she confided to Anna. 'He's been with me over a year. So good-tempered and thoughtful.'

'I can imagine it,' said Anna.

'And so *clean*!' said Mrs Armstrong, with such emphasis, that Anna felt that no adequate answer could be made. It seemed rather an odd remark. Anna began to wonder whether Mrs Armstrong's own family had *not* been so clean, or whether Tom's use of hot water was unusually excessive and made too heavy demands upon an ancient plumbing system. She felt that it was a peculiar virtue to stress to a comparative stranger, and while she was turning over these thoughts in her mind Tom came back.

'I've put some logs on,' he said. Mrs Armstrong began to pack the tea things methodically upon the tea trolley.

'Then you must both go and watch your programme. It's almost time. I shall be here if you need me,' she added, with the slight formality of a chaperon, and dismissed them with a wave of the hand.

It was snug in Tom's little room and when the programme was over Anna was very content to sit smoking and talking companionably.

There was no doubt about it, Tom was a very reassuring person to be with. And uncommonly clean, thought Anna mischievously to herself. Looking at him in the firelight Anna thought him almost handsome in an unobtrusive way. He wore good country clothes and was decidedly better groomed than his male colleagues at Elm Hill. Anna liked too his cheerful demeanour. He lacked the self-pity of Mr Foster and the arrogance of Andy Craig. Altogether she would have thought him very well settled in his job so that it was a shock when he said in the course of conversation:

'I'm thinking of leaving Elm Hill.'

'Why?' answered Anna. 'Don't you like teaching?'

'Do you?' he countered.

'I think so,' said Anna slowly. 'It's not a bit as I'd imagined it. I don't seem to have time to talk to the children individually – there are such masses of them and it makes me so tired I get cross unnecessarily. But I am liking it more as I go on. Yes, I think I'll really enjoy next term. But won't you?'

'No,' said Tom quietly. 'I'm in the wrong job and it's my own fault.'

'Tell me why,' asked Anna. There was a pause while Tom rearranged the logs. Bright flames licked up the chimney and lit up his young serious face.

'It's a fairly ordinary story, but I'll tell you if you really want to know.'

'Please,' said Anna.

'Well, my father owns a market garden between Cambridge and Bedford. It's wonderful soil – grows magnificent stuff – and he produces vegetables mainly and makes a reasonable living.' Anna noticed how his eyes lit up at the mention of the land. That's where his heart is, thought Anna, in a flash of insight.

'But it was pretty hard going in the early years. Both my father and mother were from large families. They both went to the same village school in the Fens, left at fourteen, and got married at twenty. I'm the only child and I'm afraid they've always thought far too much of me. Natural, I suppose, but as someone once said all children need a little' 'healthy neglect" which I never really had.'

'You don't appear spoilt now, if that's any comfort,' Anna assured him. Tom looked amused at her concern.

'They had very little money and both worked like beavers. I went to the grammar school near by and I helped on the home land whenever I could. After a superhuman effort my father managed to buy this market garden and I would love to work there too. But no!'

'Why not?'

'Not good enough for our son,' quoted Tom in mock solemnity. 'Can't have him soiling his hands after all that schooling. He must

73

start higher up the ladder than we did. What else have we slaved for?'

'But if you *wanted* to –' began Anna bewildered.

'Why didn't I say so?' finished Tom. 'Well, I did, in a half-hearted way, but they were so heart-broken at the idea and they'd always been so uncommonly good to me that I took the easy way out. I couldn't disappoint them. They'd set their hearts on my becoming a teacher, going on to college and bringing them credit – and so I just gave in.'

'And you're not happy?'

'I'm happy enough. I think I'd be happy anywhere. Life's pretty good, you know, wherever you find it. But I can't live without the country for ever and I'd dearly love to get back to some serious rose-growing.'

'Roses? Are they the first love?'

'They are,' said Tom enthusiastically. 'My father's started a few on the side, and they are exactly right for that soil! We could have a magnificent rose nursery in a few years there. I can't wait to start!'

'What will your parents say?'

Tom looked thoughtful.

'I don't think they'll mind so much now. I've done the college part and done some teaching. If they see I'm really determined to go back I think they'll be pleased eventually. In any case I should leave Elm Hill next summer and try for a country post.'

'You'd never get such a marvellous building,' pointed out Anna, remembering some of the rural schools in her own area.

'Nor such an army in each class,' retorted Tom. 'That's what gets me down! It's not education. It's mass-pumping, and we get nowhere with it. Who wants a palace, so overcrowded that we have to be policemen, not teachers? I tell you, I'd rather go back to my old insanitary village school with two dozen in a class and a bit of humanity. At least we'd all have time and space to get to know each other!'

The young man spoke warmly and Anna realized that he had thought long and deeply about his job. He would be a sad loss to the school, and Anna felt a small pang of pain at the thought of his going. Not that she had had time to have much to do with him, but he seemed a right-thinking, cheerful young person, who knew what he wanted of life and was now intent upon getting it.

She had food for thought as they went back to Mrs Flynn's together. They said good-bye at the gate and as Tom's footsteps receded up the road, Anna looked forlornly at the struggling lilac bush, the twigs of privet, and the six dead geraniums still planted in the centre bed cut in the sparse new grass.

If this was the best town could offer, thought Anna, fumbling for her key, she didn't blame Tom for returning to the country! Whichever he chose to raise, roses or country pupils, he would be engaged in creating something worthwhile in conditions already far more heartening than those at Elm Hill.

Feeling suddenly rebellious against life in general – too many children to teach, Tom's plan for leaving, the petty meanness of the detestable Mrs Flynn – Anna slammed the front door, made the loathsome little house shudder, and went crossly to bed.

Chapter Nine

PLAYS AND PIPE DREAMS

The bustle of Christmas preparations at school worked the children
into a state of seething excitement. They ran faster, talked more,
slammed doors, scattered blots from pens shaking with excitement,
turned over two pages instead of one, fidgeted and twisted and
turned in a fever of impatience, starry-eyed, for the glory that was
to come.

Anna, her own young spirits rising, could not help sympathizing
with their ecstasy, but found teaching them doubly hard. She
became cunning at adapting any lesson to the subject of Christmas,
using their boundless energy to further the preparations. To attempt
anything alien to this all-conquering force was asking for blood,
sweat, and tears, and Anna bowed to the inevitable.

They read about Christmas, wrote about Christmas, made up
sums about lengths of paper-chains, the cost of presents, the height
of Christmas trees, and the length of stockings. The afternoons
were devoted to rehearsals for the Christmas concert, the practising
of carols, and the eager construction of Christmas presents and
cards for their families.

Anna watched them one afternoon at their card-making, amused
by the variety of methods and materials they had chosen. Outside
the leaden sky lowered over sullen, cold fields, but in the classroom
the lights shone down upon children painting, children cutting out
bright gummed paper with energetic scissors, children tapping
frenziedly at snow scenes with agitated pencils, and children absorbed in unusually tidy lettering.

In the front desk sat George and Peter, hard at work. George
was a large, stolid, slow-moving child, no match for his skinny

volatile neighbour who kept up a running commentary on his actions. It was in keeping with George's nature that he should have chosen to paint, with a fine brush, an elaborate scene of a village inn and a stage-coach complete with four horses in intricate harness. His paint-brush moved slowly and laboriously, his tongue writhing from his mouth as he concentrated.

Beside him Peter had elected to cut out some dashing Christmas trees from gummed paper. They were done quickly he knew and would look effective. He chattered brightly to his labouring companion as he folded his own first piece of green paper, and began slashing dramatically with his scissors.

'This won't take no time, George! Bet I get six done before you've half finished that old thing!' The scissors flashed and triangles of green paper fell swiftly upon the desk.

'Six'll just do nicely,' continued Peter. 'Mum and Dad, and five aunties. How many do you want?'

George sighed heavily.

'Ten really, but I don't expect I'll have the time.' He bent again to his task and began to paint carefully the spokes of the coach wheels. Smugly his companion opened out a beautiful Christmas tree, applied a wet tongue to it back and banged it firmly down upon his folded paper.

'There!' he said triumphantly. 'One done!' George cast a morose glance upon it, but said nothing.

'I might put a setting sun or a robin or something up the corner,' meditated the irrepressible Peter, head on one side. 'Got plenty of time,' he added maddeningly.

He counted five pieces of green paper, stacked them together, and folded them over busily, thumping joyously with a small grubby fist. George began to outline the harness. The bells were going to be uncommonly tricky to manoeuvre.

'This way,' exulted Peter, 'I can cut the whole lot out at once. Won't be no time at all. Here, you'd best get a move on with all that lot to do. Bet you don't get *one* finished this lesson.'

George remained silent, but by the tightening of his lips Anna could see that this goading was almost more than he could bear.

Had he been working alone his slow-growing masterpiece would have delighted him, but the boasting mass-producer at his side wrecked all his own pleasures of creation. He plied his careful brush diligently but sadly.

Beside him Peter gave a sudden yelp of dismay. In each hand he held the fringed remnants of five decimated Christmas trees, and his face was growing slowly scarlet.

'Look at that now!' said the mass-producer, vexed. 'I've been and cut through the fold!'

A smile of infinite satisfaction spread slowly across George's countenance. With a happy sigh he raised his brush and set briskly to work upon the horses' tails.

The Christmas concert was to take place on the last two afternoons of term, for the hall was not large enough to accommodate all the parents at one performance.

A staff meeting was called about a month or so before the dates arranged in order to decide the programme. Anna sat on a hard chair at the uncomfortably crowded long table and watched Miss Enderby at the end. The headmistress gazed at them speculatively over the top of her half-glasses, tapping her pen rhythmically on the paper before her.

'Shall we take it class by class or jot down suggestions as they occur to us?' she asked.

'Suggestions!'

'Yes, suggestions!'

'Suggestions, by all means!' chorused the older members of staff emphatically, to Anna's surprise. She was soon to learn the reason for their unwonted unity.

Miss Hobbs was first to speak.

'I'll take ball games to music,' she announced firmly. 'If that seems suitable,' she added, as a concession to politeness.

'Perfectly suitable,' said Miss Enderby, scribbling smoothly. 'Ball games – Miss Hobbs. Any other ideas?'

'The Mad Hatter's Tea Party,' said Joan Berry promptly. Miss Enderby's pen flowed on.

'Carols and a tableau,' said Mr Foster, before she had finished writing 'Tea Party'.

'Mimed nursery rhymes,' whispered a mole.

'Percussion band,' whispered the other. Their whispers over-lapped and Miss Enderby's pen quickened its pace.

Anna began to feel quite bewildered. All the best ideas were being snaffled with incredible ruthlessness. The others must have been thinking things up for weeks! What on earth could her class do? Music, plays, mimes had all been whisked away before her startled eyes. What else was there? She began groping murkily about the corners of her brain. Her children were particularly quick and agile. Perhaps something to do with gymnastics?

As she fumbled with her thoughts, feeling as slow-witted as George among a number of adult Peters, Tom Drew spoke up.

'We'll have a go at gymnastics of some sort – somersaults, that sort of thing. I thought perhaps a street scene with tumblers and clowns. We could disguise the piano as an outsize barrel-organ perhaps?'

Anna could have killed him, sitting there looking so deferential and innocent, watching his suggestion being inscribed on the fast-filling sheet of paper. As slick and ruthless and self-seeking as the rest! thought Anna rebelliously, seeing her only hope whisked so neatly away from her. She fell to searching the empty cupboard of her mind yet again as the smug, bright voices echoed around her and Miss Enderby's pen scampered down the list nineteen to the dozen.

'The King's Breakfast.'

'Royalties,' said someone importantly. 'Quite impossible!'

'Oh, fiddlesticks! We did it at Brownies last year and I'm positive no mention was made of royalties!'

'Put the babies down for "Christmas Fairies – A Dance".'

'We'll have a go with our recorders!'

Anna began to feel more and more helpless. Miss Enderby's pen slowed to a stop and remained poised.

'Anyone not settled?' she asked. Her glance, bright and apprais-ing, flashed round her staff who had so efficiently acquitted themselves that only a bare twenty minutes had been needed for the concert arrangements so far.

'Me,' said Anna, in a small voice.

Everyone turned to stare at her. A number of people spoke at once. Tongues clicked with concern.

'Miss Lacey!'

'Poor dear! Now, let's think!'

'Haven't you any ideas at all?'

'What about a little play?'

'We've already got three, dear.'

'What about singing?'

'What about dancing?'

'What about a novelty number?'

A novelty number! scoffed Anna indignantly to herself. And what might that repellent name cover? She gazed round at their faces, perturbed, thoughtful, helpful and concerned, but each wearing a suspicion of smug superiority to Anna's jaundiced eyes.

'But you must have *some* idea of what your class can do,' Miss Enderby said, with a hint of impatience in her voice. It was really most annoying for a woman priding herself on her responsive staff – a credit to her own superb staff-handling – to be held up by a stupid little girl who could think of nothing for herself.

'They can do somersaults and things,' faltered Anna weakly, 'and I was going to suggest something like Mr Drew's idea –'

'Then you do that,' said Tom promptly, 'and I'll do a skit on "What's My Line". Come to think of it, I'd sooner do that.'

Anna could have shaken him. It was quite bad enough to have had her first idea frightened into the open by Miss Enderby's impatience. Now she felt a rat as well as an idiot. And how infuriating of Tom to be so maddeningly magnanimous and so bursting with ideas into the bargain! But the faces were still turned towards her, smiling and relieved, and common civility must be served. She turned a grateful smile upon Tom.

'It's very nice of you. Are you sure?'

'Positive,' said Tom cheerfully. 'I'd really prefer "What's My Line". Those somersault acts have to be really good to come off.'

Anna, still quivering with all she had endured, drew in a breath. Tom cast her a quick sideways glance and seemed to feel that something more should be added to his last remark.

'Yours will do it all splendidly!' he assured her hastily. 'And what's more, I'll thread the piano with paper for you so that it sounds like a real barrel-organ!'

Softened by such generosity Anna's rage melted away, and she was able to throw herself with renewed zest into the crazy discussion of ways and means of making the Christmas concert the biggest success that Elm Hill had ever known.

Rehearsals went on to the accompaniment of thunderous activity from the school field where the new infants' block was rising rapidly. Besides the cement mixer's throaty growl, the noise of lorries, the scream of drills, the sibilant swish of stone and gravel rushing from tip-up vehicles, the clanging of metal scaffolding, and the glad cries of several dozen workmen all made Anna's voice inaudible to the children. A near-by airfield added its quota of screaming jets to the pandemonium and Anna, at times, was forced to write her more urgent directions on the blackboard and tap lustily at them with a pointer until she had her class's attention.

This was one of the things that her college mentors had omitted to tell her. There had never been any mention of noise in her teaching duties. If anything, noise had only been spoken of as something rather desirable in class working time.

'Those dreadful, dreadful days,' Anna remembered her frail white-haired Education Lecturer saying, 'when children were told to listen to a pin drop, and to be seen and not heard! What repressed silent classes I remember seeing – little mouths shut, little fingers locked together in laps, not a sound or movement allowed! Remember, ladies, a happy busy noise means a happy, busy class.'

Anna, at times, longed for a return to those 'dreadful, dreadful days'.

She realized that more than half the racket came from outside, but even so, her exuberant class made plenty of fuss on their own. She took to having short 'silent periods' when the children must work without speaking, and these not only saved her reason but, she found, were the times when the class did its best, tidiest, and most thoughtful work. It was about time, thought Anna, watching a duffel-coated architect balancing on a plank high up on the new building, that schools were built with sound-proof walls. Any noise inside then would be legitimate and under control. It was hopeless to expect children, and adults too for that matter, to concentrate amidst such a fury of sound. She comforted herself in those last hectic weeks of term with the thought of the quiet countryside awaiting her and the blissful all-embracing silence of the widespread sleeping fields.

Meanwhile the staff room was a haven of peace, for this was on the side of the school furthest from the builders' activities, and, mercifully, the numbers present were fewer.

Anna shared it with Alan Foster for one period a week when their free time overlapped. He had sent off the children's book, he told Anna, and was now busy with another effort.

Anna looked at his bald head, across which the sparse hair was so carefully and evenly arranged in seven parallel lines with an inch of pink scalp showing between each, and wondered what new brain-child had been born within that striped bony box.

'I've been thinking about our last conversation, you know. About text-books. I think you may be right and that they are not such a good bet after all.'

'I'm afraid I've forgotten,' confessed Anna. But she need not have feared that Mr Foster's feelings were hurt. He was much too engrossed in his new venture.

'It's reference books that are needed now! Take our own class-rooms. What are the books most in use with our top class juniors?'

Anna thought, rightly, that this question was purely rhetorical and remained silent.

'Why, the encyclopedias!' exclaimed Alan Foster, thumping his hand on the table and making the marking pencils jump. 'And the dictionaries! And the reference books! "Go and look it up, boy," we say when anyone wants to know what a coelacanthus is! That's the thing to cash in on these days.'

His moist eyes fairly flashed with enthusiasm and Anna felt like a mother depriving a baby of its bottle when she said:

'But will you have the time? And won't you need an awful lot of real knowledge?'

Alan Foster's flabby face crumpled a little, but his voice remained enthusiastic.

'Plenty of other people get by and make a packet. Don't see why I shouldn't be able to do the same. Besides, I've plenty of friends I could get to do a bit of looking up for me.'

'But it isn't just a case of "making a packet" and "getting people to look up things",' insisted Anna. She felt cross and helpless and annoyed with herself for bothering to sound like a Sunday School teacher, but was determined to make her point. 'A reference book is something to rely on, something of value, something of integral worth. You can't just fling a few vague facts together – simply in the hope of raising money when people will be *relying* on the work you are doing.'

'Oh, I can see that,' replied Alan Foster airily. But Anna knew that he did not see and was not capable of seeing. There he sat, a vast, crumpled, mountain of a man, spattered with cigarette ash, too lazy even to think straightforwardly.

'You'd do better to stop smoking, if you're short of money,' said Anna downrightly, 'than sit wasting the school's time and your own on a lot of hare-brained schemes that won't come off!'

As soon as she had said it Anna was appalled. Anyone would think I was his wife, thought Anna! She began to rush in with gabbled apologies.

'I'm most terribly sorry. I shouldn't have spoken so rudely. Please –' she started.

Alan Foster turned a mild face upon her.

'Don't apologize, my dear. Actually, for a youngster you talk quite a lot of sense.' He fumbled for a cigarette in a squashed packet and lit it meditatively.

'I can't give this up,' he said, blowing a blue cloud, 'but I think perhaps the reference book might be a little too much for me. Besides, I'd have to offer my friends part of the profits, if they'd given me a hand.'

He's absolutely incorrigible! thought Anna. Afraid of giving way to another spasm of frankness, which she would later regret, she rose to put on the kettle ready for playtime tea.

'What about an anthology?' said Alan Foster, raising his voice above Anna's clatterings. 'No work at all, to speak of.'

He puffed thoughtfully, his eyes already brightening to that moist fanatic ambience which Anna was beginning to recognize as yet another sign of wish-fulfilment.

'My brother wrote several books, you know,' he added conversationally. 'Did I ever tell you?'

'Yes,' said Anna. She felt like adding, 'Several times,' but bit it back. There was no point in prodding this cloudy mass. No impression could be made.

'He got up an anthology. Modern poets, I think it was. Friends of his wrote poetry in those days.'

'Did it pay?' asked Anna bitterly, tinkling teaspoons into saucers with furious speed.

'No,' said Alan Foster, in sudden surprise. 'Come to think of it, it didn't. In fact, I believe he paid half the cost of publishing.' He sighed heavily.

In the distance the bell shrilled and the sound of children's voices could be heard. There was a clatter of footsteps outside the door as the staff flocked tea-wards.

'So that won't do,' sighed Alan Foster, piling up his unmarked books. 'What do you suggest now, young lady?'

'Please yourself,' said Anna shortly.

'They're putting the door frames in the new buildings,' said Joan Berry, between sips of near-boiling tea.

'Might get the infants in there by Easter, at this rate,' said Andy Craig.

'Ought to see the advertisement for a headmistress in the *Teacher's World* any day now,' said Tom Drew, dropping four lumps carefully into his cup. 'Going to try for it, Anna?'

'No, thanks,' answered Anna. 'I can't keep forty-odd in order, let alone four hundred.'

Andy Craig looked hastily round the staff room and seeing only five present, dropped his voice conspiratorially.

'La Belle Flo has her great luscious teeth bared to grab this juicy bone, I hear. And, what's more, she's just offered her services to the Deprived Persons' Movement which is Councillor Ormond's pet project at the moment.'

Councillor Ormond was head of the managers of Elm Hill School, but Andy's mysterious nods and winks, as he disclosed his news, had no significance for Anna. Joan Berry, however, had something to add.

'But Councillor Ormond does not like dear Flo, as you should know, my boy. They don't wear the same coloured rosettes on election day. Personally I back Marjorie Jennings.'

'Marjorie Jennings!' exploded Alan Foster. 'Why, she's ten years younger than I am!'

'Well?' asked Joan coolly.

'Well, it's just absurd! A chit of a girl like that –'

'Some chit,' said Tom Drew unchivalrously. 'Must weigh thirteen stone at least.'

'She seems a chit to me,' maintained Alan Foster. '*And* a flibberti-gibbet! Always was. Made no secret of the fact she went to Goldsmiths' for her training so that she could see plenty of the opposite sex.' He puffed out his flabby cheeks crossly.

'I was there some time before,' he added, and looked vaguely surprised at their laughter.

'If the appointments board has any sense at all it will choose a stranger,' said Tom Drew. 'There are about a dozen eligibles in this area, all as green as grass with jealousy, as far as I can make out. One of them told me on the bus this morning the past histories of two of her rivals she's known since schooldays here. It's a wonder they're not either in prison or a mental home, if all I heard was true. And what's more,' said Tom, putting his cup on the tray, 'it's a marvel *she's* not up for defamation of character.'

He shook his dark head sadly, and looked with mock seriousness at Anna.

'My, my!' he moralized. 'What ugly passions ambition doth let loose, to be sure!'

Chapter Ten

COUNTRY CHRISTMAS

The solid comfort of the Essex farmhouse was bliss to Anna after the box-like frailty and pokiness of her lodgings. Here was companionship, warmth and laughter. Besides the voices of her parents and the two young brothers home from school the house itself whispered to her in a dozen different ways. The fire crackled, the kettle sizzled, the old doors squeaked on their ancient hinges, and a loose flagstone in the hall gave a cheerful and familiar thump to the hurrying feet. It was all exactly as it should be, and Anna felt her old self again.

She had arrived at the end of term very much tireder than she realized. Small presents had been exchanged among the staff that last morning and the children had brought cards and handkerchiefs and tiny bottles of potent scent and bright pink soap and Anna had suddenly felt overwhelmingly fond of them all – even Arnold.

Most of the staff were spending Christmas with their families, but the moles, surprisingly enough, were setting off to Austria for winter sports and were almost gay with this unwonted excitement.

Miss Hobbs, answering Anna's civil inquiries about her holiday plans, flushed an unbecoming red and said that she had enrolled for a ten-day course on the teaching of infants.

'Must look ahead, you know. And if Miss Enderby gets her deserts I should like to be by her side.'

'Naturally,' said Anna, trying to hide her astonishment.

'And not a word, please, to the others, dear,' begged Miss Hobbs. 'Nothing may come of our plans. No need to broadcast all one's doing.'

Anna had promised to say nothing, though she did not think it mattered very much if Miss Hobbs's ambitions were known. After all, she was quite at liberty to go on a course, and not many of the staff would be so loyal as to give up most of their holiday for the problematical future welfare of their headmistress.

Anna was relieved to be away from them all and to slip back into the ways of home. It was a relief not to have to guard one's tongue, for Miss Hobbs's last-minute confidence was only one of dozens Anna had heard that term, but to be able to chatter and rag with the boys as they rampaged about the house busy putting up Christmas decorations. It was a relief not to worry about people's feelings, about using someone else's coat-hanger, or tea-cup, or unwittingly borrowing someone else's book. Above all, it was a relief to be with a few people in a large space for a change, and to know that no matter how much noise they made it could never be as shattering and as nerve-racking as the din at Elm Hill School.

During the cheerful bustle of Christmas preparations her father told her that he was taking on a farming pupil. He would come to live with them on the first of January.

'Do I know him?' asked Anna, busy chopping apples for fruit salad on the great kitchen table.

'Should do,' said her father. 'Edward Marchant's boy. Young Edward.'

'I thought he'd taken up engineering,' said Anna. She wrinkled her brows in heavy thought. Young Edward Marchant – a tall gangling boy whom she had met at local parties and youthful dancing classes – yes, she remembered him vaguely. The Marchants farmed a dozen or so miles away on the Suffolk border.

'He didn't take to it,' answered her father. 'He's going on to Cirencester or one of those agricultural places – can't remember which now, though Ted did tell me. Anyway, he's got to get his practical work in, and as Ted asked me I was only too pleased to have the lad. Nice family. He'll fit in here. Makes more work for your mother though, Anna, I'm afraid.'

'We've had pupils before,' said Anna comfortably, 'so I don't expect she'll mind.'

'She was younger then,' said her father. Anna felt a pang.

Somehow one never thought of mothers getting old. Other people's mothers did, of course, but one's own always seemed the same age. She stopped chopping for a moment to consider this phenomenon.

'You'll have to make it up to her in some way,' said Anna, after a pause. 'She could do with a little car of her own instead of that ramshackle old Land Rover.'

She had said the words in jest, but watched, with growing delight, her father's slow smile.

'By George!' he exclaimed, 'that's an idea! I'll think about that one, Anna. She could bob off for her shopping whenever she liked without having to come running after me for the Land Rover.'

He walked up and down the kitchen, jingling the coins in his trousers' pocket and pondering Anna's suggestion. Suddenly he stopped and turned a radiant face towards her.

'It would be jolly useful too to pull a little trailer on market days. Just the thing for a few hens or piglets. I must certainly think about this!' He hurried out into the farmyard.

'Men!' said his daughter disgustedly to the empty kitchen.

The village church, on Christmas Day, was aglow with candles, berried holly, and Christmas roses. The silver on the altar gleamed from Miss Fuller's ministrations, for she would allow no other hand to touch it. As Anna knew, the church silver was probably Miss Fuller's only real interest in life. She lived alone, on a modest income, and had admitted to Anna once, in a burst of mouse-like confidence, that she felt quite useless. Only the cleaning of the church silver gave her the feeling of being of any use to the small community, and to see her bearing it to her small cottage near by, in a clothes basket each Saturday morning, was a heart-warming and familiar sight to her neighbours.

The vicar was in his most festive robes. He gleamed with gold thread and rich embroidery as he mounted the steps to the pulpit and Anna soon found her attention wandering as his light amiable voice fluttered its way to his unusually numerous congregation. He was a happy man, an exception to the usual run of people, thought

Anna, remembering Alan Foster, Florence Enderby, Mrs Flynn, and the other odd fish of Elm Hill.

Perhaps he lacked ambition, mused Anna, and so enjoyed life as it came. Ambition, she was beginning to think, was a two-edged weapon. It could provide a motive, an interest, a spur. It could be the means of living in a state of perpetual hope. She thought of Miss Hobbs at her infants' course and of Miss Fuller at her determined silver-cleaning.

But on the other hand it could lead to self-aggrandisement and self-deception. She remembered Mrs Flynn's patronizing airs to her neighbour, and Alan Foster's literary aspirations which would never be fulfilled, and his boastings about his brother's eminence, which Anna found pitiful.

'And now to God the Father' floated from the pulpit, and Anna rose to her feet feeling uncommonly guilty, for not a word of the good vicar's homily had reached her.

But, as she greeted friends outside, she was conscious of a feeling of well-being within her and could only suppose that, by a process akin to osmosis, she had drawn in spiritual grace from her lovely surroundings.

Young Edward Marchant arrived on New Year's Day and Anna was amazed to see how massive he had grown. He towered over her tall father, his face was plump and bronzed as a pumpkin, and his hearty voice outdid those of her vociferous young brothers. These two were delighted to welcome this addition to the household and followed him about the farm marvelling at his easy strength.

'Ted lifted two sacks at a time!' gasped one with admiration.

'He carried that five-barred gate from the paddock to the stable,' said the other with awe.

Patrick Lacey certainly seemed to be lucky in his pupil. He was cheerful, willing, as strong as a horse, and eager to learn. In the house he proved himself considerate and tidy, and Margaret Lacey found herself growing very fond of him as the days passed. His prodigious appetite was a joy to her motherly heart and a challenge to her cooking prowess. It soon became a source of good-natured teasing by the Lacey family and 'Ted'll finish it up!' became a byword.

Although he was in boisterous good spirits with Anna's brothers, and natural and at ease with her parents, with Anna herself he seemed unusually shy at first. He had no sisters, she knew, and guessed that this might be the reason for his formality with her, and did her best to appear as welcoming as she could.

There was plenty of work on the farm to keep all the men busy, for early lambs were arriving thick and fast. The weather had turned cold, after a mild Christmas, with a wicked north-easter that shrivelled the grass and battered the rows of wallflowers that lined the path to the farmhouse.

One cold afternoon Anna took the pile of Christmas cards, which had decorated the house, to Miss Anderson at the village school. She had taken the used Christmas cards each year, for as far back as she could remember, and the children used them for classroom friezes, calendars, blotters, scrap-books, and all manner of things.

This year she had gone through the cards with unusual care and had selected a number for her own class's edification before setting out on the mile-long walk to the village.

It was not an inspiring day. This truly was the dead of the year. The black hedges stood stiff and splintery with the cold, the wind shrilling through their tracery. Dust and dry leaves eddied at the side of the lane, and small birds were blown sideways on the slipstream of gusty wind. Anna clutched the parcel painfully to her chest, head down and eyes streaming. With the other hand she beat upon her thigh to engender some warmth. There was no doubt about it, there would be snow before long, thought Anna, country wise.

Miss Anderson's schoolroom was a pleasant haven from the cold. An open fire roared behind a large fireguard and a half circle of children sat round it listening to *The Tailor of Gloucester*. Their faces were rosy from the heat and most of them had stretched their slippered feet towards the blaze. Anna noticed a row of outdoor shoes warming comfortably, ready for home time, and thought how cosily domestic it all seemed compared with Elm Hill's bleak cloakrooms and classrooms.

Next door she could hear the infants singing, and beyond the partition the only other class, which was the top one, appeared to be listening to a B.B.C. schools' programme.

Miss Anderson had been head teacher for years at the village school and Anna always enjoyed her visits there, but this time she looked with new interest at the little group in her charge. She knew almost all of them. There were the eight-year-old twins – sons of her father's shepherd – children from the Post Office and the grocer's shop, from farms in the neighbourhood, and houses in the village itself. They all looked as healthy as her own high-spirited young villains, she thought, but were considerably more docile. Perhaps Miss Anderson's years of teaching had something to do with it. Or maybe, she decided more ruefully, it is easier to have a spirit of serenity in a gathering of eighteen rather than forty-six.

She accepted Miss Anderson's invitation to sit and warm herself, and the children eagerly brought her a chair and shifted round to give her a central position in front of the blaze.

Miss Anderson seated herself again at the side of the hearth, book in hand, and resumed the story. Anna sat as quietly engrossed as her small neighbours as the tale unwound. With Christmas still fresh in their minds, the story of that distant snowy Gloucester where the poor old tailor tossed feverishly in his four-poster, while the sound of bells filled the narrow streets, gripped these young listeners. They tut-tutted over the wickedness of Simpkin the cat, and their sympathy, Anna was amused to see, was wholly for the mice. Simpkin's hunger was all that he deserved, it seemed to them.

They leant forward eagerly to see the beautiful little pictures as Miss Anderson held out the book for them to see. How lovely, thought Anna, to be able to show the whole class such minute illustrations without moving from one's chair! At Elm Hill she would have been forced to walk slowly round the room, letting a few at a time see the treasures, while the others fidgeted with impatience or lost interest altogether.

Yes, despite the drawbacks of Miss Anderson's village school, the dark old-fashioned building, the primitive and distant sanitation, the comparative paucity of stock which made Anna's Christmas cards all the more welcome, and the great range of age in each class, still Miss Anderson had one priceless advantage.

Her class was small, and each individual in it was known to her as if he were her own flesh and blood; known far more intimately than ever Anna could hope to know her own large brood at Elm Hill, despite the laudable efforts of the Parent–Teacher association.

She felt suddenly and insanely envious of Miss Anderson. There she sat, grey-haired, wrinkled, wrapped in a green stuff frock that was four years old and unfashionably long. The small hands that held the book were chapped and grubby from keeping the great fire fed, and her thin voice was cracked with much use. But she was a good teacher and her children returned the affection and care she gave them. They all, it seemed, had time for one another; and Anna envied her luck in having a family around her, spinster though she was.

At Elm Hill, Anna knew, the size of her class precluded any such family feeling, and thinking of next term in that chilly overcrowded palace, Anna relished the flickering firelight in the darkening schoolroom as a happy anachronism, and wondered, for the first time, if such little schools would still be found in the English countryside when she had served her apprenticeship and felt free to choose her own place.

Chapter Eleven
JOAN'S PARASITE

The walls of the new school had leapt up several feet when Anna returned, and already the gaunt framework of the roof was outlined against the sky.

It was to be a building of one storey and from Anna's high window she could now see how extensively it spread. Under the skeleton roof she watched the workmen and the duffel-coated architect thread their way along embryo corridors and into future classrooms still open to the blustering winds and unkind January skies. Her headmistress too, she noticed, made her way to the classroom windows, whenever she had occasion to call upon her, and stood gazing reflectively upon the scene of her hopes.

There was a speculative gleam in Florence Enderby's eye these days, which did not escape her staff's attention, and her public activities had increased tenfold.

She was in attendance at the Civic Ball, charity concerts, and innumerable public meetings held under the pinnacled roof of Elm Hill Town Hall; and all sorts of plans for opening her own school to the general public, as well as the pupils' parents, filled her staff with alarm tempered with amusement.

'Flo's publicity campaign,' Joan Berry remarked tartly to Anna one day, 'is going to make this place unbearable. She's just told me – politely of course – that I might be more comfortable in a fuller skirt. "Those side-slits, dear, must be draughty in this weather!"' Joan mimicked her headmistress's pontifical tones with cruel accuracy.

'I've been told to take down two wall pictures with torn corners,' observed Andy Craig, adjusting the spotted silk sling which had replaced the wrist strap during this term. 'I was told they looked slovenly.'

'Mark my words,' said Joan, 'there'll be an almighty blitz on us all until this confounded appointment's made. We'll have to face parents and all the local educational big-wigs flocking through the classrooms to see what a marvel dear Flo is.'

'Let's hope she gets it,' said Andy Craig. 'Life here won't be worth living if she doesn't. I think I'd go back in the R.A.F., if it weren't for this!'

He waved the sling bravely, winced creditably, and gave a sidelong look at Anna to see if she had noticed. Much to her annoyance, she had.

The weather continued to be bitterly cold. The muddy rutted roads were as hard as concrete and the wire netting which divided the new gardens was rimmed throughout each leaden day with whiskers of frost.

It was now that the flimsy shoddiness of Mrs Flynn's house was exposed. Wicked draughts blew under ill-fitting doors and the tiled bathroom was like a refrigerator. Condensed steam ran steadily to the floor from the chilly walls and the ventilator, already rusting high in the wall, emitted a thin scream as the wind whistled across the surrounding marshland and forced its way through the aperture.

Anna, despite a hot water bottle and a meagre smelly oil heater provided grudgingly by Mrs Flynn, could not get warm in her bedroom. The mattress was thin, and the blankets heavy but largely of cotton and smelling dismally of dog-biscuits. A lumpy eiderdown, which Mrs Flynn unearthed at Anna's timid request, added its quota of moth-ball perfume to the general unsavouriness. The weekends, in a house with two-feet thick brick walls, massive fires, and a snug bed, grew doubly precious at this time of year.

At school the children sniffed and coughed and rubbed chilblained toes and fingers. They disliked going out to play in the freezing playground and huddled, hiding, in the cloakrooms or lavatories. They became liverish and irritable, and the brisk north-easter did nothing to relieve their discomfort.

In the staff room Alan Foster displayed, with misplaced pride, a hideous cold of gargantuan proportions.

'I'b an absolute bartyre to codes,' he told the assembled company one playtime.

'You should really be in bed,' scolded Miss Hobbs.

'Card leab all the work for you good beople to do,' said Alan Foster nobly. A shattering sneeze escaped him before he could find his damp handkerchief. After several earsplitting convulsions he stood helplessly in their midst turning his bleary streaming eyes from one to the other and drawing in great gulps of air through his flabby mouth.

'Oh dear! So sorry!' he moaned thickly. His colleagues, edging back, looked at him with dislike.

'No business to be here, giving us all your germs,' said Joan Berry roundly, voicing the private feelings of them all. 'Why on earth don't you go home?'

'She's right, old chap,' said Andy Craig. 'Sorry to lose you and all that, but we'd sooner have your class than your cold – to put it brutally.'

Alan Foster gave him a cold watery glance.

'I'b nod in the habit,' he said, with ponderous dignity, 'of givig ub by job for a cobbod code. I'b still capable of teaching I hobe.'

'You're a mutton-headed old chump,' said Tom Drew, 'and a walking menace into the bargain.'

But he said it affectionately, and as he passed Mr Foster's indignant bulk on the way to the door he gave him a clap on the shoulder which appeared to comfort the sufferer.

It was during this bleak period that Anna was invited to Joan Berry's flat for the evening.

She lived nearer town, about five miles from Elm Hill, in a prosperous and pleasant suburb where lime-trees shaded the broad pavements in summer and twinkling gas lamps threw a welcoming beam upon tall evergreens and solid gateposts in winter.

Joan's flat was one of three in a comfortable red brick house set back from a quiet road. A little lantern with amber glass shed a warm glow over the deep porch as Anna waited, stamping her feet to keep them from freezing.

Joan was a cheering sight when she opened the door. She wore a bright red frock, unadorned with jewellery, which showed up her dark good looks. Anna followed her elegant legs and stiletto heels up the shallow stairs and marvelled at the warmth which enveloped the house.

A fire crackled and sparkled in the grate in Joan's sitting-room, and to Anna's surprise, a young man rose from an armchair beside it.

'This is Maurice Long,' said Joan, 'an old friend of mine. Unfortunately, he can't be with us for long, but we've time to have a drink together.'

The young man, Anna thought, looked a little put out by these words, but he smiled pleasantly enough and busied himself with preparing the drinks for Joan. He was small and very fair, with the girlish good looks which would lapse, later in life, to tubby dapperness. His manner was deprecating and Anna felt that he stood in some awe of Joan to whom he occasionally gave a fleeting glance of apprehension.

'Maurice has been working at a travel agency,' said Joan, nodding towards a pile of vivid leaflets which lay on the floor, 'and I've been torturing myself trying to choose a summer holiday.'

'Portugal!' said Maurice, firmly. 'It's quite perfect – and not outrageously expensive.'

'Oily cooking,' said Joan.

'Where have you planned to go?' asked Maurice, refilling Anna's glass neatly.

'Well, I suppose it will be Devon again,' said Anna. It sounded very unadventurous and she sought to justify such mediocrity. 'You see, my father can't get away in August, because of the harvest – he's a farmer. And my mother takes this little cottage and my brothers and I seem to go every year.'

'It sounds charming,' said Maurice with polite enthusiasm. 'Did you say your father farmed? Are there any openings in farming?'

Anna looked at his delicate hands and willowy figure, and wondered how he would fare at baling on a scorching August day, or if he could push his way, buckets in hand, through a milling mob of hefty hungry pigs in a muddy pig pen. She thought of Ted, her father's pupil, who would make two of the slight young man before her.

'Have you done any farming?' she asked cautiously.

'No. No, indeed. But there appears to be a great deal of money in it these days. And it must be a wonderfully healthy life. And I gather that the things one can slide on to the expenses account are legion. I must say it all sounds most attractive.'

'It's usual to have some practical experience first,' said Anna, ignoring the temptation to debate the financial side of farming. 'Then of course you could go on to an agricultural college for your training.'

Maurice laughed lightly and looked at Joan.

'Afraid I'm a bit long in the tooth for such things. Besides I'm an orphan boy and must earn while I learn.'

'It's almost seven o'clock,' said Joan pointedly.

There was an uncomfortable little silence. Maurice's weak mouth took on an almost mutinous line and Anna wondered what the mystery was.

'I'm not at all sure –' he began, in a voice rather high with tension.

'Maurice!' said Joan. Her voice was low and steady. It held a hint of appeal as well as warning. 'You promised, you know.'

'Oh, very well,' said Maurice pettishly. He put his empty glass on the tray and braced himself. His face was thunderous, but he did his best to smile at Anna as he bade her farewell.

'Have you got the key?' asked Joan to his departing back. Maurice hit his pockets rapidly and then nodded.

At the door he turned, and looking rather ashamed, addressed Joan.

'Good-bye, dear. Don't wait up. I may be late.'

As the door closed behind him Joan let forth a sigh of relief, blowing smoke ceilingwards.

'Poor dear!' she said affectionately. 'I didn't think he'd go, you know!'

'Where is he going?' asked Anna, as Joan seemed to be inclined to confide.

'To the Youth Club. I help there twice a week and Maurice has been coming with me while he's been here. Tom Drew comes now and again and teaches the boys to box.'

She rose to replenish the fire with small logs and Anna was glad that she could not see her astonishment. That the glamorous Joan Berry, whom Anna had dismissed as an attractive but quite selfish person, should give up two evenings a week to Youth Club work was a distinct shock to the unsophisticated country girl. She had never been inside a Youth Club herself and had vague impressions of tough Teddy boys and tougher Teddy girls jiving and jeering, between bouts of bottle-throwing and impassioned love-making. She looked at Joan with new respect.

She felt, too, extremely curious about the relationship between her hostess and Maurice Long. It seemed odd, to say the least of it, to hear Maurice announcing that he would be staying the night when, as Anna knew, there was only one bedroom containing Joan's single bed, in the little flat. Anna hoped she wasn't prudish, but it was not the sort of situation she met with in her own home background, and the blood of generations of upright East Anglians beat steadily in her veins. Somehow one didn't think of teachers – well – living in sin. She gazed, perplexed, at the dancing flames and Joan Berry, glancing at her pink bewildered face, smiled and told her more.

'Maurice is living here for a bit.' She gave a laugh, bubbling with amusement. 'Don't think, dear child, that he is living *with* me: Perish the thought! The dear boy sleeps chastely and rather uncomfortably, I suspect – on that couch over there. But he really is an old friend. I've known him since he was six and he fell off a punt at Pangbourne at the same picnic.'

'What does he do?' asked Anna, hoping to shift to safer ground. All this was really most surprising and unorthodox.

'At the moment, nothing,' said Joan and her beautiful dark eyes clouded. 'He can't stick at anything. He's had twelve jobs in the last four years and now he's just had the sack from the travel agency. That's why he's here. He's broke.'

'But surely,' Anna expostulated, 'he can find *something* to do. He can't like sponging on you!'

Joan drew a long, luxurious breath through her black cigarette holder.

'Anna, my child, I love you dearly but I must shock your innocent heart by telling you frankly that "sponging on me", as you call it, is exactly what Maurice *does* like doing.

'But no decent man –' began Anna indignantly.

'There are men and men,' said Joan equably. 'Those that you have met are doubtless good honest God-fearing types in the backwoods of Essex who fairly relish a hard day's toil. But believe you me, they're not all like that. Maurice, for one, loathes any effort. You saw his keenness to put in an hour's mild sweating at the Youth Club tonight.'

'But he may stay on indefinitely,' faltered Anna, the foundations of her calm ordered world rolling dangerously. 'And suppose he wants to get married one day?'

'How long he stays,' said Joan, 'depends on how tough I can be with him. I'm much too easy-going I know. And as for marrying, it's the best thing he could do, providing his wife can support him.'

'It all seems so dreadfully *wrong*,' persisted Anna helplessly. 'Why should a girl like you be battened on by a perfectly strong young man who can earn his own living?'

Joan smiled. To Anna she looked suddenly immensely wise and beautiful.

'It isn't really a matter of being a man or a woman, you know. The world has its weaklings in both sexes, you'll find – and Maurice is one of them. He can stay here until I really am broke myself. Then, I suspect, he'll find some other soft-headed host to be a parasite upon.'

She spoke entirely without rancour, her manner as gay and debonair as ever. Suddenly she leapt to her feet.

'But that's enough of Maurice. Let's bring the food in here and have it on our laps!'

The rest of the evening passed more lightly. They discussed the chances of Miss Enderby in what Andy Craig ribaldly called 'The New School Stakes', they talked of books and the theatre, and Anna was shown Joan Berry's extensive wardrobe which filled her with envy and delight. She tried on hats and jewellery, attempted to press her broad country feet into Joan's elegant shoes, with no success, and submitted herself to a face massage with a new expensive lotion teeming with hormones, vitamins, and moisturizers.

They played the gramophone, and listened to the radio, and Maurice's name was not mentioned again until Anna was putting on her coat and shivering already with the thought of facing the bitter night outside.

She caught sight again of the gaudy travel pamphlets which winked from the floor.

'You didn't say where you'd decided to go, you know,' she said to Joan, as she pulled on her gloves.

'I shall probably spend my summer holiday right here,' said Joan lightly. 'Don't forget I have Maurice still in my hair, and despite the economists I don't find that two can live as cheaply as one!'

As she waited for her bus in the wind-swept street Anna had food for thought. How little one knew of people! And how much finer they were when one knew more about them! She thought guiltily of her airy dismissal of Joan as a vain flibbertigibbet, of Andy Craig as a worthless show-off, of Alan Foster as a spineless windbag.

A stray cat, thin but sociable, appeared from an alley and weaved its bony length sensuously about her legs.

'Maybe I don't know much after all,' said Anna to the cat as she bent to fondle its bitten ears. 'There's one thing I've learnt tonight. Joan Berry's a greater person than ever I can hope to be!'

Chapter Twelve

MISS ENDERBY TAKES UP ARMS

Joan Berry's revelations caused Anna to look upon her colleagues with fresh understanding. The thought that Tom Drew, for instance, left the snug haven of Mrs Armstrong's house to help with boxing sessions at the Youth Club on wintry nights made her like that young man even more.

An incident occurred, too, that same week which showed Miss Enderby in a decidedly more favourable light.

One morning Anna was hearing six of her slowest children read. This was a task which she had to drive herself to do, so formidable and torturing was it. The blank bewilderment on the children's faces as they confronted their simple pages, the peculiar and unintelligible sounds which they gave forth, bearing no relation to the words before them, and their complete inability to remember Anna's kindly explanations were enough to daunt the stoutest heart.

Beyond the little circle at her desk, the rest of the class had divided itself into half a dozen groups and read noisily under the vociferous charge of their reading leaders. In the midst of this infernal bedlam, accompanied by the confusion of building noises outside, the door opened and Miss Enderby beckoned Anna mysteriously to her side.

'Can you leave them for a moment, dear?' she asked, her gaze on Arnold who, oblivious of the eye of authority, was about to hit his neighbour a satisfying wallop over the head with his *Happy Valley Reader*.

'It might be as well to leave someone in charge,' said Anna hastily, and clapped her hands thunderously.

'I'm looking for a sensible child to take charge,' announced Anna, above the hum which had succeeded the uproar. As if by magic, silence fell. Arms were folded, tongues stilled, faces became angelic and demure, and feet were placed decorously side by side. Anna, luxuriating in the sudden unaccustomed peace, let her glance wander over this band of meek cherubs.

'I think,' she said slowly, at last, 'it should be Angela.'

At once the silence was broken by the susurration of released breath and the relaxation of bodies, while Angela, a fat young lady with pigtails, bustled importantly to the front of the class.

'Them girls!' said someone in a disgruntled aside. 'Always them girls!'

'Just get on with your reading,' said Miss Enderby majestically, 'and Angela can tell Miss Lacey who has worked well when she returns.'

She bent sideways to Anna and said softly: 'The *positive* approach is always best.'

'Of course,' said Anna politely. Miss Enderby's figure stiffened, even as she spoke. Her eye had again alighted upon Arnold who was now bending back the covers of his *Happy Valley Reader* with such energy that reports like pistol shots were flying from the protesting volume.

'Of course,' said Miss Enderby, raising her voice, 'Angela is quite at liberty to report *bad behaviour* to Miss Lacey. And I shall be waiting in my room for any child who disgraces himself!'

Arnold replaced his book meekly on the desk. Miss Enderby, with a final stern glance, sailed into the corridor followed by Anna who wondered if Miss Enderby's last admonition could be called 'the negative approach' to good conduct.

It was blissfully quiet in the corridor. Miss Enderby stopped not far from Anna's room and faced her youngest member of staff. Her expression was unusually grave and Anna began to feel very uncomfortable. What could she have done? She began to rack her conscience for sins committed and omitted, and though a host of them rose at once, like so many black rooks, not one seemed to warrant the solemnity of her headmistress's demeanour.

'Now,' said Miss Enderby, looking up and down the empty corridor. 'I want you to tell me the truth, my dear.'

'Naturally,' said Anna shortly, panic flooding her. What on earth had she done? Could that light tap on the side of Betty Fellows's head last week have occasioned acute meningitis? Had that half aspirin, administered to Johnny Bates yesterday, caused his death during the night? Both children were now away from school.

Miss Enderby enlightened her before Anna could think of further unnerving possibilities.

'I have had a most serious accusation made against you by Mrs Bond.'

'Mrs Bond!' echoed Anna blankly. Janet Bond was an inoffensive little mouse of a child, with wispy fair hair and a pointed pink nose. As far as Anna could remember she had never had cause to speak an angry word to the child.

'Mrs Bond,' went on Miss Enderby solemnly, 'tells me that you swore at her daughter yesterday afternoon.'

'Swore?' squeaked Anna indignantly. 'I don't swear. At least, not in school,' she added honestly. 'But never, never at Janet Bond. There's never been any need. *Arnold* now –' Her voice trailed away.

'Mrs Bond's story is that Janet was a little late back to school in the afternoon. According to her the child was obliged to spend some time in the lavatory – some nonsense about a dose of medicine, which I don't agree with – but it meant she set out a little late.'

'Just a minute,' said Anna, light breaking. 'She did come late, *very* late. I'd closed the register and marked her absent, of course. Then she wandered in, when we'd started our paper-cutting and I believe I said she was a nuisance. She didn't appear to hear, and was certainly quite unmoved and cheerful.'

'Ah, a nuisance!' pounced Miss Enderby. 'You're sure you only said "A nuisance"?'

'I may not even have said that,' protested Anna. 'It was no more than a faint irritation that I felt – and I certainly didn't swear!'

'Mrs Bond maintains that you called her child "A blasted nuisance". Is that true?'

'Indeed it isn't,' said Anna stoutly. 'The child – or the mother – has made it up!'

Miss Enderby's face relaxed and she patted Anna's shoulder.

'As I suspected, my dear, but of course I had to make sure.' She braced her fine shoulders, her eyes sparkling.

'Follow me, dear,' she said. 'Mrs Bond's in my room and I'd like you to meet her.'

She swept, with stately tread, down the long corridor. Anna, her fears returning, although her conscience, on this score at least, was clear, wondered just what sort of monster would confront her in Miss Enderby's room. She had heard of irate parents. Now, alas, she was to meet one face to face!

Anna's overstrung imagination had envisaged an Amazon of at least six feet in height of militant aspect and powerful physique. Something red-faced, with flashing eyes, possibly brandishing a weapon, and almost certainly wearing a man's cloth cap and formidable boots was the object upon which Anna feared that she must look. It was, therefore, with a shock of relief that she first saw Mrs Bond.

She was as mouse-like as her daughter, with fair, pretty, faded good looks. A missing tooth gave an added childishness to her meek appearance as she smiled deprecatingly at Miss Enderby.

Her headmistress, Anna noticed, was now buoyantly in command. She sailed into action with considerable dash.

'This is Miss Lacey, Mrs Bond, Janet's teacher.'

'Pleased to meet you, miss,' said Mrs Bond nervously. Anna suspected that any fight which Mrs Bond had had on arrival at Miss Enderby's room had gradually run out of her heels whilst she had been left kicking them in that lady's sanctum. Could Miss Enderby have meant that to happen, Anna wondered? She must know all the strategies of parent-teacher warfare. Anna began to feel a little braver.

Miss Enderby settled herself briskly at her desk, pulled forward a clean sheet of paper and, pen poised, leant graciously towards Mrs Bond.

'Now, Mrs Bond,' she began firmly, 'in Miss Lacey's presence, would you be kind enough to repeat your allegation?'

'Repeat what?' asked Mrs Bond, eyes widening.

'Repeat your statement. Tell me again about Miss Lacey's bad language to your child in front of the class.'

Mrs Bond looked confused.

'Well, I don't hardly like –' she began uncomfortably. Miss Enderby's pen rapped peremptorily on the desk.

'Mrs Bond, will you please repeat your statement? Then I shall ask you to sign it while I ring the police and explain things.'

'The *police*?' yelped Mrs Bond, rising smartly from her seat. 'What's the police got to do with it?'

'You surely understand,' said Miss Enderby, raising her fine eyebrows, 'that you cannot come here and make allegations of such a serious nature against one of my staff without putting the whole affair into the hands of the justices. Miss Lacey, one of my most trusted members of staff, is at the beginning of a distinguished career, we all believe. If your allegation is found to be true it will seriously jeopardize her hopes later. Her good name will be damaged. I must see it cleared.'

Anna stood, marvelling at such brave tactics. Mrs Bond, looking distinctly shattered, gazed from one to the other.

'I'm not getting mixed up with no police,' she said obstinately. 'Perhaps Miss Lacey here can tell me what really happened. Children do make up things sometimes.'

'You should have thought of that before,' pointed out Miss Enderby. 'I really think you have been too hasty. I am quite willing – and so of course is Miss Lacey – to let the case come to court. We can't have accusations being made against the staff. It gives Elm Hill School a bad name. Miss Lacey, explain once more, would you, dear?'

She lay back in her armchair, eyes closed, with the tips of her beringed fingers placed judicially together, and listened to Anna's faltering account of the incident.

'Oh well,' said Mrs Bond, 'that's all right then. I see it all now. Been a mistake – that's all. You know what kids are – like to exaggerate any little thing.'

Miss Enderby sat up with a jerk.

'Mrs Bond,' she said with slow emphasis, 'this is not "a little thing". Are you satisfied with Miss Lacey's explanation?'

'Oh yes,' breathed Mrs Bond earnestly.

'And you agree that Janet has not told the truth in this matter?'

'Oh, I do, I do,' said Mrs Bond, bridling self-righteously, 'and when her dad hears about this he won't half give her what for!'

'Oh *please* –' began Anna pleadingly, horrified at any violence being done to her diminutive, if untruthful, pupil.

'You must do as you think fit,' said Miss Enderby ponderously, with a quelling sidelong glance at Anna who was struck silent. 'But if I were in your position I should say nothing of this – er – regrettable episode to my husband. You have behaved rather foolishly, you know. A quiet word to Janet should be enough to stop any further tale-bearing, and I really think that it's a case of "Least said, soonest mended".'

'Oh yes, miss: I'm sure you're right, miss,' agreed Mrs Bond hastily. 'I'm sorry I've caused such a lot of trouble. I really am.'

Miss Enderby permitted a small sad smile to curve her lips. She sighed gently and wearily.

'We're quite used to trouble, Mrs Bond. All teachers are – but we always hope for cooperation from our parents to help lighten the task. It is a great grief to us when we find ourselves attacked by those we had imagined to be our friends.'

She really is superb! thought Anna. After the running through, the sad wiping of the sword blade, with one foot still upon the victim – it was masterly! But genuine gratitude too overwhelmed young Anna. She had been most gallantly defended from her enemy and she felt a new warmth towards her headmistress.

'So, I take it, you *completely withdraw* your remarks about Miss Lacey?' pressed Miss Enderby, rising behind her desk to show that the interview had reached its end.

'Oh yes indeed,' gabbled Mrs Bond, her eyes moist with emotion. 'I won't say nothing more – not even to Harold! You've both been ever so nice about it. I can see I was a bit wrought-up like.'

Miss Enderby inclined her head graciously.

'Then we'll tear this up and forget it,' she said, raising the blank sheet of paper as though it were covered in the vilest accusations. She tore it ceremoniously across and tossed it, with superb accuracy, into the waste-paper basket.

'There!' said Miss Enderby, coming across the carpet and clasping Mrs Bond's hand, more in sorrow than in anger. 'And in future, Mrs Bond, remember that we are as devoted to your child as you are yourself, and please, I beg of you, try to *trust* us!'

There was a moving tremolo in the last sentence which caused a lurking tear to burst from Mrs Bond's eye and trickle down her mouse-like pink nose as she made her way into the corridor.

Anna waited by the desk until Miss Enderby returned from showing her visitor out. The headmistress's face glowed with righteous victory.

'It's always best to be *absolutely firm*,' she announced briskly. 'Now, child, back to your class. They've been left long enough.'

'Miss Enderby,' Anna burst out, 'thank you enormously. You were absolutely wonderful!'

'Oh tush, child,' said Miss Enderby chidingly, but she looked pleased at Anna's outburst, and admired the sapphire on her hand rather self-consciously. 'I only did what any head teacher would do – backed up my staff and my school. Can't have Elm Hill's name dragged in the mud – particularly just now.

'Of course not,' said Anna, cooling slightly. Had her headmistress, after all, only been defending her own, with no real feeling for Anna as a person? Miss Enderby had looked up and was watching her closely.

'You *didn't* swear, I suppose?' she asked softly.

'No, I didn't!' said Anna, so indignantly that it was almost a shout. 'I thought you believed me!'

'I did, my dear,' said Miss Enderby calmly. 'I still do – but I always like to be *quite sure*. Now run along and see to your class.'

Anna, much shaken by all that had happened, returned slowly to the classroom, glad of the quiet corridor's length which gave her time to compose herself.

Yes, Florence Enderby was magnificent, thought Anna, and her admiration for her had increased threefold. But still through all the storm, her headmistress had clung to her own ambition. Nothing should tarnish the name of Elm Hill – for Elm Hill was synonymous with Florence Enderby, the candidate for the new school which was now growing so rapidly beside it. By the time Anna reached her own door she faced the fact, yet again, that she was learning, not only her job, but a mighty lot about human nature at Elm Hill.

To her amazement her classroom was tranquil under the eagle eye of Angela who had ensconced herself in Anna's seat.

Anna felt a sudden rush of affection for her motley crowd of children, born of relief from tension and the return to normal working conditions. Here she was safe, here was a job to do, here she was liked and her word – if not exactly law – was, occasionally, listened to. For the first time in her teaching career Anna felt sure of herself. Could it be the knowledge that she had Miss Enderby's support behind her that gave her this blessed warmth of spirit?

Whatever it was it should be acknowledged, thought Anna happily.

'Get out the sweet tin,' she commanded the beaming Angela. 'And give *two* to everybody!'

The rapturous shout which greeted this announcement must have penetrated to Miss Enderby's sanctum, so lustily did it ring out. But Anna, full-hearted, did nothing to quell it.

Chapter Thirteen

MRS FLYNN'S TEA PARTY

As March broke, the fields of home were brushed with tender green, and Anna rejoiced to see the catkins streaming bravely in the wind and the bright crocuses following hard on the heels of the snowdrops and aconites in the farm garden.

There were young lambs in her father's fields, and two motherless ones in the stable across the yard, which she helped to feed by bottle. They were vociferously hungry, and when the bottle was emptied would suck energetically at Anna's fingers, clamping them firmly between the warm ribbed roofs of their mouths and their rough tongues.

Young Ted fed them more often than anyone and as the weeks passed they grew much attached to him, following him across the yard and greeting him with ecstatic bleatings. He christened them Gilbert and Sullivan, being a devotee of the operas, and maintained stoutly that the two lambs answered to their names.

He had settled in easily and was proving himself a conscientious and intelligent worker. Anna's parents accepted him happily as one of the family, but Anna was not completely at ease in the young man's company.

He had begun to look at her with a certain dog-like devotion that caused her some alarm. His initial shyness had been replaced by a tendency to follow her about the farm rather as Gilbert and Sullivan followed him. He made excuses to stay at the Laceys at weekends, when formerly he went home and Anna's heart dropped on many a Friday evening when she burst into the farmhouse to find Ted's great bulk rising eagerly from an armchair to greet her.

She did not dislike the boy, but she preferred to have her

parents' company undiluted at weekends. She realized that her father was only too pleased to have such willing help and that her mother probably thought that Ted's young company was pleasant to her, but in fact she found it irksome.

It could be so dangerously easy for Anna and Ted to slip into an engagement and then marriage. Nothing would appear more suitable. A farmer's daughter marrying a young farmer who would be heir to his father's neighbouring farm, known to each other, and the district, from babyhood – what could be more delightful? It was this very suitability that put Anna on her guard and made her look upon young Ted's lovesick countenance with some dismay.

Life was too full and too exciting to be tied down yet. There was so much to do and so much to learn about matters and people, as Anna was fast discovering. Such a long-term decision as choosing a husband could not possibly be undertaken yet, but Anna knew already, with a wisdom beyond her years, that Ted would never do. Sweet and slow by nature he would accept all that Anna said and did, and think it wonderful. And Anna was quite sure that to be put on a pedestal was neither right nor at all what she wanted.

The vagaries of human nature, about which Anna learnt more daily, were displayed to her fascinated gaze one spring afternoon when Mrs Flynn gave a tea party.

The fact that Mrs Flynn proposed such an extravagant act was almost unbelievable. Anna accepted the invitation to tea in the sitting-room with due solemnity and wondered what there would be to eat and who the other guests might be, in that order. She still had a healthy appetite, only half-satisfied by Mrs Flynn's meagre fare and the school dinners which left much to be desired.

On the great day she let herself in at the front door, as quietly as the obdurate piece of timber would allow, and crept upstairs to put on a fresh frock. The sound of voices raised in ladylike conversation filtered through the sitting-room door, while the largest kettle in the kitchen filled that tiny room with steam.

On entering the sitting-room she was first staggered by Mrs Flynn's unwonted smartness. She was arrayed in a checked worsted suit which Anna had never seen before. That it should be new was of course too much to hope from one of Mrs Flynn's calibre, and the fact that it had been preserved for many years was apparent from the well-padded shoulders and small lapels which dated from the military influence of the last war. There emanated too from it a faint but unmistakable smell of mothballs, and the velvet collar showed a central crease born of long folding. The blouse which she wore under it was a frothy affair of pink lace, adorned with a sparkling paste bow with only one stone missing. Anna suspected, rightly enough, that it was really a 'dicky' with a net back and elastic round the bottom, and secretly hoped that Mrs Flynn might take off her jacket in a moment of mental aberration so that she might see if she were right; though even as this delicious and irreverent thought flitted through her mind Anna realized sadly that Mrs Flynn would never forget herself to such an extent.

There were two guests, seated rather uncomfortably on Mrs Flynn's painfully 'contemporary' couch. One was a vast woman in a ruched velvet pancake of a hat, who was introduced as Mrs Porter, and the other a small dark woman, with such a large hairy mole on her chin that Anna had great difficulty in averting her gaze from it. She, Mrs Flynn explained, was Mrs Adams whose husband worked in the Council Offices.

From the way Mrs Flynn's voice took on a respectful note whilst imparting this last piece of information Anna gathered two things – firstly, that Mrs Porter had no husband, and secondly that it was Mrs Adams's husband's eminent position which gave her the status which so impressed Mrs Flynn.

They were an easy pair to entertain for Anna soon found that they much preferred talking to listening and she was very content, after a day's work, to sit back and nod and smile whilst the ladies chattered on.

An unusually hot fire warmed the sitting-room. Anna could see that the key of the gas fire was almost perpendicular which meant that it was almost fully on. Such bounty could only mean that Mrs Flynn desired to impress. The tea-table too was packed with iced buns, horribly dainty tomato sandwiches, brown bread and butter, white bread and butter, two kinds of jam, some rather nasty fish-paste, and a dish of rich fruit cake cut into cubes so minute that one might have called it diced, thought Anna, as she accepted an oblong crumb with every appearance of delight. However, this was rich fare compared with her usual Osborne-biscuits-and-weak-tea meal and she made the most of the occasion by eating as heartily as politeness and Mrs Flynn's cautious passing would allow.

Conversation turned to the vicar of the parish, led that way by Mrs Porter who was obviously a supporter of the church. How useful vicars are, thought Anna remembering other tea-parties, running as they do a close second to the weather as a conversational topic!

'He takes the service so *beautifully*,' confided Mrs Porter, her well-powdered jowls wobbling with the intensity of her utterances. 'So reverently! And of course, his voice is quite *wonderful*!'

'Really?' said Mrs Flynn, trying to appear suitably impressed and look in her guests' cups at the same time.

'My husband always said a good voice was the most important asset of a clergyman. My husband was in *oil*,' she added turning to Anna.

Anna fought down an insane desire to ask 'Boiling?' and nodded instead.

'Of course, there are a lot of people,' went on Mrs Porter, 'who *criticize* him. They say that he is too fond of *ritual* and he overdoes the incense and the genuflexions, but personally, I like it. After all, if one *doesn't*, one can always go to chapel.'

'I go to chapel,' said Mrs Adams, dangerously calm.

'Well, there you are!' said Mrs Porter, in a faintly patronizing tone. Anna was instantly aware that Mrs Porter had known this all along, and watched the scene with quickened appreciation. Here was self-aggrandizement in action again.

'And you probably enjoy it very much,' continued Mrs Porter indulgently, nodding the ruched pancake. She spoke, thought Anna, as though religion were a comfortable cup of tea, Indian or China, chosen to taste.

'Naturally,' said Mrs. Adams, turning a dusky pink. She took a deep breath as though about to defend her religious principles, but Mrs Flynn, with commendable aplomb, proffered the tomato sandwiches and spoke hastily.

'And your little boy, Mrs Adams? Is he well?'

Mrs Adams's breath expired peacefully through smiling lips.

'Very well indeed. He's the liveliest of the three. I really don't know what we'd do without him now the others are away at school.'

'Such a handsome child,' enthused Mrs Flynn, 'and devoted to you. His little face fairly lights up when he sees you.'

Mrs Adams simpered and looked gratified.

'Well, I must say he almost hero-worships me. It's "Mum this" and "Mum that". I can't do any wrong in that child's eyes.'

Anna, yet again, marvelled at the diversity of opinion on children. Beauty was certainly in the eye of the beholder. She had yet to find any child with the faintest desire to make a hero of herself but this was not the first mother she had heard claiming devoted allegiance so calmly.

'Frankly,' went on Mrs Adams, her voice getting stronger, 'I don't know how people manage *without* children. It seems so unnatural. I suppose they turn to other things for a substitute. Religion, for instance.' She gave a swift sidelong glance at Mrs Porter who, affecting complete indifference, was studying the tea-leaves at the bottom of her cup.

One all, thought Anna privately. It was Mrs Flynn who saved the situation from becoming ugly.

'It's been a great grief to us that we've never been blessed with a family,' she said, in suitably modulated tones, 'but we can't all be as lucky as you, Mrs Adams.'

Mrs Adams looked uncomfortable. It was a nasty shock to her to realize that in her anxiety to deliver a stunning blow to Mrs Porter she had inadvertently taken a side-swipe at her hostess. Anna could see, from her discomfiture, that she was wondering whether to apologize or ignore the whole concern. Mrs Porter, meanwhile, had brightened considerably at her fellow-guest's *faux pas*.

'Has Lady Parr called on you yet with tickets for the Charity Ball?' she inquired, with fresh zest, of Mrs Flynn.

'No, indeed,' said Mrs Flynn, somewhat taken aback. There was very little calling of any sort done in the muddy new roads of Elm Hill and this was the first she had heard of Lady Parr.

'Doubtless *you* will be there,' continued Mrs Porter turning her soft powdered countenance, like some mammoth marshmallow, towards Mrs Adams. 'It is to take place at the Town Hall where your husband works.'

'We don't go out in the evenings,' said Mrs Adams swiftly. 'We've the child to consider and I wouldn't dream of leaving him with a baby-sitter.'

'So devoted,' breathed Mrs Porter, 'but you really should get out occasionally. All work and no play, you know!' She gave a gay little laugh and a teaspoon slid down the steep incline of her thighs to the floor. Anna bent to retrieve it whilst the barbs flew to and fro above her head.

'I shall get Lady Parr to call specially,' continued Mrs Porter. 'She'll do anything for me – the *dearest* thing, though a little eccentric. Personally I don't mind her decorating her hats with fresh flowers, even if they *are* ox-eyed daisies; in fact, I think it shows breeding to be above petty formalities. Some people are so small-minded. I suppose it's all a matter of upbringing.'

'Oh, please don't bother her,' said Mrs Adams off-handedly. 'We live so modestly – well within our income I'm glad to say, we've both a horror of debt – that I doubt if Lady Parr would want to visit us. In your case it's quite different, of course. You have such a beautiful house and garden, it must be a pleasure for you to entertain.'

Anna was suddenly reminded of a short story that she had once read, called *The Octave of Jealousy* by Stacey Aumonier. It began with the meeting of a tramp with a labourer whom he envied. The labourer in turn envied a slightly more prosperous gamekeeper, the gamekeeper envied the neighbouring shopkeeper, and so on until the tale came full circle, and the great man, bowed down with responsibilities, looked at the carefree tramp and envied his freedom from the bottom of his heart. Here, before her, was Mrs Flynn envying the slightly exalted status of Mrs Adams whose husband was a Council official. Mrs Adams, in turn, envied Mrs Porter's more spacious house and garden and, one suspected from her remarks about her own devotion to her children, Mrs Porter's freedom from family cares. Mrs Porter, it appeared, aspired to be Lady Parr's confidante and equal. Really, thought Anna, the whole thing would be amusing if it were not so pathetic and so soul-destroying to the status-seekers.

It was with relief that she saw Mrs Porter heave herself at last from the couch to make her farewells. Mrs Adams left at the same time. Anna watched them part at the gate with much cordiality and thought what a wonderful thing civilization was.

Mrs Flynn came hurrying back flushed with the success of her tea-party.

'Well, I hope they enjoyed themselves,' said Mrs Flynn. 'They're two nice women, with a lot in common.'

And that's true enough, Anna thought. Fighters both, with eyes alert for a stranglehold! But aloud she said:

'It was a wonderful tea, Mrs Flynn,' and helped her pack the debris of this miraculous meal on to a tray.

Mrs Flynn smiled graciously at the compliment, but, even as she smiled, she bent to turn out the gas fire.

The invitation to tea at Tom Drew's had been repeated several times, and now that the evenings were getting lighter and the hint of spring could be felt even in the desert wastes of Elm Hill, they had taken to walking the few sad footpaths that still threaded the neighbourhood.

One of their favourite walks was along the tow-path of a canal. The tranquil water mirrored the raggle-taggle trees and scruffy banks, both scarred by urchins' play, and cast up a green and kindly reflection. The noise of traffic from the roads near by was always with them, and the factory hooters sent the singing blackbirds squawking in fright across their path, but it was the nearest that this country-starved couple could find to their natural background, and their pleasure in each other's company mitigated the wretched mess of their surroundings.

Anna told Tom about Mrs Flynn's famous tea-party, with a wealth of mirthful detail which amused him.

'But it's really terribly sad,' said Anna, suddenly serious. 'I mean, those poor women – making themselves so miserable, wanting things so badly! Things that really don't matter a button!'

'That's what's wrong with nine-tenths of the people you meet,' asserted Tom, with the downrightness of youth.

'As far as I can see they don't interest themselves in making things. They don't enjoy looking at plants or trees or lovely buildings –'

'Not much scope here,' pointed out Anna reasonably.

'Maybe not, but there's no need to turn exclusively to the TV and your neighbours' good luck for your interests. What beats me,' went on Tom warmly, 'is the neglect of simple pleasures and the complete loss of – well – wonder. Why, I get a thrill every time I plant something that looks like a dead flea and up comes a great, glorious, pulsing flower! Who wouldn't?'

'You've got the knack of happy living,' commented Anna. 'I think you must be like my mother who says that you aren't just given happiness. She says you have to pick it up here and there all through the day. And she does too. She smells a rose, or she marvels at a bird hanging upside down on a spray, she makes a perfect dinner. She really savours life, you know, and from it she builds up a stock of happiness.'

'She sounds as though she's discovered the secret,' said Tom. 'Have you?'

Their footsteps had slowed and they now stood by the canal. Anna bent to pick up a pebble and tossed it into the quiet water, shattering the mirrored picture into a million dancing pieces.

'Not as well,' replied Anna slowly. 'She has so many more interests, now I come to think of it. She reads a lot of poetry, for one thing.'

'She sounds quite a poet herself,' said Tom. 'She can find the essence of things.'

'And, of course, now I'm teaching there doesn't seem to be much time,' continued Anna, still perplexed. She turned to look at Tom with troubled blue eyes.

Tom laughed happily and chucked her under the chin kindly.

'Cheer up, you'll do! But take my warning. Don't you start being a specialist, young Anna, it cramps one's pleasures. So many things, as your mother says, can make happiness and thank God there are still plenty of them.'

He turned Anna round and they started to return.

'Let's run,' said Tom, 'it's getting cold. We'll hare back and light a fire. Now, there's a pleasure for you – a real elemental one. And there's a bottle of wine on the shelf!'

In great good spirits they jog-trotted along the rough towpath while the water beside them changed from green to black and the headlights on the busy highway pricked the twilight with stabbing gleaming needles.

Part Three

NEW GROWTH

Chapter Fourteen

CLASSROOM TROUBLES

As the end of her second term loomed in sight Anna began to feel more used to school life, though there were still some aspects of it which she found disconcerting.

She had not reckoned, for one thing, on the constant interruptions that would crop up during a lesson. The incidental class interruptions she soon became used to, the requests for drinks of water, trips to the lavatory, and forgotten handkerchiefs left in coat pockets. Many, she suspected, were concocted – any excuse to break the monotony of class routine – and her ignorance was being exploited by these astute young barbarians, and as she grew more experienced she squashed these classroom interruptions ruthlessly.

But interruptions from outside were incessant. Besides the constant background of building noises, there seemed to be an unending flow of children entering the classroom with some message or other demanding urgent attention, or bearing lost property.

One morning Anna had dealt with a raincoat belt which had been found and was brought in proudly by a smug infant only too pleased to be missing a Scripture lesson whilst touring the school, a scarf found in the playground, three handkerchiefs, and two notes from other teachers.

The story of Daniel in the lions' den progressed in spasmodic jerks as the door opened and shut, time and time again. The interludes followed a set pattern. The entering child planted itself before the class, held up the object needing an owner, and said importantly:

'Anyone's here?'

A full-throated chorus of:

'No! Not 'ere, mate! 'Tain't ours!' would blast the invader, who would smirk at Anna and retire to continue the pleasurable progress.

At last Anna determined to take a stand. She would finish the story of Daniel despite interruptions. She posted Janet, the militant Mrs Bond's daughter, at the door and forbade her to let anyone enter. As she did not want the child to miss the story, nor did she want Miss Enderby to see a child of hers waiting outside the door as though banished for bad behaviour she let Janet stay inside, with one hand on the door knob.

'And when I can see faces and not backs of heads, and when you've quite finished talking, David Watts, and you've finished tying up your shoe-laces, Jean Pratt – then I'll go on with the story,' said Anna tartly.

Gradually the turmoil subsided and in the fitful peace which followed, she continued.

'So Darius realized that he had been tricked by the presidents and princes, and he felt very sorry for Daniel who had been thrown to the lions –'

There was a scuffling at the door. It opened a crack and was promptly slammed back by Janet. The heads which, on the whole, had been turned towards Anna, now swivelled doorwards.

'He felt very ashamed of himself,' continued Anna doggedly, 'and spent the night praying. He could not sleep –'

A sustained thumping began at the door and some of the class began to snigger and exchange delighted glances.

'Nor could he eat, Arnold,' said Anna, glaring at the malefactor. 'And as soon as morning broke he –'

A piping sound was added to the thumping, and the door began to edge open. Janet, pressing against it with her shoulder, began to break into giggling protests.

'Can't help it, miss. He keeps all on pushing, miss. It's a infant, miss.'

'Let him in,' said Anna savagely.

Janet swung back the door to reveal a two-foot high cherub

holding a brown paper carrier bag with great care. His face was wreathed in triumphant smiles at having at last gained access.

'Stand by the cupboard till I've finished,' snapped Anna. The smiles vanished and a woebegone expression, which normally would have melted Anna's kind heart, replaced it. Bewildered but obedient he took his place, occasionally peering into the depths of the bag.

The children watched him with interest and though Anna continued with the tale of Daniel's vindication with all the narrating powers she could muster, yet she was conscious of having lost the major part of their attention.

'And so,' she wound up, 'Darius wrote the decree saying that Daniel's God was the true one, and Daniel was recognized as a very brave and honest man.'

She turned impatiently to the waiting figure.

'Let's see. Quickly now,' she said imperiously, as the child started towards her. And what might that contain this time? Anna wondered. Half-a-dozen gym shoes, all odd? A derelict train set? A couple of jigsaw puzzles, hopelessly muddled together? Anna was fast becoming acquainted with the flotsam and jetsam thrown up by the surging waves of school life.

The child, beaming again, parted the top of the bag carefully.

'Would you like to show your class –' he began, as though repeating a lesson.

'Yes, yes!' said Anna hastily, thrusting her hand into the depths. She withdrew it rapidly, with a yelp.

The bag contained a fine hedgehog.

School dinners, too, were another occupational hazard, Anna soon discovered. The noise and the children's appalling table manners almost overwhelmed her, and she certainly had very little appetite for the food which she was obliged to eat in their company.

Their home backgrounds varied, she knew, and she was prepared for a certain amount of slovenly behaviour. But almost all ate with their mouths open, displaying half-masticated food in the most nauseating way, and they crammed in great spoonfuls far beyond the comfortable capacity of their mouths. This was partly greed, she realized, and partly excitement; but she noticed in her classroom, as well as in the dining-room, that a large proportion of the children breathed through their mouths rather than their noses. When she tried to correct this she discovered that almost all the children found nasal breathing difficult, and could only suppose that this was due to a variety of reasons – possibly adenoids, possibly habitual catarrh, due in some cases, she suspected, to a diet almost exclusively of starch, and, of course, to wrong breathing habits started in babyhood and now firmly established. In any case, this common malady did nothing to help their mode of eating and even Anna's robust appetite failed her at midday dinner.

The children were allowed to talk, but their voices, raised above the clatter of their knives and forks, the crashing of plates and each other's conversation, soon reached such a crescendo of noise that the teacher in charge would ring a bell and demand silence, every now and again. Added to this the food was so badly cooked and served that it was a wonder to Anna that the children attacked it with such gusto.

Their favourite sweet was red jelly with blobs of *ersatz* cream tasting and smelling like face cream. This was greeted with roars of applause when it appeared at the serving hatch, and the long line of children bearing their plates progressed at a smarter pace than usual as each child hoped to polish off his first plateful in the expectation of a second helping. And many a grubby finger was run unhygienically round the plate and sucked loudly and lovingly to savour the last morsels of this delectable sweet.

Another problem, which Anna found a difficult one to solve, was the management of her classwork as opposed to everyday teaching and discipline.

Preparing lessons was a fairly straightforward business, undertaken in the evenings, in the comparative· peace of Mrs Flynn's establishment, and with the help of reference books, maps, pictures, and so on. Catching and holding her class's attention was becoming easier as the months passed and Anna's authority was recognized by the children and her own self-confidence grew. But there were difficulties in organizing the children's work which Anna had heard nothing of at college.

Apart from the impossibly large number in the classroom which was the arch-problem, there was the difference in speed at which children worked. Poor Anna found that she would spend most of her precious dinner hour in putting out paper and crayons for an afternoon's art lesson, would spend ten minutes or more explaining carefully that they were going to attempt to design an all-over wallpaper pattern, would show them how to fold their paper and perhaps give a few simple examples to start the more adenoidal and inartistic members of the class, and would then relax in the hope that the rest of the lesson, stretching ahead for another forty minutes, would he happily and usefully filled with artistic endeavour.

Alas for such fond hopes! Within five minutes two or three slapdash individuals would have scrawled a motif in each square, coloured it in with a frantic crayon and rushed to Anna for approval.

'Finished!' they would say proudly, sniffing cheerfully. 'Can we draw on the back?'

At first Anna would protest. The pattern was too sketchy, it was carelessly done, they must go back and improve it. And they were not to hurry. There would be no prizes, Anna said firmly, for the people who finished first.

Sometimes this worked, but with the one or two incorrigibly lazy it became simpler to let them turn over and expend what little energy and talent they had in drawing cowboys and Indians, ponies, ballet dancers, or simply a mammoth Union Jack in variegated colours – this last a firm favourite with the really backward members of the class.

At the other extreme, of course, would be the painstaking perfectionists who rubbed out as fast as they drew, and attempted designs of such intricacy and flamboyancy that only half the work was completed when the bell rang for playtime. Then there would be a great outcry for more time to finish.

'Can't we do them after play?'

'Can't we crayon while you read us *The Heroes*?'

'Can we take them home to finish them?'

'Oh, Miss! Please, miss! Oh, miss, do let's!'

It was a basic problem of class management which could only be mitigated, and never completely overcome.

Anna's severest shock, in this connexion, came one day when she decided to look through her class's work-books. Each child had one of three large paper-covered books containing English exercises, lists of spellings, general knowledge, diagrams, and pictures. The work was largely self-corrective and the advantage of the scheme was the fact that each child could work steadily at its own pace.

'Their work-books,' Miss Enderby had said casually to Anna, 'need not be taken in for correction very often. Their ordinary exercise books for arithmetic, English, nature, history, and so on, must be carefully corrected after each piece of work, and the corrections checked too.'

Anna had felt thankful that at least one of the books in each of the forty-eight desks could be left to look after itself for a week or two, and she was only too delighted to see the children busily working away, at odd times, in these books which they much enjoyed using.

The results, she found, on looking them through were disastrous. There seemed to have been a great competition going on to see how many pages could be filled up in the shortest time. Scrawls, illegible scribbles, and sometimes hasty dashes where the answer was not even attempted disfigured the pages and – worse still – the work-books designed to give useful instruction for about a term, were filled in a matter of a fortnight. What would the ratepayers think, Anna wondered, appalled, as she looked at this wantonness?

These difficulties she overcame to some extent by using odd sheets of paper made into simple one-section books one hand-work lesson by her class. These they called their 'Busy books', and when the covers had been thus lovingly inscribed, and then decorated, they were encouraged to spend the odd minutes, in which they might be waiting, in writing down useful lists, copying in short poems which they liked, items of news, or simply drawing pictures. It gave an outlet to their inventiveness and the more expensive work-books resumed their proper function.

All this took time to learn. It was experience bitterly bought, Anna found, at the cost of her own nervous energy and anxiety. Would any of these difficulties matter so much with a class of half the size, she sometimes wondered? Did Miss Anderson, at the village school at home, face quite such problems? In comparison, Anna thought, remembering her visit just after Christmas, it seemed like the land of the lotus-eaters.

An incident occurred one day which made Anna realize that size of class was indeed only comparative. Miss Enderby had opened her door one morning and in had filed a dozen or so beaming children, each clutching a chair, a pencil, several books, and other odds and ends.

'Do you mind having a few extra for today, dear?' asked Miss Enderby. Anna felt rightly that this question needed no answer and tried to look welcoming. It was at times like this that she thought enviously of the old-fashioned double desks in the village school where two small bodies could slide obligingly to one end of the bench to make room for a third without the encumbrance of extra chairs in the classroom.

The newcomers ranged themselves as neatly as they could in the little space available and held excited conversations with their friends in Anna's class who welcomed this diversion from normal routine.

'It's Mr Drew's class, dear,' said Miss Enderby. 'I'm having to divide them between four of you as I've a committee meeting at the Town Hall unfortunately. Otherwise, of course, I could take them myself.'

'Is he ill?' asked Anna in surprise. She had spent the evening before with him and he had seemed in his usual robust health then.

'His father has been taken ill. A telegram arrived this morning. A stroke, I gather, poor fellow. Mr Drew has gone straight off. It's most worrying for him.'

Poor Tom, thought Anna, it certainly would be a shock. She only hoped that things would not be as bad when he arrived as he would be imagining them on his long journey.

But her sympathy for Tom had to be put aside under the pressure of immediate circumstances. To keep over sixty children happily occupied in a confined space is not easy, especially when there are not enough desks to allow pencils and papers to be used.

They read, but those with no desks had their books at uncomfortable angles and soon fell to fidgeting. They sang, they took it in turns to recite poems and to tell stories. Anna read fairy tales to them until her throat ached. At last she could bear the oppressive mass of children no longer and, throwing the timetable to the winds she escorted her mammoth class into the playground.

It was wonderful to feel the wind on her face after the stuffy classroom. The children were unwontedly excited and rushed madly about, obeying the blasts of Anna's whistle far from promptly. How much more difficult it was to manage sixty-odd than forty-eight, thought poor Anna.

She tipped up the box of balls which she had brought out with her and the children ran hither and thither to grab one apiece. At length Anna shrilled her whistle.

'Hold them up!' she ordered.

Most of the children obeyed, but several continued to bounce or throw them and Anna had to shout against the roaring of the wind and the distant clanging of the builders at work to make herself heard.

She showed them how to walk slowly about the playground bouncing a ball steadily, keeping it under control. It was no easy job with such numbers but most of the children seemed to enjoy this exercise. Unfortunately, Arnold and his like found this an ideal opportunity for creating havoc among the more law-abiding members, and a gentle kick at someone else's ball or a determined shove at someone's back soon caused the most pleasurable complications.

Despite such subversive elements, Anna struggled manfully on, showing the children more and more manoeuvres until the time came when she knew she must return unwillingly to the over-crowded classroom.

The box had been left under the playground shed near a long bench which was secured to the wall by steel brackets under it.

'Run and put the balls back!' called Anna unthinkingly. At once the mob pelted towards the shed. They began to pile up round the box, some shouting, some protesting that they were being squashed as they bent over the box to deposit their burdens and some flinging their balls wildly from a distance in order 'to be first back'.

It was then that Anna realized what a difference a few extra children made. If she had thought forty-eight an unmanageable mob then sixty-odd certainly made a terrifying rabble. If only, she thought guiltily, she had sent back a few at a time, or moved that wretched box into the open!

She started towards the milling and vociferous crowd and at that moment heard a high-pitched shriek. The children parted and fell back aghast.

Sitting on the ground by the bench was Michael Long, his leg outstretched. A deep gash of several inches in length poured a steady flow of blood upon the grey asphalt. To Anna's horror she saw that the wound had reached the bone and was so deep that the flesh fell away leaving a sickening bleeding trough.

The child had slipped under the bench and caught his leg against the sharp steel support under the bench. He looked pale but otherwise was remarkably calm. An unnatural hush had fallen upon the rest of the children who gathered round gazing ghoulishly at this ghastly sight.

Anna pulled herself together. A dreadful sickening attack of giddiness had seized her, but this was no time for a swooning fit, she told herself fiercely, fighting against nausea.

'Run and fetch. Miss Enderby,' she told the most sensible girl present.

'She's gone out,' chorused the class. Heavens, so she had, remembered Anna!

'Miss Hobbs then,' she amended hastily. 'And run and get some mats to rest Michael on. And a rug from the sickroom!' she called after the fleeing figures, memories of first-aid classes flocking back to her.

She had never felt so pleased to see Miss Hobbs as she did on that occasion. Her sturdy figure bounded from the school door and within minutes she had taken charge.

'Take the rest in and ring the doctor, will you?' she directed. 'Four of the children can bring the stretcher and we'll carry you in, young man.'

The child smiled weakly. To Anna's relief he seemed to be feeling no pain, and almost appeared to be enjoying this unwonted attention.

Anna, much shaken, did as she was bid and before Miss Enderby returned the doctor had called, had inserted five stitches, Michael's mother had been informed, and all that remained to be done was to fill in, in triplicate, an accident form which was placed before her by Miss Hobbs's efficient hand.

But Anna could not forget the dreadful sight and could not rid herself of the terrible feeling that such accidents – and worse ones too – could happen so quickly when large numbers were in her charge. She had not quite realized, until that fateful day when Tom had been called away, how heavy her responsibilities as a teacher really were.

Chapter Fifteen

TOM MAKES PLANS

Tom was away for a week, and although Miss Enderby turned to and took the bereaved class as often as she could, the children had to be sent in batches to other classrooms whenever other matters engaged her attention.

Anna came to dread the sound of the approaching horde as it bumped and chattered its way towards her overcrowded room. The children were obedient, very lovable, and most anxious to win a handsome testimonial from their hostess in order to please Tom when he returned, but work went to the winds and Anna could not forget the accident whenever she led the throng gingerly to the playground.

Miss Enderby had had a reassuring telephone call from Tom on the evening of his departure, to say that the stroke had been slight and he hoped to return the next day. But during the night the old man had had a second, and more severe, attack. It was late in the afternoon, as the sun fell behind the flat fields he had cultivated so diligently and his labourers were slinging their legs across their bicycles to go home, when Tom's father died.

Tom had spent the next few days going mechanically about the dozens of jobs which had to be done. His mother was as shattered as he was himself, but both kept their feelings hidden as best they could in order to comfort the other. He sent messages to relations, arranged for the funeral at the small grey church whose spire was a landmark for many miles in this wide flat district, and did what he could to organize the market garden so that it would be easy for his mother to manage in the immediate future. He realized that his mother would like him to take over at once, but he wanted a little time to collect his dull wits, after the shock, before taking such a serious step. Luckily, there was a reliable man who had frequently been left in charge and who was quite capable of supervising the work of the market garden.

Anna was shaken when she first saw Tom after his return. He seemed to have grown paler and older. She had missed his presence in the school more than she had cared to admit to herself, and to see him so withdrawn and tired touched her sympathetic heart.

'Is there anything I can do?' she asked shyly, when they met in the corridor and she had stammered her words of consolation.

'Yes,' said Tom. 'Come and have tea and talk to me. I'm afraid I shan't be very good company. I feel as though my head had been thoroughly kicked. But it would be a comfort if you could bear to come.'

Anna was only too glad to hear that she would be a comfort. She scribbled a note to Mrs Flynn, gave it to a child to deliver on his way home, and accompanied Tom after school to Mrs Armstrong's.

It was a blessing, thought Anna, as she sat by Tom's fire after tea, that he was so devotedly cared for by his landlady. The room was lit by the leaping flames. The furniture shone, there were hyacinths in bloom, and everywhere proclaimed the good housekeeping of kind Mrs Armstrong.

Outside the March winds howled through the twilit garden and the rain spattered the windows; but here was a haven, and although Tom still looked unusually white and forlorn, he leant back in his armchair in a more relaxed manner. There would have been nowhere for him to relax, thought Anna grimly, if he had had the misfortune to have Mrs Flynn for a landlady, and she compared the cheap, hard, fireside – and gas fireside at that! – chair in her own sitting-room with the plump comfort of the Edwardian ones which now surrounded her. She realized that it would take more than soft chairs, good food, and Mrs Armstrong's motherly sympathy to cure the effects of Tom's shock, but they would all help in his recovery.

They smoked in comfortable silence for a time, watching the smoke spiral away into the shadows of the darkening room.

Anna did not like to press him about his plans but he spoke of them readily enough when he threw the end of his cigarette into the flames.

'I think this settles it for me, Anna,' he said. 'I had a talk to Flo this morning and I must say she is a real trump at times like this.'

'What did she say?'

'She said she thought I should go back as soon as I could if that was what I really wanted. I should have given a month's notice, I suppose. And it is what I want, as you know, but I shan't go quite so soon.'

'Why not?' said Anna. It had been the thing he wanted more than anything else, she knew, and she was puzzled by his hesitation.

'I don't think it would he fair to Flo, for one thing. She wouldn't be able to get a replacement easily at this time of year. If I teach for the rest of this term, and next, I can see my own class through and by that time the new people will be coming out of college and it will be simpler to make an appointment.'

'But what about the market garden? And your mother?'

'My mother's sister is staying with her for as long as she likes, and Albert, who's in charge, can carry on very well until July, when I take over. I shall go down as many weekends as I can. My mother has given me father's car and that will be an enormous help. I can be home by half past six or seven on a Friday night and have time to go round the place by daylight too.'

'What does your mother think?'

'She's relieved, I believe, that I haven't thrown everything overboard at once. It gives us all time to get over things and get used to the new plans. I'm sure it's wrong to make hasty decisions when there's been a death in the family. For one thing, one's not in a fit state to make a proper judgement. I think it will be best for us all to jog gently on for a bit until we return to normal.'

For a young man, thought Anna, watching his serious face as he rearranged the coals, he is remarkably wise and sweet.

And how I shall miss him! she thought with a sudden pang.

As though he could read her thoughts, Tom suddenly smiled at her, sitting back on his heels and balancing the poker in his hand. He spoke softly.

'It isn't quite the whole story, you know, of why I'm postponing my leaving Elm Hill. There are more selfish reasons. I shall miss you most horribly, Anna.'

'Me too,' said Anna, ungrammatically, in a small husky voice.

There was a pause and Tom resumed his unnecessary attentions to the fire. His face was grave.

'This isn't the time to tell you quite how much. Too much depends on it. But I'll be glad to stay until the summer when we can see how things work out.'

He replaced the poker carefully, sighed, and then shook his head as though emerging from a cold plunge.

'Let's have some music, Anna,' he said more cheerfully, and busied himself with his gramophone.

They lay back in their chairs again as the music crept and swept about the room and Anna pondered, not for the first time, on the maddening ambiguity of the English 'we'.

'We can see how things work out,' he had said. That might mean Tom and his mother, Tom and the market gardeners, Tom and his class, Tom and his headmistress. But she hoped and believed that what he had meant was Tom and Anna Lacey.

It was soon after this that Anna found herself embroiled with percussion band classes. Miss Enderby had brought this about much to Anna's dismay.

'There are some classes starting for teachers, dear,' she had said firmly, in a voice that boded no good. 'They are to show us how to take percussion band playing with the children. Miss Hobbs is going and I think it would be a good thing for you to go too. At the beginning of your career you must learn as much useful matter as you can.'

Anna had opened her mouth in weak protest, but Miss Enderby swept on.

'At half past five in our hall here, dear, on Tuesdays and Thursdays. Six lessons in all and nothing to pay!'

Really, thought Anna rebelliously, she makes it sound like a circus – which it probably will be. But much as she disliked the thought of returning to school twice a week for the next three weeks Anna acquiesced with as good a grace as she could muster. She had already escaped a gardening course, pottery-making classes, a Literary and Debating Circle which met weekly in the dejected little British Legion hut in the sad ruins of old Elm Hill, Keep-fit Classes, and a course on puppet-making, all pressed upon her by Miss Enderby and brought relentlessly to her notice by the innumerable papers which fluttered from the staff notice-board. She felt that percussion band classes would be a light price to pay for so much mercy in other directions, and presented herself cheerfully at five-thirty the next Tuesday, as a sacrifice upon the altar of Education.

The hall, which Anna saw crowded either with the entire school at morning assembly or with two classes for the rest of the day, seemed remarkably empty and tranquil. About two dozen chairs had been arranged in a half-circle and on them sat a motley collection of local teachers, mostly women, in depressingly utilitarian clothes.

In front an easel stood, and a young man of dainty appearance with long fair hair was busy arranging a large glossy chart over it. Beside him stood two large cardboard boxes filled with drums, tambourines, triangles, castanets, and cymbals. At least, thought Anna taking heart, we have to put those back at the end of the session and shan't have to bother about homework.

Miss Hobbs was already ensconced in the very middle of the half-circle, her sturdy brogues planted side by side and her thick skirt pulled well down round her plump calves. She was in animated conversation with a gaunt grey-faced woman in rimless spectacles, whom Anna recognized as a local headmistress and a possible rival to Miss Enderby for the post at the new school.

The headmistress nodded briefly to Anna, causing the curled ostrich feather which embraced her hat to flutter madly. Anna wondered why plain women were so addicted to fussy hats. Perhaps, like Arnold's habits, which Miss Enderby so despised, it was a compensatory impulse born of deprivation and inferiority.

She and Miss Hobbs were the only members from Elm Hill School, but Anna knew several of the teachers there by sight. Miss Hobbs was too busy talking to take much notice of her colleague, and Anna settled back to watch the dainty young man at his preparations and to listen to the conversation of two elderly ladies behind her. It was impossible not to hear them for they had both been infant teachers for over thirty years and their enunciation was exemplary.

'But *in Lent*!' one expostulated. 'I ask you, Hilda, *in Lent*! Not that it's any affair of mine, of course, what Mrs Appleby does with her daughter, but I should have thought a party could have waited!'

'It is her twenty-first,' pointed out the other, as one who is adding fuel to the fire, Anna suspected from the smug tone, rather than one who seeks to soothe.

'So what?' snapped the first. 'Plenty of other places to go to, if she must have a birthday in Lent, rather than the Church Hall.'

Anna felt a little sorry for the person who had been so thoughtless as to have been born in Lent.

'I had intended to give the girl something really nice – probably that silver fox fur of mother's that I've had by me in camphor since she died before the war – but now – no! I can't bring myself to.'

'You mustn't upset yourself over it,' said her companion, with obvious relish. 'You take it too much to heart.'

'I suppose I do,' admitted the first voice, somewhat mollified, 'but when one has Christian principles and a Christian outlook it makes one feel like shaking the girl and her stupid fat mother to hear of such downright wickedness during Lent! *Lent*, you know,' she persisted.

Anna was trying to reconcile the lady's Christian principles, which were obviously *her* particular prop to her self-esteem, with the severe shakings of her unfortunate neighbours which they appeared to prompt, when the young man clapped his plump pink hands, shook back a cloud of fair hair, and addressed his audience.

'Now, ladies and – gentlemen.' He flashed an arch smile at the two burly men who sat together at the end of the row and who constituted the male element in his class. They scowled back, unresponsive to this *camaraderie*.

'I want to show you the instruments first and how we hold them. This is the first and most important point.' He dived into the box at his feet and produced a tambourine.

'Come to the penitent form,' said one of the men, recovering his spirits. The young man, whose name, Anna later discovered, was Desmond Gall, threw him a coldish glance. He could give a rebuff as well as the next, it seemed to say.

'A tambourine,' said Mr Gall, holding it up with a pretty jingling. 'This is one way to use it. Another way is like this.'

He carefully threaded his left thumb into a hole in the wooden band and held the instrument edge on towards him. The class leant forward and gazed attentively. Mr Gall raised his right hand with its fingers delicately bent.

'Then I tap it gently with just the *very tips* of my fingers,' said he, pursing his lips to show how sensitive a touch would be needed. 'Like this!'

He flicked his wrist gracefully and struck the taut skin of the tambourine a light blow.

'Penny on the drum,' said the facetious man. Mr Gall ignored him.

'Don't move the *arm*, merely the *wrist*,' cautioned Mr Gall, demonstrating the movement again.

'He's really got the loveliest nails!' Anna heard one of the ladies exclaim admiringly behind her.

The lesson continued; Mr Gall demonstrated the uses of all the instruments and then gave them one apiece to practise.

It really was most satisfying, thought Anna, tinkling happily away at a triangle, and if only the wretched thing wouldn't keep turning round and round as she was about to strike it with her little metal beater, it would be quite perfect.

She looked around her at her companions and was amused to see the rapt pleasure on their ancient countenances. Miss Hobbs was banging lustily on a side drum, while Mr Gall watched with some apprehension. Her neighbour, the angular headmistress, had a beatific smile upon her thin lips as she clashed two cymbals. violently up and down together. Anna hoped that the cutting edges were not sharp and that no one would be so foolish as to lean across the path of these implements while they were in such deadly motions.

The two Christian ladies behind her were in a fine frenzy of tambourine-shaking, their eyes sparkling with zest. What with cymbals, tambourines, triangles, drums, and castanets, all being wielded by long-repressed adults, the din was incredible. Anna was quite relieved when Mr Gall requested silence and put on a gramophone record of 'Bobby Shafto'. The school radiogram emitted its usual volley of crackles, whistles, and rushing-wind noises, as well as the tune, but this was preferable to the former cacophony.

He showed them how they would learn to read the chart music which was draped over the easel, and he tapped his long pointer on the brightly-coloured notes, and sang to the music in a high light tenor. It was all most intriguing, and Anna began to feel reconciled to her lot, after all.

For the last few minutes of the lesson the class played together, with varying degrees of accuracy. 'Bobby Shafto' thumped noisily from the gramophone, while Mr Gall, now pink and perspiring, his hair cascading across his forehead like a wisp of yellow candy-floss, nodded and banged with his pointer, and rose and fell on his toes in time to his efforts.

Miss Hobbs, purple with concentration, pummelled her drum mercilessly, muttering the while: 'Bobby One-Two, Bobby One-Two! Silver One-Two, At His One-Two!' one large brogue stamping energetically on the floor. The facetious man had met his match in a twirling triangle, which he stalked intently holding his little beater aloft and smiting with a fine disregard of rhythm, whenever the triangle obligingly turned in the right direction.

It was wonderful to see two dozen grown men and women so entranced with their own efforts, and when the lesson ended Anna knew she looked as flushed and foolish as the rest.

As they made their way from the hall she heard the militant Christian talking to her friend.

'Well, I did enjoy that! I think we should be very pleased with ourselves!'

Her voice was in happy contrast to the virtuous indignation which had sharpened it earlier that evening.

Music, Anna remembered, even such poor stuff as they had made, still seemed to have charm to soothe the savage breast.

Chapter Sixteen

FRIENDS AND FRESH AIR

The end of term approached, and the Easter holidays, which had seemed to Anna like a distant speck of sunlight seen at the end of a long dark tunnel, suddenly shone splendidly near.

She would be heartily thankful to see the back of Elm Hill for a fortnight, she told herself. The term had been long and cold; darkness had closed in on many an afternoon session, and the drab darkness of the ruined countryside around her was enough to daunt even Anna's youthful spirits. Lack of air, sunshine, and exercise had worked upon both staff and children, and tempers had grown unpleasantly frayed.

Anna had not been prepared for adult tantrums and was shocked to see grown people bandying tart words and taking offence so easily. This was another aspect, and an unnerving one, of the career she had taken up. Her own family was particularly equable, and although she had seen her father and his farm hands, sweating with exhaustion, and occasionally blaspheming at some piece of recalcitrant machinery, they had remained basically even-tempered at their work. This edgy spitefulness, born of nervous tension, was a new and frightening thing to Anna. Would she get like that? Was she as viperish herself and didn't know it? It was an appalling thought.

She had overheard Miss Enderby, who normally kept her majestic façade unruffled, snap cruelly at poor Miss Hobbs, and the sight of Miss Hobbs's stricken face, looking like a child who has seen his mother drown his puppy, upset Anna considerably. Doubtless the strain of waiting for the new appointment to be made was taking its toll of her headmistress, thought Anna charitably.

Even Joan Berry had lost some of her cool urbanity as the

wearisome term dragged on, and Anna did not like to risk a rebuff by asking after Maurice, though she would dearly have loved to know if that amiable parasite was still with the same host.

The first crocuses which had begun to flower in the raw new gardens near the school seemed only to emphasize their bleak and inhospitable surroundings. The stick-like lilac which existed by Mrs Flynn's gate had put forth one or two pathetic leaves, but the little cushions of thrift with which Mrs Flynn, with unconscious irony, had chosen to edge the concrete path, had died during the winter and lay, like bunches of dead hair, in a depressing row.

Outside the blowsy greengrocer's, two or three boxes of narcissi and daffodils huddled in their blue tissue paper, and wilted in the dust which whipped around them every time a lorry screamed past. Pale pink forced rhubarb, with its yellow top-knot, arched its flabby length across the top of the boxes, and Anna thought longingly of the sturdy growth at home pressing up under the brown earthenware crocks in the farm garden and awaiting her appreciative palate. Spring at Elm Hill was a travesty of that lovely season, and it grieved her to see her children running home along those arid streets 'missing so much and so much'. Just now, the children from the village school would be searching the mossy banks on their way home for white violets and brassy celandines. Birds would be in full throat as they busied themselves with their nesting, and over the whole sweet countryside would be the benison of returning warmth and colour.

Anna had never felt so acutely all that she was missing, and had never hated Elm Hill so fiercely. Mrs Flynn's parsimony seemed to grow worse daily and Anna began to wonder if she could bear to stay much longer in that wretched house. If she had not been able to get away on a Friday evening for a weekend in comfort she felt that she would not have been able to get through the term at all.

When, finally, the last day came, and the children had gone home jubilantly clutching the Easter eggs she had provided, Anna clambered on to the first Green Line coach available, threw her case thankfully on to the rack, and lay back with her eyes closed.

It was then that she realized just how exhausted she was. She felt drained of all energy, as flat and ugly as the ruined fields around her. She felt as she had when she had once been seriously ill, curiously light and empty, and quite incapable of enjoying anything.

No wonder that the older members of the staff, many of them with household cares and ill-health added to their burden, should look as they did and snap at each other, thought Anna.

And she wondered, with a spasm of fright, if she would ever be able to stick it out.

Within two days, of course, the magic of home worked its spell, and Anna was her usual buoyant self again.

The country was beginning to flower into spring. The stark black outlines of the trees took on a softer line, as though a charcoal drawing had been lightly blurred, as millions of buds swelled and began to break their tight casings. There was a rosy smoke over the elm trees, the honeysuckle, which twined over an arch in the garden, was in small bright leaf, and the rose trees had put out little red fans of new leaves. Everything smelt of hope and growing warmth and it was impossible not to respond.

Anna's pony kicked up its heels and galloped madly round the paddock for the sheer joy of living, and Anna, watching it lovingly from the kitchen window, could have joined it. It was wonderful to be young, to have a holiday, to have the summer stretching ahead. Why, even Elm Hill, at this distance, seemed quite a pleasant place!

She found that she could answer her mother's inquiries about the job much more easily now. At first she had been so tired and so overwhelmed with the sheer ugliness of Elm Hill that she had not dared to express her true feelings for fear of upsetting her mother. But now, Elm Hill and the school were beginning to fall into place in her life, and she could talk of them more objectively.

'The staff are really jolly nice when you get to know them,' she told her mother as they prepared the large midday dinner in the kitchen. She went on to relate the story of Joan Berry's kindness to poor spineless Maurice, but carefully omitted the fact that he slept at the flat with Joan. After all, old people were easily shocked, thought Anna with newly-found sophistication, and she didn't want her mother to be embarrassed, particularly as Joan was to spend a weekend with them at the end of the holidays.

'And the children are enormous fun. Even when they're naughty,' said Anna, peeling a carrot industriously, 'it's a *nice* naughtiness – not maliciously inclined against me. Some of the bigger children, I believe, set out to be troublesome, but mine are too young for that yet.'

'And you don't find it's monotonous, teaching the same things every day?' asked her mother.

'The same things?' cried Anna. 'Why, every day's different. So many things crop up, and every child reacts in its own way, that there's always something happening. Too much, in fact, at times. You can't call teaching monotonous – if anything it's too exciting with forty-eight nine-year-olds whirling you along!'

'And you'd like to stay there?' pressed her mother. Anna lowered the carrot slowly and leant her elbows on the cool sink, gazing with unseeing eyes at the sunlit meadow beyond the quickening hedge.

'No,' she answered thoughtfully. 'Not for much longer anyway. It is marvellous experience and I'm beginning to feel that I can really teach, but after I've spent a year or so perhaps with a new head, whoever it is, I think I'll look for another post.'

'I think that might be wise,' agreed her mother, nodding sympathetically. The weariness and strain which Anna had tried to hide during the previous months had not escaped Margaret Lacey's eye, nor her husband's.

'How would you like me as headmistress of the village school here?' asked Anna, half-jokingly. 'There'll be a vacancy in the next two or three years, I should think.'

'You wouldn't get it,' said Mrs Lacey forthrightly, 'nor would you deserve it. You'd need much more experience. If you want to make a change after being at Elm Hill two or three years I should apply for a post as an assistant in a school in a country town – that is if you really think you'd like a village headship one day.'

'I think I would, you know,' said Anna slowly. 'It would probably be years ahead when I'm too old to enjoy taking the children out for nature walks and too stiff to bound about in the playground with them – but I don't think I shall ever live happily away from the country.'

Her mother laughed.

'Maybe,' she said looking at her daughter, 'you'll get married. You might possibly marry someone who lived in the country,' she added, thinking of Ted.

'So I might,' agreed Anna cheerfully, picking up the carrot again, tossing it ceilingwards and catching it again deftly. 'There's just the faintest possible chance, I suppose, that I might marry someone who lived in the country.' But she was thinking of Tom.

Joan Berry's visit was a great success. Anna's parents were instantly attracted by her gay good sense and her pretty looks, although, as Patrick Lacey told her, she 'needed to put some beef on her bones or the wind would blow her over'.

She seemed to relax and glow in the warm family atmosphere and Ted, Anna was amused to see, had eyes for no one else. He had met hosts of local girls, of varying shapes and sizes, but never before one quite so elegant and sparkling.

On the Saturday of Joan's weekend stay the local hunt held its point-to-point meeting. This took place a few miles from the Laceys' home and part of the course lay in Ted Marchant senior's fields. This was always a cheerful social occasion, when old friends met, local horses and riders were known, and everyone told everyone else the best horse to back in the next race and no one minded when it came in last.

The Laceys always made this a day's outing and the two girls helped Mrs Lacey to pack up the picnic basket during the morning. Before twelve o'clock they had parked the big shabby car in the farmers' enclosure and by twenty past Anna was not surprised to see that Ted had joined the party for lunch.

It was a wonderful April day with great white towers of clouds sailing slowly across the wide East Anglian sky. A light easterly wind brought a hint of the distant sea, and spirits were high. Farmers and farm hands, butchers and bakers, men and women who had been cooped up in offices all the week, housewives who had taken the day off, and hordes of excited children, moved hither and thither in the brilliant sunshine, and the smell of bruised young grass was everywhere.

Ted helped Joan with her bets, poring obligingly over her race-card, as this was the first time she had been to a point-to-point. Despite his advice, Joan stuck to her own choice, and much to their delight had two unexpected winners.

'A sheer fluke really,' Ted assured her. 'Neither of them should have won.'

'Nonsense!' said Joan, 'it was purely my good eye for a horse. I knew that white one would run well.'

Ted controlled his wincings at hearing a grey so ignorantly described, with his customary good humour.

It was a happy day and Anna was delighted to see her friend looking so carefree. Maurice had not been mentioned, and it was not until the next afternoon, when the two girls had gone alone to pick primroses in a near-by copse, that Anna had the opportunity to inquire after the gentleman.

'Maurice?' said Joan, sitting back on her heels and sniffing her bunch of primroses. 'Why, he's still with me.'

'For much longer?' asked Anna. Joan laughed.

'Your guess is as good as mine. He's doing a temporary job at Fraser's, the furnishers, at the moment. Someone's ill and he's standing in, but heaven knows how long that will last.'

'Does he like it?'

'Maurice, as I've told you before, my dear, dislikes any sort of work intensely. And he finds that flinging the carpets back for prospective buyers is most exhausting!'

Anna laughed with her.

'Poor Maurice!'

'Isn't it sad?' continued Joan. 'It's as much as he can do to lift one of my gin and tonics to his pallid lips in the evenings. Terribly trying to the arms, he tells me, this carpet throwing.'

'Perhaps they'll offer him a permanent post there?'

'It won't be taken,' Joan assured her. 'If he sticks a month I shall be surprised, but I must say it's very nice to have the flat to myself a little more often. He's out most evenings.'

'At the Youth Club?' asked Anna.

'Not likely! I think he has found a sympathetic female ear somewhere and enjoys pouring out his troubles. I only hope she has more influence over him than I have, and finds him another job when this one folds up.'

She moved to another rosette of primroses and began plucking busily. Anna followed her, the brittle twigs snapping underfoot and frightening a linnet who had been singing on a silver birch tree.

She bent down to pick by her friend.

'Joan, this is perhaps rather cheek, but tell me, does Maurice – well, help towards running the flat?'

Joan did not appear in the least perturbed by Anna's faltered question.

'He does when he can. But it's all in fits and starts, you know. When he first took this job he gave me three pounds a week towards expenses, but lately it's dropped to an occasional ten shillings when he feels like it.'

'But *really* –!' began Anna indignantly, but Joan stopped her

'I know, I know. It's idiotic of me, and it's downright wicked of Maurice, and it's all against your principles – but don't say it. I may be a perfect fool but I just can't turn that poor little wastrel out into the hard world while he behaves himself at the flat. Perhaps one day I'll harden my heart, but meanwhile I'm content to let things slip on from day to day.

'It's so absolutely wrong and unfair,' said Anna, tugging viciously at a twig of nodding catkins. Joan stopped picking primroses and straightened up, watching the younger girl with kindly amusement.

'Anna darling, you're sweet to get so worked up about it all. You see, you've been brought up so properly – and I don't mean that disparagingly, believe me. Your parents are absolutely straight and good. Not *goody-good*, but good in the wholesome honest way that crusty bread or fresh milk is good. This weekend has made me realize how lucky you are to have them as parents. You see it all still in black and white, partly because of their upbringing and partly because you are so deliciously young.'

'It doesn't alter the fact that Maurice is in the wrong,' persisted Anna.

'Maybe not,' rejoined Joan. 'But because I'm older and have met so many less good people than you have, I expect less from them. The more you know people the more readily you can forgive their weaknesses.'

'My mother says that,' agreed Anna wonderingly.

'Bless her, she would!' responded Joan warmly. 'And another thing, I'm terribly lazy. I'd sooner let things drift on than make a scene unnecessarily. That's why I let so many comments go by me in the staff room. If one took up every double-edged remark – particularly towards the end of term – one would be in a constant state of warfare!'

Anna, remembering those uncomfortable last few days, nodded agreement.

'What will you do if Miss Enderby goes to the new infants' school?' she asked Joan, her mind wandering back to Elm Hill. They had reached a wide glade, threaded with April sunlight, where they could walk comfortably side by side.

'I shall go with her if she'll have me,' said Joan stoutly. 'She's a grand old girl, you know, beneath that lady-of-the manor attitude she takes up to us underlings.'

'She is,' said Anna, and told her about the forthright way she had dealt with Mrs Bond on her behalf 'I suppose she's just used to coping with crises like that. She must have had all sorts of experiences. And unhappiness too,' added Anna, 'she looks terribly sad when she looks at that ring.'

Joan's laughter sent a blackbird scuttling for shelter.

'Bless your romantic young heart,' said she, 'I shall have to tell you the truth about that ring, though I'd told myself I'd keep it locked for ever in my black heart.'

'Sit on this log,' commanded Anna, taking her place promptly, 'and tell me quickly.'

'Well,' began Joan, her eyes sparkling, 'I met a Miss Evans some time ago when I was on holiday. She had been to college with Flo and they had taught together in Wolverhampton, until this Elm Hill headship had whisked them apart. Having always been unholily inquisitive about that ring I spoke of it to Miss Evans, who said –'

Here she paused tantalizingly and turned her bright gaze upon Anna's absorbed face.

'Go on! Go on!' pressed Anna.

'Who said,' continued Joan, with tormenting deliberation, 'that Flo had been left a little money by an aunt and had decided to buy that ring with some of it. In fact, she accompanied Flo to the shop and helped her to choose it. In those days she did *not* wear it on her engagement ring finger.'

'Well, I'm blowed!' said Anna inelegantly. 'What a thing! Do you think that story's true?'

'I don't see any reason for doubting it,' said Joan equably. 'She was a nice old dear, and not likely to perjure her immortal soul for my passing gratification.'

'But it's downright dishonest, if that's the case,' said Anna, beginning to see the enormity of the situation. 'I mean Flo's as good as telling a whopping great lie by letting us all believe that she was engaged once!'

'Calm down, junior,' said Joan. 'There you go again, you see. Of course, it's wrong. Of course, Flo shouldn't behave like that, but she does. And I, for one, can forgive a pathetic little sin like that quite easily. Believe you me, some of my own are pretty formidable beside that tiddy-widdly one of Flo's.'

'I wish,' said Anna slowly, 'that I were as kindhearted as you.'

'It's my great age,' answered Joan lightly, giving her companion an encouraging pat on the shoulder. 'It makes me mellow and worldly-wise, you know. Wait another five years and you'll be just as big-hearted!'

They picked up their bunches of yellow primroses and set off towards the farmhouse.

'Yes, I'll stay with Flo,' repeated Joan as they came out of the wood and paused to look upon the open countryside spread around them. 'I admire the old battle-axe tremendously. She's got pluck.

She's hard-working, she knows what she wants, and she commands respect – ring or no ring. If she gets the headship that school will be jolly well run. She hasn't really had a chance to show her form, we've been so hopelessly overcrowded.'

'I think I'll stay on, with the juniors,' said Anna. 'I like the older children better than the infants, I think, and a new head would be more experience for me but in surroundings I'm just getting used to.'

'We'd still see plenty of each other,' said Joan. 'The two schools will work together, I imagine, quite a bit. I must say I'm looking forward to Elm Hill being spread out. We can really enjoy our teaching then.'

Anna looked at her with quick interest.

'Tell me, after five years at it,' said Anna, 'do you really enjoy teaching?'

'Yes, I do,' maintained Joan stoutly. 'It gets better every year I go on. I know it's unfashionable these days to admit to enjoying children's company and to working with them, but I find teaching stimulating and amusing and jolly well worthwhile. It gives me the biggest kick in the world to see a child reading itself a story when I know that last week it could hardly put two words together without effort. Just think what's begun for that child!'

'That's cheering news!' said Anna, quickening her pace as the farmhouse came in sight.

'You don't want to believe all that you read in the library books,' continued Joan. 'Remember, my child, that for every disgruntled teacher who has burst into dismal print, there are two dozen cheerful ones who are far too busy weeding their gardens or baking a cake in their spare time, to ponder on their hard lot. And praise the Lord for that!'

As they approached the farmhouse a delicious smell of cooking floated towards them.

'Someone,' said Anna jubilantly, 'has been doing some baking in *our* house, evidently!'

Together they approached the kitchen door at a smart trot.

Chapter Seventeen

TESTING TIME

The summer term was going to be mightily disturbed, it seemed to Anna on the first day back, as she stood in front of the staff notice-board reading a long list which Miss Hobbs had just put up.

4 May   Verse-Speaking Competition
5 May   Choral Competition
15 June   Open Day
13 July   School Sports Day
20 July   Area Sports Day

So ran the list, headed in Miss Hobbs's firm hand, 'Dates to Note'.

'Don't expect to get any real work done this term,' said Joan Berry, as Miss Hobbs bustled off. 'The summer term's an absolute nightmare.'

'There are only five dates,' replied Anna reasonably. 'Surely they can't make much difference.'

'Dear, innocent, muddle-headed child,' said Joan, looking up from her minute diary in which she had been putting down the dates. 'Just think for one second. All those wretched events need weeks of practice and rehearsal. Open Day alone, at Elm Hill, shortens one's life by six months, I reckon. This year, with Flo in the last stretch of the New School Stakes, it will be even worse!'

'But what happens?' asked Anna, bewildered. 'Surely it simply means that the parents come to see the work?'

'And what work!' commented Joan darkly. 'All the cleanest bits of needlework, all the maddest pictures in the which-way-up style, all the fanciest maps, and so on, that your children have perpetrated through the year, will need to be exquisitely mounted on black paper – if the stock-cupboard runs to it – and carefully displayed. No ramming of marguerites into a Virol jar that day, my girl! Something worthy of Constance Spry has to decorate each window-sill and the cupboards must be models of tidiness!'

'Oh Lor'!' said Anna appalled.

'A few beautifully printed poems in your own best Marion Richardson hand will be expected to add a touch of culture to your walls, and I suppose I shall be spending the next six weeks making a madly gay alphabet frieze for my babies' room. And I'd better replace my notices for DOOR, CUPBOARD, and so on,' she continued morosely. 'I've had them for six years and all the corners are bent. Besides cream is out just now. A good bright scarlet might win approval. I must put in my claim for stock pretty quickly, and I advise you to do the same, my dear, before Flo is besieged by the rest of the staff. As it is, you know, she hates parting with the stuff. All stock-cupboard minders get that way. It's an occupational hazard.'

'Thanks, I will,' said Anna. 'What an outlook though,' she added. 'Is it really as bad as that?'

'Worse!' said Joan cheerfully. 'Much worse – but I don't like to depress you by telling you more just now.'

Anna knew that Joan's remark about Miss Enderby's frugality with stock was a true one. Every week it was the custom for each teacher to send to Miss Enderby a list of stock needed for class work. It usually ran something like this:

> 12 Arithmetic exercise books
> 12 Writing books
> 12 Sheets painting paper
> 24 Sheets baker's wrapping paper
>   (used for crayoning and pencil work)
> 12 pencils
> Plasticine
> Drawing pins

The last two items, Anna had found by sad experience, were best left in their stark form, for if any number of sticks of plasticine were mentioned or a whole box of drawing pins were asked for, Miss Enderby seemed to feel obliged to cut down supplies drastically.

There seemed to be something malevolent about the stock-cupboard's influence, Anna thought. Normally, Miss Enderby was an open-handed person. She delighted in presenting the staff room with flowers. Sometimes she gave a cake for her grateful staff to eat with their afternoon tea. But once in the stock cupboard she became parsimonious. Paper of most kinds she seemed to find comparatively easy to part with, but rare commodities such as thick black paper for mounting work, gummed coloured squares, so useful for cutting-out, and particularly drawing-pins she seemed most reluctant to hand out.

'I buy my own,' said Tom Drew, when Anna spoke of this particular foible of her headmistress's, one day. 'To see the spasm of pain which contorts the poor old girl's face, when I ask for a few miserable drawing-pins, is too much for my susceptible heart. It's worth a bob a term to feel magnanimous.'

With Joan's advice in mind, Anna went with some trepidation to collect her stock on the first day the cupboard was unlocked. Her list had been formidably long and included those vital drawing pins. Luckily, Miss Enderby was in an unusually benevolent mood and handed out great rolls of heavy paper, sticks of coloured chalk, and a dozen new pencils which Anna had not dared to ask for, as well as a whole new box of drawing pins. Anna congratulated herself silently on having applied early and at such a propitious time. Success made her brave enough to make a comment on the stock available.

'It must be awfully difficult to know how much you will need of everything,' she said, eyeing the shelves.

'One gets used to estimating,' answered Miss Enderby graciously, disentangling her hair-net from a hank of raffia which dangled from a high nail. 'This is the last term of the three. I shall order ready for next term, of course, for my own needs or those of my successor here.'

'I hadn't thought of that,' said Anna truthfully.

'The new school will need stock, too, but of course the new head will put in her order for that.'

'Of course,' echoed Anna, clutching her unwieldy goods to her cardigan. Miss Enderby's gaze had wandered to the window and to the distant prospect of Elm Hill Infants' School. The roof was now on, and the sounds of building were mainly from inside and mercifully muffled. She seemed to have forgotten Anna and a heavy silence fell.

Anna looked at her list and found that she had received all that she had requested.

'Thank you very much, Miss Enderby,' she murmured politely, backing quietly away with her spoils. But Miss Enderby did not seem to hear, and Anna guessed that she was already, in spirit, standing in another stock cupboard, filled with the bright necessities of an infants' school, and all of her own ordering.

But before the first of Miss Hobbs's 'Dates To Note' materialized, a more momentous day occurred for Anna.

She had hoped that the worst of her probationary troubles were now over. She had been visited by half a dozen or so educational advisers, of much the same kidney as Miss-Adams-of-the-rods, and felt that she had learnt something from their varied, and sometimes mildly fanatical suggestions.

Miss Enderby too had been a model headmistress in her handling of her new member of staff. She had come into many of Anna's lessons, sitting, as unobtrusively as a woman of her size and presence could, in a far-too-small desk at the back of the room. Afterwards she had given very fair comment on her findings and Anna had found her experience of considerable help. Miss Enderby was zealous too in examining Anna's 'Record Book' weekly. This large volume consisted of a list of subjects against which Anna made a note of the work scheduled to be done each week, so that against 'Nature', for instance, she might have: 'Hibernating Animals – Hedgehog and Squirrel.'

Too often, alas, Anna found that the heading would remain the same for two or three weeks running; for although she might have planned to have three weeks' lessons on hibernating animals, and had mentally reserved the toad, the snake, and the tortoise for one week and bats and dormice for the last, yet the pressure and upheaval of school life often ousted a lesson completely from one week's work, and it had to be carried into the next. It was her record book which gave Anna some idea of the loss of time which out-of-class interruptions occasioned. Unexpected visitors, rehearsals for plays, fire drill, searches for lost property, and dozens of other school hazards seemed to take their toll of Anna's carefully prepared lessons. The record book was both her bane – for she sometimes forgot to make it up and earned a rebuke from her headmistress – and also her prop, for with a dozen or more subjects to teach Anna often found that her head was in a whirl, and she was glad to refer to her notes to straighten her thoughts.

She had received three or four visits from inspectors, of varying degrees of helpfulness, and sincerely hoped that there were to be no more. The rest of the staff were not so optimistic.

'I'd count on half a dozen,' said Joan Berry, experimenting with gold nail varnish one playtime. She held up one finger and looked at it critically. 'What do you think of this?'

'Well –' began Anna doubtfully.

'Awful!' said Tom Drew. 'It looks like tobacco stain. Stick to the pink.'

'I believe you're right,' agreed Joan, wiping it off. 'Yes, my dear,' she resumed, 'you must expect a little visitation or two in your last term. The pace gets hotter when the tape's in sight.'

'I had a holy terror,' said Tom conversationally. 'He asked me if I could teach a class a dovetail joint and how would I set about explaining the Trinity. It was a trifle disconcerting.'

'Watch out for one called Butterworth, or Shuttleworth, or some such name,' warned Joan, screwing up the bottle of nail varnish. 'He throws the children up to the ceiling and tells them uproarious stories and generally gets them into a state of screaming hysteria and then he says: "Carry on."'

Anna's eyes widened in horror.

'Quite true!' Tom assured her, smiling at her solemn face. 'He likes to see how quickly you can restore order. Carries a stop-watch, doesn't he, Joan?'

'That's right,' agreed Joan. 'If you can get control in ten seconds flat, you're in.'

'Don't you believe a word of it, Miss Lacey,' puffed Alan Foster, who had entered and was busy spreading papers at one end of the table. 'Nothing to fear from inspectors. I was talking to one yesterday about this little project.' He waved at the mass of material before him. 'He was most interested. Said that a really worthwhile arithmetic series is exactly what's needed in the junior schools today.'

The three younger members gathered round Alan Foster's bulk and gazed at his latest work. Through the haze of cigarette smoke, which spiralled round his bald head, Anna stared at innumerable diagrams and columns of figures. It looked very much like all the other arithmetic books she had met. Alan Foster smiled proudly at it.

'Well, there it is! Good for five hundred pounds, I'd say, within the first two years, and a steady income for the rest of my life.'

'Let's hope so,' said Tom dubiously, as the bell rang. 'You're staying here for a free period, I suppose?'

'Yes,' said Alan, patting a few papers together in an efficient manner. 'I shall put in half an hour on this while I can.'

'Poor old Alan,' Tom commented to Anna as they walked together back to their classrooms. 'I doubt if putting together "many cheerful facts about the square on the hypotenuse" is going to make his fortune, but it seems to keep him happy.'

He turned into his own classroom and Anna continued along the passage to her own. The class sounded remarkably quiet, and when she entered she saw why.

A large elderly man, with forbidding black eyebrows, stood at the back of the room. In his hand he held one of the children's exercise books.

He did not appear to like what he saw in it, and Anna's heart sank.

*

'My name is North,' he said, coming towards the front of the room. 'You are Miss Lacey, I believe?'

'Yes,' faltered Anna, her eyes on the exercise book. What had she left undone there, she wondered? Whether it was Mr North's unsmiling countenance, his bass voice, or her own guilty conscience which produced her unusual inner qualms, Anna was not sure, but she had not felt so nervous with her other visitors. Perhaps the alarm felt by older members of the staff was infectious. In any case, she found herself decidedly frightened and despised herself for feeling so.

'Set them to work,' said Mr North. 'I've one or two things to ask you.'

This sounded even more ominous. At least he's not the one who wants dovetail joints and the Trinity explained, thought Anna, clinging to a straw.

She told her class to read silently or to work in their 'busy books' while she was engaged with their visitor, and was thankful to see that they set about their task in an unusually subdued way. Evidently Mr North's dour presence flung a shadow over the children's volatile spirits as well as their teacher's.

'Just look at this, will you?' asked Mr North, handing over the exercise book, when comparative peace had fallen upon the classroom.

He pointed to some corrections which Anna had blithely ticked. It was one of Miss Enderby's rules that a spelling mistake or a word wrongly used should be corrected by the teacher and copied three times by the child.

'My brother went to', had run the original sentence, which Anna had corrected to 'too'. Alas, the child had copied 'to' 'to' 'to', industriously at the end of his exercise, and poor Anna, in the press of work, had ticked it as correct. It was unforgivable, she knew, but did it really call for the solemnity of Mr North's countenance? Miserably she acknowledged her fault. Mr North's expression grew, if anything, rather more grave.

'It may seem a little thing to you,' he said heavily, 'but that child might well go through life using that word wrongly. You may find

people – colleagues of mine even – who profess to despise corrections in English work. I don't. I think that the pendulum has
swung too far and that too much slip-shod writing has resulted.'

Anna nodded dumbly. There was not much she could say in
extenuation, and if it gave him any gratification to air his opinions,
she was in no position to protest. Arnold, she noticed with some
alarm, had cut out a paper mask for himself decorated with horrible
crossed eyes and eyebrows uncommonly like Mr North's. The
resourceful child had cut a large aperture for the mouth through
which he protruded his tongue, all the more horrific as it was
bright purple from licking an indelible pencil.

Luckily, Mr North had seated himself on the front desk, with his
back to the class, and Anna prayed that Arnold would be either
unobserved or, better still, smitten by an unobtrusive bolt from
heaven and taken from their midst.

'How long do you spend in going through an exercise like this?'
persisted Mr North, rubbing a thick finger along the black brows
and turning them into herringbone stitch.

'It takes me about an hour and a half, I suppose,' answered
Anna. 'It depends of course on how much they've done. Forty-
eight books take a long time to mark,' she added apologetically.

'Forty-eight children are too many, of course,' said Mr North
casually, 'but there it is. You're no worse off than hundreds of
others, deplorable as it is.'

Anna suddenly felt furious with him and all her other tormentors
who had so glibly expressed dissatisfaction with the huge numbers,
but did not really seem to realize all that it involved. My goodness,
thought Anna warmly, if his wife were asked to mind just one child
for just one afternoon it would be something to think about, and
yet teachers are expected, not only to *mind*, but to *teach* forty or
more, week after week and year after year, and no one thinks it
remarkable at all!

'I'd like to see your record book and any notes of lessons you
may have,' went on Mr North. 'What are they supposed to be
doing now?'

'I usually tell them a story,' said Anna weakly.

'Then carry on,' said Mr North, in a doom-laden voice. Anna handed over the books he had asked for, and with a sinking heart, told the children to put away their work and get ready to listen. Arnold, she was relieved to see, had been robbed of his mask by his neighbour who, with considerable aplomb, was sitting on it. Arnold, scarlet in the face with suppressed wrath, was powerless to budge him, and though Anna feared that ugly recriminations might ensue she hoped that these might be postponed until playtime.

She began the story haltingly. She was in the throes of telling her class some Greek legends and today's was the story of Theseus and the Minotaur. She prided herself on being able to tell, rather than read, the stories, for she had found that the children listened much more eagerly. But today her nervousness made her falter and the children seemed bored. Mr North had ensconced himself on a radiator by the window and was studying the notebooks gloomily. Occasionally he made a note of his own with a very small pencil on a very small pad and looked even more morose as he did so.

Anna found it heavy going that afternoon. The clock seemed to have stopped, so slowly did the time go. The children yawned and gave sidelong glances at their silent and unsmiling visitor whenever he cleared his throat with a noise like the last trump.

At last the story drew to an end, and Mr North rose and approached Anna again. He held out a large cold hand in farewell. His dark eyes stared resignedly into Anna's.

'Good-bye, Miss Lacey,' he said heavily. 'Just do the best you can.'

And with these inspiring words he vanished from Anna's sight.

'So you've been closeted with our Mr Rochester, have you?' said Joan Berry. 'Happy little fellow, isn't he?'

'Poor chap,' said Andy Craig. 'Lives on stomach powders, I heard. Just a mass of ulcers.'

'So shall I be if he comes much more,' retorted Anna. 'He's the most unnerving person I've ever met. I don't like to think what he's put in his little notebook about me.'

'Cheer up,' said Andy Craig, tightening his wrist strap. 'Teachers are in short supply, you know. You won't get thrown out.'

The hubbub of children at play which had accompanied this conversation was suddenly and unnaturally stilled, and in the lull Anna could hear Tom Drew's voice in the playground. She knew he was on duty and went to the window to see what was happening.

Tom was addressing Arnold and his class neighbour. Both were hot and angry. Arnold's nose was dripping blood and a bruise was rapidly rising on his opponent's forehead. Recriminations were now taking place evidently.

'Ah well,' said Anna thankfully, 'it might have been a lot worse!'

Chapter Eighteen

THE MUSE VISITS ELM HILL

Another crisis arose about this time at Mrs Flynn's. It had been apparent to Anna, for some time, that her use of the sitting-room was increasingly irksome to Mrs Flynn. If her bedroom had been larger she would have suggested having a table or desk there to do her work in the evenings, for now that early summer had arrived, it was not so bitterly cold in her little cell, but it was quite impossible to jam any more furniture in it, at the moment, and Anna had endured, in silence, one or two veiled hints at the inconvenience caused by giving up the sitting-room, not knowing quite what to do about it.

Matters came to a head when Mrs Flynn entered one evening, rather flushed about the face and neck, and looking more than usually militant.

Anna guessed her errand.

'I'm afraid I shall have to ask you to give up this room entirely, Miss Lacey,' said Mrs Flynn abruptly. 'My husband said I must speak to you about it.' (Oh how useful husbands can be! thought Anna.)

'I'm sorry,' she said aloud. 'I know it must be difficult for you.'

'*Very* difficult,' said Mrs Flynn swiftly. 'Now we're getting to know more people in Elm Hill we find we must have this room to entertain them. Why, only yesterday, when you were out at tea with young Mr Drew, Mrs Porter called in – the one you met at my tea-party, remember?'

Anna did indeed remember the velvet pancake hat above the vast marshmallow face.

'And I had to ask her into the dining-room just as I'd taken tea in. And it was sprats at that!' she added bitterly.

Anna was about to ask what was wrong with a good healthy

sprat, lightly fried, but noticing Mrs Flynn's apparent chagrin, thought better of it.

'It would have been all the same, as I said to Mr Flynn when she'd gone, if she'd brought her friend Lady Parr with her. Anyway, that decided it.'

'I quite understand,' said Anna. 'But you can see my difficulty. I really have nowhere to work.'

'You'll have to manage with the top of the dressing table,' said Mrs Flynn, rising. 'Unless you prefer to get other lodgings, of course,' she added tartly.

Anna would have preferred it, but knew only too well how hard it would be to find others. She decided to temporize.

'We'll see how things work out,' she said slowly. 'Maybe I can stay late at school one or two evenings.'

But as she watched Mrs Flynn tug at the intractable door she had already made up her mind that she must seek lodgings elsewhere, and her spirits rose at the thought, though cold reason did its best to damp them down.

Now that Tom had his father's car he and Anna were more adventurous on their occasional outings. They had been to the theatre once or twice, which had been difficult to do when relying on public transport, and more frequently drove out into near-by Buckinghamshire and then enjoyed a long walk in the fresh country air after being imprisoned in the classroom.

As the evenings grew lighter they went further afield, and it was on one of these happy occasions that Anna told Tom about looking for new lodgings.

'I'd already thought of it,' said Tom. Anna looked at him in open-mouthed surprise.

'And so had Mrs Armstrong,' continued Tom calmly. 'She thinks that you're being hopelessly exploited at Mrs Flynn's, and so do I. And if you like the idea, she suggests that you take over my digs when I leave.'

'*Like* the idea!' almost shouted Anna. 'There's nothing I'd like more! It's absolutely perfect!'

Tom seemed delighted at her reaction.

'Let's go straight back,' Anna rattled on, 'and tell Mrs Armstrong how much I'd love it. It was good of her to think of me.'

In point of fact, it was Tom who had thought of it and suggested it to Mrs Armstrong. She was only too pleased to agree. The rooms were there to be let, she liked Anna, and was sorry for the girl in her present circumstances. She was sorrier still for Tom who, she guessed, was sad enough at heart in leaving Anna behind, even if it were only for a little while, and who would be somewhat comforted to know that she was being left in good hands.

Anna's relief was great. She had dreaded tramping the blowsy streets of Elm Hill, mounting unknown staircases, and battling with hard-faced landladies. Now it was all resolved for her, and the thought of Mrs Armstrong's warm comfortable house and her lavish table was inexpressibly cheering.

'I was beginning to wonder where on earth I'd be next term,' confessed Anna. 'It can be horribly depressing in the autumn at Elm Hill. But I shall be so snug at Mrs Armstrong's with a real fire with logs, and your comfortable armchair – I quite look forward to next winter now!'

'In fact,' said Tom, with a grave face, 'you'll really prefer my room to my company.'

'Oh, of *course* not!' said Anna vehemently, falling into the trap, 'I shall miss you terribly, and wish you were there too.'

'Thank you, kind child,' said Tom, 'though I did have to prompt you! In any case I shall come back often – very often. You know that surely?'

'I hope you will,' said Anna soberly.

'Of course I shall,' said Tom. 'And in any case,' he added primly, 'Mrs Armstrong has invited me particularly!'

The verse-speaking and choral competitions were now upon them, and Elm Hill, in company with a dozen or more primary schools, had entered teams for this two-day event which took place in the Town Hall.

Anna's presence was not required at the choral day, but as two of her class were entered for the verse-speaking competition, she was to take her children to hear the contestants.

Miss Hobbs had been in charge of the training, which she conducted with the same forthright vigour with which she took her 'Rhythmic Work' classes. For the past few weeks peremptory summonses had arrived at Anna's desk requesting the immediate attendance of Freda Carter and Gabrielle Pugg, the red-haired door monitor, at a rehearsal. At least, thought Anna, as the day of the competition dawned, that's one interruption less to face each day.

The morning was sparkling-bright. The 'ever-changing panorama of the heavens' which arched so magnificently above the sordid pettiness of Elm Hill, was alight with shining, fast-moving, white clouds. A brisk wind, albeit tinged with sulphurous fumes from the near-by gas-works, raised the spirits, and the thought of getting out of the frying-pan of the classroom, even if it were into the fire of the Town Hall, was invigorating.

All the junior teachers were busy in the cloakrooms seeing that their charges were well wrapped up for the half-mile walk, that socks were pulled up, shoelaces tied, and coats properly buttoned, so that Elm Hill School should appear before the public gaze as a credit to its name and its headmistress. Miss Enderby herself, in a new green suit and elegant black hat surmounted by cocks' feathers, led the party out of the school gates and towards the distant arena.

The journey was not without incident, as might be expected. The infants had been left behind, but even so half Elm Hill School presented a formidably long crocodile winding its way along the new pavements and across rutted unmade roads. Arnold had to be publicly reprimanded for helping himself to a spray of cherry blossom overhanging the pathway. Miss Hobbs, a prey to agitation, had forgotten to bring the seating plans for the hall and was forced to rush back down the length of the column to retrieve them from school, brushing aside all offers of help. Gabrielle Pugg, in an advanced state of nerves, was threatened with nose-bleeding, and made the journey with a handkerchief clutched against her face, like some poor unfortunate who has just escaped from the dentist's clutches.

It was a relief to get inside the murky Town Hall, despite its cold musty odour, and to find themselves ranged at the side of the great hall under the balcony which ran round three sides. Miss Hobbs, still perspiring from her exertions, collected her team in one special row and sat guarding them like a jealous bulldog. Gabrielle Pugg sat next to her, her head thrown back, while Miss Hobbs applied cold pennies to the nape of her neck, and called last-minute advice to the rest of the row, in a voice that could have successfully raised the dead.

Anna saw that the adjudicators were ranged at a large table on a dais at the back of the hall, facing the stage. There were three men and three women, a jumble of papers, handbags, spectacles, a glass of water, and a microphone. This was certainly more fun than arithmetic, thought Anna pleasurably, and settled back, on her uncomfortable bench, to enjoy this day's outing.

The first school to file self-consciously on to the stage was St Matthew's, a near neighbour of Elm Hill, but housed in a grimy block not far from the station. Anna had looked upon its black walls, and its arid yard enclosed behind high rusty railings, and had thanked her stars that her appointment had not been there.

St Matthew's selected verse-speaking group placed themselves neatly on the platform. They had been arranged in height and made a goodly show, their dazzling white socks catching the eye and leading it to the neat grey tunics or suits above. Their faces, all uniformly pink and gleaming with soap, registered a variety of expressions, ranging from frank alarm to smug self-importance. Their teacher, arrayed in her best navy-blue suit, with an edging of pink petticoat showing, faced them from a small dais. Her back was towards the audience, but it was quite apparent that she was rallying her band by the answering flickers and half-smiles which played upon her charges' features.

The first poem chosen by this school was:

Said the wind to the Moon, 'I will blow you out!'
  'You stare
  In the air
  Like a ghost in a chair,
  Always looking what I am about –
  I hate to be watched; I'll blow you out.'

It had never been one of Anna's favourites, and by the time St Matthew's had finished with it, she doubted if she would ever be able to face it again. Alas, it seemed more than likely that she would have to do so several times that morning, for only four poems had been put forward for selection. Two had to be chosen and it seemed, from the disparaging comments of the school behind her, that this same poem had also been chosen by them to impress the judges.

St Matthew's school had put such a wealth of expression, both of voice and countenance, into their rendering that Anna wondered how their hard-working teacher could bear it at such close quarters. Never was there such shooting forward of lips for 'moon' and 'blow' and 'out'. Never was there such vehemence as that projected into the phrase 'I hate to be watched'. There was even a concerted stamp of right legs, a uniform flashing of white socks, on the word 'hate'.

Anna felt too embarrassed to watch, and was astounded at the barrage of applause which greeted the end of this interminable ordeal. St Matthew's filed off, beaming with pride and relief, and the adjudicators conferred busily at the rostrum.

The second entry was a group from a school near the Buckinghamshire border, and they had chosen to recite 'Five Eyes'.

Despite their own and their teacher's endeavours, there remained a comforting Buckinghamshire flavour to their vowel sounds, so that the title rang out: 'Foive Oyes' and the words 'noit' and 'broight' ran with pleasant homeliness in Anna's ears attuned to country voices.

Not so their successors, whose diction was so genteel that 'Faive Ayes' was only the prelude to a painful few minutes of tortured vowel sounds. Their pink, obedient little jaws dropped so zealously that Anna had some difficulty in recognizing:

'Then dah-oon they pah-oonce, nah-oo in nah-oo ah-oot,' for the line it really was.

Elm Hill, she knew, had chosen 'Berries', and when their turn came she was amazed to find how nervous she was on their behalf. But she need have had no fears. Miss Hobbs's broad back, solidly resplendent in brown dog-tooth check, gave one a wonderful feeling of confidence. Gabrielle Pugg had quite recovered and stood in the middle of the front row, her red hair, green eyes, and raw pink nose all aflame.

They got off to a flying start and romped along in cheerful unison. Miss Hobbs had trained them well, thought Anna, and was delighted that their effort was so well received.

The morning wore on. The Town Hall grew stuffier and stuffier, despite some cruel draughts from nine massive windows set very high in the walls, each depicting one of the Muses in regrettable stained glass. The lunch break was more than welcome.

Sandwiches were provided for everybody, the teachers having collected payment beforehand for this refreshment, and while Anna was looking doubtfully at a very thick sandwich with an unidentifiable filling, Tom loomed up beside her.

'Come and have something at The Three Feathers,' he said 'Flo says we're all to get some air for a few minutes. She's going to hold the fort.'

Anna thankfully accompanied him into the bright May morning. Somewhere, above the wasteland, a lark was singing, trickling forth a cascade of bright notes as pure and clear as icy water. Anna tilted her head up to look at it, screwing up her eyes against the dazzling sunlight.

'Doesn't it make you long to rush back to the country?' she cried.

Tom looked at her, as she stood against a background of mean houses, moving traffic, and the distant factory chimneys which lined the horizon.

'You'll be there very soon,' he promised.

*

Pleasantly replete, Anna returned to the afternoon session in a state of semi-somnolence. The sun, filtered through the nine Muses, cast a variety of colours upon the hundreds sitting in the hall and, Anna watching their slow-moving beams, felt as though she were one of many tiny stones in the depths of some huge kaleidoscope.

The poems followed hard on the heels of each other. The wind blew the moon, the old woman picked blackberries, and the miller's three cats continued to pounce, occasionally giving way to an interlude for the fourth poem, which was:

'Art thou poor, yet hast thou golden slumbers?' one which, Anna decided, fitted her own case very neatly.

A professional *diseuse*, of hideous gauntness, gave a short recital of modern poems, which gave a pleasant breathing-space to the afternoon's labours, and if one closed one's eyes, Anna decided, the result was unalloyed pleasure.

The judges' comments and the awarding of places ended the day's competition and Elm Hill came second. Miss Hobbs, pink and breathless with delight, bore off a silver cup with a lid which did not quite fit; and everyone returned home in the greatest good spirits.

'How did it go?' asked Joan Berry the next day. It was the dinner hour and she and Anna were alone in the babies' room which was Joan's domain.

'Very well,' answered Anna, and proceeded to tell her all about the competition, while Joan searched through her huge new calf handbag for a lipstick.

'Drat these new-shaped bags!' said Joan, lifting out the contents and dumping them on her desk. 'Can never find a thing! Everything you want falls to the bottom. Next time I'll buy one with pockets and zips and compartments, like my mother uses.'

She took out a letter with the next assorted handful and Anna could not help noticing, with a shock of surprise, that the envelope was addressed in young Ted's unmistakable hand.

He habitually used a very fine nib and black ink and had a spidery ornate style inherited from his first school-mistress, who had been an elderly Frenchwoman. It was strangely out of keeping with Ted's large strong hands that they should wield such a ladylike pen.

Anna's narrative faltered as she averted her gaze from the letter, but Joan did not seem aware of it. She found her lipstick, plied it vigorously and replaced her property without comment.

'Is Maurice still with you?' asked Anna, for something to say. Joan's bright mouth took on a grim line.

'He won't be after tonight,' she said, with unusual force.

'Frankly, I'm jolly glad to hear it,' said Anna. 'You know how I've felt.'

'Well,' said Joan, 'I hadn't intended to spill the beans to anyone, but it would be quite a relief to get it off my chest if you could bear with me for a few minutes.'

'You know I'm all agog,' said Anna. 'It's like a serial story for me – though I know it's a good deal more than that for you, poor darling.'

Joan settled back in her hard chair, put her elegant legs up on the desk and lit a cigarette. She appeared calm, but Anna noticed that her eyes were troubled and her hand shook as she held her lighter. What had that wretched Maurice done to upset her so?

'I told you that something definite would have to happen to make me tough enough to sling Maurice out into the snow. Well, it's happened. I'm pretty sure he's pinched some money of mine.'

'No!' said Anna, aghast.

'My own fault, I suppose,' said Joan, flicking ash at the waste-paper basket under the desk. 'You know what a curse it is to get to the banks when you're teaching. They're closed after school and it cuts into the dinner hour to go then, and if you leave it till Saturday morning it's one mad spurt to fit in the shopping and washing the week's smalls before the banks close at twelve, so I normally make one sortie and keep rather a lot of money loose at home.'

'Don't you lock it up?' asked Anna.

'Not since poor old Hobbs had her month's wages pinched and a Queen Anne bureau bashed up into the bargain! No, I stuff five quid among my corsets and another five among the gloves, and a few notes in my desk drawer and some in my wallet – you know the sort of thing – but of course it was a temptation to a broken reed like Maurice. His new girl is rather predatory, I gather. I think he needs a lot of money at the moment.'

'But he's earning now –' protested Anna.

'Obviously not enough,' commented Joan. 'In any case, five pounds has disappeared overnight from my glove drawer, and I think the odd note or two has been vanishing here and there for the past few weeks, but I can't be sure.'

'I can lend you some money,' Anna said, 'if you're short.'

Joan squeezed her hand affectionately.

'Bless you, my child, but I'm still solvent. The maddening thing is that I'd seen an amethyst clip which I felt I must have. Well, now I shall just have to do without, I suppose. At least it's played its part – I feel so savage, when I think of it, I could throw Maurice out of a top window with one hand tied behind me!'

'Don't relent!' exhorted Anna, delighted to see the fires of righteous wrath so kindled in her friend. 'Do it tonight! My goodness, it should have happened months ago.'

'So everyone says, including your nice Ted,' said Joan.

'How did he know?' asked Anna. 'I didn't breathe a word.'

'I told him one day in an expansive moment,' confessed Joan. 'We've met twice in town. He's been up about some farm machinery once or twice, and he's a comforting sort of fellow to pour out one's heart to. He offered to throw Maurice out for me immediately. Said he'd simply love to!'

'He would too,' said Anna, smiling at the thought.

'A nice downright young man,' said Joan, 'very like you. You'd make a good honest pair.'

'There's no chance of that,' Anna assured her. 'I don't like him well enough.'

'Tom Drew will be relieved to hear it,' said Joan, rising to her feet and disposing of her cigarette end.

At this interesting stage of the conversation, two things happened to distract their attention. The bell shrilled, summoning them to the playground in readiness to lead in their charges for the afternoon session; and even more compelling, Miss Enderby, clad again in her neat green suit and dashing hat, could be seen making her way to her car.

Joan clutched Anna's arm.

'D'you know what? I believe Flo's off for her interview. I heard a rumour that there are three on the short list and the appointment's being made today.'

'No one's said a thing,' objected Anna. 'Surely Miss Hobbs would know?'

'Miss Hobbs's lips are sealed until she receives orders from Miss E. to unseal them,' Joan told her. 'But, mark my words, Flo's finest hour is now upon her!'

They watched their headmistress enter the car, arrange her hat, and insert the car key.

'And good luck to the old girl, say I!' continued Joan warmly, her own cares forgotten. 'Let's hope she pulls it off!'

Chapter Nineteen

MISS ENDERBY TRIUMPHS

The staff of Elm Hill School looked in vain next morning for some sign of success or failure from Miss Enderby.

Morning assembly went as smoothly as ever and the headmistress smiled imperturbably at her flock as they walked from the crowded hall to their classrooms.

'Must be hearing by post,' hissed Joan Berry in Anna's ear, as she passed her in the corridor. 'Perhaps it's a close fight!'

It was all most intriguing and Anna was amazed to find how keenly she wanted Miss Enderby to have her hopes fulfilled.

'I'm getting a thorough-going Elm-Hillite,' she thought amusedly as she settled in her wooden armchair in front of her class.

The suspense was short-lived. At playtime, the next afternoon, Florence Enderby bore into the staff room a large iced sponge-cake, which she placed on the table with a flourish.

'This is something in the nature of a celebration,' she told her expectant staff. 'I want you all to know before anyone else does.'

Her bright gaze swept round the staff room. Her cheeks were pink and she looked unusually handsome. The sapphire ring flashed as she smoothed back her white locks.

'I have been lucky enough to be appointed Head of the new school.'

There was a buzz of congratulation. Everyone was genuinely glad that Miss Enderby had succeeded, and she smiled and nodded her appreciation as the tongues wagged round her.

'The only sad thing,' she went on, when the noise had died down, 'is that I shall have to leave so many of you behind. But I hope, most earnestly, that if you are infants' teachers and would like to continue with me, you will give me your company in the new building. Please think it over. I shall want all the support I can get in this new post.'

Miss Hobbs hurried forward with a knife and Miss Enderby attacked the cake. Someone had raided the kitchen and Anna found herself with the added refinement of a plate for her slice of cake. Normally, the staff were glad enough to balance any such largesse on their saucers, but a plate apiece seemed to emphasize the auspiciousness of this particular occasion.

The post for the junior school, which Miss Enderby would vacate, was advertised in the following week's *Teacher's World* and *The Times Educational Supplement*. A headmaster was to be appointed, the advertisement said, and he would be expected to take up his appointment on 2 September.

'There'll be an ugly rush from half the heads in the area,' prophesied Andy Craig. 'Four-Eyes is making his plans already. I came with him on the bus this morning.'

Four-Eyes, Anna knew, was the ribald name given to a heavily-bespectacled headmaster at a neighbouring school.

'If you mean Mr Forbes,' said Miss Hobbs, primly, 'I doubt if he has a chance. No one's ever forgotten his outburst at the N.U.T. conference.'

'Besides,' said Alan Foster, 'he's no qualifications worth anything. He was my junior at college. And look at his wife!'

Anna thought, with amusement, how parochial school life was under its impersonal veneer. She might have been listening to gossip in her own village. Perhaps, after all, human nature remained much the same, no matter what its environment might be. Would she be any pleasanter as a person if her lot had fallen in better surroundings? The nebulous plans for a country headship one day included a vision of herself as a mellow, wise woman drawing in spiritual refreshment from the natural beauties around her. Would it really be so? Anna found that the more she discovered about people's reactions to their circumstances the more baffling it all became.

'What they want here,' said Alan Foster pontifically, 'is a lively young man in his fifties, say, with plenty of outside interests of a cultural kind – painting, for instance.'

'Or writing,' suggested Andy Craig solemnly. 'Going to apply, Alan?'

'No, no,' said Alan hastily, turning a trifle pink. 'I've too much on hand, in any case. The arithmetic series will take me a few months yet, and I think there's a positive mine for backward children waiting to be tapped. Not,' he added as an afterthought, 'that they'd consider me.'

Almost all the infants' staff had decided to transfer to the new building with their present headmistress. From outside, the school looked almost complete, though the chaos of builders' materials surrounded it still.

Anna had visited it, during the dinner hour, on several occasions, and now she went again with Joan Berry to see where that young lady would be teaching the babies, for Miss Enderby had promised her the reception class as soon as she had heard that Joan would be remaining with her.

The long corridors echoed hollowly. The walls were still of stark grey breeze blocks unadorned as yet with plaster and paint. Wood shavings swirled about their feet in the draughts which eddied from the doorless classrooms, and the cold, antiseptic smell of new wood was everywhere.

The babies' room was in the sunniest corner of the block very near the entrance hall. Joan was delighted with the windows from ceiling to floor on one side and the generous rows of low cupboards which lined the other three sides of her room. Even Anna felt a pang of envy at such wonderful surroundings.

'Well, come too!' urged Joan. 'Infants are much more fun to teach!'

'They'd kill me,' said Anna. 'It's bad enough when they can read a bit – but when they can't even do that –!'

'It's murder while you're at it,' agreed Joan. 'But there's no marking to take home in the evening, and we do end school half an hour earlier.'

'No thanks,' replied Anna firmly. 'I'll stick to the older ones. Besides the new head might be a perfect darling.'

'Better the devil you know than the rogue you don't,' quoted Joan darkly.

They stepped through the french windows on to a terrace. Near by was a paddling pool painted a delectable shade of blue. Banks of earth, later to be grassed, surrounded it, and Anna could imagine it years hence mirroring the flowering shrubs, which were only marks on the architect's plans at this stage. Where would she be then, she wondered? And where would Joan be? Wherever it was, she felt suddenly sure, they would always remain friends.

She linked her arm in Joan's and stepping over a heap of cement-caked planks, the two girls sauntered back happily to their own quarters.

Open Day, as Anna had been warned, now cast its considerable shadow before it. In her innocence, she had imagined that it was simply a normal day in which parents could come to see their children going about their normal business. That a little light refreshment might be made available seemed reasonable enough, when school finished at four o'clock, and that teachers should be willing to discuss their children's work then with interested parents; but Anna had never imagined such preparations for the event. Had all this gone on behind the scenes in her own schooldays, she wondered?

She had spent many a long hour after school mounting work for display and selecting suitable pictures for her walls, but the climax came on the morning of the day itself, when desks were finally tidied, and any superfluous furniture was trundled out to make a little more space for the visitors to circulate in the afternoon.

The noise was deafening. The children were wildly excited and threw themselves energetically into their labours. Up and down the narrow gangways they raced flinging the debris from their desks into the waste-paper basket, until Anna feared for the safety of her newly hung specimens of work on the walls.

'You are to stay in your seats!' she shouted desperately to her mad charges. 'John will bring the basket round to you. And you are not to snatch the duster from each other like that! I shall choose a sensible, quiet child to dust the desks!'

There was some slight subsidence in the din after this harangue, punctuated by the crashing of books from piles insecurely balanced on seats while their owners busily chased dust, crumbs, pellets of blotting paper, and other desk-trivia through the hole obligingly left in the corners of the desks by the makers for just this purpose. The state of the floor was deplorable but Anna made up her mind to do all the moving first before sweeping up.

'I want four large strong boys to take out these two empty desks,' she said looking round the room. Silence fell, as small chests were thrown out and young backs elongated to make their owners look impressively tough. Anna felt that she was beginning to know her job. Could those psychology lectures at college really be bearing fruit, she wondered?

She chose her henchmen and between them they heaved and hauled the desks through the door and to the end of the corridor. A formidable pile of school furniture was already assembled here, and Tom Drew was trying to put it in some semblance of order. The noise of banging wood was stupendous, and from all the classrooms rose a babel of sound from excited children.

'I'm thinking of taking up pneumatic drilling. More peaceful!' shouted Tom to Anna above the din. She nodded sympathetically before returning to the classroom and her vociferous mob.

The last object to be removed was a large model of a desert which the children had spent weeks preparing as part of their geography course. It was built in a large square sand tray, borrowed from Joan Berry's room, and was the pride of Anna's class.

Lovingly, they had constructed palm trees from green paper and straight twigs. With infinite patience they replaced them in the oasis, a bed of plasticine, whenever they toppled sideways. Arabs of various shades of brown, according to the plasticine available, had been constructed and dressed in scraps of material brought from home, and squatted by a looking-glass lake which reflected some somewhat misshapen creatures, recognized by the initiated as camels.

It had been a source of infinite interest to the children and the thought of its beauties being hidden from their parents' eyes was almost unbearable. They pleaded pathetically when Anna said that it would simply have to be moved out for the afternoon.

'But, miss, I *told* my mum to look out for it!'

'It's the best thing we've got here!'

'My dad wants to see the Arab wearing his bit of tie!'

Anna felt herself weakening. It was Gabrielle Pugg's tearful remark which made her relent finally, though she knew she would regret it during the visitation.

'I've told my mum all about my camel. She knows I call him "Charlie".'

Pressure was too great to resist and Anna succumbed. The unwieldy, dusty, much-loved object was allowed to stay, and Anna thought philosophically that parents complaining of barked shins and snagged nylons must blame them upon the eloquent tongues of their offspring.

Comparative order was now restored and Anna was relieved to hear the bell which told them that playtime was at hand. After play, she promised herself, the children would be set some really quiet work to calm them down, and she would put the finishing touches to the room with a few well-chosen flower arrangements. She looked forward to a little calm after the fury of the storm.

Anna, even now, had not yet learned the unpredictability of school life.

She returned to her classroom much refreshed for her brief break and cup of tea. There was still a buzz of chatter going on, but there was a different note to it, which Anna's ear, fast becoming sensitive to the nuances of child-noise *en masse*, was quick to notice.

A knot of children stood by her desk peering down intently at something which Arnold held. It would be Arnold, thought Anna, hastening to investigate.

The children parted to let her approach her chair and Arnold held up his trophy with pride. It was a dead slow-worm.

Country girl though she was, Anna had a natural horror of legless things, such as snakes, and even harmless worms and humble little legless lizards, such as this, filled her with revulsion, against all the dictates of her cold reasoning. It would never do, however, to let the children think that she was afraid. With commendable promptitude she praised Arnold and quickly took out a plasticine board from the cupboard.

'Put it on here, dear,' she said, quivering inwardly as the end of the dangling creature brushed her hand. 'Then you can take it round to show the others.'

There were some gasps of apprehension from some of the little girls, and squeaks of horror.

'Don't like snakes!'

'It might be poisonous!'

'Don't you bring it near me, Arnold!'

'Nonsense!' said Anna bravely. 'This is a harmless little animal. It isn't a snake, in any case, and if it were you shouldn't feel frightened of it.'

What a hypocrite I am, thought Anna! She tried to look with brisk efficiency at Arnold's treasure, coiled in an unlovely loop across the plasticine board.

'Where did you find it?' she asked.

'One of the workmen found it, miss. It was curled up in some sand. He said: "'Ere, kid, get your teacher to learn you about this!" So I brought it in.'

'It was very kind of him,' said Anna mendaciously.

Arnold, having arranged the slow-worm artistically, stood back to admire it. He smelt his hands interestedly.

'I smells awful,' he remarked, smiling proudly. Anna's distaste for the slow-worm grew, but she put a determinedly bright smile upon her lips.

'Run and wash them, and I'll take it round,' she said, screwing her courage to the sticking place. She looked round her class, putting off the evil moment.

'I shan't think of coming until I see straight backs,' said Anna firmly. The children arranged their bodies in more orthodox form, with unusual swiftness.

'This is a slow-worm,' said Anna, 'that Arnold has brought in. It is really a lizard without legs. It is absolutely harmless and if you ever see one alive you must not harm it. Slow-worms do a great deal of good.'

She paused impressively, partly to add emphasis to her short homily, but mainly to gain strength to pick up the body. It really did smell peculiar, she thought, as she reached towards it, and the sooner it was decently buried the better.

Fighting down her disgust she lifted the board. The slow-worm joggled in the most horrifyingly life-like way as she took it to the front of the class. Gabrielle Pugg backed away nervously.

'I don't want to see it, please miss,' she gasped hastily.

'There's *nothing*, absolutely *nothing*, to be frightened of,' protested Anna advancing.

At this point the slow-worm rolled, in sickening slow motion, over the edge of the board and slid down the length of Anna's frock to the floor. Stifling a scream, and frozen to the spot with horror, Anna heard the revolting plop as it hit the boards.

It was as much as she could do to look down at it, and to pick it up was beyond her. Luckily, a cheerful little boy, whose nerves presumably had been removed, leapt to his feet, scooped up the odorous corpse and dumped it with loving care upon its bier again.

Anna backed away hastily and tried to control her trembling voice.

'Thank you, John. Would you like to carry it round?'

'*Please!*' said the child, with fervour. His eyes shone as he bore it carefully up and down the aisles, and Anna, still shuddering, was able to lean against the furthest cupboard and recover.

As soon as was decently possible, the corpse was put into a paper-bag shroud and John was entrusted with its immediate burial in the school garden.

Anna watched its departure with relief, opened all the windows, sprinkled a little eau-de-Cologne on her handkerchief and mopped her brow.

'Now, children,' she said, returning to her duties, 'you can all draw a picture of the slow-worm and write a few sentences about it. The best ones can go on the wall for your parents to see this afternoon.'

They set to with a will, and peace reigned again. That pathetic, little, dead wisp of malodorous matter had served a useful purpose after all, thought Anna, watching her children's downbent heads and flying pencils. And all is grist to the mill for teachers.

The afternoon, in contrast. seemed almost leisurely. The parents, many of them known to Anna through the Parent-Teacher Association, were flatteringly pleased with all they saw and complimented Anna on the work shown on the walls and set out on the children's desks. The children were at their most endearing, anxious to show their exercise books to proud fathers and mothers and busily pointing out their own particular contributions to the splendour of the classroom.

'See that fish? No, not that one! The next one – the *good* one! That's mine!'

'Me and Bobby done that picture. Ain't it nice?'

Mrs Pugg was introduced to Charlie the camel, and Anna was relieved to see how much admired the desert model was. No doubt the parents had followed its progress daily from the first pouring in of sand until the final glory of the looking-glass water had been added. In any case they greeted it like an old friend and did not appear to mind edging their way round its awkward bulk.

Anna's heart warmed to them as they eased their way through the congestion of desks and children. Their delight was spontaneous in their children's excitement, and though they may have felt parental misgivings when confronted by some of the besmeared and inaccurate pages in their offsprings' exercise books, they were indulgent enough to keep them from Anna.

When one or two of them thanked her for her work Anna felt unaccountably humble. She was honest enough to realize that it was the parents of children who would make progress however badly taught who most readily gave her the credit, but it was heart-warming to be praised, and she was grateful.

When it was all over, and only the crumbs on the hall floor and the bruised grass in the garden bore witness to the hundreds who had invaded the premises, Anna, wearily locking her classroom cupboards, looked back upon her first Open Day. It may have meant weeks of work, it may have seemed uncommonly like 'window-dressing', and it certainly showed the school in its best silk rather than its everyday homespun; but, on the whole, she decided, remembering the parents' interested faces, it had been well worth it.

Chapter Twenty

THE YEAR'S END

The heat and glare of high summer did nothing to flatter Elm Hill and Anna found the district at its worst.

Clouds of dust, from the unmade roads and the new concrete of half-made buildings, blew endlessly across the flat wastes, covering everything with fine grit. The long light evenings kept the children late at play in their gardens and in the roads, and Anna could hear their shrill wranglings wherever she went. They swarmed about the hot pavements, many of them pot-bellied in smelly elastic bathing costumes and with reeking, slimy feet encased in hot rubber sand-shoes. Most of them clutched garish-coloured ice-lollipops in their sticky hands, and it was not surprising that as the long hot spell continued they grew increasingly fractious and inattentive in school.

Anna paid a visit to the local swimming bath, but the crowds in and around the water, the noise, the smell, and the water itself, which was unpleasantly warm and slightly viscous, filled her with such disgust that she went no more.

Walking back through the paper-strewn streets, dodging the busy shoppers and their panting dogs, Anna thought longingly of the fields of home. There the cattle would be collected in the deep shade of the elm clumps, while the heat shimmered into blue distance. It would be quiet there; quiet enough to hear a bee bumbling in and out of the Canterbury bells in the border, quiet enough to hear the whinny of her pony two fields away. The house would be drowsing in the heat, its outside walls warm to touch, but inside the stone-flagged floors and thick old walls would ensure a haven of coolness. The very presence of surrounding trees and

grass, breathing out their fragrance into the sunlight, promised
solace from the heat, but here, thought Anna, looking at the flash
of chrome and glass reflecting the glare from the tawdry shop
fronts, there was no refreshment to be found. Town life might have
to be her lot for a year or two, but of one thing she became
increasingly conscious. She must make her home in the country.
She was as lost here, in this wilderness of bricks and mortar, as any
pitiful fish lifted from the water and wilting on the bank.

She had made her way home through the old part of Elm Hill
and found herself looking once again through the gates of the
vicarage. The garden was as shabby as ever, and now, brown and
baked with the drought, presented an even more pathetic front.
There was something different about it too, thought Anna, and
then realized, with a shock of dismay, that the cedar tree, its only
touch of beauty and majesty, had been cut down.

Anna felt the tears sting her eyes as she hurried on. It seemed the
last straw. How much loveliness had been destroyed to make this
sprawling, modern, formless horror? She remembered the old man's
words, so many months ago: 'There used to be lovely beds of white
violets. Under all these pavements now, they are!' and she grieved
for the piteousness of it all.

The cedar tree had gone. Soon Tom would be gone. Elm Hill,
next term, would be a desert indeed.

As the term wore on the building activities became more and more
frenzied in the new school. Miss Enderby was a constant visitor,
and Anna, from her high window, watched her headmistress entering her new domain and surveying its growing beauties, several
times a day. Despite the heat, Florence Enderby appeared tireless.
It seemed as though this new project had given her added zest. Her
spirits were high, her smile radiant, and her staff basked in the
balmy atmosphere. Now that her hopes were fulfilled and her
energies directed towards this long-awaited venture, Miss Enderby's
tension relaxed. It certainly made the last few weeks of a gruelling
term very much pleasanter.

The new headmaster had been appointed. His name, they learnt, was Charles Willoughby, and he came from a headship in Northumberland.

'Another foreigner from the Frozen North,' said Andy Craig. 'Beats me why they all flock south when you hear from their own lips how much better everything's done up there!'

'It's sheer altruism,' said Joan Berry. 'They like to give us the benefit of their good luck.'

'It might have been Four-Eyes, don't forget,' said someone else warningly. 'At least we've been spared that.'

'Forbes would have been an excellent choice,' said Alan Foster primly. 'A good sound chap. He was thought a lot of at college, I remember.'

Anna could not help being amused at this complete *volte-face*. Last time poor Four-Eyes had been suggested, she remembered, Alan Foster's scorn had been withering.

'Mr Willoughby's coming to see the school next week,' said Miss Hobbs. 'He's putting up at The Feathers for the night. I met the landlord's wife at Choral practice last night.'

Anna felt warmed by such domestic details. She might have been back in the village, she thought happily.

'Well, I hope he brings his Keatings with him,' said Andy Craig slanderously.

Miss Hobbs raised her eyebrows significantly at Anna to show how much she deplored such vulgarity in the staff room. Andy Craig remained cheerfully impervious to this well-bred hint and rattled on.

'Poor chap! We'll have to show him round a bit. Can't have him thinking that that little flea-club is the best the south can offer. Wonder where he'll live when he moves down here?'

'If he has any sense,' said Miss Hobbs pointedly, 'he'll find somewhere at a distance from the school. And the staff!'

'Good luck to him anyway,' said Andy Craig, tossing down the dregs of his tea cup and wiping his luxuriant moustache with a gaudy silk handkerchief. 'He'll need all the northern pluck he's got to take on Elm Hill!'

*

One particularly hot afternoon, towards the end of term, Joan invited Anna to tea in her garden.

'The rent of the house is empty,' she said. 'Everyone's holidaying, lucky wretches. I'm monarch of all I survey, at the moment, and that includes a nice cool summer-house.'

It was wonderful, after the hot streets, to sit in the green shade of a matured garden and to see the sunshine filtered through the kindly screen of thick leaves. Here the bees hummed among the lime flowers, and a linnet sang from a rose bush, so that Anna might almost think she was at home. She stretched out luxuriously in the deck chair and listened to the last chapter in Maurice's brief history.

'He'd taken the money. He admitted it,' said Joan lazily. 'Not that he was contrite, of course; just simply hopping mad that I'd found out. Anyway, he said he was going to stay at dear Sandra's house, so I was spared the pain of evicting him.'

'Sandra!' commented Anna. 'It would be something like that! Is she likely to be taken in?'

'She *understands* him, dear,' said Joan mockingly. 'He has never really known security, so he tells me. I have been extraordinarily hard-hearted, I was informed, and he considers that I have no finer feelings whatsoever. He reminded me somewhat tearfully, that I laughed my head off when he fell in the river at Pangbourne. We were both about six then, and according to poor Maurice, I haven't changed a bit!'

'But what infernal cheek!' protested Anna. 'After keeping the little worm all this time. Were you furious with him?'

'Well, no,' admitted Joan. 'I'm afraid I hurt him much more than that. I laughed till I cried. He flung out of the flat, and I'm relieved to say I haven't seen him since.'

'What about his things?'

'He'd taken most of them to Sandra's already, but I sent his bath-salts and his sleeping-pills on. I must say it's wonderful to have the flat to myself.'

She rose to pack the tea things on the tray.

'Don't let's wash them now,' said Joan, sinking back after her task. 'It's too glorious to go in. Anyway, you're staying to supper and we'll face the shambles after that. I bet you'll have more to eat, even in my feckless *ménage*, than you will at Mrs Flynn's.'

'I can't wait to get to Mrs Armstrong's,' admitted Anna. 'Yesterday I was given one slice of luncheon sausage, cut as thin as paper, two lettuce leaves and half a tomato for my supper. Mrs Flynn said it was amazing how little one needed in this hot weather!'

'Never mind, you'll be home soon,' comforted Joan. 'Tell me your holiday plans.'

'Devon's off this year,' said Anna. 'The cottage roof is being taken off and put back, so we're staying at home and all helping with the harvest. My brothers are both old enough now to drive the tractor. I wondered –' She broke off and looked at Joan's elegant length doubtfully.

'Would you like to come too? Not to drive a tractor, I mean, but to stay?'

Joan sat up quickly.

'There's nothing I'd like more. But wouldn't I be a nuisance at a busy time like that?'

'You'd jolly well be made to help!' Anna assured her. 'My mother would love another pair of hands to cut sandwiches for the men. They take their lunch and tea out and they eat stacks and stacks of food.'

'It sounds heavenly,' said Joan truthfully. 'And I'd love to come.'

'And what's more,' said Anna, becoming quite excited at the prospect, 'Ted will be there.'

'That *quite* settles it, of course,' said Joan with mock gravity. But Anna could see that she was pleased.

Throughout the term Anna had had cause to remember Joan Berry's warning about the impossibility of getting much work done, but she had never quite realized how little would be accomplished in the children's class work.

The Choral Competition, the Verse-Speaking Competition, the School Sports, and Open Day were all behind her now, but the

Area Sports still loomed ahead and besides this an endless number of end-of-year chores remained to be done. Anna's record book bore witness to the lagging-behind of lessons. Far too often for her peace of mind, a prepared piece of work would have to be set aside for such things as running heats or collecting equipment.

End of term class examinations had to be fitted in, and Anna's own records of each child's progress. She found herself staying later and later at school to get her papers marked up, and her reports and marks made up. The sitting-room at Mrs Flynn's had been barred to her ever since she had given in her notice, and the atmosphere was bleaker than before in that unhappy household.

Anna wished that she had had some warning at college of the pressure of events at the end of the school year. Anxious herself about her future prospects as she approached the end of her probationary year, she found herself more and more impatient of interruptions and horrified at the unforeseen extra duties which crowded out almost all new teaching for the last half of the term.

One of her biggest headaches was stock-taking, which involved counting the many sets of books, and other apparatus, stacked in the classroom cupboards. Gabrielle Pugg seemed to be letting in and out a steady stream of her own and other people's children in search of missing property.

'Please have you got any spare *Happy Valley Readers*?'

'Miss Brown's lost six paint brushes. Have you got any?'

'Please did you return those scissors Miss Berry lent you?'

'Have you got a *Lipscombe Book 3* Arithmetic Book?'

A lighter touch was given by one of Tom Drew's boys who entered to say: 'Mr Drew's lost the globe.' Trust Tom, thought Anna, with amusement, to mislay one simple monumental article like the school globe! It reappeared finally, and inexplicably, in the caretaker's cupboard inside a new pail.

Added to Anna's labours, at this time, was the collecting of money for various things. The children not only paid for small objects which they had made in needlework or handwork lessons, but they had also been asked to contribute something towards a bouquet for Miss Enderby, as she was now to leave the juniors behind. Anna's desk drawer was ajingle with tobacco tins, supplied by Tom, each bearing its quota of money. She only hoped that in the press of events she had put the right amounts into the right tins.

It was almost a relief to get out of the chaos of her classroom to attend the Area Sports. This was to be the last out-of-school activity of the term, and Anna was heartily glad.

It was held in a large stadium about six miles from Elm Hill and the competitors were taken by bus. Anna had the onerous job of marshalling the children for each race and was nearly driven mad by absentees who had to be fetched from refreshment tents, lavatories, and distant portions of the vast stadium, in the very nick of time.

Tom Drew had an even less enviable post as Third Judge, which demanded a keen eye to see which competitor arrived in third place in each race.

'Don't you ever have doubts?' asked Anna when they met during the lunch break.

'Frequently,' said Tom, 'but I stick like glue to my decision. There'd be warfare otherwise.'

It was one of the most exhausting of Anna's teaching experiences, and the fact that the track was a cinder one added to the day's difficulties.

Black-faced, and with grit in her hair, eyes, and clothes, Anna returned to Mrs Flynn's bath ('Extra, of course,' came the echo, as she turned on the tap), and thanked her stars that another whole year would have to elapse before she need face Area Sports Day again.

On the last evening before Elm Hill School broke up, Tom came to Mrs Flynn's to help Anna collect her belongings and transfer them to his own lodgings.

It was the first time that he had met that redoubtable lady face to face, and Anna was amused to notice the alarm with which he observed Mrs Flynn's tight-lipped smile and cold bony handshake.

She accompanied them upstairs and hovered on the tiny landing as they collected the cases and books, whether for the sake of propriety or because she suspected that Tom might purloin some of her own belongings, Anna could not be quite sure. Her manner had grown increasingly off-hand as the last few hours of Anna's tenancy ran out.

'I'm sure she's been made as comfortable here as my own child,' she observed acidly, watching Tom negotiate the narrow stairs with Anna's suitcase. 'Mind the wallpaper, please. We don't want the expense of repapering *everywhere*. As it is, this bedroom will have to be done out, of course!'

She spoke as though Anna had spent her time throwing soup at her bedroom walls and stamping mud into the flimsy mat on the floor. Anna, for her part, heartily wished that she had. At least the miserable creature would have had some just cause for whining then!

Anna followed Tom into the car, and heaved a sigh of relief as Mrs Flynn slammed the front door shut at the third attempt. Despite the long hot spell all Mrs Flynn's doors remained obstinate.

'What a wicked old hay-bag!' said Tom, incensed. 'How you've stuck her all this time, I don't know! I should have hanged her from her own miserable banisters in the first week.'

'I didn't think they'd stand the strain,' said Anna candidly.

The contrast between her old quarters and the new delighted her. Tom's bedroom overlooked the leafy garden and was placed above the drawing-room where Anna had first had tea. It was a large square room, warmly carpeted and having two large cupboards, one of which, Anna noticed with approval, housed the hot water tank.

'You'll be pretty snug in the winter,' said Tom, following her gaze. 'Apart from some internal rumblings about two in the morning that old tank's very good company. I shall miss it!'

His trunk lay strapped at the foot of the bed, flanked by boxes and several grips containing the flotsam and jetsam of his time with Mrs Armstrong. Downstairs, in the little room which had been set apart for him and was now to be Anna's, stood piles of books, his gramophone, various bats, racquets, and a hockey stick.

'I'll pack the car up tonight,' he told Anna, 'so that I can flee from Elm Hill as soon as possible tomorrow.'

Mrs Armstrong was as hospitable as ever, despite her sadness at Tom's departure.

'He's a dear boy,' she told Anna repeatedly. 'A dear boy! I can't tell you how I shall miss him. It is such a comfort to me to know you are coming instead. And of course he'll come back *very often* to see you.'

Tom drove Anna back and stopped the car by Mrs Flynn's fast-expiring lilac tree.

'Dear old Mrs Armstrong!' said Tom. 'She's quite right, you know. I told you myself that I'd be coming back, didn't I?'

'You did indeed,' answered Anna. She put her hand on the door-handle, but Tom covered it with his own.

'But can I come and see you before that?' asked Tom. 'Can I come and see you at home?'

'Of course,' cried Anna.

'Often?'

'As often as you like,' Anna promised.

The last day of term was the breathless joyous time it always is, compounded of cheerful good wishes, hurried farewells, and general excitement.

Miss Enderby's bouquet of pink carnations was so large that two children were needed to bear it up the platform steps to present it to her, amidst thunderous applause, at morning assembly. She made a gracious little speech of thanks, and Anna felt quite sorry that she would not be returning to her care next term.

She had been a fine person to start work with, Anna thought, despite her oddities. She remembered the rout of Mrs Bond, the care she had taken to supervise her own first teaching steps, and her ready generosity to all the members of the staff. As Joan Berry had shown her, such trifling conceits as the sapphire ring and the insistence on somewhat archaic courtesies from the children could be readily forgiven in the light of such overwhelming virtues in a headmistress.

She looked round the hall at the staff and realized suddenly how much they had coloured her life in this last bewildering year. Each one had contributed something to her experience of human nature, and had made her, she hoped, more tolerant, and less of the prig she certainly had been.

She felt a sudden wave of affection for portly Alan Foster, still clapping politely at the conclusion of his headmistress's speech, but doubtless thinking of the next book with which to dazzle the educational world; and for Andy Craig, busily tightening the wrist-strap which would be for ever his talisman, the outward symbol of the hero-Andy he might have been.

Her gaze passed on to Joan and Tom to whom her debt was greatest. Not just for one year, but for many, she hoped humbly, would their lives be interwoven with her own.

As for the children, that excitable seething mob of hundreds, now raising the roof with three ear-splitting cheers for Miss Enderby, called for by Miss Hobbs, Anna guessed that they would remain the same dear, devilish, delicious, disarming, infuriating, and exhausting creatures wherever she met them and however long she taught. Somehow, the discovery filled her with surprising contentment.

Next morning Anna lay in the bath under the massive beams of the farm bathroom. The water was twice as deep and twice as hot as ever it was in Mrs Flynn's white-tiled cell.

The thought that she would never set foot again in that miserable establishment was enough to raise Anna's spirits; the added joy of seven weeks at home, far from Elm Hill and its inhabitants, was enough to set her singing. The smell of eggs and bacon cooking in the kitchen below began to mingle with the fragrance of the soapy water. Life was perfect!

She lay back savouring the glory of the moment. Above her, vast bright clouds of steam billowed in the morning sunshine. Outside she could hear her father talking to Ted in the yard, and in the background the voices of birds and animals rejoicing in the bounty of high summer. It was good to lie there drawing in all the pleasures of the present.

And what of the future? To Anna, wallowing gently, sluicing the water over her shoulders, and glorying in the warmth of the sun on her bare back, it all seemed as bright and nebulous as the silver steam above her. Somewhere, sometime, in the misty future, there might be a country school, a little house of her own set in quiet fields, and friends like Joan and Ted – and Tom. Of course Tom would be there.

Meanwhile it was enough to be young, to be hungry, and to be on holiday. She sprang up from the water, in a shower of silver drops, ready to face the bright day ahead.

THE MARKET SQUARE

To Olive and Philip with love

CONTENTS

Part One

Chapter One

A JUNE MORNING

It had been raining in Caxley, but now the sun was out again. A sharp summer shower had sent the shoppers into doorways, and many of the stallholders, too, from the market square, had sought more shelter than their flimsy awnings could provide.

Only fat Mrs Petty remained by her fish stall, red-faced and beaming through the veils of rain that poured from the covers above the herring and hake, the mussels and mullet. She roared a few rude and derisory remarks to her more prudent neighbours sheltering across the road, but the rain made such a drumming on the canvas, such a gurgling in the gutters, that it was impossible to hear a word.

It spun on the stones of the market square like a million silver coins. Office windows were slammed shut, shop-keepers braved the downpour to snatch in the wares they had been displaying on the pavement, and even the pigeons took cover.

It ended as suddenly as it had begun, and people emerged again into the glistening streets. The pigeons flew down from the plinths of the Corn Exchange and strutted through the shining puddles, their coral feet splashing up tiny rainbows as iridescent as their own opal necks. There was a fresh sweetness in the air, and Bender North, struggling out of his ironmongery shop with a pile of doormats in his arms, took a great thankful breath.

'Ah!' he sighed, dropping his burden on the pavement from which he had so recently rescued it. He kicked the mats deftly into a neat pile, and, hands on hips, breathed in again deeply. He was a hefty, barrel-shaped man and had been feeling the heat badly these last few days, and his much-loved garden was getting parched. This refreshing shower was welcome. He surveyed the steaming awnings in the market with an approving eye.

No one – not even Bender himself – could quite remember how he had come by his odd name. He had been christened Bertram Lewis thirty-five years earlier at the parish church across the market square. Some said that as a youth he had liked to show off his outstanding muscular strength by twisting pieces of metal in his great hands. Others, who had shared his schooldays at the old National School in Caxley High Street, maintained that he was so often called upon to 'bend over for six' that some wag had decided that 'Bender' was the perfect name for this boisterous, lusty rebel against authority. Whatever the reason, now long forgotten, for dubbing him thus, the name stuck, and if any stranger had asked in Caxley for Bertram North, rather than Bender North, he would have been met with blank countenances.

Bender watched the stallholders resuming their activities. The man who sold glue was busy smashing saucers deftly, and putting them together again with equal dexterity, while a crowd of gaping country folk watched him with wonder and amusement. Fat Mrs Petty shook a shower of silver sprats from the scale-pan into a newspaper. Tom and Fred Lawrence, who ran a market garden on the outskirts of the town, handed over bunches of young carrots and turnips, stuffed lettuces into already overcrowded baskets, weighed mounds of spring greens, broccoli, turnip tops, and potatoes, bawling with lungs of brass the while. This was Caxley at its best, thought Bender! Plenty of life, plenty of people, and plenty of money changing hands!

'A mouse trap, North,' said a voice behind him, and the ironmonger returned hastily to his own duties. He knew, before he turned to face his customer, who she was. That clipped authoritative boom could only belong to Miss Violet Hurley, and it was a voice that commanded, and unfailingly received, immediate attention.

'This way, ma'am,' said Bender, standing back to allow Miss Hurley to enter. He inclined his broad back at a respectful angle, for though the lady might buy nothing more than a mouse trap, she was a sister of Sir Edmund Hurley at Springbourne, and gentry needed careful handling.

'Sharp shower, ma'am,' he added conversationally when he was again behind the broad counter confronting his customer. She stood there, gaunt and shabby, her scrawny neck ringed with a rope of beautiful pearls, her sparse grey locks sticking out from under her dusty feathered hat like straw from beneath a ruffled hen.

'Hm!' grunted Miss Hurley shortly. Her foot tapped ominously on Bender's bare boards. This was not the day for airy nothings, Bender realized. Miss Hurley was in one of her moods. She should have found him in the shop, not dallying outside on the pavement. He reached down a large box from the shelf behind him, blew off the dust delicately, and began to display his wares.

'"The Break-back", "The Sterling", "The Invincible", "The Elite",' chanted Bender, pushing them forward in turn. He took a breath and was about to extract more models from the bottom of the box but was cut short.

'Two "Sterling",' snapped Miss Hurley. 'Send them up. Immediately, mind. Book 'em as usual.'

She wheeled off to the door, her back like a ramrod, her bony legs, in their speckled woollen stockings, bearing her swiftly out into the sunshine.

'Thank you, ma'am,' murmured Bender, bowing gracefully. 'You ol' faggot!' he added softly as he straightened up again.

He wrapped up the two jangling mouse traps, tied the parcel neatly with string, and wrote: 'Miss V. Hurley, By Hand' with a stub of flat carpenter's pencil.

'Bob!' he shouted, without looking up from his work. 'Bob! Here a minute!'

Above his head the kettles, saucepans, fly swats, and hobnail boots which hung from the varnished ceiling, shuddered in the uproar. A door burst open at the far end of the shop, and a black-haired urchin with steel spectacles fell in.

'Sir?' gasped the boy.

'Miss Hurley's. At the double,' said Bender, tossing the parcel to him. The boy caught it and vanished through the open door into the market square.

'And wipe your nose!' shouted Bender after him. Duty done, he dusted the counter with a massive hand, and followed the boy into the bustle and sunshine of the market square.

The first thing that Bender saw was Miss Violet Hurley emerging from Sep Howard's bakery at the corner of the square. Sep himself, a small taut figure in his white overall, was showing his customer out with much the same deference as the ironmonger had displayed a few minutes earlier. He held a square white box in his hands, and followed the lady round the corner.

'Taking a pork pie home, I'll be bound,' thought Bender. Howard's raised pork pies were becoming as famous as his lardy cakes. There was something particularly succulent about the glazed golden pastry that brought the customers back for more, time and time again. Pondering on the pies, watching the pigeons paddling in the wet gutter, Bender decided to stroll over and buy one for the family supper.

He met Sep at the doorway of the baker's shop. The little man was breathless and for once his pale face was pink.

'Been running, Sep?' asked Bender jocularly, looking down from his great height.

'Just serving Miss Violet,' replied Septimus. He paused as though wondering if he should say more. Unwonted excitement nudged him into further disclosures.

'She's as good as promised me the order for Miss Frances' wedding cake,' he confided. 'You could've knocked me down with a feather.'

He hurried into the shop in front of Bender and scurried behind the counter. Beaming indulgently, Bender followed with heavy tread. The air was warm and fragrant with the delicious odours from steaming pies, pasties, scones, fruit cakes and a vast dark dish of newly-baked gingerbread, glistening with fat and black treacle.

Mrs Howard was serving. Her hinds scrabbled among the wares, dropped them in paper bags, twirled the corners and received the money as though she had not a minute to lose. Howard's bakery was patronized by the stallholders as well as the town people on market day and trade was brisk.

'A pork pie, please, Sep,' said Bender. 'A big 'un. I'll pay now.'

He watched the baker inspecting the row of pies earnestly and felt amusement bubbling up in him. Same old Sep! Dead solemn whatever he was doing! Why, he'd seen him at school, years before, studying his sums with just that same patient worried look, anxious to do the right thing, fearful of causing offence.

'They all look good to me,' said Bender. 'Any of 'em'll suit me.' Lord love Almighty, he thought, we'll be here till Christmas if old Sep don't get a move on!

The baker lifted a beauty with care, put it in a bag and came round the counter to give it to Bender.

'I'll open the door for you,' he said. 'So many people pushing in you might get it broken.'

'That's what you want, ain't it?'

'You know that,' said Septimus earnestly.

They found themselves in the doorway, Sep still holding the bag.

'I should be able to let you have the last of the loan at the end of the week, Bender,' he said in a low voice.

'You don't want to fret yourself about that,' answered Bender, with rough kindness. 'No hurry as far as I'm concerned.'

'But there is as far as I am,' said Sep with dignity. 'I don't like to be beholden. Not that I'm not grateful, as you well know –'

'Say no more,' said Bender. 'Hand us the pie, man, and I'll be getting back to the shop.'

The baker handed it over and then looked about the market square as though he were seeing it for the first time.

'Nice bright day,' he said with some surprise.

'Expect it in June,' replied Bender. 'It'll be the longest day next week. Then we'll start seeing the trimmings going up. They tell me the Council's having bunting all round the square and down the High Street.'

'Well, it's over sixty years since the last Coronation,' said Septimus. 'About time we had a splash. It seems only yesterday we were decorating the town for the old Queen's Diamond Jubilee!'

'Four years ago,' commented Bender. 'That was a real do, wasn't it, Sep? Beer enough to float a battleship.'

He dug his massive elbow into the baker's thin ribs, and gave a roar of laughter that sent the pigeons fluttering. Septimus's white face grew dusky with embarrassment.

'Ah! I was forgetting you'd signed the pledge,' chuckled his tormentor. 'You'll have to change your ways now the war's over and we've got a new King. Be a bit more sporty, and enjoy life, Sep! Once we've crowned Edward the Seventh on June the twenty-sixth you'll find Caxley'll start fizzing. Keep up with the times, Sep my boy! You're not a Victorian any longer!'

Muttering some excuse the little baker hurried back to his customers, while Bender, balancing the fragrant white parcel on his great hand, strode back through the puddles and the pigeons, smiling at his secret thoughts.

Septimus stepped down into his busy shop, trying to hide the agitation this encounter had caused. Why should a brush with Bender always give him this sick fluttering in his stomach? He had known him all his life – been born within a few yards and in the same year as this man. They had shared schooldays, celebrations, football matches, and all the life of the little town, but always the rift remained.

'You're nothing but a yellow coward,' Sep told himself disgust-edly, stacking hot loaves in the window. 'Why can't you meet Bender man to man? He's no better than you are. His joking's only a bit of fun, and yet you are all aquake the minute he starts to tike a rise out of you.'

He watched Bender stopping to speak to one of the stallholders. He saw his great shoulders heave with laughter as he turned again and vanished into the murk of his shop. At once Sep's tension relaxed, and he despised himself for it. Did Bender ever guess, he wondered, how much he affected other people?

Take this morning, for instance, thought the little baker, threading his way through the customers to the comparative peace of the bakehouse at the back. Bender could never have known how much he would upset him by talking of Queen Victoria like that. The death of the old Queen had shaken many people. Septimus Howard was one of them. She was more to him than a reigning monarch. She was the mother of her people, a symbol of security, prosperity and order. She offered an example of high-minded principles and respectable family life. She was the arch-matriarch of a great nation. And Septimus loved her.

He loved her because, in his eyes, she had always been right and she had always been there, safely on the throne of England. His father and mother, staunch Methodists both, had revered the Queen with almost as much piety as the stern God they worshipped, thrice every Sunday, at the Wesleyan Chapel in the High Street. Their children, with the possible exception of flighty Louisa, shared their parents' devotion.

Septimus knew he would never forget the shock of that terrible news which Caxley had heard only a few months before. It was a dark January afternoon, the shop was empty and Sep had been engaged in cutting wrapping paper ready for the next day's supplies. He saw Tom Bellinger, the verger of St Peter's across the square, hurry up the steps and disappear inside. Within three minutes the tolling bell began to send out its sad message.

Sep put aside his knife and went to the door.

'Who's gone?' he asked Sergeant Watts, the policeman, who was striding by.

'The Queen, God rest her,' he replied. For one moment they stood facing each other in silence, then the policeman hurried on, leaving Septimus too stricken to speak. He made his way to the quiet warmth of the bakehouse and sat down, stunned, at the great scrubbed table where he made the loaves, letting the tears roll unchecked down his cheeks. Not even when his father had died had he felt such a sense of loss. This was the end of life as he knew it. An England without Queen Victoria at its head seemed utterly strange and frightening.

Septimus disliked change. He was not sure that he wanted to be an Edwardian. Something in that new word made him as nervous as he felt in Bender's presence. He suspected that the new monarch had some of Bender's qualities; his gusto, his hearty laugh, his ease of manner and his ability to know what the other fellow was thinking. The new King loved life. Septimus, his humble subject, was a little afraid of it. He mourned Victoria, not only for herself, but for all that she stood for – a way of life which had lasted for decades and which suited him, as it had suited so many of his fellow countrymen.

At the time of the Queen's Diamond Jubilee in 1897, a fund had been opened in Caxley to provide a lasting memorial of this outstanding reign. Septimus Howard was one of the first contributors. He gave as much as he could possibly afford, which was not a great deal, for times were hard with him just then, and his fourth child was about to he born. But he was proud to give, and prouder still when he stood in the market place, later that year, and watched the fine drinking fountain, surmounted by a statue of Her Majesty, being unveiled by the Mayor in his red robe of office.

Now four years later, the statue stood as an accepted landmark in Caxley. Children played on its steps and drank from the four iron cups chained at each corner of the plinth supporting the sovereign. The cheerful rogue who sold bunches of roses in the market, sprinkled his wilting blooms with water from the great basin, and Mrs Petty dipped in an enamel mug and sloshed the contents over the fish stall before the afternoon customers arrived. The fountain was much appreciated, and Caxley folk often wondered how they had managed so long without it.

But to Septimus, the statue above it gave greater comfort. He looked down upon it every morning whilst he shaved at the mahogany stand in the bedroom window. The view, it is true was shrouded a little by the lace curtains which modestly covered the windows, but that morning glimpse of Victoria meant much to the little baker.

And now, on this hot June morning, with excitement mounting everywhere at the thought of the Coronation so soon to come, Sep looked again at the small bronze crown just showing above the flapping awnings in the market square. The shop was more crowded than ever, the heat was intense, the noise deafening, but Sep had found new strength.

Bender's visit, the thought of the money he owed him, the staggering news from Miss Violet about the order for her niece's wedding cake, suddenly seemed to matter less. Somehow, Sep knew, he would be able to face everything. Surely, to have spent all the thirty-five years of one's life with the example of the Queen to follow must give a chap enough strength to recognize and perform his duties, and to welcome her son without trepidation!

He squared his shoulders, dropped six sugary buns into a paper bag and handed it down to a waiting urchin.

'Threepence, my dear,' said Mr Howard the baker briskly.

All fears had gone, and Sep was himself again.

Chapter Two

THE NORTHS AT HOME

'Nasty accident over at Beech Green,' observed Bender to his wife Hilda that evening.

'What's happened?' asked Mrs North, putting down the vast pair of trousers, belonging to her husband, which she was mending.

'Some youngster – forgotten his name – fell off the top of one of Miller's hay wagons. Young Jesse Miller was in the shop this afternoon. He told me. Just been up to see the boy at the hospital. Wheel went over his shoulder, so Jesse said. Pretty bad evidently.'

'People have no business to allow children to get into such danger,' said Hilda North firmly. 'Asking for trouble.'

Bender laughed.

'What about our kids and the boat?' he replied.

'I'm always saying,' retorted his wife, 'that I don't hold with it. One of these days one of ours will be drowned, and you'll only have yourself to blame, Bender.'

'You fret too much,' said Bender good-naturedly. 'They can all swim. What's the point in having a fine river like the Cax at the end of the garden if you don't have a bit of fun on it?'

His wife made no reply. This was an old argument and she had too much mending to get through to waste her energies that evening. Bender turned back to his desk and silence fell again in the sitting-room.

It was a vast, beautifully proportioned room on the first floor. It ran across the shop below and had three fine Georgian windows overlooking the market square. During the day, the room was flooded with sunlight, for it faced south, but now, at nine o'clock on a June evening, the room was in shadow, the gas lamp hissed gently in its globe on the ceiling, casting its light on Hilda's needlework and the great back of Bender bending over his crowded and untidy desk as he wrote out some bills.

Through the window before him he could see the last of the stallholders packing up. Two men with brooms were brushing up cabbage leaves, pieces of paper, orange peel, and all the market day débris. The setting sun shone pinkly on the upper parts of the buildings at right angles to Bender's shop. Septimus's bedroom window gleamed like a sheet of gold as it caught the last hour or so of dying sunlight. Soon its light would be doused by the creeping shadow of St Peter's spire, which lengthened and climbed steadily up the west-facing shops and houses in the market square, like some gigantic candle snuffer.

It was quiet in the great room. Bender hummed now and again and shuffled his papers, a faint squeaking from Mrs North's well-laced stays could be heard when she moved to reach more thread from her work-box, and occasionally the whirring of a pigeon's wings as it returned to roost on the parapet of the Norths' roof.

At last, Bender pushed his papers carelessly to the back of the desk, anchored them with a small ancient flat-iron, and threw himself, with a contented grunt, into the arm chair opposite his wife.

'Why you use that ugly old thing for a paper-weight I can't think!' commented Hilda. 'What's wrong with the glass one we bought at Weymouth last summer?'

'Too fiddle-faddle,' answered Bender easily. 'I like my old dad's flat-iron.'

He began to fill his black Turk's head pipe with deliberation. The fragrance of strong tobacco crept about the room as the great china tobacco jar beside him stood un-stoppered. His big roughened fingers worked delicately at his task, and when the tobacco was tamped down exactly as he liked it Bender took a long paper spill from a vase on the mantelpiece and, crossing to the gas lamp, held it above the globe until it caught fire.

Soon the room was wreathed in clouds of blue smoke, the stopper was replaced and secured with a massive brass screw on the top of the tobacco jar, and Bender was prepared for his evening relaxation.

He looked about him with pleasure. His possessions – the dearest of them still busy with her mending – gave him enormous quiet pride. He liked the grey watered silk wallpaper that had been new when they married twelve years ago, and was now comfortably grubby. He liked the sofa, the armchairs and the two prim little occasional chairs, flanking the sofa, all upholstered in good dark red velvet. He liked the heavy mahogany sideboard, richly carved, and crowded permanently with silver, china, bronze, as well as the ephemera of daily living such as letters awaiting answers, bundles of knitting, indigestion tablets, and spectacle cases.

There was something particularly satisfying too about the octagonal mahogany table which stood always by his armchair. His niece had worked the pink and red silk roses on the black satin mat, which stood plumb in the table top's centre. It was a handsome piece of work for a twelve-year-old to have accomplished, thought Bender approvingly, and she had finished it with a splendid silky fringe a good two inches in length. She had also made a companion piece which ran the length of the top of the walnut piano against the wall. Its beauties were somewhat hidden by Hilda's group of naked china cherubs and the two great nautilus shells which stood on each side of them, but the little girl's workmanship was much admired by those waiting to sing, one elbow lodged nonchalantly on the black satin runner while the accompanist was propping the music on the music rest.

No doubt about it thought Bender puffing dreamily, it looked rich, and he liked richness. His eye roamed indulgently over the crowded room, the wide wooden picture frames, the chenille curtains looped back with fine brass bands, and the cases of dried grasses and sea lavender on the corner brackets near by. It looked the sort of place a prosperous tradesman deserved, and he was indeed prospering. His wandering gaze came to rest upon his wife, now snipping busily at a frayed lining. It was to Hilda, as much as anything else, that he owed his growing prosperity. She worked as hard – harder maybe, thought Bender candidly – than he did himself. When they were first married they had thought nothing of being in the shop at seven in the morning until nine or ten at night. Somehow she had still managed to clean and cook, to sew and knit, and to bring up the family to be as industrious as she was herself.

She was a small plump young woman, fair-haired, and grey-eyed, with a pink button of a mouth, not unlike the old queen in her younger days. The bearing of three children – the first tragically stillborn – had thickened her waist a little, but tight lacing kept her figure still trim and shapely. To Bender's delight, she loved bright colours, unlike many matrons of her own age and times, and tonight she wore a lilac print frock decorated with bands of purple braid. Beneath its hem Bender could see her small black shoes adorned with cut steel buckles.

She looked across at him quickly, aware of his gaze.

'Where was Jesse Miller off to?' she inquired, harking back to the snippet of news.

'Never asked him. Beech Green, I should think. He'd done his buying at market and seen the young chap in hospital.'

'More likely to have gone up to my home,' commented Hilda. 'Pa says he's been calling to see our young Ethel lately.'

'Why not?' said Bender, smiling lazily. 'He must be twenty-odd, going to have a good farm with his brother Harold, when the old man goes aloft, and I reckon Ethel'd be lucky to get him.'

'He's a bit wild, they say,' responded Hilda, letting her mending fall into her lap and looking into the distance.

'Who's "they"?' asked Bender testily. 'There's too much gossip in Caxley. People here mind everyone else's business but their own! Makes me sick!'

He tapped out his pipe irritably.

'I'd sooner see young Ethel wed to Jesse Miller,' he continued, 'than that waster Dan Crockford she's so sweet on! What's the future in painting pictures for a living? He wants to get down to a job of work and keep his paint brushes for the week-end. If I were Dan Crockford's father I'd chuck him out to fend for himself! No, our Ethel's better off as a farmer's wife, and I hope she'll have the sense to see it!'

'Well, well, well! Don't get ratty about it,' replied his wife equably. 'They're both old enough to know their own minds, and it's time Ethel settled down.'

She rolled up the trousers briskly, and stood up, picking ends of thread from the lilac frock with quick pink fingers.

'Let's take a turn in the garden before we go up,' she said. 'It's still so hot. I wonder if the children are feeling it? Bertie was tossing and turning when I went up just now.'

Bender lumbered to his feet.

'They'll be all right. The girl's up there if they want anything. Come and look at the river, my dear.'

She led the way down the staircase, pausing on the landing, head cocked on one side for any sound from above. But all was silent. They made their way through the little parlour behind the shop, and the great shadowy store shed which housed ironmongery of every shape and size, and smelt of paint and polish, tar and turpentine, and the cold odour of stone floors, and cast iron girders.

It was almost dark when they emerged into the garden. It was small, with a brick wall on each side, and a lawn which ran gently down to the banks of the Cax. The air was soft and warm, and fragrant with the roses which climbed over the walls and the white jasmine starring the rustic arch which spanned the side path. Bender's shop might be villainously untidy and his desk chaotic. His neighbours might scoff at his muddles there, but here, in the garden, Bender kept everything in orderly beauty.

The river, lapping at the bank, kept his soil moist even in the blazing heat of such a spell as this. The Norths had always been great gardeners, and Bender was one of the best of his family. He looked about his trim flower beds with pride.

A rustic seat stood close by the river and here the two sat, while the midges hummed and a bat darted back and forth above the water. Sitting there, with the peace of the summer evening about them, was pleasantly relaxing.

'Where does it go?' asked Hilda suddenly.

'What? The river?'

'Yes. Does it go to London?'

'Must do, I suppose. The Cax runs into the Thames about fifteen to twenty miles east, so they told us at school, if I recall it aright.'

'Seems funny, doesn't it,' said Hilda dreamily, 'to think it goes past our garden and then right up to London. Sees a bit of life when it gets there. Specially just now with the streets being decked up for the Coronation. It said in the paper today that no end of royalty have arrived already, and troops from Canada and Australia for the procession. Wouldn't it he lovely if we could go, Bender? I'd give my eye teeth for a sight of the Coronation, wouldn't you?'

Bender smiled indulgently at this womanly excitement.

'I'm quite content to watch the Caxley flags and fairy-lights next week,' he replied. 'Maybe have a drink or two, and keep a lookout for the bonfire up on the beacon. We'll give the King a good send-off, you'll see, without having to traipse to London for a bit of fun.'

His wife sighed, and was about to speak when she caught sight of something white glimmering in the shadows of the fuchsia bush, and went over to investigate.

'What is it?' asked Bender following her. Hilda was turning a little white yacht in her hands.

'It must be the Howard children's,' she said. 'Bertie asked them over to bathe after tea. They've forgotten it. Another trip to make, running after them.' There was a tartness in her tone which did not escape her husband's ear.

'Only child-like,' he commented easily. 'I'm glad Bertie thought of asking them. They've nowhere to play in their baker's yard. Not much fun there for kids this weather.'

'Oh, I don't mind the *children*,' said Hilda, a trifle pettishly. 'And Septimus is all right.'

It's strange how she always calls him Septimus and not Sep, as everyone else does, thought Bender. These little primnesses about his wife never failed to amuse him. The fact that she could never bring herself to ask the butcher for belly of pork, but always asked delicately for stomach of pork, delighted Bender perennially.

'It's Edna I can't take to,' went on Hilda. 'Try as I might there's something about her – I don't know. I can't think what Septimus saw in her, respectable as he is.'

She had picked a tasselled blossom from the fuchsia bush and now tossed it petulantly into the darkening water. Bender put a massive arm round her plump shoulders.

'Are you sending your contribution to the Coronation decorations?' he asked jocularly, nodding towards the floating flower. 'It should get to Westminster in a couple of days.'

'And keep fresh in the water,' agreed his wife, smiling. Bender congratulated himself on his success in changing the subject. Once embarked on the ways of Edna Howard, Hilda could become mighty waspish for such a good-natured wife.

At that moment, the quarters chimed across the market square from St Peter's, and Hilda became agitated.

'Gracious me! That must be half past ten, and I've not had a word with Vera! You lock up, Ben, while I run upstairs.'

She flitted away from him across the grass, as light on her feet as when he first met her, thought her husband watching her depart.

He turned for a last look at the Cax before following her into the house. The twilight had deepened now into an amethyst glow. The river glided slowly round the great curve which swept eastward, shining like a silver ribbon beneath the darkening sky. Say what you like, Bender told himself, Caxley in June took a lot of beating! Let the whole world flock to London to see the King crowned! This was good enough for Bender North!

He picked up the toy boat from the rustic seat. Tomorrow he'd take it back himself to Sep's youngsters. No point in upsetting Hilda with it.

He left it on the bench in the store shed, where his eye could light on it in the morning, locked and bolted the doors of his domain, and made his way contentedly to bed.

Chapter Three

CONSTERNATION IN CAXLEY

The bunting was going up all over England, under the bright June skies. In the villages round about Caxley there was a joyful bustle of Coronation preparations. At Fairacre School an ambitious may pole dance was causing heartache to the infants' teacher there, and bewilderment to the young fry who lumbered round and round, ribbons in hand, weaving the biggest and brightest tangle ever seen in the history of the parish.

On the downs above Beech Green a great pile of faggots was outlined against the clear sky, waiting for a torch to be plunged into its heart on June the twenty-sixth. The blaze would be visible from four counties, the old men told each other, and some said that they could remember their fathers talking of the blazing beacon, on the self-same spot, which had celebrated the end of the Napoleonic Wars.

The drapers in Caxley were running short of red, white, and blue ribbon, and the little saddler in West Street was surprised to find that his horse-braid in these three colours was in demand, not only for plaiting manes and other orthodox uses, but also for decorating trestle tables, oil lamps in village halls, and even for tying patriotic children's hair now that all the ribbon had been snapped up by early shoppers.

The market square at Caxley blossomed like a rose. Strings of fairy lights were festooned round the sides of the square and tubs of red and white geraniums, edged with lobelia, flanked the steps of Queen Victoria's plinth. Less happy was the arrangement of red, white and blue ribbons radiating from an erection on the crown of Her Imperial Majesty. Like the spokes of a wheel they formed a circular canopy rather like that of Fairacre's maypole in readiness for the troublesome dance. Septimus Howard looking down on it from his bedroom window, cut-throat razor in hand, thought it looked as garish as the market place at Michaelmas Fair. He overheard an old countryman observe to his crony as he surveyed this centrepiece:

'Fair *tawdry*, 'ennit, Ern?' and, privately, Sep heartily agreed with him.

It was on the evening of the twenty-fourth that the blow fell. King Edward had been stricken with appendicitis. He was dangerously ill. The Coronation would have to be postponed. This was no time for rejoicing, but for earnest prayer for the King's recovery. There were those who said that was doubtful – but, as Bender North said stoutly – there are dismal johnnies everywhere at such times, and they should not be heeded.

It was Edna Howard who had brought the dire tidings to North's shop, and thus added yet another misdeed, in Hilda's eyes, to those already committed. The shop was closed, but Bender was still tidying shelves and sweeping odd scraps from counter to floor with a massive hand.

Hilda stood at the door, and watched Edna Howard advance across the square, with that lilting gait, and proud turn of her dark head, which irritated Hilda so unaccountably. Edna was a tall woman, large bosomed, and long-legged, with a mass of black silky hair. Her eyes were quick and dark, starred with thick black lashes, and with an odd slant to them which told of gipsy blood. For Edna Howard had been a Bryant before her marriage, the only girl among a tribe of stalwart boys. Her mother had been a true gipsy, who had left her wandering family when she married a doting farm labourer and settled near Fairacre to produce a family of her own.

There was something foreign and wild about Edna Howard which stolid Caxley inhabitants could not understand. In the country, memories are long, and despite Edna's respectable marriage, her industry in the shop and home, and her devoted care of her children, Edna's exotic streak was the first thing to be mentioned when the worthies discussed her.

'Plenty of the ol' gyppo about that 'un,' they said. 'Remember her ma? Used to come round with a basket o' pegs not so long ago.'

Edna knew very well the sort of remark that was made behind her back, and gave no hint of caring. She dressed in colours that were gaudy in comparison with those worn by her sedate neighbours. Sometimes she knotted a bright silk scarf about her throat, gipsy fashion, as though flaunting her origin, and on her wrist she jangled a coin bracelet which had once been her gipsy grandmother's.

Two other qualities added to Edna's colourful character. She possessed a thrillingly deep contralto voice and she could play the banjo. For some reason, Caxley approved of the first gift but was somewhat shocked by the second. Occasionally, Mrs Howard was invited to sing at charity concerts, by ladies who were organizing these affairs. The fact that she was an accomplished banjoist was known, but ignored, by the organizers. 'Sweet and Low', rendered by Mrs Septimus Howard to the decorous accompaniment on the pianoforte by the Vicar's son was permissible in the Corn Exchange. Edna Howard, let loose with her banjo, might prove a trifle vulgar, it was felt.

How meek little Septimus had ever managed to capture this wild bright bird was one of the mysteries of Caxley history. That Edna Bryant was 'one for the boys' was well-known. She could have picked a husband from among dozens who courted her from the time she was fifteen. Perhaps Sep's wistful shyness was the main attraction, contrasting so strongly with her own vivid confidence. In any case, the marriage had flourished, despite much early headshaking, and Edna Howard was outwardly accepted in Caxley life.

Hilda unbolted the shop door and let Edna in with a polite smile. Bender's was considerably more welcoming. He liked a handsome woman, and he didn't much mind if Hilda knew it.

'Come on in, Edna,' he shouted heartily. She rewarded him with a warm smile and a provocative glance from under her dark lashes which Hilda did her best to ignore.

'Just brought the pattern I promised you,' said Edna, holding out an envelope. 'It turned out fine for Kathy, and you only need a yard and a half.'

'Thank you,' replied Hilda. 'You shouldn't have bothered, specially leaving the children in bed.'

This was a shrewd blow, and was not missed either by Edna or Bender. Under the surface solicitude, the sentence managed to imply parental neglect and to draw attention to the fact that Edna had no resident help in the house to mind her offspring, as Hilda herself had.

'Sep's there,' said Edna shortly. She put up a dusky thin hand to brush back a wisp of hair. The coin bracelet jingled gaily.

'You heard the news?' she continued. There was a hint of excitement in her casual tone.

'What about?' said Bender, coming forward. He was frankly interested to know what was afoot. Hilda assumed an air of indifference. Really, local tittle-tattle did not interest her! She blew some dust from a box of screws with an expression of distaste.

'The King!' said Edna. 'They say he's been took bad, and the Coronation's off.'

Hilda was shaken from her lofty attitude. Her mouth fell open into a round pink O.

'You don't say! The poor dear! What's the matter?'

'The King!' echoed Bender, thunderstruck. 'You sure this is true?'

'Gospel! Had it from Lord Turley's coachman. He told him himself. Lord Turley's just got back from London on the train.'

This was news indeed.

'But what about all this 'ere?' spluttered Bender, waving a large, dirty hand at the bedecked market place.

'And the parties? And the concerts and all that?' echoed Hilda, all dignity forgotten in the face of this calamity.

'And what about poor Sep's baking?' retorted Edna. 'He's got a bakehouse chock full of iced cakes, and sausage rolls, and a great batch of dough ready for the buns. I tell you, it's ruination for us, as well as bad luck for the King!'

Bender's face grew grave. He knew, only too well, the narrow margin between Sep's solvency and his business downfall. He spoke with forced cheerfulness.

'Don't you fret about that, Edna. It won't be as bad as you think. But do the Council know? Has the Mayor been told? And what about the vicar? Ought to be summat done about a service pretty sharp.'

Edna did not know. Her cares were all for the King's condition and her husband's set-backs.

'I'll he getting back,' she said, putting the paper pattern on the counter. There was a hint of sadness now in her downcast countenance which stirred Hilda's conscience.

'No, Edna, don't you worry,' she said, with unaccustomed gentleness. 'It's a sore blow for everyone, but the one who's suffering most is poor Queen Alexandra, and the Family too. There'll be another Coronation as soon as the King's fit, you'll see, my dear, and then all our troubles will he over.' ·

She walked with Edna to the door and let her out, watching her walk back across the square beneath the fluttering flags. Hardly had she closed the door when one of the Corporation's carts, drawn by two great carthorses, clattered to the centre of the market square. Two men jumped down and began to remove the ribbons which bedizened the statue of the old Queen. At the same moment the bell of St Peter's began to ring out, calling all parishioners to prayer.

'Let's go, Bender,' said Hilda suddenly.

Without a word, Bender removed his overall, and accompanied his wife aloft to fetch jacket, hat, and gloves.

Within three minutes, the Norths with other bewildered Caxley folk, crossed the market square, fast being denuded of its finery, and, with heavy hearts, entered the sombre porch of the parish church.

From a top floor window, high above the ironmonger's shop, young Bertie North looked down upon the scene, unknown to his parents.

It is difficult to go to sleep on summer evenings when you are eight years old and put to bed firmly at seven o'clock. Bertie resented this early bed-time. Just because Winnie, two years his junior, had to go then, it seemed mighty unfair to expect a man of his advanced age to retire simply because it saved trouble for Vera, the girl. He did not make a fuss about the matter. Bertie North was a peace-loving child, and did not want to upset Vera, the fourteen-year-old country girl from Beech Green, who worked hard from seven in the morning until the North children were in bed at night.

But the injustice rankled. And tonight, as he stood at the high window in his cotton night-shirt, he felt even more resentful, for there, far below, he could see the two Howard boys. They were hopping gaily about the statue, watching all the activity of taking down the ribbons and fairy lights. Bertie had seen them bob down behind the stone plinth to hide from their mother as she made her way home from visiting his own parents.

They weren't made to go to bed so early! Of course, thought Bertie reasonably, they were much older than he was; Jim was twelve, and Leslie was ten. His particular friend, Kathy, who was only seven, had to go to bed when her little brother did, just as he did. This crumb of cold comfort went a small way towards consoling the boy gazing down at the enviable freedom of the older children.

The bell stopped ringing, and the everyday noises could be heard once more. The clop of the horses' great shaggy hooves, as they moved across the cobblestones of the market square, mingled with the screaming of swifts round the spire of St Peter's. Behind him, in one of the back bedrooms looking across the river Cax, he could hear Vera singing to herself as she darned socks.

There were four little bedrooms at the top of the tall old house. Bertie and Winnie had one each overlooking the square. Vera had another, and the fourth was known as 'the boxroom' and was filled with the most fascinating objects, from a dressmaker's model, with a formidable bust covered in red sateen and a wire skirt, to a dusty pile of framed portraits of North ancestors complete with cravats, pomaded locks, and beards.

These old be-whiskered faces intrigued young Bertie. He liked to think that he belonged to the same family; that they too had once been his age, had run across the market square with their iron hoops as he did, and floated their toy boats on the placid face of the river Cax. His father and mother had been patient in answering his questions, and he already had an idea of his respectable background. Brought up in a community which recognized the clear divisions of class, Bertie knew the Norths' place in the scale and was happy to be there.

The Norths were middle class. They were respected tradespeople, church-goers and, best of all, comfortably off. Bertie was glad he was not in the class above his – the gentry. Their children were sent away to school or had stern governesses. Their fathers and mothers seemed to be away from home a great deal. It would not have suited Bertie. Sometimes a passing pang of envy shot through him when he saw his betters on ponies of their own, for Bertie loved horses dearly. But there was always the sturdy little cob that pulled Uncle Ted's trap in the High Street, and on this the boy lavished his affection.

He was even more thankful that he did not belong to the class below, the poor. The people who lived in the low-lying area of Caxley, called 'The Marsh', were objects of pity and a certain measure of fear. Respectable children were not allowed to roam those dark narrow streets alone. On winter nights, the hissing gas lamp on the corner of the lane leading from the High Street to the marsh, simply accentuated the sinister murk of the labyrinth of alleys and small courtyards which were huddled, higgledy-piggledy, behind the gracious façade of the Georgian shop fronts.

Other people – far too many of them for Bertie's tender heart – were also poor. He saw them in his father's shop, thin, timid, unpleasantly smelly, rooting in their pockets or worn purses for the pence to pay for two screws, a cheap pudding basin, or a little kettle. They were pathetically anxious not to give any trouble.

'Don't 'ee bother to wrap it, sir,' they said to Bender deferentially.

'It don't matter if it's a mite rusty,' said another one day. ''Twill be good enough for I.'

It seemed strange to the listening boy, his head not far above the counter, that the poor whose money was so precious, should be content to accept shoddy goods, whereas those with plenty of money should make such a terrible fuss if there were the slightest fault in their purchases.

'What the hell d'you mean, North, by sending up this rubbish?' old Colonel Enderby had roared, flinging a pair of heavy gate hinges on to the counter, with such force that they skidded across, and would have crashed into young Bertie's chin if he had not ducked smartly. 'They're scratched!'

His father's politeness, in the face of this sort of behaviour, brought home to his son the necessity for knowing one's place on the social ladder. But it did not blind the child to a certain unfairness in his world's structure.

Standing at the high window, his bare feet growing more and more chilly on the cold linoleum, a new thought struck Bertie, as he watched Jim and Leslie far below. Were the Howards poor? They certainly had plenty to eat, delicious pies, new crusty loaves, and cakes in plenty; but they had very few toys, and Bertie's mother often gave Mrs Howard clothes, which Winnie had outgrown, for Kathy.

He remembered too, with some shock, that Jim's and Leslie's grandmother was old Mrs Bryant, the gipsy, who sometimes came into the shop, bent under her dirty black shawl. She certainly was poor. She spoke in a whining nasal voice and Bertie had heard her ask his father to take less than the marked price.

Did this mean that the Howard boys were on a par with the marsh children? His mother certainly spoke with some condescension about the Howards, Bertie recalled, but he knew very well that he would not be allowed to play with the marsh folk. Obviously then, the Howards were acceptable as play fellows.

It was all very puzzling, thought Bertie, resting his forehead against the cold glass. As far as he was concerned, Jim and Leslie were friends, even heroes, for when one is only eight one looks up to those of ten and twelve, especially when they are gracious enough to accept one's homage.

Through the window-pane, now misted with his breath, Bertie

saw Mrs Howard appear at the shop door and beckon her sons inside. Reluctantly, with backward glances, they obeyed and Bertie watched them vanish indoors. The shop door closed with a bang.

'Now *they've* got to go to bed!' said Bertie with satisfaction. And with this comforting thought he bounded into his own and was asleep in five minutes.

Chapter Four

FIRST ENCOUNTER

The King recovered, and the nation rejoiced. Now the Coronation would be on August the ninth. The decorations, so sadly taken down, were restored to their places, and Queen Victoria peered once more from beneath her ribbon umbrella. The bells of St Peter's rang out merrily, calling across the countryside to a hundred others pealing from tower or soaring spire, among the downs and water meadows around Caxley.

Septimus Howard was doubly thankful for the King's recovery. On the morning after Edna's visit to Bender's shop he had called there himself, pale with anxiety. Bender had ushered him into the shop-parlour and closed the door.

'Say nothing, Sep,' he said. 'I know how it is.'

'I've got to say something,' burst out poor Sep. 'I haven't had a wink all night. I stand to lose nigh on forty pounds with cancelled orders, I reckon, and I can't see my way clear to paying you back what I owe for many a week.'

He passed an agitated hand over his white face.

'Look here, Sep,' rumbled Bender, 'you've got nothing to worry about. I know my money's safe enough. It'll come back one day, and it don't matter to me just when. Your business is coming along a fair treat. These 'ere set-backs happen to us all – but you keep plodding on, boy.'

He smote the smaller man a heartening blow on the shoulder which made his teeth rattle. Sep managed to produce a wan smile.

'It's good of you, Bender,' he began, but was cut short.

'More to the point, Sep – have you got enough to tide you over? Do you want a mite more till this business is straightened out?'

222

Sep's pale face flushed. His eyes were unhappy. He looked through the glass partition between the parlour and the shop and gazed at the kettles and saucepans, dangling from the ceiling there, with unseeing eyes.

'I think so. I think so, Bender. I'll know more tomorrow, and I don't want to borrow from you if I can help it. You've been generous enough already.'

He rose from the horse-hair chair and made his way to the door.

'Must get back to the shop. Plenty to do over there. People want loaves even if they don't want Coronation cakes.'

He turned and put out a timid hand. Bender gripped it painfully and pumped his arm vigorously up and down.

'Don't let things get you down, Sep,' boomed Bender cheerfully. 'That shop o' yours will be a blooming gold mine before you know where you are. Keep at it, old chap!'

'I only hope you're right,' poor Sep had replied, hurrying back to his duties.

But by August the ninth, with Coronation orders renewed, Sep had recovered his losses and made a handsome profit besides. By the end of that month, when he settled down, with Edna beside him, to cast up his accounts, he found that for the first time he was out of debt. Bender's loan had been repaid, so that the shop, furnishings, bake-house and machinery, were now entirely their own. It was a day of thankful celebration in the Howard household.

From that moment, it seemed, fortune began to smile upon Sep and his family. The wedding cake for Miss Frances Hurley had been a creation of exquisite fragility, much commented upon by other well-born matrons at the wedding with daughters in the marriage lists. Sep's handiwork, and his competitive prices, were noted, and many an order came his way. Howard's bakery was beginning to earn the fine reputation it deserved. Sep himself could hardly believe his luck. Edna, excited by more money, needed restraining from gay and frivolous expenditure.

'Don't fritter it away,' begged poor Sep, bewildered but still prudent. ' 'Tis wrong, Edna, to be too free. There'll be plenty more rainy days to face. One swallow don't make a summer.'

With these and other cautious warnings Sep did his best to cool Edna's excitement. His strong chapel-guided principles deplored show and waste. Thrift, modesty, and humble bearing were ingrained in the little baker. He thanked his Maker for blessings received, but was too apprehensive to expect them to continue indefinitely. Nevertheless, a tidy sum began to accumulate steadily in the bank, the Howard boys had a new bicycle apiece, Edna glowed from beneath a pink hat, nodding with silk roses, as the Howards, as well as the Norths, began to share in the genial prosperity of Edward's golden reign.

It was a perfect time to be young. As the serene years slipped by, as slow and shining as the peaceful river Cax, the young Howards and Norths enjoyed all the wholesome pleasures of a small and thriving community. There was always something going on at the Corn Exchange, for this was the era of endless good works 'in aid of the poor' who were, alas, as numerous as ever. Concerts, plays, tableaux vivants, dances, socials, whist drives, and even roller-skating, followed each other in quick succession. The talent was local, the organization was local, and the appreciative audiences and participants were local too. There was something particularly warming in this family atmosphere. It had its stresses and strains, as all family relationships have, but the fact that each was known to the other, the virtues, the vices, the oddities and quirks of each individual were under common scrutiny, made for interest and amusement and bound the community at large with ties of affection and tolerance.

Bertie North now attended the town's grammar school daily and Winnie was one of the first pupils at the new girls' county school. Neither was outstandingly academic, but they were reasonably intelligent, obedient, and hardworking, and became deeply attached to their local schools, an affection which was to last a lifetime.

Despite the modest fees asked by these two establishments, and the diverse backgrounds of the pupils there, Sep could not bring himself to send his children to either, and they walked daily to the same National School in the High Street where he and Bender had been educated. The schooling was sound and the discipline strict. Bender, knowing something of Sep's finances, often argued with him to send his children elsewhere, but Sep was unwontedly stubborn on this point.

'The old school was good enough for me, Bender,' he replied. 'It'll do for my boys. No need for them to get ideas above their place.' And no amount of argument could budge him.

The children did not worry their heads about such distinctions. Life was much too full and fascinating. Every Thursday the market square's usual hum rose to a crescendo of shouting and clattering as the weekly market took place. The North and Howard children loved Thursdays. The day began very early, for long before breakfast time at seven o'clock the rumble of carts and the clop of horses' hooves woke the square. By the time the children set off for school everything was in full swing. Prudent town shoppers had already filled their baskets with fresh fruit and greens from the surrounding countryside before the country dwellers themselves arrived by trap or carrier cart to fill their own baskets with more sophisticated things. Everywhere was the sound of hooves and the sweet-sharp smell of horses.

For this was the golden age of the horse. Family coaches, some with fine crests on the doors, still rumbled through Caxley from London to the west. Glossy carriages, with equally glossy high-steppers, bore the local gentry from one tea-party to another. Broughams and landaus, gigs and phaetons, traps and governess carts tapped and stuttered, rattled and reeled, round the square and onward. In the dusty country lanes, massive hay carts and wagons piled high with sacks or sheaves, swayed like galleons, with slow majesty, behind the teams of great cart horses, shaggy of hoof and mild of eye. The music of the horse and carriage was everywhere, the thunder of wheels and hoofs acting as bass to the treble of cracked whip and jingling harness. And always, as added accompaniment, there was the cry of man to horse, the encouraging chirrup, the staccato command, the endearment, with the appreciative snort or excited whinny in reply. It was an age when the horse was king, and his stabling, fodder, and well-being were paramount. He provided transport and labour, and the calm bright world was geared to his pace. The animal kingdom from man himself, who harnessed that willing and beautiful energy, down to the lowliest sparrow which fed upon his droppings, acknowledged the horse as peer. The thought that the smelly and new-fangled motor-car might one day supersede the horse never entered the heads of ordinary folk. Wasn't it true that London made the carriages, and England supplied the horses, for all the world? Nothing could alter that invincible fact.

It was the horse, in all its infinite variety, that the three boys chiefly encountered on their bicycle rides. Within five minutes of leaving the throbbing market place, they could be in the leafy lanes that led north, south, east and west from Caxley. The wide fields were fragrant with cut hay or bean flowers, freshly ploughed earth or ripe corn according to the season. The hedges were snowy with blossom or beaded with shiny berries. Blackbirds darted across their path. Speckled thrushes sang their hearts out from sprays of pear blossom in cottage gardens. There were butterflies of every hue fluttering on the flowered verges of the roadside, and when the boys rested in the cool grass under the shade of a hedge, they could hear all around them the tiny quiet noises of the countryside. Somewhere, high above, a lark carolled. In the dark thickness of the hedge a mouse scuffled the dry leaves stealthily. A bee bumbled lazily at the orange lips of toadflax flowers, and little winged insects hummed in the sunlight. These were the long happy hours of childhood which the boys were never to forget. The gentle countryside and its quiet villages were theirs to explore, and Caxley, small and secure, the beginning and the end of every adventure. Nothing, it seemed, could ruffle Caxley's age-old order.

But something did. In the midst of this halcyon period an event occurred which was to have far-reaching consequences. It began innocently enough, as such things so often do. It began with Dan Crockford's sudden hunger for one of Sep Howard's lardy cakes.

Daniel Crockford had lived in Caxley all his life, as had generations of Crockfords before him. The family had supplied woollen cloth to the town, and to all England – and parts of Europe for that matter – from the time when Caxley, in the sixteenth century, was building its prosperity from this industry. The family still owned a mill, but now it was a flour mill, some half-mile along the bank of the Cax from the market square.

Crockfords had played their part in the town's history and were well-liked. They had been Mayors, church-wardens, sidesmen, councillors, magistrates, and generous benefactors to many causes. But not one of them, until Dan appeared, had ever had anything to do with the arts. It would be true to say that the world of the imagination was looked upon with considerable suspicion and complete lack of interest by the worthy Crockfords.

It was all the more shocking, therefore, when the adolescent Daniel proclaimed that he intended to be an artist. His father was impatient, his mother tearful. What would the neighbours say?

'They'll say you're plain stark mad,' announced his father flatly. 'The mill needs you. There's a living waiting for you. If you must paint, then have the common sense to do it in your spare time!'

'They'll say you're no better than you should be,' wailed his mother. 'You know how wild and shameless artists are! It's common knowledge! Oh, the disgrace to us all!'

The young man remained unmoved. A few uncomfortable months passed and at last his father paid for him to go to an art school in London for two years.

'Let him work it out of his system,' he growled to his wife. But Dan throve on the work, his reports were reassuring and he returned to his home determined to make painting his career. His father, seeing that the boy's mind was made up, had a studio built at the back of the house in Caxley, and let him have his way. There were other sons to take an interest in the mill, and Dan had a small income from an indulgent uncle and godfather which covered his essential needs. The Crockford family was resigned to the black sheep among the rest of the flock.

Dan sold an occasional landscape to various local people who had wall space to fill. His views of the Cax were considered very pretty and life-like. His portraits were thought unflattering, and rather too garish in colour. With photography becoming so cheap and reliable it seemed sinful to spend so much money on having a portrait painted which might not please when it was done.

But Dan worked away happily, and did not appear to mind that the stacks of paintings grew in his studio and very seldom sold. He was a large handsome man of flamboyant appearance, with a wealth of red hair and a curling red beard. He loved food, and he loved drink even more. Tales of Dan Crockford's prowess in the bars of Caxley and the country inns near by grew tall in the telling. He wore a dark wide-brimmed hat and big floppy silk ties. He had taken up the work of an artist, and he intended to make it plain. Needless to say, he was looked upon in Caxley as a somewhat worthless character, and his family, everyone said, was to be pitied.

On this particular morning, Dan had spent over an hour in cleaning his brushes and his nostrils were filled with the reek of turpentine. It was a soft May morning and the door of the studio was propped open with an old velvet-covered chair. On it, asleep in the sunshine, the family tabby cat rested a chin on its outstretched paws.

The turpentine had run out, and intrigued with the texture and markings of the cat's leonine head, Dan took a piece of charcoal and began to sketch intently. He brushed in the soft ruff, the upward sweep of grey whiskers and the fluff protruding from the pricked black ears. Delicately he sketched in the intricate frown marks of the forehead, the rows of black dots from which sprang whiskers on the upper part of the muzzle, and the bars which ran, echelon fashion, along each jaw.

He began to feel excitement rising. The sketch was good. He selected a firmer piece of charcoal and began the difficult job of emphasising the streak of each closed eye and the puckering of the mouth.

Suddenly, the cat woke, yawned, leapt down, and vanished. Furious, Dan swore, flung away the charcoal and burst from the studio into the garden. He found that he was shaking with fury. He would take a brief walk to calm himself. He picked up the empty turpentine bottle, resolved to get it filled at North's, have a quick drink and return to work.

Swinging the bottle, his great hat crammed on the back of his red head, he strode through the market place. There were several people outside the baker's shop and he was forced to step close to the window in order to pass them. A wave of spicy fragrance floated from the open door. Sep was putting a trayful of sticky brown lardy cakes in the window, and Dan realized that he was desperately hungry. He stepped down into the shop, and saw, for the first time, Edna Howard.

It was a shock as sudden and delightful as a plunge into the Cax on a hot afternoon. Dan knew beauty, when he saw it, by instinct and by training. This was the real thing, warm, gracious, dynamic. In one intent glance he noted the dark soft wings of hair, the upward sweep of the cheekbones, the angle of the small pink ears, and the most beautiful liquid brown eyes he had ever seen. Dan gazed in amazement. To think that this beauty had remained hidden from him so long!

'Sir?' asked Sep deferentially.

Dan wrenched his eyes away.

'Oh, ah!' he faltered. He fumbled in his pocket for a sixpence. 'One of your lardy cakes, if you please.'

While Sep busied himself in wrapping up his purchase in fine white paper, Dan looked again. Edna had walked across the shop to a shelf where she was stacking loaves. Her figure was as exquisite as her face, her movements supple. There was something oddly foreign about her which excited Dan.

He found Sep holding out the bag. He was looking at him curiously.

'Thanks. Good day to you,' said Dan briskly, and departed towards the river bank.

There, sitting on the grassy bank beneath a may tree, he devoured his fresh, warm lardy cake and made plans.

She must sit for him. He must go back again and ask her. She was the perfect subject for his type of portrait – full of colour, warmth, and movement. She must be Sep Howard's wife. He groped in his memory.

Of course! What had the old wives said? 'He married beneath him – a *Bryant*, you know!'

Dan leapt to his feet, and banged the crumbs from his clothes.

'"The gipsy",' he cried. 'That's what we'll call it: "The Gipsy Girl"!'

Chapter Five

DOMESTIC REBELLION

Dan fought down the impulse to return at once to Sep's shop and hurried home instead. By judicious questioning of his mother, he confirmed that the beautiful girl was indeed Sep Howard's wife.

In his studio, he wrote a brief note to say that he would give himself the pleasure of calling upon Mr and Mrs Howard that evening at eight o'clock, on a matter of business, and dispatched it by the little maid-of-all-work. The hours until that time seemed excessively tedious to the impatient artist.

'I can't think why he didn't say anything in the shop this morning,' said Sep, much puzzled, as he read the note.

'Maybe it's only just come to his mind,' suggested Edna, busy mending baby clothes and not much interested in the letter.

'Seems funny to address it to *both* of us,' went on Sep. Dan Crockford's open admiration of his wife had not escaped Sep's sensitive eye.

'He probably only wants you to do a bit of catering for a party or something,' said Edna off-handedly. She snapped the cotton with her white teeth, and folded up the baby's gown.

Prompt at eight, Dan arrived. Edna and Sep received him in the first floor parlour which was at the back of the house overlooking the yard and the distant Cax. The willows lining the banks were shimmering green and gold in their new May finery, and Edna wore a dress which matched their colour. In her presence Dan felt strangely shy, as he was introduced. Sep, who had known the Crockfords slightly for many years, was obviously ill at ease. Edna was quite unperturbed.

'I believe you want to discuss business matters,' she said, rising. 'I'll be with the children if you need me.'

Dan leapt to his feet in alarm.

'Don't go! Please, Mrs Howard, don't go! The business concerns you too, I assure you.'

Wonderingly, Edna slowly resumed her seat. Dan, still standing, wasted no more time but swiftly outlined his proposal. It would be doing him a great honour. He realized that she was very busy. Any time which would suit her convenience would suit his too. It was usual to pay sitters, and he hoped that she would name her fee. He would try to do justice to her outstanding good looks.

The words tumbled out in a vast torrent now that he had begun. Edna gazed upon him in amazement, her beautiful eyes wide and wondering. Sep grew paler as the scheme was unfolded. What impudence, what idiocy, was this?

At last Dan came to a halt, and Edna spoke shyly.

'It's very kind of you, I'm sure. I don't quite know what to think.' She looked at Sep in perplexity. Clearly, she was a little flattered, and inclined to consider the project.

Sep found his voice.

'We'll have nothing to do with it,' he said hoarsely. 'I'm not having my wife mixed up in things of this sort. We don't want the money, thank God, and my wife wouldn't want to earn it that way, I can assure you. I mean no offence, Mr Crockford. Your affairs are your own business, and good luck to your painting. But don't expect Edna to take part.'

Dan was frankly taken aback by the force of the meek little baker's attack. The thought that there would be such fierce opposition had not entered his mind. He spoke gently, controlling his temper, fearing that Edna would be surely lost to him as a sitter, if it flared up now.

'Don't close your mind to the idea, please,' he begged. 'Think about it and talk the matter over with your wife, and let me know in a few days. I fear that I have taken you too much by surprise. I very much trust that you will allow me to paint Mrs Howard. She would not need to sit for more than three or four sessions.'

Calmer, but still seething inwardly, Sep acknowledged the wisdom of discussing the matter. His old timidity towards those in the social class above him began to make itself felt again. One could not afford to offend good customers, and although his face was firmly set against Edna's acceptance, he deemed it wise to bring the interview to an outwardly civil close.

He accompanied Dan to the door and showed him out into the market square.

'We will let you know,' he said shortly, 'though I must make it plain that I don't like the idea, and very much doubt if Edna will agree.'

He watched Dan swing across the square on his homeward way. His red hair flamed in the dying sun's rays. His chin was at a defiant angle. Dan Crockford was a handsome man, thought Sep sadly, and a fighting man too.

Suddenly weary, conscious that he must return to face Edna, he caught sight of Queen Victoria, proudly defiant, despite a pigeon poised absurdly on her bronze crown.

'And what would she have thought of it?' wondered Sep morosely, turning his back on the market place.

The scene that ensued was never to be forgotten by poor Sep.

'Well, that's seen the back of that cheeky rascal!' announced Sep, on returning to the parlour. He assumed a brisk authority which he did not feel inwardly, but he intended to appear as master in his own house.

'Who says we've seen the back of him?' asked Edna, dangerously calm.

'I do. I've sent him about his business all right.'

'It was my business, too, if you remember. Strikes me you jumped in a bit sharp. Never gave me time to think it over, did you?'

'I should hope a respectable married woman like you would need no time at all to refuse that sort of invitation.' Sep spoke with a certain pomposity which brought Edna to her feet. She leant upon the table, eyes flashing, and faced her husband squarely.

'You don't appear to trust me very far, Sep Howard. I ain't proposing to stand stark naked for Mr Crockford –'

'I should hope not!' broke in Sep, much shocked.

'It was me he wanted to paint. And I should have had the chance of answering. Made me look no better than a stupid kid, snapping back at him like that, and leaving me out of things.'

Sep buttoned his mouth tightly. He had become very pale and the righteous wrath of generations of staunch chapel-goers began to make his blood boil.

'There's no more to be said, my lady. It was a shameful suggestion and I'll not see my wife flaunting herself for Dan Crockford or anyone else. I don't want to hear any more about it.'

If Sep had been in any condition to think coolly, he must have realized that this was the best way to rouse a mettlesome wife to open rebellion. But he was not capable of thinking far ahead just then. He watched the colour flood Edna's lovely face and her thin brown hands knot into tight fists.

'You don't want to hear any more about it, eh?' echoed Edna. Her voice was low, and throbbing with fury. 'Well, let me tell you, Sep Howard, you're going to! I should like to have my picture painted. Dan Crockford don't mean anything more to me than that chair there, but if he wants to paint my picture, I'm willing. You can't stop me, and you'd better not try, unless you wants to run the shop, and the home too, on your own. I won't be bossed about by you, or anyone else!'

It was at this dangerous moment in the battle that Sep should have given in completely, apologized for his arrogance, told Edna that he could not do without her, and that of course she could sit for Dan Crockford if she wanted to so desperately. Edna's defiance would have abated at once, and all would have been forgotten. But Sep made the wrong move. He thumped the table and shouted.

'I forbid –' he began in a great roaring voice which stirred the curtains.

'Forbid?' screamed Edna. 'Don't you take that tone to me, you little worm! Who d'you think you're talking to – our Kathy? I'm going up to bed now, and tomorrow morning I'm going round to Dan Crockford's to tell him I'll sit for him!'

She whirled from the room, her gold and green dress swishing, leaving Sep open-mouthed. Here was flat rebellion, and Sep knew full well that he had no weapon in his armoury to overcome it.

Morning brought no truce, and Edna set out purposefully across the square as soon as her house was set to rights. Sep watched her go, dumb with misery.

By the time market day came round again the whole of Caxley buzzed with this delicious piece of news. Fat Mrs Petty, chopping cod into cutlets, shouted boisterously above the rhythmic noise of her cleaver.

'No better'n she should be! Once a gyppo, always a gyppo, I says! And us all knows what Dan Crockford's like.'

'It's her poor husband I feel so sorry for,' nodded her customer lugubriously. Her mouth was set in a deprecating downward curve, but her eyes were gleaming with enjoyment. Gossip is always interesting, and this was a particularly exciting snippet for the good folk of Caxley.

'It won't surprise me to hear that Sep Howard turns her out,' continued the customer with relish. 'Been brought up proper strict, his lot – chapel every Sunday, Band of Hope, and all that. You never know, it might all end up in the court!'

She looked across at Caxley's Town Hall, standing beside St Peter's. Two magistrates were already mounting the steps, dignified in their good broadcloth, for the weekly sitting. Mrs Petty broke into loud laughter, holding up two fat hands, sparkling with fish-scales.

'Court?' she wheezed merrily. 'Ain't no need to take Edna Howard to court! All her husband needs is to take a strap to her!'

In this, Mrs Petty echoed most people in Caxley. If Sep's wife behaved like this, they said, then Sep was at fault. He knew what he'd taken on when he married her. He should have been firm.

The Norths watched the affair closely, and with dismay. Bender was inclined to dismiss it as 'a storm in a tea-cup'. Edna would come to her senses in time. But Hilda felt some inner triumph. Hadn't she always said that Edna wasn't to be trusted?

'One thing,' she admitted, 'it's bringing our Ethel round to seeing the truth about Dan Crockford. Pa said she was quite cool with him when they met in the street. And Jesse Miller's no fool. He's been up at Pa's every evening this week, hanging up his hat to our Ethel.'

'It don't do to make bad blood anywhere,' rumbled Bender, 'especially in a little place like Caxley. We've all got to rub along together, come fair, come foul, and the sooner this business blows over the better. No need to fan the flames now, Hilda.'

His wife bridled, but said no more.

But the flames ran everywhere, fanned smartly by the wind of gossip. That this should have happened to meek little Septimus Howard, strict chapel-goer, diligent baker, and earnest father, made the affair even more delectable. It was said that Edna went twice a week to Dan's studio, unchaperoned, in the evening, and that no one could really tell what happened there, although, of course, it was easy enough to guess.

Even the children heard the tales, and young Bertie asked the two Howard boys if their mother really had let Mr Crockford paint her picture. To his everlasting horror, one boy burst into tears and the other gave him such a swinging box on the ear that he fell into the thorn bush and was obliged to lie to his mother later about how he had become so severely scratched. Certainly, Edna's portrait created enough stir.

In actual fact the sittings were few and rather dull. They did occur, as rumour said, twice weekly and in the evening, but after six sessions Dan assured his model that he could finish it without troubling her further. Her beauty delighted him, but her dullness bored him dreadfully. Her independence having been proved, Edna was quite willing to make things up with her unhappy husband, and outwardly at least, harmony once again prevailed in the Howards' household.

But the matter did not end there.

The picture was enchanting. Dan knew in his bones that this was the best piece of work he had ever done. Edna glowed from the canvas, gay and vivid, in her gipsy costume. She made a compelling figure, for Dan had caught her warmth and grace magnificently. Furthermore, he had painted a perfect woodland background in minute detail. All the fresh haziness of a May morning sparkled behind Edna – a smoke-blue wood, with pigeons like pearls sunning themselves in the branches, above a grassy bank, starred with daisies, and almost golden in its May newness. He had caught exactly the spirit of wild young life in all its glory. Dan put it aside carefully to be sent to the Academy early next year. This one, surely, would find a place on those august walls.

Meantime, while the gossip ran rife, Howard's bakery suffered a temporary decline. A few self-righteous families refused to deal with a baker whose wife behaved so loosely. Others were embarrassed at facing Sep and preferred to slip into other bakers' establishments until the family affairs were righted. It was an unfortunate set-back for poor Sep who felt his position keenly. There were times when he longed to shut up the shop and flee from Caxley, from the sidelong glances, the whispers behind hands, the wretched knowledge that all knew his discomfiture.

He had said little to Edna after that first terrible encounter. There was so little to say which did not sound nagging, pompous, and bitter. Sep told himself that 'the least said soonest mended' and continued doggedly with his business affairs. Apart from a certain coolness, Edna continued her household duties unconcerned. When the sittings came to an end, tension between the two relaxed slightly, but, for Sep at least, things could never be quite the same again.

In time, of course, Caxley began to lose interest in the affair as other topics took the place of the portrait painting as a nine days' wonder. The scandal of the erring alderman, the bankruptcy of an old family business, the elopement of a local farmer's son with a pretty dairymaid, and many other delightful pieces of news came to the sharp eyes and ears of Caxley folk and engaged their earnest attention. It was not until the following year that the Howard scandal was suddenly revived and bathed now in miraculous sunlight instead of shadow.

For Dan Crockford's picture was accepted by the Hanging Committee of the Royal Academy and was one of the paintings of the year. *The Caxley Chronicle* printed this wonderful news on the front page, with a photograph of Dan Crockford and another of the portrait. The headline read: 'Well Deserved Success for Distinguished Local Artist', and the account mentioned 'the beauty of Mrs Septimus Howard, captured for posterity by the skill of the artist's brush.'

This put quite a different complexion on the affair, of course. If *The Caxley Chronicle* thought Dan Crockford was distinguished, then the majority of its readers were willing to believe it. And say what you like, they told each other reasonably, when they met the following week, he'd made a proper handsome picture of Sep's wife and it was a real leg-up for Caxley all round.

People now called at the bakery to see the celebrated Mrs Howard, and poor bewildered Sep found himself accepting congratulations in place of guarded condolences. It was a funny world, thought Sep, that kicked you when you were down, and patted you when you were up again, and all for the same reason.

Nevertheless, it was pleasant to find that the takings had risen sharply since the news came out. And he readily admitted that it was pleasanter still to be greeted warmly, by all and sundry, as he carried his hard-earned money across the market square to the bank. Pray God, thought Sep earnestly, things would now go smoothly for them all!

Chapter Six

LOCAL ELECTION

Things went very smoothly indeed in the early part of the century. Trade was brisk generally, and despite the high new motor-cars which began to sail majestically down Caxley High Street like galleons before the wind, though with somewhat more noise, the stablemen, coachmen, farriers, and the multitude of men engaged in ministering to the horse, still thrived.

It was true that Bill Blake's cycle shop at the marsh end of the High Street had begun repairing cars, and had taken over a yard at the side of the premises for this purpose. Under the shade of a vast sycamore tree against the rosy brick wall, Bill and his brother investigated the complicated interiors of the newcomers, surrounded by the enthusiastic small fry of Caxley. But the idea of the motor car ever superseding the ubiquitous horse was never really considered seriously by those who watched with such absorption.

The Howard boys had been among the keenest students of the early motor car, and as they grew older did their best to persuade Sep to discard the two horse-drawn vans, which now took his expanding business further afield, and to buy a motorvan. But Sep would have none of it. It would cost too much. It would break down. He preferred his horses.

By the time King Edward died in 1910 and his son George was made King, both boys were in the bakery business. Jim was now twenty-one and Leslie nineteen. Jim was like his father in looks and temperament, neat, quiet, and industrious. His presence in the shop was invaluable, and as Sep grew older, he was glad to give more responsibility to his first-born.

Leslie took after Edna, dark, volatile, and with the same devastating good looks. To be seen dancing the polka with Leslie at the Corn Exchange was something the girls of Caxley thoroughly enjoyed.

It was Leslie who bowled round the country lanes in the baker's van, touching his cap politely to the gentry as he edged Dandy the mare into the hedgerow to let a carriage – and sometimes a brand-new tonneau – pass by. It was Leslie who won the hearts of the old country women with his cheerful quips as he went on his rounds.

'A real nice lad,' they would say to each other, a warm loaf held in the crook of their arms as they watched Leslie and the mare vanish in a cloud of dust. 'Got his ma's looks, ain't he? But takes after his pa, too, let's hope.'

The growth of Sep's fortunes had brought him into the public eye. He had been persuaded to stand as a candidate in the local elections, and, much to his surprise, was successful in gaining a seat on the council. Caxley recognized the integrity and strength of character which was hidden behind his diffident appearance. His family and his business flourished, and his conduct over the portrait affair, which had been so severely criticized at the time, was now spoken of with praise.

'Sets a real example to that family of his! Look how forbearing he was with his Edna! Some would've kicked her out of doors, behaving that way. But you see, it's all turned out for the best, and she've quietened down into a thorough good wife.'

Edna certainly gained dignity as the years passed. She still sang in public, and still played her banjo in private. But memories are long in the country, and Edna was still looked upon with some suspicion by the good ladies who organized charity events. Not so Hilda North, whose help was asked for on many occasions. It gave Hilda much private satisfaction to be invited to serve on committees with the local gentry, particularly as Edna was never so invited. Their children remained firm friends, and their husbands too, but the two wives grew cooler with each other as the years passed.

Hilda, in the early days of the new reign, now had three children. Bertie was seventeen and intended going into the motor trade, Winifred fifteen, still at the High School and longing to finish there and start training as a nurse. It was on Winnie's twelfth birthday that Hilda had discovered that she was having another child – an event which she greeted with mingled dismay and pleasure, for she had thought her family complete and was looking forward to an end to cots and prams and all the paraphernalia of babyhood. But Bender was whole-heartedly delighted with the news.

'Always the best – those that aren't ordered,' he assured his wife. 'You mark my words, she'll be a beauty.'

Amazingly enough, it was indeed a girl, and a beauty. At four she was as pretty as a picture with fair curls and eyes as blue as speedwell flowers. She was also thoroughly spoilt by all the family and hair-raisingly outspoken.

When Lady Hurley called to enlist Hilda's aid in raising money for a Christmas fund for the poor of Caxley, the tea table had been laden with the best china, the silver teapot and wafer-thin bread and butter. The lightest of sponge cakes crowned a silver dish, and three sorts of jam, flanked by Gentleman's Relish, added distinction to the scene.

While Hilda was plying her honoured guest, young Mary put her head round the door and interrupted the genteel conversation.

'Our cat sicked up just before you came,' she volunteered in a clear treble voice. 'He sicked up half a mouse and a –'

'That'll do!' said poor Hilda hastily. She rang the bell and Mary was removed, protesting loudly, to the kitchen. It was a scene which the family remembered with pleasure for years, and Hilda with the deepest mortification.

Hilda's sense of propriety was strongly developed. She enjoyed her position in Caxley society and was proud to be the wife of a well-to-do tradesman, churchwarden, and well-known public figure. She liked to be seen entering St Peter's for Matins, clad in her best gown and mantle in suitably quiet colours, dove-grey perhaps, or deep mauve, with a sedate hat to match, trimmed with pansies or a wide watered-silk ribbon. She retained her trim figure over the years, and tight lacing contributed to her neat appearance.

She was proud too of her family, good-looking and robust, even if not over-blessed with brains. Winifred, now growing up fast, would never be the beauty that little Mary promised to be, but she had a fresh fairness which the boys seemed to find attractive. Somewhat to Hilda's annoyance, she suspected that Leslie Howard, old enough to have chosen someone among his numerous admirers for his particular choice, cast a roving eye upon his friend of a lifetime. An alliance with the Howard family was not to be borne. Winifred was to do much better for herself. Climbing the social ladder was an exercise which Hilda accomplished with ease and dexterity. There was no reason on earth why a girl like Winifred should not marry happily into the gentry, if the cards were played with discretion.

As for Bertie, Hilda's heart melted whenever her eye rested upon him. He had always been particularly dear, perhaps because he followed so soon upon the stillborn son who was their first child, and gave them so much comfort when it was sorely needed. At eighteen Bertie was as tall as his massive father, but long-limbed and slender. His fair hair had not darkened much with the years, and his quiet grave good looks were much admired.

There was a reserve about Bertie which set him a little apart from the rest of the Norths. Always cheerful in company, he also loved solitude. He liked to dawdle by the Cax, or hang over the bridge, watching the smooth water glide below, whispering through the reeds at the bank side and weaving ever-changing patterns across the river bed. Perhaps he had noise enough at his work at Blake's, for he had just started a course of motor engineering with that firm. It was work that absorbed him. He had patience and physical strength, and a ready grasp of mechanics. He was certain, too, in his own mind, that the motor-car had come to stay despite the scoffings of his elders. Above all, he was secretly thankful that he was not in the family business, for Bender's somewhat slap-dash methods irked him, and he was too respectful a son to criticize his father.

On the face of it, the business flourished. The Norths now owned their own horse and trap, for Uncle Ted's little cob had been sold when the old man grew too frail for driving, and it was now Bender's turn to take his elder brother on an occasional visit in the family trap. A freshly-painted skiff was moored at the end of the Norths' small garden, and once every year the shop was left in charge of Bob, now second-in-command, still with a mop of unruly black hair and steel spectacles set awry, while the family took a week's holiday at the sea. Caxley never doubted that Bender's business was as flourishing as ever.

But Bender himself knew otherwise. His turnover had not increased in the past few years, and now there was a serious threat to the business. The great firm of Tenby's, which flourished in the county town, opened a branch next door to Blake's at the marsh end of Caxley High Street. Their premises were far grander and far larger than Bender's, and the new agricultural machinery, which was beginning to make its way on to the market, was displayed and demonstrated with great ease in the commodious covered yard behind the shop.

It was Jesse Miller who brought the seriousness of the position home to Bender. He was a frequent caller now at the Norths', for he had succeeded in persuading the vacillating Ethel, Hilda North's sister, to marry him a few years earlier when Dan Crockford's behaviour appeared so reprehensible to the sterner eyes of Caxley.

The two men sat smoking in the snug murk of the shop parlour one November evening. Outside the pavements were wet with the clinging fog which wreathed its way from the Cax valley to twine itself about the gas lamps of the market place.

Above their heads the gas hissed, and a bright fire flickered cheerfully in the little round-arched grate.

'Got a good fire there,' observed Jesse, watching Bender's ministrations with the steel poker.

'Coal's cheap enough,' answered Bender, widening a crack with a smart blow. 'Can still afford that, thank God!'

Jesse Miller blew a long blue cloud towards the ceiling. He watched it disperse reflectively and then took a deep breath.

'Look, Bender! I've had something on my mind for some time and I reckon it's best to speak out. Am I right in thinking the shop's not paying its way?'

Bender's face flushed and the deep colour flooded his bull neck, but he answered equably.

'I'd not go that far, Jesse. We're not bankrupt yet, if that's what's on your mind.'

'But it's not as good as it was?' persisted Jesse, leaning forward.

'Well, no,' admitted Bender, with a sigh. He thrust out his long legs and the horse-hair chair creaked a protest. 'Bound to be a bit of a drop in takings when a shop like Tenby's first opens. People like to bob in and see what's there. They'll come back, I don't doubt.'

'I do,' said Jesse forcefully. 'You might as well face it – Tenby's are here for good, and they'll offer more than you ever can.'

Bender was about to protest, but Jesse Miller waved him aside.

'It's not only the room they've got; they've got keen chaps too. And another thing, they're quick with getting the stuff to the customer. I've had a couple of harrows on order here since Michael-mas, and where are they?'

'You know dam' well where they are,' rumbled Bender, begin-ning to look surly. 'Down in Wiltshire where they're made, and where they're too idle to put 'em on the railway! I've written to them time and time again!'

'Maybe! It don't alter the fact, Bender, that Tenby's have got a dozen stacked in their yard now, and if you can't get mine here by next week – I'm telling you straight, man – I'm going there for a couple.'

The two men glared at each other, breathing heavily. They were both fighters, and both obdurate.

'Oh, you are, are you?' growled Bender. 'Well, I daresay the old business can manage without your custom for once, though I think it's a pretty mean sort of thing for one friend to do to another.'

Jesse relaxed, and tapped his pipe out on the bars of the grate.

'See here,' he said in a softer tone, as he straightened up, 'I'm not the only chap in these parts who's feeling the same way. If you want to keep your customers you'll darn well have to put yourself out a bit more, Bender. You're too easy-going by half, and Tenby's are going to profit by it.'

'Maybe, maybe!' agreed Bender.

'And what's all this I hear about you putting up for the council? Can you spare the time?'

'That's my business. I was asked to stand, and Hilda agrees it's a good thing.'

'Against Sep Howard? He's had a good majority each time.'

'Why not against Sep Howard? We know each other well enough to play fair. Sep's quite happy about it, that I do know.'

Jesse Miller sighed, and pocketed his pipe.

'Well, Bender, you know what you're doing, I suppose, but if this business were mine, I wouldn't waste my time and energy on anything else but putting it back on its feet again.'

He rose to his feet and lifted his greatcoat from the hook on the door.

'What does young Bertie think about it all?' he asked, shrugging himself into the coat.

'He knows nothing about it,' replied Bender shortly. 'I'm not panicking simply because the takings are down a bit on last year. The business will be as good as ever when it's time for me to hand it over.'

'I wonder!' commented Jesse Miller, and vanished round the door.

Bender had cause to remember this conversation in the months that followed. Trade began to wane to such an extent that it was quite clear that many people, particularly farmers, were transferring their custom to Tenby's and would continue to do so. It was not in Bender's nature to be alarmed, but he went about his business very much more soberly.

The local election did much to distract his mind from the depressing state of affairs. The third contestant was a local school-teacher of advanced ideas, with a fine flow of rhetoric when unchecked, but having no ability to stand up to bucolic hecklers. Sep and Bender agreed that he would constitute no great menace to either of them.

When Sep had first heard that Bender was opposing him, he felt the old sick fluttering in his stomach which had afflicted him in Bender's presence ever since his school days. It was absurd, he told himself for the hundredth time, to let the man affect him in this way. Sep was now a man of some substance, although his way of life had changed little. He attended chapel as regularly as ever, accompanied by Edna and the family. Sometimes, it is true, Leslie was not present, but when you are twenty, and as attractive as Leslie Howard, it was not to be wondered at, the more indulgent matrons of Caxley told each other.

Sep had been a councillor now for several years. He looked upon this present fight as a private challenge – not between Bender and himself – but to his own courage. In chapel, his head sunk upon his hands, Sep prayed earnestly and silently for help in overcoming his own fears. He did not pray that he might win – it would have been as despicable as it was presumptuous to do so; but he prayed that he might fight the fight bravely and honourably.

There was no doubt about it, Bender was going to be a formidable opponent. He was well-liked, he had a commanding presence, and a breezy sense of humour which stood him in good stead when the heckling began. Sep knew he could not compete with Bender in this field, but he could only hope that his record of steady service to the town would keep his supporters loyal.

The boys and girls of the two families thoroughly enjoyed the excitement. They cycled up and down the Caxley streets, stuffing pamphlets through letter-boxes and nailing up election posters on doors and railings. There was no hostility between the two parties, as far as the younger generation was concerned. Winifred North and Kathy Howard accompanied each other on these expeditions, and were not above taking one side of each road and posting both notices through the boxes, with superb magnanimity.

Sep and Bender approached their electioneering in typical fashion. It was the custom to take turns in having the market place for an open-air meeting. Bender addressed the crowd in a hearty voice which could be heard clearly. His eyes sparkled, his arms waved in generous and compelling movements. Here was a man who enjoyed the publicity, the excitement, and the fight. His hearers warmed to him.

The evenings when Sep took the little platform, close by Queen Victoria, were much more sedate. Small, pale, his gentle voice scarcely audible, Sep nevertheless managed to command attention. There was a sincerity about him which appealed to his listeners, and moreover his past work was generally appreciated. It was hard to forecast which of the two men would win the election. Caxley seemed fairly equally divided in its loyalties.

On the great day, the schools were used as polling stations, much to the gratification of the local children. Bender and Sep, taking brief spells off from their businesses, ranged the town in their traps to take the infirm to register their votes. It happened to be market day in Caxley, and so the bustle was greater than ever.

By the time polling ended both men were tense and tired. Counting went on at the Town Hall next door to St Peter's. This edifice, built in the middle years of the old Queen's reign, was of a repellent fish-paste red, picked out, here and there, with a zig-zag motive in yellow tiles. It contrasted sadly with the mellow honey-coloured stone of the noble church beside it, but on this day its architectural shortcomings were ignored, for here, on the red brick balcony would be announced the name of the victorious candidate.

It was almost eleven o'clock when at last the Mayor and other officials made their entrance high above the square. The upturned faces grew suddenly still, and the noise of a distant train could be clearly heard chuffing its way rhythmically out of Caxley Station a mile away.

The three candidates stood self-consciously beside the scarlet-clad Mayor.

'John Emmanuel Abbott, two hundred and thirty-four,' read the Mayor sonorously. There was a mingled sound of cheering and booing. The little schoolteacher preserved a dignified and tight-lipped silence and bowed slightly.

'Septimus Howard, six thousand, nine hundred and two.' More cheers arose, hastily checked as the Mayor lifted his paper again.

'Bertram Lewis North, four thousand, seven hundred and twenty-two,' intoned the Mayor.

Now the cheering broke out anew, and when Septimus Howard, elected once more, stepped forward shyly, someone began to clap and shout: 'Good old Sep!' It was taken up by almost all the crowd, a spontaneous gesture of affection which was as touching as it was unexpected.

Sep bowed his thanks, spoke briefly of the honour done him, and promised to do his best to be worthy of the confidence shown in him. He turned to shake the hands of his opponents, first that of John Abbott, and then Bender's.

At that moment, their hands tightly clasped, Sep experienced a shock. Bender's smile was as broad as ever, his complexion as ruddy, but it was the expression in his eyes, the look of hurt wonderment, which shook Sep so profoundly. For the first time in his life, Sep felt pity for the great giant of a man before him, and, as well as pity, a new deep and abiding peace.

Amidst the tumult of the crowd and the dazzle of the lights, Sep became conscious of one outstanding truth. Within him, born suddenly of this strange new feeling, was an inner calm and strength. Somehow, Sep knew, it would remain there, and would colour his relationship towards Bender in the years ahead.

Chapter Seven

LOVE AFFAIRS

Like many other bluff, hearty men who seem to ride boldly through life, Bender was easily upset. The outcome of the election was a considerable shock to him. That his fellow townsmen preferred Sep's services to his own was particularly humiliating. Not that Bender disparaged Sep's industry and sincerity, but he could not help feeling a certain condescending amusement at what he called 'Sep's bible-thumping' attitude to life. As a lifelong churchgoer, Bender tended to underestimate the strength of Methodism in Caxley, and though this did not influence the outcome entirely, yet he could not help realizing that many chapel-goers had voted for Sep. His easy tolerance of nonconformists now suffered a change. Smarting secretly from his hurt, Bender was inclined to view the chapel-goers with a little more respect and, it must be admitted, with a twinge of sourness.

It was not surprising, therefore, that he was unusually waspish when Hilda told him of her fears about Leslie Howard and Winifred.

'I'm beginning to think,' Hilda said, 'that there's more to it than just being friendly. Our Winnie's at a silly age, let's face it, and Leslie's had plenty of practice turning young girls' heads.'

'Probably nothing in it,' replied Bender, pacifying womanly doubts automatically. 'But we certainly don't want our girl mixed up with the chapel lot.'

'It's not "being mixed up with the chapel lot", as you call it,' retorted Hilda, with unwonted spirit, 'but Leslie's been mixed up with too many girls already! Besides,' she continued, 'there are better fish in the sea for our Winnie than Sep Howard's boy.'

'You've no call to speak like that about Sep,' admonished Bender, secretly regretting his hasty disparagement of the Howards' religion.

'But surely you don't want anything to come of this?' demanded Hilda, putting down her crochet work as though about to do battle. Bender began to retreat. He had enough worries with the uncertainties of the business and the shock of the election without adding this problem to the list. He took a man's way out.

'You have a quiet word with Winnie, my dear. You'll handle it better than I can. And if I get a chance I'll just mention it to Sep and he can speak to Leslie. But ten chances to one, you're worrying yourself about nothing. Damn it all, Hilda, our Winnie's not nineteen!'

'I married you at that age,' pointed out Hilda tartly. She picked up her crochet work again, and stabbed sharply, in and out, with unusual ferocity.

As might be expected, Bender said nothing to Sep or anyone else about Leslie's attentions to his daughter. But Hilda approached her task with circumspection one evening when she and Winifred were alone in the kitchen. Her daughter blushed a becoming pink, twirled a tea-cloth rapidly round and round inside a jug, but said remarkably little.

Hilda, washing up busily at the sink, went a trifle further.

'Not that there's anything against the Howards, dear, or you would never have been allowed to be such good friends with the family, but it's as well to let it remain at that.'

'How d'you mean?' asked Winifred.

Really, thought Hilda, fishing exasperatedly for a teaspoon lurking in the depths, Winnie was sometimes very awkward!

'What I say! People are beginning to notice that you and Leslie dance a great deal together, and go for walks alone – all that sort of thing – and naturally they wonder if they're going to hear of an engagement.'

'You'd hear first,' said Winnie briefly.

It was not the sort of answer which gave Hilda any comfort. She began to feel that she was not making much progress.

'So I would hope! It doesn't alter the fact that Leslie is paying you a great deal of attention. He's in his twenties now, and he'll be thinking of marriage before long. You're only eighteen.'

'You were married at nineteen,' pointed out the maddening girl. Hilda tipped out the washing-up water, advanced upon the towel on the back door, and sent the wooden roller rumbling thunderously as she dried her hands energetically. It seemed that the time had come for plain speaking.

'What I'm trying to make you see, Winnie, is that there are other young men in Caxley – and *better placed* young men – who would most certainly make you happier than Leslie Howard when the time comes. Just be warned, my dear, and don't get entangled before you've had a chance to look round you. Leslie's well known as a charmer, and you don't want to be left high and dry, as so many of the others have, when Leslie's lost interest.'

Winifred continued to polish the jug. Her eyes were downcast. It was difficult to know just how she was taking this little homily, but at least she was not reacting violently. Hilda thanked her stars that Winifred had always been a placid girl. Some daughters would have answered back, or burst into tears, or flounced from the room, thought Hilda with relief.

'And you think Leslie will lose interest in me too?' queried the girl quietly.

'That's up to you,' responded Hilda. 'You certainly shouldn't encourage him. You don't want to find yourself married to a Howard, I hope.'

'Why not?' asked Winnie, setting the jug carefully on a shelf. Her back was towards her mother, so that Hilda could not see her face, but her voice was as calm as ever.

'Why not?' echoed Hilda, now too confidently embarked upon her mission. 'Because your father and I have hopes of something better for you than becoming a baker's wife when you decide to get married. We've always done our very best to introduce you to nice families. You can look higher than the Howards for a husband. Surely you can see that?'

The girl wheeled round and the determined look upon her face shook her mother into silence.

'There's one thing I can see,' said Winnie levelly, 'and that is that I've got a snob for a mother.' And before Hilda could get her breath back, Winnie walked, head-high and unhurried, from the room.

It was not only Hilda who had been perturbed by the fast-growing attachment between Leslie and Winnie. Bertie too had watched the pair with misgivings quite as strong, but of quite a different nature. His affection for the Howard boys was unchanged by the years. He was now approaching twenty-one, a thoughtful, intelligent young man, but still harbouring traces of that hero-worship he had felt as a child for the two boys who were his seniors. Jim at twenty-four, and Leslie at twenty-two, seemed to be grown men, and Leslie certainly was experienced in the ways of women. Bertie, of shyer disposition, felt that he knew too little of the world to question the Howards' actions. Nevertheless, his deep affection for Winnie put him on his guard, and he observed her growing awareness of Leslie's charms with uneasiness.

If Jim had been Winnie's choice, Bertie would have been delighted. Bertie and Jim had much in common, both being peace-loving young men, thoroughly engrossed in their jobs and enjoying the pleasant social life of Caxley in their spare time. There was a steadiness about Jim which Leslie lacked. He might be incapable of sweeping a girl off her feet, but he would make a thoroughly reliable husband. Bertie, inexperienced as he was, could not fail to see that Leslie might prove far too volatile for such a lasting institution as marriage.

But this was not the only thing which worried Bertie. He knew, only too well, that there was a streak of cruelty in Leslie. There had been birds' nesting expeditions, when they were boys, when Jim and Bertie had seen Leslie throw a young bird wantonly over a hedge. Bertie had once come upon Leslie in the baker's yard chastizing their old spaniel with unnecessary severity because it had chased a cat. Both Bertie and Jim had made their disgust plain on these occasions, but Leslie appeared unrepentant. Bertie himself remembered many a twisted arm and painful kick delivered by Leslie, for no apparent reason but self-indulgence. As he grew older, and enjoyed his successes with the girls, the same callousness showed in his attitude to those of whom he had tired. He showed not a quiver of compunction. For Leslie, when the affair was done, it was finished completely, and he passed to his next willing victim without one glance behind. It was small wonder that Bertie trembled for Winnie, so young and so vulnerable. Should he say anything to her, he wondered? Or would it simply add fuel to the fire?

He salved his conscience with the thought that almost always the pair were in company with other young people. Besides, Winnie was a sensible girl and had known Leslie and his ways long enough to realize that his affection would certainly not last long. He decided that it would be prudent to keep silence.

Other matters engaged Bertie's attention at this time, distracting him from the affairs of his sister. Kathy Howard, now nineteen and working in the family business, had long been taken for granted by Bertie as an occasional tennis partner or a useful team member when they played 'Clumps' at parties. But during the summer of 1913 Bertie began to find her presence curiously and delightfully disturbing. She was as vividly beautiful as her mother had been at the same age, and attracted as much attention from the boys. Her hair was a dusky cloud, her eyes large and luminous. She could dance all night without flagging, and had a gay recklessness which, until now, Bertie had dismissed as 'showing off'. When young Mary North, aged eight, had dared her to jump from their garden bridge fully clothed into the Cax, Kathy had done so immediately, and been reproved by Bertie. When the attic curtains blew out from the windows, high above the market square, and became caught in the guttering, it was Kathy who stood on the window-sill to release them before the three boys had pounded up the stairs after her. And it was Bertie again who remonstrated with her.

But these things had happened a year or two earlier, before Bertie's feelings had suffered a change. The very thought now of the risks that Kathy ran made Bertie tremble with apprehension. She was becoming incredibly precious to him, he realized with surprise. Meanwhile, oblivious of his feelings, Kathy continued her carelessly happy way, as dazzling as a butterfly, flitting from one pleasure to the next, with no thought of settling down. And Bertie was content to watch her with increasing delight, and to accustom himself to these new tremors which her presence excited.

He had another cause for concern. He strongly suspected that things were not well with the family finances and only wished he could ask his father openly about the situation. Somehow, it was not easy to speak to him. Bertie awaited an opportunity, half-hoping, half-fearing that his father would broach the subject, but time passed and nothing was said. It did not escape Bertie's notice, however, that his father was more preoccupied than usual, and that some of the stock was not being replaced when it was sold. He had a pretty shrewd idea that Tenby's had hit his father's trade more seriously than he would admit.

Nevertheless, the staff still numbered six, presumably were being paid, and were content with their lot. Bob, who had been at North's since leaving school, was now head assistant and Bender left more and more responsibility to him. He had grown into a harassed vague individual with a walrus moustache. His steel-rimmed spectacles screened myopic brown eyes which peered dazedly at the world about him. Despite his unprepossessing appearance the customers liked him and the staff treated him with deference. Unmarried, he lived with his old mother and seemed to have no particular vices, unless whist at the working men's club, and occasional bets on a horse, could be counted against him. Poor, plain Miss Taggerty, who was in charge of the kitchen ware at North's, openly adored him, fluttering her meagre sandy eyelashes, and displaying her distressingly protruding teeth and pink gums, in vast smiles which Bob appeared not to see. Only the very lowliest member of North's staff, young Tim, aged thirteen, sniggered at Miss Taggerty's fruitless endeavours and was soundly cuffed by the other assistants when so discovered. To them, disrespect towards Bob was tantamount to disrespect to Bender and the family. If Bob seemed satisfied with conditions in the business, Bertie told himself, why should he perturb himself unduly?

Summer slid into autumn, and the picnics and river parties gave way to concerts and dances as the days drew in. It was in October that the Caxley Orchestra gave its grandest concert each year, and in 1913 Winnie North appeared for the first time among the violinists.

Her family turned up in full force to do her honour. They sat in the front row of the balcony at the Corn Exchange.

'In case Mary wants to go out during the performance – you know what she is,' said her mother.

Mary, dressed in white silk with a wide sash of red satin, was beside herself with excitement. This was better than going to bed! Her eyes sparkled as she gazed about the crowded hall. Hilda, matronly in black velvet, did her best to quell her youngest's volatile spirits. Bender, at the end of the row, smiled indulgently upon his handsome family and their friends.

For the Howard family had been invited to join the party, and although Sep and Edna had excused themselves, and their youngest was in bed with the mumps, yet Leslie and Kathy were present and were to take Winnie and Bertie to their home for supper after the show.

As the performance went on the air grew warmer and more soporific in the balcony. Bertie found his attention wandering as the orchestra ploughed its way valiantly through Mozart's 'Eine Kleine Nachtmusik'. Along the row he could see Kathy's bronze leather shoe, wagging in time with the music, beneath the hem of her yellow skirt. Below the balcony, ranged neatly in rows each side of the wide gangway he could see the heads of almost two hundred worthy Caxley folk.

There was the mayor's bald pate, shining and pink, gleaming in the front row. Beside him were the glossy black locks, suspiciously lacking any silvery flecks or light and shade, of his sixty-year-old wife. Near him Bertie could see the bent figure of old Sir James Diller from Beech Green, his ear trumpet well in evidence and his shaking head cocked to hear every indistinct sound. Immediately behind him sat his manservant, ready to aid his ageing master if need be. In the same row were the manservant's sister and her husband, the local butcher, there to hear their two sons performing, one as a flautist and the other as a violinist.

Bertie's eyes wandered farther afield. There was the postmaster, whose son had just lost a leg as the result of a train accident. There was the cobbler who drank, the school-mistress who sang like an angel and the elderly curate of St Peter's who was father-confessor to half the parish. There was Mrs Gadd, the watchmaker's wife, who was aunt to Bob at the shop, and refused to have anything to do with him, for reasons unknown, and always demanded to be served by Bender himself. There was her cousin, known to young Caxleyites as 'old Scabby' because of his unfortunate complexion, and the chastiser of Bertie, aged six, when he had trespassed into the old man's garden in search of a lost ball. And beyond him was Louisa Howard, aunt to Kathy, and a thorn in the side of the Howard family because of her rebellious ways. Her flaming red hair and flaming red nose matched the flaming temper which scorched all with whom she came in contact.

'A vixen,' Bender called her, 'and a vicious vixen at that. If she'd been a boy she'd have been packed off to sea.'

Bertie's eyes strayed back to the platform. Husbands, wives, sons, and daughters, nieces and nephews scraped and blew, banged and squealed to the pride of their relatives in the audience. Bertie watched his sister's smooth fair head bent above her violin. Her pretty plump arm sawed energetically up and down as she concentrated on the music propped up before her.

How closely they were all tied, thought Bertie! Not only by the bonds of kinship which enlaced most of those in the Corn Exchange, but also by the bonds of shared experience. They not only knew each other, their faults and their foibles, they shared the town of Caxley. They knew the most sheltered spot to stand in the market square when the easterly wind blew sharp and keen across the cobbles. They knew where the biggest puddles had to be dodged on dark nights, and where the jasmine smelt sweetest on a summer evening. They knew where the trout rose in the Cax, where a nightingale could be heard and where lovers could wander undisturbed. They knew who sold the freshest meat, and who the stalest. They knew who made the stoutest boots, the smartest frocks and the best pork pies. In short, they were as closely knit as a family, and as lucky as villagers in a village, in that Caxley was small enough, and leisurely enough too, for them to appreciate each other and the little town which was home to them all.

Nodding gently, in the pleasant stuffiness of the balcony, Bertie gazed through half-closed eyes at his fellow-citizens and found them good.

Some chaps, mused Bertie to himself, would be itching to get away from all this at my age, but Caxley suits me!

He caught sight of Kathy's tapping toe again and sat up straight.

Yes, Caxley would certainly suit him, he decided, as 'Eine Kleine Nachtmusik' crashed triumphantly to a close, and he joined enthusiastically in Caxley's generous, and wholly biased, applause.

Chapter Eight

A TRIP TO BEECH GREEN

Winnie was flushed with excitement after the performance. Bertie had never seen her looking so pretty, nor had Leslie, it was plain.

They sat at the Howards' supper table and Bertie, hungry after three hours of Caxley music, looked with pleasure at the magnificent pork pie which stood before Sep at one end of the table, and the huge bowl of salad before Edna at the other. One of Sep's superb bread rolls, with a carefully plaited top, lay on each side plate, and Bertie broke his in two, savouring its delicious scent.

'Let us call a blessing on the food,' intoned Sep sonorously, and Bertie hastily put his erring hands in his lap and bent his shamed head. It was bad enough to look greedy. It looked even worse to appear irreverent. Cursing his luck, Bertie could only hope that the whole table had not seen his actions. But, catching the eye of Winnie across the table, he soon saw that one member of the family would tell the tale against him later on.

'Lord bless this food to our use and us to Thy service,' droned Sep, his thin hands pressed together and eyes tightly shut.

'Amen,' murmured the rest of them, and there was an uncomfortable silence, broken at last by Sep himself who picked up a large knife and fork flanking the pie and began to cut the golden crust, with almost as much reverence as his saying of grace.

Bertie, anxious to reinstate himself, passed the butter dish to Edna and complimented her on the superb vase of late roses which were the centrepiece of the table.

'Your ma gave them to me,' replied Edna. Bertie fell silent and studied the tablecloth.

It was a white damask one similar to those used in the North household, but much greyer, and badly ironed. Bertie could not imagine his mother allowing such a cloth on their own table, and certainly not such thick white plates, chipped here and there, and covered with minute cracks across the glaze where they had been left too long to heat in the oven. His knife blade wobbled on its handle, and the tines of his fork were so worn that it was difficult to spear the slippery pieces of tomato on his plate. He wondered why Sep and Edna endured such shabby adjuncts to their superb food, and also, as a rich crumb of pastry fell into his lap, why they did not think to provide table napkins. But it was positively churlish, he told himself, to think in this way at his host's table, and he set himself out to draw Edna into conversation about young Robert's mumps. He felt Kathy's eyes upon him across the table, and hoped she did not think too badly of his early gaffe.

'It's a funny thing,' Edna began energetically, 'but one side of his neck don't hardly notice, but the other's up like a football. Of course he can't swallow a thing, and his poor head's that hot you could poach an egg on it!'

Once launched, Edna sailed along readily enough, and Bertie allowed his mind to wander.

Only Winnie seemed to sparkle and Leslie too was at his gayest. Their end of the table, where Sep presided, seemed considerably livelier than Edna's where Bertie was doing his best to woo the subject from infectious diseases, but with small success. Edna had no small talk, and, as Dan Crockford had found years before, very little of interest in her beautiful head. But she liked to chatter, and the subject of mumps had led, naturally enough, to measles, whooping cough, diphtheria and other children's ailments which had caused Edna dramatic alarm over the years.

'And that young Dr Martin, who's gone over to Fairacre now – and a good thing too if you ask me – he came and had a look at our Leslie. And I said to him: "He's got yellow jaundice, doctor," and do you know what he said?'

Bertie murmured politely.

'He simply said: "And how do you know?" With that poor little ha'porth as yellow as a guinea! It didn't need much to tell a mother what was wrong with him, but doctors don't give no one any credit for having a bit of sense. Though I must say, speaking fair, he give Leslie some very strong medicine, which did him a world of good.'

She gazed down the table at her second-born, and sighed happily.

'Make a lovely couple, don't they?' she said artlessly, and Bertie felt his heart sink. Was it really becoming so obvious to everyone? Could it be that a marriage would be arranged between the two? Bertie felt cold at the thought, and even Kathy's smiles and cheerful conversation after supper could not quite dispel the chill at his heart.

They made their farewells soon after eleven and emerged into the quiet market square. The stars shone brightly from a clear sky above the tumbled Caxley roofs. In the yard of the public house a horse snorted, as it awaited its master. A few late home-goers straggled past Queen Victoria's upright figure, and somewhere, in the distance, a cat yowled in a dark alley.

Leslie had accompanied them down the stairs and opened the door at the side of the shop for them.

'Goodnight, Leslie, and thank you again,' said Bertie. But Leslie was not listening. Bertie saw that his hand held Winnie's tightly, and that the two were exchanging a look of complete love and understanding.

The Norths crossed the square, turned to wave to Leslie silhouetted against the light from his open door, and entered their own home.

Bertie made his way to bed that night with much food for thought.

It was soon after this that Bertie acquired his first motor-car, and it did much to distract the young man from his cares. It was a small two-seater, an A.C. Sociable, by name, and had been owned by young Tenby, the son of the flourishing ironmonger in Caxley High Street, since 1909 when it was in its first glory. Young Tenby, now married, with one son and another expected, had bought a larger car. It was the envy of all Caxley, a glossy new Lanchester, and Bertie was able to buy the old one at a very favourable price. One of his first trips was to Beech Green to take his mother to visit Ethel, now happily married to Jesse Miller, and also awaiting the birth of her second child.

Hilda, her hat tied on with a becoming grey motoring veil, sat very upright beside Bertie trying to hide her apprehension. But once the terrors of Caxley High Street were past, and they entered the leafy lane which climbed from the Cax valley to the downs beyond, her fears were calmed, and she looked about her at the glowing autumn trees with excited pleasure. Speech was well-nigh impossible because of noise and dust, but once they had drawn up, with a flourish, outside the farmhouse door, she complimented Bertie on his driving.

'Thank you, mamma,' said Bertie, secretly amused, 'but it's what I've been doing ever since I left school you know. I'm glad you weren't too frightened.'

While the two sisters exchanged news, Jesse Miller took Bertie round the farm. Harvest was over early that year and the stubble in Hundred Acre Field glittered like a golden sea. The two men crunched their way across it, Bertie envying his uncle's leather leggings which protected his legs from the sharp straw which pricked unmercifully through his own socks. He was glad when they approached the hedge of a cottage garden and Jesse paused to speak to the family who were working there. He bent down and removed some of the cruellest of the tormentors from the tops of his boots and his socks, and caught a glimpse through the bare hedge of a pretty girl, with her father, and a tall young man with red hair.

'Our thatcher,' said Jesse Miller, as they resumed their tour of the farm. 'Francis Clare. Just had to let him know the barn roof needs patching after last week-end's gale.'

'And the girl?'

'Dolly, his daughter. And the copper-nob's her young man, Arnold Fletcher. Getting married next year, I hear. Time you thought of it yourself, Bertie.'

'I'll remember,' promised Bertie.

The air was pure and refreshing, up here on the downs, and scented with the sweet-sad smells of autumn, the damp earth underfoot, and the dying bracken growing in the rustling hedge. Bertie paused to look about him in this lovely open place. In the Cax valley such exhilaration rarely seized him. There was something strong and uplifting in the great sweep of hills with the moving clouds gliding across their tops. He would like to live here, savouring their tranquillity, one day. Perhaps with Kathy for company, he wondered? The thought was as heady as the winds about him.

They returned to the farmhouse for a gigantic tea. A bowlful of freshly boiled brown eggs, set in the centre of the table, was only a prelude to the ham sandwiches, hot buttered scones, home made plum jam, Victoria sponge, Dundee cake, custard tartlets, and half a dozen dishes of assorted small cakes.

Ethel pressed her sister and nephew to eat heartily as they had such a long cold drive before them, and Hilda returned the compliment by persuading Ethel to eat equally well as she was 'feeding two'. Between them they managed to dispatch quite half the food arrayed on the table before setting off for home behind the hissing acetylene lamps.

Half-way between Beech Green and Caxley, a fine hare leapt from a high bank and zig-zagged along the road in front of the car, bewildered by the lights. Bertie slowed down and it stopped. He moved gently forward again and the hare continued its erratic and terrified course. At length, Hilda could bear it no longer, and motioned Bertie to stop completely, which he did in a convenient farm gateway.

The hare made off across the fields. It was very quiet with the engine at rest, and Hilda gave a little sigh.

'Bertie,' she began, 'we don't often get a little time on our own, and before we get home I want your advice.'

'My advice?' queried Bertie, genuinely startled. 'It's usually the other way round, mamma.'

'I'm worried about so many things, Bertie, and I can't discuss them all with your father. Winnie and Leslie Howard is one worry, and there's another.'

She stopped, and her voice had a little tremor which did not escape Bertie.

'There's not much one can do about Winnie,' said he gently. 'She's got plenty of sense, and father will surely have a word with Leslie if he's worried.'

'I doubt it,' responded Hilda, with a flash of spirit. 'He's got worries of his own, I suspect, which are more serious than he'll admit to me.'

She turned to him suddenly.

'Bertie, do try and talk to him. You're a man now, and can help. Something's going very wrong with the business, and he won't discuss it with me. But he's getting so unusually tight with money these days, and only this morning he said he didn't think we'd have the staff Christmas party.'

'No party?' echoed Bertie. Things must be serious indeed if this annual jollity, which Bender so much enjoyed, were to be cancelled.

'And there's a lot of other things. This car, for instance. He's really cross that you've bought it, and says we can't afford it.'

'But it's my own money,' protested Bertie, with justifiable heat. 'I saved every penny of it! Father knows that! And in any case, it's a dashed sight cheaper to run this little A.C. than to keep our horses in fodder and the trap in repair. Really, it's a bit thick!'

'Forget what I said,' said Hilda hastily, patting her son's hand. 'It's simply that he's terribly worried, and if you can help him, Bertie, he'll be so grateful, and so will I.'

'I'll do what I can, mamma,' replied Bertie, a trifle huffily, starting up the car again.

He drove home, fuming secretly at his father's criticism. Can't afford it indeed! Anyone would think he'd badgered the old man into parting with his money! For two pins he'd have it out with him the minute he got home!

But the words were never said. For when he and his mother entered the drawing-room above the shop, they found Bender

THE WORLD OF MISS READ

white-faced, his sparse hair on end, and papers and account books in confusion on the desk and floor.

'Bender,' cried Hilda, hurrying towards him, 'what on earth has happened?'

'Plenty!' replied Bender grimly. 'Bob's gone off with the cash box, and I've sent the police after him!'

Chapter Nine

THOUGHTS IN THE SNOW

The news of Bob's disappearance swept through Caxley with the speed and commotion of a forest fire.

'I've never liked the look of that fellow,' wheezed fat Mrs Petty, wise after the event. 'Had a look in his eye like this 'ere cod. Proper slimy customer, I always thought.'

The square buzzed with the gossip on that market day. Both stallholders and customers knew Bob and Bender well. It seemed a shameful thing for a man to serve his master so shabbily, wagged some of the tongues.

'We ain't heard Bob's side yet,' replied the more cautious. 'Catch the fellow first, I says. Maybe 'e never took it after all. Who's to say?'

As soon as Sep Howard heard of the affair he went across the square to see Bender. He did not relish the encounter. Bender hurt could be Bender at his most truculent, as Sep well knew, and the age-long tremors still shook the little man as he entered the ironmonger's shop.

Bender was rummaging in one of the many small drawers ranged on the wall behind the counter.

'Can you spare a minute?' asked Sep.

Bender led the way, without a word, into the shop parlour behind the shop, where private transactions were carried out. He motioned Sep to a high office stool and sat himself heavily on another.

'S'pose you've heard?' grunted Bender. 'Fine old how-d'you-do, ain't it?'

'I'm sorry,' said Sep. 'Was much taken?'

'The week's takings.'

Sep drew in his breath with a hiss. He knew what it was to face such disasters in business.

'Any chance of getting it back?'

'I doubt it, Sep, I doubt it.' Bender passed a gigantic hand over his face and head, as though to wipe away the cares that clung to him. 'There's no doubt about one thing though. The blighter's been helping himself off and on for two or three months now, and I hadn't twigged. Been too careless by half, Sep. Left too much to him, you see.'

He pushed a ledger across to him.

'See that eight? That was a three. See that nine? That was a nought. Oh, he's been having a high old time among the books just lately!'

'But what's behind it? He got a decent wage, lived pretty small, never seemed to flash the money about.'

'Betting,' said Bender briefly. 'Always liked a bob on a horse, and now it's turned into a sovereign. I've been round to see his old ma, and it all came out. I feel sorry for the poor old girl, I must say. Come to that, I feel pretty sorry for myself, Sep.'

This seemed Sep's chance to speak up, and he took it.

'If I can help, I hope you'll let me. I don't forget all you did for me, you know. You gave me a hand when I needed it most and I'd like to have the chance to help, if there's any mortal way of doing it.'

Bender's great face flushed red. There was no doubt that he was touched by the offer. He cleared his throat huskily before answering.

'Good of you, Sep. I appreciate it very much, and you'd be the first I'd turn to, if it came to it. But I ain't pushed for a pound yet, and I reckon North's will make it, Bob or no Bob.'

There was a heartiness about this reply which did not ring quite true to Sep. Bender was making light of a situation which was far more serious than he would admit. But Sep could do no more in the circumstances.

'Well, I'll be over the way if you want me any time, Bender. You know that. I hope it'll all get cleared up satisfactorily.'

He made his way from the shop feeling very worried. But in the midst of his doubts and fears, he took comfort from the words still ringing in his ears.

'You'd be the first I'd turn to, if it came to it!'

He never thought to hear Bender North utter those words to him.

A week passed, and still the villain was at large. The police had found that he was seen on the London-bound train on the evening of his disappearance. Two Caxley ladies, returning from a day's shopping in town, also remembered seeing him at Paddington station. Beyond that, there was nothing. Somewhere, Bob was lying very quietly indeed, waiting for the hue and cry to die down, it seemed.

It was almost November and a bitingly cold east wind bedevilled the town, raising tempers as well as dust. Doors banged, windows rattled, and fires smoked indoors. Outdoors it was even worse. The wind whipped off hats, stung cheeks, inflamed eyes, and screamed through the awnings of the market stalls. Dust eddied in miniature whirlwinds, raising paper, leaves, and straw, and depositing them where they were least wanted. Coughs and colds, sore throats and chapped lips plagued the populace, and it was generally agreed that it would be 'a darned good thing when the wind changed'.

Unscathed by the hostile world about them, Leslie and Winnie continued to rejoice in each other's company. Bertie had dutifully spoken to his sister, saying that their mother was worried, and that he too hoped that she was not serious about Leslie. Winnie had answered briefly. They had known the Howards all their lives. She knew what she was doing. She also knew that her mother was worried, and they had spoken about it before Bertie was approached. Bertie, having fired his warning shot, retreated in some disarray before Winnie's level defence.

Sep had suddenly realized what was afoot and secretly approved of their union. What could be more fitting than a wedding between the two families? It would be a happy bond between Bender and himself. He recalled Bender's comforting words. Sep's heart warmed to the young people. His Leslie was a fine boy and it was time he settled down. Winnie would make a good wife. As far as Sep could see the outlook was rosy. He liked the idea of the young couple finding happiness together. He liked too the idea of becoming closer to Bender. He said as much to Edna, and was disconcerted by her reply.

'You don't think *he'll* like it, do you? Nor our Hilda! She's got her eye on the gentry for her Winnie! Nothing less than a belted earl for Hilda's daughter!'

'What's wrong with Leslie? Fine upstanding youngster with a share in the business – you don't tell me that the Norths will disapprove?'

'That I do!' responded Edna flatly. 'Say what you like, Sep, the Norths have always looked down on us, and they won't let their Winnie marry Leslie without a fight.'

'You're fancying things!' muttered Sep, turning away. There was too much truth in Edna's sallies to please him, but he refused to be daunted.

'Let the young 'uns find their own way,' he pronounced at last, and hurried into the bakery before he heard any more unwelcome home truths.

There was plenty of work to distract Sep's attention from his son's affairs of the heart during the next few weeks, for Christmas was approaching, and there were scores of Christmas cakes to be made and iced.

Although Sep now employed several more workers, he still did as much himself in the bakery. The fragrance of the rich mixture, the mingled aroma of spices, candied fruits, and brown sugar, cheered Sep afresh every year. It was his own personal offering to the spirit of Christmas, and he enjoyed the festive bustle in the warmly scented bakery. It was like a sheltered haven from the bleak winds in the market square beyond the doors.

The cold spell was lasting longer than expected, and the weather-wise old folk prophesied a white Christmas in Caxley. Sure enough, in the week before Christmas, a light fall whitened the ground and powdered the rosy-tiled roofs of the town, and the lowering grey skies told of more to follow.

On Sunday afternoon, Bender set off for Beech Green with two large saw blades for Jesse Miller.

'He won't get much done in the fields,' commented Bender wrapping the blades briskly in brown paper. 'The ground's like iron. He'll be glad to set the men to sawing firewood tomorrow, and I promised him these as soon as they came.'

'Give them all my love,' said Hilda. 'I won't come with you with the weather like this. And wrap up warmly, do, my dear. Put your muffler on, and your thick gloves.'

'Never fear,' answered Bender robustly. 'I've known the downs long enough to know how to dress for them. I'll be back before dark.'

The horse trotted briskly through the town. There were very few people about and Bender was glad to be on his own, in the clean fresh air. Now he could turn over his thoughts, undisturbed by family interruptions or customers' problems. He always felt at his best driving behind a good horse. He liked the rhythm of its flying feet, the gay rattle of the bowling wheels, and the clink and squeak of the well-polished harness.

The pace slackened as Bill, the horse, approached Beech Green. The long pull up the downs was taken gently and steadily. The reins lay loosely across the glossy back, and Bender reviewed his situation as they jogged along together through the grey and white countryside.

Things were serious, that was plain. Bob had been picked up by the London police ten days earlier, and now awaited his trial at the next Assizes. He had been in possession of fourteen shillings and ninepence at the time of his arrest, and could not – or would not – give any idea of where the rest of the money had gone. Clearly, nothing would be restored to his employer.

What would he do, Bender asked himself? He could get a further loan from the bank, but would it be of any use? Had the time come to take a partner who would be willing to put money into the firm? Bender disliked the idea. He could approach both Sep Howard and

Jesse Miller who had offered help, but he hated the thought of letting Sep Howard see his straits, and he doubted whether Jesse Miller could afford to give him the sum needed to give the business a fresh start. Jesse was in partnership with his brother Harry at the farm, and times were hard for them both at the moment.

The other course was a much more drastic one. Tenby's had approached him with a tentative offer. If he ever decided to part with the business would he give them first offer? He would of course be offered a post with the firm who would be glad of his experience. They were thinking of housing their agricultural machinery department on separate premises. North's, in the market square, handy for all the farmers in the district, would suit them perfectly. They asked Bender to bear it in mind. Bender had thought of little else for two days, but had said nothing to Hilda. He knew well enough that she would be all in favour of the action, and he wanted to be sure that ·it was right before making any final decisions. Hilda, for years now, had been pressing Bender to move from the shop to one of the new houses on the hill at the south side of the town.

'It's so much healthier for the children,' asserted Hilda. 'You know how chesty Mary is – she takes after you, you know – and it's so damp right by the river here.'

'She looks all right to me,' Bender said.

'Besides,' continued his wife, changing her tactics, 'everyone's moving away from the businesses – the Loaders, the Ashtons, the Percys –'

'The Howards aren't,' pointed out Bender. Hilda tossed her head impatiently.

'Don't be awkward, Bender! Who cares what the Howards do anyway? It would be far better for Bertie and Winnie, and Mary too, later on, to have a place they can ask their friends to without feeling ashamed.'

'*Ashamed?*' echoed Bender thunderously. 'What's wrong with this place?'

'We could have a tennis court if we had a bigger garden,' said Hilda. Her blue eyes held that far-away look which Bender had come to realize was the prelude to some expense or another. 'The children could invite all sorts of nice people to tennis parties.'

'They're free to invite them here to parties – boating and otherwise – as far as I'm concerned,' said Bender. 'Don't tell me that it's the children who want to move. It's entirely your notion, my dear, and a mighty expensive one too.'

Hilda had fallen silent after that, but returned to the attack many times until Bender had begun to wonder if there was something in the idea after all. It was not social progress, though, that caused Bender to give the matter his attention, but the financial possibilities of the move.

If Tenby's made him the substantial offer he expected, he could well afford to buy Hilda the house of her dreams. There was no doubt about it that the market place living quarters were rambling and far too large for their needs. Bertie and Winnie, it was reasonable to suppose, would be married and away before long. It would be more economical, in every way, for those who were left, to live in a smaller and more up-to-date house where repairs and upkeep would probably be less than half the present sum. Also, Hilda was right in saying that they would find it healthier. Not only would they be on higher ground; it would be a good thing to leave the business behind at night and get right away from its responsibilities.

He presumed that he would be offered the managership. In that case there would be a steady income, with no worries attached. Bender, gazing unseeingly across the snowy fields, lulled almost into slumber by the rhythmic swaying of the trap, began to feel that selling North's might be the best way out of his many difficulties. But not yet, he told himself. He would hang on as long as he could, and who knows? Something might turn up. He'd been lucky often enough before. There was still hope! Bender North was always an optimist.

He put Billy into the shelter of a stable and tramped across the snowy yard to the Millers' back door.

He was greeted warmly by the family, and he was put by the fire to thaw out. The usual vast tea was offered him, but Bender ate sparingly, with one eye cocked on the grey threatening sky outside.

'I mustn't be too long,' said Bender, his mouth full of buttered toast. 'There's more snow to come before morning, or I'll eat my boots.'

They exchanged family news. Ethel's youngest was running a temperature, and was upstairs in bed, 'very fretful and scratchity', as his mother said. Jesse's pigs were not doing as well as he had hoped, and he had an idea that one of his men was taking eggs. 'Times were bad enough for farmers,' said Jesse, 'without such set-backs.'

He accompanied Bender to the stable when he set off.

'And how are your affairs?' he asked when they were out of earshot of the house. Bender gave a reassuring laugh, and clapped the other man's shoulders.

'Better than they have been, Jesse, I'm glad to say. I hope I shan't have to worry you at all.'

The look of relief that flooded Jesse's face did not escape Bender. It certainly looked as though Tenby's would be the only possible avenue of escape if the business grew worse.

Ah well, thought Bender, clattering across the cobbled yard, we must just live in hope of something turning up! He waved to Jesse and set off at a spanking pace on the downhill drive home.

The snow began to fall as Bender turned out of Jesse's gate. It came down thickly and softly, large flakes flurrying across mile upon mile of open downland, like an undulating lacy curtain. It settled rapidly upon the iron-hard ground, already sheeted in the earlier fall, and by the time Billy had covered half a mile the sound of his trotting hoofs was muffled. He snorted fiercely at the onslaught of this strange element, his breath bursting from his flaring nostrils in clouds of vapour. His dark mane was starred with snow flakes, and as he tossed his head Bender caught a glimpse of his shining eyes grotesquely ringed with glistening snow caught in his eyelashes.

His own face was equally assaulted. The snow flakes fluttered against his lips and eyes like icy moths. It was difficult to breathe. He pulled down the brim of his hard hat, and hoisted up the muffler that Hilda had insisted on his wearing, so that he could breathe in the stuffy pocket of air made by his own warmth. Already the front of his coat was plastered, and he looked like a snowman.

A flock of sheep, in a field, huddled together looking like one vast fleece ribbed with snow. The bare hedges were fast becoming blanketed, and the banks undulated past the bowling trap smoothly white, but for the occasional pock-mark of a bird's claws. The tall dry grasses bore strange exotic white flowers in their dead heads, and the branches of trees collected snowy burdens in their arms.

And all the time there was a rustling and whispering, a sibilance of snow. The air was alive with movement, the dancing and whirling of a thousand thousand individual flakes with a life as brief as the distance from leaden sky to frozen earth. At the end of their tempestuous short existence they lay together, dead and indivisible, forming a common shroud.

There was a grandeur and beauty about this snowy countryside which affected Bender deeply. Barns and houses, woods and fields were now only massive white shapes, their angles smoothed into gentle curves. He passed a cow-man returning from milking, his head and shoulders shrouded in a sack, shaped like a monk's cowl. He was white from head to foot, only his dark eyes, glancing momentarily at the passing horse, and his plodding gait distinguished him from the white shapes about him.

Bender turned to watch him vanishing into the veil of swirling flakes. Behind him, the wheels were spinning out two grey ribbons, along the snowy road. He doubted whether they would still be visible to the fellow traveller, so fast were they being covered from above.

He turned back and flicked the reins on Billy's snow-spattered satin back.

'Gee up, boy!' roared Bender cheerfully. 'We both want to get home!'

*

Sep Howard watched the snow falling from his bedroom window. His hair was rumpled from a rare afternoon nap on the bed, and he had awakened to find the window darkened with flying flakes.

He judged that it was two or three inches deep already. The steps of St Peter's and the Town Hall were heavily carpeted. The snow had blown into the cracks and jambs of doors and windows, leaving long white sticks like newly-spilt milk. A mantle of snow draped Queen Victoria's shoulders and her bronze crown supported a little white cushion which looked like ermine. Snow lay along her sceptre and in the folds of her robes. The iron cups, in the fountain at her feet, were filled to the brim with snow flakes, and the embossed lions near by peered from snow-encrusted manes.

There were very few people about for a Sunday afternoon. An old tramp, carrying his belongings in a red-spotted bundle on a stick, shuffled disconsolately past St Peter's, head bent, rheumy eyes fixed upon the snow at his feet. Two ragged urchins, no doubt from the marsh, giggled and barged each other behind him, scraping up the snow in red, wet hands to make snowballs.

Sep watched them heave them at the back of the unsuspecting old man. At the moment of impact he swung round sharply, and raised his bundle threateningly. Sep could see his red, wet, toothless mouth protesting, but could hear no word through the tightly-shut bedroom window. One boy put his thumb to his nose impudently: the other put out his tongue. But they let the old man shuffle round the corner unmolested before throwing their arms round each other's skinny shoulders and running jubilantly down an alley-way.

Momentarily the market square was empty. Not even a pigeon pattered across the snow. Only footprints of various sizes, and the yellow stain made by a horse's urine, gave any sign of life in that white world. Snow clothed the rosy bricks and sloping roofs of Caxley. It covered the hanging signs and the painted nameboards above the shops, dousing the bright colours as a candle snuffer douses a light.

What a grey and white world, thought Sep! As grey and white as an old gander, as grey and white as the swans and cygnets floating together on the Cax! The railings outside the bank stood starkly etched against the white background, each spear-top tipped with snow. There was something very soothing in this negation of colour and movement. It reminded Sep of creeping beneath the bedclothes as a child, and crouching there, in a soft, white haven, unseeing and unseen, all sounds muffled, as he relished the secrecy and security of it all.

There was a movement in St Peter's porch and a dozen or so choirboys came tumbling out into the snowy world, released from carol practice. The sight brought Sep, sighing, back into the world of Sunday afternoon.

He picked up a hair-brush and began to attack his tousled locks.

'Looks as though the weather prophets are right,' said Sep to his reflection. 'Caxley's in for a white Christmas this year.'

Chapter Ten

TROUBLE AT NORTH'S

The weather prophets were right. Caxley had a white Christmas and the good people of the town walked to church and chapel through a sugar-icing world sparkling in bright sunshine.

Edna, wrapped warmly in a new black coat trimmed with fur at the neck and hem – Sep's Christmas present to her – felt snug and happy, as she composed herself to day-dreaming whilst the minister delivered his half-hour's exhortation. Even his stern countenance was a little softened by the joyous festival, she noticed.

'New hope, a new life, a New Year,' declaimed the minister, and Edna thought how queer it would be to write 1914 so soon. It would be a relief too, in a way. She had felt a little uneasy throughout 1913. It was an unlucky number. Gipsy superstitions played a larger part in Edna's life than ever her husband suspected.

Yes, there was something reassuring about the sound of 1914. She was going to enjoy this beautiful Christmas and her beautiful new coat, and look forward to an even more prosperous New Year than ever before!

'Peace on earth, goodwill toward men,' the minister was saying, one finger upraised for attention.

Edna stroked her new fur trimming and sighed contentedly.

Hilda North also welcomed the New Year. In its early months Bender, with his mind now clear, told her of Tenby's offer and the possibility of buying the house of her dreams on Caxley's southern slopes.

Hilda was joyful and triumphant.

'Have you told Bertie?' was her first question. 'He ought to know. After all, this would have been his one day.'

Bender promised to speak to his son that evening. It was a mild spring day with soft rain falling, straight and steady over Caxley and the countryside. In his waterside garden, Bender watched the rain collecting in the cups of his fine red tulips, and dripping, drop by drop, from leaf to leaf, down the japonica bush against the workshop wall. The Cax was dimpled with rain, the rustic bridge glistened. There was a soft freshness in the whispering air that soothed, and yet saddened, the watching man. He was going to miss all this, after so many years. Would Bertie miss it too?

Bertie, at that moment, was also watching the rain. He was at Fairacre where he had been summoned by old Mr Parr whose automobile refused to start. Bertie had spent the morning repairing it, and now sat in the thatched barn which housed the car, munching a sausage roll which was his lunch. A robin splashed in a puddle near by, flirting wings and tail, bobbing its thumb-sized head, as it gloried in its bath.

A veil of drops fell steadily from the thatched roof, splashing on to the washed gravel surrounding the building. In the field next door Bertie could see sheep moving slowly and unconcernedly, their wool soaked with rain. Steam gently rose from their backs as they cropped. An old cart-horse, streaked with the wet, nodded under a horse chestnut tree, its back as shiny as the sticky buds bursting from the branches above it.

It was a good life thought Bertie, looking across at the motor-car restored to usefulness. He hoped he might never leave this absorbing occupation. It would be a sad day for him if his father decided that he should take over the family business! No – motor-cars were his own choice!

He brushed the crumbs from his clothes, stood up, and decided to visit the 'Beetle and Wedge' for a drink, before returning to Caxley.

It was a relief to the young man when Bender spoke of his affairs that evening, and he said so.

'I haven't liked to question you, Father, but I guessed things were getting more and more difficult. That business of Bob's seems to have put the lid on it.'

'Well, he's safely inside for twelve months,' replied Bender, 'and we're all a sight better off without the rascal. But North's will have to go, as far as I can see, and perhaps it's as well. I shall still be able to work here, and not have the responsibility. I tell you frankly, Bertie, I shouldn't like to go through the last year or so again.'

'You'll miss the garden,' said Bertie, looking out at the wet evening.

'There'll be another on the hill,' said Bender robustly. 'And I'm glad for your mother's sake we're making the move. It means a lot to her.'

He clapped his son on the shoulder in a dismissive way.

'Glad to have told you, Bertie. You've taken it very well. There's times I've felt I've let you all down. This used to be a real warm business, as you know. I've been a bit of a bungler, it seems to me.'

'You can put that idea out of your head,' replied Bertie. 'It's just the way things have fallen out. I, for one, won't miss the business. My heart's never been in it, as you well know.'

He made his way up to his room to change. His spirits rose as he mounted the stairs, for he was going to the Howards' and would spend the evening in Kathy's company.

He stood at the window looking down upon the glistening market square, and, for the first time since hearing the news, he felt a sudden pang.

This he would miss. He had not realized quite how much it meant to him. He could not imagine living in another house which did not look upon the market square. This scene had been the background to his entire life. He could remember being held in Vera's arms, clad in his scratchy flannel nightshirt, to watch the pigeons wheeling across the striped awnings of the market stalls. He had stood at that window in tears of fury after being banished from below for some misdemeanour. He had stood there, in quiet contemplation, soothed by the familiar shapes of the clustered buildings and the comings and goings of well-known Caxley folk.

His fears and doubts, his hopes and joys, had been experienced here in the market square. Here were his roots, here was his entire past. How would he live without the market place around him, its sights and sounds, and its bustle of people?

He looked across at Howard's bakery. How could he live so far from Kathy? The thought was insupportable. He flung away from the window and tore off his working jacket in near panic. Then he recovered his control.

He was behaving like a child. He would still be living in Caxley. Kathy would still be there, lovely and loving. Who knows? One day he might come back to live in the market square, in a house of his own, with Kathy to share it.

The news that the North family was leaving the market place came as a great shock to Caxley. The business had been there for three generations, and Bender was popular. It was sad to think of that vast figure filling a doorway no longer his own. A few self-righteous and mean-spirited citizens announced that Bender had brought this humiliation upon himself by slackness and indolence. But Bender's friends rose to his support, and cried them down.

The move was a leisurely one, much to Hilda's exasperation. She would have liked to pack up and go immediately, once the decision was made, but it was not to be. Tenby's had much to arrange with Bender, and Hilda had to content herself with daily trips up the hill to supervise the painting and decorating which went on in the red-brick villa so soon to be the family home.

As usual, on these occasions, nothing in the old house seemed to fit the new one. The curtains and carpets were either too small, too large, or too shabby. Hilda nobly did her best to keep expenses down, knowing now the truth of their financial circumstances, but she fought a losing battle. Colours clashed, walnut warred with oak, the vast mahogany dining table had to be left behind because it would not go through any door or window, and a new one bought. New chintz covers became a necessity, shrouding odd chairs in a more pleasing harmony. Two fireplaces had to be replaced, and it was deemed necessary to overhaul the gas system from the attics to the cellars. Bender began to wonder if the tidy sum from Tenby's would be enough to cover the cost of the new villa, let alone leaving him a nest egg in the bank.

His own time was occupied in clearing out the main part of the premises for Tenby's agricultural equipment. A mammoth sale of kitchen hardware took place and was long remembered in Caxley in the years to come. Many a stout bread crock or set of saucepans became known in cottage homes in the Caxley district as 'one of North's last bargains'.

Most of Tenby's men were local fellows, well known to Bender, and he found no difficulty in getting on with them in the weeks that followed. Tenby himself he disliked. He was a shrewd business man, originally from the north, and thought far more quickly than Bender ever could. His beady dark eyes ran over the possibilities of the old house, and Bender could not help feeling a qualm when he heard him discussing the advantages of ripping out the first floor walls to make one large showroom above the shop. His grey and white striped drawing-room, now standing empty, seemed to breathe a mute appeal. Where now were the red velvet chairs, the wall brackets bearing sea-lavender, and all the other familiar furnishings of his best-loved room? Bender had to admit that the new house gave him small satisfaction compared with the spacious shabby comfort of the old premises. It would be sad to see the place so altered.

It made him sadder still when he discovered that later on the firm proposed to flatten his beautiful little garden, cement it over, and to erect an enormous structure on the site to house new tractors and other large pieces of equipment. Bender could hardly bear to think about it. The pinks bordering the river bank were particularly fine in the summer of 1914, and their heady fragrance held a doomed poignancy which Bender never forgot. What had he done when he had parted with his heritage? Was it all to be destroyed?

The family was now installed on the hill. The new house was called 'Rose Lodge' which Hilda felt was refined. It took Bender years before he could write it automatically at the head of his rare letters. Somehow he always put *15 The Market Square*, before remembering the change of address.

The top two floors of the old premises were to be refurbished, 'for future staff use', as Jack Tenby said. Meanwhile, they stood empty. Sometimes Bender climbed the stairs and had a look at the bare dusty rooms. Against the walls were marks where furniture had stood for years. Here the paper had peeled where young Mary's prying fingers had been busy through the bars of her cot. There was the pale circle on the wall where Winnie's mirror had hung. And there on the corner pane were Bertie's initials, cut with his mother's diamond ring. That little escapade had earned the young ten-year-old a severe spanking, Bender recalled.

There was something infinitely pathetic in the ghostly rooms. They were full of memories. Every creak of the floorboards, every rattle of the windows, was familiar to Bender. He had not realized how tightly the old house had entwined them all, until he had cut the bonds, only to find himself still imprisoned in memories. He threw himself into the work of supervising the changes in the shop, glad to be able to forget the silence above in the hubbub of activity below.

It was not easy, as Bender discovered, as the summer slipped by. For one thing, it was excessively hot. The market place basked in one golden day after another. The Cax seemed the only cool spot in the town, and was besieged by boys and girls swimming and paddling in the evenings. For a man of Bender's weight, the weather seemed torrid, however much the younger ones might revel in it. He took to slipping out into the doomed garden to enjoy the air and to gain refreshment from the sight of the cool water rippling by. But again the pleasure was tempered by the oppressive knowledge that this might well be the last summer in which the garden would enchant him.

It was towards the end of July that the first blow came. Bender's managership had been tacitly understood, and for three months now he had done his best to get things working smoothly, under the eye of Jack Tenby, and one or two other directors of the firm, who called in from time to time to see how things were shaping.

One morning, Bender found a letter waiting for him at the office, and he read it with mounting indignation. It said that the firm had now had a chance to make plans and were reorganizing their business, both in Caxley and elsewhere. Their young Mr Parker, of Trowbridge, who had been with the firm since leaving school, would be transferred to the agricultural department of the Caxley firm and would take up residence on the premises as soon as possible. He would be in charge of the department, and they felt sure that Mr North would give him all the cooperation he had so readily shown to the firm in the last few months. They would be pleased to maintain Mr North's present rate of pay, and hoped to have the advantage of his experience for many years to come. They were 'his faithfully'.

'Faithfully!' snorted Bender, in the privacy of the shop parlour. Was this faith? Was this trust? Was it plain honesty? The truth was that it was a dam' dirty trick, to foist a young man over him in his own shop.

'His own shop.' The words echoed in his ears. Oh, the misery of it all, thought Bender! He ground one gigantic fist into the palm of the other hand, as he read the letter anew.

This was treachery. He would have it out with Jack Tenby. They should not treat Bender North like this. For two pins he would chuck the job in and let them muddle on without his help! That would show them!

But would it! Is that what they wanted? Was he simply a nuisance to be got rid of? And if he threw up this job, where would he get another? There was the family to consider. The new house was still running away with the money at an alarming rate. Dammit all, Bender groaned, ramming the letter back into its envelope, he must try and face the stark and unpleasant fact that he was no longer his own master. It was a bitter pill to swallow at any age. At forty-eight, it was doubly bitter, Bender mourned.

All that day, Bender went mechanically about his affairs in a daze. He decided not to mention the matter to Hilda until his mind was calmer. He felt that he could not bear Hilda's protestations on his behalf, her hurt pride and her ready tears. It was a day or two later, that the second unpleasant happening occurred.

Bender was adding up figures in the shop parlour with the door open into the shop. Near by, Miss Taggerty, and another woman assistant, Miss Chapman, dusted shelves and gossiped together, imagining that they were unheard.

Miss Taggerty, still faithful to the imprisoned Bob, was as plain as ever. The increasing years and private grief had speckled her sandy hair with grey, but had not added discretion to her virtues. She rattled on, blissfully unconscious of Bender's presence so close at hand, telling of scandals past and present. Bender, used to this sort of thing, let it flow over him, until a familiar name caught his attention.

'Of course it's Les Howard's! Why should the girl say it is if it isn't? A lovely boy, old Ma Tucker told my pa. Weighed nigh on ten pounds at birth, and the spitting image of Leslie – same dark eyes and all.'

'But it might be her husband's surely?' objected Miss Chapman. 'He's dark too.'

'Not *this* dark!' pronounced Miss Taggerty triumphantly. 'And it's common knowledge that Les Howard spends far too much time there on the rounds. It's pretty, lonely up Bent way. I bet she was glad of a bit of company.'

'But there's not another house in sight!' protested Miss Chapman. 'How do people know Les Howard went in?'

'There's such people as hedgers-and-ditchers, and ploughmen, and the like,' retorted Miss Taggerty. 'And they've got eyes in their heads, and wasn't born yesterday, for that matter. Besides, as I told you, the girl swears it's Leslie's and the husband swears he's going to take him to court over it.'

Bender felt it was time he made his presence known. He dropped a heavy ledger on the floor, swore, and picked it up. The clear voices stopped abruptly, to be replaced by some agitated whispering, and a muffled giggle. He heard no more of the matter, but he thought about it a great deal. If this were true, then it was time his Winnie dropped the young man pretty quickly.

In the next two days he heard the same rumour from other sources. There seemed to be some foundation for the story, and Bender's worries increased. He had half a mind to have a word with Sep about the matter, but decided to let the matter rest for a few days until he was surer of his facts.

As it happened, things came to a head precipitately within the next day or two. Although Winnie and Leslie sought each other's company still, Bender had fancied that they had seen rather less of each other since the move, and hoped that the affair might be dying a natural death. Winnie was extra busy these days at the local hospital where she was doing very well as a nurse. Her free time was scarce, and quite often she spent it lying on her bed to rest her aching legs, in the unusually hot weather.

It was now August, and as close as ever. Hilda and Bender sat in their new drawing-room with all the windows open. A pale yellow moth fluttered round the gas bracket, its wings tap-tapping on the glass globe. Bender found the noise distracting.

He was still mightily aggravated by the letter from Tenby's, and had come to realize that he was in no position to protest. Naturally, this added to his fury. He wondered, as he listened to the moth and turned the newspaper in his hands, if this were the right time to tell Hilda what had occurred. She would have to know some time about 'our young Mr Parker from Trowbridge'.

At the memory, Bender grew hotter than ever. The room seemed stifling. He undid the top button of his shirt, and turned his attention once more to the newspaper. He'd tell Hilda tomorrow. It was late. She might not sleep if he broke the news now.

There seemed mighty little comfort to be had in the paper, he reflected. All this trouble in Europe! Germany at war with Russia, and the ambassador recalled from Petersburg, and the Frenchies getting the wind up and looking to us for help! Not likely, thought Bender! Let them all get on with their squabbling safely on the other side of the English Channel!

It was at that moment that the door burst open and Leslie Howard and Winnie appeared, bright-eyed. Winnie ran to her mother, holding out her hands.

'Mummy, Leslie and I have got engaged! Look at my ring!'

Hilda's face grew rosy with mingled pleasure and wrath. What could be said in the face of such combined triumph and joy? Hilda, tears in her eyes, looked at Bender for assistance.

Something seemed to burst in Bender's head. The rumours flew back to buzz round him like stinging wasps. The heat, his private worries, the depressing newspaper, and his deep love for Winnie pressed upon him unbearably.

He flung the newspaper upon the floor and turned on Leslie.

'Engaged? That you're not, my boy, until I've had a word with you in private. Step across the hall, will you? No time like the present!'

He stormed past the young man, pale-faced, into the empty dining-room, leaving Winnie and her mother trembling.

Sep Howard did not hear of the unknown young Mr Parker's promotion until the day after Leslie's uncomfortable encounter with Bender. He did not hear, either, about that piece of news, from his son.

He was very perturbed on Bender's account. This was going to hurt him very much, and it might well mean that he would be very poorly off. Should he go once again, and offer any help that he could? It needed a certain amount of courage to face Bender at any time, but Sep remembered those words: 'You'd be the first I'd turn to, Sep,' and took heart.

He had heard the news from Jack Tenby himself, and so knew that there was no doubt about it. He decided to step across to the shop as it opened, and to do what he could.

A little nervous, as he always was when approaching Bender, yet glowing with the consciousness of doing the right thing, Sep entered North's shop. Bender glowered at him over his spectacles. His voice was gruffer than ever.

'Whatcher want?' he growled.

'A word with you, please,' answered Sep.

He followed Bender's broad back into the privacy of the shop parlour, and began, diffidently, without further ado.

'I've heard the news about the new manager, Bender. Jack Tenby mentioned it. It's very hard lines on you. Is there anything I can do?'

Bender wheeled to face him, face down, like a cornered bull, his eyes blazing and his breathing noisy. Sep began to step back in horror.

'Clear out!' said Bender, dangerously calm. 'That ain't the only news you've heard, I'll lay! You heard about that son of your'n and his goings-on?'

He threw his head up suddenly, and began to roar.

'I don't want no mealy-mouthed help from you, Sep Howard, and I don't want to see hair or hide of you or your dam' kids ever again! If Leslie comes crawling round our Winnie once more, I'll give him the hiding of his life. Clear off, clear out! And dam' well mind your own business!'

He flung open the door, bundled Sep outside, and slammed the door shut again in the little man's face. Two or three interested assistants peered furtively from behind shelves. Sep pulled his jacket straight, and walked past them with as much dignity as he could muster.

His legs trembled as he crossed the market square, and his head buzzed with the echo of Bender's shouting. He must see Leslie at once and hear his side of this shocking story. Shaken though he was by the encounter, Sep felt more pity and concern for Bender than fear, and rejoiced in his own confidence.

His eldest boy, Jim, stood immersed in the newspaper at the bakery door. His hair was white with flour, his sleeves rolled up, and his white apron fluttered in the breeze from the river near by. The boy's face was excited. His eyes sparkled as he looked up from his reading.

'Well, dad, it looks as though we're ready for 'em! Les and I should be on our travels pretty soon according to this!'

He held out the paper so that Sep could read the headlines.

'Ultimatum to Germany. War at Midnight.'

Sep's face grew graver as he read.

'I never thought it would come to this,' he said in a low voice, as though speaking to himself. He looked soberly across the paper at his son.

'But it is the right thing to do,' he said slowly. 'No matter what the consequences are, a man must always do what he knows is right.'

He turned to enter, and his son turned to watch him go, a small erect figure, bearing himself with a dignity which the young man had never noticed before.

Across the square, Bender paced up and down the shop parlour, quivering with rage. The calendar caught his eye, and he stopped to tear off yesterday's date. What had he done, he asked himself, crumpling the paper in his hand? His world seemed in ruins. He had upset Hilda, and poor Winnie, and now he had thrown his old friend from him. What straits a man could find himself in! What depths of despair still lay ahead?

Automatically he bent to read the daily motto on the new date. It said: Aug. 4, 1914 'Be strong and of a good courage'.

It was the final straw. Bender sank upon the office stool, dropped his burning head to the cold leather top of the desk, and wept.

Part Two

Chapter Eleven

OVER BY CHRISTMAS

The people of Caxley greeted the declaration of war against Germany with considerable jubilation and a certain measure of relief. Tension had been mounting steadily throughout the past week. Now that the die was cast, excitement seized them.

'That Kaiser's bin too big for 'is boots for time enough. 'E needs taking down a peg or two!' said Mrs Petty.

'Us'll daunt 'em!' declared a bewhiskered shepherd near by.

'Ah! He've got the Empire to reckon with now!' agreed his old crony, spitting a jet of tobacco juice upon the market place cobbles, with evident satisfaction. The air rang with congratulatory greetings. August Bank Holiday may have been upset a little by the news of war, but spirits were high everywhere.

The papers were full of cartoons depicting Belgium as a helpless maiden in the grip of a strong, brutal, and lustful conqueror. Chivalry flowered again in the hearts of Caxley men. Justice must be done. The weak must he protected, and who better to do it than the British, with all the might of a glorious Empire to support them? There was no possibility of failure. It was simply a question of rallying to a good cause, throwing down a despot, succouring the victims, and then returning to normal life, with the glow of work well done, and a reputation enhanced with valour.

If war had to be, then it was inspiring to he so resolutely on the right side. There was no doubt about this being a righteous cause. It was the free man's blow against slavery. It was even more exhilarating, at this time, for the common man to realize how wide-flung and mighty were the bonds of Empire. There was a sudden resurgence of pride in the colonies overseas. For some years now the word 'imperialism' had seemed tarnished. Kipling's jingoistic exhortations were out of fashion. But the older people in Caxley, including Sep and Bender, remembered the show of might at Queen Victoria's Golden and Diamond Jubilees in 1887 and 1897, and remembered it now, with fierce pride, and considerable comfort.

'You see,' Bender told Hilda, 'they'll come flocking from all over the world – black, brown, and every other colour! Wherever they salute the old Union Jack! The Kaiser hasn't a hope! It'll all be over by Christmas!'

It was the phrase which was heard on all sides: 'Over by Christmas!' As the troop trains poured through Caxley station on their way to the coast, the men shouted it jubilantly to the waving mothers and wives on the platform. Caxley had never seen such a movement of men before. This was the first European war in which England had taken part for generations, and the rumble of road and rail transport, as Haldane's Expeditionary Force moved rapidly towards France, was an inspiring sound. Between August 7th and 17th, in a period of blazing sunshine, it was said that over a hundred thousand men crossed the Channel. To the people of Caxley it seemed that most of them made their way southward through their reverberating market square.

A recruiting centre had been opened at the Town Hall and the queues waiting outside added to the noise and excitement. From all the surrounding villages and hamlets, from tumbledown cottages hidden a mile or more down leafy cart tracks, the young men found their way to the market square. They came on foot, on bicycles, on horseback and in carts, farm waggons, and motor-cars. One of the most splendid turn-outs came from Fairacre and Beech Green. Two coal-black cart horses, gleaming like jet, drew a great blue-painted waggon with red wheels into the market place. Harold Miller held the reins. His whip was decorated with red, white, and blue ribbons, and the brass work on the vehicle and the horses' harness shone like gold.

About a score of young men grinned and waved cheerfully as they clattered into the market square. Jesse Miller sat beside his brother, and among the sun-tanned men aboard could be seen the bright auburn head of Arnold Fletcher, fiancé of Dolly Clare of Fairacre. Bertie North, who had already added his name to the lengthy list, waved enthusiastically to his fellow-comrades from the doorway of his father's shop.

He had never known such deep and satisfying excitement before. Ever since he and the Howard boys had volunteered, life had assumed a purpose and meaning so far unknown to him. It was as though he had been asleep, waiting unconsciously for a call to action. Now it had come, vibrant and compelling, and Bertie, in company with thousands of other young men, responded eagerly.

Their womenfolk were not so ardent. Hilda was openly tearful. She had never made a secret of her great love for Bertie. He held a special place in her heart, and the thought of her eldest child being maimed or killed was insupportable. Winnie, though outwardly calm, was doubly anguished, for Leslie was involved, as well as Bertie.

Edna Howard, with two sons enlisted and Kathy worrying to leave home to nurse or to drive an ambulance, had her share of cares, but there was a child-like quality about her which rejoiced in the general excitement and the flags and uniforms, military bands and crowds, which enlivened Caxley at this time. It was Sep who went about his business white-faced and silent, suffering not only for his sons, but also because of his years, which denied him military action.

He grieved too for the rift which had parted him and Bender. The rebuff which he had received hurt him sorely. He was too sensitive to approach Bender again, and a quiet 'Good morning' had been greeted with a grunt and a glare from the ironmonger which froze poor Sep in his tracks. As things were, with everything in turmoil, it seemed best to leave matters alone and hope that time would bring them both some comfort.

The Corn Exchange had been turned into a medical centre, and the young men went straight there from the Town Hall. The Howard boys and Bertie were passed fit and swore to serve His Majesty the King, his heirs and successors, and the generals and the officers set over them, kissed the Bible solemnly, and looked with awed delight at the new shilling and the strip of paper bearing their army number, which each received.

'Do we get our uniform yet?' asked Jim hopefully.

''Old 'ard,' replied the sergeant, in charge of affairs. 'You ain't the only pebbles on the beach. You clear orf back to your jobs till you're wanted. You'll hear soon enough, mark my words. Now 'op it!'

Thus began the hardest part of this new adventure. Carrying on with an everyday job was galling in the extreme to these young men. But at least, they told each other, they were in. Some poor devils like Jesse Miller, for instance, had been found medically unfit.

Jesse was heart-broken.

'Flat feet and varicose veins, they said,' Jesse cried in disgust. 'I told 'em I could walk ten miles a day behind the plough without noticing it, but they'd have none of it. Makes me look a proper fool! But I'm not leaving it there. I'll try elsewhere, that I will! I'll get in by hook or by crook! If Harry goes, I go!'

He received a great deal of sympathy, as did other unfortunate volunteers who had been unsuccessful. It was Kathy who shocked everyone by stating a startling truth at this time.

'You'd think they'd be glad really. After all, I suppose lots of the others will be killed or wounded. I think *they're* the lucky ones.'

Her hearers looked at her aghast. What treason was this? Her brothers, and Bertie too, rounded on her abruptly. Had she no proper pride? Did patriotism mean nothing? Of course it was a deprivation for men like poor old Jesse Miller to be denied the glory of battle. They were amazed that she should think otherwise.

Kathy shrugged her pretty shoulders and tossed her dark head.

'It seems all topsy-turvy to me,' she replied nonchalantly. And, later, amidst the chaotic horror of a French battlefield, Bertie was to remember her words.

The sun blazed day after day throughout that golden August. The corn fields ripened early and there would be a bumper harvest. The lanes round Caxley were white with dust. The grass verges and thick hedges were powdered with the chalk raised by the unaccustomed volume of army traffic making its way southward.

It seemed unbelievable that within less than a hundred miles of Caxley, across a narrow ribbon of water, men were blasting each other to death.

Now and again in the noonday heat, which bathed the quiet downs in a shimmering haze, a shuddering rumble could be heard – the guns of distant battle. News of the retreat from Mons came through. It sounded ugly – *a retreat*. Surely, the Caxley folk told each other, the great British army should not be in *retreat*?

It was easy to explain away the unpleasantness. The army was simply moving to a better strategic position. They were luring the Kaiser's men to a sure defeat. There was nothing really to worry about. It would all be over by Christmas, they repeated.

But it was news of the retreat which resulted in action at last for the Caxley volunteers, for they were called up and sent to a training camp in Dorset at the beginning of September.

Winnie North was among those who crowded Caxley station to wave goodbye to Bertie and the Howard boys. She kissed them all in turn, but clung longer to Leslie. As the train drew away her gaze lingered upon his dwindling hand until it vanished around the great bend of the railway line. She returned, pale but calm, to Rose Lodge and her mother's tear-blotched face.

Three days later she broke some news to her father and mother.

'I'm being transferred to a naval hospital,' said Winnie abruptly. She had just come in from work, and still wore her nurse's uniform.

Her mother looked up, wide-eyed with shock. The khaki sock which she was knitting for Bertie fell neglected into her lap. Bender emerged from behind his newspaper and shot her a glance over the top of his spectacles.

'Oh, Winnie dear,' quavered Hilda, her lip trembling.

'Now, mother,' began Winnie firmly, as if speaking to a refractory patient, 'I volunteered for this as soon as war broke out, and I'm very lucky to be chosen. You must see that I can't stay behind when the boys have already gone.'

'Where is this place?' asked Bender.

Winnie told him. Bender's mouth took a truculent line.

'But that's near Bertie,' cried her mother, looking more cheerful.

'And Leslie Howard,' grunted Bender. 'It don't pull the wool over my eyes, me girl.'

'Dad,' said Winnie levelly, 'we've had all that out until I'm sick of it. Once and for all, I am engaged to Leslie, whatever you say. That disgusting rumour you persist in believing hasn't a word of truth in it —'

'Winnie,' broke in Hilda, 'you are not to speak to your father like that. He acted for the best.'

'When I need your support,' bellowed Bender to his wife, 'I'll ask for it! She's nothing but a love-sick ass, and refuses to face facts. I never thought a daughter of mine would be such a fool – but there it is!'

There was an angry silence for a moment, broken at last by Winnie.

'I'll believe Leslie, if you don't mind,' she said in a low voice. 'And it may interest you to know that I didn't choose to go to this hospital – glad though I am, of course. I'm simply being drafted there, and probably not for long.'

'When do you have to go?' asked Hilda.

'Next Saturday,' said Winnie, 'so let's bury the hatchet for these few days and have a little peace.'

She rose from the chair, went across to her mother and kissed her forehead. Five minutes later they heard the bath running and Winnie's voice uplifted in song.

Bender sighed heavily.

'I'll never understand that girl,' he muttered. 'Blinding herself to that waster's faults! Leaving a comfortable home! Defying her parents!'

'She's in love,' replied his wife simply, picking up her knitting.

*

Rose Lodge seemed sadly quiet when Winnie had departed to her new duties. Mary, the youngest, attended a sedate little private school near her home, and seemed to spend her time in fraying old pieces of sheet for army dressings.

'Pity you don't learn your multiplication tables at the same time,' commented Bender. 'Strikes me that you'll know less than the marsh lot at the National School, when it comes to leaving. And a pretty penny it's costing us too!'

'Why can't I leave then?' urged Mary. 'I could help at the hospital, couldn't I? Sweeping, and that? Kathy Howard's started there as a nurse. Did you know?'

Bender looked at Hilda. Hilda turned a little pink. Since the row with Sep he had not spoken a word to any of the Howards if he could help it, but Hilda kept in touch.

'Well, I did just happen to run across Edna at the butcher's yesterday,' admitted his wife, 'and she mentioned it. I should think she'd make a good little nurse; cheerful and quick to learn. And it does mean she can live at home,' added Hilda, rather sadly, her thoughts with her distant Winnie.

Bender made no comment, but his frown deepened, and Hilda's heart sank. If only things could be as they used to be before that horrid little Mr Parker from Trowbridge took charge of their shop! If only Bender could shake off the cares which seemed to bow him down! In the old days, nothing had worried him, it seemed. She remembered their early troubles, their set-backs, the loss of their first baby, the financial struggles of their early years in business, Bob's duplicity, and a hundred other problems. Somehow Bender had always faced things cheerfully, his great laugh had blown away her cares throughout their married life, until this last disastrous year. If only he could recover his old spirits!

She made a timid suggestion, hoping to distract his mind from the Howards' affairs and turn it to happier things.

'Shall we go and have a look at the dahlias, dear?'

'No thanks,' said Bender shortly. 'Nothing seems to do as well here as in the old garden. It's disheartening.'

He slumped back into his armchair and closed his eyes. It was, thought Hilda, as if he wanted to shut out the sight of the pretty new drawing room at Rose Lodge. Was he, in spirit, perhaps, back in the old room above the shop where they had spent so many evenings together? How helpless she felt, in the face of this silent unhappiness! Would there never be an end to it?

Letters came regularly from Winnie and Bertie during the following months. They met occasionally. Both looked extraordinarily well, they assured their parents separately. Bertie had put on almost a stone in weight, and there were rumours that his unit would be off to France before Christmas. If so, there would be leave, of course. Bertie said he would let them know just as soon as he knew himself. Hilda was buoyed up with hope, and hurried about making a hundred preparations, refusing to think further than the homecoming.

Winnie mentioned Leslie in her letters, but did not speak of her feelings. Hilda guessed that she did not want to upset her father by introducing the contentious subject.

At the beginning of December two letters arrived at Rose Lodge. Bertie's said that his week's leave began on the following day, and would his mother cook a really square meal? Winnie's said that she too had leave, and would be arriving three days after Bertie. She too could do with a square meal. Singing, Hilda made her way to the kitchen to make joyful preparations. Bender, smiling at last, stumped down the hill to the shop, which he had come to loathe, to embark on the day's work with rather more eagerness than usual.

Across the market square, Sep Howard stood in the kitchen reading a letter from Leslie. He too was smiling. Edna waited anxiously for him to finish, so that she could read it for herself.

He handed it over with a happy sigh.

'Read that, my love,' he said gently.

Edna's eyes widened as she read, and her pretty mouth fell open.

'Married?' she whispered.

'Married!' repeated Sep huskily. To Edna's surprise, she saw that there were tears in his eyes. She had never realized that Leslie had meant so much to him.

But it was not Leslie, nor his bride, that occupied Sep's thoughts. This, Sep told himself thankfully, must heal the breach between Bender and himself. At last his earnest prayers had been answered.

Chapter Twelve

AN UNWELCOME MARRIAGE

Bertie's homecoming was such a joyful occasion, he looked so fit and happy, that neither of his parents noticed a certain constraint in his manner. His appetite was enormous, his eagerness to visit his Caxley friends so keen, that Hilda was kept busy providing meals and entertainment.

Winnie was expected the following Wednesday.

'Did she tell you what time she would arrive?' asked Hilda at breakfast. 'I must go shopping this morning, but I don't want to be out when she comes.'

'I don't think she'll be here much before this evening,' said Bertie slowly.

'How late!' exclaimed Hilda. 'Won't she catch the same train as you?'

'I doubt it,' replied Bertie briefly, and escaped from the room.

All that day, Hilda went about her affairs, humming cheerfully. Bertie watched her carry a vase of late chrysanthemums up the stairs to Winnie's room. When darkness fell, she refused to draw the curtains in the drawing room, hoping to catch the first glimpse of Winnie coming up the path.

It was very quiet that evening. Bender dozed in his armchair, Hilda was stitching braid on a skirt, and Bertie flipped idly through the pages of the *Caxley Chronicle*. It was nearly eight o'clock when they heard the sound of footsteps on the gravel outside, and before Hilda could fold up her sewing and hurry out, the door opened and, Winnie, smiling and radiant, blinking in the unaccustomed light, stood on the threshold. Behind her was a tall figure.

'Leslie!' exclaimed Hilda involuntarily. The joy in her face faded to a look of apprehension. The couple came into the room and Bender awoke.

'What the devil –' he rumbled truculently, eyeing the young man. Winnie went forward swiftly, kissed him, and pushed him back again into the armchair.

'Don't say anything, Dad dear, just listen,' she pleaded. She turned to face them.

'Leslie and I are married. It's no good scolding us, either of you. So, please, *please*, forgive us and say you hope we'll be happy.'

Hilda moved forward, her face working. She took Winnie in her arms and gave her a gentle kiss, but there were tears in her eyes.

'You should have told us,' she protested. 'You should have written. This hurts us all so terribly.'

Bender had struggled to his feet. His face was red, his head thrust forward like an angry bull.

'This is a fine way to treat your mother and me,' he growled thickly. 'You'll get no forgiveness from me – either of you – whatever your mother does.'

He glared round the room and caught sight of Bertie's pale face. Something in it made him start forward.

'You knew about this,' he said accusingly. Bertie nodded.

'I stood witness, Dad,' he said. 'I'm sorry.'

There was a dreadful silence, broken only by Bender's laboured heavy breathing. At last he gave a great gasp, shouldered his way blindly across the room, and burst through the French windows into the garden, leaving them to clang behind him.

'Bender!' cried Hilda, beginning to follow, but Bertie caught her arm.

'He's better alone, Mamma,' he said quietly. 'Sit down, and I'll bring you a drink.'

He turned to the young couple.

'No doubt you'll need one too.' He moved a chair forward for Winnie and motioned the silent Leslie to another. There was an authority about him which cooled the situation.

'It would have been nice to drink a toast to your future happiness,' said Bertie, when the glasses were filled, 'but this does not seem quite the time to do it.'

Hilda, trembling, took a sip and then put down her glass carefully on the work-box beside her.

'This has been such a shock – such an awful shock! You know how your father has felt, Winnie. And as for you, Leslie, I don't think we shall ever be able to forgive you. So underhand, so sly –!' She began to fumble for a handkerchief.

'Mamma, it was no use telling you anything. Neither you nor Dad would listen. We knew that. We were determined to get married. Now we have. In a registry office. You'll simply have to get used to the idea.'

Leslie spoke at last.

'I wanted to write, but Winnie felt it was far better to come and tell you ourselves when it was all over. I promise you I'll take care of her. You must know that.'

'I don't know that,' responded Hilda with a flash of spirit, 'which is why we opposed the match. But now it's done, then all I can say is that I sincerely *hope* you will take care of her.'

Practical matters now came to the front of her distracted mind. Winnie's room lay ready for her, but what should be done with Leslie? If only Bender would return from the garden! If only he would give her some support in this dreadful moment!

As though divining her thoughts Winnie spoke.

'We're not going to stay, Mamma, as things are. Father's too upset, and it will take him a little while to get used to the idea. Aunt Edna has offered us a room and we'll call here again tomorrow morning. We'll try to have a word now with Dad before we go.'

She kissed her mother again and squeezed her gently.

'Cheer up, my love. We're so happy, don't spoil it for us. And try to persuade Father that it isn't the end of the world.'

'I'm afraid it *is* the end of the world for him,' replied Hilda sadly.

The young couple made their way into the dark garden followed by Bertie.

'Dad!' called Winnie.

'Dad!' called Bertie.

But there was no reply. Bender was a mile away, walking the shadowy streets of Caxley, his mind in torment as he looked for comfort which could not be found.

Hilda, alone in the room, wept anew. 'Aunt Edna!' It was hard to bear. That Edna Howard should be the one to whom her Winnie turned in trouble was a humiliation she had never imagined.

She thought of all her own loving preparations during the day. Winnie's bed was turned down, the sheet snowy and smooth above the pink quilt. A hot water bottle lay snugly in the depths. The late chrysanthemums scented the room with their autumnal fragrance.

Winnie married! And in a registry office too! Some dim sordid little room with no beauty about it, she supposed. All her plans for Winnie's wedding had shattered before her eyes. Where now were her dreams of a blue and white wedding, white roses, lilies, and delphiniums decorating the church, and Winnie herself a vision in bridal white?

It had all been so clear, even down to Mary's blue and white bridesmaid's frock and the posy of white rosebuds with long blue ribbons streaming from it. Somehow the bridegroom had always been a shadowy figure – just some one pleasant and kind, with a good bank balance, of course, and a natural desire for a reasonably sized family, sensibly spaced for dear Winnie's sake. That anything as catastrophic as this could happen threw Hilda's world into utter chaos. How would she ever face the other Caxley matrons? And worst of all, how could she face Edna Howard?

But this was in the future. The first thing was to comfort poor Bender. He must, somehow, be made to see that the situation must be accepted, regrettable though it was. Winnie, foolish and disobedient, was still their daughter, after all.

She mopped her eyes resolutely. All that was left for them now was to be brave, and make the best of a very bad job.

But Hilda's efforts were not to begin until the next day, for Bender did not return until the small hours of the morning, long after Hilda had taken her aching head to bed. And, as she feared, when she broached the painful subject after breakfast, Bender refused to discuss it.

'Don't speak to me about it,' he said warningly. 'I've had enough at the moment. To think that Winnie's behaved like this! And that Bertie knew about it all the time! A fine pair of children! I'd expect no more from a Howard than Leslie's shown us, but that Winnie and Bertie could treat us so shabby – well, it's like being betrayed!'

Hilda's lip began to tremble and Bender began to speak more gently.

'Let me go to the shop now, there's a love. I'll work it off, maybe, and feel better when I come home. But I can't face my family – nor that dam' scoundrel Leslie – yet awhile.'

It was Bertie who made his father face him, later that day. In these last few hours Bertie seemed to have become very grown up, and might almost be the head of the house himself, thought Hilda wonderingly, watching her son shepherd Bender into the dining room for a private talk.

'I won't keep you long, Father,' said Bertie, closing the door behind him, 'but I've only three or four days' leave left and I'm not having it spoilt by this affair. I'm sorry to have deceived you, but Winnie insisted, and frankly, I'd do it all over again, in the circumstances.'

'Bad enough deceiving me,' retorted Bender, 'but a sight worse to let a Howard marry your sister.'

'I think I know Leslie better than you do,' replied Bertie calmly. 'He's not the man I should have chosen for Winnie, but it's her choice, and I honestly think he loves her.'

Bender snorted derisively.

'He's ready to settle down,' continued Bertie levelly, 'and Winnie's the one to help him. Dash it all, Father, we've known the Howards all our lives! How would you have felt if she had run off with a complete stranger? It's happening often enough in wartime! For your own sake, as well as Winnie's and Mamma's, do try and accept this business sensibly. It does no good to keep up a useless feud, and to make the whole family unhappy.'

'It's easy to talk!' replied Bender. 'I can't forget what I know about that young man, and I can't believe he'll treat Winnie properly.'

'All the more reason why you should stand by her now,' retorted Bertie. 'If she's in trouble she'll need her home.'

'You're right, I don't doubt, my boy,' said Bender sadly. 'I'll ponder it, but I can't see much good coming of it. I wonder what Sep and Edna think of it all?'

'They're delighted,' Bertie told him. 'Made them very welcome when they arrived, Winnie said.'

A thought struck Bender. He looked shrewdly at Bertie over his spectacles.

'They knew, did they?'

'Leslie wrote on his wedding day,' said Bertie shortly. 'He knew they'd be pleased.'

'But Winnie didn't,' murmured Bender, as if to himself.

'She knew you wouldn't be,' Bertie said simply, and left his father alone with his thoughts.

That evening there was a dance at the Corn Exchange. Bertie dressed with unusual care and studied his reflection in the mirror with considerable misgivings. What a very undistinguished appearance he had! He disliked his fair hair and his blue eyes. To his mind they appeared girlish. He wondered if a moustache might improve his looks. Too late to bother about that now, anyway, he told himself, looking at his watch.

The newly-weds and Jim and Kathy were to be of the party, and Bertie was relieved to leave the heavy atmosphere of Rose Lodge behind him and stride down the hill to the market square. It was a crisp clear night, full of stars. Now and again the whiff of a dying bonfire crossed his path, that most poignant of winter smells. It was good to be back in the old town. It was better still to be on the way to meeting Kathy. Tonight he would ask her.

The Corn Exchange was gay with the flags of all nations. Ragtime music shook the hall, and there was an air of determined hilarity about the many dancers, as though, for this evening, at least, they would forget the horrors of war, and simply remember that music and rhythm, youth and excitement, also had a place in the scheme of things.

Leslie and Winnie danced together, heads close, oblivious to all about them. They had always danced well together, thought Bertie, gazing at them over the dark hair of Kathy, his own partner. They looked happy enough, in all conscience. If only he could quell the little nagging doubt at the back of his own mind! He looked into Kathy's eyes and forgot his sister's affairs.

It was agony to part from her and to watch other partners claim her. Kathy's dance programme was much too full for Bertie's liking. There was no one else in the room that he wanted to partner, but Caxley eyes were as sharp as ever, and he dutifully piloted a few young ladies about the floor, his eyes on Kathy the while. She was lovelier than ever – vivacious, sparkling, light as a feather. Had he any hope at all, wondered Bertie, stumbling over his partner's foot and apologizing abstractedly?

She was dancing with one of the Crockford boys. How unnecessarily damned handsome they were, thought Bertie crossly! When the Crockfords were not large and red-headed, they were tall, elegant and dark. This one had hair oiled till it shone like jet, a handsome black moustache, and an enviable turn of speed when he reversed. Kathy was gazing at him in a way that Bertie found infuriating. As soon as the dance was over he hurried to her side.

'Come outside for a moment,' he begged.

'Why?' asked Kathy. Her bright eyes darted everywhere about the hall. Her little satin slipper tapped the floor in time to the music. *'Hullo! Hullo! Who's your lady friend?'* throbbed through the hall, and the refrain was taken up by many voices. The noise was unbearable to Bertie.

'It's quieter,' he shouted, above the din. Kathy rose rather reluctantly, and followed him outside into the market place. It was deliciously fresh and cool after the stuffiness of the Corn Exchange, but Kathy shivered and pulled her silk shawl round her.

'Let's go and look at the river,' said Bertie.

'We'll miss the dancing.'

'Only this one,' promised Bertie. He put his arm through hers and led her past her own house and down the narrow lane leading to the tow path. The noise behind them died away. Only the plop of a fish and the quiet rippling of the Cax disturbed the silence. They made their way to the little bridge and leant over. Now that Bertie had succeeded in bringing Kathy here, he became horribly nervous. So much depended on the next few minutes. He took a deep breath and began.

'Kathy, I've wanted to ask you often. You must know how I feel about you. Do you care about me at all?'

'Of course I do,' said Kathy, with a cheerful promptness that made Bertie despair. 'I care very much about you. And Leslie and Jim, and all my friends who are fighting.'

Bertie sighed and took her hand. It was small and thin, and very cold.

'Not that way, Kathy. I meant, do you love me? I love you very much, you know. Enough to marry you. Could you ever think about that?'

Kathy laughed and withdrew her hand. It fluttered to Bertie's hot cheek and patted it affectionately.

'Oh, Bertie dear, don't talk so solemnly! I'm not thinking of marrying for years yet! Not you – or anyone else! There's too much fun to be had first I Take me back, Bertie, it's cold, and I want to dance.'

He tried once more, putting his arms round her, and tilting up her chin so that he could look into her lovely face.

'Please, Kathy,' he entreated, 'think about it. I know you're young, but I love you so much. Say you'll think about it!'

She pushed him away pettishly.

'I'm not going to promise any such thing. I want to be free, and you ought to be too!' She took his arm again and began to pull him back towards the market square.

'Come on, Bertie, I shall miss the next dance and it's a military two-step. Don't be stuffy, there's a love. You're a dear old stick really!'

They walked back to the Corn Exchange, Bertie in silence, Kathy chattering of he knew not what. At the doorway he stopped.

'I won't come in,' he said. 'I've a headache. Go and enjoy yourself.'

She tripped in without once looking back, arms outstretched to her waiting partner.

Bertie turned away, and made his way blindly to the drinking fountain in the middle of the square. He filled one of the iron cups and drank the icy water. The feel of the cold iron chain running through his hot palm reminded him of the times he had sought refreshment here as a boy.

He leant his head against the comforting cold plinth beneath the Queen's bronze skirts, and looked across the square towards his old house. If only he could turn back the years! If only he could be a boy again, with none of a man's troubles to torture him!

It was almost a relief to return to his unit. The prospect of going overseas was one to look forward to after the unhappy events of this disastrous leave. He was glad to let other people make the decisions for him. Whatever the future held could give Bertie no more pain, he felt sure, than the grief of his family and the bitter disappointment of Kathy's complete disregard of his feelings.

In the crowded railway carriage rattling to Dorset through the darkening winter afternoon, Bertie re-lived again those moments with Kathy. To be called a 'dear old stick!' He shuddered at the remembrance. What hope was there ever for him, if those were her feelings? He remembered his last glimpse of her at Caxley Station. To his surprise she had come to see off the three of them, for Winnie and Leslie too were on the train.

She had kissed them all in turn. He felt her kisses still upon his cheek, as cold and light as moths, and his heart turned over. One thing he knew, whatever happened to him here, or in France, now or in the future, there would be nobody else for him but Kathy. Always, and only, Kathy.

He closed his eyes. The train roared through a cutting, carrying him unprotesting to whatever the future might hold.

Chapter Thirteen

CAXLEY AT WAR

The bells of St Peter's rang out across the market square and the rosy roofs of Caxley on Christmas morning. Bender, Hilda, and Mary hurried up the steps and made their way to their usual pew.

The church was unusually full. Across the aisle the Crockford family filled two pews. They must have a houseful for Christmas, thought Hilda, with a pang of envy. Dan was making one of his rare appearances in church, his leonine head glowing against the murky shadows of the old building.

As the organ played the voluntary, Hilda gazed up the long nave and let her sad thoughts wander. If only Bertie and Winnie were here! But Bertie and the Howard boys and the rest of their company were somewhere in France, and Winnie was still nursing at the hospital in Dorset.

If only Winnie could have chosen someone else to marry! What a wedding Hilda had planned for her, with this noble church as its setting! She could see it so clearly in her mind's eye – the lilies on the altar, where now the Christmas roses and the scarlet-berried holly glowed, the smilax and white rosebuds where now the glossy ivy trailed its dark beauty. And there, at the altar, her dear Winnie in the beautiful wedding gown with the long train which she had so often visualized!

Tears blurred Hilda's eyes. The nave and chancel swam mistily before her, and she was glad to hear the gentle meanderings of the organist turn to the loud joyful strains of 'Adeste Fideles' as the choir entered, singing, and the congregation rose to join in praise.

'Please, God,' prayed Hilda desperately, as she struggled to her feet, 'let us all be together next Christmas, and let us all be happy again!'

Not far away, Edna Howard, beside Sep in the chilly chapel, wondered too about her two children in a foreign land. To think that this time last year she was positively looking forward to 1914! It had brought nothing but trouble!

The minister's voice droned on, but Edna did not attend to his exhortations. Sometimes she doubted if there were really any God to speak to. Sep said there was, and seemed to be comforted by the knowledge, and Edna had never expressed any of her own doubts. It would have upset Sep so much. But when you heard of the terrible things that the Germans were doing, then surely there couldn't be a God or he would never let it happen?

Edna mused vaguely on her uncomfortable bench, until her attention was caught by a white thread on the sleeve of her coat. She plucked it away neatly, let it flutter to the scrubbed floor boards so near her painful knees, and stroked the fur of her cuffs lovingly. It was wearing very well, she thought. After all, she had had it a whole year now, and it still looked as good as new. How kind Sep was to her! She stole a glance at his pale face beside her. His eyes were shut fast, his dark lashes making little crescents. His lips were pressed together with the intensity of his concentration. He was in communion with his Maker, and for Sep the world had ceased to exist.

Perhaps, thought Edna, returning to the contemplation of her coat, it could be turned in a few years' time. It was good stuff . . .

It was during the next week that Hilda heard how Bertie had spent his Christmas Day in the front line somewhere south of Armentières. His letter read:

Dearest Mamma,

I opened your parcel on Christmas morning and everything in it was first-class. Thank you all very much. The cake was shared with some of the other Caxley chaps who appreciated it very much.

The queerest thing happened here. Just before dawn we heard the Germans in their trench opposite singing carols. They sang 'Silent Night, Holy Night' – only in German, of course, and we joined in. After a bit, one of our officers went into no-man's-land and met one of theirs, and gradually we all climbed out and wished each other 'Happy Christmas' and exchanged cigarettes. Some were from your parcel, Mamma, and I hope you don't mind a few of them going to the enemy. I can assure you, they did not seem like enemies on Christmas morning. We kept the truce up long enough to bring in our dead.

Further down the line, we heard, both sides had a game of football together. It makes you realize what a farce war is – nobody wants it. But it looks as though it will drag on for a long time yet, I'm afraid.

My love to you and to all the family,

Your loving son,

Bertie

Bertie's fears were echoed by all at home. The cheerful cry: 'Over by Christmas' was heard no more. Fighting was going on in all parts of the world, and the news from the western front grew grimmer weekly. It was here that the local men were engaged, and anxious eyes read the columns of 'Dead, Wounded, and Missing' which were published regularly in the *Caxley Chronicle*. It was a sad New Year for many families in Caxley, as 1915 came in, and the knowledge that losses must continue to be very heavy was too terrible to contemplate.

For Bender, at least, the war had brought one small consolation. He was again in charge of the old shop, and all alterations had been postponed. Young Mr Parker was serving in the Navy, one or two of the assistants had also gone to the war and Bender struggled on with Miss Taggerty and a chuckle-headed boy from Springbourne, called Ralph Pringle, as his only support.

It suited Bender. Trade was slack, so that he was not overworked, and he had time to look after the shabby empty rooms of his late home, and to keep the beloved garden tidy. It was a reprieve for North's, Bender thought, and he was thankful.

He had recovered some of his old zest, doing his best to cheer Hilda now that Bertie was away from home. They spoke little of the disastrous marriage. The subject was too painful, but time and the background of war did much to lessen the tension. Hilda held weekly sewing parties in her new drawing room and busied herself in packing up the results to be sent to the Front.

Bender joined the local branch of the Home Defence Corps and thoroughly enjoyed his evenings at the Corn Exchange or in the market square. He, in company with other Caxley men too old for military service, drilled rigorously. Stiff joints and creaking knee-caps gave off reports as loud as the guns they longed to have, and although they knew in their hearts that their contribution was pitifully inadequate, yet they enjoyed the comradeship, the exercise, and the feeling of being alert.

Sep Howard was not among them. He had joined the Red Cross at the outbreak of war, and spent many nights at Caxley Station tending the wounded on their way to hospital from the battle front. He never forgot those tragic hours.

Between trains, Caxley station lay dim and quiet in the hollow by the river. The waiting room had been turned into a canteen. Urns bubbled, sandwiches were stacked and the helpers' tongues were as busy as their willing hands. Sometimes Sep left the warm fugginess to pace the deserted dark platform. Alone under the stars he walked up and down, watching the gleam of rails vanishing into the distance, and listening for the rumble of the next train bearing its load of broken men. His compassion had quickly overcome the physical nausea which blood and vomit inevitably aroused. He had become used to limbs frighteningly awry, to empty sleeves, and to heads so muffled in cotton wool and bandages that nothing emerged from them but screams.

Sep was recognized as one of the most tireless workers, with an uncanny gift of easing pain.

'I'm used to working at night,' he said simply, 'and I try to move the chaps the way my mother handled me when I was ill. She was a good nurse.'

He gained great satisfaction from the voluntary work. He recoiled from the martial side of war and even more from the pomp and glory of its trappings. Military bands, flags fluttering, soldiers in splendid array, all gave Sep a cold sickness in his heart. He had viewed with tears the jubilant crowd outside the Town Hall at the outbreak of war. The boisterous zeal of the elderly Home Defence Corps was not to Sep's liking. He found himself nearer the truth of war in those dark pain-filled hours at Caxley station.

He had seen Bender stepping out bravely with his fellows as they marched through the streets of Caxley to some military exercise on one of the surrounding commons. After the terrible scene in Bender's office, Sep had purposely kept out of his way, but had longed for things to be easier between them.

He had never been able to find out the truth about the ugly rumour of the girl at Bent. Leslie had denied the whole thing roundly when he had asked him about the matter. Sep was still troubled about the affair, and could not wholly believe his son, but was too proud to do more than accept Leslie's word. In any case, both he and Edna were delighted with his marriage to Winnie, and welcomed the couple whenever they could manage a brief visit. One must look forward, not back, Sep told himself.

As the early weeks of 1915 passed, Sep was relieved to see Bender looking more cheerful. Now they spoke when they met. Topics were kept general, inquiries were made about each other's families, but no mention was ever made of Winnie and Leslie between the two men. There was still a constraint about each meeting, but at least the ice was broken, and Sep hoped earnestly that one day he and Bender would be completely at ease with each other. The families did not meet so readily these days. Since the move, and since the war began, they had grown apart. The younger children did not mix as readily as the older ones had done when they lived so near each other in the market place, and the marriage had proved another barrier, much to Sep's grief.

It was in February that the Howard family had its first blow. Two local men had been killed near the Ypres Canal, and one of them was Jim Howard. The other was Arnold Fletcher, the gardener at Beech Green, and the fiancé of Dolly Clare who taught at Fairacre.

Sep received the news with numbed dignity, Edna with torrents of tears and furious lamentations. Sep grieved for her, but secretly envied the ease of her outbursts, for they were so exhausting that she slept soundly at nights. He went about his affairs pale and silent, and refused to give up his Red Cross vigils, even on the night of the news. Each man that he tended was Jim to him, and from this he gained strength.

Bender heard the news as the wintry sun was setting behind St Peter's. Without a word he made his way across the square, still clad in his shop overall, and went into the bake-house in the yard. As he had suspected, Sep was there alone, stacking tins automatically, his face stricken.

'Sep,' muttered Bender, putting one massive hand on each side of Sep's thin shoulders and gazing down at him. 'What can I say?'

Sep shook his head dolefully. He did not trust himself to speak.

'I feel it very much,' went on Bender gruffly. 'And so will Hilda. We were always very fond of your Jim – a fine boy.'

Sep bit his quivering lip but remained silent. Bender dropped his hands and sat down heavily on the great scrubbed table, sighing gustily.

'This bloody war,' he growled, 'is going to cause more heartache than we reckoned, Sep. Who'd have thought, when our kids were playing round the old Queen out there, that it would have come to this?'

He gazed unseeingly at the brick floor and his two great black boots set upon it. After a minute's silence he shook himself back into the present, and began to make his way to the door. It was then that Sep found his voice.

'It was good of you to come, Bender. I've missed you.'

'Well, we've had our ups and downs, Sep,' replied Bender, turning in the doorway, 'and there's some things we'll never see eye to eye about. But in times like this we forget 'em.'

His voice dropped suddenly.

'God's truth, Sep, I'm sorry about this. I'm sorry for all of us with sons these days.'

And before Sep could reply he had turned the corner and vanished.

The war dragged on. Food was getting short, and the posters everywhere exhorted men and women to save every crumb and to guard against waste. Caxley did not feel the want of food as harshly as the larger towns. Set amidst countryside, with the Cax meandering through it, vegetables, fruit, eggs, milk, and river fish were comparatively easy to come by. There was a shortage of sugar, and sweets, and Mary North was told never to ask for such things when they were visiting.

'People haven't enough for themselves,' pointed out Hilda. 'Just say you aren't very hungry.'

'But I'm *always* hungry for sweets,' protested Mary. 'You wouldn't want me to lie?'

'There are such things as *white* lies!' responded Hilda. 'And in wartime you'll have to make use of them.'

Certainly there were minor hardships as well as the dreadful losses overseas which cast their shadows. But the spirit of the people was high, and many of the women were tasting independence for the first time. They set off daily to munitions factories or shops, enjoying company and the heady pleasure of earning money of their own. They did not intend to throw this freedom away when the war ended. As they worked they talked and laughed, as they had never done cooped up in their own homes, and snippets of news about local fighting men were always the first to be exchanged. So often they were sad items, but now and again there was good news, and there was great excitement in 1916 when Caxley heard that Harold Miller had been commissioned at Thiepval after displaying great gallantry. His brother, Jesse, still struggling with the farm and with very little help, received many congratulations on market day that week.

It was towards the end of the same year that Hilda had a letter from Winnie to say that a baby was expected the next summer. She sounded happy and well. She was living in a small flat near the hospital, where she was going to remain at work for as long as possible. There were also plans for her to have the baby there in a small maternity wing attached to the main hospital.

Leslie was still in France and had taken to army life very well. He made a good soldier, quick, obedient, and cheerful, and had received his commission about the same time as Harold Miller. He did not write to Winnie as often as she would have liked, but as things were, she readily forgave him. Now that the baby was coming, she longed for the war to end, so that they could settle down together as a family.

Hilda was delighted with the news and even Bender softened at the idea of a grandchild in the family. The Howards were even more pleased, but Sep had the sense to resist mentioning it when he and Bender met. Let him make the first move, thought Sep!

One wet November day when the market square was lashed with rain and the wet leaves fluttered about the garden of Rose Lodge, the postman arrived at the Norths' door with another letter.

Bender took it in and tore it open. His face grew pale as he read the message and he put a hand on the door for support.

Hilda came up the hall to him, perplexed. He handed her the flimsy paper in silence.

Trembling, Hilda read it aloud.

'We regret to inform you that your son has been wounded and is receiving medical attention at the above military hospital. He may be visited at any time.'

Wonderingly she raised her face and looked at her husband. His expression was grim and determined.

'Put on your coat, my dear. We'll go at once.'

Chapter Fourteen

CAXLEY GREETS THE ARMISTICE

The hospital lay a little way from Bath, some sixty miles or so from Caxley. Bill Blake, who owned the motor firm where Bertie worked in peace time, drove them there himself.

There was little talking on the journey. Hilda gazed through the rain-spattered windscreen at the wind-blown countryside. The sky was grey and hopeless, the trees bowed, the grass flattened. Long puddles lined the road reflecting the dull skies above. They passed little on the long agonizing journey, except an occasional army lorry which only reminded them more sharply of their purpose.

In happier days the hospital was a country mansion. The three mounted the long flight of steps, dreading what lay ahead. Within a few minutes, formalities were over and they found themselves at Bertie's bedside. He was barely conscious and very pale, but he smiled when he saw them.

They had been told that one leg was badly shattered and that a bullet had gone clean through his upper arm. Loss of blood was the chief cause for concern. He had lain for several hours in the mud before he had reached a field station.

Bender never forgot Hilda's bravery at that time. Not a tear fell. She smiled as encouragingly at her son as she had done years before when he was bed-bound by some childish ailment.

'You'll be home again soon, my dear,' she whispered to him, as she kissed his waxen face gently. 'Back safely in Caxley, you remember?'

He nodded very slightly, his blue eyes bemused. She could not know that the word 'Caxley' brought back a vision of the market square to him, framed in the familiar curtains of his old Caxley bedroom.

They were only allowed to stay for two or three minutes before being ushered out by the nurse.

'The doctor thinks he will be able to operate tomorrow or the next day,' the sister told them later. 'Of course he's gravely ill, but he's a strong young man and all should go well, we hope.'

With this guarded encouragement to give them cold comfort, the three made their farewells, and returned sadly along the road to Caxley.

The hours seemed endless when they reached home, and there was little sleep for Hilda and Bender in the next two nights. Bender rang the hospital twice a day, and at last he spoke to the surgeon who had operated that afternoon.

'He's doing fine,' said the voice, warm and hearty at the other end of the line. 'The arm should be as good as new in a few weeks. Just a little stiffness maybe.'

'And the leg?' Bender pressed the receiver closer to his ear. Hilda stood beside him and he clasped her hand with his free one. She could only hear the distant murmur of the surgeon's voice, but her eyes scanned Bender's face anxiously. His grip tightened, he swallowed noisily, and his voice was husky when he said the final words.

'I'm sure you did. Quite sure you did. It's a sore blow, but you know we're grateful to you. Good-bye.'

He hung up and turned to his wife.

'The leg is not as bad as they feared, but his foot, Hilda . . . His foot has had to come off . . .'

Bender had expected tears, but they did not come. For all her pallor, Hilda looked calm.

'I'm thankful,' she said in a low tone. 'Honestly thankful! Now he'll never have to go back. He'll be safe at home for always.'

Women, thought Bender in wonderment, were truly unpredictable.

Bertie's lengthy convalescence took place at a riverside nursing home within fifteen miles of Caxley. He made slow but steady progress, but endured great pain, and had to learn to walk again with an artificial foot.

Lying in bed, or in a chair on the green lawn sloping down to the river, he had plenty of time for thought. In many ways he regretted the end of his soldiering days, but he was realistic enough to be grateful that he need not return to active fighting. He had seen enough of war's squalor and agony to sicken him, and had often remembered Kathy's remarks about 'the lucky ones who were left at home'. He did not think she was wholly right, but he could see her point more clearly now.

But what of the future? Bill Blake had guaranteed him a job in the firm – possibly a partnership after the war. He looked forward to returning. There was no place like Caxley and no business like the motor business. It should be more flourishing than ever when the war ended. He supposed he would live at Rose Lodge as before, but he longed to have a place of his own. If only he could have gone back to the old home!

He thought, as he so often did, of Kathy. He had never met another girl to touch her, and felt positive that he never would. But how could he ask any girl to marry such an old crock? He was irritable when he was in pain, which was most of the time, and devilish slow in making progress with the new foot. He must simply persevere and hope that things grew easier. Meanwhile, he received many Caxley friends, and learnt all he could about Kathy's circumstances. She was still nursing at Caxley Hospital, he heard, and having as gay a time as war allowed in the evenings.

Bill Blake, who knew what was in Bertie's mind without being told, offered to bring Kathy over one afternoon when she was free, and was as good as his word.

Bertie watched the clock anxiously all the morning. By two o'clock when she was due, he was in a state of feverish excitement. He sat in a wicker chair on the lawn waiting impatiently.

She was as lovely as ever when she finally arrived, clad in a pink fluttery frock with pearls at her throat. Her dark hair was piled on top, her great eyes danced as gaily as ever. She gave him a light kiss, making his head swim, and settled herself in a chair beside him. Bill, the soul of tact, vanished to make some imaginary adjustment to the car which had brought them.

They fell into conversation as easily as ever. Kathy told Bertie all about her life at the hospital. She chattered of the patients, the staff, the doctors. She talked of the Howards and the fun of looking forward to being aunt to Leslie's baby. Only when she spoke of Jim did her lovely face cloud over, and she let Bertie take her hand. But within a minute she was happy again, and Bertie thought how like her mother she was, with the same gaiety and the same ability to throw off trouble. Could it be lack of feeling? Sadly, listening to the welcome prattling, Bertie realized that it could, but he would not have her any different. Kathy was perfect.

'Want to see me walk?' asked Bertie suddenly. Kathy leapt to her feet. They made careful progress along a path beside the river.

'It reminds me of the Cax,' said Bertie, shading his eyes with his hand and gazing along the shining water. 'It makes me think of you. I still do you know.'

Kathy squeezed his arm, her smile mischievous.

'Bertie, don't think of me any more. I wasn't going to say anything. Nobody knows – not a soul. But I'm going to tell you, because somehow I can tell you everything. I'm going to be engaged any day now. We shall tell our families this week.'

It was as well that Kathy's arm supported him for Bertie could have fallen with the shock. It was really no great surprise. He had known that Kathy must marry one day and that his own case was now doubly hopeless. She had never felt for him in that way, and now his injuries made him shy of asking her again. But now that the blow had fallen it was hard to bear.

'Say you're pleased, Bertie dear. I shall be so miserable if you're not pleased. I'm very fond of you. I want you to like Henry. Shall I bring him next time?'

Bertie did his best to rally. She was gazing at him anxiously for his approval. He could deny her nothing, and told her sincerely that he hoped she would always be happy. The unknown Henry he loathed with all his being at the moment, but supposed he would feel less savage when he got used to the idea. But God help him if he was not good to Kathy!

He let Kathy tell him more, glad to be silent to regain his composure. Henry was very tall, and big, with red hair. He was in a Scottish regiment. (That damned kilt, groaned Anglo-Saxon Bertie inwardly! What havoc it caused among susceptible young women!) He was as brave as a lion, and always happy. (Who wouldn't be with Kathy beside him, thought poor Bertie?) His home was in Edinburgh and he had shown her pictures of the great castle there. He would take her to see it, on his next leave, and then she would stay with his parents. They hoped to marry in the spring.

It was small wonder that Bill Blake thought Bertie looked a bit off colour when he returned to take tea on the lawn. He commented on it with some concern, adding that there were bound to be ups and downs in a long illness.

'In life too!' agreed Bertie simply, smiling across at Kathy.

Winnie's baby, a boy, was born soon after Kathy's visit to Bertie, and he was glad to hear of this event for his mother's sake as well as Winnie's. It diverted attention from his own affairs and enabled him to get a grip on life. Now that Kathy was irretrievably lost to him, he set his mind on getting back to his unit as quickly as his tardy body would allow.

But it was autumn before he was discharged, and no medical board would pass him fit for military service. Philosophically, Bertie returned to Rose Lodge, the raptures of Hilda, and the welcome routine of the motor trade. He undertook more voluntary work than Hilda felt he should, but he gained in strength and seemed happy enough in his sober way.

The Norths received an invitation to Kathy's splendid wedding in the spring, and surprisingly, Hilda insisted on going, but she went alone. Bender pleaded overwork. Bertie simply stated flatly that he was unable to accompany her. There was a stricken look about Bertie's face, when he told her this, that gave Hilda her first suspicion of his feelings towards Kathy. Not another Howard, surely! She dismissed the thought almost as soon as it had come to life, and dwelt with relief on Kathy's union with another and her probable abode in the northern fastness of Edinburgh. The further away the better, thought Hilda privately. The Howards brought them nothing but trouble, one way or another.

As it happened, Kathy did not move away immediately. Whilst the war still ground on remorselessly, Kathy lived with her parents in the market square and continued nursing. Bertie often saw her as he drove his little A.C. to work in the morning, and his heart turned over as disconcertingly as it had ever done. She looked so pretty and trim in her nurse's uniform, and Bertie envied the lucky patients who would spend their day in her presence.

In the early days of November 1918 it became apparent that, at last, victory was near. After four years of suffering it was hard to believe, but on Monday, November 11th, there were excited murmurs in the streets of Caxley.

'It's true, Mr North,' said an old woman across the counter in his shop. 'The war's over!'

'Who told you that yarn?' quipped Bender. 'The papers don't say so.'

'The paper shop does though,' she retorted. She shook her umbrella at Bender's unbelieving face. 'He's put up a notice saying "Yes! Yes!" that must mean it's true!'

After she had departed Bender made his way out into the drizzling morning. Little knots of people had gathered and were asking questions. A cheer went up as several bell-ringers were seen to run up the steps into St Peter's.

'Where are the flags?' yelled one. As if in answer to his question the cross of St George began to mount the flag staff on top of the church.

'The Post Office should know if it's true,' Bender said to fat Mrs Petty who stopped to get news. He resolved to walk there and make enquiries. Miss Taggerty and young Pringle could cope with slack Monday morning trade for once.

There was no confirmation yet of the rumours, the official at the Post Office said austerely. As soon as anything was known it would be posted publicly. Bender made his way back across the market square. By now there was quite a crowd. Some wag had lashed a

Union Jack to Queen Victoria's hand and tied a red, white, and blue bow on her crown. Sep, standing at his shop window, would normally have felt shocked at such sacrilege, but today he was sure Her Majesty would have forgiven this little frivolity had she known the circumstances.

The children began to pour out of school. It was twelve o'clock, and they gathered round the statue to enjoy the fun before racing home to Monday's meagre cold meat or wartime rissoles. At twelve-thirty the suspense was over. A notice was put up in the Post Office window. It said: 'Armistice signed. Hostilities ceased this morning.'

Now Caxley rejoiced. The flag was run up over the Town Hall. The bells of St Peter's rang out and people left their homes to run through the streets to the market square. The crowd joined hands and danced in a gigantic ring round Queen Victoria. Overhead, an aeroplane flew back and forth, very low, over the town, the pilot waving madly to the crowd. Someone had wrapped himself in a Union Jack and rode majestically through the streets on a high old-fashioned bicycle, acknowledging the cheers of the throng.

The town band was gathered hastily and marched through the pouring rain, blowing away at their instruments with gusto. Outside the hospital, an effigy of the Kaiser dangled from the portico, and a bonfire was being prepared for his funeral pyre in the grounds by enthusiastic patients.

Union Jacks waved everywhere. Buttonholes and hair ribbons of red, white, and blue blossomed on all sides. The pouring rain did nothing to dampen the spirits of Caxley folks on their great day. After dark came the greatest thrill of all – the street lamps were lit for the first time for years, and children gaped in amazement at the wonderful sight. Fireworks were let off by the river, and as the rockets soared and swooshed, and the Catherine wheels whirled in dizzy splendour, Caxley celebrated victory with frenzied excitement which lasted till the small hours. Now it was over – the suffering, the parting, the misery! Let all the world rejoice!

But not all could rejoice. Not all could forget. Some like Sep, thankful though they were that the war was over, mourned the loss of a son. Standing outside his shop in the dark market place that night, Sep watched the surging crowds with mingled joy and sorrow. The flags fluttered bravely, the bells rang out, beer flowed freely, singing and laughter echoed through the square. And above all, indomitable and unchanging, Queen Victoria surveyed her people from beneath her beribboned crown. She too, thought Sep, had seen war and victories. She too had lost sons. She would have understood his own mixed feelings.

Poor Jim, dear Jim! But it was no use grieving. Leslie was still spared to him, and Winnie, and the new baby. Kathy too and her husband, and young Robert at large somewhere in the town, and enjoying all the fun with a twelve-year-old's zest for it.

He turned to go in and caught sight of Bertie North limping resolutely along the pavement towards the firework display. What was Bender feeling, Sep wondered as he mounted the stairs? Despite the jubilation in the streets, Sep guessed that there was mourning in many hearts today, not only for a million dead, but for many more damaged in mind and body.

It was going to be hard, thought Sep, to build the new world the papers spoke of so hopefully, but somehow it must be done. Resolutely, Sep looked to the future.

Chapter Fifteen

POST-WAR TROUBLES

The men came back with relief and with expectations of unalloyed bliss. But things were not as simple as that. The first flush of joy necessarily cooled a little. Wives who had enjoyed freedom found the kitchen routine irksome. Children born during their father's absence resented the intrusion of the stranger in their homes. Food was still short and jobs were hard to get. But families shook down together again as well as they could, and it was good to see young men again in the fields and on the farms and working in the shops, and in the market square of Caxley.

About a third of them did not return, and some came back only to succumb to the plague called Spanish influenza which swept the country in 1918 and 1919. Among them, tragically, was Harry Miller so recently returned to his Beech Green farm, covered in honours. Once more Jesse Miller was left to farm alone.

Sep Howard, his Red Cross work having dwindled, threw himself with added concentration into his council duties. He had been made chairman of the local housing committee and found plenty to occupy him, for many new homes were needed for the returning men. Leslie was back in the business and doing well. He and Winnie were living in a small cottage which Sep had bought some years earlier for Edna's mother. Now that the old lady was dead it provided the young couple with an attractive little home, strategically placed at a distance from the parents of both.

The Howards had cheerful letters from Kathy now settled in Edinburgh with the stalwart Henry and expecting their first child. Henry was the only son of a fairly prosperous printer in the city, and Kathy enjoyed some social standing at the local functions. It looked as though Kathy was lost to Caxley for ever, and Bertie tried to persuade himself that it was all for the best.

His father was less quixotic about his circumstances. Young Mr Parker had returned from the war, full of zeal, and was turning North's upside down with his plans for the business. Worse still, from Bender's point of view, his wife and family had joined him and all were to live above the shop in Bender's old premises. It was some comfort to know that his children were numerous and that, for the time being, anyway, he would need all the living accommodation available. At least, thought Bender, his old drawing room would remain intact, and not house dairy equipment and rolls of chicken wire as had once been suggested.

It was in 1921 that Winnie's second child was born. Hilda had begged her to come to Rose Lodge for the confinement, but Winnie preferred to remain at the cottage attended by the local district nurse and a good-natured neighbour. Family affairs were difficult for Leslie and Winnie. The Howards always welcomed them and they visited the market square house frequently, but Bender refused to have Leslie at Rose Lodge although he wanted Winnie as often as she could manage it, and adored his grandchild, Edward. Winnie paid most of her visits home in the afternoon, when Leslie was at work, or called at the shop to see her father whenever she was in town.

A pair of enterprising brothers had started a motorbus service from Caxley to the surrounding villages, after the war, and this proved a blessing. Winnie frequently used it to travel to Caxley, and Edna often hopped on the bus outside her door and paid a surprise visit to her mother's old cottage.

Hilda came less often. It grieved her to see Winnie living in such modest surroundings.

'You can perfectly well afford something better,' she scolded her daughter. 'Leslie's a partner now, and Howard's is an absolute gold-mine.'

'There's time enough for something bigger when the family grows,' replied Winnie. 'Besides, I love it here, and it's healthier for Edward.'

She did not add that money was not as plentiful as Hilda supposed. Leslie never seemed to have much, despite the modest way they lived, and she too had wondered if Howard's were as flourishing as local people asserted. If so, just where was the money going? It made Winnie uneasy.

All through the long hot summer of 1921 she had plenty of time to think. Leslie bad never been a home-lover, and now he seemed to spend most of his evenings out. He pleaded work at the shop, but Winnie wondered. She lay in a deck chair in the shade of the damson tree in the cottage garden and tried to put these tormenting questions out of her mind, as she awaited the birth of the baby.

The heat was overpowering. Day after day of blazing sunshine scorched the grass and turned the chalky lane outside the gate into a white dust bath for the sparrows. Streams dried up, and the Cax shrank to half its size, leaving muddy banks criss-crossed with cracks and smelling abominably.

Water was short everywhere. Wells ran dry, and water carts trundled the lanes doling out a little to each householder. People ran down their paths, buckets in hands, and watched jealously to see that they received as much as their neighbours.

Edward, now a lively four-year-old, grew fractious in the heat and demanded more attention than his unwieldy mother could give him. It was a relief to Winnie when at last her pains began and Leslie took Edward to work with him, as arranged. She knew Edward would be thoroughly spoilt and happy with his grandparents, and she was free to get on with the vital job in hand.

The birth was easy, and by tea-time Leslie was at home again with his new daughter in his arms. She was to be called Joan.

For a few months after the baby's arrival, things seemed to be happier. Leslie was kinder and more thoughtful, and Winnie began to hope that Leslie was beginning to take his family responsibilities more seriously. But, as the autumn approached, his absences from home became more and more frequent. Winnie found herself sitting by the fire, the two children in bed above, alone with her thoughts from six o'clock until eleven or twelve when Leslie returned. He was always in good spirits, with ready and plausible excuses, but Winnie was fast becoming aware that her husband was a glib liar, and that her father, and Bertie too, had known more about his true nature than she had done.

One afternoon, just before Christmas, Hilda was busy decorating the Christmas tree at Rose Lodge. She was alone in the drawing room. On the table beside her was the box of bright baubles which had appeared annually ever since her marriage. Here was the spun glass bird with the long red tail which was Bertie's favourite. She hung it carefully towards the front of the tree. Here was a tiny silver lantern made by Winnie as a child. If only they were all young again! How they had always enjoyed dressing the tree! Now she was doing it alone. She threaded the little lantern on to a dark branch. The broken needles of fir gave out an aroma in the warmth from the crackling fire. At that moment the door opened, and Winnie appeared with the baby in her arms and Edward beside her.

'What a lovely surprise!' cried Hilda. She settled Winnie by the fire. The girl looked cold and shaky. Edward made straight for the box of bright decorations. Hilda removed it hastily, and then began to take off the baby's shawl.

'We'll have tea now, dear,' said Hilda. 'You look tired. Vera's here this afternoon, polishing the silver ready for Christmas. I'll get her to make it.'

'I've got a lot to tell you, Mamma,' said Winnie. Edward's bright eyes were fixed upon her hopefully. 'But little pitchers you know . . .'

'Edward, you can have tea with Vera in the kitchen,' said his grandmother promptly. 'Come along, and we'll see her.'

Ten minutes later, while the baby slept on the sofa, and Winnie neglected her tea, the tale unfolded. To Hilda, it came as no great surprise, but she grieved for Winnie telling it with a stony face.

She had taxed Leslie last night with his neglect of her and the children. Without a trace of shame he had admitted that there was another woman and that he fully intended to leave home to live with her.

'His actual words,' said Winnie bitterly, 'were: "I owe it to her. She was always first with me." He goes there today.'

'Very nice!' commented Hilda drily. 'I suppose it's the woman at Bent?'

Winnie nodded. Her hands turned her teacup round and round ceaselessly. A little muscle twitched by her mouth, but her eyes remained dry.

'Well, this has shown him in his true colours,' said Hilda grimly.

'For God's sake don't say "I told you so!",' cried Winnie. 'I don't think I could bear it! The thing is – what happens to me and the children?'

'You come here,' said Hilda promptly.

Winnie shook her head.

'It would never do, Mamma, and you know it. Father might not say anything in front of me, but I should know he was thinking about Leslie. It's not fair to either of you. Besides there's not enough room.'

'What would you like to do?' asked Hilda. 'Are you prepared to have him back if he can be persuaded?'

'He won't be. He said so, and he means it.'

There was silence. A robin outside whistled in the grey afternoon and the fire rustled companionably.

'Do the Howards know?' asked Hilda.

'I've no idea. I doubt it. But I shall tell them, of course. Tomorrow probably. I can't face much more today.'

'You must stay the night here. Tomorrow too. For as long as you like, my dear. This is your home.'

'No, Mamma, it isn't,' replied Winnie gently. 'The cottage is my home, even if Leslie's left it. I must go back.'

'Not tonight,' said Hilda with all her old authority. 'This has been a terrible shock. We'll look after the children, and you must have an early night.'

'Very well,' agreed Winnie, in a low tone. She passed her hand across her face, with the same gesture as her father's when he was worried and bemused.

Hilda began to stack the tray. Before it was done she looked across at Winnie. The girl lay back, eyes closed, as white as death and as quiet as the baby asleep nearby.

Hilda lifted the tray and crept stealthily from the room.

But the Howards knew already – at least Sep did. At about the same time as Winnie's arrival at Rose Lodge, Sep and Leslie were alone in the bakehouse.

'You may as well know, Dad, that Winnie and I have parted company,' announced Leslie. He was wiping shelves and kept his back carefully towards his father.

Sep stood stock still by the great scrubbed table. Had he heard aright?

'Whose idea is this?' he asked.

'Well, mine I suppose,' said Leslie with assumed lightness.

'Am I to understand,' said Sep thunderously, 'that you are seriously proposing to leave your wife and children?'

Leslie continued to rub at the shelves. For once he was silent.

'Face me!' commanded Sep. Obediently, Leslie turned. He was a child again, caught out in some misdemeanour, and awaiting retribution. Sep, filled with righteous wrath, commanded respect, despite his small stature.

'What lies behind this? What has happened?'

'Well, Winnie and I haven't seen eye to eye for some time. She's been off-hand most of this year. She –'

'She has been carrying a child,' Sep broke in. '*Your* child. What do you expect?'

Leslie flushed. He opened his mouth to speak, but Sep was first.

'There is another woman.' It was a statement not a question. Leslie nodded, eyes cast down.

'The one at Bent?' asked Sep, his voice dangerously calm.

'Yes, Dad.'

There was a dreadful silence, broken only by the heavy breathing of the older man. His hands were clenched on the surface of the table.

'Then you did lie to me. I feared it.'

Leslie threw up his head. Now he was angry, with the anger of a cornered animal. He shouted wildly.

'So what? Why shouldn't I lie? I was driven to it, in this bible-thumping house – and so was Jim, if you did but know it! He wasn't the stained-glass saint you tried to make out!'

'You'll do no good trying to blacken your dead brother's name,' cried Sep. 'Answer for yourself! What hold has this woman on you?'

'She's got my child –'

'Winnie's got two of your children.'

'She came first. She always did. We suit each other. And now her husband's left her. I've got to help her.'

Suddenly, the younger man crumpled, slumping on to the wooden stool by the table. Sep, standing, surveyed him grimly.

'You knew your responsibilities before marrying Winnie North. You've wrecked her life, and this woman's – and her husband's too. No good ever came of giving way to sin.'

Leslie raised his head from his arms.

'It's too late for chapel talk now,' he said bitterly.

'It's never too late for true repentance,' said Sep gravely. 'You must think again. Don't break up your marriage. Go back to Winnie. She'll forgive you. Break with this woman for good. If she knows there is no chance of seeing you, their marriage may be mended. For pity's sake, Leslie, think about it!'

'I have thought. I will never go back to Winnie. She'd never forgive me. At heart she's her father all over again. I'm starting afresh, and taking Milly with me. I should have married her years ago.'

Sep began to pace the bakehouse.

'I'm not going to discuss it with you further today. Go home and turn over my advice. Think of Edward and Joan. What sort of life will they have without a father? And tomorrow we'll talk again. I shall say nothing to your mother about this.'

Leslie struggled to his feet.

'Whatever you say, Dad, will make no difference. I'll see you tomorrow morning as usual. But there's no hope, I tell you.'

'There's always hope,' said Sep soberly, as his son went through the door.

*

There was little sleep for Sep that night, while Leslie packed his bags in the empty cottage and Winnie tossed and turned under her parents' roof.

The next morning father and son faced each other again. Leslie's expression was mutinous.

'I've nothing to add,' he said with finality. His jaw was set at an obstinate angle.

'But I have,' responded Sep. He leant across the table and spoke firmly. 'If you have decided to go forward with this wickedness, then you must leave the business and leave your home too.'

Leslie looked up, startled.

'I won't have you setting a bad example to the workmen or to young Robert. You know my views. I won't countenance such behaviour. Finish the week here, and meanwhile look for another job.'

'But, Dad –' began Leslie.

'I am putting a hundred pounds into your bank account today,' went on Sep. 'Our partnership will be dissolved. You must make your own way. Don't appear here for help if you find yourself in a mess. You've chosen your own road – you must travel it alone.'

Later that evening he had to break the news to Edna and face the expected storm. She could not believe that Leslie had behaved so badly. It would pass. This other woman could be paid off. Why didn't Sep think of it? After all, lots of boys had these passing infatuations. The war had unsettled poor Leslie.

Sep let her ramble wildly on for a time, and then spoke sternly. Leslie was a man. He knew what he was doing. He, as his father, was not prepared to connive in such despicable conduct. He had his duty to Robert, to his wife and to his work people. Leslie must go.

Edna looked up at him with wet eyes. Another thought had flitted through her head.

'What will happen to poor Winnie and darling Edward and the baby? How will they live if you've stopped Leslie's wages? Why should they suffer?'

'I have thought of that,' replied Sep. 'They will be looked after.'

Unable to bear more he made his way upstairs to the peace of the bedroom. In the market square they were erecting the town's Christmas tree. The season of peace and goodwill towards men, thought Sep bitterly, and he had just banished a son!

Beside the tree, dwarfed by its dusky height, Queen Victoria gazed regally across the cobbles.

'She would have approved,' Sep murmured aloud. 'Yes, she would have approved.'

Nevertheless, it was cold comfort.

Chapter Sixteen

BERTIE FINDS A HOME

Christmas was a muted affair, for both the Howard and North families. There was the usual visit to church and chapel, the mammoth Christmas dinner, the ritual of the tree at tea time, and for those at Rose Lodge the welcome diversion of Edward's excitement.

On Boxing Day Winnie and the children went to tea in the market square and it was then that she learnt of Sep's generous provision for her family. Leslie's salary would be paid automatically into her bank account. The cottage was hers, rent free, for as long as she cared to make use of it.

Sep explained it all to her in the privacy of the dining room when the rest of the party were playing 'Hunt the Thimble', for Edward's benefit, next door. The table was still littered with the remains of Christmas crackers and tea time debris. The magnificent cake, made by Sep's own hands, towered amid the wreckage, the candles still gave out a faint acrid whiff.

Winnie was greatly touched by this overwhelming generosity, and tried to say so, but Sep would not hear her.

'It's little enough,' he said, 'and my pleasure'.

Winnie broke the news to her parents as soon as she returned home. They too were loud in their praises of Sep's conduct. Secretly, Hilda felt a pang of shame for her past off-handedness towards Sep and Edna. She must do what she could to make amends, she determined.

Bender's first feeling was of great relief. He had been much worried by his responsibilities towards Winnie and her children.

She was welcome to make her home with them, though the house would be devilishly cramped, he had to admit. But his salary simply could not he stretched to giving Winnie an allowance, and the thought of Edward's education and Joan's in the years to come had made him shudder. He was on the point of going to Sep and telling him to force his son to pay a weekly maintenance sum. Thank goodness he had never done it! In the face of this liberal open-handedness, Bender was overcome. He had never thought to be beholden to Sep Howard, but he was glad to be, in the circumstances.

It was now that Bertie came forward with his proposal. He had been thinking for some time of buying a house. Now that Mary was growing up, and her hobbies took up a large amount of room, he felt that it was time he provided for himself. Hilda began to protest when he broached the subject, but Bertie was firm.

'Mamma, I have reached the ripe old age of twenty-eight. You were good enough to take me in and look after me when I really needed it. But I've no excuse now. I'm as fit as the rest of you and I should dearly love to have a little place of my own to invite you to whenever you wanted to come.'

Hilda was partly mollified, and when he went on to point out that he would need advice on furnishing his establishment, she began to be quite reconciled to the idea.

Bertie went on to suggest that Winnie might like to housekeep for him. They had always got on well together, and he would do his best to keep a fatherly eye on Edward and Joan. He had been told of a house for sale just off Caxley High Street, with a small garden sloping down to the Cax. It was not far from his work, and would be convenient for Winnie for shopping and visiting her Caxley friends.

'And remember,' continued Bertie, 'young Edward will be starting school in a few months' time. There is plenty of choice in Caxley. He's a good two miles to walk if he stays at the cottage.'

This was perfectly true, and had not occurred to Winnie in her present distraught condition. She liked the idea immensely, and appreciated Bertie's kindness. There would be no quarrelling in the household, she felt sure.

And so it was arranged. The house that Bertie had found was approached from a little lane off the busy High Street. It was a red-brick, four square house, solidly built with good rooms and large windows. It was certainly more commodious than a bachelor would normally choose, and Winnie realized that it had been bought mainly for her benefit.

She told Sep at once about Bertie's proposal and he agreed that it was the best possible arrangement. The cottage would be welcomed by one of his men, he knew, but Winnie's needs had come first.

She had hardly left him before Bender crossed the market square and entered the shop.

'Come through,' said Sep, guessing his errand. The two men settled themselves in Sep's tiny office. It was hardly big enough to house the neat oak desk and the rows of books on the shelves around the walls, but at least they had privacy.

'You know why I'm here, Sep. You're being uncommonly good to our Winnie. It's appreciated, you know. To tell the truth, I couldn't help her much myself, as things are.'

'Say nothing, please. I'm too much ashamed of Leslie's behaviour to talk about it. This is the least I can do. She may be your daughter, Bender, but her children are my grandchildren. I do it for their sakes as much as Winnie's.'

'Ah! It's a bad business!' agreed Bender, shaking his massive head. 'And no hope of patching it up, as far as I can see.'

'Perhaps it's as well,' replied Sep. 'I blinded myself to the boy's faults. I face that now. He'll be no good to any woman, as that poor creature he's with will soon find out. No, I think Winnie's well rid of him.'

'And you've heard of Bertie's plans?'

'Yes, indeed. Winnie's just been here, and I'm all in favour! That boy of yours is solid gold, Bender.'

'He's a good chap,' nodded Bender. 'Bit of an old stick-in-the-mud, I sometimes think, but better that way than the other!'

'Definitely,' replied Sep, with a little chilliness. Bender felt that he may have put his foot in it. He rose hastily.

'Must get back to the shop.' He held out his hand and ground Sep's small one painfully in it.

'Bless you, Sep. We've got every reason to be grateful. Winnie's happiness means a lot to us.'

'I'm glad to be able to help,' said Sep sincerely, putting his damaged hand behind him and opening the door with the other.

He watched the vast figure cross the market place, then hurried hack soberly to his duties, well content. For the first time in his life he had been able to succour Bender.

After weeks of occupation by bricklayers, carpenters, plumbers, plasterers, decorators, and their assorted minions, the house was ready and Bertie and Winnie moved in.

The garden was still a tangle of weeds and overgrown plants, but tall tulips peered from the undergrowth in the borders and the lilac was in fine bloom. Bertie strolled about his new kingdom in proud happiness. It was a fine place to own and the neglected garden would give him a rewarding hobby. He paced down the mossy gravel path to the tall hedge at the end. Let into it was a wooden gate, in sore need of painting, which opened on to the tow-path of the winding Cax.

It was this aspect of his property that gave Bertie the greatest satisfaction. All his life he had loved the river. Its rippling had soothed him to sleep as a boy. In the dark, pain-filled nights of the war, when his absent foot throbbed and leapt as though it were still in the bed with him, he had imagined himself sitting by the shining water, cooling his feet among the waving reeds and the silver bubbles which encrusted them. Its memory had helped to keep him sane in the nightmare world. Now it was here for him to enjoy for the rest of his life. He gazed at it with affection. Here he would saunter in the evenings while the gnats danced above the surface and the swallows skimmed after them. Here he would sit on long hot afternoons listening to the noisy boys splashing in the distance. He might take up fishing seriously. It was a good occupation for a man with a gammy leg and young Edward already had a taste for trout.

He returned to the garden and made his way towards the house. Someone was hanging curtains upstairs and for one wild ecstatic moment he imagined that it was Kathy. If only it could be! But he thrust the thought from him. No use crying for the moon! He was damned lucky to have all this – and dear old Winnie to keep him company.

He waved affectionately to the figure in the window and limped into his own house thankfully.

Thus began a period of great pleasure and tranquillity, for the brother and sister. It gave them both time to recover from the shocks they had received, and to gain strength to enjoy the pleasant familiar world of Caxley again.

They had always been fond of each other. They were both placid and good-natured in temperament, and shared the same circle of friends. Occasionally they went to a concert or spent an evening with neighbours or at Rose Lodge or at Sep's. Vera, their old maid, lived close by, and loved to bring her knitting and sit with the children. To many people in Caxley it seemed a remarkably humdrum existence. Why on earth didn't they each find a partner, they wondered? Bertie was charming, gentle, and handsome – eminently suited to matrimony, the speculative matrons with daughters told each other. Winnie was free now that her divorce from Leslie had gone through.

The older generation, including the Howards and the Norths, could not help being rather shocked at divorce. To their minds, attuned to good Queen Victoria's proprieties, a woman – even if she were the injured party – was somehow besmirched if she had appeared in the divorce court. Happily, those of Winnie's generation took a more realistic view of her position and sincerely hoped that in time she would find a partner who would appreciate her company and prove a good father to her two attractive children.

There was little news of Leslie and his new wife. They had moved far west into Devon where he was working as a car salesman. With his smart good looks and plausible tongue, Winnie felt he was well equipped to make a success of this career. She never ceased to be thankful that he had gone, and hoped never to set eyes on him again.

Every year that passed made the children dearer to her. Edward attended a small school in the High Street and was to go to Caxley Grammar School when he was nine. One of his friends was Tim Parker, the youngest child of the Parkers at his grandfather's old home.

He had always known the shop well, for he had visited Bender there for as long as he could remember, but he had not been familiar with the premises above until he was invited to play with Tim. From the first, he was enchanted. To stand at the windows of the great drawing room and to look out at the bustle of the market square was a constant joy. There was so much to watch – the cheapjacks, flashing cutlery and crockery, their wives spreading gaudy materials over their buxom arms and doing their best to persuade cautious housewives to part with their money.

And even if it were not market day when the square was gay with stalls, there were always familiar figures to be seen going about their daily affairs. He saw the tall dignified figure of the Town Clerk enter the Town Hall, the vicar running up the steps of St Peter's, the one-legged sweeper wielding his besom broom round the plinth of the Queen's statue. Sometimes he saw his grandfather in his white baker's clothes, or Grandma Howard in one of her pretty hats, tripping across to buy chops for dinner. In sunshine, or rain, winter or summer, the view fascinated him. There was always something happening there. It was as good as a serial story – a story which would never end.

He tried to tell his Uncle Bertie about his feelings and found a sympathetic listener. Bertie told him old tales of their childhood above the shop, and on his next visit Edward searched for, and found, the scratched initials on the window pane which had resulted in a beating for poor Uncle Bertie. He told the child about the beauties of the old drawing room – the red plush furniture, the sea lavender on the wall brackets, the hissing gas lamps, and Edward longed to be able to go back in time and see its ancient glory.

He was, naturally, more familiar with the Howards' house for here he was one of the family and not just a guest. He adored Sep and Edna, and felt much more at ease with them than with Bender, of whom he was a little afraid. Grandma North he was fond of, but conscious that he must behave 'like a little gentleman'. Ears were inspected, nail-biting was deplored, and his dress had to he immaculate at Rose Lodge. At the baker's house so much was going on that such niceties were overlooked. Here he was happy with the company, but the house itself had not the same power of enchantment for him as the rooms above North's old shop. With a child's disconcerting frankness he said as much to Sep one day.

'It's a lovely house,' agreed Sep gravely. 'And your grandpa and grandma North always made it very pretty and comfortable. But we have the same view, you know. In fact, I often think there is I better view of the market square from here.'

Edward pondered the point, and lit upon the truth.

'But the sun's wrong. You only get it when it's going down behind the church. Over there, at Tim's, it shines into the rooms from morning till afternoon. That's what makes it so nice.'

Sep agreed again. The child was right. North's aspect was much more favourable than their own. He was amused to see how much the old house meant to the boy. Of course, he had heard all sorts of tales from his mother and uncle about the good old days there and this must lend a certain fascination to the place. But it was not a good thing to dwell too much in the past, thought Sep. A young boy should be living in the present, and looking forward to the future.

'What about giving me a hand in the bakehouse?' asked Sep. The child's eyes shone. He loved the warmth, the fragrance and the bustle as dearly as he loved the square outside. And, who knows ? There might be a hot lardy cake or a spiced bun waiting for him.

He danced ahead of Sep towards the treasure house, and Sep, following sedately, recalled with a pang the days when two small boys, now lost to him, had led the same way to happiness.

Chapter Seventeen

SEP MAKES A DECISION

It was in the January of 1930 that Bender had his first serious illness. Hilda found him a most refractory patient.

'It's only a chest cold, I tell you,' he wheezed, waving away inhalants, cough sweets and all other panaceas that his poor wife brought. The very idea of calling the doctor sent up his temperature.

'He'll only send me to bed,' he gasped. 'I'm much better off down here by the fire. Don't fuss so, Hilda.'

But after a day or two he had such violent pains in his chest, and his breathing was so laboured that Hilda slipped out of the house and rang up the doctor from a neighbour's. Within an hour Bender was in Caxley Cottage Hospital.

Sep heard about it at dinner time and rang the hospital for news. He was in some discomfort, he was told, but making progress. He would not be allowed visitors for some time.

Sep was deeply shaken. For the next few days he went about his affairs silent and depressed. The market square was not the same without Bender's huge figure in the doorway of North's, and his great laugh sending the pigeons flying. Sep rang Hilda and kept in touch. He did not like to call at the house. Since the Norths had moved he had seldom visited them. Any meeting with bender had taken place at the shop, or, by chance, in the market place or street.

As soon as Bender was allowed visitors Sep went to see him. It was a cold night of sharp frost, and the railings and lamp posts were hoary with rime. It was good to get inside the warmth of the hospital, despite the reek of disinfectant which always upset Sep's stomach.

Bender looked mountainous in bed. His face against the pillow had an unnatural pallor which shocked Sep. Clearly, Bender had been very ill indeed. Beside his bed was another visitor, and as Sep approached he saw that it was Jack Tenby. The man rose as Sep came near.

'Don't go, Jack,' said Bender. 'Sit you down, man. I'm allowed two visitors at a time. Stay till Hilda comes.'

He held out a hand to Sep and gripped him with the same old firmness with which Sep was familiar.

'Good to see you, Sep. How's things?'

The three men exchanged news of Caxley friends. Someone had moved, someone else had taken up motor-racing, a third was to be made Mayor next year. The bridge was being repainted. A new bus service had been started to the county town. There was talk of a housing estate in the field behind the park.

Bender listened eagerly to all these topics, but he seemed tired, Sep thought, and when Hilda appeared bearing fruit and flowers, the two men made their farewells and left the hospital together.

The cold air caught their breath as they emerged. Above them the stairs were brilliant. Their footsteps rang on the frosty pavement as they descended the gentle slope into the town together.

'How d'you think he looks?' asked Jack Tenby.

'Pretty weak,' admitted Sep.

'I agree. His wife was telling me the other day that the doctor says he should retire.'

They had reached the crossroads where their ways divided and paused beneath the lamp post to continue their conversation. In the light from the gas above them their breath rose in clouds.

'I haven't said anything to Bender about this yet, but I know it will go no further if I tell you about my plans. I'm pulling out of the market place.'

Sep was taken aback.

'For good, do you mean? What's gone wrong?'

'Nothing particularly. It's time I retired myself. It's been thought over and it seems best to sell up all but the original shop. Things aren't easy and are going to get worse. Staffing's a constant headache. I'm not getting any younger. If I collect the cash now and bank it, I reckon I can tick over comfortably until I die. The family's out in the world and it's time my wife and I had a bit of a rest.'

Sep nodded. All this was sensible. But what would Bender feel about it? And what would happen to his old home?

'What about North's?' he asked.

'It'll be put on the market,' replied Tenby. 'Good position like that should help its sale.'

'Jack,' said Sep suddenly, laying a hand on the other's arm, 'let me know when you finally decide. I should like to think about it.'

'I'll do that,' promised Tenby. 'It's going to happen before long. You shall be the first to know my plans.'

He raised hand and set off at a brisk pace, leaving Sep to gaze at his dwindling figure.

Sep moved off more slowly. He had plenty of food for thought, and he would digest it undisturbed as he walked the streets of Caxley.

How oddly things had turned out! For over a year now Sep had been trying to find new premises in which to expand his thriving business. All Caxley said that Howard's was a gold mine. Only Sep knew how prosperous the business really was. He had saved regularly. His way of life had altered little over the years. As a result of this, and of his foresight and industry, Sep's bank account was extremely satisfactory. It was time that he put some of this money into another business, he decided, and it looked now as if one of his pipe dreams might come true. If North's were to come on the market it would the the perfect place for Howard's restaurant which he and Edna had thought about for so long.

He turned aside down a quiet lane which led to the river. Firelight flickered on the curtains of a cottage. A tabby cat streaked across his path. The smoke from Caxley's chimneys rose straight into the motionless night. Sep seemed to he the only person abroad as he paced along deep in thought.

He could see it all so clearly in his mind's eye. There would be one great room running from front to back on the ground floor, with french windows leading into Bender's garden. A garden had always been one of the highlights of Sep's dream. Here, in the summer, the Caxley folk could eat at little white tables, sipping their coffee or tea and choosing those delectable pastries made at Sep's shop over the way. There had been a need for a good class restaurant in Caxley for many years. Who better to supply it than Sep, who could provide the best cakes and pies in the neighbourhood?

If this property really became his how wonderful it would be! His own premises had been cramped for many years now. True, he had been able to buy the yard next door which belonged to the old herbalist who ran the dusty little shop beside Sep's own. Here he was able to keep the vans and some of his stores. He had often thought about buying out the herbalist, but the property was small and inconvenient, and although old Mr White was in his seventies, and looked as though a puff of wind would blow him away like thistledown, he continued to bumble about among his elixirs and nostrums with remarkable energy for one so frail.

Strangely enough, the possibility of North's ever becoming free had never occurred to Sep when thinking about his restaurant. Somehow, North's belonged to Bender still in Sep's mind, and was inviolate. If it should become his, thought Sep, quickening his pace as he reached the tow path, he would see that Bender's garden was restored as nearly as possible to its former glory. It would be a perfect setting for teas on the sloping lawns with the Cax rippling by.

And what about the house above the restaurant? He and Edna would not want to live there. They were far too comfortable in their own home, and even such a short move would be repugnant to Sep. Would Bender want to return? Would he rebuff any offer of Sep's yet again, if he were to suggest it?

Sep stopped by a willow tree, stretching its skinny arms to the stars above. Bender's waxen face as he had seen it that evening, floated before him. It was no use blinking the fact, thought Sep, suddenly becoming conscious of the icy cold, Bender had not many years before him, either at Rose Lodge or anywhere else. But if it lay in his power, Sep swore to himself, Bender should have his old home again, if he so wished.

And after? Sep turned up his coat collar and set his face towards the market square. Well, if this dream should become reality, then one day, far in the future, Bender's home should go to one of his own – one who would love it as Bender had done.

It should be Edward's.

Sep kept his thought to himself, and said nothing of Tenby's disclosures to Edna or anyone else. Bender made very slow progress, and the crocuses were out before he was allowed to return to Rose Lodge.

He found convalescence even more tedious than hospital life. At least there had been a routine there, a succession of small happenings and a constant stream of people, nurses, doctors, fellow-patients, and visitors. It was too cold to go in the garden. He was forbidden to work in the greenhouse, which was his latest joy, in case he lifted something too heavy or stood too long on his weak legs. Books tired his eyes, radio programmes his ears. Food was a bore, drink was restricted, and smoking too. Visitors were his only distraction, and Hilda welcomed them for it gave her a brief respite from her patient's claims on her time.

Bertie and Winnie and the children called in every day. Occasionally Winnie stayed the night and Bertie took his mother out to friends or for drive in the countryside to refresh her. She had borne up wonderfully during these tiring months, but to Bertie's eyes she looked years older.

'He frets to get back to the shop,' said Hilda on one of their outings, 'but the doctor won't hear of it yet. I do so wish he would retire. Do try and make him see sense, Bertie.'

'I'll have a word with him when I can,' promised Bertie dutifully.

But there was no need for Bertie to exercise his persuasive powers. When they returned they found that Jack Tenby had called and had told Bender all his plans for the future. So there had been something in the rumours flying round Caxley, thought Bertie.

His father looked pale and shaken.

'That settles it,' he said heavily. 'I'm finished for good now. The old place to be sold, and no job for me even if I could do it.'

Hilda straightened the cushion behind his aching head, and spoke with spirit.

'Don't be so full of self-pity! This is the best news I've heard for a long time. Now perhaps you'll make the best of being a retired man, and stop worrying about that wretched shop.'

'What have I got to look forward to?' asked Bender, half-enjoying his sad plight.

'Looking after me,' said his wife promptly. 'Pottering about in the greenhouse. Planning the garden for the summer. Helping your grandchildren with their homework. Being a little more welcoming to Mary's boy friends when she brings them home. Dozens of things.'

Despite himself, Bender had to smile.

'Have I been such a trial?' he asked.

'You've been *terrible*!' cried Hilda, with such fervour that Bender laughed aloud, and then began to wheeze. Bertie went forward in alarm, but was waved back vigorously.

'I'm all right, boy. Haven't been so right for weeks! Dammit all, now it's come to it, I believe I'm going to settle back and enjoy my old age!'

It was a month later that Sep called at Rose Lodge – a month that had been hectic for the little baker. He and Edna had talked far into the nights about the restaurant. There had been discussions with the bank, with surveyors, builders, solicitors, and dozens of people concerned in the exchange of property. Meanwhile, his own business had to be carried on, and all the time the problem of broaching the subject to Bender was uppermost in Sep's mind. Now the time had come. The deal was virtually done, and the property his.

He had gone about the affair as discreetly as possible and was confident that Bender had heard nothing. He wanted to break the news himself. It was unthinkable that he should hear of it from any other source.

Hilda let him in with a smile.

'He'll be so glad to see you. He's in the greenhouse watering the plants.'

Sep made his way into the garden. The greenhouse was warm and scented. Little beads of perspiration glistened on Bender's forehead. He put down the watering can and sank on to an upturned wooden box, motioning Sep to do the same.

'Good to see you, Sep. What's the news?'

'I'm not sure how you'll take it. But it's news you're bound to hear before long, and I wanted to be the one to bring it.'

'Well, get on with it then. Is it about Edna? Or has that new baby of Kathy's arrived?'

'Not yet – any day now, I believe. But it's not exactly family affairs I've come to talk about, but business ones.'

'Oh ah!' said Bender, yawning.

He did not seem to be particularly interested. At least, thought Sep, it should not be too great a shock.

'It's about your shop, Bender.'

'Has it gone yet? Jack Tenby said something about an auction if it didn't sell.'

'It has been sold,' said Sep. He ran a finger round the rough rim of a flowerpot, his eyes downcast.

'That's quick work!' commented Bender with more interest. 'Anyone we know bought it?'

'As a matter of fact,' said Sep, looking up from the flowerpot, 'I've bought it.'

There was silence in the heat of the greenhouse, and then Bender took a deep breath.

'Well, I'm damned,' he said softly. Then, leaning forward, he smote Sep's knee with something of his old heartiness.

'Well, don't be so deuced apologetic about it, boy! I'm glad you're having it, and that's the truth! Could have been bought by some sharp lad from London, simply to sell at a profit. Tell me more.'

Sep began. Once started it became easier to tell of his search for premises, for the hope of restaurant and the general expansion of Howard's. Bender listened intently.

'And the garden?' he asked, when Sep paused to take breath.

'I want to keep it as you used to have it,' said Sep, 'when the children played there. It was at its best then, I always think.'

'It was,' agreed Bender. 'Tell you what, I'll try and remember how it was we had it, and let you have the plants to set it up again. I'd like to do that for the old place.'

His face was cheerful, and he picked up the watering can again.

'Well, well, well!' he muttered bending over his seedlings. 'So you're going to be the owner of North's!'

He looked across at Sep.

'Ever going to live there?'

'No,' replied Sep. 'Young Parker is going to set up on his own in the High Street. Starting a china shop, evidently, but there's no accommodation there. I've told him he can stay where he is for the time being.'

Bender nodded, and continued his watering. Was this the time, Sep wondered, with beating heart, to broach the question of Bender's return? Not yet, perhaps. Enough had happened today. He would wait a little.

But Bender forestalled him.

'It's a good house. We had some happy times there, didn't we, Sep? And some rotten ones too, but that's how it goes – and somehow it's only the happy ones we remember, thank God. I wouldn't want to go back there – not for all the tea in China. Too many memories, Sep. Far too many! Hilda and I are better off here.'

He put down the can resolutely.

'But it's good to think of it going to friends, Sep. I'm glad things have turned out this way.'

He opened the door of the greenhouse and gulped the cool air.

'Let's go and get Hilda to give us a cup of tea. Ain't no point in offering you anything stronger I suppose?'

Wheezing and laughing, he made his way to the house, relishing the news he had to give his wife. And behind him, thankful in heart, followed Sep.

That night, lying sleepless in bed, Bender pondered on the changes of fortune. Who would have thought, when they were boys together in the rough and tumble of the old National School, that frightened little Sep Howard with holes in his boots would beat him – the cock o' the walk – as he had done?

There was Sep now, hale and hearty while he lay a crock of a man. Sep was a prosperous tradesman, a councillor, a pillar of the chapel, and now the owner of his old home. Not that he grudged him any of it. He'd earned it all, he supposed – funny little old Sep!

Well, that's how it went on life's see-saw, thought Bender philosophically. One went up, while the other went down! Nothing to be done about it, especially when you were as tired as he was. But who would have thought it, eh? Who would have thought it?

He turned his cheek into the plump comfort of his pillow, and fell asleep.

Chapter Eighteen

WHAT OF THE FUTURE?

As usual, there were innumerable delays in starting work on Sep's new restaurant. But one windy autumn day the workmen moved in and the sound of picks and shovels was music in Sep's ears.

It was market day, and he watched the first stages of the work to the accompaniment of all the familiar market noises. Cheapjacks yelled, awnings flapped and crackled in the wind, leaves and paper rustled over the cobbles, dogs barked, children screamed, and everywhere there was bustling activity.

Caxley was becoming busier than ever, thought Sep, picking his way through the debris underfoot. Cars and vans streamed along the western side of the square to continue on their way into the High Street. There would be plenty of travellers needing refreshment at the new restaurant, particularly in the summer. By that time it should be going well. There were plenty of local people too who would fill the tables at midday. He had already planned to have a simple three-course luncheon, modestly priced, to suit the time and tastes of the business people nearby. This should provide steady trade for all the year, and he hoped that he would be able to cater for evening functions as well. As Caxley expanded – and it was doing so fast in the early thirties – there should be plenty of scope for Howard's restaurant.

Sep made a daily inspection of the work. Never before had he felt such deep satisfaction in a project. This was building for the future. The thought of Edward living in the house in the years to come filled Sep with joy. The union of the two families, which Bender had refused to recognize in the marriage of Leslie and Winnie, would be assured when Edward took his joint heritage in the property.

One foggy November afternoon Sep returned from his inspection to find the evening paper on the counter as usual. His eye was caught by a photograph of two trains, hideously telescoped, toppling down the side of an embankment. The headline said : 'Scottish Rail Disaster'. Sep read on.

In the dense fog which covered the entire British Isles this morning, an express train from London crashed into the rear of a local train three miles outside Edinburgh. Twenty-four people are known to be dead. It is feared that almost fifty are injured.

It went on to describe the valiant efforts of volunteers who scrambled up the steep embankment to help the victims. Fog and ice hampered rescuers. Survivors were being treated at local hospitals. It was estimated that it would take twenty-four hours to clear the wreckage from the track.

A terrible affair, thought Sep. So many other people affected too – wives and mothers, husbands and sons. A number of children were among the dead, for the accident had occurred soon after eight in the morning, when people were going to work and children to school.

The shop bell tinkled, and Jesse Miller came in to buy buns to take back to the farm for tea. Twisting the corners of the paper bag, and asking Jesse about his affairs, Sep forgot the news he had been reading.

It was not until the next day that the Howards learnt that Kathy's Henry, on his way to the printing business, had been killed and now lay in an Edinburgh mortuary with the others so tragically dead.

It was young Robert Howard who escorted Edna to Scotland to comfort Kathy, and to attend the funeral, for Sep could not leave the business or the supervision of the new building.

The news was soon known in Caxley and Sep received many messages of sympathy. Kathy had always been popular, and Henry, so stalwart and handsome, had impressed the neighbourhood during his short time there. It was Winnie who told Bertie the news. His face turned so ashen that she thought that he would faint, but he remained calm and very quiet.

Inwardly he was in turmoil. He would like to have snatched his coat, leapt in the car and headed for Scotland to comfort her. The thought of Kathy in trouble, in tears, lonely and broken was insupportable. But it could not be. Instead he sat at his desk and wrote, offering all help possible. He would come at once if it were of any assistance. Please let him help in any way possible. He wrote on, feeling all the time how inadequate it was, but the best that he could do in the circumstances.

Kathy's reply arrived in a few days. She was so touched by everyone's kindness, Bertie's particularly, but she was being well looked after. Her mother and Robert were still with her, and Henry's family lived close by and were taking care of everything. She was planning to come to Caxley when the weather improved and looked forward to meeting all her friends again.

This letter, Winnie noticed, was put into Bertie's pocket-book and was carried with him, but she made no comment.

Some days after Robert's and Edna's return, Sep walked up the hill to visit Bender. The shops were beginning to dress their windows for Christmas. Blobs of cotton wool, representing snow flakes, adorned the grocer's, tinsel glittered in the chemist's, and a massive holly wreath was propped tastefully against a grave vase in the local undertaker's. Sep shuddered as he passed. Death was too near just now.

He found Bender sitting in his high-backed winged armchair by the fire. He looked suddenly very old and his massive frame seemed to have shrunk, but his eyes lit up when he saw his visitor and his greeting was as hearty as ever.

'Hilda's down at Winnie's,' said Bender. 'They're making a party frock or some such nonsense for young Joan. She won't be long. Nice to have a bit of company, Sep.'

The two men warmed their feet by the fire. The kettle purred on the trivet. Chrysanthemums scented the firelit room. Hilda had always had the knack of making a house attractive, thought Sep. It was something that Edna had never really managed to do.

'Terrible business of Kathy's,' said Bender. 'I can't tell you how shocked we were to hear it. How's the poor girl getting on? And the children?'

Sep give him what news he could. The little boy was the hardest one to console – just old enough to understand . The baby girl was thriving. She should be a great comfort to Kathy. They hoped to see them all in the spring for a long visit. They might even persuade Kathy to stay for good, but she was very attached to Edinburgh and to Henry's people. It was too early to make decisions yet.

Bender listened and nodded, sipping a glass of brandy and water.

'And the shop?' asked Bender, turning the conversation to more hopeful things. Sep's face lit up.

'We've taken down the wall between the shop and the parlour,' began Sep enthusiastically and went on to explain the plans he had for the interior decoration. Bender thought he had never seen him so animated. Howard's restaurant would not lack care and affection, he thought, as he listened to Sep running on.

'You're looking ahead,' he commented when Sep paused for breath, 'and a good thing too. Young Robert will have a fine business to carry on when you want to give up.'

'The business will be his,' agreed Sep, 'but not the house. Our own place will go to him, no doubt.'

'And what about North's?'

'He doesn't know yet,' said Sep slowly, 'but it's to be Edward's.'

A long silence fell. A coal tumbled out of the fire, and Bender replaced it carefully. The tongs shook in his hands, his breathing was laboured. At last he sat back and gazed across at Sep.

'That pleases me more than I can say, Sep. The old house will stay in the family – in *both* our families – after all!'

He picked up his glass again, raised it silently to Sep, and drained it.

It was at that moment they heard a car draw up at the front door and the sound of voices. Hilda hurried into the room followed by Bertie and Edward.

'Bertie brought me back,' said Hilda, when greetings were over, 'and I want him to stay to supper, but he won't.'

'I can't, Mamma. I've three business letters to write and young Edward has his Latin prep. to do. We promised Winnie we'd go straight back.'

Hilda looked rather put out, but made no further demur, and Sep watching them thought how well Bertie handled his parents. He was, in truth, the head of the family now, with an air of authority which was not entirely hidden by his gentle and affectionate manner. Edward began to make obediently for the door.

'Can I sit in the front, Uncle Bertie? I wish I could drive! I could if it were allowed, you know. Uncle Bertie says he'll let me have a go in a field one day.'

'You must take care –' began Hilda.

'Don't worry, Grandma. A car's easy. I'm going to fly an aeroplane as soon as I get the chance.'

'Really, Edward!' expostulated Hilda, laughing.

'No, I mean it. I've told Uncle Bertie, haven't I? I'm going into the Air Force, and in the next war I shall be a pilot.'

'Time enough to think of that later,' put in Sep. 'You're only fourteen. You may change your mind.'

'Can I give you a lift?' asked Bertie, turning to Sep.

They made their farewells to Hilda and Bender and went out into the starlit night. An owl was hooting from a nearby garden, and another one answered from the distant common. The scent of a dying bonfire hung in the air. It smelt very wintry, thought Sep, as they drove down the hill to the market square.

Bertie dropped him by St Peter's and drive off. Obeying an impulse, Sep mounted the steps and opened the door. He rarely went inside the church, but was proud of its history and its beauty. It was dimly lit and Sep guessed that the cleaners were somewhere at work. There were sounds of chairs being moved in the vestry at the far end of the church.

Sep sat down in a pew near the door and gazed up at the lofty roof. Tattered flags hung there, relics of the Boer War and earlier wars. He thought of Edward's excitement as he talked of a future war in which he proposed to fly. Would there ever be an end to this misery and wrong thinking? Would the League of Nations really be able to have the last sane word if trouble brewed?

And there certainly was trouble brewing, if the papers were right. Not only between nations, but here on our own doorstep. What would be the result of these desperate hunger marches, some of which Sep had seen himself? It was an affront to human dignity to be without means to live. A man must have work. A man must have hope. What happened if he had neither? Life, thought Sep, chafing his cold fingers, was a succession of problems, and only some of them could be solved by personal effort.

He sighed and rose to his feet. His boots made a loud noise on the tiled floor as he made his way to the door. Across the market place the lights of his home glowed comfortingly. On his left shone the three great windows of young Mr Parker's drawing room above the gaunt black emptiness of the future Howard's Restaurant.

Warmth suddenly flooded Sep's cold frame. A man could only do so much! He had set his hand to this particular plough and he must continue in the furrow which it made. What use was it to try to set the whole world to rights? He must travel his own insignificant path with constancy and courage. It might not lead to the heights of Olympus, but it should afford him interest, exercise, and happiness as he went along. And, Sep felt sure, there would be joy at the end.

As Sep was crossing the market square to his home, Bertie sat at his desk, pen in hand, and a blank sheet of writing paper before him.

His thoughts were centred on Edward who sat at the table, head bent over in inky exercise book. His dark hair shone in the light from the lamp. His eyes, when he looked up, were just as Bertie remembered Leslie's at the same age. He was going to have the good looks of his father and his grandmother – vivacious, dusky, and devastating.

And so he wanted to fly, mused Bertie! There was no reason on earth why he shouldn't. Bertie thought it was an excellent idea and would do all in his power to help him. Flying was going to develop more rapidly than people imagined. With the world shrinking so fast, surely the nations must settle down amicably together! Edward's calm assumption that there would be another war did not fill Bertie with quite the same horror as it had Sep. Bertie could not believe that the world would go to war again. The memory of 1914–18 was too close. Even now, years after its ending, scenes came back to Bertie as he drifted off to sleep at nights, waking him again. It had been a war to end war. Thank God, Edward's flying would be used for more constructive ends!

He pulled the blank paper towards him and began to write the neglected letter.

Chapter Nineteen

SEP LOSES A FRIEND

Christmas came and went. The tree in the market square grew bedraggled, the tinsel in the shop windows tarnished. It was a relief when Twelfth Night came and everything could be tidied away. Down came the brittle holly, the withered mistletoe. Into the rubbish bins went the dusty Christmas cards, the broken baubles, and the turkey bones, and into the cupboards went some unwanted Christmas presents, placed there by the more frugal for future raffles and bazaars.

It grew iron-cold as the New Year broke and little work could be done on the site of the restaurant. Sep did his best to be patient, but it was almost more than he could endure. This was the great year when he would open his new venture. He wanted everything ready by the spring, down to the napkins and the flowers on the tables. From Easter onwards he looked forward to a growing volume of trade. These delays irked Sep sorely.

In the midst of his frustration he heard that Bender was again in hospital with pleurisy. Sep went at once. He was deeply shocked at Bender's appearance. He had not seen him since his visit to Rose Lodge before Christmas. His eyes were sunken, and he moved his head restlessly on the pillow. His hand, as he took Sep's, felt hot and damp. Now there was no vigour in his grip. He could barely speak.

Sep tried to hide his distress, and talked gently of things which he felt might interest the sick man. Bender scarcely seemed to hear him. He began to wheeze alarmingly, and a young nurse hurried towards him and tried to hoist him higher on the pillow.

'Let me,' said Sep, sliding an arm under Bender's shoulders. All his memories of wounded men at Caxley station in wartime flooded back to him.

'You've got a good touch, Sep,' wheezed Bender. 'Got a knack you have. That's better now!'

'That's the spirit!' rallied the young nurse, tucking in the bed-clothes with painful vigour. 'Not dead yet, you know!'

'It's not death I'm afraid of,' responded Bender, with a flash of his old spirit, 'but living on with this dam' pain!'

He put a hand to his side and lay silent for a minute.

'Tell me,' he managed to say it last, 'tell me, Sep, about the shop. The plants are ready in the greenhouse whenever it's fit to put them out in the garden. Hilda'll let you have them. And Sep, the jasmine wants trimming back at that old arbour. Makes a deal of growth every year, that stuff.'

Sep promised to attend to it. Suddenly Bender's eyelids drooped and his head fell back. The nurse hurried forward.

'He's asleep again. I think you'd better leave now, Mr Howard. He's having drugs, you know, to relieve the pain.'

Sep nodded and rose to go. There was something pathetic and defenceless about the sleeping man, a look of the boy that Sep remembered years ago. He stood silent, loth to leave him, loth to turn away.

The nurse touched his arm, and he moved unseeingly towards the door. He knew now, with utter desolation, that he would not look upon Bender's face again.

It was very cold that night. The market square glistened with frost. Icicles hung from the lions' mouths on the old Queen's fountain. The pigeons, roosting on the ledges of the Town Hall, tucked their heads more deeply into their feathers. The stars above were diamond-bright, the air piercingly sharp.

The ward where Bender lay was dim and shadowy. The young night nurse, on duty, sat at the table at the end near the corridor, a pool of light upon her papers. She shivered in the draught and wrapped her cloak more tightly around her.

It was deathly quiet. Only the sound of laboured breathing, and an occasional moan from the red-blanketed beds, broke the stillness. It was the time of night, as the nurse well knew, when life was at its lowest ebb.

She raised her head, suddenly aware of a change in the ward. Someone, somewhere, had ceased breathing. There was a chill in the air, which was not wholly natural.

Quietly she rose and glided swiftly to Bender's bedside. His eyes were closed, his mouth slightly open in a smile which was infinitely young and gentle. The nurse held the warm wrist and put her ear to the quiet breast.

At last, she straightened herself, crossed Bender's arms and covered his face with the sheet.

The day of Bender's funeral was cold and bright. It happened to be market day, and Sep, as he crossed the bustling square, thought how Bender would have liked that last touch.

St Peter's was crowded with mourners, many of them from the stalls outside. Bender had been known and respected, not only in Caxley, but for many miles around. His great figure was as much a part of the market scene as the bronze statue which dominated the place. Bender was going to be sadly missed.

The church looked very lovely. The candles wavered and flick-ered – now tall as golden crocuses, now small and round as buttercups, as the breeze caught them. On the coffin, at the chancel steps, a great cross of bronze chrysanthemums glowed in the candlelight. The family mourners sat, straight-backed and sad-faced. Among them, Sep was surprised to see, was young Edward.

Winnie and Bertie had not wanted the children to be present, feeling that the occasion was too harrowing for them, but Edward had pleaded passionately to be allowed to attend.

'He's my grandfather. I want to be with him till the end,' announced Edward, his mouth stubborn. 'I'm not a child any more. You must let me go.'

Winnie had been about to protest, but Bertie restrained her.

'The boy's right,' be said quietly. 'He's part of the family. Let him take his place.'

And so Edward was the youngest mourner present. Sep and Edna sat towards the back, and Sep couldn't help noticing how old and bent many of the congregation were. It was a shock to realize that he would be seventy in a few years' time and that these people were his and Bender's contemporaries. Did he too look so old, Sep wondered? He did not feel any older than he had when he had first taken his lovely Edna to live in the market square, and together they had worked so hard to build up the business.

And that would not have been possible, thought Sep, his eyes on the coffin, if it had not been for Bender's timely help. He had a debt to him which he could never repay – and it was not only a material debt. His whole life had been inextricably bound up with that of the dead man. Bender's influence upon him had been immeasurable. To say that he would miss him was only stating a tenth of the effect which Bender's passing meant to him.

What was it, Sep mused in the shadowy church, that created the bond between them? They had shared schooldays, manhood, and all the joys, troubles, and setbacks of war and peace. Together they had played their parts in the life of Caxley. The market square had been their stage – the kaleidoscopic background to tragedy and farce. Their families had intermarried, their grandchildren were shared.

But that was not all.

Sep felt for Bender – and always had – a variety of emotions: fear, affection, pity, hero-worship, and, at times, distaste for his ebullience and ruthlessness. Perhaps he could best sum up these mingled feelings as awareness. Whatever happened to Bender affected Sep. Whatever had happened to Sep was measured for him by Bender's possible reaction to it. He could never remember a time when he had been entirely independent of the other man. Bender mattered. What Bender thought of Sep mattered, and reason, principles, codes of conduct – even religion itself – could not entirely guide Sep's actions while Bender lived.

A vital part of Sep had died too when Bender died. From now on the stuff of Sep's life would be woven in more muted hues. The brightest, the strongest, and the most vivid thread in the fabric would be missing.

That afternoon Sep made his way alone to the old garden behind the restaurant. It was sadly neglected. The workmen had trodden down the borders, the lawn was bare and muddy, the shrubs splashed with lime and paint where the men had plied their brushes carelessly.

Sep stood in silence, taking stock. With care, before long, it should look as it did in Bender's day. The grey spiky foliage of pinks still lined the edge of the path. The lilac bush already showed buds as large and green as peas. Dead seed-pods of irises and lupins made rattling spires above the low growing pansies and periwinkles at their feet. It should all be as it was, vowed Sep, silently surveying the scene of decay.

He made his way to the ancient arbour which was covered with jasmine. It had been made years earlier for Bender's mother to sit in and enjoy the sunshine. Now it was damp and mouldering. Sep sat down on the rickety bench. Bright spots of coral fungus decorated the woodwork, and splashes of bird droppings made white arabesques on the floor. An untidy nest spilt grass and moss from the rustic work at the corners of the doorway. Broken snails' shells surrounding a large flint by the entrance showed where the thrushes used their anvil. The brick floor was slimy and interlaced with vivid lines of green moss and the silver trails of slugs.

It was very tranquil. The river whispered nearby and the overgrown jasmine rustled gently in the little breeze from the water. Tomorrow, thought Sep, he would bring his shears and trim back the waving fronds as Bender had directed.

He rose to go, and then caught sight of something white half-hidden in the shadows under the seat. He bent down to retrieve it and carried it into the dying light of the winter afternoon.

It was a toy boat. It must belong to one of the Parker children, he supposed, but it was exactly like the boat he had once bought for Leslie long ago. Money had been short, he remembered, but the boy had looked at it with such longing in his dark eyes, that Sep had gone into the ship and paid a shilling for the little yacht. How it brought it all back!

Sep stroked the rusty hull, and straightened the crumpled sail. How many generations had sailed their boats on the Cax's placid surface? And how many more would do so in the future?

With the first flush of warmth that he had felt that day, Sep remembered Edward. One day his children – Sep's great-grand-children – would carry their boats across this now deserted garden and set them hopefully upon the water.

Smiling now, Sep made his way from the peace of the riverside to the noise and confusion of the emerging restaurant. He paused to set the little yacht on the foot of the stairs leading to Bender's old home, where its young owner would find it – safely in harbour.

The short afternoon was rapidly merging into twilight. The stall-holders were beginning to pack up now. The children from the marsh were already skimming round the stalls, like hungry swifts, and screaming with much the same shrill excitement. This was the time when the stallholders gave away the leavings, when a battered cabbage or a brown banana or two were tossed to eager hands. Many a prudent Caxley housewife was there too, glad to get a joint or some home-made cheese or butter at half price.

The dust vans were already beginning to collect the litter. The dustmen's brooms, a yard wide, pushed peelings, straw and paper before them. Colour from all over the world was collected and tossed into the waiting vans – squashed oranges from Spain, bruised scarlet tomatoes from Jersey, yellow banana skins from Jamaica, the vibrant purplish-pink tissue paper which had swathed the Italian grapes – all were mingled with the gentler colours of the straw, the walnut shells and the marbled cabbage leaves from the Caxley countryside.

Already the sun had sunk behind St Peter's, where earlier in the day Sep had watched part of his life put quietly away. The air was beginning to grow chilly, and the market people redoubled their efforts and their clamour to get their work finished before nightfall.

Sep turned at his doorway to watch them. For them, it was the end of just another market day. For him, it was the end of an era.

He let his eyes roam over the darkening scene. In an hour's time the market folk would have departed – folk as colourful and ephemeral as summer butterflies.

But the market square would remain, solid and enduring, a place of flint and brick, iron and cobbles, shabby and familiar, ugly and beloved. There was no other place quite like it. Caxley life might pulse throughout the network of streets and alleys on each side of the slow-running Cax, but here, in the market square, was the heart of the town.

Here sprang the spirit, here the hope. Sep looked across at the dark shell of Bender's old shop, awaiting its future life, and was comforted.

Chapter Twenty

HOPES REALIZED

In the weeks that followed, Sep's spirits rose. An unusually mild spell gave the workmen a chance to make progress unhindered by frost. If things continued at this pace, he would certainly open on time.

Whenever he could spare a few moments from his own shop, Sep was at the new premises watching with a keen eye all that was being done. He took a particular interest in the remaking of the garden. He knew little about gardening. He had never owned one, and had been too busy to acquire much knowledge of plants and flowers, but Bertie proved to have the North flair for gardening, and he and Edward offered to help in the work.

Bertie's own garden was a constant joy to him. He was very proud of his property and liked to do jobs himself. Since his father's death Winnie was often at Rose Lodge with the children, and Bertie was left undisturbed to enjoy his gardening and his attempts at carpentering and decorating.

Bertie had tried to persuade his mother to make her home with him, but she disliked the idea of becoming dependent upon the next generation. She had always felt a fierce pride in possessions, and would not consider parting with any of the things which made Rose Lodge so dear to her.

'It would break my heart to have to sell, Bertie, and that's what I'd have to do. There simply wouldn't be room for everything, and every single piece means so much to me. That desk of your father's, for instance – and that ugly old flat-iron to hold down his papers! Why, I can't throw that away! And that chair – I used to sit on it to change your nappies, dear. Just the right height for me. No, it can't be done! I shall stop here until I'm too old and doddery to cope, and you must all come and see me as often as you can.'

And so it had been settled. After the first shock of grief had gone, Hilda set about running the house and her many charitable activities with all her old zest and efficiency. She went out and about to friends and relations in Caxley, and delighted in her grandchildren. But she was thankful to settle by her own fireside at Rose Lodge each evening, with all the dear souvenirs of a happy life around her.

Bertie was glad to see her so independent and was relieved too that she need not face the upheaval of another move. His own house was pretty full and he would have had to sacrifice his sitting room to accommodate his mother if she had wanted to come. This he was prepared to do willingly. Winnie had suggested that she should go and live with Hilda, so that she would not be alone, but it was done half-heartedly for she did not want to leave Bertie, and the children were happy in the house. It seemed best to let things go on as they were, and so far everything had gone very smoothly.

Winnie heard from Kathy occasionally. They usually wrote when one of the children had a birthday, and then exchanged news of Caxley and Edinburgh. Kathy had been left comfortably off, and her parents-in-law were kind and understanding. She was beginning to meet people again. Her visit to Caxley was planned to coincide with the opening of Sep's restaurant in April, and she told Winnie that she hoped to stay with her parents for several weeks.

Winnie never suspected the turmoil which went on behind her brother's calm countenance when she read these letters to him. Kathy was never far from Bertie's thoughts. Henry's parents, whom he had never met, he viewed with mixed feelings – gratitude for their care of Kathy and alarm at their solicitude for her future. It sometimes seemed to Bertie that they were busy looking for another handsome Scot for his Kathy. Would she never return? Should he take the plunge and go north to see her? Natural shyness restrained him. Her loss was so recent. She must be given time to find herself again. He must await her coming to Caxley with all the patience he could muster, and speak to her then. He had nothing to lose: everything – everything in the world to gain! Bertie watched the calendar as avidly as a homesick schoolboy.

She came soon after Easter, three days before the party to celebrate the opening of Howard's restaurant. Winnie and Bertie were invited to supper the day after her arrival, and as they sat at the great table, waiting for Sep to carve a handsome round of cold beef, Bertie remembered all the other meals he had eaten in this room and with this family. Robert sat now where Jim used to sit. Mary was beside him. Kathy sat opposite, lovelier than ever, but thinner than he remembered. Life had dealt both of them some pretty shrewd knocks, thought Bertie, and they were both a good deal older and more battered than when he had sat there bringing shame upon the Norths by starting to eat his roll before Sep had said grace. Bertie smiled now at the recollection – but how he had smarted then!

Kathy's children were asleep in her old bedroom, but Winnie insisted on creeping up to see them and Bertie went with her. The boy was a Howard, dark and handsome. The baby already displayed a few wisps of auburn hair and the fresh complexion of her Scottish father.

'What do you think of 'em?' asked Sep proudly, when they returned. 'I'm all for having 'em at the party, but Kathy won't hear of it. Everyone else in the family will be there. Seems a pity to me!'

Excitement was in the air. The party was to take place on Saturday evening. The restaurant opened on Monday. All those connected with the building and creation of the new premises were invited. Old Caxley friends and the whole of the Howard family would be present. This grand affair was to start at seven o'clock, and the party would sit down to a superb dinner of Sep's devising at seven thirty.

'Now, do keep an eye on the time, Edward,' begged Winnie at lunch time. He was going fishing with Tim Parker, and when thus engaged the hours flew by unnoticed. 'You must be back by six at the latest to get cleaned up.'

Edward nodded absentmindedly. Uncle Bertie had promised to

inquire about a rod in Petter's shop window. Had he done it, asked the boy?

'Sorry, Edward. it slipped my mind. I have to go out this afternoon. I'll call in then. If he's asking a reasonable price you can come in with me later on and see if it suits you.'

Edward's face lit up. The rod he used now had once been Bender's and was sadly the worse for wear. A new one was the height of Edward's ambition. He could scarcely wait to tell Tim the good news.

As Winnie had feared, it was half past six before the boy returned on his bicycle, drenched, muddy, but supremely happy. He was pushed swiftly into the bathroom and exhorted to hurry. Winnie fluttered back and forth between her own room and Joan's, arranging curls, fastening necklaces, and smoothing stockings.

At last the party set off, Edward still damp from his bath, his hair as sleek as a seal's. He gazed in admiration at his uncle's neat figure.

'You've got a new suit!'

'Do you like it?'

'Very much. It makes you look quite young, Uncle Bertie.'

'Thank you, Edward. How do I usually look?'

'Well, not exactly old, but –'

'Middle-aged?'

'That's it! But not in that suit. I suppose it's because it's more up-to-date than your others.'

And with this modified praise, Bertie had to be content.

The restaurant was ablaze with lights, although the evening was bright with sunshine. Sep had chosen white and gold for the interior of his new premises, and vases of daffodils added to the freshness. The tables had been put together to form two long ones down each side of the room with another across the end. The new table linen glistened like a fresh fall of snow, the glass winked like diamonds, the silver reflected the gay colours of the women's frocks and the golden lamps on the tables.

Through the french windows could be seen the green sunlit lawn running down to the Cax. More daffodils nodded here, and a row of scarlet tulips stood erect like guardsmen. The Cax caught the rays of the sun, flashing and sparkling as it wound its way eastward under Bender's rustic bridge. There was no doubt about it, Sep's dream had come true, and this evening he rejoiced in its fulfilment.

The meal was as sumptuous as one might guess with Sep as host, and although he himself drank only lemonade, he saw that his guests were served generously with wine. One of the waiters poured out some sparkling white wine for Edward, unnoticed by his elders, and the boy drank it discreetly. It looked remarkably like Joan's fizzy lemonade across the table, he noticed with considerable complacency, but tasted very much better. This was the life!

He caught sight of his Uncle Bertie at the other end of the table and remembered his fishing rod. He was too far away to call to – he must catch him later. Meanwhile it was enough to sip his wine, and see if he could find room for cheese and biscuits after all the courses he had managed already. He eyed the pyramids of fruit ranged down the tables for dessert. Somehow he doubted if he would have room for fruit as well . . .

Now his grandfather was standing up to make a speech – and heavens! – how loudly the people were clapping and cheering him! And how pretty grandma Howard looked tonight in her pink silk frock – as pretty as she looked in the picture Dan Crockford had painted long before Edward was born. Edward leant back in his chair and let the room revolve gently round him, too dizzy and happy to listen to speeches, too bemused to see anyone in focus.

When, finally, the guests moved from the tables and coffee was being served, Edward was obliged to look for the lavatory. His head throbbed so violently that he could not be bothered to seek out the luxurious accommodation provided for the restaurant, but slipped up the familiar stairs to the Parkers' bathroom. It was blissfully cool there after the heat and cigar smoke below. Edward splashed his burning face with cold water and began to feel better.

He leant his forehead against the cold window panes and gazed at the market place below. Queen Victoria was bathed in a rosy glow from the setting sun. Her bronze features gleamed as though she had been rubbed with butter. A car or two went by, and a girl on a piebald pony. A man with a violin case hurried into the Corn Exchange. How peaceful it was, thought Edward!

Below him he could hear the hum of the party. He must go back again before he was missed . . . back into that strange noisy grown-up world where men smoked and drank wine and clapped his pale little grandfather. It was good to have escaped for a few minutes, to have found a brief refuge in the old familiar quietness above.

But it was good, too, to go back, to join his family, to be one of the Howards and one of the Norths too, to be doubly a man of Caxley. He belonged both upstairs and down in this ancient building.

Swaggering slightly, Edward descended the stairs.

An hour or so later, as the guests were beginning to depart, Edward remembered his fishing rod and looked for his Uncle Bertie.

'He went into the garden,' said his mother. But Edward could not find him there.

'Maybe be stepped into the market place,' suggested Grandma North. There was no sign of him there either.

'Have a piece of crystallized ginger,' advised his sister Joan. 'You can see Uncle Bertie any day. You won't see this gorgeous stuff tomorrow.' Edward shelved the problem of his Uncle Bertie's disappearance and joined his sister at the sweet dish.

At last only a few of the family were left. It was beginning to get dark. The evening star had slid up from the Cax and hung like a jewel on the dusky horizon.

'Cut along home, my boy,' said his grandfather's voice. 'To our place, I mean. Your mother's just gone across. I'll be there in a few minutes.'

Obediently, he set off across the darkening square. A child was filling one of the iron cups with water, and Edward realized how thirsty he was himself. He made his way to the next lion, and pressed the cold button in its head. Out gushed the water from the lion's mouth, giving him the same joy which it had always done.

He let it play over his sticky fingers and hot wrists before filling the cup. He tilted it against his parched mouth and enjoyed the feeling of the drops spilling down his chin. Wine was all right to boast about, but water was the real stuff to drink!

At that moment he heard his grandfather approach and turned to greet him. At the same time he saw Uncle Bertie and Aunt Kathy emerge from the doorway of Howard's Restaurant. How young Uncle Bertie looked tonight! It must be the suit. And how happy! That must be the wine, surmised Edward, unusually sophisticated.

He suddenly remembered his fishing rod.

'Uncle Bertie!' be shouted towards the couple. 'What about my fishing rod? *Uncle Bertie? Uncle Bertie!*'

Sep's hand came down upon his shoulder.

'He doesn't hear me!' protested Edward, trying to break free.

'No, he doesn't,' agreed Sep equably.

The boy stopped struggling and watched the pair making their way towards the river. There was something in their faces that made him aware of great happenings. This was not the time to ask about his fishing rod, it seemed.

He gave a great tired sigh. It had been a long day.

Sep took his wet hand as he had done when he was a little boy. They turned to cross the market square together.

'There's always tomorrow, Edward,' Sep said consolingly. 'Always tomorrow . . .'

THE HOWARDS OF CAXLEY

To Pat and John with love

CONTENTS

Part One

1939–1945

Chapter One

HAPPY INDEPENDENCE

It was six o'clock on a fine May morning.

The market square was deserted. Long shadows lay across the cobblestones, reaching almost to the steps of St Peter's church. Pink sunlight trembled across its old grey stone, gilding the splendid spire and warming the hoary saints in their niches. A thin black cat, in a sheltered angle of the porch, washed one upthrust leg, its body as round and curved as an elegant shell. Not even the pigeons disturbed its solitude, for they still slept, roosting in scores on the ledges of the Corn Exchange and the Victorian Town Hall.

A hundred yards away, the river Cax, swollen with spring rains, swept in a shining arc through the buttercup fields. The haze of early hours lay over all the countryside which surrounded the little market town, veiling the motionless clumps of elm trees in the fields and the cottages still sleeping among their dewy gardens.

The minute hand of St Peter's clock began its slow downhill journey from the gilded twelve, and Edward Howard, pyjama-clad at his bedroom window near by, watched it with mounting exhilaration. This was the life! How wonderful to be alive on such a morning, to be twenty-one and – best of all – to have a place of one's own!

He flung up the window and leaned out, snuffing the morning air like a young puppy. The sun touched his face with gentle warmth. It was going to be a real scorcher, he thought to himself happily. He laughed aloud and the thin cat, arrested in the midst of its toilet, gazed up at him, a tongue as pink as a rose petal still protruding from its mouth.

'Good morning!' called Edward civilly to the only other waking inhabitant of the market square. The cat stared at him disdainfully, shrugged, and then continued with its washing.

And Edward, turning towards the bathroom, followed its good example.

Lying in the warm water, he ran an appraising eye round the bathroom and mused upon his good fortune. At this time last year he had been living at Rose Lodge, a mile away on the hill south of Caxley, with his mother and grandmother North. It had been his home for seven or eight years, and he had, he supposed, been reasonably happy there in the company of the two women. But these last few months of bachelor independence made him realize the restrictions which he had suffered earlier. Now there was no one to question his comings and goings. If he cared to stay out until two in the morning, there was no waiting tray, complete with hot chocolate in a vacuum flask, to reproach him, No parental note reminded him to bolt the door and switch off the landing light. It wasn't that he didn't love them, poor dear old things, thought Edward indulgently as he added more hot water to his bath, but simply that he had outgrown them.

'God bless Grandpa Howard!' said Edward aloud, as he sank back again.

It was good to be living in Caxley market square where his grandparents on both sides had built up their businesses. Here, in this house, of which he was now the proud owner, Bender North and his wife Hilda had lived for many years over their ironmongery shop. Edward could see his grandfather clearly now, in his mind's eye, a vast figure in a brown coat-overall striding among the coal scuttles and patty pans, the spades and milking pails, which jostled together beneath the pairs of hob-nailed boots and hurricane lamps that swung from the ceiling above him. Soon afterwards, Bender and his wife had moved to Rose Lodge – a far more genteel address to Hilda's mind – and the glories of the great drawing room over the shop were no more. But Winnie, Edward's mother, and his Uncle Bertie North had described the red plush furniture, the plethora of ornaments and the floral arrangements of dried grasses and sea-lavender, with such vivid detail, that he felt quite familiar with the Edwardian splendour which had now vanished.

He knew, equally well, the sad story of the decline of Bender's business. It had been bought by a larger firm in the town and, later still, his grandfather Septimus Howard had taken it over. Sep still lived in the market square above his thriving bakery. The whole of the ground floor at North's he had transformed into a restaurant, almost ten years ago. It was, according to Caxley gossip, 'an absolute gold-mine', but there were few who grudged Sep Howard his success. Hardworking, modest, a pillar of the local chapel, and a councillor, the little baker's worth was appreciated by his fellow townsmen.

The business was to go to his son Robert, already a vigorous partner, when Sep could carry on no longer. Sep was now, in the early summer of 1939, a spry seventy-three, and there was no sign of his relinquishing his hold on family affairs. The acquisition of Bender's old home and the growth of the restaurant had given Sep an added interest in life. It was typical of his generosity, said his neighbours, that he had given Edward the house which had been Bender's when the boy attained the age of twenty-one. The restaurant, on the ground floor, would be Robert's in time, and the more shrewd of Caxley's citizens wondered why Sep could not foresee that there might be friction between Edward and his young uncle in the years to come.

But on this bright May morning all was well in Edward's world. It had needed courage to tell his two women-folk that he proposed to set up his own establishment, and even now, when he looked back on the scene at Rose Lodge, Edward winced.

15 The Market Square, still generally known in Caxley as 'North's', had fallen empty at Michaelmas 1938. The Parker family, who had been tenants for several years, had prospered, and bought a house in the village of Beech Green a few miles away. The property had become Edward's that same year on his twenty-first birthday. It was the most splendid present imaginable, for the boy had loved the house as long as he could remember. The idea of living there one day had been with him for many years, a secret joyous hope which he fully intended to turn into reality.

'It's a big responsibility for a young man in your position,' Grandma North quavered, when the old home was first made over to him. 'I know your Grandpa Howard has arranged for a sum of money to keep the place in repair, but what happens when he's gone? You may have a wife and family to keep by then.'

'We'll all live there,' cried Edward cheerfully, 'and you shall come and tell us how badly we keep it, compared with your days.'

'Well, you may laugh about it now, my boy,' said the old lady, a little querulously, 'but I know what a big place that is to keep going. The stairs alone are a morning's work, and no one ever managed to keep that back attic free from damp. Your Grandpa Howard's never lived there as I have. He's no notion of what it means in upkeep.'

Hilda North had never liked Septimus Howard. She had watched him rise as her own husband had steadily declined. Old age did not mellow her feelings towards this neighbour of a lifetime, and the marriage of her darling son Bertie to Kathy Howard and the earlier marriage of her daughter Winnie to Leslie, Edward's ne'er-do-well father, did nothing to allay the acrimony which she felt towards the Howard family.

'Thank God,' she said often to Edward, 'that you take after the North side of the family, despite your name. Your dear mother's been both father and mother to you. Really, I sometimes think it was a blessing your father left her. She's better without him.'

Edward was wise enough to keep a silent tongue when the old lady ran on in this vein. He knew quite well that there was a strong streak of the Howards in his make-up. He hoped, in all humility, that he had something of Sep Howard's strength of character. He was beginning to guess, with some astonishment, that he might possess some of his erring father's attraction for the opposite sex.

He often wondered about his father. It was impossible to get a clear picture of him from either side of the family, and his own memories were hazy. Leslie Howard had decamped with an earlier love when Edward was four and the second child, Joan, only a few months old. As far as was known, he flourished, as the wicked so often do, in a Devonshire town. He had never been seen in Caxley again.

'Too ashamed, let's hope!' said Edward's grandmother North tartly, but Edward sometimes wondered. What was the result of that flight from the family? He had never heard his father's side of the affair. It was as tantalizing as a tale half-read. Would he ever know the end of the story?

Edward had dropped the bombshell on a mellow September evening, a week or two before Michaelmas Day, when the Parkers were to vacate his newly acquired property. The two women were sitting in the evening sunshine admiring the brave show of scarlet dahlias. Around them, the gnats hummed. Above them, on the telephone wires, were ranged two or three dozen swallows like notes on staves of music. Soon they would be off to find stronger sunshine.

It was too bad to shatter such tranquillity, thought Edward, pacing restlessly about the garden, but it had to be done. He spoke as gently as his taut nerves allowed.

'Mother! Grandma!' He stopped before the two placid figures. Sun-steeped, vague and sleepy, they gazed at him with mild expectancy. Edward's heart smote him, but he took the plunge.

'Don't let this be too much of a shock, but I'm thinking about living in the market square myself when the Parkers leave.'

His mother's pretty mouth dropped open. His grandmother did not appear to have heard him. He raised his voice slightly.

'At the old house, Grandma dear. I want to move in at Michaelmas.'

'I heard you,' said the old lady shortly.

'But why, Edward? Why?' quavered his mother. 'Aren't you happy here?'

To Edward's alarm he saw tears welling in his mother's blue eyes. Just as he thought, there was going to be the devil of a scene. No help for it then, but to soldier on. He sat down on the iron arm of the curly garden seat upon which the two were reclining, and put a reassuring arm about his mother's shoulders.

'Of course I'm happy here –' he began.

'Then say no more,' broke in his mother swiftly. 'What should we do without a man in the house? We're so nicely settled, Edward, don't go upsetting things.'

'What's put this in your head?' queried his grandmother. 'Getting married, are you?'

'You know I'm not,' muttered Edward, rising from his perch and resuming his prowlings. 'It's simply that the house is now mine, it's empty, and I want to live there.'

'But it will be far too big for you alone, Edward,' protested his mother. 'And far too expensive.'

'I've worked it all out and I can manage quite well. I don't intend to use all the house, simply the top floor. The rest can be let, and bring me in a regular income.'

'Well, I must say,' cried his mother reproachfully, 'you seem to have been planning this move for some time! I can't tell you what a shock it is! I'd no idea you felt like this about things. What about poor Grandma? How do you think she is going to like it when there are only women left alone to cope with everything here?'

Winnie produced a handkerchief and mopped her eyes. Her mother, made of sterner stuff, sniffed militantly and Edward prepared to hear the old lady's vituperation in support of her daughter. What a hornet's nest he had disturbed, to be sure! But a surprise was in store.

'Let him go!' snapped old Mrs North testily. 'If he wants to go and ruin himself in that damp old shop by the river, then let him, silly young fool! I've lived alone before, and I won't be beholden to my grandchildren. He doesn't know when he's well off. Let him try managing that great place for a bit! He'll soon learn. And for pity's sake, Winnie, stop snivelling. Anyone'd think he was off to Australia the way you're carrying on!'

It had been too much to expect an ally at Rose Lodge, but the old lady's impatient dismissal of the affair greatly helped Edward. After a few uncomfortable days, whilst Edward tried to avoid his mother's martyred gaze and the sound of intermittent argument about the subject between the two women, he managed to make them see that he was adamant in his decision.

'Dash it all, I'm less than a mile away. I shall be in and out of Rose Lodge until you'll probably get fed up with me. I can do any odd jobs, and Tom comes twice a week for the garden. He's promised me to keep an eye on things. And you'll see Joan as regularly as you always do.'

Joan, Edward's sister, now eighteen, was in London, training to teach young children. Her vacations were lengthy and just occasionally she managed to get home on a Sunday during term-time. Edward had written to her telling of his plans and had received enthusiastic support. There was an unusually strong bond of affection between the brother and sister, forged in part by the absence of a father. Certainly, during the stormy period which preceded Edward's move, he was doubly grateful for Joan's encouragement.

As soon as the Parkers had gone to their new home, Edward put his plans into action. He decided to make the attic floor into his own domain, and the four rooms became a bedroom and sitting-room, both overlooking the market square and facing south, and a kitchen and bathroom at the back. He had papered and painted the rooms himself, and although the paper was askew in places and a suspicion of rust was already becoming apparent on the bathroom pipes, the whole effect was fresh and light.

Surveying his handiwork from the bath Edward felt a glow of pride. This was all his own. At times he could scarcely believe his good luck. The spacious rooms below were already occupied by a young bank clerk who had been at Caxley Grammar school with Edward some years before. He and his wife seemed careful tenants, likely to remain there for some time. Their first child was due in the autumn.

The future looked pretty bright, decided Edward, reviewing the situation. He enjoyed his work as an agricultural engineer at the county town some fifteen miles away, and promotion seemed likely before long. The family appeared to have come round completely to the idea of his living apart and no one could possibly realise how exciting he found his newly-won independence.

And then there was his flying. He had joined the R.A.F.V.R. when he was eighteen and had first flown solo on a bright spring day over two years ago. It was the culmination of an ambition which had grown steadily in fervour since he was ten. Now most weekends were spent at the aerodrome west of Caxley and his yearly holiday was earmarked for annual training. He liked the men he met there, their cheerful company and their predictable jokes, but better still he liked the machines with their fascinatingly complicated engines and their breathtakingly flimsy superstructure.

In a few hours he would be in the air again, he thought joyfully, looking down on the patchwork of brown and green fields far below. For this was one of the blessed Sundays when he set off early in his two-seater Morris in his carefully casual new sports jacket and a silk scarf knotted about his neck in place of the workaday tie.

He stood up in the bath and began to towel himself vigorously. A pigeon cooed on the gutter above the steamy window. Edward could see the curve of its grey breast against the sky.

'Two rashers and two eggs,' called Edward to the bird, above the gurgle of the bath water swirling down the waste pipe, 'and then I'm off!'

A thought struck him. The car's spare tyre was at Uncle Bertie's garage. He must remember to pick it up on his way. The possibility of a puncture somewhere on Salisbury Plain, even on a fine May morning such as this, was not to be borne, especially on a day dedicated to flying.

He shrugged himself into his shabby camel-hair dressing-gown and went, whistling, in search of the frying pan.

Chapter Two

THE SHADOW OF WAR

Edward's Uncle Bertie was his mother's brother and now the head of the North family. He lived in a four-square red-brick house some yards from the busy High Street of Caxley where his motor business flourished.

One approached Bertie's house by way of a narrow lane. It started as a paved alley between two fine old Georgian buildings which fronted the pavements, but gradually widened into a grav-elled track which led eventually to the towpath by the river Cax. Edward always enjoyed the sudden change from the noise of the street as he turned into this quiet backwater.

As he guessed, Bertie was already at work in the garden. Oil can in hand, he was bending over the mower when his nephew arrived. He straightened up and limped purposefully towards him, waving the oil can cheerfully. For a man who had lost one foot in the war, thought Edward, he moved with remarkable agility.

'You want your spare wheel,' said Bertie. 'I'll give you the garage key and you can help yourself.'

They moved towards the house, but Bertie checked suddenly to point out a thriving rose which was growing against the wall.

'Look at that, my boy! I planted it when your Aunt Kathy and I married. Just look at the growth it's made in these few years!'

Edward looked obediently, but he was already impatient to be off to his flying. Catching sight of the expression on his handsome nephew's dark young face, Bertie threw back his head and laughed.

'You're no gardener, Edward! I forgot. Too bad to hold you up. Come and say "Hello" to the family before you set off.'

His Aunt Kathy was beating eggs in a big yellow basin. Her dark hair was tucked into a band round her head so that she looked as if she were wearing a coronet. How pretty she was, thought Edward, as slim and brown as a gipsy! No wonder Uncle Bertie had waited patiently for her all those years. He remembered Grandma North's tart comments to his mother on the marriage.

'I should've thought Bertie would have had more sense than to marry into the Howard family. Look what it brought you – nothing but unhappiness! And a widow too. Those two children will never take to a stepfather – even one as doting as dear Bertie. I can see nothing but misery ahead for that poor boy!'

' "That poor boy" is nearly forty,' his mother had replied with considerable vigour, 'and he's loved her all his life. Long faces and sharp tongues won't harm that marriage, you'll see.'

And all Caxley had seen. Bertie and Kathy, with her son and daughter by her first husband, were living proof of mature happiness, and when a son was born a year or so later, the little town rejoiced with them. Even Grandma North agreed grudgingly that it was all running along extraordinarily smoothly and put it down entirely to Bertie's exceptionally sweet North disposition.

'Where are the children?' asked Edward.

'Fishing,' replied Kathy, smiling. 'Unless you mean Andrew. He's asleep, I hope. He woke us at four this morning with train noises – shunting mostly. It makes an awful din.'

'That boy wants to look forward, not backwards,' observed Edward. 'He wants to get his mind on aeroplanes.'

'I think one air fanatic in the family is enough,' commented Bertie, handing over the key to the garage. 'Off you go. Have a good day.'

And Edward departed on the first stage of his journey westward.

'It would never surprise me,' said Bertie to his wife, when Edward had gone, 'to hear that Edward had decided to join the R.A.F. His heart's in aeroplanes, not tractors and binders.'

'But what about our business?' queried Kathy. 'I thought you'd planned for him to become a partner?'

'I shan't press the boy. We've two of our own to follow on if they want to.'

'But *flying*,' protested Kathy, sifting flour energetically into the beaten eggs. 'It's so dangerous, Bertie. Edward might be killed!'

'He might indeed,' observed Bertie soberly. And thousands more like him, he thought privately. He watched his pretty wife at her work, and thought, not for the first time, how much there was which he could not discuss with her. Did she ever, for one fleeting moment, face the fact that war was looming closer and closer? This uneasy peace which Chamberlain had procured at Munich could not last long. There was menace on every side. It must be met soon. Bertie knew in his bones that it was inevitable.

'What a long face!' laughed Kathy, suddenly looking up from her cooking. 'You look as though you'd lost a penny and found a halfpenny.'

She crossed the kitchen towards the oven, shooing him out of the way as if he were one of the children.

'It's time this sponge was in,' she cried. 'Don't forget Mum and Dad are coming to tea this afternoon. You'd better get on in the garden while the sun's out.'

She paused briefly by the window to gaze at the shining morning.

'Isn't it lovely, Bertie? When it's like this I can't believe it will ever be any different – just sunshine all the time. Do you feel that way too, Bertie?'

'I don't think I'm quite such an incurable optimist,' answered Bertie, lightly. 'More's the pity maybe.'

He made his way back to the mower, his thoughts still with him. The grass was still too wet to cut, he decided. He would take a stroll along the towpath and watch the river flowing gently eastward beneath the cloudless sky. There was something very comforting about flowing water when one's spirits were troubled.

He turned left outside his garden gate, his back to the town, and limped steadily towards the tunnel of green shade made by a dozen or so massive chestnut trees, now lit with hundreds of flower-candles, which lined the banks some quarter of a mile away. The sunshine was warm upon his back, and broke into a thousand fragments upon the surface of the running water, dazzling to the eye. Just before the dark cavern formed by the chestnut trees, the river was shallow, split by a long narrow island, the haven of moorhen and coot.

Here Bertie paused to rest his leg and to enjoy the sparkle of the fretted water and the rustling of the willow leaves on the islet. The shallows here were spangled with the white flowers of duckweed, their starry fragility all the more evident by contrast with a black dabchick who searched busily for food among them, undisturbed by Bertie's presence.

The mud at the side of the water glistened like brown satin and gave forth that peculiarly poignant river-smell which is never forgotten. A bee flew close to Bertie's ear and plopped down on the mud, edging its way to the brink of the water to drink. A water-vole, sunning itself nearby, took to the stream, and making for the safety of the island left an echelon of ripples behind its small furry head.

The change in temperature beneath the great chestnut trees was amazing. Here the air struck cold upon Bertie's damp forehead. The path was dark, the stones treacherously slimy and green with moss. There was something dark and secret about this part of the Cax. No wonder that the children loved to explore its banks at this spot! It was the perfect setting for adventure. To look back through the tunnel to the bright world which he had just traversed was an eerie experience. There it was all light, gaiety and warmth – a Kathy's world, he thought suddenly – where no terrors were permitted.

But here there was chill in the air, foreboding, and a sense of doom. He put a hand upon the rough bark of a massive trunk beside him and shuddered at its implacable coldness. Was this his world, at the moment, hostile, menacing, full of unaccountable fears?

He was getting fanciful, he told himself, retracing his steps. It was good to get back into the sunshine, among the darting birds and the shimmering insects which played above the kindly Cax. He would put his morbid thoughts behind him and return to the pleasures of the moment. There was the lawn to be cut and the dead daffodils to be tied up. He quickened his pace, advancing into the sunshine.

In the market square the bells of St Peter's called the citizens of Caxley to Matins. Under the approving eyes of the bronze Queen Victoria whose statue dominated the market place, a trickle of men, women and children made their way from the dazzling heat into the cool nave of the old church. The children looked back reluctantly as they mounted the steps. A whole hour of inaction, clad in white socks, tight Sunday clothes, and only the hat elastic wearing a pink groove under one's chin to provide entertainment and furtive nourishment, loomed ahead. What a wicked waste of fresh air and sunshine!

Septimus Howard and his wife Edna crossed the square from his bakery as the bells clamoured above them, but they were making their way to the chapel in the High Street where Sep and his forebears had worshipped regularly for many years.

Automatically, he glanced across at Howard's Restaurant which occupied the entire ground floor beneath Edward's abode. The linen blinds were pulled down, the CLOSED card hung neatly in the door. His son Robert had done his work properly and left all ship-shape for the weekend. It was to be hoped, thought Sep, that he would be in chapel this morning. He was far too lax, in Sep's opinion, in his chapel-going. It set a poor example to the work people.

Edward's presence he could not hope to expect, for he and his sister Joan were church-goers, taking after the North side of the family. Not that they made many attendances, as Sep was well aware. He sympathized with Edward's passion for flying, but would have liked to see it indulged after he had done his duty to his Maker.

The congregation was sparse. No doubt many were gardening or had taken advantage of the warmth to drive with their families for a day at the sea. It was understandable, Sep mused, but indicative of the general slackening of discipline. Or was it perhaps an unconscious desire to snatch at happiness while it was still there?

After the grim aftermath of the war, and the grimmer times of the early thirties, the present conditions seemed sweet. Who could blame people for living for the present?

Beside him Edna stirred on the hard seat. Her dark hair, scarcely touched with grey, despite her seventy years, curled against her cheek beneath a yellow straw hat nodding with silk roses and a golden haze of veiling. To Sep's eye it was not really suitable headgear for the Sabbath, but it was impossible to curb Edna's exuberance when it came to clothes, and he readily admitted that it set off her undimmed beauty. He never ceased to wonder at the good fortune which had brought into his own quiet life this gay creature, whose presence gave him such comfort.

Now the minister was praying for peace in their time. Sep, remembering with infinite sadness the loss of his first-born Jim in the last war, prayed with fervent sincerity. What would happen to the Howards if war came again, as he feared it must? Robert, in his thirties, would go. Edward, no doubt, would be called up at once to the Royal Air Force. Leslie, his absent son whom he had not seen since he left Caxley and his wife Winnie years earlier, would be too old to be needed.

And he himself, at seventy-three? Thank God, he was still fit and active. He could continue to carry on his business and the restaurant too, and he would find time to work, as he had done earlier, for the Red Cross.

What dreadful thoughts for a bright May morning! Sep looked at the sunshine spilling lozenges of bright colour through the narrow windows across the floor of the chapel, and squared his shoulders.

He must trust in God. He was good and merciful. A way must surely be found for peace between nations. That man of wickedness, Adolf Hitler, would be put down in God's good time. He had reached the limit of his powers.

He followed Edna's nodding roses out into the sunny street. Someone passed with an armful Of lilac, and its fragrance seemed the essence of early summer. Opposite, at the end of one of the roads leading to the Cax. he could see a magnificent copper beech tree, its young thin leaves making a haze of pink against the brilliant sky.

It was a wonderful day. It was a wonderful world. Surely, for men of faith, all would be well, thought Sep, retracing his steps to the market square.

But despite the warmth around him, there was a little chill in the old man's heart, as though the shadow of things to come had begun to fall across a fine Sunday in May in the year 1939.

Chapter Three

EVACUEES IN CAXLEY

As the summer advanced, so did the menacing shadow of war. It was plain that Germany intended to subdue Poland, and Caxley people, in common with the rest of Britain, welcomed the Prime Minister's guarantee that Britain would stand by the threatened country. The memory of Czechoslovakia's fate still aroused shame.

'Hitler's for it if he tries that game again with Poland,' said one worthy to another in the market square.

'If we gets the Russians on our side,' observed his crony, 'he don't stand a chance.'

There was a growing unity of purpose in the country. The ties with France, so vividly remembered by the older generation who had fought in the Great War, were being strengthened daily. If only the Government could come to favourable terms with Russia, then surely this tripartite alliance could settle Hitler's ambitions, and curb his alarming progress in Europe.

Meanwhile, plans went ahead for the evacuation of children, the issue of gas masks, the digging of shelters from air attacks, and all the civilian defence precautions which, if not particularly reassuring, kept people busy and certainly hardened their resolve to show Hitler that they meant business.

The three generations in the Howard and North families faced the threat of war typically. Septimus Howard, who had been in his fifties during the Great War of 1914–18, was sad but resolute.

'It's a relief,' he said, voicing the sentiments of all who heard him, 'to know where we stand, and to know that we are acting in the right way. That poor man Chamberlain has been sorely hood-winked. He's not alone. There are mighty few people today who will believe that evil is still abroad and active. But now his eyes are opened, and he can see Hitler for what he is – a liar, and worse still, a madman.'

Bertie North, who had fought in France as a young man and had lost a foot as a result, knew that the war ahead would involve his family in Caxley as completely as it would engage the armed men. This, to him, was the real horror, and the thought of a gas attack, which seemed highly probable, filled him with fury and nausea. Part of him longed to send Kathy and the three children overseas to comparative safety, but he could not ignore that inward voice which told him that this would be the coward's way. Not that Kathy would go anyway – she had made that plain from the start. Where Bertie was, there the family would be, she maintained stoutly, and nothing would shake her.

Only two things gave Bertie any comfort in this dark time. First, he would return to the army, despite his one foot.

'Must be masses of paper work to do,' he told Sep. 'I can do that if they won't let me do anything more martial, and free another chap.'

The second thing was the attitude of mind, in which the young men most involved faced the situation. Bertie remembered with bitter pain the heroic dedication with which his own generation had entered the war. High ideals, noble sacrifices, chivalry, honour and patriotism had been the words – and not only the words – which sent a gallant and gay generation into battle. The awful aftermath had been doubly poignant.

Today there was as much courage and as much resolution. But the young men were not blinded by shining ideals. This would be a grim battle, probably a long one. There was no insouciant cry of 'Over by Christmas', as there had been in 1914. They were of a generation which knew that it was fighting for survival, and one which knew too that in modern warfare there is no real victor. Whatever the outcome it would be a long road to recovery when the war itself was past.

Nevertheless, for Edward and his friends, hearts beat a little faster as action appeared imminent. What if Hitler had annexed an alarming amount of Europe? The Low Countries and France would resist to a man, and the English Channel presented almost as great an obstacle to an invader today as it did to Napoleon. This year had given England time to get ahead with preparations. The uneasy peace, bought by Mr Chamberlain at Munich a year earlier, may have been a bad thing, but at least it had provided a breathing space.

'Thank God I'm trained for something!' cried Edward to his mother. 'Think of all those poor devils who will be shunted into the army and sent foot-slogging all over Europe! At least I shall have some idea of what I'm to do.'

He spent as much time training now as he could possibly manage. He had a purpose. It was a sober one, but it gave him inward courage. Whatever happened, he intended to be as ready and fit as youth, good health and steady application to his flying would allow.

Edward, most certainly, was the happiest man in the family despite the fact that he was the most vulnerable.

During the last week of August it became known that all hope of an alliance with Russia had gone. Triumphantly the Nazis announced a pact with the Soviet Union. Things looked black indeed for England and her allies, but assurances went out again. Whatever happened, Britain would stand by her obligations to Poland. After a period of anxiety over Russia's negotiations, it was good to know the truth.

On 24 August the Emergency Powers Bill was passed, together with various formalities for calling up the armed forces. Edward's spirits rose when he heard the news at six o'clock. How soon, he wondered, before he set off?

It was a few days later that the House of Commons met again. The question facing the country, said one speaker, was: 'Shall one man or one country be allowed to dominate Europe?' To that question there could be only one answer.

People in Caxley now prepared to receive evacuees from London and another nearby vulnerable town into their midst. No one could pretend that this move was wholeheartedly welcome. The genuine desire to help people in danger and to afford them a port in a storm, was tempered with doubts. Would strangers fit into the home? Would they be content? Would they be co-operative?

Sep and Edna had offered to take in six boys of school age. If they could have squeezed in more they would have done. Frankly, Edna welcomed the idea of children in the house again. The thought that they might be unruly, disobedient or difficult to handle, simply did not enter her head or Sep's.

'It is the least we can do,' said Sep gravely. 'How should we feel if we had ever had to send our children to strangers?'

Bertie and Kathy expected a mother and baby to be billeted with them in the house by the river. The fate of Edward's flat was undecided at the moment, and the future of Rose Lodge hung in the balance. There was talk of its being requisitioned as a nurses' hostel, in which case Winnie and her mother might move back to Edward's new domain in the market square.

'Proper ol' muddle, ennit?' observed the dustman to Edward. 'Still, we've got to show that Hitler.' He sighed gustily.

'Wicked ol' rat,' continued the dustman, 'getting 'is planes filled up with gas bombs, no doubt. You see, that's what'll 'appen first go off. You wants to keep your gas mask 'andy as soon as the balloon goes up. Can't think what them Germans were playing at ever to vote 'im in.'

He replaced the dustbin lid with a resounding clang.

'Ah, well,' he said indulgently, 'they're easy taken in – foreigners!'

And with true British superiority he mounted the rear step of the dust lorry and rode away.

It was on Friday, 1 September that evacuation began and Caxley prepared for the invasion. Beds were aired, toys brought down from attics, welcoming nosegays lodged on bedroom mantelpieces and pies and cakes baked for the doubtless starving visitors.

'Isn't it odd,' remarked Joan Howard to her mother, as she staggered from the doorstep with a double supply of milk, 'how we expect evacuees to be extra cold and extra hungry? We've put twice as many blankets on their beds as ours, and we've got in enough food to feed an army.'

'I know,' agreed Winnie. 'It's on a par with woollies and shoes. Have you noticed how everyone is buying one or two stout pairs of walking shoes and knitting thick sweaters like mad? I suppose we subconsciously think we'll be marching away westward when war comes, with only a good thick sweater to keep out the cold when we're asleep under a hedge at night.'

'Very sensible,' approved old Mrs North, who was busy repairing a dilapidated golliwog which had once been Joan's. 'I can't think why you don't take my advice and stock up with Chilprufe underclothes. You'll regret it this time next year. Why I remember asking Grandpa North for five pounds when war broke out in 1914, and I laid it out on vests, combinations, stockings, tea towels and pillow slips – and never ceased to be thankful!'

Joan laughed. Despite the horrors which must surely lie ahead, life was very good at the moment. She had just obtained a teaching post at an infants' school in the town and was glad to be living at home to keep an eye on her mother and grandmother. As soon as things were more settled, however, she secretly hoped to join the W.A.A.F. or the A.T.S. Who knows? She might be posted somewhere near Edward.

It was not yet known if Rose Lodge would be wanted to house an influx of nurses. Meanwhile, the three women had prepared two bedrooms for their evacuees.

Winnie and Joan left the house in charge of old Mrs North and made their way towards the station. The local Reception Officer was in charge there, assisted by a dozen or so local teachers. Winnie and her daughter were bound for a school which stood nearby. Here the children would come with their teachers to collect their rations for forty-eight hours and to rest before setting off for their new homes. Winnie was attached to the Women's Voluntary Service Corps and as Joan's school was closed for the time being she had offered to go and help.

A train had just arrived at the station, and the children were being marshalled into some semblance of order by harassed teachers.

The children looked pathetic, Joan thought, clutching bundles and cases, and each wearing a label. A gas mask, in a neat cardboard box, bounced on every back or front, and one's first impression was of a band of refugees, pale and shabby.

But, on looking more closely, Joan noticed the cheeks which bulged with sweets, the occasional smile which lightened a tired face and the efficient mothering by little girls of children smaller than themselves. Given a good night's rest, Joan decided, these young ones would turn out to be as cheerful and resilient a lot as she had ever met during her training in London.

Inside the school hall an army of helpers coped with earlier arrivals. To Joan's secret delight, and her mother's obvious consternation, she saw that Miss Mobbs was in charge. This formidable individual had once been a hospital sister in the Midlands but retired to Caxley to look after a bachelor brother some years before.

'Poor man,' Caxley said. 'Heaven knows what he's done to deserve it! There's no peace now for him.'

But running a home and cowing a brother were not enough for Miss Mobbs. Within a few weeks she was a driving force in several local organisations, and the scourge of those who preferred a quiet life.

At the moment she was in her element. Clad in nurse's costume, her fourteen-stone figure dominated the room as she swept from table to table and queue to queue, rallying her forces.

'That's the way, kiddies,' she boomed. 'Hurry along. Put your tins in your carrier bags and don't keep the ladies waiting!'

'Old boss-pot,' muttered one eight-year-old to her companion, much to Joan's joy. ''Ope 'Itler gets 'er.'

Miss Mobbs bore down upon Winnie.

'We've been looking for you, Mrs Howard. This way. A tin of meat for every child and your daughter can do the packets of sugar.'

Joan observed, with mingled annoyance and amusement, that her mother looked as flustered and apologetic as any little probationer nurse and then remembered that, of course, years ago her mother really had been one. Obviously the voice of authority still twanged long-silent chords.

'Better late than never,' remarked Miss Mobbs with false heartiness. But her strongly disapproving countenance made it quite apparent that the Howards were in disgrace.

Glasses flashing, she sailed briskly across the room to chivvy two exhausted teachers into line, leaving Joan wondering how many more women were adding thus odiously to the horrors of warfare.

She and her mother worked steadily from ten until four, handing out rations to schoolchildren and their teachers and to mothers with babies. A brief lull midday enabled them to sip a cup of very unpleasant coffee and to eat a thinly spread fishpaste sandwich. Joan, whose youthful appetite was lusty, thought wistfully of the toothsome little chicken casserole her mother had left in the oven for Grandma North, and was unwise enough to mention it in Miss Mobbs' hearing.

'It won't hurt some of us to tighten our belts,' claimed that redoubtable lady, clapping a large hand over her own stiff leather one. Joan noticed, uncharitably, that it was fastened at the last hole already.

'We shan't beat Hitler without a few sacrifices,' she continued, putting three spoonfuls of sugar into her coffee, 'and we must be glad of this chance of doing our bit.'

Really, thought Joan, speechless with nausea, it was surprising that Miss Mobbs had not been lynched, and could only suppose that the preoccupation of those present, and perhaps a more tolerant attitude towards this ghastly specimen than her own, accounted for Miss Mobbs' preservation.

At four o'clock they returned to Rose Lodge to find that their own evacuees had arrived and were already unpacking. Two women teachers, one a middle-aged widow, and the other a girl not much older than Joan, were sharing Edward's former room, and a young mother with a toddler and a six-week-old baby occupied the larger bedroom at the back of the house which had been Joan's until recently.

Grandmother North, trim and neat, her silver hair carefully

waved and her gold locket pinned upon her dark silk blouse, was prepairing tea. She looked as serene and competent as if she were entertaining one or two of her excitement at this invasion.

'Where are we having it?' asked Joan, lifting the tray.

'In the drawing-room, of course,' responded her grandmother. 'Where else?'

'I thought – with so many of us,' faltered Joan, 'that we might have it here, or set it in the dining-room.'

'Just because we're about to go to war,' said Grandma North with hauteur, 'it doesn't matter follow that we have to lower our standards.'

She poured boiling water into the silver tea pot, and Joan could not help remembering the advertisement which she had read in *The Caxley Chronicle* that morning. Side by side with injunctions to do without, and to tackle one's own repairs in order to leave men free for war work, was the usual story from a local employment agency.

'Patronized by the Nobility and Gentry,' ran the heading, followed by:

'Titled lady requires reliable butler and housekeeper. 4 in family. 3 resident staff.'

There was a touch of this divine lunacy about her grandmother, thought Joan with amusement, and gave her a quick peck of appreciation.

'Mind my hair, dear,' said Mrs North automatically, and picking up the teapot she advanced to meet her guests.

'We're going to be a pretty rum household,' was Joan's private and unspoken comment as she surveyed the party when they were gathered together. Grandma North sat very upright behind the tea tray. Her mother, plump and kindly, carried food to the visitors, while she herself did her best to put the young mother at her ease and to cope with Bobby's insatiable demands for attention. This fat two-year-old was going to cause more damage at Rose Lodge than the rest of them put together, Joan surmised.

Already he had wiped a wet chocolate biscuit along the cream chintz of the armchair, and tipped a generous dollop of milk into his mother's lap, his own shoes and Joan's. Now he was busy hammering bread and butter into the carpet with a small, greasy and powerful fist. His mother made pathetic and ineffectual attempts to control him.

'Oh, you are a naughty boy, Bobby! Look at the lady's floor! Give over now!'

'Please don't worry,' said Grandma North, a shade frostily. 'We can easily clean it up later.'

Joan felt sorry for the young mother. Exhausted with travelling, parted from a husband who had rejoined his ship the day before, and wholly overwhelmed by all that had befallen her, she seemed near to tears. As soon as was decently possible, she hurried Bobby upstairs to bed and made her escape.

Mrs Forbes, the older teacher, seemed a sensible pleasant person, though from the glint in her eye as she surveyed Bobby's tea-time activities, it was plain that she would have made use of a sharp slap or two to restrain that young gentleman. Her companion, Maisie Hunter, was a fresh-faced curly-haired individual whose appetite, Joan noticed, was as healthy as her own.

How would they all shake down together, she wondered, six women, and two babies – well, one baby and a two-year-old fiend might be a more precise definition – under the roof of Rose Lodge? Time alone would tell.

Chapter Four

WAR BREAKS OUT

By Sunday morning, the visitors at Rose Lodge appeared to have settled down. This was by no means general in Caxley. Already, much to the billeting authorities' dismay, some mothers and children were making their way back to the danger zone in preference to the dullness of country living. Others were making plans to be fetched back to civilization during the week. Their hosts were torn between relief and the guilty feeling that they had failed in their allotted task of welcoming those in need.

The early news on the wireless said that the Prime Minister would speak at eleven-fifteen, and Mrs North invited the household to assemble in the drawing-room.

'I suppose this is it,' said Joan.

'And about time too,' rapped out the old lady. 'All this shilly-shallying!'

She, with Winnie and Joan, was going to lunch at Bertie's. The parents of the young mother, Nora Baker, were coming to spend the day, and Mrs Forbes' son was paying a last visit before setting off to an army camp in the north.

'Let them have the house to themselves for the day,' Bertie said, 'and come and see us.'

And so it had been arranged.

Just before the broadcast, the inhabitants of Rose Lodge settled themselves in the drawing-room. Bobby, mercifully, had been put into his cot for his morning sleep, but the baby, freshly-bathed and fed, kicked happily on the floor enjoying the admiration of so many women.

By now it was known that an ultimatum had been handed to

Germany to expire at 11 a.m. There was a feeling of awful solemnity when finally the Prime Minister's voice echoed through the room. There had been no reply to the ultimatum, he told his anxious listeners, and in consequence we were already at war.

Joan felt a cold shiver run down her hack. She shot a glance at the older women around her. Their faces were grave and intent. Only Nora Baker and her baby seemed unaffected by the terrible words. The baby gazed with blue, unfocused eyes at the ceiling, and its mother nodded and smiled gently.

'It is the evil things we shall be fighting against,' said Mr Chamberlain, 'brute force, bad faith, injustice, oppression and persecution.'

Old Mrs North nodded emphatically. A little nerve twitched at the corner of her mouth, but otherwise she looked calm and approving.

The speech ended and she turned off the set.

'Thank goodness, that poor man has done the right thing at last,' she said.

'Well, we know where we are,' agreed Mrs Forbes.

She had hardly finished speaking when the sound of wailing came from the distance, to be followed, seconds later, with a similar sound, five times as loud, as the air-raid siren at the Fire Station sent out its spine-chilling alarm.

'It *can't* be an air raid,' whispered Winnie. They all gazed at each other in incredulous perplexity.

'Trust the Germans,' said Mrs Norah briskly. 'Too efficient by half. And where did I leave my gas mask?'

'Gas!' gasped little Mrs Baker, snatching up the baby. She had become a greenish colour, and the child's pink face close to hers made her appear more terror-stricken than ever.

'I'll go and get the gas masks,' said Joan, and began methodically to shut the windows. How idiotic and unreal it all seemed, she thought, suddenly calm.

'I must get Bobby,' cried the young mother. 'Oh, my Gawd, who'd think we'd get gassed so soon?'

'I'll fetch him,' said Winnie. She and Joan ran upstairs to collect their gas masks, a bottle of brandy and – no one quite knew why – a rug and a box of barley sugar. Meanwhile the two teachers ran around the house closing windows and looking anxiously up into the sky for enemy invaders.

They were hardly back in the drawing-room before the sirens sounded again, but this time on one long sustained note which, they were to learn, heralded safety.

'That's the "All clear",' cried Joan. 'What can have happened?'

'Very confusing,' said her grandmother severely. 'It was far better arranged in our war, with the Boy Scouts blowing bugles.'

'No doubt someone pressed the wrong button,' said Winnie. 'What a fright to give us all!'

Mrs Baker, her baby clutched to her bosom and a very disgruntled and sleepy Bobby clinging to her skirt, had tears running down her face. The others did their best to comfort her, and Joan insisted on administering a dose of brandy. It seemed a pity to have brought it all the way downstairs, she thought, and to take it back again unopened.

'D'you think it's safe to put them upstairs to sleep?' asked Mrs Baker pathetically.

'Perfectly,' said old Mrs North. 'Take my word for it, that stupid fellow Taggerty's at the bottom of this. Fancy putting him in charge at the A.R.P. place! If he's anything like that foolish cousin of his we had in the shop, he'll lose his head on every possible occasion. I hope he gets thoroughly reprimanded.'

'I don't think Taggerty has anything to do with it,' began Winnie. But her mother was already across the hall and beginning to mount the stairs.

'We must hurry,' she was saying. 'Bertie asked us there for twelve and we mustn't keep the dear boy waiting.'

If they had just ejected a troublesome wasp from the drawing-room she could not have been less concerned, thought Joan in admiration, following her small, upright figure aloft.

To Joan's and Winnie's delight, Edward was at Bertie's.

'We tried to ring you last night,' cried his mother, 'but there was no reply. How did you get on?'

'Don't talk about it,' said Edward, throwing up his hands despairingly. 'I trotted along to report at the town centre and I'm on *indefinite leave*, if you please! *Indefinite leave!*'

'What exactly does that mean, dear?' asked Winnie anxiously.

'It means that I go back to work as usual, and sit on my bum waiting to be called up.'

'Language, Edward, language!' interjected his grandmother severely. 'There's no need to be vulgar just because you're disappointed.'

'No uniform?' said Joan.

'Only when I report each week,' said Edward. 'It seems the training units are bunged up at present. I suppose our turn'll come, but it's the hell of a nuisance, this hanging about.'

'At least you know what you will be doing when you do get started,' comforted Bertie. 'How are your evacuees, Mamma?'

'Very pleasant people,' said the old lady firmly. 'And yours?'

'Gone home,' said Kathy entering. 'Took one look at the bedroom and said it wasn't what they were used to.'

'Now, I wonder how you take that?' queried Joan.

'With a sigh of relief,' said Bertie, taking up the carving knife. 'She was quite the ugliest woman I've ever clapped eyes on, and the babies were something fearful. Enough to give us all night terrors.'

'Now, Bertie!' said his mother reprovingly. 'Don't exaggerate!'

'The trouble is,' said Edward, looking at his Aunt Kathy, 'your standards are too high. You don't know when you're well off.'

Bertie made no reply. But he smiled as he tackled the joint.

During the next few weeks, Caxley folk and their visitors did their best to shake down together, while the seasonal work went on in the mellow September sunshine. The harvest was gathered in, corn stacked, apples picked. In the kitchens frugal housewives made stores of jam and preserves, bottled their fruit and tomatoes and put eggs to keep in great buckets of isinglass.

Those who remembered the food shortages of the earlier war told gruesome tales to younger women.

'And I had to feed my family on puddings made of chicken

maize on more than one occasion,' said one elderly evacuee. 'And not a spoonful of sugar to be had. You stock up with all you can. Rationing'll be tighter still this time.'

There was general dismay among farmers who had lost land to the defence departments. 'Where corn used to grow for hundreds of years,' *The Caxley Chronicle* reported one as saying, 'camps are now sprouting in profusion. Thousands of acres of good farmland have been sterilized for artillery ranges, exercise grounds for tanks, barracks and aerodromes.'

Edward, reading this at his solitary breakfast table snorted impatiently. They'd got to train *somewhere*, hadn't they? Oh, if only he could get started!

He flipped over the page.

'Petrol rationing hits delivery vans,' he read. 'Old cycles being brought out again.'

His eye caught a more bizarre morsel of wartime news.

'New Forest ponies may be painted with white stripes to make them more visible to motorists in the black-out.'

Edward laughed aloud.

'Good old *Caxley Chronicle*! And what's on at the flicks this week?'

Will Hay in *Ask a Policeman* and Jessie Matthews in *Climbing High*, he read with approval. Below the announcement was a new wartime column headed 'Your Garden and Allotment in Wartime.'

'Thank God I'm spared that,' exclaimed Edward, throwing the paper into a chair. But the caption had reminded him that he had promised his Uncle Robert, who so lovingly tended the garden of their shared premises, that he would give him a lift this morning on his way to work.

Edward's Uncle Robert was the youngest of Sep Howard's children and only eleven years older than Edward. He felt towards this youthful uncle rather as he did towards the youngest child of Bender and Hilda North, his attractive aunt Mary, who was much the same age as Robert. They seemed more like an older brother and sister than members of an earlier generation.

Aunt Mary he saw seldom these days, which was a pity. She was a moderately successful actress, better endowed with dazzling good looks than brain, but hard working and with the good health and even temper which all three North children enjoyed.

'A messy sort of life,' Grandpa Sep Howard had commented once. 'I'm glad no child of mine wanted to take it up.' To Sep, staunch chapel-goer, there was still something of the scarlet woman about an actress.

Robert, of course, Edward saw almost daily. He did part of the supervision of Howard's bakery at the corner of the market square, but spent the major part of his time in running the restaurant on the ground floor below Edward's establishment.

Howard's Restaurant had flourished from the first and had now been in existence for about eight years. Sep's dream of little white tables and chairs set out on the lawn at the back of the property had come true. The garden, which had been Bender North's joy, remained as trim and gay as ever and added considerably to Caxley's attractions in the summer.

'I suppose you won't be running this little bus much longer,' observed Robert as they sped along.

'I've just enough petrol to keep her going for about a fortnight. With any luck I'll be posted by then.'

Robert was silent. Edward would dearly have liked to know Robert's feelings about the war, but he did not like to ask. No doubt Robert's job would be considered as a highly necessary one and he would be more advantageously employed there than in some humdrum post in one of the services. Nevertheless, Edward had not heard him mention volunteering or offering his services in any more martial capacity, despite the fact that he was only in his early thirties. In some ways, Edward mused, Robert was a rum fish.

Take this stupid business of his tenants, the couple who lived below his own flat and above Robert's restaurant, thought Edward. They were quiet people, taking care to be unobtrusive, but Robert had complained bitterly to Edward that the ceiling of the café was flaking and that this was due to the 'banging about upstairs.'

'And they had the cheek to say that the cooking smells from my restaurant went up into their sitting-room,' asserted Robert.

'Daresay they do, too,' said Edward equably. 'There's a pretty high stink of frying sometimes. I can even get a whiff on the floor above them.'

Robert's face had darkened.

'Well, you knew what to expect when you came to live over a restaurant,' he said shortly. 'The old man was a fool ever to think the property could be divided. The floors above my bit should have been kept for storing things.'

Edward had been amazed at the depth of feeling with which Robert spoke. For the first time in his carefree life, Edward realised that he was encountering jealousy, and a very unpleasant sight it was. Luckily, he had inherited a goodly portion of the Norths' equanimity and could reply evenly. But the barb stuck, nevertheless.

He dropped Robert now at his wholesaler's and drove on to the office. If only his posting would come through! There was no interest in his work during these tedious waiting days, and he was getting thoroughly tired of Caxley too, as it was at present. He was fed up with hearing petty tales about evacuees' headlice and wet beds; and fed up too with the pomposity of some of the Caxleyites in positions of wartime authority. Somehow, in these last few weeks Caxley had become insupportable. He felt like a caged bird, frantic to try his wings, in more ways than one.

Ah well, sighed Edward philosophically as he turned into the yard at the side of the office, it couldn't be long now. Meanwhile, Will Hay and Jessie Matthews were on at the flicks. He would ask that nice little teacher, Maisie something-or-other at Rose Lodge, to accompany him. At least it was a new face in dull old Caxley.

Edward was not alone in his frustration. This was the beginning of a period which later became known as 'the phoney war', when the Allied forces and those of the Germans faced each other in their fortresses and nothing seemed to happen.

The Caxley Chronicle echoed the general unease. 'Don't eat these berries!' said one heading. Foster parents should make sure that their charges knew what deadly nightshade looked like. Could they distinguish between mushrooms and toadstools?

The Post Office issued a tart announcement pointing out that it had a much depleted staff and far more work than usual.

Someone wrote to say that country people were being exploited. Why should a farm labourer, with about thirty shillings a week left after paying his insurance, feed the parents of his two evacuees when they spent Sundays with them? And who was expected to pay for the new mattress that was needed? There was no doubt about it – the heroic spirit in which the nation had faced the outbreak of war was fast evaporating, in this anticlimax of domestic chaos and interminable waiting.

'If anyone else tells me to Stand By or to Remain Alert,' said Bertie dangerously, 'I shall not answer for the consequences.

'It's better than being told We're All In It Together,' consoled Kathy.

Joan, meanwhile, had started her new job, for the schools had reopened. A London school's nursery unit had been attached to the combined infants' school and this was housed in the Friends' Meeting House, a pleasant red-brick building perched on a little grassy knoll on the northern outskirts of Caxley. A Viennese teacher, who had escaped a few months before Austria was overrun by the Nazis, was in charge, and Joan was her willing assistant.

She loved the chattering children in their blue and white checked overalls. The day seemed one mad rush from crisis to crisis. There was milk to be administered, potties to empty, dozens of small hands and faces to wash, tears to be quenched, passions to be calmed and a hundred activities to take part in.

She loved, too, the atmosphere of the old premises. It was an agreeably proportioned building with high arched windows along each side. Round the walls were dozens of large wooden hat pegs used by Quakers of past generations. The floor was of scrubbed boards, charming to look at but dangerously splintery for young hands and knees.

Outside was a grassy plot. In one half stood a dozen or so small headstones over the graves of good men and women now departed.

There was something very engaging, Joan thought, to see the babies tumbling about on the grass, and supporting themselves by the little headstones. Here the living and the dead met companionably in the autumn sunlight, and the war seemed very far away indeed.

A steep flight of stone steps led from the road to the top of the grassy mound upon which the Meeting House stood. An old iron lamp, on an arched bracket, hung above the steps, and Joan often thought what a pleasant picture the children made as they swarmed up the steps beneath its graceful curve, clad in their blue and white.

Her mother came on two afternoons a week to help with the children. Three afternoons were spent at the hospital, for Winnie did not want to tie herself to a regular full-time job, but preferred to do voluntary service when and where she could. There was her mother to consider and the evacuees. Winnie determined to keep Rose Lodge running as smoothly as she could, and only prayed that the proposal that it should be turned into a nurses hostel would be quietly forgotten.

She found the small children amusing but thoroughly exhausting. The nursing afternoons were far less wearing.

She said as much to Joan as they walked home together one afternoon, scuffling the fallen leaves which were beginning to dapple the footpath with red and gold.

'I suppose it's because I was trained to nurse,' she remarked.

'Rather you than me,' responded Joan. 'It's bad enough mopping up a grazed knee. Anything worse would floor me completely.'

They turned into the drive of Rose Lodge and saw old Mrs North at the open front door. She was smiling.

'You've just missed Edward on the telephone. He's as pleased as a dog with two tails. He's posted at last to – now, what was it? – a flying training school in Gloucestershire.'

'Well,' said Joan thankfully, 'there's one happy fellow in Caxley tonight!'

Chapter Five

GRIM NEWS

Edward arrived at the flying training school on a dispiritingly bleak October afternoon. The aerodrome lay on a windswept upland, not unlike his own downland country. In the distance, against the pewter-grey sky, a line of woods appeared like a navy-blue smudge on the horizon; but for mile upon mile the broad fields spread on every side, some a faded green, some ashen with bleached stubble and some newly-furrowed with recent ploughing.

Edward surveyed the landscape from a window by his bed. His sleeping quarters were grimly austere. A long army hut, with about ten iron beds on each side, was now his bedroom. A locker stood by each bed, and the grey blankets which served as coverlets did nothing to enliven the general gloom.

But at any rate, thought Edward hopefully, he had a window by his allotted place and the hut was warm.

There was an old man working some twenty yards from the window where a shallow ditch skirted a corner of the aerodrome. A row of pollarded willows marked the line of the waterway, and the old man was engaged in slashing back the long straight boughs. His coat was grey and faded in patches, his face lined and thin. He wore no hat, and as he lunged with the bill-hook, his sparse grey hair rose and fell in the wind. It reminded Edward of the grey wool which catches on barbed wire, fluttering night and day throughout the changing seasons.

He seemed to be part of the bleached and colourless background – as gnarled and knotty as the willow boles among which he worked, as dry and wispy as the dead grass which rustled against his muddy rubber boots. But there was an intensity of purpose in his rhythmic slashing which reminded Edward, with a sudden pang, of his grandfather Sep Howard, so far away.

He turned abruptly from the window, straightened his tunic, and set off through the wind to the sergeants' mess.

He entered a large room furnished with plenty of small tables, armchairs, magazines and a bar. The aerodrome was one of the many built during the thirties, and still had, at the outbreak of war, its initial spruceness and comfort.

Edward fetched himself some tea, bought some cigarettes, and made his way towards a chair strategically placed by a bronze radiator. He intended to start the crossword puzzle in the newspaper which was tucked securely under his elbow. There were only five or six other men in the mess, none of whom he knew. But he had scarcely drunk half his tea and pencilled in three words of the puzzle before he was accosted by a newcomer.

'So you're here too?' cried his fellow sergeant pilot. Edward's heart sank.

There was nothing, he supposed, violently wrong with Dickie Bridges, but he was such a confoundedly noisy ass. He had met him first during voluntary training and found him pleasant enough company on his own, but unbearably boastful and excitable when a few of his contemporaries appeared. When parties began to get out of hand you could bet your boots that Dickie Bridges would be among the first to sling a glass across the room with a carefree whoop. He was, in peacetime, an articled clerk with a firm of solicitors in Edward's county town. Rumour had it that their office was dark and musty, the partners, who still wore wing collars and cravats, were approaching eighty, one was almost blind and the other deaf. However, as they saw their clients together, one was able to hear them and the other to see them, and the office continued to function in a delightfully Dickensian muddle. Edward could only suppose that with such a restricting background it was natural that Dickie should effervesce when he escaped.

Edward made welcoming noises and made room on the table for Dickie's tea cup. Typical of life, he commented to himself, that of all the chaps he knew in the Volunteer Reserve, it should be old

Dickie who turned up! Nevertheless, it was good to see a familiar face in these strange surroundings and he settled back to hear the news.

'Know this part of the world?' asked Dickie, tapping one of Edward's cigarettes on the table top.

'No. First time here.'

'Couple of decent little pubs within three miles,' Dickie assured him. 'But twenty-odd miles to any bright lights – not that we'll see much of those with the blackout, and I hear we're kept down to it pretty well here.'

'Better than kicking about at home,' said Edward. 'I would have been round the bend in another fortnight.'

'Me too,' agreed Dickie.

Edward remembered the two old partners in Dickie's professional life and inquired after them.

'They've both offered their military services,' chuckled Dickie, 'but have been asked to stand by for a bit. If they can't get into the front line they have hopes of being able to man a barrage balloon in the local park. Even the blind one says he can see *that*!'

Edward, amused, suddenly felt a lift of spirits. Could Hitler ever hope to win against such delicious and lunatic determination? He found himself warming towards Dickie, and agreeing to try one of the two decent little pubs the next evening.

Back at Caxley the winter winds were beginning to whistle about the market square, and people were looking forward to their first wartime Christmas with some misgiving. The news was not good. A number of merchant ships had been sunk and it was clear that Hitler intended to try to cut the nation's life-lines with his U-boats.

Cruisers, battleships and destroyers had all been recent casualties, and there seemed to be no more encouraging news from the B.E.F. in France.

The evacuees were flocking back to their homes and the people of Caxley folded sheets and took down beds wondering the while how soon they would be needed again. Petrol rationing, food rationing and the vexatious blackout aggravated the misery of 'the phoney war'. In particular, men like Bertie, who had served in the First World War and were anxious to serve in the present conflict, could get no satisfaction about their future plans.

Sep Howard had added worries. His supplies were cut down drastically, and some of his finest ingredients, such as preserved fruit and nuts, were now impossible to obtain. It grieved Sep to use inferior material, but it was plain that there was no alternative. 'Quality', or 'carriage trade', as he still thought of it, had virtually gone, although basic fare such as bread and buns had increased in volume because of the evacuees in Caxley. His workers were reduced in numbers, and petrol rationing severely hampered deliveries.

But business worries were not all. His wife Edna was far from well and refused to see a doctor. Since the outbreak of war she had served in the shop, looked after the six evacuee boys, and run her home with practically no help. She attacked everything with gay gusto and made light of the giddiness which attacked her more and more frequently.

''Tis nothing,' she assured the anxious Sep. 'Indigestion probably. Nothing that a cup of herb tea won't cure.'

The very suggestion of a doctor's visit put her into a panic.

'He'll have me in hospital in two shakes, and I'd die there! Don't you dare fetch a doctor to me, Sep.'

It was as though, with advancing age, she was returning to the gipsy suspicions and distrust of her forebears. She had always loved to be outside, and now, even on the coldest night, would lie beneath a wide-open window with the wind blowing in upon her. Sep could do nothing with the wilful woman whom he adored, but watch over her with growing anxiety.

One Sunday evening they returned from chapel as the full moon rose. In the darkened town its silvery light was more welcome than ever, and Edna stopped to gaze at its beauty behind the pattern of interlaced branches. She was like a child still, thought Sep, watching her wide dark eyes.

'It makes me feel excited,' whispered Edna. 'It always has done, ever since I was little.'

She put her hand through Sep's arm and they paced homeward companionably, Edna's eyes upon the moon.

It was so bright that night that Sep was unable to sleep. Beside him Edna's dark hair stirred in the breeze from the window. Her breathing was light and even. A finger of moonlight glimmered on the brass handles of the oak chest of drawers which had stood in the same position for all their married life. Upon it stood their wedding photograph, Edna small and enchantingly gay, Sep pale and very solemn. The glass gleamed in the silvery light.

It was very quiet. Only the bare branches stirred outside the window, and very faintly, with an ear long attuned to its murmur, Sep could distinguish the distant rippling of the Cax.

An owl screeched and at that moment Edna awoke. She sat up, looking like a startled child in her little white nightgown, and began to cough. Sep raised himself.

'It hurts,' she gasped, turning towards him, her face puckered with astonishment. Sep put his arms round her thin shoulders. She seemed as light-boned as a bird.

She turned her head to look at the great glowing face of the moon shining full and strong at the open window. Sighing, she fell softly back against Sep's shoulder, her cloud of dark hair brushing his mouth. A shudder shook her body and her breath escaped with a queer bubbling sound.

In the cold moonlit silence of the bedroom, Sep knew with awful certainty that he held in his arms the dead body of his wife.

In the months that followed Sep drifted about his affairs like a small pale ghost. He attended to the shop, the restaurant, his chapel matters and council affairs with the same grave courtesy which was customary, but the spirit seemed to have gone from him, and people told each other that Sep had only half his mind on things these days. He was the object of sincere sympathy. Edna Howard had not been universally liked – she was too wild a bird to be accepted in the Caxley hen-runs – but the marriage had been a happy one, and it was sad to see Sep so bereft.

Kathy was the one who gave him most comfort. If only Jim had been alive, Sep thought to himself! But Jim, his firstborn, lay somewhere in Ypres, and Leslie, his second son, was also lost to him. They had not met since Leslie left Winnie and went to live in the south-west with the woman of his choice.

Sep would have been desolate indeed without Kathy and Bertie's company. He spent most of his evenings there when the shop was closed, sitting quietly in a corner taking comfort from the children and the benison of a happy home. But he refused to sleep there, despite pressing invitations. Always he returned through the dark streets to the market square, passing the bronze statue of good Queen Victoria, before mounting the stairs to his lonely bedroom.

As the days grew longer the news became more and more sombre. The invasion of neutral Norway in April 1940 angered Caxley and the rest of the country. The costly attempts to recapture Narvik from the enemy, in the weeks that followed, brought outspoken criticism of Mr Chamberlain's leadership. Events were moving with such savagery and speed that it was clear that the time had arrived for a coalition government, and on May 10 Mr Churchill became Prime Minister.

Earlier, on the same day, Hitler invaded Holland. The news was black indeed. Before long it was known that a large part of the British Army had retreated to Dunkirk. The question 'How long can France hold out?' was on everyone's lips.

'They'll never give in,' declared Bertie to Sep, one glorious June evening in his garden. 'I've seen the French in action. They'll fight like tigers.'

The roses were already looking lovely. It was going to be a long hot summer, said the weatherwise of Caxley, and they were to be proved right. It did not seem possible, as the two men paced the grass, that across a narrow strip of water a powerful enemy waited to invade their land.

'They'll never get here,' said Bertie robustly. 'Napoleon was beaten by the Channel and so will Hitler be. The Navy will see to that.'

'At times I half-hope they will get here,' said Sep with a flash of spirit. 'There will be a warm welcome! I've never known people so spoiling for an encounter.'

Bertie was enrolled as a Local Defence Volunteer, soon to he renamed the Home Guard, and enjoyed his activities. One day, he hoped, he would return to army duties, but meanwhile there was plenty to organize in the face of imminent invasion.

Edward, now commissioned, had been posted to a squadron of Bomber Command in the north of England and was engaged in night bombing. Dickie Bridges was one of his crew. His letters showed such elation of spirit that the family's fears for him were partly calmed. Edward, it was plain, was doing exactly what he wanted to do – he was flying, he was in the thick of things, he was at the peak of his powers and deeply happy. The mention of a girl called Angela became more frequent. She was a Waaf on the same station and Winnie surmised that much of Edward's happiness came from her propinquity.

On a glorious hot June day, while haymaking was in full spate in the fields around Caxley and children refreshed themselves by splashing in the river Cax, the black news came over the radio that France had fallen. Joan Howard heard it in a little paper shop near the nursery school at dinner time. The old man who kept the shop beckoned her to the other side of the counter, and she stood, holding aside a hideous bead curtain which screened the tiny living-room from the shop, listening to the unbelievable news. She grew colder and colder. What would happen now?

The old man switched off the set when the announcement was over and turned to face her. To Joan's amazement his expression was buoyant.

'Now we're on our own,' he exclaimed with intense satisfaction. 'Never trusted them froggies for all old Winston said. We're better off without 'em, my dear. What was you asking for? *The Caxley Chronicle?* Thank you, dear. That's threepence. And now I'm off to get me Dad's old shot-gun polished up!'

She returned up the steep hill to the nursery school with the dreadful news. Miss Schmidt, the Viennese warden, always so gay and elegant, seemed to crumple into a frail old lady when Joan told her what she had heard.

'He is unbeatable,' she cried, and covered her face with her hands. Joan remembered the man in the paper shop and felt courage welling up in her.

'Rubbish!' she said stoutly. 'He's got us to reckon with. We'll never give in!'

'That is what my people said,' Miss Schmidt murmured, 'and the Poles and the Dutch. All of us – and now the French. The devil himself is with that man. He will rule the world.'

'You must not think that!' cried Joan. 'You know what the Prime Minister has said: "We'll fight on for years, if necessary alone," and it's true! We've all the Empire behind us. We can't lose, we can't!'

A child came up at this moment clamouring urgently for attention, and Miss Schmidt wiped away her tears and returned to her duties. But Joan could see that she could not believe that there was any hope for this small island where she had found brief refuge.

As for Joan herself, in some strange way her spirits grew more buoyant as the day wore on. Walking home that afternoon, through the brilliant sunshine, the confident words of the old man echoed in her ears: 'Now we're on our own. Better off without 'em, my dear!' They were as exhilarating as a marching song.

All Caxley seemed to share her mood, she discovered during the next few days. There was a fierce joy in the air, the relish of a fight.

'I'm sharpening up my filleting knife,' said Bill Petty at the fish stall in the market. The son of fat Mrs Petty, now dead, who had served there for years, Bill was a cripple who could never hope to see active service. His gaiety was infectious.

'I'll crown that Hitler with a jerry!' cried his neighbour at the crockery stall. 'Very suitable, don't you think?'

The spirit of Caxley was typical of the whole nation, roused, alert and ready to fight. As Doctor Johnson said: 'When a man knows he is going to be hanged in a fortnight, it concentrates his mind wonderfully.' Caxley concentrated to the full. Feverishly, defence plans went forward, old weapons were unearthed from cupboards and attics, and everyone intended to make it a fight to the finish.

'The Pry Minister,' said the B.B.C. announcer, 'will speak to the nation at half-past nine tonight.' And the nation, listening, rejoiced to hear that brave belligerent voice saying: 'What has happened in France makes no difference to our actions and purpose. We have become the sole champions now in arms to defend the world-cause. We shall fight on unconquerable until the curse of Hitler is lifted from the brows of mankind. We are sure that in the end all will come right.'

And somehow, despite the disaster of Dunkirk, the shortage of weapons, and the acknowledged might of the enemy, the people felt sure that all would come right.

It was two days later that a letter arrived at Rose Lodge from Edward. It was short and to the point.

Angela and I have just got engaged. So happy. Will bring her down to see you next weekend.
    Love to you all,
    Edward.

Chapter Six

EDWARD IN LOVE

She would never do, thought Winnie, gazing at Angela. She would never do at all. And yet, what was to be done about it? There was Edward, his dark eyes – so like his father's – fixed upon the girl, and his face wearing the expression which her mother so aptly described as 'the-cat's-got-at-the-cream'.

The memory of her own disastrous infatuation rushed at her from across the years. Was Edward about to make such an error of judgement? Or was she herself over-sensitive to the circumstances?

She tried to rationalize her feelings as she poured tea in the drawing-room at Rose Lodge. After all, she did not really know the girl. She must have faith in Edward's judgement. He was twenty-three, quite old enough to know his own mind. He was certainly very much in love, by the look of things. But – was she?

It was impossible to tell from Angela's cool, polite demeanour. She was small and very fair, with the neat good looks which would remain unchanged for many years. Just so had Winnie's mother been, trim and upright, and only recently had come the grey hair and wrinkles of old age to mar the picture. Old Mrs North's sharp blue eyes were now assessing the girl before them and Winnie wondered what she would have to say when at last they were free to speak together.

She did not have long to wait. Edward took Angela to meet Bertie and Kathy and to show her something of Caxley. Winnie and her mother washed up the rarely-used fragile best china while their tongues wagged. Old Mrs North was surprisingly dispassionate. She loved Edward dearly and Winnie quite expected fierce criticism of his choice.

'Seems a ladylike sort of gal,' declared the old lady, dextrously exploring the inside of the teapot with the linen towel. 'And got her head screwed on, I don't doubt.'

'That's what worries me a bit,' confessed Winnie. 'Do you think she's in love with him? I think Edward's rather romantic, for all his shyness.'

'Hardly surprising,' commented her mother drily. 'And I'd sooner see the girl level-headed about this business than getting foolishly infatuated. Let's face it, Winnie – we've seen what happens in that sort of situation in our own family.'

Winnie flushed. It was all so true, and yet, despite the wisdom of her mother's words, the nagging doubt remained. Was this girl the sort who could make Edward happy? She could only hope so.

They were married in August in a little grey church in the village by the aerodrome. Winnie and Joan had a nightmarish railway journey involving many changes and delays. They were the only representatives of Edward's family, for Bertie was now back in the army, blissfully happy in charge of fleets of army lorries at a maintenance unit. Kathy could not leave her family, and Sep and Robert were inextricably tied up with their business commitments.

Angela's mother was there. Her husband had left her some years before, but she was in the company of a prosperous-looking sixty-year-old who was introduced as 'a very dear friend'. Winnie disliked both on sight. Angela's mother was an older edition of the daughter, taut of figure, well dressed, with curls of unnaturally bright gold escaping from the smart forward-tilting hat. Her fashionable shoes, with their thick cork soles and heels, made Winnie's plain court shoes look very provincial. She sported a marcasite brooch in the shape of a basket of flowers on the lapel of her grey flannel suit, and spoke to Joan and Winnie in a faintly patronizing way which they both found intolerable.

She had travelled from Pinner in the friend's car, and Winnie would dearly have loved to inquire about the source of the petrol for this journey, but common decency forbade it.

The service was simple, the wedding breakfast at the local public house was informal, and the pair left for a two-day honeymoon somewhere in the Yorkshire dales. On their return the bridegroom would continue his bombing of Wilhelmshaven, Kiel or Bremen. How idiotic and unreal it all seemed, thought Winnie, making her way back to the station. The only real crumb of comfort was the memory of Edward's face, alight with happiness.

The golden summer wore on, and the blue skies above Caxley and the southern counties were crisscrossed with trails and spirals of silver vapour as the Battle of Britain raged in the air above the island. This was truly a battle for life and freedom as opposed to death and slavery at the hands of the Nazis. Across the channel the enemy amassed his armies of invasion, and by night and day sent waves of bombers to attack London and the south-east. The achievements of the R.A.F. gave the nation unparalleled hope of ultimate victory – long though it might be in coming.

The raids now began in earnest. The phoney war was at an end and the evacuees again began to stream from the stricken towns. Many of them spent the rest of the war away from their own homes. Many had no homes to return to. Many adopted the town of their refuge, grew up, married and became happy countrymen for the rest of their lives.

Sep's six boys had been found new billets when Edna died. Now he was anxious to have at least two back with him, despite the fact that his household help was sketchy. It was old Mrs North who thought of Miss Taggerty as housekeeper.

Miss Taggerty, almost as old as Sep, had once been in charge of Bender North's kitchenware department. She retired to look after an exasperating old father who was bed-ridden when being watched and remarkably spry on his pins when not, and who lived until the age of ninety-seven in a state of ever-growing demand. On his death, his cottage was due for demolition and poor, plain Miss Taggerty was to be made homeless.

The family had been anxious about Sep for some time. Joan very often called in to see her grandfather on the way home from school. He was touchingly grateful for her visits and Joan grew to love him, during this summer, more deeply than ever before. Bit by bit she began to realize how much Edna had meant to this lonely old man.

They sat together one hot afternoon in the little yard by the bakehouse, and Sep spoke of his lost wife. On the grey cobbles, near their outstretched legs, a beautiful peacock butterfly settled, opening and closing its bright powdery wings in the sunshine.

'Edna was like that,' said Sep in a low voice, almost as if he spoke to himself. 'As bright and lovely. I never cease to wonder that she settled with me – someone as humdrum and grey as that old cobblestone there. She could have had anyone in the world, she was so gay and pretty. I'd nothing to give her.'

'Perhaps,' said Joan, 'she liked to be near something solid and enduring, just as that butterfly does. If you are fragile and volatile then you are attracted to something stable. Surely that's why you and Grandma were so happy. You gave each other what the other lacked.'

'Maybe, maybe!' agreed Sep absently. There was a little pause and then he turned to look at his grandchild.

'You're a wise girl,' he said. 'Stay wise. Particularly when you fall in love, Joan. You need to consult your head as well as your heart when you start to think of marrying – and so many people will give you advice. Listen to them, but let your own heart and head give you the final answer.'

'I will,' promised Joan.

Later she was to remember this conversation. And Sep, with infinite sadness, was to remember it too.

Meanwhile, it was arranged for Miss Taggerty to take up her abode at Sep's house. The family was relieved to think that Sep would be properly looked after at last. With winter approaching, such things as well-aired sheets, good fires and a hot steak and kidney pudding made from rationed meat now and again, were matters of some domestic importance. With Miss Taggerty in the market square house the two evacuee boys could return, and Sep would be glad to feel that he was doing his war-time bit as well as having the pleasure of young company. As for Miss Taggerty, her cup of happiness was full. Used to a life of service, a gentle master such as Sep was a god indeed after the Moloch of her late father.

The winter of 1940 was indeed a bitter one. The war grew fiercer. Britain stood alone, at bay, the hope of the conquered nations and the inspiration of those who would later join in the struggle. The weather was unduly cold, fuel was short and food too. In Caxley, as elsewhere, this Christmas promised to be a bleak one.

But December brought one great glow of hope. The Lend-Lease Bill was prepared for submission to the United States' Congress. It meant that Britain could shape long-term plans of defence and attack with all the mighty resources of America behind her. It was a heart-warming thought in a chilly world.

Rose Lodge was to be the rendezvous for as many members of the Howard and North families as could manage it that Christmas. It looked as though it might be the last time that they would meet there, for, with the renewal of fighting, the question of turning the house into a nurses' hostel once again cropped up. This time it seemed most probable that it would be needed early in the New Year, and Winnie and her mother planned to move into the top floor of their old home, now Edward's, in the market square, for the duration of the war. At the moment, Robert was being allowed to use the flat as storage space. The thought of moving out his supplies was something of a headache but, as Sep pointed out rather sternly, it must be done.

Edward and Angela arrived late on Christmas Eve. He had three days' leave and they had been lucky enough to get a lift down in a brother officer's car, three jammed in the back and three in the front. They were to return in the same fashion on Boxing Night.

They were in great good spirits when they burst in at the door. It was almost midnight but old Mrs North insisted on waiting up and the two women had a tray of food ready by the fire.

'If only I had a lemon,' cried Winnie, pouring out gin and tonic for the pair, 'I think I miss lemons and oranges more than anything else. And Edward always says gin and tonic without lemon is like a currant bun with no currants!'

'Not these days, mum,' said Edward stoutly. 'Gin alone, tonic alone would be marvellous. To have the two together in one glass in war-time is absolutely perfect.'

'And how do you find domestic life?' Winnie asked her daughter-in-law.

'Wonderful, after those awful days in the W.A.A.F.,' said Angela. 'I potter about in my own time, and it's lovely to compare notes with the other girls who pop in sometimes when they're off-duty.'

She went on to describe the two rooms in which she and Edward now lived in the village near the aerodrome. Life in the services had obviously never appealed to Angela and her present circumstances, though cramped and somewhat lonely, were infinitely preferable.

'If only Edward hadn't to go on those ghastly raids,' claimed his wife: 'I stay up all night sometimes, too worried to go to bed. Luckily, there's a phone in the house, and I ring up the mess every so often to see if he's back.'

'You'd do better to go straight to bed with some hot milk,' observed Winnie. 'It would be better for you and far better for Edward too, to know that you were being sensible. It only adds to his worries if he thinks you are miserable.'

'I'm surprised you are allowed to ring up,' said Mrs North.

'Oh, they don't exactly *like* it,' said Angela, 'but what do they expect?'

Edward changed the subject abruptly. He had tried to argue with Angela before on much the same lines, and with as little effect.

'Shall we see all the family tomorrow?'

'Bertie and Kathy and the children are coming to tea. They're bringing your grandfather too. He misses Grandma, particularly at Christmas, and they will all be together for Christmas dinner at Bertie's.'

'And there's just a chance,' added his grandmother North, 'that Aunt Mary may look in. She starts in pantomime one day this week, and may be able to come over for the day.'

Edward stretched himself luxuriously.

'It's wonderful to be back,' he said contentedly. 'Nowhere like

Caxley. I can't wait for this bloody war to be over to get back again.'

'Language, dear!' rebuked his grandmother automatically, rising to go up to bed.

Before one o'clock on Christmas morning all the inhabitants of Rose Lodge were asleep.

All but one.

Edward lay on his back, his hands clasped behind his head, staring at the ceiling. Beside him Angela slept peacefully. He was having one of his 'black half-hours' as he secretly called them. What hopes had he of survival? What slender chances of returning to Caxley to live? Losses in Bomber Command were pretty hair-raising, and likely to become worse. He could view the thing fairly dispassionately for himself, although the thought of death at twenty-four was not what he looked for. But for Angela? How would she fare if anything happened to him? Thank God there were no babies on the way at the moment. He'd seen too many widows with young children recently to embark lightly on a family of his own.

The memory of his last raid on Kiel came back to him with sickening clarity. They had encountered heavy anti-aircraft fire as they approached their target and the Wellington had been hit. Luckily not much damage was done. They dropped their load and Edward wheeled for home. But several jagged pieces of metal, razor-sharp, had flown across the aircraft from one side to the other, and Dickie Bridges was appallingly cut across the face and neck.

One of the crew had been a first-year medical student when he joined up, and tied swabs across a spouting artery and staunched the blood as best he could. Nevertheless, Dickie grew greyer and greyer as the Wellington sped back to base and it was obvious that something was hideously wrong with his breathing. Some obstruction in the throat caused him to gasp with a whistling sound which Edward felt he would remember until his dying day.

As they circled the aerodrome he was relieved to see the ambulance – known, grimly, as 'the blood cart' – waiting by the runway. Sick and scared, Edward touched down as gently as he could and watched Dickie carried into the ambulance. He knew, with awful certainty, that he would never see him alive again.

Dickie Bridges died as they were getting him ready for a blood transfusion, and next day Edward sat down with a heavy heart and wrote to his crippled mother. He had been her only child.

Damn all wars! thought Edward turning over violently in bed. If only he could be living in the market square, sharing his flat with Angela, starting a family, flying when he wanted to, pottering about with his friends and family in Caxley – what a blissful existence it would be!

And here he was, on Christmas morning too, full of rebellion when he should be thinking of peace and goodwill to all men. Somehow it hardly fitted in with total war, Edward decided sardonically.

He thought of all the other Christmas mornings he had spent under this roof, a pillowcase waiting at the end of the bed, fat with knobbly parcels and all the joy of Christmas Day spread out before him. They had been grand times.

Would this be the last Christmas for him? He put the cold thought from him absolutely. His luck had held so far. It would continue. It was best to live from day to day, 'soldiering on', as they said. Enough that it was Christmas time, he was in Caxley, and with Angela!

He pitched suddenly into sleep as if he were a pebble thrown into a deep pond. Outside, in the silent night, a thousand stars twinkled above the frost-rimed roofs of the little town of Caxley.

Chapter Seven

THE MARKET SQUARE AGAIN

The New Year of 1941 arrived, and the people of Caxley, in company with the rest of the beleaguered British, took stock and found some comfort. The year which had passed gave reason for hope. Britain had held her own. Across the Atlantic the United States was arming fast and sending weapons in a steady stream to the Allied forces.

Even more cheering was the immediate news from Bardia in North Africa where the Australians were collecting twenty thousand Italian prisoners after one of the decisive battles in the heartening campaign which was to become known as the Desert Victory.

'The longer we hangs on the more chance we has of licking 'em!' pronounced an old farmer, knocking out his cherrywood pipe on the plinth of Queen Victoria's statue in the market square. He bent painfully and retrieved the small ball of spent tobacco which lay on the cobbles, picked one or two minute strands from it and replaced them carefully in his pipe.

'Not that we've got cause to get *careless*, mark you,' he added severely to his companion, who was watching the stubby finger ramming home the treasure trove. 'We've got to harbour our resources like Winston said – like what I'm doin' now – and then be ready to give them Germans what for whenever we gets the chance.'

And this, in essence, was echoed by the whole nation. 'Hanging on,' was the main thing, people told each other, and putting up with short commons as cheerfully as possible. It was not easy. As the months went by, 'making-do-and-mending' became more and more depressing, and sometimes well-nigh impossible. Another irritating feature of war-time life was the unbearable attitude of some of those in posts of officialdom.

It was Edward who noticed this particularly on one of his rare leaves in Caxley. It occurred one Saturday afternoon when the banks were closed and he needed some ready money. Luckily he had his Post Office savings book with him and thrust his way boisterously through the swing doors, book in hand. Behind the counter stood a red-haired girl whose protruding teeth rivalled Miss Taggerty's.

Edward remembered her perfectly. They had attended the same school as small children and he had played a golliwog to her fairy doll in the Christmas concert one year. On this occasion, however, she ignored his gay greeting, and thrust a withdrawal form disdainfully below the grille, her face impassive. Edward scribbled diligently and pushed it back with his book, whereupon the girl turned back the pages importantly in order to scrutinize the signature in the front and compare it with that on the form. For Edward, impatient to be away, it was too much.

'Come off it, Foof-teeth!' he burst out in exasperation, using the nickname of their schooldays. And only then did she melt enough to give him a still-frosty smile with the three pound notes.

There were equally trying people in Caxley, and elsewhere, who attained positions of petty importance and drove their neighbours to distraction: air raid wardens who seemed to relish every inadvertent chink of light in the blackout curtains, shop assistants rejoicing in the shortage of custard-powder, bus conductors harrying sodden queues, all added their pinpricks to the difficulties of everyday living, and these people little knew that such irritating officiousness would be remembered by their fellow-citizens for many years to come, just as the many little kindnesses, also occurring daily, held their place as indelibly in their neighbours' memories. Friends, and enemies, were made for life during war-time.

Howard's Restaurant continued to flourish despite shortages of good quality food stuffs which wrung Sep's heart. Robert failed his medical examination when his call-up occurred. Defective eyesight and some chest weakness sent him back to running the restaurant.

Secretly, he was relieved. He had dreaded the discipline and the regulations almost more than the dangers of active service. He was content to plough along his familiar furrow, fraught though it was with snags and pitfalls, and asked only to be left in peace. He said little to his father about his feelings, but Sep was too wise not to know what went on in his son's head.

The boy was a disappointment to him, Sep admitted to himself. Sometimes he wondered why his three sons had brought so much unhappiness in their wake. Jim's death in the First World War had taken his favourite from him. Leslie, the gay lady-killer, had betrayed his trust and vanished westward to live with someone whom Sep still thought of as 'a wanton woman', despite her subsequent marriage to his son.

And now, Robert. Without wife or child, curiously secretive and timid, lacking all forms of courage, it seemed, he appeared to Sep a purely negative character. He ran the restaurant ably, to be sure, but he lacked friends and had no other interests in the town. Perhaps, if marriage claimed him one day, he would come to life. As it was he continued his way, primly and circumspectly, a spinsterish sort of fellow, with a streak of petty spite to which Sep was not blind.

His greatest comfort now was Kathy. He saw more of her now than ever, for Bertie was away in the army, and she and the children were almost daily visitors to the house in the market square. She grew more like her dear mother, thought Sep, with every year that passed. She had the same imperishable beauty, the flashing dark eyes, the grace of movement and dazzling smile which would remain with her throughout her life.

Yes, he was lucky to have such a daughter – and such wonderful grandchildren! He loved them all, but knew in his secret heart that it was Edward who held pride of place. There was something of Leslie – the *best* of Leslie, he liked to think – something of the Norths, and a strong dash of himself in this beloved grandson. He longed to see children of Edward's before he grew too old to enjoy their company. Did his wife, that beautiful but rather distant Angela, really know what a fine man she had picked? Sometimes

Sep had his doubts, but times were difficult for everyone, and for newly-weds in particular. With the coming of peace would come the joy of a family, Sep felt sure.

And for Joan too, he hoped. She was a North, despite her name, if ever there was one, and the Norths were made for domesticity. There flashed into the old man's mind a picture of his dead friend Bender North, sitting at ease in his Edwardian drawing-room, above the shop which was now Howard's Restaurant. He saw him now, contented and prosperous, surveying the red-plush furniture, the gleaming sideboard decked with silver, smoking his Turk's-head pipe, at peace with the world. Just as contentedly had Bertie settled down with Kathy. He prayed that Joan, in her turn, might find as felicitous a future in a happy marriage. It was good, when one grew old, to see the younger generations arranging their affairs, and planning a world which surely would be better than that in which Sep had grown up.

Joan was indeed planning her future, unknown to her family. She was still absorbed in her work at the nursery school and as the months of war crept by it became apparent that the chances of joining the W.A.A.F. became slighter.

For one thing, the numbers at the school increased rapidly. As local factories stepped-up their output more young women were needed, and their children were left in the care of the school. And then the Viennese warden was asked to take over the job of organizing nursery work for the whole county, and Joan, trembling a little at such sudden responsibility, was put in charge.

She need not have worried. Despite her youth, she was well-trained, and had had varied experience. Allied to this, her equable North temperament and her genuine affection for the children, made her ideally suited to the post. Two women had been added to the staff, one of them being Maisie Hunter who had arrived at the beginning of the war as an evacuee at Rose Lodge and who had remained in the neighbourhood. She was a tower of strength to Joan. The second teacher was a wispy young girl straight from college, anxious to do the right thing, and still with the words of her child-psychology lecturer ringing ire her ears. Joan could only hope that face-to-face encounters with healthy three-year-olds would in time bring her down to earth a little, and give her confidence.

All this made Joan realize that her duty really lay with these young children and the job with which she had been landed. In some ways she regretted it. Her dream of being posted somewhere near Edward, perhaps even learning to fly one day, was doomed to fade. Nevertheless, this job was one equally valuable, and one which she knew she could tackle. It meant too that she could keep an eye on her mother and grandmother. Winnie was more active than ever, it seemed, but there were times when old Mrs North looked suddenly frail, and her memory, until now so acute, was often at fault. The oven would be left on, telephone messages were forgotten, spectacles and bags mislaid a dozen times a day and, worse still, the autocratic old lady would never admit that any of these little mishaps were her own fault. Physically, she was as active as ever, mounting the steep stairs to the flat in the market square as lightly as she had done when she lived there as mistress of the house so many years before.

All three women found the quarters somewhat cramped after Rose Lodge, but they all enjoyed living again in the heart of Caxley, close to their neighbours, and with the weekly market to enliven the scene each Thursday. They were handy too for the shops and for Sep's restaurant down below where they frequently called for a meal.

They found too that they were admirably placed to receive visits from their family and friends. Buses were few and far between, but the market square was a main shopping point, and friends and relations from the villages could call easily. Old Mrs North's sister, Ethel Miller, whose husband farmed at Beech Green, frequently came to see them bearing farm eggs, butter, an occasional chicken or duck – treasures indeed in wartime.

It was her Aunt Ethel who first introduced Michael to Joan. He was one of three junior army officers billeted at the farm, and Joan had heard a little about them all. They seemed to be a cheerful high-spirited trio and her aunt was devoted to them – indeed, so fulsome was she in her praise, that Joan had tended to think that their charms must be considerably overrated.

'Michael is picking me up at six o'clock,' said Aunt Ethel, glancing at the timepiece on the mantelpiece. She had been ensconced on the sofa when Joan came in from school at tea-time.

'He's had to collect some equipment from the station in the truck,' she explained, 'and offered me a lift.'

At ten past six they heard the sound of footsteps pounding up the stairs and Joan opened the door to admit the young man. He was full of apologies for being late, but he did not look particularly downcast, Joan observed. Aunt Ethel, anxious to get back to the family and the farm, made hurried farewells, and the two vanished after a few brief civilities. Joan, in spite of herself, was most impressed with the stranger.

He was exceptionally tall, a few inches over six feet, slender and dark. He had grey bright eyes with thick black lashes, and his face was lantern-jawed and pale. He was an Irishman, Joan knew, and he looked it. In the few words which he had spoken, Joan had recognized the soft brogue and the intonation full of Irish charm. A heart-breaker, if ever there was one, commented Joan amusedly to herself!

They did not meet again for some time, but one Saturday early in October, Joan offered to take some wool to the farm for her aunt.

'It will do me good to get some exercise,' she said, trundling out her bicycle from the shed where Bender had once kept mangles and dustbins, buckets and baths, in the old days.

It was a still misty day. Cobwebs were slung along the hedges like miniature hammocks. Droplets hung on the ends of wet twigs. There was a smell of autumn in the air, a poignant mixture of dead leaves, damp earth and the whiff of a distant bonfire.

Halfway to Beech Green a sharp hill caused Joan to dismount She stood still for a moment to get back her breath. Above her a massive oak tree spread gnarled wet arms. Looking up into its intricacies of pattern against the soft pale sky she noticed dozens of cobwebs draped like scraps of grey chiffon between the rough bark of the sturdy trunk and the branches. Far away, hidden in the mist, a train hooted. Near at hand, a blackbird scrabbled among papery brown leaves beneath the hedge. Otherwise silence enveloped the girl and she realized, with a shock, how seldom these days she enjoyed complete solitude.

What a long time it was too, she thought, since she had consciously observed such everyday natural miracles as the cobwebs and the blackbird's liquid eye! Engrossed with the children and their mothers, walking to and from the nursery school along the pavements of Caxley, restricted by war from much outside activity, she had quite forgotten the pleasure which flowers and trees, birds and animals had subconsciously supplied. She free-wheeled down the long hill to the farm, exhilarated by her unaccustomed outing.

Her aunt was busy making a new chicken-run and, with a quickening of the heart, Joan saw that Michael was wielding the mallet which drove in the stakes.

'You dear girl,' exclaimed Aunt Ethel, proffering a cold damp cheek to be kissed, while her fingers ripped open the package. 'Four whole ounces! I can't believe it! Now I shall be able to knit Jesse a good thick pair of winter socks. How on earth did Hilda manage it?'

'Sheer favouritism,' replied Joan. 'It was under-the-counter stuff, and passed over with much secrecy, I understand. They only had two pounds of wool altogether, Grandma said, and you had to be a real old blue-blooded Caxleyite to nobble an ounce or two.'

Michael laughed at this, and Joan found him more attractive than ever.

'Now hold the end of this wire,' directed Aunt Ethel, returning to the business in hand, 'and we'll be done in no time. Then you must stop and have lunch. It's rabbit casserole with lots of carrots.'

'S'posed to keep off night-blindness, whatever that is,' said Michael jerkily, between powerful blows with the mallet.

When the job was done and the excellent rabbit demolished, Michael and Joan sat in the warm farm kitchen and talked. Uncle Jesse was in the yard attempting to repair a wiring fault in his ancient Ford, while Aunt Ethel had gone upstairs 'to sort the laundry', she explained, although Joan knew very well that she was having the nap which she refused to admit she took every afternoon.

Michael talked easily. He told her about his home in Dublin and his family there.

'My old man keeps a hotel. Nothing in the five-star range, you know. Just a little place where the commercials stay overnight – but we've a quiet decent little house there and a grand garden.'

He had two sisters and a brother, he told her. His mother was an invalid, and he wanted to get back soon to see her.

'And what do you do,' asked Joan, 'when you're not in the army?'

'I'm not too sure,' answered Michael. 'You see, I'd just got my degree at Trinity College when war broke out. Maybe I'll teach. I read modern languages. Oh, there now, I can't tell you what I'll do, and that's the truth!'

Joan was intrigued with the way the last word came out as 'troot'. Despite his vagueness about the future, it was apparent that he intended to do something worthwhile. She told him a little about her own work and he seemed deeply interested.

'You're lucky,' he said. 'You know where you're going. Maybe I'll know too before long, but let's get the war over first, I think. Somehow, it's difficult to, make plans when you may be blown to smithereens tomorrow.'

He spoke cheerfully, his wide smile making a joke of the grim words.

'I wish I could see you home,' he said when at last Joan rose to go. 'But I'm on duty in half an hour. Can I ring you one day soon? Are you ever free?'

'I'm completely free,' Joan said.

'Good!' replied the young man with evident satisfaction.

They walked together to the front door of the farmhouse. Joan's dilapidated bicycle stood propped against the massive door-scraper which had served generations of muddy-booted Millers.

Across the lawn a copper beech tree stood against the grey fawn sky, like some old sepia photograph, framed in the oblong of the doorway.

'It's a grand country,' said Michael softly.

'Lovelier than Ireland?'

'Ah, I'm not saying that! Have you never been?'

'Never.'

'You must go one day when the war's over. I'll look forward to showing it to you.'

'That would be lovely,' said Joan, primly polite. She mounted the bicycle and smiled her farewells. He saluted very smartly, eyes twinkling, and watched her ride away.

She reported on her visit to her mother and grandmother as they sat by the fire that evening, saying little about Michael. She was more deeply attracted than she cared to admit, and felt that she could not face any family probings.

Old Mrs North's sharp eye, however, missed nothing.

'An attractive young man, that Michael,' she said, briskly tugging at her embroidery needle. 'Even if he is Irish.'

Joan smiled.

'Pity he's a Roman Catholic,' continued the old lady. 'Off to seven o'clock mass as regular as clockwork, Ethel says. But there,' she added indulgently, 'I expect it keeps him out of mischief.'

Joan nodded. But her smile had gone.

Chapter Eight

THE INVASION

Edward had been posted yet again. This time it was to a station in Wales where he would be a staff pilot, instructing others in the art of flying bombers. This was a rest period, for six months or possibly longer, between operational tours.

Angela was more than usually disgruntled at the move. She insisted on accompanying her husband wherever he might be, and was beginning to get heartily sick of other people's houses and unending domestic problems. As the war dragged on, she became steadily more discontented with her lot, and Edward was sincerely sorry for her. He knew how long the days were, cooped in two rooms, in someone else's home. He realized, only too well, the anxiety she suffered when he was on operations. And he was beginning to see that Angela had very few inner resources to give her refreshment and strength to combat her tedium.

She seemed to spend most of her time in the company of other young wives as bored as she was herself. They met for innumerable coffee parties and games of bridge. Edward had suggested more fruitful ways of spending the time. There was plenty of voluntary work to be done, helping in hospitals, schools, A.R.P. centres and so on but Angela's answer had been disturbing and illuminating.

'I married you to get out of the W.A.A.F. Why the devil should I put my head into another noose?'

It was not very reassuring to a newly-married man, and as the months lengthened into years Edward began to realize that Angela had meant every word of that remark. Perhaps they should have started a family, foolhardy though it seemed. Would things have been more satisfactory? He doubted it. Edward was too wise to pin his hopes on motherhood as a panacea to all marital ills, and he had observed other young couples' problems with babies in wartime. It was difficult enough to obtain accommodation without children. Those who had them were definitely at a disadvantage.

No, thought Edward, they had been right to wait. But would the time ever come when they both looked forward to children? With a heavy heart, he began to face the fact that Angela might have waited too long.

It was at the end of May when Edward and Angela made their next visit to Caxley.

'No family yet then?' Mrs North greeted them, with devastating directness. 'Why's that?'

Angela pointedly ignored the question. Edward laughed, hugged his diminutive grandmother and pointed out of the window to the market square.

'That partly,' he replied.

A steady flow of army transport was travelling across the square heading south to the ports. Lorries, armoured cars and tanks had been pouring through Caxley for days now, and the thunder of their passage shook the old house and caused headaches among the inhabitants.

But there was no heart-ache. This, they knew, was the start of a great invasion – an invasion in reverse. The time had come when this mighty Allied force could cross the Channel and begin the task of liberating oppressed Europe. Who would have thought it? they bellowed to each other, against the din. Four years ago it was the British Isles which awaited invasion! The tables were turned indeed.

Edward was now stationed within eighty miles of Caxley and was back on operational duty. He had no doubt that he would be busy bombing supply bases and cutting the communications of the retreating enemy. He should see plenty of activity, he told himself. It would be good to support an attacking army in Europe.

'Make no mistake,' he told his family, 'we're on the last lap now. Then back to Caxley and peace-time!'

That afternoon, while Angela was at the hairdresser's, he walked through the throbbing town to see Bertie who was also on brief leave. He found him pushing the lawn mower, his fair hair turning more and more ashen as the grey hairs increased, but still lissom in figure and with the same gentle good looks.

They greeted each other warmly.

'Kathy's out on some W.V.S. ploy,' said Bertie, 'and the children are still at school. Come and have a look at the river. It's quieter there than anywhere else in Caxley at the moment. But, by God, what a welcome sound, Edward, eh? Great days before us, my boy!'

It was indeed peaceful by the Cax. The shining water slipped along reflecting the blue and white sky. Here and there it was spangled with tiny white flowers which drifted gently to and fro with the current. On the tow path, across the river, a cyclist pedalled slowly by, and his reflection, upside down, kept pace with him swiftly and silently. The moment was timeless and unforgettable.

'Tell me,' said Bertie, 'has Joan said anything to you about Michael?'

'Not much,' replied Edward, startled from his reverie by something in his uncle's tone. 'Why, what's up?'

'They're very much in love,' said Bertie slowly. 'And to my mind would make a very good pair. He's a Catholic, of course, but it doesn't worry me. I wondered if it would complicate matters with the family.'

'Grandfather'd hate it,' admitted Edward bluntly. 'And probably Grandma North. I can't see anyone else losing much sleep over it. Surely, it's their affair.'

'I agree,' said Bertie. They paced the path slowly. Edward noticed that Bertie's limp was more accentuated these days and remembered, with a slight shock, that his uncle must now be over fifty.

'After all,' continued Edward ruminatively, 'you can't call the Norths a deeply religious family – and Joan and I, for all we're called Howard, take after the Norths in that way. I can't truthfully say I'm a believer, you know. There's too much to accept in church teaching – I boggle at a lot of it. But for those who really are believers, well, it's probably better to go the whole hog and be a Catholic. You know where you are, don't you?'

'Meaning what?' asked Bertie smiling at Edward's honest, if inelegant, reasoning.

'Well, if Joan is as luke-warm as I am, and yet she recognizes that Michael has something in his faith which means something to him, then she may be willing for the children to be brought up in the same way. I just don't know. I've never talked of such things with her.'

They turned in their tracks and made their way slowly back. A kingfisher, a vivid arrow of blue and green, streaked across the water and vanished into the tunnel made by the thick-growing chestnut trees.

'Lucky omen!' commented Bertie.

'In love or war?' asked Edward, gazing after it.

'Both, I predict,' said Bertie confidently, limping purposefully homeward.

It was at the end of that same week that Michael and Joan mounted the stairs to the flat and told Winnie and her mother that they were engaged.

Edward and Bertie were back on duty, Michael was moving to the coast the next day with his unit. The young couple did not blind themselves to the risks of the next few days. The casualties would be heavy, and it was likely that the army would bear the brunt of the attack. But nothing could dim their happiness, and Winnie and old Mrs North were glad to give them their blessing.

When at last Michael had gone and Joan returned, pink and a little damp-eyed from making her farewells, Mrs North spoke briskly the thoughts which were shared, but would have been left unuttered, by Winnie.

'Well, dear, I'm very happy for you. I've always liked Michael, as you know, and as long as you face the fact that there will be a new baby every twelve months or so I'm sure it will work out well. You'll stay C. of E. I suppose?'

'No, Grandma,' replied Joan composedly. 'I shall become a Roman Catholic, like all those babies-to-be.'

'Pity!' said the old lady. 'Well, you know your own business best, I suppose. Sleep well, and remember to take that ring off whenever you put your hands in water. Goodnight, dears.'

She put up her soft papery cheek to be kissed as usual, and went off to bed.

Winnie looked at her daughter. She looked tired out. Who wouldn't, thought Winnie, with all she had been through, and with Michael off to battle at first light? And yet there was a calmness about her which seemed unshakeable. Just so had she herself been when breaking the news of her engagement to Joan's father. Please, she prayed suddenly, let her marriage be happier than mine! And happier than Edward's! It was the first time, she realized suddenly, that she had admitted to herself that Edward's marriage was heading for the rocks. Were they all to be doomed to unhappiness with their partners?

She put the dark fear from her and kissed her daughter affectionately.

'Bed, my love,' she said.

It was Sep, of course, who felt it most. Joan told him the news herself the next day. She found him pottering about in his bakehouse, stacking tins and wiping the already spotless shelves.

She thought how little the place had changed since she was a child. The same great scrubbed table stood squarely in the middle of the red-tiled floor. The same comfortable warmth embraced one, and the same wholesome smell of flour and newly-baked bread pervaded the huge building. And Sep too, at first sight, seemed as little changed. Small, neat, quiet and deft in his movements, his grey hair was as thick as ever, his eyes as kindly as Joan always remembered them.

'Sit 'ee down, sit 'ee down,' cried Sep welcomingly, pulling forward a tall wooden stool. 'And what brings you here, my dear?'

Joan told him, twisting Michael's beautiful sapphire ring about her finger as she spoke. Sep heard her in silence to the end.

'I know you can't approve wholeheartedly, Grandpa,' said Joan, looking up at his grave face, 'but don't let it come between us, please.'

Sep sighed.

'Nothing can,' he said gently. 'You are part of my family, and a very dear part, as you know. And you're a wise child, I've always said so. Do you remember how you comforted me when your dear grandmother died?'

'You asked me then to choose wisely when I got married,' nodded Joan. 'I remember it very well. Do you think that I've chosen unwisely after all?'

'You have chosen a good man; I have no doubt of that,' replied Sep. 'But I cannot be happy to see you embracing his faith. You know my feelings on the subject. It is a religion which I find absolutely abhorrent, battening on the poor and ignorant, and assuming in its arrogance that all other believers are heretics.'

'Michael would tell you that it is the one gleam of hope in the lives of many of those poor and ignorant people,' replied Joan.

'Naturally he would,' responded Sep shortly. 'He is a devout Catholic. He believes what he is told to believe.'

He turned away and stood, framed in the doorway, looking with unseeing eyes at the cobbled yard behind the bakehouse. The clock on the wall gave out its measured tick. Something in one of the ovens hissed quietly. To Joan the silence seemed ominous. Her grandfather wheeled round and came back to where she sat, perched high on the wooden stool.

'We'll say no more. There must be no quarrels between us two. You will do whatever you think is right, I know, without being swayed by people round you. But think, my dear, I beg of you. Think, and pray. There are your children to consider.'

'I have thought,' replied Joan soberly.

'And whatever your decision,' continued Sep, as though he had not heard her interjection, 'we shall remain as we've always been. I want you to feel that you can come to me at any time. Don't let anything – ever – come between us, Joan.'

She rose from the stool and bent to kiss the little man's forehead.

'Nothing can,' she assured him. 'Nothing, Grandpa.'

But as she crossed the market square, and paused by Queen Victoria's statue to let the war-time traffic thunder by, her heart was torn by the remembrance of Sep's small kind face, suddenly shrivelled and old. That she, who loved him so dearly, could have wrought such a change, was almost more than she could bear.

On the night of 5 June in that summer of 1944 a great armada sailed from the English ports along the channels already swept clear of mines. By dawn the next day the ships stood ready off the Normandy coast for the biggest amphibious operation of the war – the invasion of Europe.

Edward was engaged in attacking enemy coast-defence guns, flying a heavy bomber. As the first light crept across the sky, the amazing scene was revealed to him as he flew back to base. The line upon line of ships, great and small, might have been drawn up ready for a review. A surge of pride swept him as he looked from above. The fleet in all its wartime strength was an exhilarating sight. Edward, for one, had not the faintest doubt in his mind that by the end of this vital day victory would be within sight.

Excitement ran high in the country. News had just been received of the liberation of Rome under General Alexander's command, but people were agog to know what was going on across the strip of water which had so long kept their island inviolate.

At midday the Prime Minister gave welcome news to the House of Commons. 'An immense armada of upwards of four thousand ships, together with several thousand smaller craft, crossed the Channel,' he told them and went on to say that reports coming in showed that everything was proceeding according to plan. 'And what a plan!' he added.

It was the success of this vast enterprise, on sea and land simultaneously, which gripped the imagination of the country. Napoleon had been daunted by the Channel. Hitler, for all his threats, had been unable to cross it. The success of the allied British and American armies in this colossal undertaking was therefore doubly exciting.

The inhabitants of Caxley kept their radio sets switched on, eager to hear every scrap of news which came through. Joan longed to know where Michael was and how he was faring. There must have been heavy casualties, she knew, and the suspense was agonizing.

The Norths and Howards knew where their other fighting men were. Bertie was stationed not far from Poole, and Edward was based in Kent. They did not expect to hear or see much of the pair of them in these exciting times, but the fortunes of Michael, now somewhere in the thick of things in Normandy were the focus of their thoughts.

As the days went by they grieved for Joan watching anxiously for the postman's visits. There was sobering news during the next week, about stubborn enemy resistance at the town of Caen. It was apparent that failure to capture this key-point would mean that a large force of allied troops would be needed there for some time. Could the enemy make a come-back?

One sunny morning the longed-for letter arrived and Joan tore it open in the privacy of her bedroom. She read it swiftly.

My Darling Joan,

All's well here. Tough going, but not a scratch, and a grand set of chaps. We are constantly on the move – but in the right direction, Berlin-wards. The people here are being wonderful to us.

I can't wait to get home again. Look after yourself. I'll write again as soon as I get a chance.

All my love,
Michael

Joan sat down hard on the side of the bed and began to cry. There was a tap at the door and her grandmother locked in. Tears were rolling steadily down the girl's cheeks, splashing upon the letter in her hands.

A chill foreboding gripped the old lady. In a flash she remembered the dreadful day during the First World War when she had heard the news that Bertie was seriously wounded in hospital. The memory of that nightmare drive to see him was as fresh in her mind as if it had happened yesterday.

She advanced towards her granddaughter, arms outstretched to comfort.

'Oh, Joan,' she whispered. 'Bad news then?'

The girl, sniffing in the most unladylike way, held out the letter.

'No, Grandma,' she quavered. 'It's good news. He's safe.'

And she wept afresh.

Chapter Nine

EDWARD AND ANGELA

It was the beginning of the end of the war, and everyone knew it. Perhaps this was the most hopeful moment of the long conflict. The free world still survived. Within a year Europe would be liberated, and two or three months later, hostilities would cease in the Far East. Meanwhile, a world which knew nothing yet of Belsen and Hiroshima, rejoiced in the victory which was bound to come.

It was the beginning of the end too, Edward realized, of his marriage. Things had gone from bad to worse. No longer could he blind himself with excuses for Angela's estrangement. Indifference had led to recriminations, petty squabbles, and now to an implacable malice on his wife's part. Edward, shaken to the core, had no idea how to cope with the situation now that things had become so bleakly impossible.

Any gesture of affection, any attempt on his part to heal the breach, was savagely rebuffed. Anything sterner was greeted with hysterical scorn. If he was silent he was accused of sulking, if he spoke he was told he was a bore.

It was about this time that an old admirer of Angela's appeared. She and Edward had been invited to a party at a friend's house. There was very little social life in the small Kentish town where they were then living, and Angela accepted eagerly. Edward preferred to be at home on the rare occasions when that was possible. He dreaded too the eyes which watched them, and knew that the break-up of their marriage was becoming all too apparent. But he went with good grace and secretly hoped that they would be able to get away fairly early.

It was a decorous, almost stuffy, affair. About twenty people, the local doctor and his wife, a schoolmaster, a few elderly worthies as well as one or two service couples, stood about the poorly-heated drawing-room and made falsely animated conversation. Their hostess was a large kindhearted lady swathed in black crêpe caught on the hip with a black satin bow. She was afflicted with deafness but courageously carried on loud conversations with every guest in turn. As the rest of the company raised their voices in order to make themselves heard, the din was overwhelming. Edward, overwrought and touchy, suddenly had a vision of the leafy tunnel of chestnut trees which arched above the Cax, and longed with all his soul to be there with only the whisper of the water in his ears.

As it was, he stood holding his weak whisky and water, his eyes smarting with smoke and his face frozen in a stiff mask of polite enjoyment. The doctor's wife was telling him a long and involved story about a daughter in Nairobi, of which Edward heard about one word in ten. Across the room he could see Angela, unusually gay, talking to an army officer whom he had not seen before.

They certainly seemed to enjoy each other's company, thought Edward, with a pang of envy. How pretty Angela was tonight! If only she would look at him like that – so happily and easily! The tale of the Nairobi daughter wound on interminably, and just as Edward was wondering how on earth he could extricate himself, he saw Angela's companion look across, touch Angela's arm, and together they began to make their way towards him.

At the same moment the doctor's wife was claimed by a faded little woman in a droopy-hemmed stockinette frock. They pecked each other's cheeks and squawked ecstatically. Thankfully, Edward moved towards his wife.

'Can you believe it?' cried Angela, 'I've found Billy again, after all these years! Billy Sylvester, my husband.'

'How d'you do?' said the men together.

'Billy has digs at the doctor's,' Angela prattled on excitedly. Edward wondered if he had heard all about the daughter in Nairobi, and felt a wave of sympathy towards the newcomer.

'We used to belong to the same sports club years ago,' continued

Angela, 'before Bill went into the army. Heavens, what a lot of news we've got to exchange!'

'Mine's pretty dull,' said Billy with a smile. He began to talk to Edward, as the daughter of the house moved across to replenish their glasses. He had been in the town now for about a month it transpired, and was in charge of stores at his camp.

'Any chance of going overseas?' asked Edward.

'Not very likely,' replied Billy, 'I'm getting a bit long in the tooth, and my next move will be either up north or west, as far as I can gather.'

Edward watched him with interest, as they sipped amidst the din. He was probably nearing forty, squarely built, with a large rather heavy face, and plenty of sleek black hair. He spoke with a pleasing Yorkshire accent, and gave the impression of being a sound business man, which was indeed the case. He did not appear to be the sort of man who would flutter female hearts, but Angela's blue eyes were fixed upon him in such a challenging manner, that Edward wondered what lay hidden from him in the past. Probably nothing more serious than a schoolgirl's crush on the star tennis player at the club, he decided. Or, even more likely, yet another gambit to annoy an unwanted husband. He was getting weary of such pinpricks, he had to admit.

Nevertheless, he liked the fellow. He liked his air of unpretentious solidity, the fact that his deep voice could be heard clearly amidst the clamour around them, and the way in which he seemed oblivious of Angela's advances.

After some time, Edward saw one of his friends across the room. He was newly-married and his young shy wife was looking well out of her depth.

'Let's go and have a word with Tommy,' said Edward to Angela.

'You go,' she responded. 'I'll stay with Bill.'

And stay she did, much to the interest of the company, for the rest of the evening.

Edward saw very little of Billy Sylvester after that. Occasionally, they came across each other in the town, and on one bitterly cold morning they collided in the doorway of 'The Goat and Compasses'. Angela, Edward knew, had seen something of him, but he had no idea how often they met. Angela spoke less and less, but she had let out that Billy had parted from his wife before the war, and that he had two boys away at boarding school.

Air attacks in support of the Allied forces were being intensified and Edward was glad to have so much to occupy him. He had been promoted again, and was beginning to wonder if he would stay in the Air Force after the war. In some ways he wanted to. On the other hand the restrictions of service life, which he had endured cheerfully enough in war-time, he knew would prove irksome and certainly Angela would be against the idea. He was beginning to long for roots, a home, a family, something to see growing. In his more sanguine moments he saw Angela in the Caxley flat, refurbishing it with him, starting life afresh. Or perhaps buying a cottage near the town, on the hilly slopes towards Beech Green, say, or in the pleasant southern outskirts of Caxley near the village of Bent? And then the cold truth would press in upon him. In his heart of hearts he knew that there could never be a future with Angela. She had already left him. The outlook was desolate. Meanwhile, one must live from day to day, and let the future take care of itself.

He returned home one wet February afternoon to find the flat empty. This did not perturb him, as Angela was often out. He threw himself into an armchair and began to read the newspaper. Suddenly he was conscious of something unusual. There was no companionable ticking from Angela's little clock on the mantelpiece. It had vanished. No doubt it had gone to be repaired, thought Edward, turning a page. He looked at his watch. It had stopped. Throwing down the paper, he went into the bedroom to see the time by the bedside alarm clock. The door of the clothes cupboard stood open and there were gaps where Angela's frocks and coats had hung.

Propped against the table lamp was a letter. Edward felt suddenly sick. It had come at last. His hands trembled as he tore it open.

Dear Edward,

Billy and I have gone away together. Don't try to follow us. Nothing you can do or say will ever bring me back. I don't suppose you'll miss me anyway.

Angela

At least, thought Edward irrelevantly, she was honest enough not to add 'Love'. What was to be done? He thrust the letter into his pocket and paced up and down the bedroom. He must go after her, despite her message. She was his wife. She must be made to return.

He stopped short and gazed out into the dripping garden. The tree trunks glistened with rain. Drops patterned on the speckled leaves of a laurel bush, and a thrush shook its feathers below.

Why must she be made to return? He was thinking as Sep might think, he suddenly realized. Angela was not a chattel. And what sort of life could they hope to live if he insisted on it? It was best to face it. It was the end.

The thrush pounced suddenly and pulled out a worm from the soil. It struggled gamely, stretched into a taut pink rubbery line. The thrush tugged resolutely. Poor devil, thought Edward, watching the drama with heightened sensibilities. He knew how the worm felt – caught, and about to be finished. The bird gave a final heave. The worm thrashed for a moment on the surface and was systematically jabbed to death by the ruthless beak above. Just so, thought Edward, have I been wounded, and just so, watching the thrush gobble down its meal, have I been wiped out. He watched the thrush running delicately across the wet grass, its head cocked sideways, searching for another victim.

He threw himself upon the bed and buried his face in the coverlet. There was a faint scent of the perfume which Angela used and his stomach was twisted with sudden pain. One's body, it seemed, lagged behind one's mind when it came to parting. This was the betrayer – one's weak flesh. A drink was what he needed, but he felt unable to move, drained of all strength, a frail shell shaken with nausea.

Suddenly, as though he had been hit on the back of the head, he fell asleep. When he awoke, hours later, it was dark, and he was shivering with the cold. His head was curiously heavy, as though he were suffering from a hangover, but he knew, the moment that he awoke, what had caused this collapse. Angela had gone.

The world would never be quite as warm and fair, ever again.

Meanwhile, in Caxley, Joan was receiving instruction from the local Roman Catholic priest, much to her own satisfaction and to her grandfather's secret sorrow.

The wedding was planned for the end of April, when Michael expected leave, and would take place in the small shabby Catholic church at the northern end of Caxley.

Old Mrs North made no secret of her disappointment.

'I've always hoped for a family wedding at St Peter's,' she said regretfully to Joan. 'Your dear mother would have made a lovely bride. I so often planned it. The nave is particularly suitable for a wedding. I hoped Winnie would have a train. Nothing more dignified – in good lace, of course. And the flowers! They always look so beautiful at the entrance to the chancel. Lady Hurley's daughter looked a picture flanked by arum lilies and yellow roses! D'you remember, Winnie dear? It must have been in 1929. I suppose there's no hope of you changing your mind, dear, and having the wedding at dear old St Peter's?'

'None at all,' smiled Joan. 'Of course, if I'd met Michael four or five hundred years ago we should have been married in St Peter's. But thanks to Henry the Eighth I must make do with the present arrangements.'

'Now, that's a funny thing,' confessed her grandmother. 'It never occurred to me that St Peter's was once Roman Catholic! It really gives one quite a turn, doesn't it?'

Preparations went on steadily. Joan got together a sizeable quantity of linen and household goods. Kind friends and relatives parted with precious clothing coupons and she was able to buy a modest trousseau. Sep made the most elegant wedding cake consistent with war-time restrictions and embellished it, touchingly, with the decorations from his own wedding cake which Edna had treasured.

He had given Joan a generous dowry.

'You will want a house of your own one day,' he told her. 'This will be a start. I hope it won't be far from Caxley, my dear, but I suppose it depends on Michael. But I hope it won't be in Ireland. Too far for an old man like me to visit you.'

Joan could not say. Somehow she thought that Ireland would be her home in the future. As Sep said, it all depended on Michael.

One thing grieved her, in the midst of her hopeful preparations. Sep would be present at the reception, but he could not face the ceremony in the Catholic church. His staunch chapel principles would not allow him to put a foot over the threshold.

In the midst of the bustle came Edward's catastrophic news. Joan, herself so happy, was shocked and bewildered. The bond between Edward and herself was a strong one, doubly so perhaps, because they had been brought up without a father. She had never shared her mother's and grandmother's misgivings about Angela, for somehow she had felt sure that anyone must be happy with Edward, so cheerful, so dependable as he was. This blow made her suddenly unsure of her judgement. Loyalty to her brother made her put the blame squarely on Angela's shoulders. On the other hand, a small doubting voice reminded her of the old saw that it takes two to make a marriage.

Had Edward been at fault? Or was this tragedy just another side-effect of war? She prayed that she and Michael would be more fortunate.

Her mother took the news soberly and philosophically. She had known from the first that Angela would never do. Much as she grieved for Edward, it was better that they should part now, and she thanked Heaven that no children were involved in the parting.

It was old Mrs North, strangely enough, who seemed most upset. Normally, her tart good sense strengthened the family in times of crisis. This time she seemed suddenly old – unable to bear any more blows. The truth was that the ancient wound caused by Winnie's unhappy marriage to Leslie Howard, was opened again. With the controversial marriage of Joan imminent, the old lady's spirits drooped at this fresh assault. Edward was very dear to her.

He could do no wrong. In her eyes, Angela was a thoroughly wicked woman, and Edward was well rid of her. But would any of her family find married happiness? Would poor Joan? Sometimes she began to doubt it, and looked back upon her own long years with Bender as something rare and strange.

Edward was at the wedding to give the bride away. He looked thinner and older, and to Joan's way of thinking, handsomer than ever. He refused to speak of his own affairs, and set himself out to make Joan's wedding day the happiest one of her life.

With the exception of Sep and Robert the rest of Joan's relations were there with Kathy's auburn-haired daughter as bridesmaid, and Bertie and Kathy's small son as an inattentive page. Michael's mother was too ill to travel and his father too was absent, but a sister and brother, with the same devastating Irish good looks as the bridegroom, were present, and impressed old Mrs North very much by their piety in church.

'I must say,' she said to Winnie, in tones far too audible for her daughter's comfort, 'the Catholics do know how to behave in church. Not afraid to bend the knee when called for!'

Winnie was glad that something pleased the old lady, for she knew that she found the small church woefully lacking in amenities compared with Caxley's noble parish church built and made beautiful with the proceeds of the wool trade, so many centuries earlier.

There were few Roman Catholics in Caxley. One or two families from the marsh, descended from Irish labourers who had built the local railway line, attended the church. Two ancient landed families came in each Sunday from the countryside south of the town, but there was little money to make the church beautiful. To old Mrs North the depressing green paint, the dingy pews and, above all, the crucified figure of Christ stretched bleeding high above the nave, were wholly distasteful. A church, she thought, should be a dignified and beautiful place, a true house of God, and a proper setting for the three great dramas of one's life, one's christening, one's marriage and one's funeral. This poor substitute was just not good enough, she decided firmly, as they waited for the bride.

Her eyes rested meditatively upon the bridegroom and his

brother, and her heart, old but still susceptible, warmed suddenly. No doubt about it, they were a fine-looking family. One could quite see the attraction.

There was a flurry at the end of the church and the bride came slowly down the aisle on her brother's arm. Old Mrs North struggled to her feet, and looking at her granddaughter's radiant face, forgot her fears, If she knew anything about anything, this was one marriage in the Howard family which would turn out well!

Chapter Ten

VICTORY

The honeymoon was spent at Burford and the sun shone for them. The old town had never looked lovelier, Joan thought, for she had visited it often before the war. This was Michael's first glimpse of the Cotswolds. He could not have seen Burford at a better time. The trees lining the steep High Street were in young leaf. The cottage gardens nodded with daffodils, and aubretia and arabis hung their bright carpets over the grey stone walls.

As May broke, they returned to Caxley and to neglected news of the world of war. Much had happened. A photograph of the ghastly end of Mussolini and his mistress, Signorina Petacci, shocked them as it had shocked the world. And now, the suicide of Hitler was announced. On the last day of April, as Joan and Michael had wandered along the river bank at Burford, Hitler and his newly-married wife, Eva Braun, had done themselves to death, with pistol and poison.

A week later came the unconditional surrender of the enemy. By that time, Michael was back with his regiment, and Joan watched the celebrations of victory with her family in the market square.

The cross of St George fluttered on the flag pole of St Peter's, close by the flapping Union Jack at the Town Hall. The Corn Exchange was draped with bunting and some irreverent reveller had propped a flag in Queen Victoria's hand. The public houses were busy, sounds of singing were abroad and everywhere people stopped to congratulate each other and share their relief.

But there was still the knowledge that the war was not completely finished, and Joan listened with her family to the voice of Churchill giving the nation grave thoughts in the midst of rejoicing.

'I wish,' he said, 'I could tell you tonight that all our toils and troubles were over. But, on the contrary, I must warn you that there is still a lot to do, and that you must be prepared for further efforts of mind and body.' He went on to point out that 'Beyond all lurks Japan, harassed and failing, but still a people of a hundred millions, for whose warriors death has few terrors.'

He was listened to with attention; but the moment was too happy to darken with sober warnings. For most of his hearers one splendid fact dazzled them. Victory in Europe was accomplished. Victory in the rest of the world must follow soon. And then, after six bloody years, they would have peace at last.

In the months that followed, old Mrs North spoke joyfully of returning to Rose Lodge. Winnie had her doubts about the wisdom of this step. Now that there were only the two of them to consider, the house seemed over-large, and they must face the problem of little or no help in running it. Mrs North refused to be persuaded.

'I absolutely set my face against finding another place,' she declared flatly. 'Rose Lodge is my home, bought for me by your dear father. The nurses are moving out in a month or two. There's no reason at all why we shouldn't get out the old furniture from store and move in right away. Besides, Edward will want this flat again the minute he's demobbed. We must leave everything ready for him.'

Winnie was wise enough to drop the subject for the time being, but returned to the attack whenever she had a chance. It was no use. The old lady was unshakeable in her determination.

'Go back,' Bertie advised his sister. 'Dash it all, she's getting on for eighty! She may as well enjoy her own for the rest of her time. Rose Lodge was all she ever wanted when she lived in the market place, and she's had to do without it for years.'

'I suppose we must,' sighed Winnie. 'But I shall shut off some of the rooms. It's a house that eats fuel, as you know, I really don't think I can cope with the cleaning single-handed.

'We're all getting old,' agreed Bertie cheerfully. 'But I bet

Mamma will be in and out of the locked rooms smartly enough with a duster.'

Soon after this Edward had a few days' leave, and within twenty-four hours was thanking his stars that his stay would be a short one. If anyone had ever told him that Caxley would pall, he would have denied it stoutly. But it was so.

He knew that he was under strain. He knew that Angela's desertion was a greater shock than he cared to admit. He was torn with remorse, with guilt, with what he might have left undone. He had thrown himself, with even more concentration, into his flying duties and now lived on the station, hoping, in part, to forget his trouble. All this added to the tension.

Perhaps he had relied too much on the healing powers of his native town. Perhaps, after all, he had outgrown the childhood instinct to return home when hurt. Perhaps the people of Caxley, his own family included, were as spent as he was after six years of lean times and anxiety. Whatever the causes, the results for Edward were plain. He could not return to Caxley to live, as things were.

His womenfolk said very little to him, but there was a false brightness in their tones when they did, and a sad brooding look of inner pain when they watched him. Edward found both unendurable. Bertie was the only person he could talk to, and to him he unburdened his heart.

'I just can't face it,' he said savagely, kicking the gravel on Bertie's garden path. 'Anyone'd think I was suddenly an idiot. They talk to me as though I'm a child who is ill. And then I snap at them, and feel an utter heel. God, what's going to be the end of it?'

'It's the hardest thing in the world,' observed Bertie, 'to accept pity gracefully. It's easy enough to give it.'

'It isn't only pity,' retorted Edward. 'There were two old cats whispering behind their hands in the restaurant, and I've had one or two pretty unpleasant remarks chucked at me. The top and bottom of it is that Caxley's little and mean, and I never saw it before. I feel stifled here – as though everyone has known and watched the Howards for generations. We're simply actors to them

– people to look at, people to feed their own cheap desire for a bit of drama.

'If you haven't realized that until now,' said Bertie calmly, 'you're a good deal more naïve than I thought. We all have to take our turn at being a nine days' wonder. It's yours now, and damned unpleasant too – but you'll be forgotten by next week when someone else crops up for the place in the limelight.'

'You're right,' agreed Edward bitterly. 'But it makes no difference to me for good, even if other people forget in a day or two. In any case I shall get a job elsewhere for a year or two, and then see how I feel about Caxley. What is there to bring me back?'

'Nothing,' said Bertie. 'Except us. I'm not trying to wring your withers and all that – but when this has blown over, I hope you'll want to come back to the family again.'

'Maybe I will. Maybe I won't. All I need now is to thrash about a bit and see other places and find a useful job. One thing, I'm alone now, and I'll take good care I stay that way. I've had enough of women's ways to last me a lifetime.'

Bertie observed his nephew's devastating, if sulky, good looks with a quizzical eye, but forbore to comment on his last remark.

'There's a chap in the mess at the moment,' continued Edward, 'whose father runs a factory for making plastic things – a sort of progression from perspex and that type of thing. He says there should be a great future in plastic materials. Might even make them strong enough for use in building and ships and so on.

'Would you want to go in for that sort of thing?'

'I'm interested,' nodded Edward. 'Jim took me to meet the old boy a few weeks ago. I liked him. He's got ideas and he works hard. I know he wants to build up the works as soon as he can. If he offered me a job, I think I'd take it.'

'Where would it be?'

'Near Ruislip. I'd rather like to be near London, too.'

'It sounds a good idea,' agreed Bertie, glad to see that his companion could still be kindled into life. 'I hope it comes off.'

They wandered through the garden gate to the tow path. The Cax reflected the blue and white sky above it. In the distance a fisherman sat immobile upon the opposite bank. Edward looked upon the tranquil scene with dislike, and skimmed a pebble viciously across the surface of the water towards the town.

'And at least I'd get away from here,' was his final comment.

The Cax flowed on placidly. It had seen centuries of men's tantrums. One more made very little difference.

That evening the occupants of the flat above Howard's Restaurant descended for their dinner. They did this occasionally when the restaurant was shut, and Robert was agreeable. He waited on them himself and joined the family party at coffee afterwards.

Sep came across and Bertie too was present. It was a cheerful gathering. Although the curtains were drawn across the windows looking on to the market place, those at the back of the building remained pulled back, and the sky still glowed with the remains of a fine July sunset. The little white tables and chairs, set out upon the grassy lawn sloping down gently to the Cax, glimmered in the twilight. It was comfortably familiar to Edward, and even his frayed nerves were soothed by the view which had remained the same now for years.

It was Joan who brought up the subject of Edward's return to the flat.

'How soon, do you think,' she asked, 'before you can come home again?'

Better now than later, decided Edward.

'I don't think that I shall come back to Caxley for a while,' he answered deliberately.

'Why ever not?' exclaimed old Mrs North. 'It's your home, isn't it?'

Edward drew a crescent very carefully on the white tablecloth with the edge of a spoon, and was silent.

'Edward's quite old enough to do as he pleases, Mamma,' said Bertie quietly.

'I hope you will come back, dear boy,' said Sep, putting a frail old hand on his grandson's sleeve.

'One day, perhaps,' said Edward, putting his own hand upon his grandfather's. 'But I want to have a spell elsewhere. You understand?'

'I understand,' said the old man gravely. 'You know what is best for you.'

'There's no need to feel that you are pushing us out,' began his mother, not quite understanding the situation. 'You know that we shall go back to Rose Lodge very soon.'

'Yes, dear, I do know that,' replied Edward, as patiently as he could. He drew a circle round the crescent, turning the whole into a plump face with a large mouth. He became conscious of Robert's eyes fixed upon him, and put down the spoon hastily, like a child caught out in some misdemeanour. But it was not the mutilation of the white starched surface which gave Robert that intent look, as Edward was soon to discover.

It was now almost dark and Sep rose to go, pleading a slight headache.

'I shall see you again before you leave,' he said to Edward, turning at the door. Edward watched him cross the market square, his heart full of affection for the small figure treading its familiar way homeward.

The ladies too had decided to retire. Good-nights were said, and Bertie, Edward and Robert were alone at the table. Robert carefully refilled the three coffee cups. His face was thoughtful.

'Have you any idea,' he asked 'when you'll come back to Caxley?'

'None,' said Edward shortly. 'At the moment I feel as though I want to turn my back on it for good.'

A sudden glint came into Robert's eyes. It was not unnoticed by the watchful Bertie.

'In that case,' said Robert swiftly, 'you won't want the rooms upstairs. Would you think of letting me have them? I would give you a good price to buy the whole of this property outright.'

Edward looked at Robert in astonishment. His Uncle Bertie's face had grown pink with concern.

'Thanks for the offer,' said Edward shortly, 'but I wouldn't do anything to upset Grandpa Howard. And in any case, I don't intend to part with the property.

'You've no business to make such a suggestion,' exclaimed Bertie. His blue eyes flashed with unaccustomed fire. Edward had never seen his uncle so angry, and a very intimidating sight he found it.

'If he doesn't want it, why hang on to it?' demanded Robert. A little nerve twitched at the corner of his mouth, and he glared across the table at his brother-in-law.

'He may want it one day,' pointed out Bertie, 'as well you know. It is unfair to take advantage of the boy at a time like this. More than unfair – it's outrageous!'

'He's being nothing more nor less than a dog in the manger,' retorted Robert heatedly. 'He doesn't want it, but he'll dam' well see I don't have it! Why on earth the old man ever made such a barmy arrangement I shall never know! I'm his son, aren't I? How does he expect me to run this place with no storage rooms above it? The old fool gets nearer his dotage daily – and others profit by it!'

Edward, who had grown tired of listening to the two men arguing his affairs as though he were not present, felt that he could stand no more.

'Oh, shut up, both of you,' he cried. 'We'll keep Grandpa out of this, if you don't mind. And forget the whole thing. You can take it from me, Robert, the house remains mine as he intended, whether I live here or not, and you must like it or lump it.'

He rose from the table, looking suddenly intensely weary.

'I'm off to bed. See you in the morning. Goodnight!'

'I'm off too,' said Bertie grimly. He limped towards the door of the restaurant as Edward began to mount the stairs to his own apartment.

He heard the door crash behind his uncle, and then two sounds, like pistol shots, as Robert viciously slammed the bolts home.

The sooner I get out of this, the better, determined Edward, taking the last flight of stairs two at a time.

The next morning he made his round of farewells cheerfully.

Robert seemed to have forgotten the previous evening's unpleasantness and wished him well. Sep's handshake was as loving as ever. He called last of all on Bertie.

'I'm sorry I lost my temper last night,' Bertie greeted him. 'I hate to say this, Edward, but you must be wary of Robert. He's a man with a grievance, and to my mind he gets odder as the years go by.'

'I'll watch out,' smiled Edward, making light of it.

'He's let this separation of the house and the restaurant become an obsession,' continued Bertie, 'and he's decidedly unbalanced when the subject crops up. Hang on to your own, my boy. It would break Sep's heart if he thought you'd broken with Caxley for good.'

'I know that,' said Edward quietly.

They parted amicably, glad to know each other's feelings, and Edward made his way up Caxley High Street noticing the placards on the buildings and in shop windows exhorting the good people of Caxley to support rival candidates in the coming election. Not that there would be much of a fight in this secure Conservative seat, thought Edward. The outcome was a foregone conclusion. And so, he felt sure, was the return of the Conservative party to power. The hero of the hour was Winston Churchill. It was unthinkable that he should not lead the nation in peacetime, and as bravely as he had in these last five years of grim warfare.

He was right about Caxley's decision. The Conservative candidate was returned, but by a majority so small that his supporters were considerably shaken. When at last the nation's wishes were made known, and the Socialists were returned with a large majority, Edward was flabbergasted and disgusted, and said so in the mess.

Back in Caxley old Mrs North summed up the feelings of many of her compatriots, as she studied the newspaper on the morning of 27 July.

'To think that dear Mr Churchill has got to go after all he's done for the nation! The ungrateful lot! I'm thoroughly ashamed of them. The poor man will take this very hard, and you can't wonder at it, can you? I shall sit straight down, Winnie dear, and write to him.'

And, with back straight as a ramrod and blue eyes afire, she did.

The end of the conflict was now very close. Millions of leaflets demanding surrender were showered on the inhabitants of Japan. The last warning of 'complete and utter destruction' was given on 5 August. On the following day the first atomic bomb was cast upon Hiroshima, and on 9 August a second one was dropped on the city of Nagasaki. Within a week the terms set out by the Allied governments were accepted, and the new Prime Minister, Mr Attlee, broadcast the news at midnight.

Overwhelming relief was, of course, the first reaction. There were still a few places in the Far East where fighting continued, but virtually this was the end of the war. Soon the men would be back, and life would return to normal.

Sep surveyed the happy crowds from his bedroom window, and thought of that other victory, nearly thirty years earlier, when the flags had fluttered and the people of Caxley had greeted peace with a frenzy of rejoicing. Today there was less madness, less hysteria. It had been a long bitter struggle, and there had been many casualties, but the numbers had been less than in that earlier cruel war.

He remembered how he had stood grieving for his dead son amidst his neighbours' cheers. Thank God that his family had been spared this time! He looked down upon the bronze crown of Queen Victoria below him, and wondered inconsequently what she would make of a victory finally won by an atomic bomb. The descriptions of its ghastly power had affected Sep deeply. Now that such forces were known to the world, what did the future hold for mankind? What if such a weapon fell into the hands of a maniac like Hitler? Would the world ever be safe again?

Four young men, aflame with bonhomie and beer, had caught each other by the coat tails and were stamping round Queen Victoria's plinth shouting rhythmically 'Victory for us! Victory for us! Victory for us!' to the delight of the crowd.

Sep turned sadly from the window. Victory indeed, but at what a price, mourned the old man, at what a price!

Part Two

1945–1950

Chapter Eleven

EDWARD STARTS FRESH

The return to Rose lodge was accompanied by the usual frustrations
and set-backs. The decorators waited for the plasterers' work to be
completed. The electricians waited for the plumbers to finish their
part. A chimney was faulty. Damp patches had appeared mysteriously on the landing ceiling. The paintwork inside and out showed
the neglect of six years of war and hard wear.

At times Winnie wished that she had stuck to her guns and
refused point blank to return. But her mother's joy was not a whit
dampened by the delays, and she threw herself with zest into the
job of choosing wallpaper and curtaining from the meagre stocks
available. Tirelessly she searched the shops for all the odds and
ends needed to refurbish her home. One morning she would be
matching fringe for the curtains, or gimp for a newly upholstered
chair; on the next she would be comparing prices of coke and
anthracite for the kitchen boiler. She was just as busy and excited as
she had been years ago, Winnie recalled, when the family moved to
Rose Lodge for the first time. Bertie had been quite right. Rose
Lodge meant everything to their mother, and it was obviously best
that she should spend the rest of her days there.

They moved from the market square on a blustery November
day. Ragged low clouds raced across the sky. The Caxley folk,
cowering beneath shuddering umbrellas, battled against the wind
that buffeted them. Vicious showers of rain slanted across the
streets, and the removal men dripped rivulets from their shiny
macintoshes as they heaved the furniture down the stairs and into
the van.

But, by the evening, Winnie and her mother sat exhausted but triumphant one on each side of the familiar drawing-room hearth.

'Home, at last,' sighed the old lady happily, looking about her. It was still far from perfect. The curtains hung stiffly, the carpet had some extraordinary billows in it, the removal men had scraped the paint by the door and chipped a corner of the china cabinet, but she was content.

'And to think,' she continued, 'that Edward will be demobilized in a few weeks' time, and dear Bertie, and perhaps Michael, and we can all have a proper family Christmas here together. The first peacetime Christmas!'

'I wonder how Joan's managing,' answered Winnie, still bemused from the day's happenings. 'I hope she won't feel lonely.'

'Lonely?' echoed her mother. 'In the market place? Take my word for it, she's as right as ninepence with the flat to play with and her own nice new things to arrange. She'll thoroughly enjoy having a place of her own.'

'You're probably right, Mamma,' said Winnie. 'Early bed for us tonight. There are muscles aching in my back and arms which I never knew I had before.'

By ten o'clock Rose Lodge was in darkness and its two occupants slept the sleep of the happy and exhausted.

It was Joan who had written to Edward to ask if she and Michael might have the flat temporarily, and he was delighted to think of it being of use to the young couple. He had been offered a good post in the plastics firm, as he had hoped, and was already looking forward to finding a flat or a house somewhere near London and the job.

This suited Joan and Michael admirably. It was plain that the nursery school would close now that the war was over, despite the recommendations of the Education Act of 1944. Joan grieved at the thought, but numbers were dwindling steadily, as the men came back, and the evacuees moved away from Caxley. By Easter the school would be no more, and the Quaker meeting house which had echoed to the cries and mirth of the babies, tumbling about the scrubbed floor in their blue-checked overalls, would once more be silent and empty, but for the decorous meetings of the children's war-time hosts, the Friends.

She was glad, though, that she had a job to do, for it transpired that Michael's demobilization would be deferred. He was now in Berlin, and his fluency in German was of great use. He had been given further promotion and been asked to stay on until the spring, but he had Christmas leave and the two spent a wonderful week arranging their wedding presents and buying furniture for the future.

'None of this blasted utility stuff,' declared Michael flatly. 'I'm sick of that sign anyway. We'll pick up second-hand pieces as we go – things we shall always like.' And so they went to two sales, and haunted the furniture shops in Caxley High Street which offered the old with the new.

Christmas Day was spent at Rose Lodge to please Mrs North. Edward and Bertie, recently demobilized, were in high spirits. All the conversation was of the future and Winnie, surveying the Norths and Howards filling the great drawing-room, thought how right it was that it should be so. The immediate past was bleak and tragic; and, for her particularly, earlier years in this house held sad memories. She remembered arriving with Joan as a baby and Edward as a toddler to find her mother dressing the Christmas tree in just the same place as the present one. Leslie had left her, and the long lonely years had just begun. She often wondered what had become of him – the handsome charmer whose son was so shatteringly like him in looks – but hoped never to see him again. He had hurt her too cruelly.

One evening before Michael returned to Germany, Joan and he talked over their plans for the future. At one time he had thought of following up his Dublin degree with a year's training for his teacher's diploma, but now he had his doubts about this course.

'I don't think I could face sitting at a desk and poring over books again. The war's unsettled me – I want to start doing something more practical. I've talked to other fellows who broke their university course, or who had just finished, like me, and there are mighty few who have got the guts to return to the academic grind again. Somehow one's brain gets jerked out of the learning groove. I know for a fact mine has.'

He faced Joan with a smile.

'Besides,' he continued, 'I've a wife and a future family to support now. I must earn some money to keep the home together. We shan't want to stay in Caxley all our lives, you know, and we shall have to buy a house before long.'

'But what do you want to do?' asked his wife earnestly. 'I do understand about not wanting to go back to school, I couldn't face it myself. But what else have you thought of? It seems a pity not to use your languages.'

'I wouldn't mind doing the same sort of thing that my father does – hotel work. Here or abroad. I'm easy. And perhaps, one day, owning our own hotel. Or a chain of them.'

His eyes were sparkling. He spoke lightly, but Joan could see that there was an element of serious purpose behind the words.

'Or I could stay in the army. That's been put to me. What do you feel about that, my sweet?'

'Horrible,' said Joan flatly. 'I've had enough of the army; and the idea of moving from one army camp to another doesn't appeal to me one little bit. And you know how *backward* army children are, poor dears, shunted from pillar to post and just getting the hang of one reading method when they're faced with an entirely different one.'

Michael laughed at this practical teacher's approach.

'I can't say I'm keen to stay myself,' he agreed. 'Six years is enough for me. We'd be better off, of course, but is it worth it?'

'Never,' declared Joan stoutly. 'Let's be poor and lead our own lives.'

And with that brave dictum they shelved the future for the remainder of his leave.

Meanwhile, Edward had been finding out just how difficult it was to get somewhere to live near London. He tried two sets of digs whilst he was flat hunting and swore that he would never entertain the thought of lodgings again. The only possible hotel within striking distance of the factory was expensive, noisy, and decidedly seedy.

It was Jim, the son of his employer, who saved him at last.

'I've got a house,' he cried triumphantly one morning, bursting into the office which he shared with Edward. 'It's scruffy, it's jerry-built, but it's got three bedrooms and a garden. Eileen is off her head with delight. Now the boy can have a bedroom of his own, and the baby too when it arrives.'

Edward congratulated him warmly. Then a thought struck him.

'And what about the flat?'

'A queue for that as long as your arm,' began Jim. He stopped pacing the floor and looked suddenly at his colleague. 'Want it?' he asked, 'because if you do, it could be yours. The others can wait. I'll have a word with the old man.'

After a little negotiation, it was arranged, and Edward moved in one blue and white March day. A speculative builder, an old school friend of Edward's employer, had acquired the site a few years before the war, and had erected two pairs of presumably semi-detached houses, well placed in one large garden. Each house was divided into two self-contained flats, so that there were eight households all told in about an acre of ground.

The plot was situated at the side of an old tree-lined lane and was not far from a golf course. A cluster of fir trees and a mature high hedge screened the flats from the view of passers-by. The ground-floor tenants agreed to keep the front part of the garden in order, the upstairs tenants the back.

The rent was pretty, steep, Edward privately considered, by Caxley standards, but he liked the flat and its secluded position and would have paid even more for the chance of escaping from digs and hotels. He surveyed his new domain thankfully. He had a sitting-room, one bedroom, a kitchen, a bathroom and a gloriously large cupboard for trunks, tennis racquets, picnic baskets and all the other awkward objects which need to be housed. He was well content.

He saw little of his neighbours in the first few weeks, and learned more about them from Jim than from his own brief encounters. His own flat was on the ground-floor, and immediately beside him lived a middle-aged couple, distantly related to the owner, and now retired. Edward liked the look of them. The wife had wished him 'Good morning' in a brisk Scots brogue and her husband reminded him slightly of his grandfather, Bender North.

Above them lived a sensible-looking woman, a little older than Edward himself, who mounted a spruce bicycle each morning and pedalled energetically away. Edward had decided that she was an efficient secretary in one of the nearby factories, but Jim told him otherwise.

'Headmistress of an infants' school,' he informed him. 'Miss Hedges – a nice old bird. She was awfully kind to Eileen when she was having our first. And the two above you are secretaries, or so they say. I'd put them as shorthand-typists myself, but no doubt they'll rise in the scale before very long. Flighty, but harmless, you'll find.'

'And decorative,' added Edward. 'And much addicted to bathing. One at night and one in the morning, I've worked out. There s a cascade by my ear soon after eleven and another just after seven each morning, down the waste pipe.'

'Come to think of it,' said Jim, 'I believe you're right. Trust a countryman to find out all the details of his neighbours' affairs! It had never occurred to me, I must admit.'

'It's a pity my grandmother can't spend an afternoon there,' replied Edward. 'She'd have the life history of every one of us at her finger tips before the sun set! Now, Jim, let's get down to work.'

The first Caxley visitors to the flat were his Uncle Bertie and Aunt Kathy, on their way to meet friends in London.

'You look so happy!' exclaimed his aunt, kissing him. She stood back and surveyed him with her sparkling dark eyes. 'And so smart!' she added.

'My demob suit,' said Edward, with a grimace. 'And tie, too.'

'Well, at least the tie's wearable,' observed Bertie. 'At the end of my war, I was offered the choice of a hideous tie or "a very nice neckerchief". How d'you like that?'

Edward pressed them for all the Caxley news. Bertie noticed that he was eager for every detail of the family. How soon, he wondered, before he would return? Certainly, he had visited Rose Lodge on several occasions, and his present home was conveniently near Western Avenue for him to make his way to Caxley within a short time. At the moment, however, it looked as though Edward was comfortably settled. His decree nisi was already through; before the end of the year he should be free, but as things were, it seemed pretty plain that his nephew was happy to return to a bachelor's existence.

The greatest piece of news they had to offer was that Joan was expecting a child in the late summer, and that Michael, now demobilized, had decided to learn more about the catering trade by working for a time in Howard's Restaurant. Sep had suggested this move, and although Michael realized that there might be difficulties, he was glad to accept the work as a temporary measure, until the baby arrived.

'And how has Robert taken it?' asked Edward, after expressing his delight at the prospect of becoming an uncle.

'Fairly quietly, so far. I don't think it would be very satisfactory permanently though. His temper is getting more and more unpredictable. Two waitresses have left in the last month. It's my belief he's ill, but he flatly refuses to see the doctor.'

'He's a queer customer,' agreed Edward, 'but times are difficult. He must have a devil of a job getting supplies. Food seems to be shorter now than during the war – unless it's because I'm a stranger here and don't get anything tucked away under the counter for me. I'd starve if it weren't for the works' canteen midday, and some of the stuff they dish up there is enough to make you shudder.'

'Father says that people mind most about bread rationing,' said Kathy. '"Never had it in our lives before," they said, really shocked, you know. And poor dear, he *will* get all these wretched bits of paper, bread units, *absolutely* right. You know what a stickler he is. I was in the shop the other day helping him. People leave their pages with him and then have a regular order for a cake, using so many each week. It makes an enormous amount of book work for the poor old darling. Sometimes I try to persuade him to give up. He's practically eighty, after all.'

'He won't,' commented Bertie, 'he'll die in harness, and like it that way. And Robert's more of a liability than a help at the moment. He resents the fact that Sep didn't hand over the business to him outright, when he gave you the house. It's beginning to become more of an obsession than ever, I'm afraid.'

'He was always dam' awkward about that,' said Edward shortly. 'Good heavens! Surely Grandpa can do as he likes with his own? If there's anything I detest it's this waiting for other men's shoes – like a vulture.'

'Vultures don't wear shoes,' pointed out Kathy, surveying her own neat pair. 'And whatever it is that screws up our poor Robert it makes things downright unpleasant for us all, particularly Father.'

'And Michael and Joan?'

'Michael's such a good-tempered fellow,' said Bertie, 'that he'll stand a lot. And Joan's at the blissfully broody stage just now. I caught her winding wool with Maisie Hunter the other evening with a positively maudlin expression on her face.'

'Maisie Hunter?' echoed Edward. 'I thought she'd got married.'

'Her husband-to-be crashed on landing at Brize Norton, about six weeks before the war ended.'

'I never heard that,' Edward said slowly. 'Poor Maisie.'

Bertie glanced at his watch and rose to go.

'Come along, my dear,' he said, hauling Kathy to her feet. 'We shall meet all the homegoing traffic, if we don't look out.'

Edward accompanied them to the gate and waved good-bye as the car rounded the bend in the lane. It was strange, he thought, how little he envied them returning to Caxley. It was another world, and one which held no attraction for him. Much as he loved his family, he was glad that he was free of the tensions and squabbles in which they seemed now involved.

He bent down to pull a few weeds from the garden bed which bordered the path, musing the while on his change of outlook. He revelled in his present anonymous role. It was wonderful to know that one's neighbours took so little interest in one's affairs. It was refreshing to be able to shut the door and be absolutely unmolested in the flat, to eat alone, to sleep alone, and to be happy or sad as the spirit moved one, without involving other people's feelings. It was purely selfish, of course, he knew that, but it was exactly what he needed.

He straightened his aching back and looked aloft. An aeroplane had taken off from nearby Northolt aerodrome and he felt the old rush of pleasure in its soaring power. And yet, here again, there was a difference. He felt not the slightest desire to fly now. Would the longing ever return? Or would this numb apathy which affected him remain always with him, dulling pleasure and nullifying pain?

It was useless to try to answer these questions. He must be thankful for the interest of the new job, and for this present quietness in which to lick his wounds. Perhaps happiness and warmth, ambition and purpose, would return to him one day. Meanwhile, he must try and believe all the tiresome people who kept reminding him that 'Time was the Great Healer'.

Perhaps, they might, just possibly, be right.

Chapter Twelve

A FAMILY TRAGEDY

As the summer advanced, affairs in the market place went from bad to worse. The aftermath of the war – general fatigue – was felt everywhere. Food was not the only thing in short supply. Men returning from active service found it desperately hard to find somewhere to live. Women, longing for new clothes, for colour, for gaiety, still had to give coupons for garments and for material for making them, as well as for all the soft furnishings needed. 'Makes you wonder who won the war!' observed someone bitterly, watching Sep clip out the precious snippets of paper entitling her to three loaves, and the feeling was everywhere.

Sep, hard-pressed with work and smaller than ever in old age, maintained his high standards of service steadily. But he was a worried man. The shop was doing as well as ever, but the returns from the restaurant showed a slight decline as the weeks went by, and Sep knew quite well that Robert was at fault. It was becoming more and more difficult to keep staff. Robert was short with the waitresses in front of customers, and impatient and sarcastic with the kitchen staff. How long, wondered Sep, before Michael, who was working so wonderfully well, found conditions unendurable?

He made up his mind to take Robert aside privately and have a talk with him. The fellow was touchy and might sulk, as he had so often done as a boy, but at the rate he was going on Howard's Restaurant would soon be in Queer Street. Sep did not relish the task, but he had never shirked his duty in his life, and it was plain that this unpleasant encounter must take place.

He crossed the square from the shop as the Town Hall clock struck eight. The restaurant was closed, the staff had gone and

Robert was alone in the kitchen reading *The Caxley Chronicle*. Sep sat down opposite him.

'My boy, I'll come straight to the point. Business is slipping, as you know. Any particular reason?'

'Only that I'm expected to run this place with a set of fools,' muttered Robert, scowling at his clenched hands on the table top.

'I'm worried more about you than the business,' said Sep gently. 'You've been over-doing it. Why not take a holiday? We could manage, you know, for a week, say.'

Robert jumped to his feet, his face flushing.

'And let Michael worm his way in? Is that what you want? It's to be Edward all over again, I can see. What's wrong with me – your own son – that you should slight me all the time?'

'My boy –' began Sep, protesting, but he was overwhelmed by Robert's passionate outburst.

'What chance have I ever had? Edward has the house given him at twenty-one. The house that should have been mine anyway. Do I get given anything? Oh no! I can wait – wait till I'm old and useless, with nothing to call my own.'

His face was dark and congested, the words spluttered from his mouth. To Sep's horror he saw tears welling in his son's eyes and trickling down his cheeks. The pent-up resentment of years was bursting forth and Sep could do nothing to quell the violence.

'I've never had a fair deal from the day I was born. Jim was a hero because he got himself killed. No one was ever allowed to mention Leslie, though he was the kindest of the lot to me, and I missed him more than any of you. Kath's been the spoilt baby all her life, and I've been general dog's body. Work's all I've ever had, with no time for anything else. The rest of the family have homes and children. I've been too busy for girls. Edward and Bertie and Michael came back from the war jingling with medals. What did I get for sticking here as a slave? I'm despised, I tell you! Despised! Laughed at – by all Caxley –'

By now he was sobbing with self-pity, beating his palms against his forehead in a childish gesture which wrung his father's heart. Who would have dreamt that such hidden fires had smouldered for so long beneath that timid exterior? And what could be done to comfort him and to give him back pride in himself?

Sep let the storm subside a little before he spoke. His voice was gentle.

'I'm sorry that you should feel this way, my boy. You've let your mind dwell on all sorts of imagined slights. You were always as dear to me and your mother as the other children – more so, perhaps, as the youngest. No one blames you for not going to the war. You were rejected through no fault of your own. Everyone here knows that you've done your part by sticking to your job here.'

Robert's sobbing had ceased, but he scowled across the table mutinously.

'It's a lie! Everyone here hates me. People watch me wherever I go. They talk about me behind my back. I know, I tell you, I know! They say I couldn't get a girl if I tried. They say no one wants me. They say I'm under my dad's thumb – afraid to stand on my own feet – afraid to answer back! I'm a failure. That's what they say, watching and whispering about me, day in and day out!'

Sep stood up, small, straight and stern.

'Robert, you are over-wrought, and don't know what you are saying. But I won't hear you accusing innocent people of malice. All this is in your own mind. You must see this, surely?'

Robert approached his father. There was a strange light in his glittering eyes. He thrust his face very close to the old man's.

'My mind?' he echoed. 'Are you trying to say I'm out of my mind? I know well enough what people are saying about me. I hear them. But I hear other voices too – *private* voices that tell me I'm right, that the whisperers in Caxley will be confounded, and that the time will come when they have to give in and admit that Robert Howard was right all the time. They'll see me one day, the owner of this business here, the owner of the shop, the biggest man in the market square, the head of the Howard family!'

His voice had risen with excitement, his eyes were wild. From weeping self-pity he had swung in the space of minutes to a state of manic euphoria. He began to pace the floor, head up, nostrils flaring, as he gulped for breath.

'You'll be gone by then,' he cried triumphantly, 'and I'll see that Edward goes too. There will be one Howard only in charge. Just one. One to give orders. One to be the boss!'

'Robert!' thundered Sep, in the voice which he had used but rarely in his life. There was no response. Robert was in another world, oblivious of his father and his surroundings.

'They'll see,' he continued, pacing even more swiftly. 'My time will come. My voices know. They tell me the truth. "The persecutors shall become the persecuted!" That's what my voices tell me.'

Sep walked round the table and confronted his son. He took hold of his elbows and looked steadily into that distorted face a little above his own.

'Robert,' he said clearly, as though to a distraught child. 'We are going home now, and you are going to bed.'

The young man's gaze began to soften. His eyes turned slowly towards his father's. He looked as though he were returning from a long, strange journey.

'Very well, Father,' he said. The voice was exhausted, but held a certain odd pride, as though remnants of glimpsed grandeur still clung to him.

He watched his father lock up. Sep, white-faced and silent, walked beside his son across the market square, watching him anxiously.

Robert, head high, looked to the left and right as he strode proudly over the cobbles. He might have been a king acknowledging the homage of his people, except that, to Sep's relief, the square was empty. When they reached their door Robert entered first, as of right, and swept regally up the stairs to his room, without a word.

When faithful old Miss Taggerty brought in Sep's bedtime milk, she found her master sitting pale and motionless.

'You don't look yourself, sir,' she said with concern. 'Shall I bring you anything? An aspirin, perhaps?'

'I'm all right. Just a little tired.'

'Shall I fetch Mr Robert?'

'No, no! Don't worry about me. I'm off to bed immediately.'

They wished each other good night. Sep watched the door close quietly behind the good-hearted creature, and resumed his ponderings.

What was to be done? Tonight had made plain something which he had long suspected. Robert's mind was giving way under inner torment. He was obsessed with a wrongful sense of grievance against himself, and worse still, a gnawing jealousy, aimed chiefly against Edward. These two evils had become his masters. These were the 'voices' which he claimed to hear, and which were driving him beyond the brink of sanity.

To Sep's generation, insanity in the family was something to be kept from the knowledge of outsiders. One pitied the afflicted, but one kept the matter as quiet as possible. So often, he knew from experience, attacks passed and, within a few months, rest and perhaps a change of scene, brought mental health again. It might be so with Robert.

He disliked the idea of calling in a doctor to the boy. Suppose that Robert were sent to a mental home? Would he ever come out again? Did doctors really know what went on in the human brain, and could they cure 'a mind diseased'? Wouldn't the mere fact of consulting a doctor upset his poor son's condition even more?

And yet the boy was in need of help, and he was the last person to be able to give it. How terrible it had been to hear that awful indictment of himself as a father! Was he really to blame? Had he loved him less? In all humility he felt that he could truthfully claim to have loved all his children equally – even Leslie, who had betrayed him.

And those fearful indications of a deluded mind – the assumption of omnipotence, of grandeur, to what might they lead? Would he become violent if he were ridiculed in one of these moods? Sep remembered the menacing glitter in his son's eyes, and trembled for him. What did the future hold for Robert?

He took his milk with him to the bedroom. The blinds were

drawn against the familiar view of the market square and the indomitable figure of Queen Victoria. Miss Taggerty had turned the bedclothes back into a neat white triangle. Sep knelt beside the bed and prayed for guidance.

When he arose his mind was clear. He would sleep on this problem and see how things fared in the morning. There was no need to rush for help to the rest of the family. This was something to be borne alone if possible, so that Robert should be spared further indignities. He had suffered enough, thought Sep, torn with pity.

For a few weeks things went more smoothly. Robert never referred to that dreadful outburst. It was as though it had been wiped completely from his memory. For Sep, the incident was unforgettable, but he said nothing.

Nevertheless, it was obvious that the young man was in a precarious state of mind. Sep did what he could to relieve the pressure of work at the restaurant, and Michael's efforts ensured the smooth running of the place. His cheerfulness and good looks soon made him popular, which was good for trade but not, as Sep realized, for Robert's esteem.

Kathy, knowing that staff were hard to get at the restaurant offered to help whenever possible. She and Bertie realized that Robert was under strain, although they had no idea of the seriousness of his malaise.

'You'd be more use, my dear, in the shop,' said Sep. 'It would leave me free to go across to Robert's more often, and you know exactly where everything is at home.'

'I was brought up to it,' laughed Kathy. 'I'd enjoy it, you know, and now that the children are off my hands, it will give me an interest.'

Her presence was a great comfort to Sep, and meant that he could keep a discreet, if anxious, eye on affairs across the square.

During these uneasy weeks Joan's baby was born. It was a girl, and the family were all delighted. She was born in the nursing home to the north of Caxley, on the road to Beech Green and

Fairacre, where so many other Caxley citizens had first seen the light. Michael was enormously pleased and visited his wife and daughter every evening.

Joan remained there for a fortnight. It was decided that she should go for a week or two to Rose Lodge to regain her strength, and submit to the welcome cossetings of her mother and grandmother. The house was certainly more convenient than the flat, and the baby would have the benefit of the garden air as well as the doting care of three women. She was to be christened Sarah.

'No hope of the poor little darling being christened at St Peter's, I suppose?' sighed Mrs North.

'You know there isn't,' replied Joan, smiling at her grandmother's naughtiness.

'I never seem to have any luck with family ceremonies,' commented the old lady. She brightened as a thought crossed her mind. 'Perhaps Kathy's girl one day?'

Soon after Joan returned to the flat trouble began again. Robert's antagonism towards Michael was renewed in a hundred minor insults. Despite his easy-going disposition, Michael's Irish blood was roused.

'The fellow's off his rocker,' declared Michael roundly one evening in the privacy of the flat. 'He's beginning to talk as though he's the King of England. Sometimes I wonder if we should stay.'

Letters from his family in Dublin had also unsettled him. His father was in failing health and it was plain that he longed for his son to return to carry on the hotel, although he did not press the boy to come if his prospects were brighter in Caxley. Joan did not know how to advise her husband. She herself half-feared the uprooting and the break with the family, especially with a young child to consider. On the other hand it was right that Michael should obey his conscience, and she would do whatever he felt was best. Certainly, as things were, there was nothing but petty frustrations for Michael in his work, and he had obviously learned all that could be learned from the comparatively small Caxley restaurant. It was time he took on something bigger, giving him scope for his ability.

She told her problem to her old friend Maisie Hunter, who was to be godmother to Sarah. Her answer was straightforward.

'Michael's trying to spare you. Tell him you'll be happy to go to Dublin, and then watch his face. I'm sure he wants to go back home, and he's bound to do well.'

She was right, and the couple had almost decided to break the news to Sep and Robert and to write to Michael's father, when two things happened to clinch the matter.

Joan had put her daughter to sleep in the pram in the little garden sloping down to the Cax, when Robert burst from the restaurant in a state of fury.

'I won't have that thing out here,' he said, kicking at a wheel. 'This is part of my restaurant, as you well know. You can clear off!'

'Robert!' protested Joan, much shocked. 'I've always used the garden. What on earth has come over you?'

Two or three curious customers, taking morning coffee, gazed with interest upon the scene from the restaurant windows. Joan was horribly aware of their presence, and took Robert's arm to lead him further away. He flung her from him with such violence that she fell across the pram. The child broke into crying, and Joan, now thoroughly alarmed, lifted her from the pram.

'You'll use the garden no more,' shouted Robert. 'You're trespassing on my property. And if you leave that contraption here I shall throw it in the river!'

At this moment, Michael arrived, and took in the situation at a glance.

'Take the baby upstairs,' he said quietly. 'I'll deal with this.'

He propelled the struggling and protesting Robert into the little office at the end of the restaurant and slammed the door, much to the disappointment of the interested customers. He thrust Robert into an arm chair, and turned to get him a drink from the cupboard. He was white with fury, and his hand shook as he poured out a stiff tot, but he was in command of himself and the situation. He was facing an ill man, and a dangerous one, he realized.

Robert leapt from the chair, as Michael put the glass on the desk, and tried to make for the door. Michael administered a hard slap to each cheek, as one would to an hysterical patient, and Robert slumped again into the chair.

'Drink this slowly,' commanded Michael, 'and wait here until I get back.'

He left the office, turned the key in the lock, and told good old John Bush who had been in Sep's employ for forty years, to take charge while he saw to his wife and let Sep know what was happening.

Later that evening Sep, Bertie and Michael held counsel.

'We must get a doctor to see him,' said Bertie firmly. 'I'll ring Dr Rogers tonight.'

'I blame myself,' said Sep heavily. 'He has not been himself for months. We should have got help earlier. It must be done now. I fear for Joan and the child if he is going to get these attacks of violence.'

'I want them to go back to Rose Lodge, but Joan is very much against it,' said Michael. 'But it's going to be impossible to stay over the restaurant, if he doesn't change his ways.

'Let's get the doctor's verdict before we do anything more,' said Bertie.

Dr Rogers said little when he had examined his patient, but his grave looks alarmed Sep.

'Will he get better?' he asked anxiously. 'He's such a young man – so many years before him. What do you think?'

Dr Rogers would not commit himself, but provided various bottles of pills and promised to visit frequently. Meanwhile, he asked the family to call him in immediately if the symptoms of excessive excitement occurred again.

A few days later a letter arrived from Ireland from Michael's invalid mother. His father was sinking. Could he return? And was there any hope of him taking over the hotel?

'This settles it,' said Joan, looking at Michael's worried face as he read the letter again.

'But what about Howard's Restaurant? How will Sep manage?'

'John Bush can run the place blindfold. And Aunt Kathy would help, I know. Go and tell Sep what has happened. Take the letter.'

She knew full well how Sep would react.

'Of course you must go, my boy. Your father comes first, and your mother needs your presence at a time like this. You've been of enormous help to us here, but it's right that you should start a life of your own.'

And so, within two days, Michael returned to Dublin, and Joan and the baby were to join him as soon as possible. It was Bertie who drove them to Holyhead to catch the boat to Dun Laoghaire. Saying farewell to the family had been ineffably sad.

'I'll be back soon for a holiday,' she told them all bravely. It was hardest to say good-bye to Sep and Grandma North. They looked so old, so shattered at the parting.

'You are doing the right thing,' Sep assured her firmly. 'I'm sure you have a wonderful future in Ireland.'

Her grandmother was less hopeful and inclined to be tearful.

'Such a *long* way off, and a very wild sort of people, I hear. The thought of all those poor babies of yours being brought up in such *strange* ways quite upsets me. Do boil all the water, dear, whatever you do.'

Joan promised, and kissed her, hardly knowing whether to laugh or cry. Funny, exasperating, old Grandma! How long before she saw her again?

Dr Rogers' treatment seemed to have only a small sedative effect on Robert, but Sep tried to assure himself that the cure was bound to take a long time, and that his son's youth and a lessening of his work would finally ensure his recovery.

Kathy insisted on taking over the financial affairs of the restaurant while John Bush coped with the practical side. She was as quick at figures as her mother, Edna Howard, had been, and soon proved a competent business woman.

It was quite apparent that Robert resented her intrusion into his affairs, and Kathy ignored the snubs and sarcastic comments which punctuated the day's work. Robert was sick. Soon he would be better, and he would be happy again, she thought.

She was totally unprepared, therefore, for a sudden attack of the mania which had so appalled Sep months before. It happened, luckily, soon after the restaurant had closed and Kathy was checking the money. Perhaps the clinking of the coins reminded him of the fact that the business was not his. Perhaps the sight of his sister, sitting in the chair which had always been his own, inflamed him. No one would ever know; but resentment flared again, his voice grew loud and strident as he screamed his hatred of his family and his intention to get rid of them.

'My voices told me,' he roared at the terrified Kathy. 'They told me I would triumph, and I shall! Michael and Joan have gone. Old Bush will go, and you will go! There will be no one left but me – the unbeatable – the true heir!'

His lips were flecked with saliva, his eyes demented, as he bore down upon her. Dropping the money on the floor, Kathy tore open the door, and fled across the square to find help, the jingle of the rolling coins ringing in her ears.

The next day an ambulance took Robert and his attendants to the county mental hospital some twenty miles away. Sep, shattered, sat trying to understand Dr Rogers' explanation of his son's illness. He heard but one phrase in four and many of those were inexplicable to him. 'A progressively worsening condition,' he understood painfully well, but such terms as 'manic depressive' and the seriousness of 'hearing voices', as symptoms, meant nothing to the desolate old man.

To Sep, who knew his Bible, 'the voices' were simply Robert's demons – the outcome of the twin evils of jealousy and self-pity. Robert had been weak. He had succumbed to the temptations of his demons. His madness was, in part, a punishment for flying in the face of Providence.

When the doctor had gone, Sep stood at the back window and looked upon the row of willows lining the bank of the Cax. Three sons had once been his, gay little boys who had tumbled about the yard and moulded pastry in the bakehouse in their small fat hands.

One was long dead, one long-estranged, and now the last of the three was mad. Sep's life had been long and hard, but that moment by the window was the most desolate and despairing he had ever known.

Chapter Thirteen

NEW HORIZONS

Edward heard the news about Robert in a letter from his mother. He was deeply shocked, and very anxious about the effect this blow might have on his grandfather. He was thankful to know that his Aunt Kathy and John Bush were coping so ably with the restaurant, and glad to give permission to the faithful old employee to use his flat on the top floor. It would be some relief for Sep to know that there was someone reliable living on the premises.

He telephoned to the mental hospital that morning to hear how Robert was, but learnt very little more than his mother's letter had told him. He had the chance, however, of talking to the doctor in charge of the case, and asked to be kept informed of his progress, explaining his own relationship and his desire to do anything to spare the patient's very old father.

As he replaced the receiver Edward noted, with a start of surprise, how anxious he was. Robert had never been very close to him. They were eleven years and a generation apart. By temperament they were opposed, and resentment, which had no place in Edward's life, ruled his young uncle's. But this was a blow at the whole family, and Edward's reaction had been swift and instinctive. It was all very well to decide to cut loose, he admitted somewhat wryly to himself, but the old tag about blood being thicker than water held good, as this shock had proved.

He resolved to go to Caxley at the weekend to see how things were for himself. Sep was pathetically delighted with the surprise visit, and Edward was glad to find that he was taking Robert's illness so bravely.

'I should have insisted on getting medical advice earlier,' he told

Edward. 'Robert is certainly having proper treatment now, and perhaps a spell away from us will quicken his recovery.'

They talked of many things. Edward had never known him quite so forthcoming about the business. Perhaps he realized that Edward himself was now a keen and purposeful businessman. It certainly amazed the younger man to realize how profitable the old-established shop and the newer restaurant were, and what a grasp his grandfather had of every small detail in running them. Since Robert's departure, trade had improved. There were now no staff troubles with Kathy and John Bush in charge, and after a long day visiting his mother and grandmother, Bertie and Kathy, Edward drove back to London very much happier in mind.

His own business affairs he found engrossing. He was now a partner in the firm, responsible chiefly for production and design. At his suggestion they had expanded their range of plastic kitchen equipment and were now experimenting with domestic refrigerators and larger deep-freeze receptacles for shops. This venture was proving amazingly successful and Edward found himself more and more absorbed and excited by the firm's development. Suddenly, after the apathy which had gripped him, he had found some purpose in life. He discovered a latent flair for design, an appreciation of line and form put to practical use, which gave him much inward satisfaction. The costing of a project had always interested him. He was, after all, the grandson of Bender North and Sep Howard, both men of business. He enjoyed planning a new design and then juggling with its economic possibilities. It was a fusion of two ways of thought and a new challenge every time it was undertaken.

He paid one or two visits to the continent to compare methods of production. He visited firms in Brussels and Paris who were engaged in much the same work as his own, and returned full of ideas. Jim and his father recognized that Edward was the most able of the three for this part of the business. His gaiety and charm, fast returning under the stimulus of new work, helped him to easy friendship. He had the ability to select ideas which could be adapted to their own business, and the power to explain them on his return to his partners. With Edward's drive, the firm was advancing rapidly.

In the early summer of 1947 Edward set off for a fortnight's visit to two firms in Milan. There were plumes of lilac blowing in the suburban gardens as the train rumbled towards the coast, and the girls were out and about in their pretty summer frocks. Edward approved of this 'new look' which brought back full skirts, neat waists, and gave women back the attractive curves which had been lost in the square military styles of wartime fashion. It was good to see colour and life returning to war-scarred England, to watch new houses being built, and see fresh paint brightening the old ones. There was hope again in the air, and the breezy rollicking tunes of the new musical *Oklahoma* exactly caught the spirit of the times – the looking-ahead of a great people to a future full of promise.

From Milan he made the long train journey to Venice, there to spend the last few days meeting an Italian industrial designer who lived there, and sight-seeing. From the moment that he emerged from the station into the pellucid brilliance of Venetian sunlight, he fell under the city's spell. The quality of the light, which revealed the details of brickwork and carving, exhilarated him. To take a gondola to one's hotel, instead of a prosaic bus or taxi, was wholly delightful. If only he could stay four months instead of four days!

His hotel was an agreeable one just off St Mark's Square. He looked from his window upon a gondola station. There were twenty or more black high-prowed beauties jostling together upon the water. Their owners were busy mopping and polishing, shouting, laughing and gesticulating. Edward liked their energy, their raffish good looks and the torrents of words of which he only understood one in ten.

Picturesque though the scene was he was to find that its position had its drawbacks. The noise went on until one or two in the morning and began again about six. Luckily, Edward, healthily tired with walking about this enchanted place, did not lose much sleep.

On the last morning he awoke with a start. He was in the grip of some inexplicable fear. He found himself bathed in perspiration and his mind was perturbed with thoughts of Robert. He tossed back the bed clothes and lay watching the trembling reflections of the sun on water flickering across the ceiling. Against this undulating background he could see the face of Robert – a sad, haunted face, infinitely moving.

Outside, the gondoliers exchanged voluble jests in the bright Italian sunshine. The waters of Venice lapped against the walls and slapped the bottoms of the gondolas rhythmically. An Italian tenor poured forth a cascade of music from someone's wireless set.

But Edward was oblivious of his surroundings. In that instant he was hundreds of miles away in the cool early dawn of an English market square. What was happening at home?

After breakfast he felt calmer. He packed his bags and paid his bill, glad to be occupied with small everyday matters and telling himself that he had simply suffered from a nightmare. But the nagging horror stayed with him throughout the long journey to England, and as soon as he arrived he rang his Uncle Bertie for news.

'Bad, I'm afraid,' said Bertie's voice, 'as you'll see when my letter arrives. Robert was found dead in the hospital grounds. They think he had a heart attack. We'll know more later.'

'When was this?' asked Edward.

Bertie told him. He must have died, thought Edward, as he had suspected, at the moment when he himself awoke so tormentedly in the hotel bedroom.

This uncanny experience had a lasting effect upon Edward's outlook. Hitherto impatient of anything occult, he, the least psychic of men, had discovered that not all occurrences could be rationally explained. It was to make him more sympathetic in the years to come and more humble in his approach to matters unseen.

Robert's tragic death had another effect on Edward's future. Unknown to him, Sep, when his first grief had passed, crossed the market square to enter the offices of Lovejoy and Lovejoy, his solicitors. There, the will which he had drafted so long ago was drastically revised, and when Sep returned to the bakery he was well content.

It was about this time that Edward heard that his ex-wife Angela had had a son by Billy Sylvester, her second husband. Edward was glad to hear the news. It should make Angela a happier person. Despite the misery which she had inflicted upon him, Edward felt no resentment. He soberly faced the fact that he could not exempt himself from blame. They had never had much in common, and it was largely physical attraction which had drawn them together. Now, with the baby to think of, she would have some interest in the future. Nevertheless, Edward felt a pang when he thought about the child. He might have had a son of his own if things had worked out.

But domesticity did not play much part in his present affairs, although he enjoyed running the little flat. He took most of his meals out, and he grew increasingly fond of London. His lifelong love of the theatre could now be indulged, and by a lucky chance he was able to meet a number of theatrical people.

His Aunt Mary, younger sister of Bertie and his mother Winnie, and the acknowledged beauty of the family, had a small part in a well-written light comedy which had already run for eight months and looked as though it were settled in the West End for another two years. It was one of those inexplicable successes. No great names glittered in the cast, the play itself was not outstanding; but it was gay, the dialogue crisp, the settings and the costumes ravishing. It was just what theatre-goers seemed to want, and Aunt Mary hoped that they would continue to do so.

Edward took her out on several occasions after the show. He had always enjoyed her company, and found something exhilarating in the mixture of North common-sense, typified by his good-humoured Uncle Bertie, and the racy sophistication which her mode of life had added to it.

Two husbands, little mourned, lay in Aunt Mary's past. Many good friends of both sexes enlivened her present. She often brought one or more to Edward's supper parties, and he grew very fond of this animated company of friends, admiring the outward nonchalance which masked the resilience and dedication necessary to survive the ruthless competition of the stage world. They had something in common with businessmen, Edward decided. They needed to be long-sighted, ambitious and capable of grasping opportunity when it came. And, when times were hard, they must show the world a brave face to inspire confidence.

He liked to take out one or two of the pretty girls occasionally. It was good to laugh again, to be amused and to amuse in turn. He began to realize how little feminine company he had enjoyed. The war, early marriage, and the restrictions put upon him whilst awaiting his divorce, had combined with his temporary inner weariness to make him solitary. But although he enjoyed their company, there was not one among them with whom he would like to spend the rest of his days. The fact that they were equally heart-whole rendered them the more attractive.

More disturbing were the attentions of one of the girls who shared the flat above his own. As time passed, they had become better acquainted. Edward had used their telephone one evening when his own was out of order. He had stayed to coffee. Some evenings later they came to have a drink. From these small beginnings, not greatly encouraged by Edward, who enjoyed his domestic privacy, came more frequent visits by the girls.

Susan was engaged to a monosyllabic mountain of muscle who played Rugby football regularly on Wednesdays and Saturdays, and squash or badminton in between to keep himself fit for his place in the front row of the forwards. It was Elizabeth who was the more persistent of the two. She was small and dark, with an engaging cackling laugh, and Edward enjoyed her occasional company.

It was Elizabeth who called from the windows when he was gardening, offering him a drink. It was she who took in the parcels and delivered them to Edward when he returned from the office. And when he took to his bed with a short sharp bout of influenza it was Elizabeth who offered to telephone for the doctor and brought aspirins and drinks.

Edward, engrossed in his expanding business and intrigued with

Aunt Mary's friends, had little idea of Elizabeth's growing affection. She was ardently stage-struck, and when she knew that Edward sometimes met people connected with the theatre, she grew pink with excitement. Edward found her touchingly young and un-sophisticated. He invited her to come with him one evening to Aunt Mary's play, and to meet her afterwards.

It was a warm spring evening with London at its most seductive. A lingering sunset turned the sky to amethyst and turquoise. The costers' barrows were bright with daffodils, tulips and the first mimosa. In the brilliant shop windows, Easter brides trailed satin and lace. Hats as frothy as whipped egg-white, or as colourful as a handful of spring flowers, attracted the bemused window-gazers.

The play seemed to improve as its run lengthened, Edward thought. Aunt Mary queened it as becomingly as ever in all three acts. She was at her most sparkling afterwards at supper and brought a famous couple with her to dazzle Edward's young friend.

Later, while Edward was dancing with the actress and her husband was at the other side of the room talking with a friend, she watched Elizabeth's fond gaze follow Edward's handsome figure round the floor. He certainly was a personable young man, thought Aunt Mary, with family pride. He would have had a fine stage presence if he had cared to take up the profession.

'How well Edward fits into this sort of life,' said Elizabeth sighing. 'You can see that he loves London, and people, and a gay time.'

Aunt Mary, whose bright blue eyes missed nothing, either around her or in the human heart, seized her opportunity.

'I don't think you know Edward very well. He seems happy enough in town at the moment, but his roots are elsewhere. He doesn't know it yet himself, but Caxley will pull him back again before long. Of that I'm positive.'

'How can you say that?' protested Elizabeth. She looked affronted and hurt. 'What would Edward find in a poky little country town?'

'Everything worthwhile,' replied Aunt Mary composedly. 'He's his two Caxley grandfathers rolled into one, with a strong dash of my darling brother Bertie thrown in. That mixture is going to make a Caxley patriarch one day out of our dashing young Edward!'

'I don't believe it,' replied Elizabeth.

'Wait another ten years or so and you'll see,' promised Aunt Mary. But she felt quite certain that the pretty young thing beside her would not be prepared to wait at all. The role of country mouse would never do for her.

And that, thought Aunt Mary in her wisdom, was exactly as it should be.

Chapter Fourteen

INTERLUDE IN IRELAND

While Edward enjoyed the spring in London, the good people of Caxley greeted the returning warmth just as heartily. At Rose Lodge, the clumps of daffodils and pheasant-eyed narcissi which Bender had planted, so long ago, were in splendid bloom. Bertie's garden, close by the Cax, was vivid with grape hyacinths and crocuses beneath the budding trees. Even Sep's small flagged yard, behind the bakehouse, sported a white-painted tub of early red tulips, put there by Kathy's hand.

Pale-pink sticks of rhubarb with yellow topknots, the first pullets' eggs and bunches of primroses graced the market stalls. People were buying bright packets of flower seeds and discussing the rival merits of early potatoes. Felt hats were brushed and put away on top shelves, and straw ones came forth refurbished with new ribbon and flowers.

In the wide fields around Caxley the farmers were busy drilling and planting. Dim lights shone from lonely shepherds' huts as lambing continued. Along the hedges the honeysuckle and hawthorn put out their rosettes and fans of green, among the tattered tassels of the hazel catkins, and hidden beneath, the blue and white violets gave out the exquisite scent of spring from among their heart-shaped leaves.

Bertie, driving his mother to Beech Green one spring afternoon to visit her sister Ethel Miller, noticed the encouraging sights and sounds with a great sense of comfort. He always enjoyed being in this familiar countryside and remembered the long bicycle rides which he and the Howard brothers took when these same lanes were white with chalky dust and most of the traffic was horse-drawn.

It grieved him to see the new estates going up on the slopes flanking Caxley. People must be housed, but the gracelessness of the straight roads, the box-like structures packed too closely together, the narrow raw strips of gardens and the complete lack of privacy, saddened him. He would hate to have to live in a house like that, he thought, passing one garishly-painted one with a board outside saying: SHOW HOUSE, and he guessed that many future occupants would feel the same way, but be forced by circumstances to make the best of a bad job. It seemed to Bertie that for so little extra cost and care something lovely might have been built upon the fields he remembered, to give pleasure and pride to the dwellers there as well as to the town as a whole. As it was, this new development, in Bertie's opinion, was nothing but an eyesore and, as a block of houses embellished with moulded concrete weatherboarding came into view, he put his foot heavily on the accelerator to reach the sanctuary of leafy lanes beyond, unaltered since his boyhood.

It was good to arrive at the old farmhouse. Nothing seemed to have changed in the square panelled room which the Millers still called 'the parlour', and through the windows the copper beech, pink with young leaf, lifted its arms against the background of the mighty downs. Only such an observant eye as Bertie's would notice significant details of a fast-changing way of farming. Sacks of chemical fertilizer were stacked in a nearby barn. Strange new machinery had its place beside the old harvest binder which Bertie remembered his Uncle Jesse buying at a distant sale. Jesse's sons, it seemed, were abreast of modern methods.

The two old ladies gossiped of family affairs. There had been a letter that morning from Joan in Dublin.

'She's invited Edward to visit them later in the summer. That's the best of having a hotel, isn't it?'

'It could work both ways,' Bertie pointed out, amused at his mother's matter-of-fact approach. 'Suppose all your relations wanted to come for the summer. You wouldn't make much profit, would you?'

'Don't be tiresome, dear,' said his mother automatically, in the tone she had used ever since he could remember. Bertie smiled, and sampled his aunt's gingerbread in contented silence.

'Will he go?' asked Ethel. 'Who knows? He might meet a nice Irish girl.'

'Heaven forbid, Ethel! We've had quite enough mixed marriages in our family as it is!'

'They're not *all* Catholics over there,' said her sister with asperity. 'I know very well that quite a few of them are Christians.'

'You mean *Protestants*, surely, Aunt Ethel,' put in Bertie mildly. The old lady looked at him frostily and then transferred her gaze to her sister.

'That boy of yours, Hilda,' she observed severely, 'interrupts his elders and betters even more than he used to.'

'I'm so sorry,' said Bertie with due humility, and sat back with his gingerbread to play the role of listener only.

But, driving home again through the thickening twilight, Mrs North said:

'You mustn't mind what Ethel says, dear.'

'I don't, Mamma,' replied Bertie calmly.

'She's getting old, you know, and a little peculiar in her ways.'

Bertie was about to say that Ethel was some years younger than she was herself, but had the sense to hold his tongue.

'Fancy suggesting that Edward might marry an *Irish* girl!' There was an outraged air about this remark which amused Bertie. If Aunt Ethel had suggested that Edward was considering marriage with an aborigine, his mamma could not have sounded more affronted.

'Irish girls are quite famous for their charm and good looks,' said Bertie. 'But I don't think you need to worry about Edward. No doubt he can find a wife when he wants one.'

'If ever!' snapped old Mrs North shortly. Bridling, she turned to watch the hedges flying by, and spoke no more until Bertie deposited her again at Rose Lodge.

The invitation to Ireland pleased Edward mightily. He missed his sister Joan, for despite their promises to visit each other, various reasons had prevented them from meeting and it was now eighteen months since they bad seen each other.

Business affairs would keep Edward ceaselessly engaged for the next two or three months, but he promised to cross to Ireland during the last week of August. It would be his first visit to a country which had always intrigued him. He hoped, if he could arrange matters satisfactorily at the factory, to go on from Dublin to see something of the west coast. He looked forward eagerly to the trip.

When the time came he set off in high spirits. He was to make the crossing from Holyhead to Dun Laoghaire, and as the train rattled across Wales, Edward thought how little he knew of the countries which marched with his own. The war had fettered him, and for the last few years London had claimed him, apart from the occasional business trips abroad. Catching glimpses of Welsh mountains, and tumbling rivers so different from the placid Cax of home, he made up his mind that he would explore Wales and Scotland before he grew much older.

He slept soundly during the night crossing, and awoke to find the mailboat rocking gently in the great harbour of Dun Laoghaire, or Kingstown, as the old people at home still called it. Beyond the massive curves of the granite breakwaters, the little town basked in the morning sunshine. Gulls screamed above the glittering water. A maid twirled a mop from a window of the Royal Marine Hotel. A train, with a plume of smoke, chugged along the coast to Dublin. Edward's first glimpse of Ireland did not disappoint him.

He breakfasted aboard before meeting Joan and Michael who had driven the seven miles from Dublin to meet him.

'You both look younger – and fatter!' cried Edward with delight.

'It's Irish air and Irish food,' replied Joan, 'You see! You'll he twice the man at the end of your holiday.'

There was so much news to exchange on the drive to Dublin that Edward scarcely noticed his surroundings; but the soft, warm Irish air on his cheeks was strange and delicious.

Michael's father had died recently but his mother still made her home with them. Edward found her a gender edition of his grandmother North, with some deafness which rendered her endearingly vague. Sarah, not yet two years old, with red curls and a snub nose, flirted outrageously with her uncle from the instant they met. She was in the care of a good.looking young nursemaid whose broad Irish speech Edward found entirely incomprehensible. She was equally incapable of understanding Edward, and for the duration of his stay they relied on smiles, and occasional interpretation from the family, for communication.

The hotel was small, but well placed in one of the quiet streets near Stephen's Green. Joan and Michael worked hard here and the business was thriving. Edward explored Dublin, mainly on his own, browsing at the bookstalls along the quays by the River Liffey, and admiring the hump-backed bridges which crossed its broad waters. Michael took time off from his duties to show him Trinity College, not far from the hotel, and Edward thought that the vast eighteenth-century library, its sombre beauty lit by slanting rays of sunlight, was one of the most impressive places he had ever seen.

On the third morning Joan received a letter which she read at the breakfast table with evident satisfaction.

'She can come. Isn't that good?' she said to her husband.

'Maisie Hunter,' she told Edward. 'She's staying with an aunt in Belfast and said she would come down if she could manage it. She's arriving tomorrow by train.'

Although Edward liked Maisie, he felt a slight pang of regret. He was so much enjoying his present circumstances in this new place and among the friendly people who always seemed to have time to stop and talk with a curious stranger. At the moment he was content to forget Caxley and all its inmates. He chided himself for such selfishness and offered to meet Joan's friend at the station.

'Take the car,' said Michael. 'She's bound to have a mountain of luggage.'

But all Maisie carried were two neat matching cases when

Edward first saw her, in the distance, stepping from the train. She was thinner than he remembered her, and her brown hair, which used to hang to her shoulders, was now short and softly curled. It suited her very well, thought Edward, hurrying to meet her. Her obvious surprise delighted him.

'I'd no idea you were here! What a nice surprise.'

Her smile was warm, lighting up her sun-tanned face and grey eyes. No one could call Maisie Hunter a beauty: her features were not regular enough for such a description, but her skin and hair were perfect, and she had a vivacity of expression, combined with a low and lovely voice, which made her most attractive. Edward was now wholeheartedly glad to see her again.

'I've had a standing invitation to visit Joan,' she explained, as they drove towards Stephen's Green, 'and this seemed the right time to come. My aunt has her son and daughter arriving for a week's stay. But I didn't realize that I was interrupting a family reunion.'

Edward assured her truthfully that they were all delighted that she had come, and constituted himself as guide on this her first visit to Dublin.

'A case of the blind leading the blind,' he added, drawing up outside the hotel. 'But it's amazing how ready people are to drop what they are doing and take you wherever you want to go. Time stands still over here. That's Ireland's attraction to me.'

'You know what they say? "God made all the time in the world, and left most of it in Ireland." Now, where's my god-daughter?'

The next two or three days passed pleasantly. Edward and Maisie discovered the varied delights of Phoenix Park, revelling in the long walks across the windy central plain, watching the fine race-horses exercise and the little boys flying their kites in the warm summer breezes.

It was Michael who suggested that they took his car and set off to explore the western part of Ireland.

'I've a good friend who has a little pub on the shores of Lough Corrib,' he told them. 'There's no such modern nonsenses as telephones there, but tell him I sent you. He'll find room for you, without doubt, and the views there will charm your hearts from your breasts.'

Michael, waxing lyrical in the Celtic fashion, always amused Edward. Ireland was the finest place in the world, Michael maintained, and it was a positive sin not to see as much of its glories as possible during Edward's short stay. Persuaded, the two set out in the borrowed car, promising to return in a few days.

Edward had envisaged hiring a car and making this journey on his own. He had secretly looked forward to this solitary trip, stopping when and where he liked, sight.seeing or not as the mood took him. But now that he had a companion he found that he was enjoying himself quite as much. They were easy together, sometimes talking animatedly, sharing memories of Caxley characters, or sometimes content to relax in silence and watch the rolling green fields of Ireland's central plain slide past.

The welcome at 'The Star' was as warm as Michael had promised. It was a small whitewashed pub, set on a little knoll above the dark waters which reflected it. The sun was setting when they arrived, and long shadows streaked the calm surface of the lake. Edward thought that he had never seen such tranquillity. His bedroom window looked across an expanse of grass, close-cropped by a dozen or so fine geese, to the lake. Here and there on the broad waters were islets, misty-blue against the darkening sky. Moored against the bank were three white skiffs, and Edward made up his mind to take one in the morning to explore those secret magical places fast slipping into the veils of twilight.

But now the welcome scent of fried bacon and eggs came drifting from below, and he hurried down, trying to dodge the low beams which threatened his head, to find Maisie and their waiting meal.

Their brief holiday passed blissfully. They explored Galway and made a trip to the Aran Islands in driving rain, and lost their hearts, just as Michael said they would, to the sad grey-green mountains and the silver beaches of Connemara. But it was the waters of Lough Corrib, lapping beneath their windows at night and supplying them with the most delicious trout and salmon of their lives, which had the strongest allure.

On their last day they took a picnic and set off in the boat to row across to one of the many islands. Maisie was taking a turn at the oars and Edward, eyes screwed up against the dazzling sunshine, watched her square brown hands tugging competently and thought how much he would miss her. He had been happier in her company than he would have thought possible. He tried to explain to himself why this should be. Of course they had known each other, off and on, for almost ten years, so that they had slipped into this unexpected companionship with perfect ease. And then there was no tiresome coquetry about the girl, no playing on her femininity. She had tackled the long walks, the stony mountain tracks, and the quagmires too, with enthusiasm and with no useless grieving over ruined shoes. He remembered an occasion when they descended a steep muddy lane beside a tiny farm, lured by the distant prospect far below of a shining beach. Out of the cottage had run a stout Irishwoman who threw up her hands in horror to see their struggles through the mud.

'Come away now,' she cried, 'and go down through our farm yard. You'll be destroyed that way!'

He laughed aloud at the memory.

'What now?' queried Maisie, resting on her oars. Bright drops slid down their length and plopped into the lake. He told her.

'Once when I was out with Philip,' she began animatedly, and then stopped. Edward watched her expression change swiftly from gaiety to sadness. This was the first time that she had mentioned her dead fiancé's name. They had not talked of their past at all during these few lovely days.

She looked away across the lake and spoke in a low but steady voice, as though she bad made up her mind to speak without restraint.

'Once when I was out with Philip,' she repeated, and continued with the anecdote. But Edward did not hear it, He was too engrossed with his own thoughts, From his own experience, he guessed that this moment was one of great advance for Maisie's progress towards full recovery from her grief. If Ireland had been able to thaw the ice which held her heart, then that alone would make this holiday unforgettable.

He became conscious that she was silent, and smiling at him,

'You haven't heard a word, have you?' she asked, 'Don't fib. I don't mind. D'you know that something wonderful has just happened to me?'

'Yes,' said Edward gently. 'I can guess.'

'I've never spoken about him. I couldn't. But somehow, here, with nothing but lake and sky, it seems easy. My family mind so much for me, I don't dare to talk of it. I can't face the emotion it brings forth.'

'I've had my share of that,' replied Edward. 'Someone – I think it was Uncle Bertie – told me once that it's the hardest thing in the world to receive pity. The damnable thing is that it takes so many forms – and all of them hell for the victim.'

He found himself telling the girl about his own family's attitude to his broken marriage, and the comfort he had found in his solitary life.

'We've been lucky in having that,' agreed Maisie. 'My Caxley flat has been a haven, I should have gone mad if I had been living at home. There's a lot to be said for a single existence. Wasn't it Katherine Mansfield who said that living alone had its compensations? And that if you found a hair in your honey it was a comfort to know it was your own?'

An oar slipped from its rowlock and the boat rocked.

'Here, let me row for a bit,' said Edward, restored to the present. They crept gingerly past each other exchanging places, and Edward pulled steadily towards the nearest island.

They picnicked on salmon and cucumber sandwiches and hard-boiled eggs, afterwards lying replete in the sun. A moor-hen piped from the reeds nearby. The sun was warm upon their closed eyes. A little breeze shivered upon the surface of the lake and ruffled their hair.

'Damn going back,' said Edward lazily. 'I could stay here for ever.

'Me too,' said Maisie ungrammatically. 'I feel quite different. You've been a great help, letting me talk about Philip. It was a thousand pities we never married, in more ways than one. Somehow one tends to build up a sort of deity from the person one's lost, and I think that is wrong. If we'd had a few years of married ups and downs perhaps I should have been able to bear it more bravely.'

'In some ways,' said Edward, 'you miss them more.' He remembered, with sharp poignancy, the perfume which Angela had used and how terribly it had affected him after their parting.

He propped himself on one elbow and looked down upon his companion. She looked very young and vulnerable, a long grass clamped between her teeth, her eyes shut against the sunlight. She'd had a tough road to travel, just as he had. Fortunately, he was further along that stony track, and knew that, in the end, it grew easier. He tried to tell her this.

'It gets better, you know, as you go on. All that guff about Time, the Great Healer, which irritates one so when one's still raw – well, it's perfectly true. I've just got out of the let-me-lick-my-wound-in-solitude state, which you're still in, and all the things which wise old people like Sep told me are coming true. Hope comes back, and purpose, and a desire to do something worthwhile – and, best of all, the perfectly proper feeling that it is *right* to be happy, and not to feel guilty when cheerfulness breaks in.'

Maisie opened her grey eyes, threw aside the grass and smiled at him.

'Dear Edward,' she said, 'you are an enormous comfort.'

They returned reluctantly to Dublin. Edward was to go back the next day to England. Maisie was going to her aunt's for a little longer.

'When do you go back to Caxley?' asked Edward, through the car window as Michael prepared to drive him to the station.

'Term starts on September the twelfth,' said Maisie. 'A Thursday. I'll probably go back on Tuesday or Wednesday.'

'I shall be down on Friday evening for the weekend,' said Edward with decision. 'Keep it free. Promise?'

'Promise,' nodded Maisie, as the car drove away.

Chapter Fifteen

EDWARD AND MAISIE

During the golden autumn months that followed Edward's visit to Ireland, work at the factory quickened its pace. Edward was as enthusiastic and conscientious as ever, but it did not escape the eyes of his partners that all his weekends were now spent at Caxley.

Elizabeth, in the flat above, watched Edward's car roar away early on Saturday mornings, or sometimes on Friday evenings, when pressure of work allowed. Aunt Mary, it seemed, was right when she predicted that Caxley would pull her attractive nephew homeward. What was she like, Elizabeth wondered, this Caxley girl who had succeeded where she had failed?

Not that she cared very much, she told herself defiantly. There were just as good fish in the sea, and the thought of spending her life in a tin-pot little dump like Caxley appalled her.

If Edward wanted to bury himself alive in a place like that, then she was glad that nothing had come of their affair. It was only, she admitted wistfully, that he was so extraordinarily handsome, and made such a wonderful escort. Meanwhile, it was no good grieving over her losses. Sensibly, she turned her attention to the other young men in her life. They might not have quite the same high standard of good looks and general eligibility as dear, lost Edward, but they were certainly more attainable.

In Caxley, of course, the tongues wagged briskly. The Howards had provided gossip of one sort or another for generations. There was that deliciously spicy affair of Sep's wife Edna, the Caxley folk reminded each other, when Dan Crockford painted her portrait and the shameless hussy had sat for it *unchaperoned*. True, she was fully dressed, they added, with some disappointment in their tones, but

Sep had been very upset about it at the time. It had happened years ago, in the reign of King Edward the Seventh in fact, but was still fresh in the memories of many old stalwarts of the market square.

Sep's rise in fortune was remembered too, and the buying of Bender North's old property, but there were few who grudged Sep his success. He bore himself modestly and his high principles were respected. Besides, he had faced enough trouble in his life with the death of his first-born in the war, and the goings on of his second son Leslie. It must be hard to banish one's child, as Sep had done. Did he ever regret it, they asked each other? And then this last tragedy of poor Robert's! What a burden Sep had carried to be sure!

But this latest tit-bit was a pleasant one. It was a pity, of course, that Maisie Hunter was not a true-bred Caxley girl, but only a war-time arrival. On the other hand, as one pointed out to her neighbour over the garden hedge, a bit of fresh blood worked wonders in these old inter-married families of Caxley. And say what you like, if Maisie Hunter had chosen to stay all these years in Caxley, it proved that she had good sense and that she was worthy to marry into their own circle. It was to be hoped, though, that the children would take after Edward for looks. Maisie Hunter was *healthy* enough, no doubt, but certainly no oil painting – too skinny by half.

Thus flowed the gossip, but one important point was overlooked by the interested bystanders. It was taken for granted that Maisie Hunter would accept such a fine suitor with alacrity. The truth was that Edward's ardent and straightforward wooing was meeting with severe set-backs. Maisie was beset with doubts and fears which were as surprising to Edward as they were painful to the girl herself.

Was he truly in love with her, or simply ready for domesticity? Was he prompted by pity for her circumstances? The questions beat round and round in her brain, and she could find no answer.

She wondered about her own response. In the solitude of the little flat which had become so dear to her, she weighed the pros and cons of the step before her, in a tumult of confusion. She was now twenty-nine, and Edward was two years older. There was a lot to give up if she married. She was at the peak of a career she enjoyed. The idea of financial dependence was a little daunting, and she would hate to leave Caxley. She was not at all sure that she wanted to embark on the troubled seas of motherhood as soon as she married, and yet it would be best for any children they might have to start a family before she and Edward were much older.

And then, to be a *second* wife was so much more difficult than to be a *first*. Marriage, for Edward, had been such an unhappy episode. Could she make him as happy as he deserved to be? Would he secretly compare her with his first wife? Would he find her equally disappointing and demanding? Wouldn't it be safer if they didn't marry after all, she wondered, in despair?

It had all been so much simpler when she had become engaged to Philip. They had both been very young. Love, marriage, and children had seemed so simple and straightforward then. Now everything was beset with doubts and complications. Philip's death had shaken her world so deeply, that any decision was difficult to make. Edward's patience with her vacillations made her feel doubly guilty. It was not fair to subject him to such suspense, but she could not commit herself while she was so tormented.

Thus the autumn passed for Maisie in a strange blur of intense happiness and horrid indecision. Edward came to see her each weekend, and often she travelled to London to meet him after school. In his company she was at peace, but as soon as she returned to Caxley the nagging questions began again. The Howards and Norths were dismayed at the delay in Edward's plans. It was quite apparent that he was in love. What on earth could Maisie be thinking of to shilly-shally in this way? Wasn't their Edward good enough for her?

November fogs shrouded the market square. The Cax flowed sluggishly, reflecting sullen skies as grey as pewter. People hurried home to their firesides, looked out hot-water bottles, took to mufflers, complained of rheumatic twinges, and faced the long winter months with resignation. The gloom was pierced on November 14 that year by the news of the birth of a son to the Princess

Elizabeth. The church bells rang in the market square, and from village towers and steeples in the countryside around. Their joyous clamour was in Maisie's ears as she pushed a letter to Joan into the pillar box at the corner of the market place.

It had taken her a long time to write, but even longer to decide if it should be written at all. But it was done, and now relief flooded her. All the things which she had been unable to tell Edward, she had written to his sister, and she begged for advice as unbiased as possible in the circumstances. Maisie respected Joan's good sense. In these last few agitated weeks, she had longed to talk with her, to discuss her doubts with someone of her own sex, age and background.

She awaited the reply from Ireland with as much patience as she could muster. No doubt Joan would take as much time and trouble with her answer as she herself had taken in setting out her problems. As the days passed, she began to wonder if it had been kind to press Joan on the matter. After all, she was an exceptionally busy person, and young Sarah took much of her attention.

At last the letter came. Maisie sped to the door, her breakfast coffee untasted. It lay, a square white envelope with the Irish stamp, alone on the door mat. Trembling, Maisie bent to pick it up. It was thin and light. Obviously, whatever message Joan sent was going to prove terse and to the point. She tore it open. Joan's neat handwriting covered only one side of the paper.

You darling ass,

All your ifs and buts are on Edward's account, I notice. Let him shoulder his own worries, if he has any, which I doubt – and please say 'Yes.' Go ahead and just be happy, both of you.

All our love,
Joan

P.S. Dr Kelly has just confirmed our hopes. Prepare for a christening next April.

Suddenly, the bleak November morning seemed flooded with warmth and light. This was exactly the right sort of message to receive – straightforward, loving and wise. How terrible, Maisie realized, it would have been to receive a long screed putting points for and against the marriage – merely a prolongation of the dreary debate which had bedevilled her life lately. Joan had summed up the situation at once, had recognized the nervous tension which grew more intense as time passed and had made Maisie's decision impossible. In a few lines she had pointed out something simple and fundamental to which worry had blinded her friend. Edward knew what he was undertaking. Maisie recalled his saying one evening, with a wry smile: 'You might give me credit for some sense. I've thought about it too, you know.'

She folded the letter, put it in her handbag like a talisman, and set off, smiling, for school.

'No long engagement for us,' said Edward firmly next weekend. 'You might change your mind again, and that I couldn't face.'

They had spent the winter afternoon visiting the family to tell them of their engagement and their future plans.

At Rose Lodge it was Grandma North who received the news with the greatest display of excitement.

'At last, a wedding in St Peter's!' she exclaimed, clapping her thin papery old hands together. Edward shook his head.

'Afraid not. For one thing we neither of us want it. And I don't think our vicar would relish a divorced man at his altar.'

'Not a church wedding?' faltered the old lady. 'Oh, what a disappointment! Really, it does seem hard!'

She rallied a little, and her mouth took on the obstinate curve which Edward knew so well.

'I'll have a word with the vicar myself, dear boy. Bender and I worked for the church all our lives, and the least he can do is to put on a nice little wedding service for our grandson.' She spoke as if the vicar would be arranging a lantern lecture in the church hall – something innocuous and sociable – with coffee and Marie biscuits to follow.

Edward broke into laughter. His grandmother began to pout, and he crossed the room in three strides and kissed her heartily.

Unwillingly, she began to smile, and Winnie, watching them both, thought how easily Edward managed the wilful old lady whose autocratic ways grew more pronounced and embarrassing as the years passed.

'No, no church this time, but a wonderful wedding party at Sep's. He's already planning the cake decorations, and we shall expect your prettiest bonnet on the day.'

Mrs North appeared mollified, and turned her attention to more practical matters concerning linen, silver and china. It was clear that she was going to be busily engaged in the wedding preparations from now on.

And this time, thought Winnie, her eyes upon Edward and Maisie, there is happiness ahead. For a fleeting moment she remembered her first encounter with Angela, and the dreadful premonition of disaster to come. Now, just as deeply, she felt that this time all would be well for them both.

Sep too, had shared the same feeling when he had held their hands that afternoon and congratulated them.

'Dear boy, dear boy!' he repeated, much moved. His welcome to Maisie was equally warm. He had known and liked her for many years now. She would make Edward a good wife.

He accompanied them down the stairs from his parlour above the shop and said good-bye to them in front of the bow windows which displayed the delicious products of his bakehouse at the back. When they were out of sight, he glanced across at the fine windows above his restaurant across the square. Would Edward ever return there, he wondered? Would his children gaze down one day upon the varied delights of market day, as Edward had done, and his friend Bender's children had done, so long ago, when horses had clip-clopped across the cobbles and Edward the Seventh was on the throne?

He turned to look with affection at that monarch's mother, small and dignified, surveying the passing traffic from her plinth.

'No one like her,' exclaimed Sep involuntarily. 'No one to touch her, before or since.'

Two schoolgirls, chewing toffee, giggled together and nudged each other. What a silly old man, talking to himself! They passed on, unseen by Sep.

He entered the shop, glad to be greeted by its fragrant warmth after the raw cold outside. For four reigns now he had served in this his own small kingdom. Sometimes, lately, he had wondered if he could rule for much longer, but now, with Edward's good news ringing in his ears, he felt new strength to face the future.

'I'll take some crumpets for tea,' he said to the assistant behind the scrubbed counter.

He mounted the stairs slowly, bearing his paper bag to Miss Taggerty. This, after all, he told himself, was the right way for a baker to celebrate.

The wedding was to be in January, and meanwhile Edward searched for a house or a larger flat than the one in which he now lived. Maisie accompanied him as often as her school work would allow.

It was a dispiriting task. New houses had gone up in abundance near Edward's factory, but neither he nor Maisie could face their stark ugliness, the slabs of raw earth waiting to be transformed into tiny gardens and the complete lack of privacy. Older houses, in matured gardens, never seemed to be for sale.

Back in Edward's little flat after an exhausting foray, Maisie kicked off her shoes and gazed round the room.

'What's wrong with this?' she asked.

'Why, nothing,' said Edward, 'except that it's hardly big enough for one, let alone two.'

'We haven't seen anything as comfortable as this,' replied Maisie. 'I'll be happy here, if you will. Let's start here anyway. If it becomes impossible we'll think again – but I simply can't look at any more places just now. I can't think why we didn't settle for this in the first place.'

Edward agreed, with relief. It might not be ideal, but the flat was quiet with an outlook upon grass and trees, and it would be simple for Maisie to run. He would like to have found something more splendid for his new wife, but their recent expeditions had proved daunting, to say the least. Maybe, in time, they could move much further away, to the pleasant greenness of Buckinghamshire, perhaps, where property was attractive and the daily journey to work would not be too arduous. Meanwhile, Edward's tiny flat, refurbished a little by Maisie, would be their first home.

There was snow on the ground on their wedding day, but the sun shone from a pale-blue cloudless sky. Steps and window sills were edged with white, and the pigeons' coral feet made hieroglyphics on the snowy pavements. Edward and Maisie emerged from the registrar's office into the market place, dazzled with the sunshine, the snow and their own happiness.

'I suppose,' said Mrs North to Bertie, as they followed the pair, 'that it's *legal*. I mean they *really are* married?'

'Perfectly legal, Mamma,' Bertie assured her.

'It seems so quick,' protested the old lady. 'I do so hope you're right, Bertie. It would be terrible for them to find they were living in sin.'

The registrar, coming upon the scene and overhearing this remark, gave a frosty bow and marched stiffly away.

'Now you've offended him,' said Bertie, smiling.

'Hm!' snorted the old lady, unrepentant. 'Marrying people without even a surplice! Small wonder he hurries away!'

It was a gay party that gathered in Sep's restaurant. The wedding cake stood on a table by the windows which overlooked the snowy garden. The dark waters of the Cax gleamed against the white banks, and a robin perching upon a twig peered curiously at the array of food inside the window.

Edward gazed contentedly about him. Sep and his grandmother were nodding sagely across the table. Her wedding hat was composed of velvet pansies in shades of blue and violet. She had certainly succeeded in finding a beauty, thought Edward affectionately.

His mother and Bertie were in animated conversation. Aunt Kathy, gorgeous in rose-pink, glowed at the corner of the table, her children nearby. If only Joan could have been here it would have been perfect, but he and Maisie were to see her before long as they returned from their honeymoon.

He turned to look at his new wife. She wore a soft yellow suit and looked unusually demure. He laughed and took her hand. Another Howard had joined the family in the market square.

Far away, the quiet waters of Lough Corrib reflected the bare winter trees growing at the lake side.

There was no snow here. A gentle wind rustled the dry reeds, and the three white skiffs lay upside down on the bank, covered by a tarpaulin for the winter. The grey and white geese converged upon the back door of the inn, necks outstretched, demanding food.

A plume of blue smoke curled lazily towards the winter sky. Timeless and tranquil, 'The Star' gazed at its reflection in the water, and awaited its guests.

Chapter Sixteen

HARVEST LOAVES

One bright Sunday morning in April, Sep awoke with curious constriction in his chest. He lay still, massaging it gently with a small bony hand. He was not greatly perturbed. A man in his eighties expects a few aches and pains, and Sep had always made light of his ailments.

It was fortunate, he thought, that it was Sunday. On weekdays he continued to rise betimes, despite his family's protests, but on Sunday he allowed himself some latitude and Miss Taggerty prepared breakfast for eight o'clock.

Always, when he awoke, his first thoughts were of Edna. He lay now, remembering just such a shining morning, when he and Edna had taken the two boys for a picnic in the woods at Beech Green. Robert and Kathy were not born then, and Jim and Leslie had frisked before them like young lambs, along the lane dappled with sunshine and shadow. They had picked bunches of primroses, and eaten their sandwiches in a little clearing. Sep could see the young birch trees now, fuzzy with green-gold leaf. A pair of blackbirds had flown back and forth to their nestlings, and a young rabbit had lolloped across the clearing, its fur silvered and its translucent ears pink, in the bright sunshine.

Perhaps he remembered it so clearly, thought Sep, because they so rarely had a day out together. The shop had always come first. Edna must have found it a great tie sometimes, but he could not recall her complaining. She had been a wonderful wife. He missed her more and more. It was hard to grow old alone.

He sat up, suddenly impatient with his own self-pity, and a spasm of pain shot through him. It was so sharp and unexpected that he gasped in dismay. When it had abated a little, he lay back gingerly against the pillow. The bells of St Peter's were ringing for early service. It would soon be seven-thirty.

'Indigestion,' Sep told himself aloud. He tried to remember if he had eaten anything unusual on the previous day, but failed. His appetite was small, and he had never been in the habit of eating a heavy meal in the evening. Perhaps he had put too much sugar in his Horlicks. As he grew older he found himself becoming increasingly fond of sweet things. He must not be so self-indulgent.

He sat up carefully. The pain was dwindling, and he crossed slowly to the window. A few church-goers were mounting the steps of St Peter's. A milkman's float clanged and jangled on the opposite side of the square. It was a typical Sunday morning in Caxley – a scene which he had looked upon hundreds of times and always taken for granted.

But today, suddenly, it had a poignant significance for Sep. Would he see many more Sundays? Death must come soon, and he was unafraid – but Caxley was very dear, and hard to leave behind.

He shaved and dressed carefully in his sober Sunday suit in readiness for chapel, and in his mind there beat a line of poetry which he had heard only that week.

> Look thy last on all things lovely,
> Every hour –

It was good sense, Sep decided, descending the stairs slowly, as well as good poetry.

In the weeks that followed, the pain recurred. Sep found that his head swam sometimes when he bent down, or if he lifted a heavy pan in the bakehouse. He told no one of the disability, dismissing it as a passing ailment, unworthy of serious attention. He brushed aside Miss Taggerty's anxious inquiries. There was little affecting her master which her keen old eyes missed, but natural timidity kept her from expressing her fears to the rest of the family. Sep would brook no tale-telling, she knew well.

But the secret could not be kept for long. One warm May

evening Sep set off along the tow path to see Kathy and Bertie. Half a dozen naked boys splashed and shouted by the further bank. Clouds of midges drifted above the river, and swallows swooped back and forth, like dark blue arrows. From the oak tree near Bertie's garden gate, minute green caterpillars jerked on their gossamer threads. It was sultry, with a mass of dark clouds building up menacingly on the horizon. Soon there would be thunder, and the boys would scramble for home, leaving the placid surface of the river to be pitted with thousands of drops.

Bertie was in his vegetable garden, spraying the blackfly from his broad beans. Sep heard the rhythmic squish-squish of the syringe. Bertie was hidden from sight by a hawthorn hedge which divided the lawn from the kitchen garden. A blackbird flew out, squawking frenziedly, as Sep brushed the hedge. There were probably a dozen or more nests secreted in its length, Sep surmised, looking at it with interest. He turned to watch his son-in-law, still unaware of his presence, intent on washing away the sticky black pest.

Bertie wore well, he thought affectionately. His figure had thickened slightly, and his hair, still plentiful, had turned to silver. But his complexion was fresh and his blue eyes as bright as ever. He was becoming more like Bender as he grew older, but would never have the girth, or the bluster, of his father. Bender's ebullience had made Sep nervous at times. There was nothing to fear in his son.

At last he straightened up, and started when he saw Sep's slight figure at the end of the row.

'Good heavens! I didn't hear you arrive! How are you? Let me put this thing away and we'll go indoors.'

'No, no, my boy. Finish the job. There's rain on the way and there's no hurry on my account.'

Obediently, Bertie refilled his syringe and set off along the last row, Sep following. A flourishing plant of groundsel caught the old man's eye and he bent to pull it up. Immediately, the pain in his chest had him in its grip with such intensity that his head thumped. The rosette of groundsel, the damp earth and the pale green stalks of the bean plants whirled round and round together, growing darker and darker, as the blood pounded in his head.

Bertie ran to pick up the old man who was in a dead faint and gasping alarmingly. His cheek and the grey hair at one temple were muddied by the wet soil. With difficulty Bertie managed to lift him in his arms and limped towards the house, calling for Kathy. Sep was as light as a bird, Bertie noticed, despite his agitation – lighter by far than his own young son, Andrew.

They put him on the couch and Kathy ran for smelling salts, while Bertie chafed the frail hands and watched him anxiously.

'We must call the doctor,' he said. As he spoke, Sep opened his eyes and shook his head slowly and wearily.

'No. No doctor,' he whispered.

'Some brandy?' urged Bertie.

'No, thank you,' said Sep, with a touch of his old austerity. Bertie realized that he had blundered.

'Some tea then?'

Sep nodded and closed his eyes again. Kathy ran to the kitchen and Bertie followed her.

'Whatever he says, I'm ringing for the doctor. This is something serious, I feel sure.'

Within ten minutes the doctor had arrived. There was no demur from Sep who, with the tea untasted, lay frail and shrunken against Kathy's bright cushions, with a blanket tucked around him. The examination over, the doctor spoke with false heartiness.

'You'll see us all out, Mr Howard. Just a tired heart, but if you take care of yourself, you'll be as sound as a bell for years yet. I'll write you a prescription.'

Bertie accompanied him into the lane, well out of ear-shot.

'Tell me the truth, doctor. How is he?'

'As I said. If he takes his pills regularly and avoids excessive exercise, he can tick over for a few more years. Your job is to persuade him to take things easily.'

'That's one of the hardest things in the world to ask me to do, but I'll try. Should he spend the night here?'

'It would be best. Tell him to stay there until I call again in the morning.'

Sep submitted to the doctor's orders with unusual docility, and as soon as he was settled in Kathy's spare room Bertie hurried to the market square to tell the news to Miss Taggerty.

It grieved Sep, in the months that followed, to lead such a comparatively inactive life. True, he rose at the usual time and supervised the shop, the restaurant, and the bakehouse, as he had always done, but he walked from place to place more slowly now, and tried not to mount his steep stairs more than was necessary. The doctor had advised him to rest after his midday dinner, and now that the weather was warm, he took to sitting in the old arbour by the river at the rear of the restaurant. This had been his old friend Bender's favourite spot, and Sep had made sure that it was kept as spruce as Bender would have wished.

Jasmine starred and scented its rustic entrance, and an Albertine rose added its splendour. Kathy made the rough seat comfortable with cushions, and provided a footstool and rug. It was a perfect sun trap, and as she went about her affairs in the restaurant, she could watch Sep dozing in sheltered warmth, or gazing at his life-long companion, the river Cax.

The family called to see Sep more often than usual. Hilda North took to paying Sep an occasional afternoon visit. Winnie drove her down the hill from Rose Lodge and left her to keep the old man company while she shopped in the town.

The two old people, who shared so many common memories, were closer now than ever they had been, and as they took tea together in the arbour they enjoyed reminiscing about their early days in the market square when their children had played together in this same garden, and floated their toy boats on the river before them.

Edward and Maisie spent as many weekends in Caxley as they could, but both were busy, for Maisie had taken a part-time teaching post. Miss Hedges, the middle-aged headmistress who lived in a neighbouring flat, had soon discovered that Maisie was a trained teacher, and had no difficulty in persuading her to accompany her three mornings a week to school. Here Maisie helped children who were backward in reading and thoroughly enjoyed the work.

'But we don't call them 'backward' these days, my dear,' said Miss Hedges with a twinkle. "Less able' is the most forthright term we are allowed to use in these namby-pamby times!'

Maisie was glad to be doing something worthwhile again. She and Edward were blissfully happy, but he was off to work before half-past eight, the tiny flat was set to rights soon after, and Maisie was beginning to find time hanging heavily on her hands when Miss Hedges had appeared. It was a happy arrangement for them all.

Maisie found her new life absorbing. She looked back now upon her doubts and fears with amusement and incredulity. How right Joan had been, and how lucky she was to have found Edward! They had much in common. As a Londoner, Maisie shared Edward's love of the theatre and they spent many evenings there. Aunt Mary, going from strength to strength as she became better known as a character actress, saw them frequently, and was loud in her approval of Edward's choice.

'And when are you going to Caxley?' she inquired one September evening, after the play. She was in her dressing-room removing make-up with rapid expert strokes.

'The weekend after next,' replied Edward.

'I meant for good,' said his aunt. She noted Edward's surprise.

'Hadn't really thought about it,' said Edward frankly. 'This job is growing daily, and the journey from Caxley would take too long. We're still hoping for a house in the country somewhere, but it will have to be nearer than Caxley.'

Aunt Mary did not pursue the subject. How it would come about she did not know, but in her bones she felt quite sure that Edward and his Maisie were destined for Caxley one day.

She rose from her seat before the dressing table and kissed them unexpectedly.

'Give the old place my love,' she said. 'And all the people who remember me there. Particularly Sep – yes, particularly Sep!'

The last Friday in September was as warm and golden as the harvest fields through which Edward and Maisie drove to Caxley.

It had been a good crop this year and the weather had been favourable. Most of the fields were already cut, and the bright stubble bristled cleanly in the sunshine.

Winnie was staking Michaelmas daisies in the garden of Rose Lodge when they arrived. Edward thought how well she looked, and his grandmother too, as they sipped their sherry and exchanged news.

'And Sep?' asked Edward.

'Fairly well,' said his grandmother. 'I had tea with him yesterday afternoon and he's looking forward to seeing you.'

'I'll go and have a word with him now,' said Edward. 'Coming?' he asked Maisie.

'Tell him I'll look in tomorrow morning,' she answered. 'I'll unpack and help here.'

'Don't be long,' called Winnie as he made for the car.

'There's a chicken in the oven, and it will be ready by eight o' clock.'

'That's a date,' shouted Edward cheerfully, driving off.

The long shadow of St Peter's spire stretched across the market place, but the sun still gleamed warmly upon Sep's shop and the windows of his house above it. Edward parked the car and looked around him with satisfaction. Choir practice was in session and he could hear the singers running through the old familiar harvest hymns. Queen Victoria wore a pigeon on her crown and looked disapproving. At the window of his own flat he could see old John Bush, peering at a newspaper held up to the light. This was the time of day when Sep's house had the best of it, Edward thought, and remembered how, as a boy, he had explained to his grandfather why he preferred Bender's old home to Sep's.

'It gets the sun most of the day,' he had told the old man. 'You only get it in the evening.'

But how it glorified everything, to be sure! The western rays burnished Sep's side of the square, gilding steps and door-frames and turning the glass to sheets of fire. Edward ran up the stairs, at the side of the closed shop, and called to his grandfather. Miss Taggerty greeted him warmly.

'He's pottering about downstairs, Mr Edward, having a final look at the Harvest Festival loaves, no doubt. The chapel folk are fetching them tomorrow morning for the decorations. Lovely they are! He did them himself. You'll find him there, you'll see.'

Edward made his way to the bakehouse. There was no one about at this time of day and the yard was very quiet. He entered the bakehouse and was greeted by the clean fragrance of newly-baked bread which had been familiar to him all his life. Ranged against the white wall stood two splendid loaves in the shape of sheaves of corn, with smaller ones neatly lined up beside them. There were long plaited loaves, fat round ones, Coburg, cottage, split-top – a beautiful array of every pattern known to a master baker.

And sitting before them, at the great table white and ribbed with a lifetime's scrubbing, was their creator. He was leaning back in his wooden arm chair, his hands upon the table top and his gaze upon his handiwork. He looked well content.

But when Edward came to him he saw that the eyes were sightless and the small hands cold in death. There, in the centre of his world, his lovely work about him and his duty done, Sep rested at last.

Dazed and devastated, an arm about his grandfather's frail shoulders, Edward became conscious of the eerie silence of the room. Across the square the sound of singing drifted as the boys in St Peter's choir practised their final hymn.

'*All is safely gathered in,*' they shrilled triumphantly, as the long shadows reached towards Sep's home.

Chapter Seventeen

PROBLEMS FOR EDWARD

In the bewildered hours that followed Sep's death, the family began to realize just how deeply they would miss his presence. He had played a vital part in the life of each one. He had been the lynch-pin holding the Norths and Howards together, and his going moved them all profoundly.

After the first shock was over, Edward and Bertie spent the weekend making necessary arrangements for the funeral, writing to friends and relatives, drafting a notice for *The Caxley Chronicle* and coping with the many messages of sympathy from the townsfolk who had known Sep all his life.

As they sat at their task, one at each end of Bertie's dining-room table, Bertie looked across at Edward. The younger man was engrossed in his writing, head bent and eyes lowered. His expression was unusually solemn, and in that moment Bertie realized how very like Sep's was his cast of countenance. There was something in the slant of the cheekbone and the set of the ear which recalled the dead man clearly. Age would strengthen the likeness as Edward's hair lost its colour and his face grew thinner.

There was also, thought Bertie, the same concentration on the job in band. Edward had assumed this sudden responsibility so naturally that, for the first time, he felt dependent upon the younger man. He bad slipped into his position of authority uncon-sciously, and it was clear to Bertie that Edward henceforth would be the head of the family. It was a thought which flooded Bertie with rejoicing and relief. It was all that Sep had hoped for in his wisdom.

The chapel in the High Street was full on the occasion of Sep's funeral. Edward had not realized how many activities Sep had taken part in in the town. He was a councillor for many years. He had been a member of the hospital board, the Red Cross committee, the Boys' Brigade, and a trustee of several local charities. All these duties he had performed conscientiously and unobtrusively. It was plain, from the large congregation, that Sep's influence was widely felt and that he would be sorely missed in Caxley's public life.

The coffin bore the golden flowers of autumn. The chapel was still decorated with the corn and trailing berries of Harvest Festival. Edward, standing between Maisie and his mother, with Kathy beautiful in black nearby, was deeply moved, and when, later, Sep was lowered into the grave beside his adored wife, the dark cypress trees and bright flowers of Caxley's burial ground were blurred by unaccustomed tears. Sep had been a father as well as a grandfather to him. It was doubly hard to say farewell.

But, driving back to Bertie and Kathy's after the ceremony, he became conscious of a feeling of inner calm. This was death as it should be – rest after work well done, port after storm. Death, as Edward had met it first during the war, was violent and unnatural, the brutal and premature end of men still young. Sep had stayed his course, and the memory of that serene dead face gave his grandson comfort now, and hope for the future.

He and Maisie said little on the journey back to town, but later that evening Maisie spoke tentatively.

'Did you wish – did you feel – that your father should have been there, Edward?'

'Yes, I did,' replied Edward seriously. 'As a matter of fact, I wrote to him and told him.'

'Where is he then? I'd no idea you knew where he was!'

'I haven't. Mother would never speak of him – nor, of course, would Sep. But I found an address among his papers when Uncle Bertie and I were putting things straight. Somewhere in Devon. Heaven alone knows if he's still there, but it might be sent on to him, if he's moved. I felt he should know.'

It was the first time that his father had been mentioned, though

Maisie knew well the story of Leslie Howard's flight with an earlier love when Edward was only four and Joan still a baby in arms.

'Do you remember him?'

'Hardly at all. I can remember that he used to swing me up high over his head, which I liked. The general impression is a happy one, strangely enough. He was full of high spirits – probably slightly drunk – but willing to have the sort of rough-and-tumble that little boys enjoy.'

'And you've never wanted to see him again?'

'Sometimes, yes. Particularly when I was about sixteen or so. Luckily, Uncle Bertie was at hand always, so he got landed with my problems then. And I knew mother would have hated to see him again, or to know that I'd been in touch. As for Grandma North, I think she would have strangled my father with her bare hands if she'd clapped eyes on him again! He certainly behaved very badly to his family. Sep minded more than anyone. That's why he never spoke of him. He was such a kind man that I always thought it was extraordinary how ruthlessly he dealt with my father.'

'Sep was a man with exceptionally high principles,' said Maisie. She crossed the room to switch on the wireless, and paused on her way back to her chair to look down upon Edward. He was so solemn that she ruffled his thick hair teasingly.

'And a Victorian,' added Edward, still far away, 'with a good Victorian's rigid mode of conduct. It must have made life very simple in some ways. You knew exactly where you were.'

'You're going grey,' said Maisie, peering at the crown of his head, and Edward laughed.

'It's marriage,' he said, pulling her down beside him.

One morning, a week or so later, a long envelope with a Caxley postmark arrived for Edward. It was the only letter for him, but Maisie had a long one from Joan, full of news about the baby and Sarah's recovery from measles. Sipping her breakfast coffee, and engrossed in the letter from Ireland, she was unaware of the effect that Edward's correspondence was making upon him, until he pushed away his half-eaten breakfast and got up hastily. He looked white and bewildered, and rubbed his forehead as he always did when perplexed.

'Not more bad news?' cried Maisie.

'No. Not really. I suppose one should say quite the opposite – but the hell of a shock.'

He handed her the letter and paced the room while she read it.

'He's left you *everything*?' queried Maisie in a whisper. 'But what about Aunt Kathy and your father and the other grandchildren? I don't understand it.'

'They're all provided for – except for my father, which one would expect – by incredibly large sums of money. But the two businesses are for me, evidently.'

'Didn't he ever mention this to you?'

'Never. It honestly never entered my head. It's amazingly generous, but a terrific responsibility. I thought everything would be Aunt Kathy's, with perhaps a few bequests to the others. He'd already given me the house above the restaurant. This is staggering.'

'But lovely,' exclaimed Maisie. 'Dear Sep! He always wanted you in the market square.'

Edward paused in his pacing and looked at her in astonishment.

'Do you seriously suggest that I should run the business myself? I don't know the first thing about baking – or catering for that matter.'

'You could learn,' pointed out Maisie. 'And running one business must be very like running another. And just think – to live in Caxley!' Her eyes were bright.

Edward continued to look distracted. His eye caught sight of the time and he gave a cry of dismay.

'I must be off. This will need a lot of thought. Lovejoy wants to see me anyway to sign some papers. We'll talk this over this evening, and go down again this weekend.'

'Don't look so worried,' comforted Maisie. 'Anyone would think you'd been sentenced to death! In fact, you've been sentenced to a new life.'

'Not so fast, please,' begged Edward, collecting his belongings frenziedly. 'There's a great deal to consider – Sep's wishes, the family's reactions, whether we can cope with the business ourselves or get people in to manage it properly – a hundred problems! And what about my job here? I can't let Jim down after all he's done for me.'

Maisie pushed her agitated husband through the front door.

'Tell Jim what's happened,' she said soothingly. 'And calm down. I'm going back to celebrate in a second cup of coffee.'

The day seemed to drag by very slowly for Maisie. There was no school for her that morning, and although she was glad to have some time to collect her thoughts, she longed for Edward to return so that they could discuss this miraculous news.

For her own part she welcomed a return to Caxley. To live in the market square, either in Edward's house or in Sep's, would give her enormous pleasure. Her friends were there, and the thought of living so near all her in-laws, which might daunt many young wives, did not worry Maisie who had known the Howards and Norths now for so many years. She longed too to have a sizeable house to furnish and decorate. Here, in the tiny flat, she had found small scope for her talents. It would be lovely to choose curtains and wallpaper and to bring either of the two fine old houses to life again.

And what better place to raise a Howard family than in the heart of Caxley where their roots ran so deeply? This would mean too the end of the fruitless house-hunting which depressed them both. As she went mechanically about her household tasks, Maisie hoped desperately that Edward would be able to wind up the job satisfactorily here, and return to Caxley with a clear conscience and zest for what lay ahead.

Edward returned, looking less agitated than when he had departed for the office that morning.

'Jim is as pleased as if it had happened to him,' said he. 'We've gone into things as thoroughly as we can at this stage. He's quite happy for me to go whenever I like, but we've all sorts of negotiations going on at the moment, started by me mainly, and I must see those wound up before I'd feel free.'

'And when would that be?'

'I can't say. Probably in a few months' time.'

'A few *months*!' echoed Maisie, trying to keep the disappointment from her voice.

Edward looked across at her and laughed.

'You want to go back very badly, don't you?'

Maisie nodded.

'I'm beginning to think that I do, too, but I must clear up things at this end first. We'll see what Lovejoy says at the weekend, and how the family feels. Who knows? We may be back in the market square by the New Year. That is if I've mastered the bakery business by that time!'

As they drove to Caxley that weekend, Edward had some private misgivings. How would Aunt Kathy feel about the will? She had taken an active part in the business, and it seemed hard that no share in it had been left to her. It was true that Sep's bequest to her and her children had been characteristically generous, and of a magnitude which staggered Edward, but it was not quite the same as having a part in a thriving concern. And how would the rest of the family view his amazing good fortune? Edward had seen many united families rent assunder by wills, and could only hope that the Howards and Norths would be spared this ignominy. He approached Caxley with some trepidation.

His mother and grandmother greeted them with unfeigned delight.

'Which house would you settle in, dear?' asked Mrs North with the shattering directness of old age. She refused to believe that Edward did not know yet if he would be able to return to Caxley at all.

'But you must have known, dear, that Sep intended you to have the business?'

'I hadn't a clue, Grandma, and that's the plain truth.'

'Neither had I,' said his mother.

'Well, he spoke to me about it, towards the end,' maintained Mrs North trenchantly, 'and I agreed that it was an excellent idea.'

'Grandma, you are incorrigible!' exclaimed Edward, amused.

'It's high time you came back anyway, to look after your mother and me. And what about your own family? Married for nearly a year and no baby on the way! It's deplorable! What you need is some invigorating Caxley air.'

Edward and Maisie exchanged delighted glances.

'Yes, Grandma,' said Edward meekly.

He walked up the familiar path to Bertie and Kathy's house with a nervousness he had never felt before. Kathy opened the door to him, put her arms round his neck, and kissed him soundly. All Edward's worries fled in the face of this warm embrace.

'We're all very pleased about it,' Bertie assured him, when they were settled by the fire. 'Although Sep never said a word about his settlements we guessed that this would be the way he wanted it.'

'Would you come in with me as a partner?' asked Edward of his aunt. She smiled and shook her head.

'You're a dear to think of it, but I'm fifty-six next birthday and shall be quite glad to be away from it all. Father's left us money, as you know, and I'm glad the business is yours – still in the family, with "Howard" over the door – but not giving me any more worries.'

They talked of Edward's plans, and he explained the necessity of staying in town to clear up his affairs at the factory.

'And I'm still not absolutely sure if I ought to come back to run the shop and restaurant myself, or whether I should try and get someone to manage them.'

'John Bush and I can hold the fort until you decide,' offered Kathy. 'But *please* think about taking it on yourself. You could do it easily, and think how pleased Sep would have been.'

'And Maisie will be,' added Bertie. 'Off you go to your appointment with Lovejoy! See what he advises.'

Mr Lovejoy, pink and voluble, succeeded in confusing Edward even more, by presenting him with a host of incomprehensible documents to peruse, and a torrent of explanation.

From amidst the chaos one thing emerged clearly to Edward. He was going to be a man of some wealth. Death duties would amount to a considerable sum, but if the business continued at its present rate he could expect an income far in excess of that which he now earned. He had no doubt, in his own mind, that with some rebuilding and more modern equipment, the two businesses could become even more lucrative.

He thanked Mr Lovejoy for his help and emerged into the pale October sunlight. Hardly knowing what he was about, he passed Howard's Restaurant and crossed to Sep's old shop. It was strange to think that all this now belonged to him.

He stepped into the shop in a daze. A young new assistant, unknown to him, asked him what he would like. Edward tried to pull himself together.

'Oh, a loaf,' he said desperately. 'Just a loaf.'

She picked out a stout crusty cottage loaf from the window, shrouded it in a piece of white tissue paper, and thrust it into his arms like a warm baby.

Edward gave her a florin, and she slapped some coins into his palm in return. He studied them with interest. It was time he knew the price of bread.

Still bemused, and clutching his awkward burden, he made his way towards the Cax. What had possessed him to buy a loaf, he wondered, exasperation overcoming his numbness!

He strode now with more purpose towards the tow path. The families of mallards and moorhens paddled busily at the edge of the water, as they had always done. Today, thought Edward, they should celebrate his inheritance.

He broke pieces of the loaf and threw them joyfully upon the Cax. Squawking, quacking, piping, the birds rushed this way and that, wings flapping, streaking the water with their bright feet, as they fought for this largesse.

Exhilarated, Edward tossed the pieces this way and that, laughing at the birds' antics and his own incredible good fortune. What was it that the Scriptures said about 'casting thy bread upon the waters'? He would ask Grandma North when he returned.

He thrust the last delicious morsel into his mouth, dusted his hands, and walked home, whistling.

Chapter Eighteen

EDWARD MEETS HIS FATHER

The first frosts of autumn blackened the bright dahlias in the suburban gardens and began to strip the golden trees. Children were scuffling through the carpet of dead leaves as Edward drove to the factory one morning.

In his pocket lay a letter from his father. It was the first communication he had ever received from him, and it provided food for thought.

He studied it again in the privacy of his office. It was written on cheap ruled paper, but the writing was clear and well-formed. It had come from an address in Lincolnshire, and said:

My dear Edward,

Thank you for writing to tell me of the death of your grandfather.

To be frank, I had already seen a notice of it in *The Caxley Chronicle* which has been sent to me ever since I left the town.

I could not have attended the funeral, even if I had wished to do so, as the expense of the fare to Caxley made the trip impossible. I live alone here, in very straitened circumstances, my second wife having died two years ago.

I should very much like to see your mother again and, of course, you too, but I shall understand if it is not convenient. The contents of your grandfather's will are unknown to me, but I take it that he was stubbornly against me to the end.

Affectionately,
Leslie Howard

It was pretty plain, thought Edward, from the letter before him, that his father was as bitter as ever against Sep. Not once did he speak of him as 'my father' – but as 'your grandfather', and the final reference to the will disclosed a disappointed man. Nevertheless, Edward experienced a strong feeling of mingled pity and curiosity. His father must be getting on in years. He was certainly older than Uncle Bertie, and must now be approaching sixty. He sounded lonely too, as well as hard up.

He began to wonder how he lived. There had been two children by the second marriage, as far as he remembered. Was he perhaps living with one of them in Lincolnshire? He felt fairly certain that his mother would not wish to meet his father again, but he himself was suddenly drawn to the idea of seeing him. He turned the notion over in his mind, deciding not to do anything precipitous which might upset the family.

At the weekend, when he went once more to Caxley, he showed his mother the letter when they were alone. The vehemence of her reaction astonished him.

'He wrote to me at much the same time,' she told Edward, her face working. 'I tore up the letter. He's hurt me too much in the past, Edward. If anything, the bitterness has grown with the years. I wouldn't lift a finger to help him. He treated us all abominably, and if it hadn't been for his own father we should have been very hard up indeed. And now he has the nerve to approach us and – more than that – to expect money from Sep! The whole thing is despicable.'

It was obviously not the moment to tell his mother that he felt like visiting his father; but before he and Maisie left for home he broached the subject tentatively. He had already told Kathy and Bertie about Leslie's letter, and about the possibility of travelling to Lincoln to see how his father fared. They had both been sympathetic towards Edward's project, but had no desire to meet Leslie themselves.

'He's a charmer – or was –' said Bertie plainly, 'and a sponger. So be warned, my boy. And if your mother objects, I advise you to chuck up the idea. No point in opening old wounds.'

'I see that well enough,' responded Edward. 'But I don't like to think of him in want, when Sep has left us all so comfortably off.'

'Your feelings do you credit,' replied Bertie, 'but don't let yourself in for embarrassment in the future. Leslie might well have developed into an old-man-of-the-sea, always demanding more and more.'

As his nephew vanished up the lane to the High Street, Kathy looked at Bertie.

'Will he really go, do you think?'

'He'll go,' said Bertie. 'He feels it's his duty. He's Sep all over again when it comes to it – and the sooner we all realize it, the better.'

Luckily, Winnie's reactions to Edward's proposal were less violent than he had imagined.

'I can understand that you want to see him,' she said, rather wearily. 'He is your father after all. But I absolutely refuse to have any more to do with him. And nothing of this is to be mentioned to Grandma. She is too old for this sort of shock.'

Edward promised to be discreet, kissed his mother good-bye and drove back to London well content.

The next few weeks were unusually busy for Edward, and it was early December before the trip northwards could be arranged.

The clearing-up process at the factory was going well, but Edward was to remain one of the directors and there were a number of legal matters to arrange. Every other weekend he spent at Caxley, studying the business, and going through the accounts and staff arrangements with Kathy and John Bush. It was clear that they longed to hand over the responsibilities of the shop and restaurant which they had so bravely borne, and Edward hoped to move back to his own house as soon as the tenants in the floors below could find alternative accommodation. John Bush had been offered the little cottage where Edward and Joan had been born. A daughter, recently widowed, was to share it with him, and the old man made no secret of looking forward now to complete retirement.

Maisie was in her element choosing papers for the walls and material for curtains and covers. She went with Winnie to one or two furniture sales and acquired some fine pieces. Old Mrs North gave her the tea service which had graced her own table at the house in the market square, and Maisie liked to think of it in its own home again.

At the end of November she was delighted to discover that she was to have a baby in the early summer.

'We *must* get in before long,' she implored Edward. 'I must get everything ready for it while I'm still mobile.'

The family was as pleased as they were themselves at the news, and Mrs North's comment amused them all.

'At last,' she cried, 'we'll have a *christening* at St Peter's. Don't tell me you've anything against that?'

She was reassured, and set to work to knit half a dozen first-size vests with enthusiasm.

Edward set out alone on his journey, starting very early, as he wanted to make the return trip in the day.

It was cold and overcast when he set out, and rain began to fall heavily after an hour or so on the road. He had looked forward to this visit, but now a certain depression invaded him, due in part to the dismal weather and to general fatigue. Although he had made up his mind to return to the market square and to take up the duties laid upon him by Sep, he still had moments of doubt.

True, as Maisie had said, running one business was very like running another, but he was going to miss his trips abroad and his growing skill in designing. Life in London had been pleasant. Would he find Caxley too parochial after wider horizons? He could only hope that he was doing the right thing. In any case the thought of the baby being born in Caxley gave him enormous pleasure, and he looked forward to introducing it to all the varied delights of the Cax running through the garden.

He reached the town where his father lived a little before noon. Rain slashed against the side windows, and passing vehicles sent up showers of water across the windscreen. Wet grey-slated roofs and drab houses stretched desolately in all directions. Bedraggled people, bent behind dripping umbrellas, looked as wretched as their surroundings. Edward drove through the centre of the town and followed the route which his father's last letter had given.

He found the road, the house, switched off the car's engine and sat looking about him. It was less gloomy than parts of the town he had just traversed, but pretty dispiriting, nevertheless. The houses were semidetached, and built, Edward guessed, sometime in the thirties. They were brick below and pebble-dash above, each having an arched porch with a red-tiled floor to it. The front gardens, now leafless, were very small. Here and there a wispy ornamental cherry tree, or an etiolated rowan, struggled for existence in the teeth of the winds which came from the North Sea.

The sharp air took his breath away as he made his way to the door. It was opened so quickly that Edward felt sure that his arrival had been watched. A plump breathless woman of middle age greeted him with an air of excitement. She wore a flowered overall and carried a duster.

'Come to see your dad?' she greeted him. 'He's been waiting for you. Come in. You must be shrammed.'

Edward, who had never heard this attractive word, supposed, rightly, that it meant that he must be cold, and followed her into the small hall. An overpowering smell of floor polish pervaded the house and everything which could be burnished, from brass stair rods to the chain of the cuckoo clock on the wall, gleamed on every side.

The door on the right opened and there stood a slight figure, taller than Sep, but less tall than Edward, gazing at him with the bright dark eyes of the Howards.

'Your son's come,' announced the woman. The words dropped into the sudden silence like pebbles into a still pool.

'Come in, my boy,' said Leslie quietly, and they went into the sitting-room together.

The meeting had stirred Edward deeply, and for a moment or two he could find nothing to say. His father was fumbling at the catch of a cupboard.

'Like a drink?'

'Thank you.'

'Whisky, sherry or beer?'

'Sherry, please.'

Edward watched his father pouring the liquid. He was very like Aunt Kathy. His hair was still thick, but now more grey than black. He had the same dark, rather highly arched, eyebrows, and the pronounced lines from nose to the corner of the upper lip which all the Howards seemed to have inherited from Sep. He was dressed in a tweed suit, warm but shabby, and his shirt was so dazzlingly white that Edward felt sure that his landlady attended to his linen.

The room was over-filled with large furniture and numerous knick-knacks, but a good fire warmed all, and old-fashioned red wallpaper, overpowering in normal circumstances, gave some cheer on a morning as bleak as this.

'You seem very comfortable here,' ventured Edward, glass in hand.

'They're good people,' said Leslie. 'He's a railway man, due to retire soon. I have two rooms. I sold up when the wife died. Came up here from the west country, and took a job with a car firm.'

'Are you still with them?' asked Edward.

'No,' replied Leslie briefly. 'Tell me about the family.'

Edward told him all that he could. He appeared quite unaffected by Robert's tragic end and his father's recent death, but Edward noticed that mention of his mother brought a smile.

'But she won't see me, eh?'

'I'm afraid not. I hope you won't try.'

'Don't worry. I treated her badly. Can't blame her for giving me the cold shoulder now. I shan't come to Caxley. I thought of it when I read of the old man's death, but decided against it. If there were any pickings I reckoned Lovejoy would let me know.'

There was something so casually callous about this last utterance, that Edward stiffened.

'Did you imagine that there would be?' he inquired. There must have been an edge to his tone, for the older man shot him a quick glance.

'Can't say I did, but hope springs eternal, you know.'

He placed his glass carefully on the table beside him, and turned to face Edward.

'This looks like the only time I'll be able to put my side of the story, so I may as well tell it now. You knew my father well enough, I know, but only as an older man when he'd mellowed a bit. When Jim and I were boys he was too dam' strict by half. Chapel three times on Sundays and Lord knows how many Bible meetings of one sort or another during the week. Jim stuck it all better than I did – and then, as we got older, he didn't have the same eye for the girls as I had. He was more like Dad – I was like Mum. I don't think I ever loved my father. He said "No" too often.'

'But I know he was fond of all his children,' broke in Edward.

'Had a funny way of showing it,' observed his father bitterly. 'He drove me to deceit, and that's the truth. He was a narrow-minded bigoted old fool bent on getting to heaven at any cost. I can't forgive him.' He was breathing heavily.

'He was also brave, honest and generous,' said Edward levelly. His father seemed not to hear.

'And he poisoned Winnie's mind against me later. There was no hope of reconciliation while Father was alive.'

'That's not true,' said Edward, anger rising in him. 'My mother's mind was made up from the moment you parted!'

'Maybe,' replied Leslie indifferently. 'She was a North – as obstinate as her old man.' He laughed suddenly, and his face was transformed. Now Edward could see why Leslie Howard was remembered in Caxley as a charmer.

'Don't let's squabble,' he pleaded. 'We've a lot to talk over. Let's come out to a pub I know for our grub. Mrs Jones here is a dab hand with housecleaning but her cooking's of the baked cod-and-flaked-rice variety. I told her we'd go out.'

Edward was secretly sorry to leave the good fire and over-stuffed armchair, but dutifully drove through the relentless rain to a small public house situated two or three miles away on a wind-swept plain. Over an excellent mixed grill Edward learnt a little more of his father's life.

'My boy was killed in France,' said Leslie, 'and the girl is married and out in Australia.'

It was queer, thought Edward, to hear of this half-brother and sister whom he had never seen. His father spoke of them with affection. Naturally, they were closer to him than he and Joan could ever have been.

'And then Ellen was ill for so long – three or four years, before she died. I got to hate that place in Devon. We had a garage there, you know. Dam' hard work and mighty little return for it.'

'What happened to it?' asked Edward.

'Sold everything up when Ellen went. Paid my debts – and they were plenty – and found this place. I wanted a change, and besides, the doctor told me to live somewhere flat. I've got a dicky heart. Same thing that took off my poor mum, I daresay.'

Gradually, Edward began to see the kind of life which was now his father's lot. He had fallen out with the car firm. It was obvious that he disliked being an employee after running his own business. It was also plain to Edward that if he did not have some regular employment he would very soon drift into a pointless existence in which drink would play a major part. Nevertheless, it seemed that there were grounds for believing that he had some heart complaint. The woman behind the bar, who seemed to be an old friend, had inquired about 'his attacks' with some concern, and both his parents had suffered from heart trouble.

For the past week he had been without work for the first time. He had heard of two book-keeping jobs in local firms and proposed to apply for them. Edward thought it sounded hopeful. As far as he could gather, his father's financial resources consisted of fifty pounds or so in the bank. This amount would not last long even in such modest lodgings as Mrs Jones'. This urgency to earn was a spur in the right direction, Edward surmised.

He paid the bill and drove his father home. The matter which had been uppermost in his mind was more complicated than he had first thought. He was determined to see that his father was not in want. Now that he had met him he was equally sure that this was not the time to offer financial help. If he did, the chances of Leslie's helping himself grew considerably slighter. Prudently, Edward postponed a decision, but made his father promise to let him know the outcome of his job-hunting.

'I'll write to you in a week or so,' said Leslie as they parted. 'I don't suppose we'll meet again, my boy. Better to make this the last time, I think. It was good of you to make the journey. Tell those who are interested how I am. I've got a soft spot for old Bertie. I wonder if he ever regretted marrying a Howard?'

'Never,' said Edward stoutly, driving off, and left his Father laughing.

Driving back along the wet roads Edward pondered on the day's encounter. He was satisfied now that he had seen his father. He was well looked after, in fairly good health, and obviously as happy as he would be anywhere.

As soon as he heard that he was in work again he would make adequate provision against the future. He wanted to feel that there was a sum in the bank which would be available if the old man fell on hard times. But he must have a job – no matter how small the return – which would keep him actively occupied. His father's worst enemy, Edward saw, was himself. Too much solitude would breed self-pity and self-indulgence. He could see why Sep had never had much time for him. There was a streak of weakness which Sep would never have been able to understand or forgive.

'A rum lot, the Howards!' said Edward aloud, and putting his foot down on the accelerator, sped home.

Chapter Nineteen

RETURN TO THE MARKET SQUARE

Edward found a surprising lack of interest in Leslie's welfare among the family. Aunt Kathy was perfunctory in her inquiries. His mother refused to discuss the matter. Maisie, naturally enough, was only vaguely interested in someone she had never met. Uncle Bertie alone seemed concerned, and listened attentively to Edward's account of all that had happened. He approved of Edward's decision to wait and see if a job materialized.

In the week before Christmas the awaited letter arrived. Leslie wrote enthusiastically. The post was in a large baker's. 'Back where I began,' was how he put it. He not only looked after the accounts but also took the van out twice a week to relieve other roundsmen. His weekly wage was modest but enough for his needs, he wrote.

Edward replied congratulating him, and telling him that he was paying the sum of two hundred and fifty pounds into his bank account which he hoped he would accept as a nest-egg and a Christmas present. He posted the letter with some misgivings. Was he simply trying to salve his conscience by handing over this money? He hoped not. What would Sep have thought? Well, maybe Sep would not have approved, but Edward had his own decisions to make now, he told himself firmly. He felt sure that it was right to supply his father with a bulwark against future storms. He felt equally sure that it had been right to wait until he was established in a suitable job before providing that bulwark. Now it was up to his father.

Everything was now planned for their removal from the flat to the market square. After innumerable delays, the old house was free of workmen and, freshly decorated, awaited its owners.

Maisie had enjoyed refurbishing the fine old rooms. The great drawing-room, with its three windows looking out upon the market place, was painted in the palest green, a colour which would show up well the mahogany pieces which she had bought at the sales. It was a splendid room, high and airy. Bender North had always appreciated it, admiring its fine proportions and its red plush furnishings, after a day in the shop below. Now his grandson would find equal domestic pleasure in the same room.

On the same floor, at the back of the building, were the dining room and kitchen, overlooking the small garden and the river Cax. Above them were three bedrooms and a bathroom, while on the top floor, in the old attics, Edward's flat remained much as it was, except that his sitting-room had been converted into a nursery for the newcomer.

'You'll have to put the window bars back again,' said Uncle Bertie when he inspected the premises. 'There were three to each window when I slept there. You took them out too hastily, Edward my boy!'

Edward and Maisie spent the last weekend in January at Rose Lodge. She was to see the furniture in on the Monday, with Winnie's help, while Edward would return to the flat to arrange things at that end. It was bitterly cold, and as she and Winnie directed operations on Monday morning, and dodged rolls of carpet and bedsteads, Maisie was thankful that they had faced the expense of central heating for the house. With the open market square before, and the river Cax behind, it had always felt cold. Now, with new warmth, the house seemed to come to life.

She took a particular interest in the larger of the back bedrooms, for here she planned to have the baby. She was determined that it should be born in the old house in the market square, and had already engaged the monthly nurse who was to sleep in the bedroom adjoining her own.

The view from the windows on this bleak January day was grey and cheerless. The pollarded willows lining the Cax pointed gaunt fingers towards the leaden sky. The distant tunnel of horse chestnut trees made a dark smudge above the river mist, but Maisie could imagine it in May when the baby was due to arrive. Then the willows would be a golden green above the sparkling water. The chestnut leaves would be bursting from their sticky buds. The kingfisher – harbinger of good fortune – should be flashing over the water, and on the lawn below the window the crocuses, yellow, purple and white, would be giving way to daffodils and tulips.

It was past nine o'clock when Edward arrived. Both of them were excited but exhausted, and went early to bed in the bedroom overlooking the market square. Maisie fell asleep almost immediately, but Edward lay on his back watching the pattern on the ceiling, made by the lamps in the market place.

Now and again the old house creaked, as wood expanded gently in the unaccustomed heat. Someone crossed the cobbles, singing, pausing in his tune to call good night to a fellow wayfarer. There was a country burr in the tone which pleased Edward.

How often, he wondered, had Grandfather North lain in this same room listening to the sounds of the square by night? He thought of Uncle Bertie and his own mother, sleeping, as children, on the floor above, where soon his own child would be bedded. It gave him a queer feeling of wonder and pride.

Tomorrow, he told himself, he must wake early and go downstairs to the restaurant and then across to the bakery. He was a market square man now, with a reputation for diligence to keep up! Smiling at the thought, he turned his face into the pillow and fell asleep.

Caxley watched Edward's progress, in the ensuing weeks, with considerable interest. On the whole, his efforts met with approval. He was applying himself zealously to the new work, and people were glad to see a young man in charge.

The assistants in the shop and restaurant spoke well of him, and the grape-vine of the closely-knit little town hummed busily with day-to-day reports – mainly favourable. Young Edward was taking on two new counter-hands. He was going to enlarge the storage sheds at the back of the bakery He was talking of keeping the restaurant open later at night. He was applying for a liquor licence.

Think of that! The more sedate chapel-goers could imagine Sep turning in his grave at the thought, but the majority of Caxley's citizens approved.

Edward himself was beginning to enjoy it all enormously. The years of solitary living, which had been all that he desired after the break-up of his first marriage, were behind him. He began to flourish in this new gregarious life and found pleasure in joining some of the local activities and meeting boyhood friends again. The Crockfords, grandchildren of the famous Dan who had painted Edna Howard so long ago, lived within walking distance and were frequent visitors. William Crockford, the present owner of the family mill which supplied Edward with much of his flour, introduced him to the Rotary Club and Edward became an energetic member. He also took up cricket again. He sometimes went dutifully with Maisie to concerts at the Corn Exchange which she, who was musical, thoroughly enjoyed, while Edward, who was not, leant back and planned future business projects while local talent provided mingled harmony and discord.

For there was, indeed, a great deal to plan. Edward, the product of two business families, saw clearly the possibilities of the future. Times were becoming more prosperous after the lean forties. People were buying more, and demanding more luxurious goods. Caxley families were prepared to dine out in the evenings. Caxley businessmen took their lunches in the town much more frequently. What is more, they brought their clients, and talked over deals at Howard's Restaurant.

There were more cars on the road, more wayfarers travelling from London westward, and from the Midlands southward. Caxley was a convenient stopping-place, as it had been in the days of the stage-coach. The restaurant trade was booming. It could become even more thriving with judicious re-organization.

Edward was so engrossed with his present commitments and his plans for the future that a letter which arrived for him one April morning came as a bolt from the blue. He could hardly believe his eyes as he read the document.

It was from the managing director of a firm of departmental

stores well known to Edward. They were proposing to set up several more branches in provincial towns. The two sites belonging to Edward would be suitable for their purpose. The larger site would be used for their drapery and furnishing departments. Their Food Hall would probably be accommodated on the present bakery site. Perhaps Mr Howard would consider taking up a position of responsibility in this department, the salary to be arranged by mutual agreement? Naturally, there was a great deal to consider on both sides, but his firm had in mind the sum of – (here followed a figure so large that Edward seriously wondered if a nought or two too many had been added) and their agents were Messrs Ginn, Hope & Toddy of Piccadilly who would be glad to hear from Mr Howard if he were interested.

Edward handed the letter to Maisie in silence.

'Well?' she said, looking up at last.

'Some hopes!' said Edward flatly, stuffing it in his pocket. 'This is ours. We stay.'

As a matter of interest he showed the letter to the family before replying to it. As he expected, Bertie wholeheartedly agreed with his decision, but Kathy and the two ladies at Rose Lodge had doubts. This surprised Edward. The two properties had been their homes and livelihoods for so long that he had felt sure that they would be as forthright in their rejection of the offer as he was himself. How strange women were!

'It's such a lot of money,' said old Mrs North. 'After all, with that amount you could start up another business anywhere, or go back to the plastics place, dear, couldn't you?'

'Or simply invest it, and have a nice little income and a long holiday somewhere,' said his mother. 'There's no need to feel tied to Caxley simply because the business has been left to you.'

'But I *want* to be tied to Caxley!' Edward almost shouted. 'This is *our* business – the *Howard* business! Dammit all, it's the work and worry of three generations we're considering! Doesn't that mean anything?'

'Really,' tutted Mrs North, in some exasperation, 'men are so romantic about everything – even currant buns, it seems!'

'All we're trying to say,' said Winnie, more patiently, 'is that we should quite understand if you felt like accepting the offer, and I'm sure the rest of the family would agree.

'Well, I don't intend to, and that's flat,' retorted Edward. He had not felt so out of patience with his womenfolk for years, and took a childish pleasure in slamming the front door as he departed.

He walked back through a little park, and sat down on one of the seats to cool off. Beds of velvety wallflowers scented the evening air, and some small children screamed on the swings, or chased each other round and round the lime trees. A few middle-aged couples strolled about, admiring the flowers and taking a little gentle exercise. It was the sort of unremarkable scene being enacted a hundred-fold all over the country on this mild spring evening, but to Edward, in his mood of tension, it had a poignant significance.

Here, years ago, he had swung and raced. Before long, his own children would know this pleasant plot. These people before him, old and young, were of Caxley as he was himself. They all played their parts in the same setting, and with their neighbours as fellow-actors. And the centre of that stage was Caxley's market square. How lucky he was to have his place so firmly there – his by birthright, and now by choice as well! Nothing should make him give up this inheritance.

A very old man shuffled up to Edward's bench and sat down gingerly. His pale blue eyes watered, and a shining drop trickled down his lined cheeks into the far from clean beard which hid his mouth and chin.

His clothes were shabby, his boots broken. Edward guessed that he was making his way to the workhouse on the hill. He held a paper bag, and thrusting a claw-like hand inside, he produced a meat pasty. He gazed unseeingly before him as he munched, the pastry flaking into a shower of light crumbs which sprinkled his deplorable beard and greasy coat.

But it was not so much the old man who engaged Edward's attention as the blue and white paper bag which he held. It was very familiar to him. He had seen such bags since his earliest days –

bright and clean, with 'Howard's Bakery' printed diagonally across the checked surface. Tonight, the sight of it filled him with a surge of pride. Here, he was, face to face with one of his customers, watching his own product from his own paper bag being consumed with smackings of satisfaction! Who would give up such rewards? He felt a sudden love for this dirty unknown, and rising swiftly, fumbled in his pocket and pressed half a crown into the grimy paw.

'Have a drink with it,' he said.

'Ta, mate,' answered the tramp laconically. 'Needs summat to wash this muck down.'

Edward walked home, savouring the delicious incident to the full. It warmed the evening for him. It added to his growing zest for life in Caxley, and to the enjoyment he felt, later that evening, when he pulled a piece of writing paper towards him and wrote a short, polite, but absolute rejection of the store's offer.

It was dark as he crossed the square to post it. He balanced the white envelope on his hand before tipping it, with satisfaction, into the pillar box. Now it was done, he felt singularly light-hearted, and walked jauntily back across the cobbles, smiling at Queen Victoria's implacable bulk outlined against the night sky.

At his doorway he turned to take a last breath of fresh air. The moon slid out from behind a ragged cloud, and touched the market square with sudden beauty.

Edward gave the scene a conspiratorial wink, opened his own door, mounted his own stairs and made his way to bed.

Chapter Twenty

JOHN SEPTIMUS HOWARD

It was six o'clock on a fine May morning.

The market square was deserted. Long shadows lay across the cobblestones, reaching almost to the steps of St Peter's church. At the window of his bedroom, in a crumpled suit, and with tousled hair, stood Edward. It had been one of the longest nights that he had ever known, but now peace, and the dawn, had arrived.

The monthly nurse, Mrs porter, had been in the house with them for eight days. That she was expert in her profession, Edward had no doubt, but as a member of the household he had found her sorely trying. Her shiny red face and crackling starched cuffs and apron dominated every meal. She ate very slowly, but needed a large amount of food to keep her well-corseted bulk going, so that Maisie and Edward seemed to spend three times as long at the table.

Maisie was worried because the baby was overdue. Nurse Porter added to her anxiety by consulting the calendar daily and talking gloomily of her timetable which might well be completely thrown out by Maisie's tardy offspring. Her next engagement was in a noble household in the shires, a fact which gave her considerable satisfaction.

'And the Duchess,' she told Maisie daily, 'is *never* late. The two little boys arrived on the dot, and the little girl was two days early. You'll have to hurry up, my dear, or the Duchess will beat you to it.'

But yesterday, when Edward returned from the shop after tea, Maisie and the nurse were in the bedroom, and all, according to Nurse Porter, was going well. Maisie's comments, in the midst of her pains, were less euphemistic.

'Shall I stay with you?' asked Edward solicitously.

'Good heavens, no!' exclaimed Maisie crossly. 'It's quite bad enough as it is, without having to put a good front on it. Go a long way away – to Rose Lodge or somewhere, so that I can have a good yell when I want to.'

Thus banished, Edward took himself to the restaurant below, and pottered aimlessly about. Thank God, he thought honestly, Maisie was not one of the modern brigade who wanted a husband's support at this time! Although he intended to stay with her had she so wished, he was frankly terrified of seeing her in pain, and squeamish at the sight of blood. Dear, oh dear, thought Edward, rubbing his forehead anxiously, what poor tools men were when it came to it!'

He had no intention of going to Rose Lodge or anywhere else for that matter, until the child was born. He would stay as close as he could while it all went on. He suffered the common terrifying qualms about his wife's safety, and to calm his agitation set himself to such mechanical tasks as sorting out the cutlery and inspecting the table linen for possible repairs.

He could settle to nothing for long, however, and walked into the little garden on the dew-wet grass beside the river, looking up at the lighted window where the drama was being enacted. Every so often he mounted the stairs quietly and listened, but there was nothing to hear. On one of these sorties he encountered the nurse, and she took pity on him.

'She's doing splendidly,' she said. 'Come and have a look.'

Maisie looked far from splendid to Edward's eyes. She looked white and exhausted, but seemed glad to see him.

'Not long now,' said Nurse Porter, with what, to Edward, seemed callous indifference to her patient's condition. 'It should be here by morning.'

'By *morning*?' echoed Edward, appalled. The hands of the clock stood at a little before two. Would Maisie live as long, he wondered desperately?

'Go and make us all a nice pot of tea,' suggested the nurse, and Edward obediently went to the kitchen to perform his task. How parents could have faced ten, fifteen and even twenty such ordeals in days gone by, he could not imagine! He decided to have a whisky and soda when he had delivered the tea-tray to his task-mistress.

Later, as the first light crept across the countryside, he dozed in the arm chair, dreaming uneasily of white boats floating upon dark water. Could they be the little boats he floated as a boy upon the Cax? Or were they the white boats 'that sailed like swans asleep' on the enchanted waters of Lough Corrib? And where was Maisie? She should be with him. Had she slipped beneath the black and shivering water? Would he see her again?

A little before five Nurse Porter woke him. Her red face glowed like the rising sun, broad and triumphant. She held a white bundle which she displayed proudly to Edward.

'Want to see your son?' she asked. 'Six and a half pounds, and a perfect beauty.'

Edward looked upon his firstborn. A pink mottled face, no bigger than one of his own buns, topped by wispy damp hair, was all that could be seen in the aperture of the snowy shawl. Nurse porter's idea of beauty, Edward thought, differed from his own, but the child looked healthy and inordinately wise.

'How's Maisie?' said Edward, now wide awake. 'Can I see her?'

'Asleep. You shall go in later. She's fine, but needs her rest.'

At that moment the baby opened his mouth in a yawn. Edward gazed at it, fascinated. There was something wonderfully clever about such an achievement when one considered that the child was less than an hour old. Edward felt a pang of paternal pride for the first time.

'He seems a very forward child to me,' said Edward.

'Naturally!' responded Nurse Porter with sardonic amusement, and took her bundle back to the bedroom.

That was an hour ago. Since then he had seen his Maisie, well, but drowsy, drunk a pot of coffee and tried to marshal his incoherent thoughts. As soon as possible, he would telephone to Rose Lodge, but six o'clock calls might alarm the household. He must let Bertie and Kathy know too as soon as they were astir.

Meanwhile, he gazed upon the market place, pink in the growing sunlight. A thin black cat, in a sheltered angle of St Peter's porch, washed one upthrust leg, its body as round and curved as an elegant shell, and suddenly Edward was back in time, over ten long years ago, when he had stood thus, watching the same familiar scene.

What a lifetime ago it seemed! Since then he had experienced war, an unhappy marriage and personal desolation. He had watched Robert's tragic decline and death, and lost Sep, his guide and example. He had shared, with his fellows, the bitterness of war, and the numbing poverty of its aftermath.

But that was the darker side of the picture. There was a better and brighter one. He had found Maisie, he had refound Caxley, and in doing so he had found himself at last.

A wisp of blue smoke rose from Sep's old house. Miss Taggerty was making up the kitchen boiler, thought Edward affectionately. In the bakehouse, work would already have started. The little town was stirring, and he must prepare, too, for another Caxley day. It was good to look ahead. It was good too, to think that John Septimus Howard, his son, would be the fourth generation to know this old house as home.

What was it that Sep used to say? 'There's always tomorrow, my boy. Always tomorrow.'

And with that thought to cheer him, Edward went to look, once more, upon the new heir to the market square.

MRS PRINGLE

To Vicki and Horace with love

CONTENTS

Chapter One

FACE TO FACE

It is snowing again. We shall certainly have a white Christmas this year, a rare occurrence even in this downland village of Fairacre.

I have been the head teacher of Fairacre School for more years than I care to remember, and the school house, where I write this, has been my home for all that time. It is particularly snug at the moment: the fire blazes, the cat is stretched out in front of it, and Christmas cards line the mantelpiece. Very soon the school breaks up for the Christmas holidays, and what a comforting thought that is!

Comfort is needed, not only from the snowflakes which whisper at the window, but also from the aftermath of a recent skirmish with Mrs Pringle, our school cleaner, who has lived in the village even longer than I have.

She does her job superbly, but is a sore trial. It is generally agreed that she is 'difficult', the vicar's expression, and 'a proper tartar', as Bob Willet our handyman and school caretaker puts it.

During term time our paths cross on most days. It is no wonder that I relish the school holidays and the peace that they bring. How long, I muse, putting another log on the fire, will I be able to stand her aggression? Stroking Tibby's warm stomach, I look back through the years at my tempestuous relationship at Fairacre School with the doughty Mrs Pringle.

I first encountered Mrs Pringle one thundery July afternoon.

It was a Friday, I remember. The vicar, the Reverend Gerald Partridge who was chairman of the school governors, had invited me to tea before looking over the school house which was to become my home at the end of the month. I had recently been appointed head mistress of Fairacre School.

There were puddles in the playground, and we splashed through them on our way to the school house. A strange mooing noise, as of a cow or calf in distress, was coming from the deserted school building. The children of Fairacre had already started their summer holiday.

'That,' said Mr Partridge, 'is Mrs Pringle, our school cleaner. It sounds as though she is singing a hymn. She is in the church choir.'

We paused for a moment, listening to the distant voice and the plop of raindrops into puddles.

'I don't recognise it,' I ventured.

'Probably the descant,' replied the vicar. He did not sound very sure. 'In any case, perhaps I should take you to meet her before we visit the house.'

We changed direction, and the vicar pushed open the door into the lobby.

Mrs Pringle, bucket at her feet and floor cloth in her hand, stood before us. She was short and stout. Her expression was dour. She made no attempt to smile, offer a hand, or make any other gesture of welcome as the vicar introduced us.

Eventually, she jerked her head towards the floor where our feet had made wet prints.

'I just done that,' she remarked, the four words dropping as cold and flat as the stones upon which we stood.

Although I did not know it at the time, it was the first shot in a war which was to last for many years.

I was the first woman to be appointed head teacher of Fairacre School, and I looked forward eagerly to taking up my duties.

The downland village and the market town of Caxley were known to me, for my good friend Amy who had been with me at college, had married and lived south of Caxley in the village of Bent. On my frequent weekend visits we explored the countryside, and often drove up to the downs for a picnic and an exhilarating walk. We drove through the villages of Beech Green and Fairacre and sometimes stopped to look round their churches, or to buy something from Beech Green's village shop.

When I had seen the headship of Fairacre School advertised in *The Times Educational Supplement* I had applied for the post.

'I'm not likely to get it,' I said to Amy, 'I doubt if I shall even get called to an interview.'

'Rubbish!' said Amy stoutly. 'You are better qualified than most, and I'm positive you'll get the job.'

Although I was grateful for this display of support, biased though it was, I had private misgivings. Consequently, when I was appointed, I felt both pride and trepidation. Could I fulfil the governors' hopes, and would the children and parents be co-operative?

I need not have worried.

Any initial suspicions or doubts on the part of the inhabitants of Fairacre were soon hidden from me, and as the years passed I was accepted as part of the village community. I could never expect to be in the same category as a native, born and bred in Fairacre, but to be welcomed was quite enough for me.

But on that humid thundery afternoon I was still at the apprehensive stage, and my encounter with the school cleaner aroused my fears.

I tried to put them aside as I followed the vicar round my new home. It was a snug well-built house with a good-sized sitting room, and a decent kitchen flanked by a small dining room. Upstairs were two bedrooms and a tiny box room, later destined to be a bathroom.

At that time the house was empty, for my predecessor, Mr Fortescue, had moved out just before his retirement. It was Mrs Pringle, the vicar told me, who had a key and kept the premises clean.

'In fact,' went on the vicar, 'she has cared for this house for many years.'

'I see,' I said, my heart sinking.

'Of course, it is entirely up to you, but if you felt like continuing to employ her, I am sure she would carry on.'

'Thank you for telling me.'

'She is really a wonderful worker,' persisted the vicar as we went out into the dripping garden. 'Her manner is a little off-putting, I know, but she is diligent and honest, and has always taken a great pride in her work.'

I did not reply, determined not to commit myself at this stage to being hostess to Mrs Pringle for years to come.

'What a lovely garden!' I said, changing the subject.

There were a few mature fruit trees displaying small unripe apples, plums and pears, and an impressive herbaceous border flaunting lupins, delphiniums and oriental poppies.

The flowers were looking rather battered from the recent rain, the border was undoubtedly weedy and the lawn shaggy, but basically it was a splendid garden, and my spirits rose.

'Yes, Mr Willet gives a hand,' said the vicar. 'In fact, he gives a hand at most of our activities, as you will find.'

He drew out a watch from his waistcoat pocket.

'Dear, dear! I think we should get back to the vicarage. My wife will have tea ready.'

We retraced our steps to rejoin Mrs Partridge and Amy who had brought me over, and who had spent the time, I learned later, in unravelling the sleeve of a cardigan which the vicar's wife was engaged upon. She had misread the directions for increasing, and the sleeve was ballooning out in an alarming fashion, to say nothing of using up all the wool before the whole thing was finished.

As the vicar and I walked up the drive to our tea he returned to the subject of Mrs Pringle.

'Do consider the matter of employing her,' he urged. 'I feel sure she is expecting it.'

He sounded, I thought, somewhat nervous. Was he *frightened* of the lady, I wondered? Was she really as fearsome as she undoubtedly looked? It only strengthened my determination not to commit myself.

'I'll certainly consider it,' I assured him, as he opened the front door.

'Ah, good!' he replied, sounding much relieved. 'And good again, I think I can smell toasted teacakes.'

On the way back to Bent, I prattled happily to Amy about the school house and garden, and how much I looked forward to living there.

'You must let me give you a hand in getting it ready,' said Amy, hooting at a pheasant who strolled haughtily across the road intent on suicide.

'I should enjoy your company,' I replied.

'It's not so much my *company*,' said Amy severely, 'as my *advice* you will need. You know you've never been much good at measuring accurately, and I haven't much opinion of your sense of colour.'

'Thank you,' I said, trying not to sound nettled. That is the worst of friends who have known you from youth. They remember all those faults which one has done one's best to eradicate over the years. However, Amy always means well, despite her undoubted bossiness, and on this occasion I managed not to answer back.

In any case, I reminded myself, I had quite a few memories of Amy's early indiscretions, and should have no hesitation in using them if she continued to rake up the infirmities in my own past.

But I was too euphoric about my future to take serious offence as Amy's car swished through the puddles. The sky remained lowering, and it was obvious that the thunderstorm was not yet over.

'Of course, the garden needs tidying,' I continued, 'but the vicar seems to think that someone called Bob Willet will give a hand. I must get in touch with him.'

'And what about the house?'

I felt a slight pang as I recalled Mrs Pringle's visage, quite as dark and menacing as the sky overhead.

'Well,' I began, 'the school cleaner seems to have looked after the head teacher's house before, but I didn't really take to her.'

'Taking to her or not,' said Amy, 'is beside the point. You're not exactly the model housewife, as you well know. I should advise you to take whatever domestic help is offered.'

'But, Amy,' I protested, 'you haven't seen this Mrs Pringle. She's quite formidable. Why, I believe the vicar himself is afraid of her, and after all he's girt about with righteousness and all the other Christian armament. What hope for a defenceless woman like me?'

'You exaggerate,' replied Amy, swinging neatly into her drive. 'I'll come over with you next time and meet the lady.'

And what a clash of the dinosaurs that could be, I thought with some relish as I clambered from the car.

James, Amy's husband, proved to be a welcome ally later that evening when the subject of help in my new abode cropped up.

'I shouldn't saddle myself with that lady if I were you,' he said. 'Fob her off. Say you want to see how things work out. Play for time.'

'My feelings entirely,' I responded. 'I didn't like to press Mr Partridge too much. He seems so anxious not to offend her, but perhaps a few discreet inquiries among other villagers would be useful. This Bob Willet might be helpful.'

'There are no such things as *discreet inquiries* in a village,' said James. 'Everything is known within a flash. I should make up your own mind. Keep your ears open, by all means, but your mouth shut. I was brought up in a village and I know what I'm talking about.'

'I've had some experience of living in a village myself,' I responded, 'but not as one of the pillars of society as I suppose I will be in Fairacre. I shall have to watch my step.'

'If you are going to be a public figure,' remarked Amy, 'and an example of right living to the children and their parents, I should think that a clean house might be the first step in the right direction.'

She sounded rather waspish, I thought, probably rather cross with James for taking my part.

'Well, I haven't turned down Mrs Pringle absolutely flat,' I pointed out, 'but I'm not being rushed into anything.'

'Wise girl,' commented James.

Amy gave a snort.

In bed later, I recalled the pleasures of my first sight of the school house and garden. It gave me great joy to remember the pleasant rooms awaiting my furniture, and the pretty garden awaiting urgent attention by both Bob Willet and me.

I refused to be put off by the malevolent shade of Mrs Pringle.

'A mere fly in the ointment,' I said aloud, settling into my pillow.

I fell asleep within minutes.

Chapter Two

SETTLING IN

What with one thing and another, it was the beginning of August before I could make my next visit to Fairacre.

Amy, hospitable as ever, was going to put me up, but I made the journey by train, and then caught one of the rare buses which went from Caxley to Fairacre.

It was market day in the little town, and the stall holders were doing a brisk trade in the square. It was hot and noisy, and my case was heavy. I was glad to climb aboard the bus and find a seat.

Fairacre was several miles distant, and the bus chugged gently uphill from the valley of the river Cax, stopping at the villages for laden shoppers to alight.

At Beech Green, the village before Fairacre, the bus stopped beside the village school, and I wondered who my next door colleague might be.

It was a scorching afternoon, the very best time to see this downland country. In some distant fields, harvest had already started, combines crawling like gigantic toys around the fields.

The hedges were heavy with summer foliage, still starred here and there with late wild roses and the creamy flat heads of elder-flowers. The grass on the roadside banks was sun-bleached, and as the bus swished by it undulated like ripe corn before a strong wind.

Amy was coming to pick me up at the school house at half past four, and meanwhile I had over two hours in which to visit Mr Willet, the Post Office and, best of all, my new house and garden.

It was no wonder that my spirits were high as we rattled towards Fairacre.

*

Mr Willet was hoeing in his remarkably neat vegetable patch. Despite the heat he was wearing a cap, and although he was in his shirt sleeves he had a tweed waistcoat as his outer garment.

After greetings and my compliments on his vegetables, I broached the subject of help in the garden at the school house.

'Now I was hopin' you'd be along,' said Mr Willet. 'I've looked after that for more years than I can count. It may look a bit rough at the moment, as I didn't like to be too forward and trespass-like in there when I'd not been given permission.'

'But you'll come?'

'Of course I'll come. Be up tomorrow evenin' if you like. There's a row of shallots should be lifted by now. I wondered if I ought to do that, but thought Mrs Pringle might catch sight of me and tell all and sundry I was pinchin' 'em.'

This gave me an opening for further enquiries.

Mr Willet pushed back his cap and leant heavily on the hoe.

'Let's put it this way. I don't like to speak ill of anyone,' he began, obviously about to do just that, 'but you wants to start as you means to go on with that one. I'm not sayin' she's all bad. She done a lot for us when my Alice was took ill one winter, but she's a proper moaner. If you gets a smile out of her, you'll be the first as has.'

'Well, thank you for telling me. Forewarned is forearmed, so they say.'

'It isn't *arms* as is the trouble with her. It's *legs*. She's got one that gives her a mort of trouble, so she says, and everyone else too come to that, when she's crossed in any way. Ah, yes! Mrs Pringle's leg is a force to be reckoned with, as you'll find.'

We walked together to the gate.

'You lettin' her do your house-cleanin'?' he asked, coming to the point with a directness I already respected.

'I haven't decided . . .'

'You think it over well, Miss Read. 'Tis easy enough to ask people in, and a durn sight more tricky to get 'em out. Not that she isn't a good worker, I will say that,' he added.

'I'll be over tomorrow evening,' I promised, 'and we'll look at the garden together.'

'I'll tell Alice you called. She's over at Springbourne on some W.I. lark. She'll want to hear all about you.'

And so will the rest of Fairacre, I surmised, as I made my way to the Post Office.

After the few obligatory comments on the weather (nice to see the sun, but the peas need some rain to plump up), I introduced myself to Mr Lamb.

'Hope you'll be very happy here,' he said, shaking my hand. 'Thought it was you getting off the bus. Been to see Bob Willet?'

'As a matter of fact I have.'

'Good chap, Bob. Going to give you a hand in the garden?'

'I hope so.'

'Nothing that chap can't turn his hand to. Looks after the school a fair treat, and the church and graveyard. And always cheery.'

He stopped suddenly. 'You met Mrs Pringle yet?'

I said that I had.

'She'll be cleaning the school still, I suppose?'

I said that I hoped so.

'Excuse me asking, but is she going to work for you too? In the house, I mean?'

I said that I had not yet made up my mind.

Mr Lamb gave a sigh. It sounded like one of relief.

'Yes, well. She's a good worker, I'll grant, but I'd take time in deciding to have her regular myself.'

I thanked him, bought some stamps and a packet of biscuits, and made my way to the school house.

Amy had already arrived, and was wandering about the garden. She was smiling in a dreamy fashion.

'What a blissful spot. Absolute peace!'

There was an ancient bench lodged against the house wall. It looked as though it had once been part of the furnishings of Fairacre School in Queen Victoria's reign. We settled ourselves upon it, turning our faces up to the sun.

Some shaggy Mrs Sinkins pinks wafted their scent towards us.

Two inquisitive chaffinches surveyed us within a yard of our feet, and far away some sheep bleated from the downland.

'"To sit in the shade and look upon verdure,"' I quoted.

'Except that we're not in the shade,' Amy pointed out, 'and I shall be done to a frizzle if I stay here too long. By the way, I brought a flask of tea.'

'You marvellous girl! And I've got some Rich Tea biscuits.'

'My word, you are going it,' commented Amy.

'Well, it was either Rich Tea or Garibaldi from the Post Office, so I settled for Rich Tea. After all, they'll do for cheese as well.'

'Very prudent,' said Amy.

She went to the car to fetch the flask, and I hastily shifted my weight to the centre of the bench, which bucked alarmingly when Amy left it.

'We could have it inside,' I said. 'I've got the key.'

'Better out here,' Amy replied, 'besides, I don't suppose there's anything to sit on in there.'

She was quite right – of course.

We sipped our tea. The chaffinches had flown to a nearby plum tree, but kept a sharp lookout for crumbs.

'Of course, you'll have to put in a lot of work on this garden,' said Amy, becoming her usual brisk self, 'it's been terribly neglected.'

I told her about my visit to Mr Willet.

'Sounds hopeful,' she conceded. 'And this Mrs Pringle?'

As if on cue, I heard the click of the garden gate and round the corner of the house stumped a thickset figure with a black oilcloth bag over her arm.

Mrs Pringle had arrived.

I made the necessary introductions and awaited the outcome with some interest.

We had both risen at the approach of our visitor and I invited her to share the bench.

'I wish I could offer you tea,' I apologised, 'but I'm afraid it's all gone. Have a biscuit.'

Mrs Pringle held up a hand as if she were stopping the traffic. 'I don't eat between meals. It don't do the digestion any good.'

There seemed to be no adequate reply to this dictum.

'I was just passing,' went on the lady, 'and thought I'd put this week's *Caxley Chronicle* through your door. No doubt you'd like to be up to date with what's happening. Fairacre news is on page six.'

'Thank you. Very kind of you. I will let you have it back.'

'No need for that. I've read all I want. I always turns to the Deaths first, and then the Wills, and if anybody local's up in Caxley court I sees what they've got. Not much usually. Probation or some such let-off, when a nice bit of flogging would be more to the point.'

I put the newspaper on the small space between Amy and me, and resolutely avoided catching my old friend's eye.

'Garden looks a real mess,' she continued lugubriously. 'I happened to see you going into Bob Willet's just now, so I suppose he'll be up to give you a hand.'

'That's right.'

'So I heard at the Post Office when I called in just now.'

The bench shuddered at Amy's ill-concealed mirth.

'Would you like to look round the garden?' I asked.

'Well, I knows it like the back of my hand, of course,' replied Mrs Pringle, 'but it'd be nice to get out of this blazing sun for a few minutes, and there should be a few gooseberries about still.'

Amy accompanied us. Despite the heat, the long grass was damp, and Amy examined her elegant sandals.

'Hot or not,' observed Mrs Pringle, 'I always wears good sensible shoes. My mother brought us up to respect our feet. "Nothing strappy or silly," she used to say, "or you'll be storing up trouble for your old age." And she was right.'

At this double insult to her footwear and her advancing years Amy could only respond with some heavy breathing. So far, I thought, Mrs Pringle was winning hands down.

There certainly were some fine late gooseberries at the end of the garden, yellow translucent beauties dangling from the thorny branches.

Mrs Pringle eyed them greedily.

'Do help yourself to a picking,' I said, 'if you could use some.'

'Very nice of you,' she replied, still unsmiling. 'Lucky I brought my bag.'

Amy and I helped, but Mrs Pringle's speed at gooseberrypicking was amazing. Within ten minutes, three bushes were stripped and the oilcloth bag almost full.

She straightened up reluctantly. 'I must say I like a nice gooseberry pie,' she said, 'and now I'd best be off. Pringle gets in about now.'

At the gate she stopped.

'I take it you'll need me on a Wednesday afternoon to do your house over? Been doing it for years now. If Wednesdays don't suit, what about Tuesdays?'

I took a deep breath. 'Can I let you know? I should like to see if I can manage on my own for a bit. But thank you for the offer.'

For the first time that afternoon, she looked taken aback. 'Are you saying you don't want me?'

'Not at the moment. Let's see how things go.'

Without a word she opened the gate and set off down the lane, her heavy bag swinging dangerously.

'Well!' exploded Amy. 'What a miserable old faggot!'

This archaic expression from my childhood days made me laugh.

'So *rude*,' continued Amy, 'criticizing my sandals! And greedy too! Why, she's got enough gooseberries there to make *two dozen* pies.'

'So you don't take to Mrs P? She did offer to help in the house, you know.'

'I thought you handled that very well,' said Amy, with rare praise. 'Personally, I wouldn't employ her for a pension, the wicked old harridan.'

'Let's unlock the house and have a look round. It might lower our blood pressure after that encounter.'

'We certainly need something,' agreed Amy, following me.

*

Later that evening we discussed the afternoon's events, and made our plans for the next few days.

Amy had volunteered to help me paint the downstairs walls. Upstairs, we agreed, could wait until later. We proposed to go into Caxley in the morning and choose emulsion paint and brushes, and also to buy curtaining material for the main living room, at present my predecessor's dining room. For all Amy's elegance, she was a great one for practical pursuits and I welcomed her co-operation in the decorating project.

My furniture was due to arrive at the end of the week and, all being well, we should have the house clean and ready for it.

'Without Mrs Pringle's assistance?' queried James, much amused by his wife's volte-face on the employment of Mrs Pringle in my house.

'Absolutely without!' snapped Amy.

'I bet she comes along to see what we're doing though,' I prophesied.

'If I know anything about village life, she won't be the only one,' rejoined James.

He was right. Over the next few days, as Amy and I toiled with our brushes and some rather exquisite pale grey paint, we had several visitors.

The first was more than welcome, for it was Bob Willet.

'I really come up to get your twitch out,' he volunteered.

It sounded rather a medical matter until Amy said she had far too much couch grass in her border, and I remembered the country name for this wretched weed.

'But I could give you a hand in here instead,' he offered, looking at the half-done walls and then the floor boards.

'You wants to wipe up with a bit of damp rag as you go,' he said. 'Shall I take a turn?'

'No, no,' we protested, 'you carry on in the garden, and we'll muddle along in here.'

He went rather reluctantly.

Our next visitor was the milkman, a cheerful young man with a splendid black beard, who said he would come on Monday, Wednesday and Saturday if that was all right?

We said it was.

'And if I was you,' he added, looking at the floor, 'I'd wipe up that paint as it falls.'

An hour later, Mrs Partridge, the vicar's wife, called in and gave us a welcome invitation to tea any time between four and five.

'Just when you've finished one wall, or something,' she said vaguely, 'in fact whenever it's convenient to stop.'

She admired our handiwork in a most satisfactory way, and only noticed the floor as she went out.

'Ah now! I believe Bob Willet carries a piece of wet cloth with him when he does work for us, and he wipes up the paint as he goes along. He says it saves a lot of trouble later.'

We said that he had been kind enough to pass on this tip already.

At two-thirty, Mrs Pringle appeared, paused on the threshold, and drew a deep breath.

'Oh dear, oh dear!' she groaned, shaking her head. 'My poor floor!'

I did not like to point out that it was in fact *my* floor, but invited her in to see our efforts. She approached gingerly, stepping over the larger blobs of paint with exaggerated care.

'I didn't come in here to pry,' she said unnecessarily, 'but as I was going over to the school to check the supplies was all right for next term, I thought I'd just look in.'

'Well, what do you think of it?' I asked, inviting the bolt from the blue.

'It'll show the dirt,' she said, and departed.

The rest of the summer holiday was spent mainly in getting the house to rights. As all those who have moved house know, nothing was straightforward.

Two of the windows were stuck fast, and needed Mr Willet and a hefty friend to release them, breaking one pane in the process. It meant a trip to Caxley for more glass.

The man who laid the stair carpet forgot to put the underlay down first, the excuse being that his wife had given birth to twins in the early hours of the morning and it had unsettled him. I wondered what it had done to his wife.

The removal men were three hours late and made a mark on the beautiful new dove-grey paint. A nasty scratch had appeared on the side of my dressing table, but the men assured me that if I put it 'best side to London', meaning with that side against a wall, where I did not want it, then all would be well.

I never did find the tea cosy or the egg timer. My guess is that they went back in the van.

But gradually things were sorted out, and I grew fonder and fonder of my home as the days passed. Callers still dropped in with some excuse or other, and I was proud to show them over my new abode.

I also paid a few calls myself, and one of them was to see Miss Clare who lived at Beech Green, and would be my only member of staff and sole companion in our labours together. I had taken to her at first sight, when I had come for the interview some months earlier. It had been a great comfort to know that Miss Clare, who had taught at Fairacre for many years, would be there as my support when I took up the post.

Her cottage could have graced any of the 'Beautiful Britain' type of calendar. It had been thatched first by her father, and the straw renewed by a young local man who was making his name as a master thatcher.

The garden was the perfect cottage mixture of summer flowers at the front and a vegetable patch and lawn at the back. There were even hollyhocks doing their best to reach up to the eaves, with pansies and pinks at their feet.

In the distance, the downs shimmered in a blue haze of heat, and I was glad to prop my bicycle against the fence, and to sit in the cool sitting room. A fat tabby cat basked on the window sill, a lark poured forth a torrent of song above the field beyond the garden, and I could understand the inner peace which gave Dolly Clare such strength and calm.

She was a tall slender woman, dressed this afternoon in a dark blue linen frock which high-lighted her white hair and pale skin.

She had been a pupil at Fairacre School, and had then gone on to become a pupil teacher, encouraged by the head master of that time Mr Wardle, who recognised in this quiet fourteen-year-old the makings of a first-class teacher. She and her life-long friend Emily Davis had trained together, and both taught locally for many years, known officially as 'uncertificated teachers' but, like so many thus designated, were efficient, dedicated and much loved by pupils and parents.

The vicar had told me all this. It was plain that he had a high regard for Miss Clare, as I had too.

We discussed a few practical matters concerned with the timetable and then, inevitably, the subject of Mrs Pringle cropped up. I told her that I had decided to postpone any firm invitation to the lady about working in the school house, and she nodded approval.

'She's not an easy person, as no doubt you've guessed. In any case, the position now is rather different. When we had a head master it was the wife who coped with the domestic side. Now you have to deal with her at school and in your home. Very wise to take it step by step.'

'Why is she so difficult?'

Miss Clare smiled. 'I expect present-day psychologists would blame some childhood drama, or even heredity, as no one these days seems to accept the fact that evil is as rife today as ever it was.'

'I wouldn't have labelled Mrs P. as evil,' I protested, 'just a bit of a misery.'

'That's true. But why she is such a misery is a mystery. I suppose I've known her longer than most people in Fairacre.'

'Did you teach her?'

'No. She was brought up in Caxley. Born there too, I believe, and was the first child. But she had relations in Fairacre, an aunt and uncle, though whether they were blood relatives or simply friends of her parents, I don't know, but they used to have her for visits during the school holidays, so I used to see her about.'

'What was she like as a child?'

'Much the same as she is today,' said Dolly Clare, looking amused. 'The first time I came across her, she had been sent to this aunt because the next child was coming into the world. She was particularly resentful, but we all put it down to temporary jealousy, quite common on these occasions.'

'Did it pass?'

'No, I can't say it did. And when another baby turned up, it made things worse. Mind you, I don't think the two younger children were the reason for Maud being so gloomy. I realise now that she was that by nature, and time has proved it.'

'Well, I'm glad to know that my reaction to the lady is pretty general. And I'm glad to know her name is Maud!'

'But don't dare to call her by it,' warned Miss Clare. 'She would look upon that as terribly familiar! No, "Mrs Pringle" it must be, I assure you.'

I promised to remember.

On the night before term began, as I prepared for bed, I thought how lucky I was to have obtained this post in Fairacre. I had already made friends with Dolly Clare, Bob Willet, the kind vicar and his wife, and was on nodding terms with most of the other local inhabitants.

My house was as straight as one could reasonably expect in the time, although the new curtains, being made by someone Amy had recommended, were still not done, and there was a strange ticking noise at night which I could not track down, and only prayed that it was not something gruesome like death watch beetle at work.

The school gleamed from Mrs Pringle's labours, and a strong smell of yellow soap, mingled with carbolic disinfectant, greeted one as the door opened.

The stocks of books, stationery, and educational apparatus seemed adequate, but I had been busy with a list of further requirements which I hoped would soon be forthcoming.

All in all, I climbed into bed that night in a hopeful frame of mind. Amy had once said: 'Will you feel lonely out there in the wilds?' I could truthfully say that I had been so enchanted with my house and garden, the village and the glorious countryside surrounding it, that I had not felt the faintest qualm of loneliness.

And tomorrow, I had no doubt that I should have other responsibilities which were equally absorbing. I was not so euphoric as to imagine that all would go smoothly. There would be frustrations and annoyances, possibly hostility from parents who preferred Mr Fortescue's régime, but these thoughts did not stop me from sleeping from ten o'clock until nearly seven the next morning.

Chapter Three

BOB WILLET REMEMBERS

There was no doubt about it, as all agreed, Mrs Pringle was a good worker.

Her chief passion was a fierce proprietary love of the two coke-burning stoves which dominated the infants' room and my own. These monsters had heated the school throughout many winters extremely efficiently. Each was surrounded by a sturdy fireguard which had a brass top running round it. On this we dried gloves, socks, tea towels, scarves and very useful it was.

In bitterly cold weather I warmed the children's milk in a saucepan kept for the purpose. Children with earache or toothache were placed with the afflicted area close to the stove's blessed warmth. All in all, each provided the classroom with much varied comfort.

But Mrs Pringle's attitude towards these charges of hers went far beyond our general gratitude and affection. Like the Romans, she had her household gods, and top of the list were Fairacre School's two coke stoves.

She did her duty conscientiously with the desks, cupboards, floors and so on, and also came to wash up the dinner things. Everything sparkled, tea towels were snowy, the zeal with which she laboured was highly commendable. But it was the stoves which meant most to her.

At the beginning of the term they had shone like jet with lots of blacklead and Mrs Pringle's elbow grease. The cast-iron lids were much indented with a pattern, and by dint of skilful use of a blacklead brush these ornamentations stood out splendidly.

A light dusting was really all that was needed to keep them in pristine condition for the first few weeks. Even so, I noticed that the blacklead brush appeared now and again to keep them just as Mrs Pringle wanted.

We were lucky with the weather, and it was not until half term that the first chill winds of October began to blow.

I had been looking forward to tidying up the garden. Fallen leaves were strewn everywhere, and the dead spires of lupins, delphiniums and other summer plants needed cutting down. The lawns were in need of mowing and edging, and the plum tree had surpassed itself with a harvest of yellow fruit which bade fair to nourish the whole village.

But my plans were frustrated by the weather. Rain lashed across the garden, the distant downs were invisible, and it was so cold that I lit a fire in my sitting room.

Amy rang to see how I was getting on, and I vented my frustration into her listening ear.

'As Burns says: "The best laid schemes of mice and men gang aft agley",' she quoted.

I was not comforted. 'Well my schemes certainly have "ganged agley",' I told her. 'What about yours?'

'We're off to a wedding tomorrow, and apart from a mackintosh, wellingtons and a sou-wester, I can't think what to wear.'

'Thermal underwear for a start, and then anything warm under the mac.'

'I expect you're right. And how are things with you? Is Mrs Pringle still playing up?'

'Mrs Pringle,' I said forcefully, 'will be lighting the school stoves this week, come hell or high water, if this weather lasts.'

'Attagirl!' said Amy, putting down the receiver.

School began on the Tuesday. I saw Mrs Pringle sloshing through the puddles in the playground soon after eight that morning. She was wearing a raincoat, wellingtons and a shiny plastic head square, and carried the usual oilcloth bag on her arm.

I snatched a coat from the peg on the kitchen door and sped after her. She was busy unlocking the school when I caught up.

'Mrs Pringle! Let's get inside and out of this downpour.'

We gained the comparative peace of my classroom. A pool of water lay on the floor immediately below the skylight in the roof. It was my first encounter with a problem which would be with me throughout my teaching years at Fairacre School.

'Good heavens!' I exclaimed. 'We must get this seen to.'

Mrs Pringle gave something between a snort and a sarcastic laugh.

'That there skylight *has been seen to* more times than I can remember,' she told me, with considerable satisfaction, 'and nothing don't make no difference.'

'Do you mean it has leaked for years?'

'Every winter. Every drop of rain. Every storm. Every snow shower . . .'

'But it can't be beyond the wit of man to put it to rights,' I broke in before Mrs Pringle called upon all the armoury of the heavens to prove her point.

'It's beyond the wit of Bob Willet,' she said, 'and if he can't fathom it, there's none else can. Why, we've even had people out from Caxley, *sent by The Office* what's more, and they've been beat.'

'Well, we shall have to try again,' I said. 'It was sheer luck that it didn't drip all over my desk.'

'Most head teachers have shifted this 'ere desk along a bit when it starts raining. Only needs a bit of forethought,' she said rudely.

I ignored the thrust, and gave one of my own.

'I came over early to say we'd better have the stoves alight now.'

'The stoves? *Alight?*' gasped the lady. 'What, in this weather?'

'Particularly in this weather.'

'But it's still October!'

'I really don't care if it is June, Mrs Pringle. The children can't work in this temperature, and I don't intend to let them try.'

'But what will The Office say?"

'What the Office says I can well answer,' I said, beginning to lose patience. 'All I am asking is that you will be good enough to put a match to each of the stoves. I know you have set them already, and Mr Willet has brought in coke.'

Mrs Pringle's face began to be suffused with an unpleasant shade of red, and her bosom heaved as busily as a Regency heroine's. I began to wonder, with some alarm, how one dealt with an apoplectic fit, and wished, not for the first time, that I had undertaken that course in first-aid which I kept postponing.

But her voice came out steadily and with such malevolence that Miss Clare's talk of evil rushed into my mind.

'You knows what you are starting, I suppose? It's not just *a match* as is needed, it's cleaning out, setting again, clearing up the mess, heaving in the coke, day in and day out for months to come. And all when there's *no need*.'

'But there is need,' I said as bravely as I could under this onslaught. I was ashamed to feel my legs beginning to shake, and my inside becoming decidedly queasy. There was no doubt about it, Mrs Pringle was a formidable enemy. I could see how she barged her way, like a tank, through village affairs.

'And what about my poor leg?' she thundered, thrusting her furious face close to mine.

I retreated hastily, stepping into the puddle. 'What about it?' I countered.

'Doctor Martin says I'm to respect my leg. It flares up if I overdoes it, and seeing to these stoves isn't going to help.'

I summoned all my failing strength. 'In that case, should you be doing this job? I've no wish to impose on an invalid, but these stoves must be lit this morning.'

Mrs Pringle drew in an outraged breath, ready for a renewed attack, but I made a swift exit with as much dignity as I could muster, and was thankful to return to my kitchen, and a cup of coffee which did little to calm my shattered nerves.

But the stoves were lit.

I was conscious that Mrs Pringle's leg was being dragged along heavily for the rest of the day, and an ominous silence hung over any chance meeting we had, but I refused to offer an olive branch. If she wanted to sulk then that suited me; as long as she did her work that was really all that mattered. I was not going to pander to Mrs Pringle's feelings, or her leg.

Mr Willet came up that evening bearing two large marrows which would have been enough for a family of twelve, let alone one spinster. I thanked him effusively and invited him in.

'Well, just for half a minute,' he said, wiping his boots vigorously on the kitchen mat. 'I see you've managed to get the stoves goin'.'

I had suspected that this visit was not only to deliver two marrows. Now I knew his real motive.

'Well, it was cold enough,' I said. I was careful to remain unforthcoming. Village prattle grows as it spreads, like bindweed.

'But I bet you had a battle with our Mrs Sunshine,' responded Mr Willet, unabashed.

I confessed that I had.

'You don't want to worry overmuch about her feelin's,' he said, sturdily. 'She's been the same since she was so high.'

He held a horny hand six inches from the floor.

'Always a tartar, that one. Why, I can tell you how I first rumbled our Mrs Pringle, and I bet she remembers it as well as I do.'

'But I oughtn't to keep you,' I began weakly.

Bob Willet settled back in his chair. 'It was like this,' he said.

As a child, Bob Willet had lived in a cottage between the villages of Springbourne and Fairacre. There were several children, and Bob's mother was well known as a fine disciplinarian, a good mother and an exemplary housewife.

In Springbourne itself was another family, the Picketts, who did not come up to Mrs Willet's high standards. One of the sons, Ted Pickett, attended Fairacre School and often called on his way to pick up the Willet children.

Mrs Willet senior was not best pleased at this attention, and hoped that Bob's obvious admiration for Ted, a year or two older than he was, would soon fade. But the friendship grew stronger as the days passed, and Bob's mother resigned herself to the inevitable.

One day, in the summer holidays when Bob was about eight and

Ted nearing ten, the two boys wandered into Fairacre and sat on a sunny bank by the roadside.

In those days there was a sizeable duck pond in Fairacre, and the boys watched the ducks going about their lawful occasions. It was too hot to be energetic, and the lads were content to loll back chewing grass and wishing they had a penny, or even a halfpenny, to buy liquorice strips or four gob-stoppers from the village shop.

Before long, a little girl about Bob's age appeared on the other side of the pond where a duck board sloped from the further bank into the water. She took up her position at the top of the board and made clucking noises. The ducks, excited and trusting, rushed towards her in a flurry of wings and water.

'Wotcher!' shouted Ted, languidly.

'Who is she?' asked Bob.

'That Maud.'

'What Maud?'

'Comes to stop with the Bakers. Auntie or something.'

Bob knew the Bakers. They were an elderly childless couple living in a neat bungalow at the other end of Springbourne. No one knew much about them, and they 'kept themselves to themselves' as the villagers said, usually with approval.

The general feeling was that it was good of them to have young Maud Gordon now and again, to give her mother a rest. She was a singularly unattractive child which made their kindness even more laudable. Mrs Baker and Mrs Gordon, it was understood, had been in service together and had remained friends.

'Them ducks wants some bread,' yelled Ted, hands behind his head and legs stretched out in the sunshine.

Maud tossed her head, and then put out her tongue.

'Watch it!' shouted Ted. 'You'll be stuck like it if the wind changes!'

Bob was a silent admirer of these witticisms from his hero, but did not attempt to add his share.

Maud squatted down on the board and began to splash water over the milling crowd of ducks. They quacked and flapped but did not retreat, still hoping, no doubt, that food would soon be forthcoming.

'Watch your step, Maudie!' bawled Ted, and at that the girl stood up, slipped on the slimy board and landed with one leg sunk deep into the muddy water and one outstretched on the duckboard. Her cotton skirt was stained and dripping, and she was gasping with shock.

Bob was half-frightened although he could see that very little had happened to the girl. But Ted put back his head and roared his amusement to the blue sky above.

'That'll learn you,' he wheezed. 'Teasin' them poor birds! Serves you right. Now run home and tell yer auntie. She'll give you what for!'

Maud struggled out of the pond, and stumped furiously past the boys. Her face was scarlet and one shoe squelched as she made for home.

'You wait, Ted Pickett!' she stormed. 'I'll tell on you!'

Mr Willet paused and looked at my kitchen clock.

'Here I sits natterin' on, and I expect I'm keepin' you from somethin'. Ironin' and that, say?'

'Far from it,' I assured him. 'Go on. Did she tell?'

'That she did, the little besom,' said Mr Willet. 'She went straight home, and she knew damn well she'd get into trouble over that mucky frock, so she said Ted Pickett had pushed her in.'

'No!'

'Yes! The little liar! Why, Ted and me hadn't stirred from that bank. It was much too hot to muck about.'

'What happened?'

'Our Maud told the tale all right, tears and all, and Mrs Baker came storming up to the Picketts' place, breathin' fire and brimstone, so poor old Ted was sent upstairs to wait for his Dad to come home and use his belt.'

'Ted wasn't believed?'

'No. And I didn't know until the next day when Ted showed me his behind – begging your pardon, miss.'

I assured him that I was not shocked.

'And even if I had stuck up for Ted that afternoon, I don't suppose them Picketts would have believed me. After all, boys hangs together at times like that. No, poor old Ted fairly copped it, and all through our Mrs Pringle. Ted's dad was a hefty bloke, and when he used the strap you knew it all right.'

Mr Willet sighed heavily at things remembered, and got to his feet.

'Poor old Ted,' he repeated. 'We stayed friends right up to the outbreak of war, though my old ma never really approved. We joined up the same day in Caxley, but Ted never got back from Dunkirk.'

'That's a sad ending.'

'Sad for both of us,' admitted Bob Willet. 'I always touches his name when I pass the war memorial by the church gate. I miss him still, poor old Ted.'

I accompanied him out of the front door, and thanked him again for the marrows and his story.

'Well, I only told you because I don't want you to worry about Maud Pringle's little ways. She was born a tartar, and she's stayed that way. All Fairacre knows it, so you keep a stout heart.'

I promised that I would, and went back into my house much comforted.

To my secret relief, Mrs Pringle kept the stoves going throughout this unreasonably chilly spell. She even bent so far as to address me now and again, and her leg was not dragged quite so heavily as the days passed. I was not so sanguine as to imagine that all was forgiven, but at least our relationship was civil, if not exactly cordial.

A week or two after our clash over the stoves, Mrs Pringle spoke of Fairacre Women's Institute, and urged me to join.

'It sounds a good idea,' I told her, 'it means that I shall get to know more people.'

'Well, that's a mixed blessing,' was her gloomy reply. 'There's some in this village as should be drummed out, to my way of thinking. Like them Coggses.'

I had heard about Arthur Coggs already, evidently the village ne'er-do-well, and a strong supporter of 'The Beetle and Wedge'. His young and fast-growing family, not to mention his down-trodden wife, went in fear of him. Later I was to have his son Joseph as a pupil.

'But apart from them undesirables,' continued Mrs Pringle, 'there's a lot of good folk you'd like. Mrs Partridge is President. She looks after us a fair treat.'

I could imagine that she would, brave, fair-minded and tactful woman that she was. A vicar's wife must get plenty of day-to-day training in diplomacy.

Consequently, I took myself along to the next meeting and was welcomed with surprising warmth.

We all sang 'Jerusalem' with varied success, listened to interminable arrangements about various activities to which no one apparently wanted to go, and voted on paper for our choice of Christmas treat, Caxley pantomime, tea-party with magician in the village hall, or coach trip to London for Christmas shopping. I plumped for the last, and had visions of going straight to Harrods Food Hall and buying almost all my Christmas presents there in one fell swoop.

After that, a very nervous flower-arranger who was inaudible except to those of us in the front row, showed us how to make 'The Best of our Late Blooms'. The response was lack-lustre, I felt, and only the knitters behind me, busy clicking their needles, really benefited.

But tea time was the real highlight. Despite the fact that it was past eight o'clock in the evening, we all fell upon home-made sponges, wedges of treacle tart, shortbread fingers, and squares of sticky gingerbread, as though we had not seen food for weeks.

I met a host of cheerful women, several of them with children at the school, and many of them former pupils, and went home as a fully paid-up member of Fairacre's W.I.

It will not surprise any newcomer to a village to know that I was also committed to supplying a contribution to the next month's tea table, and had agreed to stand in for the Treasurer when she had her baby.

Of such stuff is village life made. And very nice, too.

Chapter Four

MRS WILLET GOES FARTHER

One of the nicest women I met at our local Women's Institute was Alice Willet, wife of Bob. She had been at our school as a child, and had many memories of Fairacre folk including Maud Gordon when she visited her adopted uncle and aunt during the school holidays.

'Mind you,' she said, 'I could never take to her. She was a year or two older than me, and bossy with it. I kept out of her way when she was around in Fairacre.'

Some years later, it seems, Miss Parr, who lived at the largest house in Fairacre, was looking for a housemaid to replace her well-trained Mary who had been with her for over twenty years and had had the effrontery to get married.

Miss Parr was a great power in the village. She had, in fact, been the most venerable of the school governors who had appointed me to the headship of Fairacre School, and so I was particularly interested in her history.

Her family, it appears, came from Lancashire where innumerable cotton mills had brought them much wealth in the last century. Hard-headed and shrewd, the money had been invested, not only in enlarging the mills, but in divers other money-making ventures. Miss Parr had inherited a fortune, as well as the commonsense of her forebears, and lived in style in the Queen Anne house in Fairacre.

She employed a head gardener and an under-gardener, and a chauffeur to look after her limousine. Indoors, a cook and a housemaid coped with most of the chores, although a succession of what Miss Parr termed 'village women' came in to help with 'the rough' and the laundry work.

Those she employed spoke well of her, and stayed in her service. She was not lavish in her payments but they were paid on the dot, and in those hard times one was lucky to have a job at all. Also, when the garden was producing more than one lone lady and her staff could consume, the gardeners and the daily helpers could take home this welcome largesse to their families.

'She kept a sharp eye on things, of course,' said Mrs Willet. 'I mean, her people had made their money by looking after the pennies, and she took after them. And when she found old Biddy Stamper had helped herself to a bunch of grapes and some peaches from the hot-house, and was trying to smuggle them out with the washing, she got the sack there and then, and never set foot in the house again.'

Mrs Willet nodded her approval before continuing. 'Well, when Mary left, Mrs Pringle's auntie, Mrs Baker, she went up to Miss Parr's to see if she could put in a word for her Maud. Mrs Baker was one of the women that helped with the ironing each week, so she knew the house and all that. Miss Parr thought a lot of her. She was a dab hand with the ironing, and could use a goffering iron.'

'I've never heard of such a thing!' I exclaimed.

'Oh, it was what you used to crimp the edges of things. Mary's afternoon caps had to be goffered, and some collars too that she wore. I believe some people even goffered the frills round their pillow cases. Anyway, Mrs Baker was famous for her goffering, and Miss Parr had a soft spot for anyone as was good at their particular job.'

Thus it was that Miss Parr agreed to see Maud, and up the girl went, all dressed neat-but-not-gaudy, to the big house one evening.

'And did she get the job?'

'She did. We was all a bit surprised seeing that Maud was so much younger than Mary, but she'd had a good bit of experience at the Howards' place in Caxley, both in their house and the restaurant, so top and bottom of it was she was taken on.'

'And gave satisfaction obviously.'

'That's right. Well, you know yourself, our Mrs Pringle is a good worker, despite her funny little ways. No one can touch her for cleaning brass, and she can get any bit of furniture up to look like satin. The only snag was Henry.'

'Henry?' I queried.

'The chauffeur. He was a real knock-out. All us girls were a bit soft on Henry.'

Mrs Willet's pale cheeks were suffused with a becoming blush, and her eyes grew misty with memories. Henry, I surmised, must have been a real lady-killer.

'He had dark wavy hair,' continued Mrs Willet, looking dreamily towards the window as if he still lingered in the village outside. 'And one of them Ronald Colman moustaches. And I've never seen such eye-lashes on anyone, girl or boy. He was nice with it, too. Very soft-spoken, and kind to everyone. Miss Parr thought the world of him, and we did too.'

'Mrs Pringle as well?' I asked, my mind boggling at the thought of Mrs Pringle being undone by love.

'Worse than any of us,' asserted Mrs Willet. 'She was forever making sheep's eyes at him. I was going steady at the time with Bob, so I didn't see a lot of Maud, but all the village was talking about her.'

'What about Henry? It must have been embarrassing for him working at the same place.'

'Nothing worried Henry. He was as nice to Maud as he was to everybody, but he did try and keep out of her way. He didn't want to lose his job after all.'

'Did Miss Parr know?'

'She guessed something was up when she saw Maud coming out of the bothy.'

'The bothy?'

'The room near the coach-house where Henry lived,' explained Mrs Willet. 'Maud had the cheek to take a cake over there for him. Of course, the bothy was out of bounds to women, just as the attics where the maids slept was out of bounds to the men. When Miss Parr caught her, she gave her a fine old dressing-down, but Maud wriggled out of it that time, and was allowed to stay on.'

'She was lucky.'

'But Henry wasn't. Miss Parr had him up in the drawing room that evening and cook heard it all.'

'How?'

'Well, I take it she was passing at the time,' said Mrs Willet, looking slightly confused, 'and then they was both shouting, cook said, so she couldn't help hearing.'

'And what did she hear?'

'Not as much from Miss Parr as she did from Henry, but I gather he fairly let fly when Miss Parr as good as told him that he'd been leading Maud on. "Such a young innocent girl too!" Cook heard her say. And evidently that tore it.'

Mrs Willet paused to find a snowy handkerchief in her sleeve. 'He told Miss Parr it was the other way round. Maud had been pestering him. And then he went on to say what he thought of Maud, in the most dreadful language that I wouldn't repeat to you, though Cook never turned a hair when she repeated it to all and sundry in Fairacre. My Bob told her to wash out her mouth with carbolic, I remember.'

'So Henry was sacked?'

'No. He gave in his notice there and then, and left at the end of the week. I think Miss Parr regretted the whole affair, but of course it was easier to get a good chauffeur than a good worker like Maud in those days. But how we all missed him!'

Mrs Willet sighed. 'He had a green uniform to match the car. Very trim figure he was in that. What with his smile and his nice ways, he was a real gentleman.'

'What happened to him?'

'He got a job in foreign parts.'

I imagined that trim green-suited figure driving wealthy Americans about, or being snapped up by an Indian rajah.

'Northampton, I think it was,' said Mrs Willet, 'or maybe Leicester. We never saw him again.'

She sounded wistful.

'And Mrs Pringle?'

'Well, with Henry gone she turned her attention to the next best thing on the premises, and that was the under-gardener.'

'What about the head gardener?'

'He was married already, but the under one was easy game. And anyway the head gardener moved off soon after Henry to open a nursery garden of his own, so the under-gardener was promoted and had a rise in wages.'

'How did he respond to Maud's advances?'

'Didn't stand a chance. It was Fred Pringle, you see. He soon knuckled under, and he's stayed that way ever since.'

It was a few days later that Bob Willet continued this enthralling episode in Fairacre's history.

'You could've knocked us down with a feather when we heard poor old Fred was engaged to Maud. Not that he had a chance, of course, but Maud was so high and mighty and the Pringles had a bad name.'

'Why?'

'They was all a bit harum-scarum, and Josh Pringle, Fred's brother, was a proper bad lot – poachin', pinchin', fightin' – always in trouble and turnin' up in Caxley court. No end of kids, and half of them not his wife's, if you follow me.'

I said I did.

'The Bakers was upset about it, but couldn't do much. After all, Maud was of age – *over* age, come to that – and she and Fred got married in Caxley where her parents lived, so us Fairacre folk didn't see or hear much about the weddin'. All this was before the war, of course.'

'But I take it they came to live in Fairacre?'

'Oh yes! In one of Miss Parr's cottages, near where they are now. Fred did the garden and Maud helped in the house until John was on the way when she stopped workin' at Miss Parr's. She used to give a hand once a week to the Hopes who were livin' here at the school house, and then the Bensons when Mr Benson took over. That's when she became school cleaner.'

Mr Willet paused, blowing out his cheeks. 'Still,' he went on, rallying slightly, 'I suppose she's done a good job, considerin'. She done it all through the war, while Fred was away. We all reckoned it did poor old Fred a power of good to get away from Maud during the war. He looked much fresher when he come back.'

'I haven't seen Mr Pringle yet.'

'Nor likely to,' responded Bob Willet. 'After the war he got a job up the Atomic, and he's still at it. Gets the Atomic bus soon after seven, and when he gets home he spends most of the time in that shed of his at the end of the garden.'

'What does he do there?'

'Keeps out of her ladyship's way, I shouldn't wonder, but he makes things with matchsticks as well.'

'Matchsticks?' I exclaimed, my mind boggling.

'Models and that. Fairacre Church he done once, and it was on show at the village fête. Then he done a piano – not life size, of course – and that was a real masterpiece, and a set of chairs for a dolls' house. He's a clever chap in his way, although he don't say much. Come to think of it, I suppose he can't get a word in edgeways with his missus, so he's driven to matchsticks.'

He made for the door. 'Best have another tidy up of the coke pile. Them little varmints can't leave well alone.'

And he departed, leaving me to mull over the story of Mrs Pringle's love life.

During these early days at Fairacre I had a great deal to learn, not only about my new job, but also about the people of the village.

Mrs Pringle herself enlightened me on many aspects of life in the country. At that time the village had no piped water, and rain barrels stood by the houses collecting rainwater from the roofs.

I soon learnt to appreciate this precious fluid, and Mrs Pringle was my chief adviser. What she called 'the top quality', that is the filtered water which supplied the school house, was used for drinking and cooking. The rainwater from the barrels was used for bathing, hair washing, laundering and other household activities, but still had other uses which Mrs Pringle explained to me.

'The soapy water from the washing does for the floors,' she told me, 'and then after that you can use some for pouring over the flagstones on the path, and give them a good brushing with a stiff broom. And what's left you throws over the cabbages and such-like in the garden. There's no need,' she continued, turning a fierce eye upon me, 'to waste a drop!'

In times of drought the villagers were hard-pressed, and Fair-acre pond furnished a few precious bucketfuls for cleaning operations. Mr Roberts, the local farmer, had put in a bore to keep his cattle watered, and he let each household have a bucket or two of fresh water from this well for drinking when things became serious.

Of necessity we had earth closets, and thanks to Bob Willet and Mrs Pringle these were kept as hygienic as such primitive amenities could be, but it was a great relief to everyone when water was piped to the village some years after my arrival.

Even so, the old ways persisted, and I noticed that Mrs Pringle transferred what she termed 'lovely suds' from the new wash basins to a pail, in readiness to wash over the lobby floor.

Considering the somewhat primitive hygiene which the Fairacre folk had perforce to endure, it was surprising to see what a healthy lot we all were.

I suppose the air had something to do with it. Even on a still summer's day there is a freshness in this downland air, and in the winter the winds can be ferocious, blowing away not only cobwebs but any germs hovering about, I suspect.

Doctor Martin, who looks after the local population, does not get called upon unnecessarily. Accidents on the farms, unlucky tractor drivers pinned beneath overturned vehicles, men carelessly wielding scythes, hedge slashers and other dangerous implements may get Doctor Martin's ready attention, but minor ailments are usually dealt with at home.

Some of these remedies sound horrific, and over the years Mrs Pringle has curdled my blood with her first-aid tips.

'My young nephew,' she told me once, 'had the whooping cough something dreadful. Nearly coughed his heart up, and Doctor's medicine never done him a bit of good. In the end, it was Bob Willet's old mother as suggested the fried mouse.'

'Fried mouse?' I quavered.

'Oh, it's a good old cure, is fried mouse. You want a *fresh* one, of course. And it's best to skin it, and then try and eat it whole.'

I must have looked as horrified as I felt.

'It does sound *unpleasant*, don't it?' said Mrs Pringle, with evident satisfaction. 'But no end of people swear by it.'

'Did it help your nephew?'

'Well, no, it didn't seem to work with him, but old Mrs Willet's cure for chilblains was always a winner.'

'And what was that?'

'A thorough thrashing with stinging nettles. Worked like a charm. Always.'

Pondering on this, after Mrs Pringle had left to resume her duties, I could only suppose that the stings from the nettles acted as a counter-irritant to the itching of the chilblains, but it all seemed unnecessarily violent to me, and I resolved to treat any chilblains I might suffer with more orthodox methods.

But in my early days at the school, I soon discovered that apart from the inevitable childish complaints such as measles and chicken-pox, my thirty-odd pupils were a hardy lot, only succumbing occasionally to a bout of toothache or earache, or an upset tummy, the latter usually in August or September when the apples and plums were unripe.

The first-aid box, on the wall above the map cupboard, was seldom used; a bottle of disinfectant, lint and bandages for scraped knees and cut fingers were the things most often in demand and, as I pointed out, if the children kept off the coke pile half the injuries would never occur at all.

But I might just as well have saved my breath.

It was Mrs Pringle who first pointed out to me that it was traditional at Fairacre School to give a Christmas party to parents and friends.

'I thought as how it should be *mentioned*,' she told me, 'so's you can decide if you want to go on with it. Alice Willet usually bakes a cake – and very nice it is too,' she added graciously.

I said that I thought it was an excellent idea and would start planning straightaway.

Miss Clare confirmed Mrs Pringle's information, and was slightly amused at her early pronouncement.

'I meant to tell you in good time,' she said, 'but Mrs P. has got there first.'

I was careful to find out how things were traditionally done. One has to tread warily in a village, particularly if one is a newcomer. Mrs Willet, it seemed, had the largest square baking tin in the village, and was adept at producing enormous square cakes, ideal for cutting into neat fingers on festive occasions.

'Her coronation cake,' Mrs Pringle told me, 'was a real master-piece, with a Union Jack piped on it in icing. And *waving* at that!'

It was Miss Clare who told me that it was right and proper for Mrs Willet to be given the ingredients for such an expensive product, but this had to be done with great diplomacy, and the money was usually taken from the school funds.

I negotiated these perils as well as I could, and rather dreaded my meeting with Alice Willet to arrange about making the cake, but my fears were groundless.

One misty November day I called at her cottage after school to broach the subject, but she greeted me with a smile.

'The cake? Why, I made it nearly a month ago. It's not iced yet, of course, but the cake itself needs a few weeks to mature nicely. I always put a spoonful of brandy in it, but I don't tell Bob. He's a strict teetotaller, you see. I don't drink either, but I think a spot of brandy in a good fruit cake, a little drop of sherry in a trifle, makes all the difference.'

I began to make a halting speech about the cost of the cake, and Mrs Willet opened a corner cupboard and took out a neat list which she handed me. It showed all the ingredients and the prices, and the total was shown clearly between two neatly-ruled lines. It seemed extraordinarily modest to me.

I studied the list again.

'But you haven't put in eggs,' I said, feeling rather proud of my perspicacity.

Mrs Willet looked shocked. 'Oh, I wouldn't dream of charging for the eggs! They come from our own chickens, you see.'

'But all the more reason why you should charge for such a first-class product.'

'No, no. I've never done that in all these years. Call it my contribution to Christmas, if you like.'

And with that I had to be content.

The Christmas party took place during the last week of term. The schoolroom was garlanded with home-made paper chains, and a Christmas tree glittered in the corner.

The children acted as hosts to their parents and friends of the school, the stoves roared merrily, and Mrs Willet's Christmas cake was the centre piece of the long tea table. In its centre stood a snowman, some over-large robins and a tiny Christmas tree, and the children were loud in their admiration of Mrs Willet's handiwork.

Among our visitors was Amy, who was quite the most elegant figure among us, and also one of the most appreciative.

At the end of the proceedings, when we had waved goodbye to the children and their guests, we turned back into the quiet school-room, crumbs and chaos about us, but also a blessed silence after the junketings.

'Well,' said Amy, 'I don't know when I have enjoyed a party more. You certainly know how to do things in Fairacre.'

I was just beginning to glow with pride at these kind words when the door was flung open and Mrs Pringle stood there surveying the scene.

'Humph!' said the lady, 'about time I made a start, I can see.'

Suddenly chilled, Amy and I made our escape to the school house.

Chapter Five

WARTIME MEMORIES

As time passed, Mrs Pringle and I established a precarious truce. Every now and again she would broach the question of cleaning my house, but I resisted her offers as civilly as I could. Mrs Pringle during school hours was quite enough for me. I hoped that I could keep my home out of that lady's clutches.

There were occasional clashes, of course, and after each one Mrs Pringle's combustible leg would 'flare up', and oblige her to drag the suffering limb about her duties with many a sigh and a wince. I grew very skilled at ignoring these manifestations of Mrs Pringle's umbrage.

The stoves were the usual source of trouble. For some reason, pencil sharpenings near these monsters, usually inside their fire-guards, were a major source of irritation. The milk saucepan sometimes left a ring on the jet-black surface, and this too caused sharp comment.

Wet footmarks, coke crunched in, bubble gum, crumbs from lunch packets and any other hazards to Mrs Pringle's floors were also severely criticised and, up to a point, she had my support.

She was indeed a sore trial, but I reminded myself that she was a superb cleaner, as I was always being told, and that Fairacre School was a model of hygiene in the area.

I also remembered Mr Willet's advice. 'You don't want to worry about her funny ways. She's always been a tartar since a girl. All Fairacre knows that.'

It was some comfort in times of crisis.

Mrs Pringle's bossiness had been well to the fore during the war years it seems. Fairacre, in company with most rural communities, had its fair share of evacuees, and Mrs Pringle was lucky in that the couple billeted upon her were a middle-aged self-effacing pair who inhabited one room of her semi-detached cottage, and who were careful to creep into the kitchen when Mrs Pringle had finished her labours there.

Next door there lived a middle-aged lady, Jane Morgan, who was not as fortunate as Mrs Pringle in her evacuees, Mrs Jarman and her four boisterous children.

They ruled the roost, and soon clashed with Mrs Pringle next door. At the time, Jane Morgan's husband and Fred Pringle were both away in the army. Mrs Jarman's husband had been killed in the blitz of May 1941. It was then that the three solitary women, the four Jarman children, and Mrs Pringle's schoolboy son John were fated to meet at close quarters.

The Jarman family was an indomitable one. Despite the loss of a husband and father, not to mention their home and all that was in it, the Jarmans' cockney spirit remained irrepressible. The children took to taunting Mrs Pringle over the hedge, and when that lady reported the matter to their mother, Mrs Jarman joined battle with equal zest. For once, it seemed, Mrs Pringle was on the losing side.

One of their skirmishes took place in the village hall. During wartime this building was in constant use for a great many village functions, and also as an extra classroom on weekdays to accommodate the London children evacuated to Fairacre.

It was on the occasion of a local jumble sale that the clash between Mrs Pringle and Mrs Jarman was observed by some dozen or so Fairacre ladies who were sorting out the contributions ready for the Saturday afternoon sale.

Mrs Jarman and Mrs Pringle had entered the hall together. Mrs Pringle deposited a large bundle on the floor before making her way with ponderous dignity to her stall, marked 'Junk', and starting to arrange chipped vases, moulting cushions, lidless saucepans and innumerable objects of china or tarnished metal to which no one could give a name.

Meanwhile, Mrs Jarman had fallen to her knees beside the

bundle dropped by her neighbour, and was holding up threadbare underpants, cardigans washed so often that they resembled felt, and a number of men's shirts. She kept up a running commentary as she sorted out the garments. Some of the comments were ribald enough to shock a few of the Fairacre folk, but on the whole there was secret delight in seeing Mrs Pringle discomfited.

'Look at these then!' shrieked Mrs Jarman, scrabbling among the shirts. 'Not a button between them. Who's pinched them, eh?'

Mrs Pringle's voice boomed from her corner. 'I cut them off to use again, as any one would in wartime. There's such a thing as *thrift* which a lot of people not a hundred miles from here don't ever seem to have heard of!'

This lofty speech did nothing to curb Mrs Jarman's spirit.

'How mean can you get!' she yelled back.

'Nothing *mean* about it,' returned Mrs Pringle, putting a headless garden gnome to best advantage on the stall. 'I simply collect shirt buttons. They're bound to be needed.'

'I'll remember that,' cried Mrs Jarman, unearthing a moth-eaten strip of fur. 'Ah, I wonder what sort of skin disease this ratty old collar would give you!'

'Now that's enough,' said Mrs Partridge, the vicar's wife, who had just arrived. 'Time's getting short, and we must get on.'

Even Mrs Jarman took some notice of Mrs Partridge, and curbed her tongue. Work continued apace, with considerably more decorum, and all the stalls were ready by half past twelve.

The helpers returned to their homes to dish up spam, whale meat, a piece of unidentifiable fish or some other wartime delicacy, before returning to the fray at two-thirty.

The open warfare between Mrs Jarman and Mrs Pringle was a source of much pleasure to all who witnessed it, and each skirmish was noted with interest.

It was generally felt that the Battle of the Buttons would have some repercussions, probably on that same day, but there was no sign of anything other than disdain on Mrs Pringle's side and raucous laughter on Mrs Jarman's. Both ladies, in any case, were kept busy with the throng of customers snapping up old shoes, stained waistcoats and cracked crockery throughout the afternoon. Those who had witnessed the earlier exchange were slightly disappointed.

Over the months the shirt button incident was forgotten, and it was not until after Christmas that the sequel to the quarrel became general knowledge in Fairacre.

One of the uses to which the village hall's large copper was put during war time was the communal boiling of the village's Christmas puddings. Each basin was clearly labelled with its owner's name, and all were lodged securely in the capacious boiler.

Naturally, the water had to be topped up at intervals, and a list of ladies was pinned up on the wall. The afternoon session was designated thus:

2.30 Mrs Pringle
3.30 Miss Parr (only that would really be her maid carry-
       ing out her elderly mistress's orders)
4.30 Mrs Jarman
5.30 Everyone welcome

This was when the puddings would be claimed by their owners, the boiler turned off, and the village hall locked for the night. The precious puddings, of course, were then carefully stored away in Fairacre larders to await Christmas Day.

It was innocent little Mrs Morgan, unwilling hostess to the Jarman family, who spread the news of Mrs Pringle's remarkable Christmas pudding about the village of Fairacre.

It so happened that Mrs Pringle had invited her sister and niece to share the Christmas festivities with her son John and herself. Corporal Fred Pringle was on military duty, and so was Jane Morgan's husband.

The Jarmans had invited a horde of relatives and friends to spend the day with them, and Mrs Pringle, prompted more by malice against the Jarmans rather than neighbourliness to Jane Morgan, hastened to invite that lady to share their Christmas dinner. As Jane and Mrs Pringle's sister were old friends, the invitation was gratefully accepted.

The roast duck was delicious, the vegetables beautifully cooked, and everyone was most complimentary.

The Christmas pudding, steaming and aromatic, awaited Mrs Pringle's knife. It was apparent, as soon as the first slice was removed, that a number of foreign bodies mingled with the glutinous mixture.

'Threepenny bits!' shouted John.

'Sixpences!' squeaked his cousin excitedly.

Mrs Pringle's bewilderment was apparent. 'I don't hold with metal objects in a pudding,' she said austerely, passing plates.

'Quite right,' agreed Jane. 'My mother always said the same, but she did put little china dolls in when we were small. We used to wash them afterwards and put them in the dolls' house.'

But no one was listening to her reminiscences. Forks and spoons were busy pushing the pudding this way and that, and on the rim of each plate a pile of assorted shirt buttons grew larger.

'*Someone*,' said Mrs Pringle with a face like thunder, 'has been playing tricks on us, and I know just who it is!'

At that moment, a particularly loud yell of half-tipsy laughter could be heard through the wall.

Mrs Pringle rose majestically and went to open the last precious tin of pineapple chunks to augment the despoiled Christmas pudding.

Boxing Day had hardly passed before the sequel to the Battle of the Buttons was known to all Fairacre. But Mrs Jarman denied any knowledge of it.

It was Mrs Willet who told me this tale. She and many other Fairacre folk had happy memories of the evacuees, and the relationship was kept fresh by an annual reunion in our village hall each summer.

Soon after I had settled in Fairacre, I was invited to help in getting preparations ready for the visitors. As you can imagine, I looked out for Mrs Jarman, and there she was, a little sharp-faced woman with unnaturally blonde hair and lots of make-up. Her shrill laugh rang out over the general hubbub, and I saw Mrs Pringle sail by with face averted. Mrs Jarman made some comment which was greeted with half-scandalised tittering from the cronies around her. Could it have been some quip about shirt buttons, I wondered?

I could quite understand the affection which had grown up between our country women and their town guests during the dark days of war. Mrs Jarman epitomised the cockney effervescence which had survived the blitz, and defied threats and even death itself.

Mrs Willet and I walked home together when the party was over and our visitors had boarded their coaches.

Mrs Willet spoke wistfully. 'I always liked those Londoners. They were a real larky lot!'

I had just arrived home, and was sitting on the couch with my feet up, wondering if I had the strength to switch on the kettle after my labours, when Amy arrived looking as chic as ever.

'You look terrible,' she said in that downright tone old friends use when making wounding remarks. 'Honestly, you look ten years older than when I saw you last.'

'So would you,' I retorted, 'if you had spent the day coping with evacuees.'

'Good grief! Don't say another war's started!'

'No, just a hang-over from the last,' and I went on to explain.

'I expect you'd like a cup of tea,' I added, suddenly remembering my duties as hostess, and wondering if I could ever move from the couch.

'Well . . .' began Amy, and then stopped as I began to laugh. 'What's the joke?'

'Do you remember a wartime cartoon in *Punch*? The hostess is saying: "If you *do* take milk in your tea, it is absolutely no bother for me to get out my bike and cycle three miles to the farm." Well, I feel a bit like that.'

'I'll put on the kettle,' said Amy kindly, and went to do so.

I stirred myself to follow her after a few minutes, and found her peering into three tins, each containing tea.

'Which do I use? You really should have these labelled, you know.'

'Well, *I* know which is which, so it would be a waste of time and labels. That blue one has Earl Grey, the red one holds Indian, and the black one has Darjeeling in it – I think, but I'm not sure, so I hardly ever use it. Anyway it takes ages to get to the right colour.'

'You really are hopelessly disorganised,' said Amy, spooning Indian tea into the teapot. 'I'll write you three labels myself when we've had this.'

'Wicked waste of paper,' I told her, 'cutting down all those forests to make labels.'

We carried our mugs into the sitting room and smiled at each other over the steam.

'How's James?' I asked.

'Off to Amsterdam at the end of the week.'

'He might bring you back some diamonds,' I said.

'An Edam cheese, more likely,' responded Amy. 'He can eat it by the pound, but I find it too rubbery.'

She began to look about her in an enquiring way. 'Have you got a mat, or a tile, or something for me to put this hot mug on? I don't like standing it on the table. Even yours,' she added unnecessarily.

'Oh, don't be so fussy!' I retorted. 'Bung it down on the corner of the newspaper.'

'Well, it may mark the television programmes for this evening, but I don't suppose that's any great loss. I pine to have a play about ordinary normal people instead of all these programmes about unfortunates who can't see, or can't hear, or have other disabilities.'

'I know. I'm getting tired too of having my withers wrung every time I switch on. If it isn't flood or famine, it's more sophisticated ways of killing each other.'

Amy moved her mug to the edge of the newspaper and studied the evening's offerings.

'There's an hour of medical horrors, including a blow-by-blow, or perhaps cut-by-cut might be a better description, of a hip replacement operation. On another channel there's a jolly half-hour entitled "How to Succeed despite Degenerative Diseases", and there's a discussion on the radio about "The Horrors of our Geriatric Wards"!'

'Mrs Pringle should be all right tonight then,' I said. 'She told me she loves a good operation on the telly.'

'And how is the lady? Is her leg still in a state of spontaneous combustion?'

'It's fairly quiescent at the moment, although she did roll down her stocking yesterday, when the children were out in the playground, to show me her varicose veins.'

'I hope you studied them with due reverence.'

'One glance was more than enough,' I confessed. 'I think she thought me very callous not to spend longer poring over them. Her parting shot was to the effect that Veins Come To Us All, and that my time would soon come.'

'Ah well,' said Amy, 'she may be right at that. Now, are you going to let me label those tea tins before I go?'

'No, Amy dear. I'll just muddle along as usual.'

'You know,' she remarked, flicking a dead leaf from the window sill, 'having Mrs Pringle once a week might be a good thing in this place. Why don't you think about it?'

'I have. Nothing doing. You know yourself what a pain in the neck she is.'

'Yes, but sometimes this house . . .' She let her voice trail away into something like despair.

I put my arm comfortingly round her shoulders as we went out to the car. 'Don't worry about me. I'm managing perfectly well on my own,' I told her.

Later I was to remember this conversation.

As time passed I began to realise that Mrs Pringle was slightly more approachable during the summer months than the winter ones. I put this down to the fact that her cleaning duties were considerably lighter. For one thing, the treasured stoves were not in use, and so less mess was caused by the carrying of coke to and fro.

Naturally, a certain amount was scrunched into the school floorboards by miscreants who had disobeyed rules and had run up and down the coke pile in the playground. Mrs Pringle's eagle eye soon noticed any traces of the offending fuel and complained bitterly.

I sometimes thought too that she missed her cosseting of the stoves during the summer months. A flick with a duster night and morning was all that was needed, and it seemed to me that, in some perverse way, she regretted the ministrations with blacklead and brush which dominated the winter months.

Nevertheless, on the whole, she appeared marginally more cheerful in the summer. The light evenings gave her more scope in arranging her cleaning activities, and I frequently heard her singing some lugubrious hymn as she went about her work when I was in the garden after school hours.

It so happened that one particular April was unseasonably warm, and I decreed that the stoves could be allowed to go out.

'Well, I'm not arguing about that,' said Mrs Pringle. 'Dear knows I've got enough to do in this place, and it'll be a treat not to have coke all over the floor.'

She walked quite briskly about the classroom, dusting energetically without a trace of a limp, before the children came into morning prayers.

'I'll put the stoves to rights this evening,' she told me as she departed. 'See you midday.'

She always returned in the early afternoon to wash up the school dinner things. Usually our paths did not cross then, for I was teaching and she was alone in the lobby.

On this particular day I heard her at her labours. At the same time, the bell of St Patrick's church next door began to toll. The children looked up from their work and there was some whispering.

I went out to the lobby to see if Mrs Pringle could enlighten me. Obviously, someone of local importance had died. Mrs Pringle was standing in the steamy lobby, her hands red and puffy from her task. To my amazement she was trembling and there were tears in her eyes.

'It's Miss Parr,' she said, before I could make any enquiry, 'went sudden about five this morning.'

'It has upset you,' I replied, as much in wonderment as in sympathy. This was the first time I had seen Mrs Pringle in a weak condition. I was much moved.

'She was good to me. I was in service with her before I married.'

'I did know that.'

'Gave me this and that quite frequent, but that weren't all.'

'What else?'

'She took my word against others when I was in trouble once. I never forgot that. I might have lost my job, but she stood by me.'

Two tears rolled down her cheeks, and I found myself patting her substantial shoulder.

'Well, this won't do,' she said, sniffing loudly, 'can't bring back the dead, can you? Best get on with my job.'

She sounded much more like her tough old self, and I left her smoothing the tea towels over the still-warm boiler to dry.

But I noticed that her puffy hands still trembled.

Later that evening I pondered over this surprising episode. I remembered Alice Willet's account of the row over the chauffeur and his fierce denial of any interest in the love-lorn Maud, and his consequent departure to foreign parts.

It looked as though Mrs Pringle still had feelings of guilt over her part in the proceedings. Did she regret her faults as poignantly as she mourned the loss of the dashing Henry in his bottle-green uniform? And had Fred Pringle, the next best thing, ever given her any comfort in the years between?

So much must remain conjecture, but one thing was certain. Mrs Pringle, my arch enemy, had some human feelings after all. Those few sad minutes in the steamy lobby had been a revelation to me, and I felt a new regard for her.

Chapter Six

JOSEPH COGGS AND MRS PRINGLE

Every community has its problem families. At Springbourne, our neighbouring village, the black sheep was Fred Pringle's brother Josh and his unfortunate relations.

In Fairacre we had the Coggs family. As in the case of Josh Pringle, all blame for the situation lay squarely on the shoulders of Arthur Coggs, the father. By nature he was lazy and of low intelligence. Added to that was his addiction to drink which made him boastful and belligerent when in his cups. It also made him a petty thief for he could not do without his beer, and was very seldom treated; Arthur Coggs, it was soon discovered, never stood his round.

He had various jobs, none of which lasted very long. He occasionally found casual work as a labourer on a building site, or as a roadman for the Caxley council. But absence, arriving late, and taking time off to visit the nearest pub soon ended his employment.

Mr Roberts, the Fairacre farmer, had done his best to give him work. He pitied Arthur's poor down-trodden wife, and the fast-growing family, but Arthur's feckless ways soon exhausted his employer's patience, and apart from a little spasmodic field work at the appropriate time, Mr Roberts could do no more.

The village folk looked upon the Coggses with mingled pity and exasperation.

'If that gel of Arthur's had taken the rolling pin to him early on,' said Mr Willet roundly, 'she'd have done the right thing.'

'But he could easily have killed her,' I cried. 'She's a poor wispy little thing and must be terrified of him.'

'Bullies is always cowards,' replied Mr Willet trenchantly. 'Arthur's got away with it too easy, that's his trouble.'

Naturally, Mrs Pringle was the loudest in her condemnation of the slatternly ways of Mrs Coggs and her husband. As a strict teetotaller she also deplored Arthur's drunken habits.

'I know for a fact he signed the pledge, same as dozens of us years ago. A fat lot of good that done him. He's a proper waster, and we're all sorry for his poor wife. Not that she does much to help herself or that row of kids. She may be short of money, I give you that, but soap and water cost nothing, and those children and the house are a disgrace.'

'She doesn't have much of a chance,' I observed, opening the register and looking pointedly at the wall clock which said ten to nine.

'Those as behaves like doormats,' quoth Mrs Pringle, 'gets treated like 'em!'

As usual, she had the last word, and swept out into the lobby, meeting the rush of children who were swarming into school.

I had been at Fairacre School some five or six years when Joseph Coggs became a pupil. I liked the child from the start. He was dark-haired and dark-skinned, with large mournful eyes. Somewhere in the past there had been gipsy forebears. He was appreciative of all that happened in school, and seemed to settle into an ordered way of life for which his early years could not have trained him.

He was in Miss Clare's class in the infants' room, so that I did not see a great deal of him. But he was an enthusiastic eater, and demolished his plates of school dinner with a joy which I shared whilst watching him.

The Coggs family lived in a broken-down cottage, one of four collectively called Tyler's Row. Their landlord was an old soldier who could not afford to keep the property in good heart, and it was widely thought that it would be better to see the whole place pulled down, and the families rehoused.

Not that all four cottages were as deplorable as the Coggs' establishment. The Waites next door kept their identical accommodation as neat as a new pin. An elderly couple in the first cottage were also house-proud, and Mrs Fowler who lived in the last one, although feared by all for her violent temper, was certainly house-proud to the point of fanaticism.

It was not surprising that the Coggses were a source of trouble to their close neighbours. Arthur Coggs's habit of roaring home when the pubs had closed did not make him popular. The neglected garden sent its weeds into the neighbouring neat plots, and the cries of unhappy children were clearly heard through the thin dividing walls.

'I wouldn't live near them Coggses for a bag of gold,' Mrs Pringle told me. 'They get more help than the rest of the village put together, but what good does that do 'em? All goes down Arthur's throat, that's what!'

As usual, she was right of course. Mrs Partridge, our vicar's wife, had told me of the kindness of people in the village who had provided clothes, bed linen, furniture and even pots and pans for the pathetic family.

'Most of the stuff,' said Mrs Partridge, 'was never seen again. Arthur exchanged all he could with his cronies and put the money on the bar counter. Gerald has taken him to task on many occasions, and I think he tries for a day or two, but soon falls back into his old bad habits. He was put on probation after one court appearance, and things were slightly better when the probation officer kept an eye on the family. But it really is a hopeless task.'

Mrs Pringle's attitude to Joseph Coggs on his arrival as a pupil was one of lofty disdain. Anyone, or anything, as grubby as the little boy was unwelcome. Not that she said anything to hurt the child's feelings, but he was ignored rather pointedly, I considered, and my affection for him was obviously deplored.

Not long after his entry into the school, there was a most disturbing incident. Mr Roberts, the farmer who is also one of Fairacre School's governors, had been missing eggs from the nest-boxes. He suspected that one of the children had been taking them, and very reluctantly asked me if he could look through the pockets of the coats hanging in the lobby.

Poor man! He was most unhappy about it all. We asked the

children if they knew anything about it, but there was no response. Consequently, Mr Roberts and I went through their pockets and found three marked eggs in young Eric's pocket.

When faced with this, the boy confessed tearfully that he had indeed been taking the eggs, and on several occasions.

'And I give some to little Joe Coggs,' he sniffled abjectly. 'He saw me, and I never wanted him to tell.'

We dealt with the malefactor fairly leniently as he obviously was suffering much, though not as severely as Mr Roberts himself who was far more agitated than Eric or young Joseph when I confronted the little boy later. He had handed the eggs to his mother, who must have guessed that they were obtained by stealing, but was too delighted with the gift to take the matter further.

Mrs Pringle's attitude to the incident was predictable. 'What do you expect from that lot?' she asked dismissively.

'It won't happen again,' I assured her, 'both boys were very contrite.'

'It's easy enough to be *contrite*, as you call it, when you've been found out. But in my opinion, that Joe wants watching. Them Coggses is all tarred with the same brush.'

All the new entrants settled in quickly that term under Miss Clare's kindly guidance, and Joseph, although not particularly bright academically, proved to be a helpful and happy little boy.

The weather remained quite warm all through September and the early part of October, but suddenly the chill of autumn struck with clammy fog which veiled the downs and misted the school windows.

Our building is old and damp, and the skylight an ever-present trouble to us, admitting rain in wet weather and a howling draught at all times.

'Better start the stoves,' I said to Mrs Pringle, and waited for the usual delaying tactics.

'Bob Willet hasn't done me any kindling wood.'

'I'll see him at dinner time.'

'One of the coke hods is broken at the bottom.'

'I'll indent for another one. You should have told me before.'

'Matches is short, too.'

'I'll bring you a box from the house at play time.'

Then, her final thrust: 'What will The Office say?'

'I can deal with the Office. *Just light the stoves!*'

Mrs Pringle, bristling with umbrage and muttering darkly, left my presence limping heavily.

We needed those stoves in the weeks that followed for winter seemed to have arrived early. A sharp east wind blew away the fog after some days, and draughts whistled round the classrooms. Every time the door opened, papers fluttered to the floor and top-heavy vases, stuffed with branches of autumn foliage, capsized and spilt water, berries and leaves everywhere. It was impossible to dodge the draught from the skylight, and I had a stiff neck only partially eased by a scarf tied round it.

The children wore their winter woollies or dungarees. Summer sandals were exchanged for wellingtons or stout shoes. The shabbiest of all the children was Joseph, but even he had an extra cardigan – once owned by a girl if the buttoning was anything to go by – and I noticed that Miss Clare had moved him to a desk close to the stove.

The infants went home a quarter of an hour earlier than my class, but on one particularly bitter afternoon, as I was seeing my children out, I saw that Joseph was still in the playground.

'I was waitin' for Ernest,' he said gruffly in reply to my questioning. 'I goes a bit of the way with him.'

The child's hands were red with the cold, and he was sniffing lustily. I handed him a tissue from my pocket supply.

'No gloves?' I asked.

'No, miss.'

At that moment Ernest appeared.

'Well put your hands in your pockets,' I advised, 'and run along together to get warm.'

A few days later I had occasion to go into Miss Clare's classroom. As in my own, a row of damp scarves and gloves steamed gently over the top rail of the fireguard round the tortoise stove. Among the motley collection was a pair of thick red woollen gloves, obviously expertly knitted in double-knitting wool. I turned them over to help the drying process.

Joseph, from his nearby desk, looked up with pride. 'They's mine,' he said, 'Mrs Pringle give 'em to me.'

I exchanged puzzled glances with Miss Clare.

'I'll tell you later,' she whispered.

It all happened evidently on the afternoon when I had despatched Ernest and Joseph homeward in the bitter cold.

When Ernest had turned into his cottage, not far from the school, Joseph had continued on his solitary way. Most of his schoolfellows had run homeward, keen to get to the fireside and some welcoming food. Joseph, whose home was short of both comforts, dawdled along the village street, occasionally looking through a lighted window for interest.

As he came to the Post Office, which stood back from the village street, he was surprised, and a little alarmed, to hear a shout from Mr Lamb standing in his doorway.

'Joe! Come here a minute, boy.'

Wondering if he had done anything wrong, Joe approached. Grown-ups meant authority, and young Joseph was wary of tangling with those in power, used as he was to his parents' attitude to the police, the probation officer and even the kindly vicar himself.

Mr Lamb, unaware of the trepidation in young Joe's heart, was holding out a large door key.

'Can you nip round to Mrs Pringle's, Joe? She left the school key here when she dropped in for some stamps just now. She'll need it to get in for her cleaning any time now.'

Joseph, much relieved, and somewhat flattered to be entrusted with this task, nodded his assent and Mr Lamb put the heavy key into the small cold palm, folding the fingers over it.

'Don't drop it, will you? Be a fine old to-do if that got lost. I can't leave the shop, or I'd pop down myself, but it's not much beyond your place.'

'That's all right,' replied Joseph, and set off, clutching his burden.

His trepidation returned when he got to Mrs Pringle's back door. No one in his station of life would dare to knock at the front one, and Joseph automatically trotted round to the rear door, knocked timidly, and waited.

Mrs Pringle, who had seen the little figure coming up the path, appeared in the doorway. Mutely, Joseph held out the key. Here was authority at its most formidable, and the child was struck dumb.

'Well, I'm blowed!' said Mrs Pringle, dignity abandoned in her shock. 'Where did you get that, Joe?'

'Mr Lamb,' faltered Joseph. 'You left it in the Post Office.'

'I've been looking all over for it,' said Mrs Pringle, 'and been worrying about where it could be. Been through my oil-cloth bag times without number, and was just going to search the street.'

She took the key from the child's hand, and felt how cold it was, as cold as the heavy key itself.

'Where's your gloves, boy?'

'Ain't got none.'

'Not at home even?'

'No.'

Mrs Pringle snorted, and Joseph felt his fear returning. Was it so wrong not to have gloves?

'Well, you're a good boy to have brought my key back. You run along home now before it gets dark, and thank you.'

The child turned without a word, cold hands thrust into the pockets of his dilapidated raincoat, and made his way homeward.

Later in the day when I had first seen Joe's new gloves, Mrs Pringle and I were alone in the classroom. The children had gone home and all was quiet.

I locked my desk drawers while Mrs Pringle dusted window sills and hummed 'Lead kindly light, amid the encircling gloom', rather flat.

The key in my hand reminded me of Joseph Coggs. Curiosity prompted me to broach the subject.

'Young Joe has a splendid pair of winter gloves,' I observed.

The humming stopped, and Mrs Pringle faced me, looking disconcerted, which was a rare occurrence.

'Well, time he had! No child should be out in this weather with his hands bare.'

'No,' I agreed. She was about to resume her dusting, but I wanted to know more.

'And were you the kind soul who knitted them?'

Mrs Pringle sat heavily on a desk which creaked in protest.

'The child did me a good turn,' she said. 'I been and left the school key on Mr Lamb's counter, and he give it to Joe to bring along to me. And that child's hands!'

Here Mrs Pringle raised her own podgy ones in horror. 'Cold as clams, they was. A perishing day it was, as well I know, having to get these stoves going far too early. I don't hold with encouraging them Coggses in their slatternly ways, but there's such a thing as Christian Kindness, and seeing how young Joe had helped me out, I thought: "One good turn deserves another" and I got down to the knitting that same evening.'

'It was very good of you,' I said sincerely.

'Well, I had a bit of double-knitting over from our John's sweater, and it did just nicely. The boy seemed grateful. I slipped them to him a morning or two later, and told him to keep them out of his dad's sight.'

'Surely he wouldn't take those?'

'Arthur Coggs,' said Mrs Pringle, 'would drink the coat off your back, if you gave him a chance. And now, if I don't get this dusting done I shan't be back in time to get Pringle's tea.'

Thus dismissed, I left her to her cleaning. She was still humming as I closed the door – it sounded like 'Abide with me', rather sharp.

Whether it was the inescapable draught from the skylight, the wintry weather, or simply what the medical profession calls 'a virus' these days, the result was the same. I went down with an appalling cold.

It was one of those which cannot be ignored. For several days I had been at the tickly throat stage with an occasional polite blow into a handkerchief, but one night, soon after my conversation with Mrs Pringle, all the germs rose up in a body and attacked me.

By morning every joint ached, eyes streamed, head throbbed and I was too cowardly to take my temperature. It was quite clear that I should be unable to go over to the school, for as well as being highly infectious and pretty useless, I was what Mr Willet described once as 'giddy as a whelk'.

I scribbled a note to Miss Clare, and dropped it from my bedroom window to the first responsible child to appear in the playground.

At twenty to nine, my gallant assistant appeared at the bedroom door.

'Don't come any nearer,' I croaked. 'I'm absolutely leprous. I'm so sorry about this. As soon as it is nine o'clock I'll ring the Office and see if we can get a supply teacher for a couple of days.'

'I shall ring the Office,' said Miss Clare, with great authority, 'and I shall bring you a cup of tea and some aspirins, and see that Doctor Martin calls.'

I was too weak to argue and accepted her help gratefully.

After my cup of tea I must have fallen asleep, for the next I knew was the sound of Doctor Martin's voice as he came up-stairs. As always, he was cheerful, practical and brooked no argument.

'When did this start?' he asked when he had put the thermometer into my mouth.

I wondered, not for the first time, why doctors and dentists ask questions when you are effectively gagged by the tools of their trade.

'About two or three days ago,' I replied, when released from the thermometer.

'You should have called me then,' he said severely. How is it, I wondered, that doctors can so quickly put you in the wrong?

Relenting, he patted my shoulder. 'You'll do. I'll just write you a prescription and you are to stay in bed until I come again.'

'And when will that be?' I asked, much alarmed.

'The day after tomorrow. But I shan't let you loose until that temperature's gone down.'

He collected his bits and pieces, gave me a beaming smile, and vanished.

I resumed my interrupted slumbers.

It was getting dark when I awoke, and I could hear the children running across the playground on their way home. I could also hear movements downstairs, and wondered if Miss Clare had come over again on a mission of mercy, but to my surprise, it was Amy who appeared, bearing a tea tray.

I struggled up, wheezing a welcome.

'Dolly Clare rang me,' she said, 'and as James is in Budapest, or it may be Bucharest, I was delighted to come. What's more, I've collected your prescription, and pretty dire it looks and smells.'

She deposited a bottle of dark brown liquid on the bedside table.

'I may not need it,' I said, 'after a good cup of tea.'

'You'll do as you're told,' replied Amy firmly, 'and take your nice medicine as Doctor Martin said.'

We sipped our tea in amicable silence, and then Amy told me that she intended to stay until the doctor called again.

'But what about the school? I can't leave Miss Clare to cope alone.'

'Someone's coming out tomorrow, I gather, and in any case, I could do a hand's turn. I *am* a trained teacher, if you remember, and did rather better than you did in our final grades.'

She vanished to make up the spare bed, and left me to my muddled thoughts for some time. I thought I heard her talking outside in the playground. but decided it must be Miss Clare or even Mrs Pringle going about their affairs.

When Amy reappeared, the clock said half past seven.

'I can't think what's happened to today,' I complained, 'I must keep falling asleep.'

'You do,' she assured me, 'and a good thing too.'

'But there's such a lot to do. The kitchen's in a fine mess. I left yesterday's washing up, and the grate hasn't been cleared.'

'Oh yes, it has! Mrs Pringle came over after she'd finished at the school. She had it all spick and span in half an hour.'

'Amy,' I squeaked, 'you haven't asked *Mrs Pringle* to help! You know how I've resisted all this time.'

'And what's more,' went on Amy imperturbably, 'she is quite willing to come every Wednesday afternoon, if you need her.'

'Traitor!' I said, but I was secretly amused and relieved.

'Time for medicine,' replied Amy, advancing on the bottle.

Chapter Seven

CHRISTMAS

As so often happens in the wake of nervous apprehension, reality proved less severe than my fears.

The advent of Mrs Pringle into my personal affairs had its advantages. For one thing, the house benefited immediately from her ministrations. Furniture gleamed like satin, windows were crystal clear, copper and brass objects were dazzling, and even door knobs on cupboards, which had never hitherto seen a spot of Brasso, were transformed.

The beauty of it was, from my point of view, that I hardly came across the lady when she was at her labours. She chose to come on a Wednesday afternoon. (Mrs Hope, that paragon of domestic virtue who had been an earlier occupant in the school house, had always preferred Wednesdays, according to Mrs Pringle.) So Wednesday it was.

She went straight from her washing up in the school lobby to my house, and worked from half past one until four o'clock. As I was teaching then it meant that I seldom saw her in the house, but simply marvelled at the shining surfaces when I returned.

Occasionally, of course, I ran into her and we would share a pot of tea before she set off for home.

It was on one of these tea-drinking sessions that she first told me about her niece, Minnie Pringle, daughter of the black sheep of the family, Josh Pringle of Springbourne.

'She come up this morning to see if I'd got any jumble for their W.I. sale next week. At least, that's what *she said* she'd come for, but it was money she was after for herself.'

I knew that the girl had two small children, so enquired innocently if her husband was out of work.

'*Work?* A *husband?*' cried Mrs Pringle. 'Minnie never had a husband. These two brats of hers is nothing more than you-know-what beginning with a B but I wouldn't soil my lips with saying it.'

'Oh dear,' I said feebly. 'I didn't realise . . .'

'And another on the way, as far as I could see this morning. One is one thing, most people give a girl the benefit of the doubt. But two is taking things too far, especially when the silly girl can't say for sure who the father is.'

'She must have *some* idea.'

'Not Minnie, 'she's that feckless she just wouldn't remember. Not that she's entirely to blame. That father of hers, our Josh — though I'm ashamed to claim him as part of the Pringle family — he's an out and out waster, and his poor wife is as weak-minded as our Minnie. Nothing but a useless drudge, and never gave Minnie any idea of Right and Wrong.'

'But surely —' I began, but was swept aside by Mrs Pringle's rhetoric. Mrs P. in full spate is unstoppable.

'I told her once, "If you can't tell that girl of yours the facts of life, then send her to church regular. She'll soon find out all about adultery."'

It seemed a somewhat narrow approach to the church's teachings but I did not have the strength to argue.

'More tea?' I asked.

Mrs Pringle raised a massive hand, rather as if she were holding up the traffic. 'Thank you, no. I'm awash. Must get along to fetch my washing in. It looks as though there's rain to come.'

I accompanied her to the gate. A few children were still in the playground taking their time to go home.

'Mind you,' said Mrs Pringle, dropping her voice to a conspiratorial whisper in deference, I presumed, to the innocent ears so near us, 'if there *is* another on the way, I shan't put myself out with more baby knitting. Minnie don't have any idea how to wash knitted things. It's my belief she *boils them!*'

*

As Christmas approached that term, the school began to deck itself ready for the festival.

In the infants' room a Christmas frieze running around the walls kept Miss Briggs's children busy. Santa Claus, decked in plenty of cotton wool, Christmas trees, reindeer resembling rabbits, otters, large dogs and other denizens of the animal world, as well as sacks of toys, Christmas puddings, Christmas stockings and various other domestic signs of celebration were put in place by the young teacher's careful hands, and glitter was sprayed plentifully at strategic points.

At least, the stuff was supposed to be at strategic points such as the branches of the Christmas trees, but glitter being what it is we found it everywhere. It appeared on the floor, on the window sills, in the cracks of desks, and sometimes a gleam would catch our eyes in the school dinner, blown there, no doubt, by the draught from the door. The stoves suffered too, much to Mrs Pringle's disgust.

In my own room, glitter was banned on the grounds that we had quite enough from the room next door, but we had a large picture of a Christmas tree, on which the children stuck their own bright paintings. We also made dozens of Christmas cards for home consumption, and some rather tricky boxes to hold sweets.

I bought the sweets, a nice straightforward approach to Christmas jollifications. The construction of the boxes, which appeared such a simple operation from the diagram in *The Teachers' World*, was not so easy. Half the boxes burst open at the seams whilst being stuck together. The rest looked decidedly drunken. By the time we had substituted a household glue for the paste we had so hopefully mixed up, the place reeked with an unpleasant fishy smell and I was apprehensive about the sweets although they were wrapped.

However, nothing could quell the high spirits of the children, and the traditional Christmas party for their parents and friends of the school was its usual jubilant occasion on the last afternoon.

We all wished each other a happy Christmas as our guests made their way out into the December dark. I waved goodbye until the last figure had disappeared, locked the school door upon the chaos within – plentifully besprinkled with glitter – and returned thankfully to the peace of the school house.

Tomorrow, I had told Mrs Pringle, would be soon enough to tackle the clearing up, and I would give her a hand.

Meanwhile, I was content to sit down in my armchair and to let the blessed quietness of my home surround and soothe me.

I slept like a log, and then ate a hearty breakfast, much cheered by the thought that it was the first day of the holidays.

Amy had invited me to her house at Bent for Christmas, and as it fell conveniently on a Sunday this year I should have a wonderful weekend amidst the luxury of Amy and James's home.

Meanwhile, I remembered my duty to Mrs Pringle, and hurried across the playground to the school to set about taking down the decorations and putting away some of the Christmas pictures.

I half expected to hear Mrs Pringle's morose singing as I approached. Instead, I heard her scolding someone, and thought that she might have surprised a child returning to collect something it had forgotten in the excitement of the Christmas party.

But it was not one of my schoolchildren who was being harangued. A little boy of three or four years was sucking his thumb and gazing at the school cleaner. He did not appear to be at all upset.

'Ah, Miss Read,' cried Mrs Pringle, 'I'm sorry to be burdened with *this*, today of all days, but our Minnie has had to catch the Caxley, and there was only me to mind this 'un.'

'The Caxley' is the term used in our downland villages for either the bus which goes to Caxley, as in this case, or for the local newspaper *The Caxley Chronicle*.

'You must have seen it in the *Caxley*,' we say. 'There was a wedding photo in the *Caxley*,' and so on.

'Our Min's taken the other child to *hospital*,' continued Mrs Pringle, giving full weight and reverence to the last word. 'There was an *accident*!'

'Oh dear! What happened?'

Mrs Pringle eyed the little boy who was idly wiping his wet thumb along the edge of my desk.

'Give over!' bellowed Mrs Pringle, nearly making me jump out of my skin. The child appeared unmoved.

'I'll give him something to do,' I said hastily, always the teacher, and went to the cupboard for paper and crayons. We settled the child in a distant desk, and I prepared to listen to Mrs Pringle's account.

For the sake of appearances I took a few drawing pins out of the pictures pinned to the wooden partition, and dropped them back into their tin.

'That Minnie,' said Mrs Pringle in a wrathful whisper, 'brought these two in first thing this morning with some cock-and-bull story about collecting evergreens and ivy and that for Springbourne church. As if Springbourne hasn't got ivy enough without coming all the way to Fairacre!'

'Quite,' I said.

'Well, I'd just put some dried peas to soak for tomorrow's dinner, and before you could say Jack Robinson that dratted first kid of hers had the bowl over and was fiddling about on the floor, getting in everyone's way as we started to pick up the mess. Then what?'

She stopped dramatically. The silence was split by the sound of an appalling sniff from our visitor. Automatically I handed him a tissue from my permanent store, and returned to Mrs Pringle.

'We'd hardly got the peas back in the bowl and put fresh water on 'em, when that child started grizzling, and fidgeting with his ear-'ole. D'you know what that little varmint had done?'

'Stuffed a pea in his ear,' I said, 'it often happens. With beads too, if they are small enough. And I once had a child push a hazelnut up its nose, from the nature table –'

But my tale was cut short by my fellow storyteller. She disliked having her thunder stolen.

'*One in each ear!*' roared Mrs Pringle. 'And I daresay he would have put more in his nose, and *elsewhere*, if we hadn't caught him. And could we get them out?'

I guessed correctly that this was only a rhetorical question intended to heighten the dramatic effect.

'With them being wet, you see,' resumed the lady, 'they was beginning to plump up – the peas, I mean, not his ears – and we tried everything, fingernails, pen knife, even a skewer –'

I must have shuddered.

'Well, we had to *try*,' said Mrs Pringle grumpily.

'Of course, of course.' I began to roll up a picture of a sleigh pulled by reindeer.

'So I said to Minnie, "It's no good you standing there hollering. Get on the Caxley with him and cut up to the Casualty. They'll have instruments for getting peas out of ear-'oles." Must be at it daily up there.'

'The best thing,' I agreed, still envisaging a meat skewer being twisted in the child's ear.

'So here I am, ten minutes late, and *hampered*, as you see.'

She cast a malevolent glance at the silent child who was now engrossed in scribbling energetically with his crayons. As far as I could see, he was drawing a tangle of multi-coloured wool, but it kept him quiet.

'I told Minnie I'd keep him till she got back, but there isn't another Fairacre till midday, unless she gets the Beech Green and walks the rest.'

She gave a sigh which rustled the pictures still on the wall. 'Children!' she groaned. 'D'you want them wash basins done too?'

'Yes please,' I said.

She pushed herself up from the desk where she had seated herself during the recital of her woes, and limped towards the lobby.

We continued our labours in silence.

It was good to go to Amy's. Dearly as I love my own home and the village of Fairacre, it is exciting to have a change of scenery and company.

Tibby, my spoilt cat, was in the care of Mr Willet who had promised to come up night and morning to see that all was well.

'Strikes me,' he had said, on being shown the pile of tins left for Tibby's sustenance, 'that that cat of yours eats a damn sight better than we do.'

'Well, it is *Christmas*,' I said weakly.

'I'll bring him up a slice of turkey,' replied Mr Willet, 'or ain't that good enough?'

I was not sure if he was being heavily sarcastic, or meant what he said, so I contented myself with sincere thanks, handing over a jar of stem ginger at the same time. I had once heard Mrs Willet say that they were 'both very partial' to ginger.

As always, it was bliss to stay at Amy's. Her house is quiet and beautiful, and looks out upon a southern-sloping garden and the Hampshire hills in the distance. My bedroom had the same aspect, and a bowl of early pale pink hyacinths scented the room.

'How clever of you to get them in bloom by Christmas!' I said. 'Mine are only an inch high, and they were planted at the beginning of term.'

'Choose Anne-Marie,' advised Amy, 'and leave them in the dark for at least two months. Then they roar ahead once you get them into the light.'

They obviously did for Amy, I thought, but would they for me?

Bent church, where Amy and James were regular attenders, was splendidly decorated on Christmas Day with arum lilies as well as Christmas roses and the usual evergreens. There was an air of opulence about the building which our modest St Patrick's lacked at Fairacre. A rich carpet covered the chancel, and the vicar's vestments were embroidered in gold thread, so much more ornate than the simple white cassock, laundered by Mrs Willet, which clothed Gerald Partridge.

But Bent church itself had a cathedral-like splendour, with side chapels and a roof of fan-vaulting. The choir was twice the size of our own, and obviously more musically proficient. The processional hymn had a beautiful and intricate descant which soared to the equally beautiful and intricate roof above, and raised all our spirits with it. Altogether, the service was gloriously inspiring, and I said so to Amy as we walked back.

'Our vicar,' said James, 'always excels himself at the major church festivals, and puts on a good show.'

It was said quite seriously, but I was rather taken aback by the last few words. Was there something theatrical about the service? Was there a display of pomp and ceremony which would not have been in order at St Patrick's?

And what if there were? The whole service had been to the glory of God and surely, I thought, it was only right and proper for the finest music and the most splendid flowers and vestments to be used to heighten the impact of the best-loved of all church festivals.

We needed a rest after our Christmas dinner, but as soon as we could move again Amy suggested that we all went for a walk before it grew dark.

James was always at his gayest in the open air. As a young man he had been a great sportsman, and even now had the litheness and spring of a twenty-year-old. He was a handsome fellow, and I quite understood how he had appealed to Amy.

He had the knack of making any woman feel that she was the only person in the world that interested him. He had a way of gazing intently into one's face, and although I was pretty sure that it was because he was short-sighted and too vain to wear spectacles, the result was still very pleasant.

The countryside south of Caxley was more wooded than that around Fairacre, and we scuffed our shoes amongst drifts of dead leaves as we threaded our way through a nearby copse. The bare branches creaked and rustled in a light breeze above us, and on the ground the rosettes of primrose leaves were already showing. It was heartening to see that the honeysuckle was already in tiny leaf, and blackbirds were calling to each other as if this mild weather were really spring.

We emerged from the wood into a wide meadow where sheep grazed. The grass was pale and dry, but the animals ate steadily, only raising their heads briefly to survey us as, jaws rotating methodically, they gazed at us without interest.

There was a stile before us which James vaulted in fine fashion, but Amy and I rested our arms upon it and gazed at the view. The horizon was the sort of blue one sees in Japanese prints, and beyond that, we knew, was the sea some seventy miles away. It was so peaceful and quiet that we might have been looking at a landscape by John Constable, all thought of towns, traffic and the madness of men left far behind.

'Are you coming?' called James from the distance.

Amy looked at me questioningly.

'As you like,' I said.

'We're going back,' she shouted.

James nodded and retraced his steps. He made another gallant attempt to clear the stile, but caught his foot on the top bar and fell.

He was unhurt, and lay on the ground laughing.

'You shouldn't show off at your age,' said Amy sternly.

But she was kind enough to haul him upright.

On Boxing Day Amy announced that a few old friends were coming for a midday drink.

'Everyone will be having cold turkey anyway,' she said, 'so that no one will have to worry about rushing back to see if all's well in the oven.'

'But they might have mince pies,' I pointed out.

'That's their lookout,' replied my friend, filling up delectable little silver receptacles, which my grandmother used to call 'bonbon dishes', with roasted almonds, cashew nuts and minute cheesy morsels.

'Do I know any of them?'

'John and Mary from next door. Bella and Bob from down the lane, and two very nice bachelors I wanted you to meet.'

My heart sank. Amy is an inveterate matchmaker, and after years of patient – and impatient – explanations on my part, she still harbours the hope that she will one day turn me into a middle-aged bride.

I forbore to question her more on the matter, but carried the little dishes into the sitting room and disposed them in strategic positions, only to watch Amy positioning them elsewhere when she came in.

The guests duly arrived. The married couples I had met before, and we greeted each other affectionately. We all agreed that the weather was unseasonably mild – and quoted: 'a green Christmas makes a full churchyard' – but what a blessing there was no snow! (Who, apart from Bing Crosby, we said, wanted a white Christmas?)

Both bachelors were of a suitable age to be married to me one day should any of the three of us feel inclined, but they were cheerful company, and prattled away about ski-ing and cheese dishes.

I was not much help to the one who was going ski-ing, but his companion, who had been given nearly three pounds of cheese for Christmas, was given a few recipes from my memory.

'Would you like some?' he asked eagerly. 'I could easily run over to Fairacre with a lump of Cheddar or Stilton – no bother at all.'

'It's terribly kind of you,' I replied, 'but I've been given quite a lot of cheese too, and shall have the deuce of a time eating it up.'

Afterwards, when all our guests had gone home to their cold turkey, and possibly over-cooked mince pies, Amy chided me for turning down Osbert's kind offer.

'It would have been so nice for you to meet again,' she said, 'I'm sure he was hoping to see you in the New Year.'

'He'll probably be giving a bumper cheese and wine party,' I said.

'That's possible,' agreed Amy, looking pleased. 'Good! You're bound to be asked.'

I left James and Amy after lunch on Wednesday so that I could drive home in the light.

I found Mrs Pringle just about to go home after putting my house to rights.

'And you had a good Christmas?' I enquired.

'A bit of an upset early on,' said she, 'but Christmas Day and Boxing Day went well, considering.'

I did not ask about the 'bit of an upset' in case it took too long to recount, but turned to wider issues.

'And all's well in Fairacre?'

'You'll be sorry to hear that Mr Mawne has gone to hospital.'

'Oh dear! What's wrong?'

A mulish look came over Mrs Pringle's countenance. 'That,' she said, 'I am not prepared to say.'

'Not prepared to say?' I echoed, absolutely dumbfounded.

If there is one thing Mrs Pringle loves beyond all others, it is the recounting, with nauseating details, of any ailment which has cropped up. As a squeamish woman I have suffered often in this way, and the thought that Mrs Pringle was willing to pass up a golden opportunity to discomfit me was more than I could comprehend.

My undisguised surprise prompted her to continue, however. 'It's a *gentleman's* complaint,' she said austerely, 'and farther than that I will not go.'

'I quite understand,' I managed to say. I was certainly not agog to hear about Henry Mawne's afflictions, gentlemanly or otherwise, and offered to run her home to change the subject.

'Thank you, but no! I have to go to the Post Office for my pension, and Alice Willet's for a sheet she's sides-to-middling for me.'

I accompanied her to the door. There she turned, and fixed me with a glinting eye. 'As well you know, I do my best not to speak Mr Mawne's name after *all that bother*, but I thought it was only Christian to mention it.'

'Oh, all that's forgiven and forgotten ages ago,' I said easily.

'Not by me it isn't,' said she implacably, and swept out to her errands.

Chapter Eight

TROUBLE FOR JOSH PRINGLE

'All that bother' to which Mrs Pringle referred had happened some months before.

After Miss Parr's death, her nephew John Parr inherited her lovely house. It was turned into three flats, and he kept the ground floor one.

As he was abroad on business a great deal, and later got married and moved away, Fairacre did not see much of John Parr but he had let the first floor flat to an acquaintance of his, a retired schoolmaster called Henry Mawne.

The village took to Henry Mawne. He was a friendly soul, and the vicar soon became grateful to him for his ease with figures and his willingness to straighten out some church accounts which had become sadly entangled by our highly literate, but completely innumerate, vicar.

He was a great bird-lover and had written several books on ornithology. He contributed to *The Caxley Chronicle* on topical nature matters, and altogether was considered a most welcome inhabitant of Fairacre.

He lived alone, and of course the usual rumours flew around:

(1) He was a widower, and his wife had died of cancer,

(2) He was a widower, and his wife had been killed in (a) a car crash (b) a train crash (c) a plane crash,

(3) He was a bachelor and had looked after his aged mother until matrimony seemed out of the question,

(4) He had been married but his wife had left him, and he was now (a) divorced (b) in a state of secret and well-hidden grief.

It was not long before the village made up its corporate mind that Henry Mawne and I should make a match of it. It was some time before this embarrassing fact percolated my innocent head and was then very difficult to ignore.

Mrs Pringle made arch remarks. Even Gerald Partridge meandered on about the happy outcome of marriages made 'when the partners are of mature years' and I began to get quite alarmed.

To give Henry Mawne his due, he seemed to be unaware of the gossip flying about, and apart from accompanying me to a concert in Caxley and bringing me a rather untidy bunch of daffodils picked from the thousands in his garden in the spring, he did not pay me any particularly ardent attentions.

But one day Mrs Pringle had gone too far. After telling me how much 'poor Mr Mawne' could do with a woman about the place, she told me that 'he was fair eating his heart out – and the whole village knew it.'

That did it. I told her that to repeat idle gossip could not only be hurtful but scandalous, and that I should have to consider consulting my solicitor.

At this, Mrs Pringle retaliated by giving in her notice – much to my secret relief.

She was away for a little over a week on this occasion, and very pleasant it was without her morose presence. Her niece Minnie, as mad as a March hare, came 'to oblige' in the school, but it was obvious that she could never be allowed to take on permanent duties.

In the end, of course, my old sparring partner returned, but I had been so fierce with her that she did her best never to mention Henry Mawne's name again in my presence.

In fact, Henry's wife turned up some time later, much to my relief and the disappointment of Fairacre in general. They had had their differences, and evidently had lived apart for some two years, but had decided to throw in their lot together again. It appeared to work, and I grew very fond of vociferous Mrs Mawne as the years passed.

But at that time, I was the unwilling recipient of a great deal of sympathy from neighbours who thought I might be heartbroken.

Mrs Pringle's silent tribute to my feelings expressed itself in a fine plump partridge, ready for roasting. I accepted it partly as an expression of condolence, but also as a peace-offering, and very good it was when it was dished up.

'The bit of an upset' which had preceded Mrs Pringle's Christmas that year, was recounted to me by Mr Willet. It involved the black sheep of the Pringle family, Josh Pringle from Springbourne.

It seems that as Christmas approached, his numerous children began to clamour for such things as a Christmas tree, a turkey, and, above all, presents.

Josh shook off these scandalous demands until his wife, unusually outspoken, added her weight to the children's.

'Of course you must get 'em something,' she told Josh when the children were in bed. 'Pity you never paid into a club like most people do, then we could have a few sweets and oranges and that to put in their stockings.'

'They gets all they need,' replied Josh. 'Anyway, clubs is your business. You gets the housekeeping.'

His wife gave a sarcastic laugh. 'That'll be the day! You give me what's in your pocket now and I'll see what I can do.'

'There ain't nothing in my pocket.'

'Gone on beer, I suppose. Self, self, self, and them poor kids without a present between them.'

Josh swore, rose from his armchair and walked out into the night to get a bit of peace.

As he mooched along the dark lanes, he pondered about Christmas and its expense. He supposed he would have to provide the minimum for the festivities or he would never hear the last of it. The thing was, where to get the money?

He had been given two weeks' work on a building site and the wages had gone already. Not only on beer, but also on one of those 'dead certs' in the three-thirty at Newbury which had unseated its rider in the first fifty yards, and run happily unencumbered, with its fellow racers, finishing well down the field.

Turning over the uncertainties of life in general, Josh plodded along the miry lane until he found himself on the outskirts of Fairacre. It was then that he remembered his brother Fred. Could he possibly touch him for a quid or two? He knew better than to approach Maud Pringle – she wouldn't give anyone a brass farthing, and a clump on the ear might well be collected by an importuning relative, Christmas or no Christmas. It had happened to Josh before, and he was not going to ask for another.

By this time he had reached Fred Pringle's house. He walked silently to the back door, his feet making no noise. Josh was not a poacher for nothing, and had deceived many a gamekeeper with his noiseless movements.

He could see Maud at her ironing through the kitchen window. She was late at her task, although Josh was not to know that, for Minnie had not returned from the hospital on the bus expected. She had arrived with the patient, happily freed from peas in his ears, two hours later than intended, and by that time Mrs Pringle had had more than enough of Josh's family. Some paper chains made the room gay, and a large red paper bell hung close above his sister-in-law's head.

There was no sign of Fred, but he might well be in the sitting room watching telly. Having come this far, Josh decided to knock and trust his luck. He would certainly stay well back out of arm's length of Fred's wife. He doubted if the Christmas spirit of peace on earth and goodwill to all men would extend to embrace him in Maud's eyes.

When the door opened Mrs Pringle gave a gasp. 'And what do *you* want?'

'Just passing. Thought I'd wish you a merry Christmas.'

Mrs Pringle snorted. 'You'd better see Fred. He's down the shed. I'm busy.'

With that the door slammed. It was no more than Josh had expected, and at least he had not been injured. He made his way down the concrete path, beneath the clothes line, to Fred's shed at the bottom of the garden, hard by the chicken run.

There was a queer droning noise coming from behind the

broken door. Josh listened for a moment, decided it was only his brother humming and knocked.

The droning stopped abruptly.

'What's up?' Fred sounded startled. Josh opened the door.

'Good lord! What brings you here?' said Fred.

'Just thought I'd wish you a merry Christmas,' replied Josh, 'happened to be passing like.'

'My Maud seen you?'

'She spoke to me at the back door.'

'I wonder you didn't get a clip round the ear.'

'What you up to?' said Josh, feeling it was wise to change the subject.

A pile of matchsticks, some stout cardboard and a pot of evil-smelling glue lay on the bench before his brother. He was sitting on a backless kitchen chair which looked vaguely familiar. It must have come from their old home, he decided. Funny that Fred should have kept it, and funnier still that Maud had not thrown it out.

'Calendars!' replied Fred. 'See, I makes one of them little wooden houses – *chalets*, they call 'em. It stands out in relief like and I hangs a calendar underneath. Go like hot cakes down "The Beetle and Wedge" for three bob a time. Not that I dares go in there with our Maud, but the landlord sends the money down.'

The mention of 'The Beetle and Wedge' combined with money acted as a spur to Josh's intentions.

'Very nice,' he said ingratiatingly, 'specially at Christmas. Could do with a bit of cash myself to tell the truth.'

'Oh ah!'

'The kids, you know. Need a few things, and I'm fair strapped for money. Times have been hard lately.'

'Thought you had work at Bailey's yard.'

'Ah! All that went on bills that come in.'

There was silence while Fred stuck on another matchstick.

'So you've come here for a loan, have you?'

'Well, if you could see your way clear, Fred, I'd be much

obliged. I've got some beating coming up after Christmas. Three big shoots – ought to make me a bit. I could pay you back early in the New Year.'

Again silence fell. A hen squawked nearby. A large vehicle rumbled in the village street.

'That's the last Caxley,' observed Fred, picking up another matchstick. 'Must be half past seven.'

Josh was content to wait. He knew old Fred. Everything took time to decide.

'I see you've got one of our Mum's old chairs,' he remarked.

'Ah! Just the right height for this job. Maud was all for chucking it out, but I brought it down here.'

'We had good times as kids,' said Josh. There was a sentimental whine in his tone, and Fred was not deceived. Best get rid of him he supposed, stirring the glue pot, before he started crying over old times. At this rate he'd never get the roof done, let alone the doorway.

'I've got mighty little myself,' said Fred, dismissing the old memories bit, 'but you can have two quid.'

He rummaged in a back pocket and handed over two crumpled pound notes.

'You're a good sort, Fred. I won't forget.'

'You'd better not! It's a loan, not a Christmas present. You see you pay me back after your beating.'

'I'll do that, Fred. That I will. That's a promise.'

He held out a dirty hand. Reluctantly Fred shook it.

'Now I've been and dropped that matchstick, blast it!' he said.

'Best not let Maud hear you a-swearing,' laughed Josh and made his way into the night.

When Fred Pringle finally emerged from his haven, leaving two calendars to dry on the bench, his wife was waiting for him in the living room.

'And what did that waster want?'

'Old Josh? Oh, he just dropped in, you know. Christmas, and all that.'

Fred's airy tone did not deceive Maud.

'I asked what he *wanted*,' persisted the lady. 'Did you give him money?'

Fred had a sudden coughing attack.

'You'd best have your cocoa now,' said Mrs Pringle, 'we'll talk then.'

She departed into the kitchen and soon returned with two steaming mugs on a tray, and the usual pair of digestive biscuits which constituted their bed-time snack.

'Now, let's have the truth, Fred Pringle,' she said flatly. 'How much, and why?'

'Two quid, and because he's my brother,' replied Fred, who thought he might as well get the whole business over and done with.

'You're a bigger fool than I thought,' was his wife's comment, stirring two spoonfuls of sugar into Fred's mug. 'You'll never see that again!'

'He knows it's only a loan. He's got money due from beating after Christmas.'

'If I was a betting woman,' said Mrs Pringle, 'which I am glad to say I'm not, I would bet my last penny that Josh Pringle will never pay you back. You're a fool, Fred, and weak with it. You should have sent him packing.'

'At Christmas time?'

'Particularly at Christmas time,' said Mrs Pringle, 'that's when he needs it most. If I know that good-for-nothing brother of yours he's already in "The Beetle and Wedge" drinking his way through your cash.'

'I was thinking of his poor kids.'

'His *poor kids*,' replied Maud, who had seen more than enough of them that day, 'are Josh's affair, not yours. Let him provide for his own.'

And with that she banged the two empty mugs on the tray, and swept out into the kitchen.

She was right of course.

Josh Pringle had gone to the pub in Fairacre's High Street, and there quaffed three pints of beer before closing time. He was not drunk when he emerged from the pub, but the path was slippery. He crashed to the ground outside Mr Willet's gate, letting out a great bellow.

Bob Willet, busy shutting up his hen house, heard the cry and went to investigate and, seeing who it was, assumed that Josh was drunk.

'Here, give us your hand,' he said, 'and remember to take more water with it.'

Josh staggered to his feet, gave a yelp of pain, and flung his arms round Mr Willet for support.

'It's me ankle,' gasped Josh, 'bin and done it in.'

He was certainly in pain and, although he smelt of beer, Mr Willet was pretty sure he was not completely intoxicated.

'You'd best come in a minute, and let Alice have a look.'

Leaning heavily on the shorter man, Josh hobbled up the path.

Alice Willet, who was getting ready for bed and had already taken down her bun and transformed it into a wispy grey plait, was not pleased to see their guest.

'Josh has done somethin' to his ankle,' explained Bob, depositing the patient in an armchair with a sigh of relief.

'Better let me see,' said Alice resignedly.

The state of Josh's socks gave her far more of a shock than his injuries. The former were tattered and decidedly noisome. His ankle was already beginning to swell.

'It's only a sprain,' said Alice. 'I'll tie a wet bandage round it.'

She departed into the kitchen and Bob Willet decided to open a window. When his wife returned, the air was much fresher.

'See if you can stand on it,' said Alice, 'before I strap you up.'

Josh heaved himself upright, gave a yell and collapsed back into the chair.

'I reckon I've bin and broke it,' he despaired. 'And I've got beating to do next week.'

'You'll be all right by then,' said Bob. 'Just have to keep it up over the next couple of days.'

Alice knelt down and began to swathe the ankle with a long strip of clean linen which had once been part of one of Bob's shirts.

'Gawd!' yelped the patient. On seeing Alice's scandalised face, he apologised.

'You'll have to put up with a bit of pain,' said his nurse.

'But how am I going to get home?'

Bob and Alice exchanged glances. Getting him home was the ardent desire of both, but it was now ten-thirty, and who would be going to Springbourne at that time?

Inspiration came to Mr Willet as his wife secured the last two inches of the wet bandage.

'What about Chalky White? I believe he's on night shift at the signal box this week. I'll nip round and see. Won't be a tick.'

He vanished through the door leaving Josh and Alice surveying each other.

'I'm real sorry about this,' began Josh. 'Your old man thought I was drunk, I believe.'

'Well, it wouldn't be the first time,' commented Alice tartly. She was longing for her bed, but her natural kindness triumphed, and she asked if Josh would like a cup of tea. Good for shock, she said.

'No thanks, duck. You done enough.'

They sank into silence.

Meanwhile, some hundred yards away, Bob Willet was explaining his problem to Chalky, who owned a battered Ford of uncertain age because his hours of work as a signalman were erratic.

'It would be Josh, wouldn't it?' he groaned. 'Fair reeking of ale, no doubt. And a good half mile out of my way. How's the time?'

He looked at the clock on the mantelpiece, then hauled out a silver pocket watch from his uniform waistcoat pocket. He looked carefully from one to the other, while Bob secretly fumed. Chalky always took his time.

'Well, it's like this,' said Chalky at last, 'I have to be at Fox Bottom at midnight to relieve young Skinner. Now I reckons to get there at *five to* at the outside – *ten to* would be better – and I've got to have a bite before I go while Mother cuts me sandwiches. D'you follow?'

Bob said that yes, yes, he followed.

'So if you can get him here before, let's say, eleven-fifteen pip emma, I'll deliver him to Springbourne.'

Bob broke into a torrent of thanks, but Chalky White raised a hand for silence.

'I'm not doing it *willingly*, I don't mind admitting, but to oblige you and Alice.'

'Very grateful we are too, Chalky,' Bob assured him, and hurried back with the good news.

Their visitor seemed quite lively, but his poor Alice, thought Bob, looked ready to drop. He went into action at once.

'Chalky'll drop you home, Josh. We'll take it easy. One arm round my shoulders, and my old blackthorn stick in the other hand. Let's try it.'

In this fashion, Josh limped to the door, then turned to Alice. 'Thanks for the help. I'm real grateful, Mrs Willet.' He held up the stick. 'See you when I return this.'

'No need to return it,' said Bob, urging him through the door. 'Keep it as a Christmas present. I've got half a dozen walkin' sticks. Now, watch the step, and put your weight on me.'

Alice watched them out of sight, put up the fireguard and went thankfully upstairs to bed.

Half an hour later, Bob Willet fell into bed beside her.

'What an evenin'! Thank heavens we got him to old Chalky's. I'll take a few eggs round to them tomorrow to thank him for helpin' us out.'

'That Josh!' murmured Alice. 'The yarns he tells! He'd been to see Fred, he said, and Fred had given him two pounds.'

'Bet that didn't go farther than "The Beetle",' observed Bob, with a mighty yawn.

'I don't think you should've given him that stick, you know, Bob. You was always fond of it.'

'I'd never see it again, anyway,' said her husband. 'No point in *lendin'* anything to our Josh. You'd never get it back.'

'Well, he said Fred Pringle *lent* him the two pounds.'

'Fred Pringle,' said Mr Willet, 'is a fool, and always was. Well, look who he married!'

Chapter Nine

SPINSTERS, 'SPLASHEM' AND SPRING

Although Mrs Pringle did her best to distance herself from what she termed 'that Springbourne lot', Minnie Pringle turned up far more frequently than her aunt-by-marriage wished.

In the fullness of time, the third child born out of wedlock arrived, and not long afterwards Mrs Pringle told me some surprising news.

'Believe it or not, Miss Read, but that Minnie is getting married.'

'Good heavens! It hardly seems worth the bother, does it?'

I was squatting down by the map cupboard, trying to extricate a large piece of cardboard which I needed for mounting the children's pictures.

The map cupboard is a dangerous place to work in: furled maps, ranging from 'Great Britain's Possessions Overseas' (somewhat out of date) to 'The Disposition of the Tribes of Israel' (equally out of date) not to mention 'Aids to Resuscitation in case of Inhalation of Gas' (fat chance in Fairacre where we have no gas) to 'The Muscular System of the Human Body'.

As well as these aids to education, all the awkward objects which have no real home seem to find their way into this cupboard: odd shoes, a broken croquet mallet, a moth-eaten rug, an archaic oil lamp and a cardboard box containing a jumble of jigsaw pieces which have lost their way over the years and share the space with an assortment of stray building bricks, bone counters, odd dominoes and the like.

'That cupboard,' remarked Mrs, Pringle, 'is a menace. That great Union Jack fell out on me Monday afternoon, and brought up a lump the size of a pigeon's egg.'

She put a hand to her head dramatically, while I tugged out the cardboard sheet successfully, wondering meanwhile why it is always a *pigeon's* egg. Why not a bantam's, or an owl's or even an everyday hen's egg?

'So who's the lucky man?' I asked, dusting myself down. It seemed rather silly to get married when Minnie had been doing as nicely as she was capable of, without benefit of the clergy, all this time.

'Quite a nice steady chap,' said Mrs Pringle. 'A widower with five children, called Ern.'

I began to see the reason for this marriage.

'But will Minnie be able to cope with such a large family? That will make eight altogether, won't it?'

'Well, one or two are off his hands now, married or working in Caxley, so there will only be a few home to sleep, and the biggest girl's quite helpful. And you see, he's got a council house, so Minnie will be getting a place of her own at last.'

It sounded as though it would be uncomfortably crowded, but Mrs Pringle seemed to think the whole affair was a good arrangement.

'Minnie wanted a white wedding,' she went on, 'with some of the small children as bridesmaids and pages and that. She was all for bells and the organ as well, but her mum pointed out it would cost a pretty penny.'

'I should have thought a quiet wedding at Caxley Registry Office would have suited the occasion.'

'That's just it! It *is* an occasion! After all, every girl likes to remember her wedding day. I can quite see why Minnie wanted it all nice and lovely.'

I did not feel that this was the right time to remind Mrs Pringle that a bride in white was meant to represent virginity, and that Minnie could hardly be included in that state with three young children in attendance.

'So what with one thing or another, our Minnie's got a blue dress with a matching coat, and making do with a white hat she got at the Plymouth Brethren jumble last month.'

'Sounds splendid.'

'And I'm lending her my white confirmation Bible to carry.'

I privately hoped she would hold it the right way up. Minnie cannot read, but probably there would be no need to refer to it during the ceremony so the Bible would be for effect only.

'That's the *borrowed*,' said Mrs Pringle.

'The borrowed what?' I asked bewildered.

Mrs Pringle tut-tutted crossly.

'Something old,

Something new,

Something borrowed

And something blue', she quoted. 'Well, my Bible's the *borrowed*, see?'

At this moment, Joe Coggs rushed in to say that Ernest had got himself locked in the lavatory, and was hollering something awful.

Minnie's nuptials were forgotten as I went to investigate.

I did not come across Mrs Pringle during the rest of the day so heard no more of Minnie's plans for some time.

But that evening Amy called on her way back from Oxford, and while we were drinking coffee and admiring her purchases, the subject of matrimony cropped up. It often does with Amy.

'This is such a dear little house,' she said, 'such a shame that it only has you living in it.'

'It doesn't complain,' I retorted, 'and neither do I.'

'You know, the older you get,' continued Amy, changing tactics slightly, 'the more difficult it is going to be to find somebody suitable.'

'Don't worry about it. I honestly prefer to be single.'

'Of course you feel that way now. But what about the time when you retire? You're bound to be lonely.'

'Don't you believe it! I shall kick up my heels and nip off to foreign parts, squandering my hard-earned pension in all directions.'

'But again, it would be so much more fun if you had a companion.'

'Why? They might want to do the things I don't want to do. Now I can please myself.'

'That's a very *selfish* point of view,' said Amy severely. 'Anyway, it's not just holidays I'm thinking of. It's the general day-to-day companionship you need. Besides,' she added, catching sight of an untidy pile of books by the sofa, 'it might make you tidier, if you had someone else to consider.'

'Mrs Pringle comes tomorrow,' I comforted her. 'I shall be thoroughly "bottomed", and not be able to find anything.'

'Haven't you ever met anyone who attracts you? You were quite pretty when we were at college.'

'Thanks for the compliment. And yes, of course I've seen lots of men who are attractive. Your James, for one, but you snapped him up first.'

Amy looked smug. 'Yes, I did, didn't I? And I don't regret it.' She began to look pensive and then added: 'Really,' rather doubtfully.

To cheer her up I told her about Minnie's wedding.

'I'm glad to hear she's been persuaded from wearing white,' she said. 'What are you giving her for a wedding present?'

'I didn't propose to give her anything. Mrs Pringle is giving her a set of saucepans and her old mincer, if she can find the wing nut that holds all the blades together.'

'Is Minnie capable of managing a mincer?'

'I shouldn't think so for a minute, and if she does get it to work, I'm sure it will be Minnie's fingers that will go first through the contraption.'

'What coffee is this?' asked Amy, swilling the dregs of her cup round and round.

'This Week's Offer from the shop in the village.'

'As I thought,' said Amy, and drank no more.

After Amy had gone I pottered about my domestic duties. There was a blouse to iron, some clothes to wash, the window box to water and Tibby's belated supper to put down for that fastidious animal.

Rain had set in, and I went about my affairs to the accompaniment of raindrops pattering against the window, and a musical trickling of water into the butt outside the kitchen door.

It was all very peaceful. I relish my time alone in the school house, dealing rather inefficiently with my chores. This evening I pondered on Amy's urgings towards matrimony.

I am, far too often for my liking, the object of my friends' solicitude. Why this overwhelming desire to see everyone married? Quite a few of us, both men and women, are perfectly satisfied with the single state and seem to lead useful and happy lives.

At this point, doubts assailed me. Was this being too smug and selfish? Certainly we did not have to consider other people in the home – husbands, children and so on. So were we really leading useful lives?

Well, I jolly well am, I told myself robustly. I run my school with fair success. I do my best to help in the village, handing over clothes to the jumble sale (which I almost always regret later, as I could have done with them myself), I occasionally stand in for the organist, I do my stint of washing up at the Women's Institute, and a bit of sitting-in for friends with young children. I help at local fêtes and concerts, stick up posters, deliver leaflets for worthy causes, and lend an ear to those who come to me for advice, and give them coffee as well.

At this point, my mind veered to This Week's Offer. Was it really as dreadful as Amy seemed to think? It had tasted all right to me, but then I did not have Amy's rarefied palate.

Perhaps Amy was right – not just about the coffee, but the selfish and narrow life I lead. But what could I do? I was in no position to put the world to rights. There was no way in which I could feed the Third World, stop global warfare, cope with sea, air and land pollution and other immense problems, except for adding my signature to the appropriate forms.

No, I decided, it was just a case of soldiering on from day to day in one's own little sphere.

'You in your small corner, and I in mine,' I sang to Tibby. The cat, startled, shot out of the window.

Of course, it was nice of Amy, I thought charitably, to be so concerned about my solitary state, but also decidedly irritating. She *would* dredge up those middle-aged men! As bad as Mrs Pringle and the others in Fairacre, who had made my life uncomfortable over Henry Mawne.

I began to put out the breakfast things on the kitchen table, ready for the morning, still pondering on the mentality of those who are intent on pressing matrimony upon those who don't need it. Had Minnie's approaching nuptials really set off a whole evening's train of thought?

The clock struck ten, and I pulled myself together. Hot milk, and bed with a book. What bliss! Why, if I had a husband he might want the light off, or dislike me sipping hot milk! He would probably snore too.

Feeling delightfully smug I surveyed the kitchen table. I saw that I had picked up Tibby's plate, still decorated with the remains of Pussi-luv, and set it carefully at my breakfast place.

'That's what comes of thinking,' I said aloud, and went to bed.

The wet weather continued for weeks. Mrs Pringle grew more and more morose as wet footmarks sullied the floors, and raincoats dripped from their pegs.

Most days we were unable to let the children play outside. The consequence was that they grew peevish with being cooped up all day. The dog-eared comics grew even shabbier, the 'playtime toys' grubbier, and the children longed to rush about in the fresh air as keenly as I wanted them to do so.

Occasionally, when the rain stopped at the appropriate time, I let them out, with terrible threats about what would happen to them if they played 'Splashem'.

This game, which cannot be Fairacre's alone, is simplicity itself. All it needs is some puddles and plenty of unsuspecting victims.

The idea is to wait until a child strays near a puddle and then to jump heavily into the water, sending a cascade over the victim. The harder you jump, the higher the spray, and it has been known to drench a small child from the neck down. Wild cries of 'Splashem' accompany this simple pursuit, and roars of laughter. It is a game which I forbid in the playground, with some success, but what happens on the way home I shudder to think, despite my exhortations.

Mrs Pringle, of course, is as equally opposed to 'Splashem' as I am, but with her floors rather than the unhappy victims in mind.

'I see that Jimmy Waites and Joe Coggs jumping about in that long puddle by the Post Office. Their shoes was fair sopped. It's time the Council done something about that puddle. What do we pay rates for, I'd like to know?'

'I hope you ticked them off.'

'I done my best, but kids these days gets away with murder.'

She bent down to scrape something sticky from the classroom floor with her finger nail.

'Blessed bubble gum!' she grumbled. 'Our Minnie used to give it to hers until I told her I wouldn't have the stuff in my house.'

'I meant to ask you, how did the wedding go?'

She straightened up, wheezing heavily, and seated herself on the front desk. To my surprise, a maudlin smile spread over her face.

'Oh, it was a real lovely wedding! Minnie looked a treat in blue, and she had his youngest girl as bridesmaid. It wouldn't have looked too good to have had her own children.'

'Quite,' I said.

'I left the baby in the pram just outside the church porch, and looked after the other two in the back pew. They wasn't too bad, considering. His four was further up the church. Not very well turned out, I thought, and no hats.'

'People don't seem to bother about hats these days.'

'Well, I certainly do. I bought a real beauty in Caxley. Navy blue straw with a white feather ornament. Very smart. I always think navy and white looks *classy*, and it don't date.'

'Did you have a wedding breakfast?'

'We did indeed! In Springbourne village hall, and though the toilet arrangements there are not what they should be, we had some lovely ham and salad.'

'So now Minnie is really settling down,' I said, one eye on the clock, and hoping to see my school cleaner depart.

'Well, she's *married*,' she said cautiously, 'but *settled* I'd not like to say. You can never tell with Minnie.'

And with this ominous comment she made her way into the lobby to see that the doormat was thoroughly used by the children.

Much to the relief of everyone in Fairacre, the wet spell of weather was followed by days of sunshine.

Blankets and quilts, coats and curtains blew on the clothes lines. Mats and rugs were draped over hedges ready for thorough beating, as the long delayed spring cleaning got on its way.

Mrs Pringle caught the fever and insisted on tackling my house room by room. I took to staying a little longer in school to miss the severe censure I faced about my housekeeping methods.

She started on the bedrooms and I was unfortunate enough to encounter her on the first occasion.

'I've been droring my finger along the top of this pelmet,' she told me, from her vantage post on a bedroom chair, 'and you could write your name in the dust, that you could. When Mrs Hope was here, she had a feather broom in *constant use*! Tops of doors, picture rails, curtain tops, she done 'em all regular. Everything smelt as sweet as a nut.'

'It doesn't *smell*,' I protested.

'You gets used to it,' she retorted. 'Living in your own mess, you gets used to it. Like pigs,' she added malevolently.

I was about to retire worsted in this battle, but Mrs Pringle called me back.

'I'll take these curtains home with me and give the poor things a bit of soap and water. So you'd better let me have your summer ones to put up while I'm here.'

'I don't have any summer ones,' I told her, 'those are simply *The Curtains*. They stay up all the year round.'

Mrs Pringle gasped, and nearly fell off the chair with shock.

'You mean to say you've no spares in the linen cupboard?'

'That's right.' I was beginning to enjoy myself.

'The gentry,' said Mrs Pringle, 'always has two sets, winter and summer.'

'I'm not gentry.'

'That's *quite* plain,' she said offensively, 'but even poor Mrs Hope had velvet for winter and sprigged cotton for summer. Made them herself too,' she added for good measure, 'and her a chronic invalid.'

When Mrs Hope's name is invoked I know that I don't stand a chance. My predecessor in the school house must have been a perfect housewife.

'Well, take them by all means,' I said, 'they are probably ready for a wash.'

'That's more than true,' she panted, beginning to struggle with the hooks, 'but what about bed time, when you're undressing?'

'No one will be watching,' I assured her, 'only the birds in the garden, and they'll be roosting by the time I go to bed.'

'My old mother,' she said, 'would have been scandalised at having no curtains to the bedroom windows.'

Mrs Pringle's mother has been dead for many years, so I forbore to comment on her possible disapproval and made for the door.

'Mrs Hope –' began Mrs Pringle.

But by that time I was well out of earshot.

School, in this balmy spell of weather, returned to normal and 'Splashem' was a thing of the past.

We had rather more nature walks than the timetable allowed, and thoroughly enjoyed finding spring flowers for the nature table. Celandines and primroses starred the banks and coppices, and white and blue violets hid themselves in the dry grass under Mr Roberts' hedgerows.

Birds were already nesting, and some still building, flying across our path trailing long grasses or struggling with beaks full of moss or feathers. Soon the swallows would be back, searching in cottage porches and barns for the nests they left behind the autumn before.

It was a time of great hope. There were lambs in the fields, the sun was warm, and the hedges were showing a tender green.

Our little procession was in high spirits, and people waved to us from their gardens or windows, deserting their hoeing or dusting for a few minutes to watch us on our way to the windy downs.

It is at times like this that I relish my life as a teacher in a country school. For me, there is nothing so satisfying as life in a village. It is good to know everybody, and good to be known. Occasionally, I resent the interest in my affairs, as in the case of Henry Mawne's attentions, but it is far better, I tell myself, to know that I am of interest rather than to be ignored.

And then the job itself is so varied. How many people could walk away from their desks, their papers, their telephones, and take a refreshing stroll among grass and trees, with rooks cawing overhead?

I thought of the glimpses one gets from the train, running into London, showing vast open-plan offices with row upon row of desks, strong overhead lighting and a regiment of workers, as confined as battery hens. No doubt these soulless places had windows hermetically sealed, and a system of air-conditioning liable to give the unfortunate inmates sinus trouble, sore throats and headaches. How much better to have one's shoes clogged with the pale chalky mud of the downs – despite the wrath of Mrs Pringle. At least our lungs were filled with exhilarating fresh air, and we were bursting with energy.

There was something terrifying too about the vast numbers of people glimpsed in those offices and factories. The pressure on space, seen possibly at its worst on the platforms of stations at rush hour, was incredibly depressing and frightening. Here at Fairacre, our little school numbered less than thirty children, and it looked as if those numbers would fall again before long, a fact which brought its own problems, but fortunately not that of over-crowding and its attendant ills.

By this time, the nature walk had left the village, and had taken a steep muddy track uphill. On our right a flock of Mr Roberts' sheep grazed on the close-bitten grass. Above us the skylarks vied with each other, pouring down their lively trickle of song, as they pushed higher and higher towards the blue sky.

We sat down on a bank to get our breath. Most of the children were content, as I was, to sit in silence, studying the village spread out below us like a pictorial map.

The spire of St Patrick's was the salient feature, and even at this distance we could catch the gleam of the weathercock on its tip, pointing to the south-west.

Hard by the church stood our school, its playground now empty, as the infants were still in their classroom while we played truant. The vicarage and John Parr's house were hidden by the trees in their gardens, but the cottages lining the village street were visible, their thatched or weatherbeaten tiled roofs blending into the greys and browns of gardens and fields.

Beyond the church we could see Mr Roberts' herd of black and white Friesians in one field, and in the next his bay hunter cropping as industriously as the cattle. They might have been farmhouse toys at this distance, I thought. It only needed a farmer in a smock, and a milkmaid carrying a stool and pail to take one back a century.

A glance at my watch brought me to my feet.

'Nearly dinner time,' I shouted to the few stragglers in the distance, and reluctantly we gathered for our return.

I took another look at the view spread before us as we waited for the last two or three to join us. How idyllic it looked, that village of Fairacre! A stranger, gazing at it as we had done, would be forgiven for imagining that all was peace and plenty in that little community. Those of us who lived there knew better.

Arthur Coggs's house held fear and poverty for his wife and children. At the Post Office, Mr Lamb's old mother was dying, slowly and painfully, from cancer. Next door there were money troubles, and the wife was threatening to leave home. It was not all rapture in Fairacre, any more than it was elsewhere.

But at least we had space, we had wide views, we had almost unpolluted air and water and most of us had the inestimable blessing of robust health.

We began to slither down the slope, each clutching the treasures so recently collected. As well as little bunches of spring flowers, Jimmy had found three empty snail shells, large and bleached white by the weather, and I told the children that I had heard that the Romans used to collect them and eat the contents when they lived in these parts.

Eileen Burton had a rook's feather stuck behind her ear. Linda Moffat had found some late catkins and the front of her coat was yellow with pollen.

But Joseph Coggs had the most prized possession: an old nest damp from the recent rains, but still a miracle of bird-building and lined snugly with moss, feathers and shreds of wool from Mr Roberts' sheep.

He held it close to his shabby coat and his eyes were shining as he looked up at me.

'I'm going to find some little stones to put in it, like eggs,' he said.

'A good idea,' I told him, hoping he would have the sense to keep his treasure out of his father's sight. Joe had lost things like that before.

Ernest, at the head of our procession, set up a yell.

'Dinner van's just gone up street, Miss!'

Spurred into action, we fairly sprinted up the road. First things first, we told ourselves, as we puffed dinnerward.

Chapter Ten

MRS PRINGLE GOES TO HOSPITAL

Over the years, I grew quite astute at gauging Mrs Pringle's state of mind by the barometer of her bad leg. Dragging the afflicted limb with many a sigh, heavy limping and the occasional yelp of pain on moving, all betokened umbrage on Mrs Pringle's part. I really did not think there was anything much the matter physically, but when she told me that she had to visit Caxley Cottage Hospital for some tests, I presumed that it must be something to do with her leg. Not that she said as much. I tended to hurry away with some excuse or other as I could not face the gruesome details of real or imagined symptoms.

So I only had myself to blame for my ignorance when she informed me that she had to have two or three days in hospital, or 'up the Cottage', as it is affectionately known in these parts. (We locals often have to catch 'the Caxley' to attend 'up the Cottage'.)

'Got to be there Wednesday evening, and they do me Thursday.'

'I suppose they are going to try some physiotherapy,' I said, 'or traction, or something like that.'

'*Traction!*' boomed Mrs Pringle. 'What, with my complaint?'

'They do use traction on legs, I believe.'

'And who said anything about legs?' she demanded.

I began to falter. Mrs Pringle's beetling brows and flashing eyes would intimidate the bravest person.

'Well, I just thought –' I began.

'*You just thought,*' echoed the lady witheringly. 'I've told you time and again I've been having Inner Trouble.'

'I'm sorry. I quite thought it was your leg giving trouble.'

'My leg,' she said, 'is always giving me trouble, but I have learnt to live with it.'

She began to limp about the classroom flicking a duster over cupboards and desks, while her last remark reminded me of a poignant little rhyme dealing with old age, which I had heard recently. It went something like this:

> 'I can manage my bifocals,
> To my dentures I'm resigned,
> I can cope with my arthritis,
> But how I miss my mind!'

Whether Mrs Pringle wanted to enlighten me about the true nature of her illness I was never to know, for the children came in at that moment, and she simply called out:

'I'll let you know times and that when I comes up midday,' and departed.

The whole incident had slipped from my mind during the morning's multifarious activities, but Mrs Pringle buttonholed me in the lobby as she washed up after school dinner.

'I'll be up to do this next Wednesday, as usual. Don't have to be there till six, and Mr Partridge is giving me a lift in as the Caxley's no good that time of day. He's got to go to some Economical Council meeting, he says, so it's no bother. A real gentleman, isn't he?'

'Indeed he is.'

'But you'll have to do without me here for the rest of the week. One thing, the stoves don't need doing. With any luck, I'll be all right by the Monday, but I expect they'll say "No heavy work", like lifting desks and that, after Inner Trouble.'

'Naturally. And don't come back too soon,' I said, trying to sound solicitous rather than pleased.

'I knows my duty,' said Mrs Pringle, 'and *all being well* I should be fit for light work by then. It all depends on what they find, and if the scar is a long one.'

And on this ominous note she dropped the subject.

*

I met Mrs Partridge that evening as I walked to post an urgent letter, and she enlightened me a little more, but not much.

'How will you manage without Mrs Pringle?' she began.

'It's only for a few days, she tells me. We shall be all right.'

'Yes. As far as I can gather, it's only one of these little routine women's affairs. Quite straightforward.'

The phrase 'routine women's affairs' reminded me of Henry Mawne's 'gentleman's complaint', but naturally I forbore to comment.

In any case, I did not propose to enquire further. Mrs Partridge has had some nursing experience, and is apt to enlarge on symptoms and their treatment in unpleasantly explicit detail, and if Mrs Pringle's trouble were *'inner'*, then it would involve a conglomeration of tubes, I imagined, which would knock me cold at once.

'How's your garden?' I asked.

'Full of blossom,' she said. 'Come back with me and have a look.'

But I excused myself saying that I had books to mark and some ironing to do. This was perfectly true, but I was pretty certain that both activities would be shelved while I did that day's crossword.

A day or two later I fetched Miss Clare from Beech Green to spend the evening with me.

A few hours of Dolly Clare's company is a real refreshment of spirits. Always calm, wise and dignified, old age seems to have increased these attributes, and her memories of Fairacre School are always fascinating.

'We used to drink a lot of cocoa when I taught here before the war. Only in the winter, of course, but the children enjoyed it. Somehow, cocoa seems to have gone out of fashion.'

'School milk took over, I expect,' I said. 'And some avant-garde mothers are already saying it's too fattening.'

'There weren't many over-weight children when I started teaching,' responded Dolly. 'In fact, just the other way. The farm labourers' children were definitely under-nourished, on the whole. Plenty of garden produce, of course, but mighty little meat. And somehow fish was never much relished in these parts, and so often the eggs were sold to bring in a few pence. "Us has the cracked 'uns" the children used to say.'

'Well, I'm just about to crack some for our omelettes,' I told her. 'Cheese, tomato or both, for a filling?'

She pondered for a moment and then gave me her slow sweet smile.

'Both, please. And I hear that Mrs Pringle is going to be away for a few days. Will you be able to cope?'

'Very happily, believe me.'

'Well, it can't be anything very serious if she expects to be back on the Monday.'

I thought, not for the first time, how efficiently a village grape-vine works. I supposed that absolutely everyone in Beech Green and Fairacre, if not Caxley itself, knew that Mrs Pringle was due at 'the Cottage' next Wednesday. Probably they knew why too, which was more than I did.

'It can't be appendicitis,' mused Dolly, 'she had that done some time ago. Probably just one of those tiresome women's things.'

'Mrs Partridge thinks so too,' I informed her. 'Now, do you like spring onions in your salad?'

'I shall come and help,' said Dolly, rising from her chair.

We spoke no more of Mrs Pringle.

'So we're going to be without Madam Sunshine, for a day or two,' said Mr Willet. 'Do you reckon we can manage?'

He gave me a sly grin.

'One thing,' he went on, 'they won't keep her any longer than they need. Hospitals these days gets you in just long enough to slit you up, stitch you up and get you up. Needs the beds, see.

'Well, no one wants to linger anyway,' I replied.

'Linger where?' asked Mrs Pringle, appearing from the lobby.

Neither of us replied, and Bob Willet departed, rather smartly.

'One thing does worry me,' said my cleaner. 'that house of yours. I could easily give it a quick doing-over before I went in with the vicar.'

'We've had all this out already,' I told her. 'You'll have enough to do at your own place, and I can perfectly well cope for two Wednesdays.'

'I could ask Minnie,' she said. My blood ran cold. Out of pity, some time before, I had let Minnie loose in my house so that she could earn a little money, but she had nearly wrecked the place. The tea towels had been put to soak in neat bleach. She had tried to clean the windows with the stuff one uses for the insides of particularly black ovens, and I never did find the furniture polish, or the screw which holds the floor-cleaner together.

'No, don't bother Minnie,' I said hastily. 'I managed alone for years perfectly well.'

'That's as maybe,' retorted Mrs Pringle. '"Managed" perhaps. I wouldn't say "perfectly well". Never have I seen such a cupboard as that one of yours under the stairs. But there it is. Some are born tidy, and some isn't.'

I decided to be charitable and ignore these remarks.

'I shall ring the hospital on Thursday and see if you are fit to see visitors,' I replied. 'Anyway, good luck and we'll see you back on duty when you feel up to it.'

On Friday mornings, our vicar takes prayers in the school, gives a simple homily, discusses any problems with me and, all in all, is a welcome visitor.

I was able to tell him that the news from the hospital, about Mrs Pringle's affairs, was good, and that I proposed to visit her on Saturday afternoon.

He expressed relief, and then invited me to call at the vicarage after morning service on Sunday.

'Just a few old friends,' he said vaguely. 'I think you know them all, and the garden is looking at its best. Cordelia wants you to see her irises. She was so disappointed that you couldn't come the other evening.'

This, of course, caused intense feelings of guilt on my part, as I remembered my excuses about ironing and marking exercise books, when all I had attempted was the crossword, and a fine hash I had made of it, I recalled.

I promised to come and said how much I should look forward to seeing the irises, and mentally arranged a Sunday lunch which could be left to look after itself. Cold meat, or something in a casserole? Two boiled eggs would go down well, and one of the joys of living alone was the pleasure of making one's Sunday lunch as simple as that. No doubt a husband would expect a roast joint, two or three vegetables and a substantial pudding to follow. Oh, blessed spinsterhood!

On Saturday afternoon I set out for Caxley Cottage Hospital. It is situated on the outskirts of the town which is a good thing, particularly on a Saturday when Caxley High Street is choked with traffic and hundreds of shoppers intent upon committing hara-kiri by crossing the road inches in front of moving cars.

I took the back route which involves waiting at a level crossing and having a view of a small tributary of the river Kennet which runs nearby.

It is always peaceful waiting for the train to come. Small animals rustle in the reeds by the water. Wood anemones star a little copse, and in the summer meadowsweet grows in the marshy ground sending out its heady scent. In the autumn, there are some wonderful sprays of luscious blackberries at this spot, but it is hopeless to try and pick them, for no sooner are you out of the car than the gates soar up, and it is time to push on again.

This particular afternoon, the waiting was enhanced by a mallard duck who crossed the road with six yellow ducklings, halting now and again to make sure that all were in attendance. Her beady eyes looked this way and that, not I think through fear, but because she wanted to be sure that we knew that we had to wait for her. And, meekly, we did.

The hospital car park was uncomfortably full, and the usual number of thickheads had parked diagonally so that they took up two spaces instead of one. However, I edged mine beside a magnificent Mercedes and hoped for the best.

Mrs Pringle was looking resplendent in a pale blue nightgown and bright pink bed jacket. The ward seemed stiflingly hot after the fresh air, but she appeared to be quite comfortable.

'I'm doing very well considering,' she replied in answer to my enquiry into her health. 'Should be out on Monday, the sister says.'

'Will you need fetching?'

'No, my John's coming for me soon after six, and he'll run me home. Fred's been told what to get ready for me.'

I bet he has, I thought.

'I have to see the doctor on Monday morning, just to make sure everything's holding up. Then I can have my lay-down in the afternoon, and my tea, and be ready to go home when John comes.'

I was busy gazing at the other patients during this conversation, and felt that I ought to know one woman in a nearby bed. After all, you can hardly enter 'the Cottage' without seeing someone you know. It is part of its attraction, unlike the enormous town hospitals where everyone is strange.

'Used to work in Boots,' replied Mrs Pringle in answer to my query. 'Then went on to the pork butcher's on the bridge. Nice girl. Had a brother with a hare lip.'

I returned the distant lady's smile with more confidence.

'And that woman in the next bed to her,' said Mrs Pringle, 'thinks herself the Queen of the Ward just because she's had her gall bladder out. Gets all the attention. Not that she's any worse than the rest of us, and sleeps like a log at nights, but you see she's got all her gall stones in that jam jar on the top of her cupboard, so everyone goes across to see them.'

Mrs Pringle sounded resentful of this claim to fame.

'Not that they're much to write home about,' she continued. 'Why, my Uncle Perce had one much bigger than hers, and had it on his mantelpiece. Big as a walnut it was. Always attracted notice. Made a talking point, as people say.'

'Not at meal times, I hope,' I said.

'The meals aren't bad,' said Mrs Pringle, luckily mis-hearing me, 'not for a hospital, I mean. We had scrambled egg for breakfast. A bit too dry, but scrambled eggs is a bit tricky if they have to be kept warm. And fish in parsley sauce for our dinner just now. At least, they said it was parsley sauce but the parsley was pretty thin on the ground. Might just as well have been cigarette ash, and maybe it was.'

I put my little offering of spring flowers on her bedspread, and there was a slight lifting of the corners of her down-turned mouth.

'Well, thank you. Not that they'll stand a chance in this heat, but it's the thought that counts, isn't it?'

'You're not in any pain, I hope?'

'Not but what I can't bear,' she said, with a martyred sigh, 'I don't take no pain-killers at night. Not like *some*!'

She cast a malevolent glance across to the gall-bladder sufferer who was now holding up her jam jar for the admiration of half a dozen visitors.

'So you'll be back on Monday,' I said hastily, to change the subject.

'Not for *work*!' she cried.

'No, no. I know you won't be fit for work for some time —' I began.

'For *some time*?' she echoed. 'Of course, I'll be back the minute I can put one foot before the other. When have you ever seen me *shirking*?'

I began to feel that I could never say the right thing, and that possibly I was making Mrs Pringle's condition worse than when I arrived.

'You *never* shirk,' I said stoutly.

'I will say one thing for this place. It may be noisy and too hot, and the pain is something cruel at times, but at least it's giving my leg a rest.'

'That's splendid,' I said. I looked at my watch. I had been by the bedside for over twenty minutes, and I felt we should both enjoy a rest from each other's company.

'I'm not going to stay any longer,' I said, 'because you need all the rest you can get. I'll pop in and see you when you have settled back at home.'

She nodded her agreement, and picked up the bunch of flowers, holding them up to her nose.

'That really do smell like Fairacre,' she cried. 'You couldn't have brought anything nicer.'

And with this rare display of grace and gratitude, she waved me away.

The next morning I gave my shoes an extra polish, my clothes an extra brush, looked out my prayer book, found finally among the cookery books, and went to morning service.

As the head mistress of a church school I ought to go every Sunday, but somehow it does not work out that way. Friends tend to invite me to share their Sunday roast, or other friends come to me from some distance, so that I do not visit St Patrick's as often as I should. Dear Gerald Partridge, however, never upbraids me, and I am grateful for his Christian forbearance.

The church, even on this sunny morning, was chilly, and I envied the sensible women who had put on knitted or tweed skirts and would be withstanding the clammy chill of the wooden pews more successfully than I was.

But the peace of the place soon exerted its customary soothing influence. The monument to Sir Charles Dagbury, who had worshipped here a few hundred years before, was as commanding as ever, but his marble curls, which cascaded to his lace collar, could have done with a dusting. Mrs Hope's little feather duster could have been useful here, I thought.

Our church is a simple structure, white-washed inside, and with a roof of stout oak beams. I remembered the magnificent fanvaulting of Bent church at Christmas time, the beautiful carpets and the vicar's vestments.

Now Mr Partridge emerged from the vestry, followed by the ten or twelve souls forming our church choir. The four boys were all my pupils, and uncommonly angelic they looked in their snowy surplices and their hair sleeked down with a wet brush.

We began the service, and in due time settled down on our cold seats for the first lesson read by Henry Mawne.

My gaze roamed around the church. On the altar were bright garden flowers and, on each side, on the floor of the chancel, stood two large vases filled with blossom, probably from the vicarage.

I remembered the arum lilies which had flanked the chancel steps at Bent, and the plethora of exotic hothouse flowers which had scented the church that day.

St. Patrick's had no such grandeur, but it was just as moving in its homely simplicity. In both cases, honour and glory were being given.

It seemed particularly appropriate when the vicar announced the next hymn:

> 'Let us with a gladsome mind,
> Praise the Lord for He is kind.'

It was good to get out into the sunshine again as the church clock struck twelve.

Mrs Partridge caught up with me and took my arm, waving the while with her free hand at Henry Mawne and his wife. Evidently they, and also Peter and Diana Hale from Tyler's Row, were making their way to the vicarage.

'I have my sister Edith and her husband with us for a few days,' she said, as we crunched up her drive. 'She's not been too fit, so she didn't come to church this morning. It's one of those sick headache maladies.'

I hoped she would not go into further details, and was spared as the sister in question and her husband came out of the drawing room to greet us. Both, I was relieved to see, appeared to be in robust health.

Peter Hale drifted over to me. He used to teach at Caxley Grammar School in the days when it went under that honourable name.

'This is quite a scholastic gathering, isn't it?' he said waving towards Henry Mawne with a dangerously full sherry glass, 'Cordelia's sister used to teach too, I hear.'

I enquired after his house and garden. He had bought all four cottages which comprised Tyler's Row, and was now spending his retirement improving his property.

'I must say it's absolutely engrossing, though terribly hard work.

But so much more satisfying than teaching. I'd far rather lay bricks than discuss the Unification of Italy.'

'And you are now free of neighbours,' I commented. He and Diana had suffered much when they first bought the property, for Mrs Fowler, a virago of a widow, had lived next door in the end cottage, and had made their lives a misery.

'Thank heaven for that!' he said. 'I hear she is living in Caxley, and I don't envy her neighbours there, I must say.'

At this point the Mawnes came up and enquired after Mrs Pringle. I told them about my visit, sticking to the fact of the lady's good recovery, and her hopes to be home the next day.

'Not a bad hospital that,' commented Henry. 'They did a good job on my hydraulic system.'

'Well, we don't want to hear about *that*, Henry,' said his wife severely. He seemed unabashed.

'Then I'll tell you about a spotted woodpecker that comes regularly to our bird table,' he said with a smile. And he did.

Soon Mrs Partridge led us into the garden. She is one of those gardeners, maddening to the rest of us, who never seem to have any set-backs – if Cordelia Partridge plants anything, it grows. Even those most tricky of bulbs, the nerines, which bloom in October and November, flourish in the vicarage garden and supply the house with beautiful pink blooms when the rest of Fairacre is doing its best with hardy chrysanthemums.

The irises, of course, were superb. I was not expecting anything quite so foreign-looking as the dark brown and yellow, the burgundy and cream, and even a two-coloured beauty in pale mauve which delighted our eyes. Cordelia Partridge was suitably smug with the praise heaped upon her, and we were allowed to wander at will after we had paid our respects to the iris bed.

I found myself by the rockery in the company of Diana Hale.

'It must be a mixed blessing for you having Mrs Pringle back again.'

'That's true,' I admitted.

'One thing about her,' went on Diana Hale, 'she is the only person I ever met who could compete with our awful Mrs Fowler.

They crossed swords once outside the Post Office, and I've never seen such a clash! I slunk home the other way, too scared to go near them. But I must say, it did my heart good to see Mrs Fowler being trounced.'

'Oh, she's a doughty fighter, is Mrs Pringle,' I said. 'I know that to my cost.'

But somehow, I thought as I made my way home to a late lunch, I should be quite glad to see the old harridan when she deigned to turn up.

It dawned on me later that I still had no idea of the cause of Mrs Pringle's visit to 'the Cottage'.

What is more, I had no intention of enquiring.

Chapter Eleven

RUMOURS AND CONFLICTS

As it happened, Mrs Pringle did not appear again until the week after her return.

Apart from the limp she seemed as tough as ever, and quite disappointed to find that both the school and my house had survived without her attentions.

However, she cheered up when she studied the children's wash basins which she pronounced 'a death trap swarming with germs', and attacked them with Vim and plenty of elbow grease. She was positively genial when this task was over, and told me that the hospital had given her a diet sheet.

'The doctor there said I was to lose two stone. But if I stuck to his diet I'd be in my grave by Christmas. All greenery and acid fruit, and what they calls "roughage" and I calls 'animal feed'. All them oats and raw carrots and apples! Never heard the like. I told him flat: "My sister was warned against just such a diet when she had colitis. Funny we never hear about colitis these days – just this 'ere roughage."'

'And what did he say?'

'Oh, you know doctors! He just waved it aside, and said to keep off sugar, fat and starches. And I said: "And what does that leave, pray, for a hard-working woman?" He simply walked away. I mean, it's so *rude*. Some of these so-called educated men what's been to college and that, haven't got any more manners than Minnie Pringle's boy Basil. And that's saying something.'

I was foolish enough to enquire after Minnie, and Mrs Pringle's face grew sourer than ever.

'Her husband Ern's playing up,' she said, 'getting home late, and sometimes staying out all night. He's been seen in Caxley too.'

She made Caxley sound like Sodom and Gomorrah rolled into one.

'Mind you,' she continued, 'our Minnie's no home-maker, and you can't blame the chap in some ways. You should see Minnie's cooking! Burnt pies, addled custard, potatoes full of eyes, and the house filthy with it.'

'Still, that's no excuse for neglecting a wife, surely?'

'It's plain you don't know *nothing* about *men*!' she retorted, and limped away.

Later that morning some rhythmic thuds which disturbed the comparative peace of our Arithmetic lesson took me into the playground to investigate.

I found Mr Willet, mallet in hand, thumping at the gatepost.

'Bit out of true,' he told me, desisting for a moment. 'Why, can you hear me in there?'

'That's why I've come out,' I said. 'I wondered if Mr Roberts had got one of those confounded bangers going in the field.'

'What, a bird-scarer?'

'That's right.'

'Don't do a ha'porth of good, them things. Besides it's the wrong time of year for that lark.'

'I'd better get back,' I said, 'before there's a riot.'

'Heard about the Russells?'

These were fairly recent arrivals in Fairacre, and I had three of their children at school.

'No. What?'

'Been made redundant, if that's the right word. Stood off anyway. Last come, first go, evidently.'

'I didn't quite take in what he did do.'

'Something to do with machines in Caxley. Make the bits they do there, in some back alley running down to the river.'

'That's tough on him,' I said, 'and I shall miss the children. They're a nice little lot.'

Bob Willet looked at me with an unusually solemn expression.

'You knows what this means? The numbers get fewer every term. Looks to me as though the office will be closing us down. We'll both be out of a job, you'll see. Like poor Stan Russell.'

'I doubt it,' I told him. 'And anyway, this school has been threatened with closure ever since I've been here. We've always fought it off. We'll do it again if need be.'

I could hear the sound of voices coming from my classroom. No doubt warfare was about to break out.

'Must go,' I said, and hastened away to quell the riot.

Despite my brave words to Bob Willet, I felt a certain tremor about this latest piece of news, and wondered what the future would hold.

During the next few hours I heard the same tale from the vicar, Mr Lamb and Mrs Pringle. All three added their own gloomy prognostications about the possibility of Fairacre School closing if numbers fell further.

The evening was overcast, and now that the autumn was upon us the days were shorter. I could not rid myself of a feeling of foreboding as I sat, red pencil in hand, correcting essays and changing 'brids' to 'birds' and 'grils' to 'girls' with depressing regularity. 'Off of', 'meet up with' and 'never had none', also cropped up here and there, and after a while I put aside my work and made myself a cup of coffee. It was supposed to be a stimulant, and I could do with it.

I faced the various possibilities which my future might hold if Mr Willet's forecast proved correct. The obvious one would be a transfer to another school, or I could apply for a post elsewhere. On the other hand, I could take early retirement, but should I really like that?

I lived in a tied house which went with the job. Presumably the education authority would put it up for sale, as it would the school building itself.

Normally this would have been the most serious blow, for I had certainly not enough money to buy another, and had been foolish enough not to acquire one over the years, as some prudent teachers did when contemplating retirement.

But this worry was spared me, for a year or two earlier Dolly Clare had told me that she had left her Beech Green cottage to me in her will. This overwhelmingly generous deed had lifted the fears of the future from my undeserving shoulders. I should not be homeless whenever the blow fell, for Dolly had stipulated that I could stay with her whenever I liked, and however short the notice. To be so spoilt touched me deeply, and I knew that I should never be able to repay my old friend as she deserved.

Naturally, we had agreed that nothing would be said by either of us. Miss Clare's solicitor had the legal side of the transaction drawn up, but Dolly and I preserved strict silence about the matter.

Nevertheless, as the months passed, I grew conscious of the fact that the disposition of Dolly's main asset was known in the neighbourhood. How, or why, or by whom this knowledge was transmitted, neither of us could imagine. But we had both heard a remark here and there, noticed a knowing look, a nod of the head and so on, which made it clear that this piece of news was airborne like the seeds of thistledown, and lodged just as tenaciously wherever it happened to alight. Was *everything* known in a village, I wondered, sipping my coffee?

Echo answered: 'Of course it is!'

I was about to take my worries to bed when the telephone rang. It was Amy, offering me early plums.

'Rather sharp, from a funny old tree, but they make lovely jelly. Like some?'

I said that I should.

'You sound mopey,' said Amy. 'Are you ill or something?'

'No, no. Just tired. I've been marking essays.'

'Well, you should be used to that. I'll pop over tomorrow after school and bring the plums. What's more, I'll bring some crumpets for tea. It's getting quite nippy when the sun goes down, and crumpets are wonderfully cheering.'

'You are a stout friend,' I told her sincerely, 'and I'll look forward to seeing you and the crumpets tomorrow.'

'I'd better warn you, I have a new car. It's automatic, and I only hope I can manage it from Bent to Fairacre. I'll come the back way, so if I'm not with you by four-thirty you'll know where to direct the search party.'

And on this practical note I went to bed, much cheered.

By the morning, of course, I was feeling much more hopeful. As I had said to Bob Willet, we were quite accustomed to the threat of closure, and there was no reason to suppose that the departure of the three Russell children would make much difference. With any luck, I told myself in my present buoyant mood, we should have another family with children moving into Fairacre.

I might have guessed that Fate was waiting to have another crack at me. My assistant, who had been in the infants' classroom as Miss Briggs for some time, was now Mrs Richards, and still doing sterling work.

She now approached me with unusual diffidence and told me that the doctor had confirmed her hopes and that she was pregnant.

'Oh dear!' I said involuntarily, and then hastily added congratulations, and asked when the baby was due.

'Early March,' she said. 'If all goes well, I thought I could work until half-term in February, and then give up.'

'But you'll come back later?' I queried. She was a good teacher and we had always got on well together. In a two-teacher school this relationship is extra important, and I must admit I have had so many changes over the years that I dreaded yet another.

'I'm not sure,' she said, 'it all depends on how I feel when the time comes. I shall certainly take the full maternity leave, but of course I'll be in touch to let you know how things are going.'

'Fair enough,' I replied. 'But I hope you will return. I've enjoyed your company.'

'That goes for me too,' she said, 'and Wayne says will you be godmother?'

'My goodness,' I cried, quite overcome by this, 'I think it's a bit early to decide on that, but yes, if you still feel the same way next March I should count it an honour.'

'We shan't change our minds.'

'Well, I think you should choose the hymn this morning in celebration.'

'What about "Praise to the Holiest in the height"?' she replied with a smile.

'Very suitable,' I agreed, putting my fears behind me. Trust *Hymns Ancient and Modern* to come up with something fitting!

It was good to see Amy, as always. She arrived at ten past four, complete with plums and crumpets, so that I did not have to organise a search party as we had feared.

The car was discreetly opulent as befitted a tycoon's wife and I was greatly intrigued with the automatic controls.

'Jolly useful if you break your left leg,' I said, 'or your left arm for that matter.'

'It might well be your right, of course,' commented Amy, 'or both. Then what would you do?'

'I should sell it, and put the money aside for taxis,' I told her. 'Let's go and toast these crumpets.'

'Now tell me what was worrying you yesterday,' said Amy later, licking a buttery finger.

I told her about the Russell children and Mr Willet's gloomy forecast.

'Well, that's something that's been hanging over you for years,' she said. 'The snag is, you'd have to give up this house, I suppose.'

'I don't think I should actually be thrown out. I'd have plenty of time to look around. The office is pretty humane, and I've been here for long enough for them to know me.'

I always feel guilty about keeping my secret from Amy, but I stick to the sensible principle of letting no one – no matter how trustworthy – learn of something which one does not want disclosed. In all innocence it can be let out, and it is a burden which one should not lay on anyone's shoulders. The old adage: 'Least said, soonest mended' is one I live by, and as a villager it is doubly true. Of course, this is a puny adversary compared with the local grapevine but it is a useful principle to adopt.

'You should have bought something years ago,' said Amy, with a return of her usual bossy tone.

'I know,' I said meekly.

'Well, if you do get the push,' she continued, helping herself to another crumpet, 'there's always our spare bedroom. The curtains clash rather with the carpet, but I don't suppose you'd notice.'

As we washed up, she admired a large bowl of red and green tomatoes which Alice Willet had brought for me.

'For chutney?' she asked.

'Only the green ones. I shall freeze a few of the red ones, and have a feast for the next few days with the others. Would you like some?'

'Please. It's funny, I could never bear tomatoes as a child, or beetroot, or swedes. Now I dote on all three.'

'I can't face the last,' I said, 'nothing more than shredded soap. We get far too many swedes at school dinners during the winter, but thank heaven the children like them.'

'When you are out of work,' said Amy, hanging up the tea towel, 'and begging in the wintry streets of Caxley, you'll be glad of a nice plate of hot swedes handed out at the soup kitchen.'

'I'll just ask for the soup.'

'You'll have what you are given,' Amy told me severely, 'as our mothers used to say.'

'As long as our benefactors don't add that old bit about "thousands of poor children",' I answered, 'I'll accept anything gratefully, but I draw the line at swedes.'

It was about this time that Mrs Pringle's limp became so apparent that I was impelled to ask after her leg.

'Too much to do. that's my trouble,' she told me. 'Top and bottom of it is Minnie.'

'Hasn't Ern come back?'

'No. He's still in Caxley, and the worst of it is that Bert's hanging around her again – always was dead set on Minnie.'

'She must send him packing.'

'Fat chance of that. I can see the girl's lonely without Ern, but she's far too soft to give Bert the push. And what's more, she's everlasting coming up to my place, mooning about with all those kids. I've had more than enough, I can tell you. The minute I finds out where Ern is in Caxley I'm going to fetch him back.'

'Can't the police trace him?'

'No one wants to get mixed up with *the police*,' she said, with such disgust that one felt that she looked upon that noble force as being on a par with some virulent germ.

'Well, I should make sure Minnie doesn't worry you,' I said, 'after all, you haven't got your strength back yet from the operation.'

This seemed to mollify the lady, and she nodded her head in agreement.

'Well, we must see what comes to pass,' she said, attacking my Victorian ink stand with a dab of Brasso.

What came to pass was the appearance of Mrs Pringle, a few days later, with a scratch on one cheek, bruises on her face, and a bump on her head.

'Have you had a fall?' I asked, much alarmed. 'I think you should see a doctor.'

'No need for that. These wounds was come by in Righteous Battle,' she replied. 'And my enemy come off worse, I can tell you.'

'But who?'

She settled herself on the front desk and folded her arms across the flowered overall which is her working garb.

'It was like this. Minnie suddenly let out that Ern was staying in Caxley with – you'll never guess!'

She looked at me bright-eyed.

'His mother?' I hazarded.

She snorted with disgust.

'Ern's mother has been dead these ten years. No, I tell a lie. Must be nearer twelve, because she came to the chapel centenary, and very poorly she looked then, we all thought.'

'Then I've no idea,' I said firmly. I set about looking for a pen knife I needed in the desk drawer. This withdrawal of my interest spurred Mrs Pringle into action again.

'That Mrs Fowler! You know, as used to be at Tyler's Row before it was prettied up. I never could stand that woman, and she was proper insulting to me on more than one occasion.'

'Did Minnie get in touch with her somehow?'

'No. I said I'd get in touch!' Mrs Pringle's tone was triumphant. 'That Minnie wouldn't say boo to a goose. But the minute she told me Ern was there as a lodger – *so-called* – I thought I'll get that fellow back before the night's out. I've had enough of Minnie and her tribe under my feet all day. If Ern's back, he'll have to look after them, and he can see off that good-for-nothing Bert who's hanging round Minnie all the time, and confusing her.'

In my opinion, Minnie's state of confusion is permanent, but I forbore to comment.

'So,' said Mrs Pringle, sitting down heavily on the creaking desk, 'I caught the Caxley and went straight to her place. When she opened the door I said I wanted Ern and wasn't going until she handed him over.'

'Was he there then? I should have thought he would be at work.'

Mrs Pringle tut-tutted at this interruption, and I fell silent.

'She said she hadn't got him, had never wanted him, he never paid the rent, and he was at "The Barleycorn" round the corner. And then she said something *so rude* about me I wouldn't soil my lips by repeating. So I slapped her face.'

'That was very . . .' I paused, not knowing whether to say 'brave' or 'foolhardy', and Mrs Pringle rushed on.

'So she grabbed at me and that's where I got this nasty scratch on my face, the vixen. It was then I clawed out a good handful of her hair. She shrieked something terrible, but I told her she'd asked for it.'

Joseph Coggs put his head round the classroom door at this point, asking if he could ring the bell. We waved him away.

'I was just going down the path to the gate when that besom opened the top window and flung Ern's case out. It hit me on the top of my head. Might have killed me as I told her at the time. That's what brought up this wicked great lump on my head.'

'Did you find Ern?'

'I did indeed. He was at "The Barleycorn" all right, with a lot of his layabout cronies. I shoved the case at him and brought him home. Just caught the last Fairacre luckily.'

My mind boggled at such meekness on Ern's part, and I said so.

'I never had a mite of trouble with him,' Mrs Pringle said, standing up and stroking down her flowered overall. 'Ern's a great coward for all his bluster. To tell the truth, I reckon I went there at just the right time. He and Mrs Fowler was at loggerheads already, and he was scared to go back there, I reckon. That woman can be quite violent at times.'

I looked at Mrs Pringle's battle scars and agreed.

'So you think he'll settle down again with Minnie?'

'Who's to say?' She began to set off for the lobby. 'But I done my bit last night. It's up to them to make it up.'

A rare smile crossed her battered countenance.

'One thing, that Mrs Fowler won't be feeling too grand today. I smote her good and proper, like they did the wicked in the Bible.'

'Tell Joe he can come in and ring the bell,' I called after her.

And about time too, I thought, looking at the clock.

I had just returned to the school house that afternoon, and had decided to light the fire as a nasty little cold wind had blown up when I heard tapping at the back door.

There stood Minnie Pringle. For once, she was unencumbered with a pram and toddlers. She looked remarkably waif-like shivering in the wind.

'Come in,' I cried. 'Do you want Mrs Pringle? She doesn't come here on a Friday, you know.'

'Auntie don't know about me coming,' she replied.

'Sit down, while I put a match to this fire,' I said.

She obeyed, sitting primly on the edge of a Victorian buttoned chair which is liable to tip forward unless its occupier sits well back.

I pointed this out to Minnie but it seemed to have no meaning to her, and she remained dangerously perched.

'Well, what brings you here today, Minnie? And where are the children?'

'My mum at Springbourne has 'em Friday afternoons. She does the ironing from the Manor then. She irons lovely.'

'Lovelily,' I corrected automatically, ever the teacher. It did not sound right.

'Beautifully,' I amended hastily.

'That's right. Lovely,' agreed Minnie. I let it pass.

'Ern's back,' she said, after a pause.

'Good,' I said, wondering whether to commiserate or congratulate.

'Bert don't like it,' she added.

This, I felt, was hardly surprising, but made a noncommittal noise. I was tired, cold and dying for a cup of tea.

'I'm about to make tea,' I said, facing the fact that Minnie would be with me for some time yet, 'would you like a cup?'

'Lovely,' said Minnie. 'Shall I help?'

'No, no. You sit there and get warm.'

I looked at the lightweight suit she was wearing. It was a dazzling turquoise blue with grubby white trimmings. Her stick-like arms, mottled with the cold, protruded from the sleeves. It could have done with Minnie's mother's ironing expertise.

'You should have put on a coat,' I said, as I waited for the kettle to come to my rescue.

'It's on the baby's pram,' she replied. Whether it was there to keep the baby warm, or because Minnie had put it there and forgotten to retrieve it, I was never to know, for the kettle whistled and I attended to my duties as hostess.

Over our steaming cups and a ginger biscuit apiece, Minnie became more relaxed.

'I wondered if I could come and work for you Fridays,' she said.

My heart sank.

'Isn't there somewhere nearer to find work?' I said, playing for time. 'Surely you used to have a job at Springbourne Manor?'

'They don't want nobody at that house,' she said.

And I don't want nobody at this house, I thought. It all seemed pretty hard. Dash it all, I already suffered Mrs Pringle on a Wednesday. To have Friday afternoon commandeered as well was really rather much. In any case, what on earth could I let Minnie do which she could manage without causing irreparable damage? I had faced this problem before, with small success.

'You see,' said Minnie, placing her tea-cup in the hearth by the side, rather than on the saucer, 'I run up a bill at Springbourne Stores when Ern was away, and I needs the money.'

'Can't Ern pay it?'

'He says I done it and I got to pay it back.'

I looked at the pinched face, the tousled red hair, the cheap flimsy shoes. She might have been taken for an under-nourished child of twelve, rather than a wife and mother of three.

I began to feel my tough old heart softening a little. After all, she had had the initiative to walk from Springbourne and to apply for a job.

'It's like this, Minnie,' I told her, 'I can really only afford to have you for an hour on a Friday. Your Aunt Maud does all that's really needed on Wednesday, as I'm sure you know.'

'That'd suit me fine,' said Minnie, looking more cheerful.

'And I'm not making it a permanent arrangement,' I went on, gaining strength. 'If you like to come, say, until we break up for Christmas, then you are welcome, but I don't want too much help over the holidays.'

'What time?' said Minnie, beginning to stand up ready for departure. 'My cousin comes up to help in the garden at Mr Mawne's Friday afternoons. He'd give me a lift in his van. Has to be there at two o'clock.'

'That will suit me,' I said, 'then you can go at three.'

That way, I figured, I should not have to share the house with her. At the same time, I reminded myself, I should probably have to spend half an hour or so clearing up after Minnie's labours.

A gust of wind flung a spattering of dry leaves against the window as I showed her to the door.

'Lor!' said Minnie, flinching from the cold wind as we opened the back door.

'Hang on,' I said, 'you'd better have a cardigan.'

I scrabbled under the stairs in the cupboard which Mrs Pringle so greatly deplores, and emerged with a thick cardigan which was there with other garments waiting for the next local jumble sale.

'Thanks ever so,' cried Minnie, when safely enveloped, 'I'll bring it back Friday. See you then.'

She gave me her mad grin and teetered down the path in the dilapidated shoes.

'Tibby,' I said to the cat who was stretched in comfort before the fire, 'I am not only an ass, but what Mr Willet rightly calls "a soft touch".'

And what, I suddenly thought with alarm, should I say to Mrs Pringle?

Chapter Twelve

THE END OF THE YEAR

I need not have worried. Mrs Pringle knew all about Minnie's new job when our paths crossed on Monday morning, and she was far from pleased.

'I suppose you knows what you are doing,' was her opening gambit, 'but what, pray, are you going to find for Minnie to do on a Friday?'

This problem had been facing me over the weekend, and I trotted out a few ideas.

'She can wash the porch floors,' I said, 'those quarry tiles are pretty tough. And she could do the kitchen floor while she's about it. It would save you doing it.'

Mrs Pringle snorted. 'Minnie's not to be let loose on my kitchen floor, and anyway she'd ruin that squeegie-thing you got me. If Minnie does the kitchen floor, I goes, I tell you flat.'

'Very well, if that's how you feel,' I said, with what dignity I could muster, 'but she's certainly going to do the porches. And I'm sure she could manage the brass and copper. And even the silver,' I added, getting bolder.

'In that case, you'd have to put it out separate,' she said. 'Brasso, copper and brass one week. Silvo and the silver next, or you'll be in a fine old mess. Worse than usual, I mean,' she added vindictively.

'Well, it's only for a few weeks,' I said, 'just up until Christmas. She seemed to need the money, and I thought it was very resourceful of her to come and try her luck.'

'You'll rue it!' she said darkly, waddling off to the infants' room.

*

For the next few Fridays I tried to nip across from the school to the house to see that Minnie was safely started on her set jobs. Washing the floors of the front and back porch she managed very well, but I had to be sure that she only used harmless but efficient soap liquid. This was the only bottle I left out for her, and I forbade her to take anything from the cleaning cupboard.

I knew that she could not read, so hid such dangerous things as disinfectant, bleach and scouring agents in case she used – or even drank – them during her labours.

By dint of putting out the Brasso, copper and brass together on the kitchen table one week, and Silvo and my meagre collection of silver and plated articles the next, as advised by Mrs Pringle, things went fairly smoothly, but there were some aspects of Minnie's ministrations which I was unable to alter.

Long before I had met her, she had been taught to wash her dusters and to leave them to dry before returning home. This excellent training had stuck in Minnie's feather brain, and the dusters were always spotless when I returned from school.

Unfortunately, I was unable to get it into Minnie's thick skull that they should be hung on a little line outside the back door to dry. In Minnie's past, dusters were always put to dry indoors, and I found my own draped over the edge of the dining room table, the banisters, and even over the backs of upholstered chairs.

I always intended to point this out to Minnie, but often, by the next Friday, I had forgotten. It was useless to leave notes for her as she could not read, but I had not really taken in the fact that she could not tell the time, until I found her still in the house well after the hour when she should have departed.

'Well, I never sort of mastered the clock,' she said vaguely, implying that there were a great many other things which she *had* mastered in her time.

'But how do you manage?' I enquired, genuinely interested.

'I looks out for the Caxley,' she replied. 'It gets to the church about the hour.'

'But not *every* hour,' I pointed out.

'There's the kids coming out of school, too,' she explained.

'It still seems rather hit and miss,' I said, 'and there are lots of places where you can't see the bus, or the children for that matter. Has Springbourne Church got a striking clock? Can you hear it at home?'

'I never bothers to count,' replied Minnie. 'Sometimes I misses the first note or so.'

It began to seem more and more difficult to me.

'Actually,' said Minnie, 'I just asks somebody the time.'

I did not have to wait long before the comments on Minnie Pringle's return arrived.

Mr Willet was the first.

'You could've knocked me down with a feather when Alice told me Minnie was back. "Never!" I said to her. "Miss Read had enough last time. She's got too much savvy to have Minnie back again." But there you are! I see you've been taken advantage of.'

This last sentence annoyed me on two counts. Firstly, it was ungrammatical, ending with a preposition as it did. Secondly, it seemed to put me on a par with all those gullible girls who are the victims of predatory males.

'It's only until Christmas,' I told him rather coldly.

'She can do plenty of damage before then,' he commented, and continued with his coke-sweeping.

The vicar said that it was a great credit to me to employ Minnie and that he was sure the girl must be most grateful.

Mrs Partridge, more of a realist, begged me to keep any breakables out of Minnie's clutches.

'She *once* – and I stress *once*,' she told me, 'helped wash up after a Fur and Feather Whist Drive in the village hall, and we lost four plates, three cups and a sandwich dish which unfortunately belonged to Mrs Pringle. I had a great deal of trouble trying to replace it, and she did not seem to appreciate it when we did track one down.'

I said that I could well believe it.

Mr Lamb said Minnie was a very lucky girl. Mrs Willet said Bob could have been knocked down with a feather. Mrs Richards, now in a capacious maternity smock, confessed herself amazed, Amy, on the telephone, responded to my news with: 'What on earth are you thinking about?', and even gentle Miss Clare, when I visited her, advised me not to let my heart rule my head.

It was all pretty hard to bear, but I only had myself to blame, and comforted myself with the thought that Christmas would soon be here, and my bonds would be broken.

It began to grow very cold. Rough winds which had chased the dead leaves round and round the playground, and sent their most searching draughts down the skylight, now gave way to still weather of biting chill.

I shivered in my bedroom as I dressed each morning by the inadequate heat of an electric fire, and thought of Amy and many other lucky women, who had central heating in their homes.

I routed out my warmest clothes, regretting the thick cardigan which I had given to Minnie as the only one which had really matched my thickest skirt. This sort of thing is always happening.

And ten to one, I told myself, as I had never seen Minnie wearing my garment, it was on the baby's pram with her own coat. Unless, of course, she too had passed it on to a jumble sale.

It was good to get home after school and to settle in by a roaring fire, knowing that the frost was sparkling outside behind the drawn curtains.

I even changed my late night cup of coffee for one of milky cocoa, remembering Dolly Clare's account of this warming drink so much appreciated by long-ago Fairacre children.

Tibby enjoyed this too, and lapped at a saucerful in the hearth while I sipped mine with my feet up on the sofa.

'You wants to take your spade inside tonight,' Bob Willet called out to me one afternoon. 'You see! There'll be snow afore mornin'.'

I have a great respect for Mr Willet's weather lore, and although I did not take the garden spade indoors, I certainly found the coal shovel and put it ready with my wellington boots.

He was right, of course. It was a white world in the morning. The trees were bowed with their burden, the garden beds hidden beneath their white blanket, and the distant downs shrouded as far as the eye could see.

Snow was still falling. It lay thick upon the window sills, and crusted the ledges of each windowpane. I dressed hurriedly, congratulating myself on looking out that shovel which I should need to get out of the back door.

Nothing moved in the garden. No birds hovered round the bird table. No doubt they were sheltering from the snow flakes in the hedgerows and buildings.

From the kitchen window, as I prepared porridge for breakfast as the best possible warmer on such a day, I could see Tibby's footmarks, a ribbon of rosettes in the snow, leading to the cat flap. The cat's fur was still flecked with melting flakes when we greeted each other.

I cleared the back and front steps just enough to let me open the doors, but I could see it was going to be love's labour lost with the snow still falling. With wellingtons on, my thickest coat buttoned up, and an umbrella atop, I fought my way over the virgin wastes to the school.

Footsteps led from the road into the building, and Mrs Pringle was already there stoking the stoves.

'No children yet,' I observed.

'Nor likely to be,' she replied, 'there's a fair old drift at the end of the lane. Mr Roberts give me a lift up in his Land Rover.'

Here was a dilemma. How was I to get her back after her labours? I knew that I should never be able to dig the snow away from my garage doors, let alone negotiate the drift in the lane with my small car.

As if she could read my thoughts, she continued: 'Mr Roberts and his shepherd's going by with the Land Rover in half an hour, when Mr Roberts has had his breakfast. Says I can squeeze in the cab with them two.'

A squeeze, I thought, it certainly would be.

'Why not go over to the school house,' I said, 'when you have done here. The fire's going, and as soon as this snow lets up, I'll get you home somehow.'

'No, no. I'll go with Mr Roberts. I've got to get back. I've got Fred in bed with his chest.'

He would hardly be in bed without it, I commented mentally, but kept this flippancy to myself.

She bustled about humming some dirge while I found the register and wondered if I should have any attendances to mark in it.

At that moment the telephone rang and I snatched it from the cupboard top to hear Mrs Richards' voice.

'Absolutely impossible to make it,' she said, 'even in Wayne's van. The road between Beech Green and Fairacre's waist deep.'

I told her not to worry, and said that I did not think we should have many pupils, and that I should be ringing the office after nine to say that I intended to close the school.

'And what about my stoves?' demanded Mrs Pringle, who should not have been eavesdropping on the conversation. 'Another full week we've got before end of term. Who's to keep 'em going? Or do we let 'em out?'

'Look,' I said, 'be reasonable. How do I know? All I propose to do is to play it by ear. I shall stay here until mid-morning in case some children do get through, and they can have a bite to eat in my house, as obviously the dinner van will never make it. I shall ring the office any minute now, as *you heard*,' I added pointedly, 'and I'll tell you before you go home.'

At that moment there was a flurry at the door and Ernest, who lives nearest to the school, appeared caked in snow all down his coat, but with a pink shining face and bright eyes.

'Get out!' shouted Mrs Pringle.

'Shake your coat outside,' I said more mildly, 'and leave your wellingtons in the lobby. Then come and get warm.'

Sniffing cheerfully, he obeyed.

'I shoved along under the hedge,' he said, when he was holding his hands over the stove. 'It ain't too bad there, in the shelter, see?'

'Anyone else in sight?'

'Not a sausage,' said my lone pupil.

The telephone rang again. It was a message from the office to say that closure of the schools in our downland area was inevitable. We chatted about the weather conditions: a bus had overturned in Caxley High Street making everyday confusion even more confounded, no one could get over the downs to Oxford in the north or Winchester in the south, the farmers were fearing for their sheep, and the best thing to do was to sit by the fire.

I relayed this invigorating news to Mrs Pringle who began to swathe herself in layers of clothing ready for her homeward ride. There was a sound of voices shouting and a well-revved engine chugging, and Mrs Pringle set off for the door.

'Expect me when you see me,' she boomed, 'and look after yourself.'

It was very quiet when she had gone. Ernest looked apprehensive. 'D'you reckon any of the others will get here?'

'I doubt it, Ernest. Is your mother at home?'

'Not till ten. She goes down the Post Office to help with old Mrs Lamb, nine till ten. Blanket bath and that.'

I remembered that Ernest's mother had once been a district nurse.

'Well, you go and find something to read from the cupboard,' I said, 'and I'll see you home just after ten.'

I had a brainwave and rang the Post Office.

'Yes,' said Mr Lamb, 'Ern's mum made it across the back field. Jolly stout effort. We'll get her home, never fear, by ten.'

'Any sign of children coming to school?'

'Not one,' he told me.

'Spread the news that school's closed till further notice,' I said.

We exchanged pleasurably dramatic news. Up to the eaves down Pig Lane where the wind caught it. Two abandoned cars outside 'The Beetle and Wedge'. Bob Willet had sent a message to say he'd be up school as soon as he could make it. Some old tramp had been found sleeping in the church porch, and the vicar had taken him home; Mrs Vicar wasn't best pleased; fleas and that. No sign of Mr Roberts' sheep in Long Meadow, probably under the snow.

He rang off at last, leaving me with hazy memories of *Lorna Doone* and gurt Jan Ridd rescuing his flock.

'Makes a bit of fun, don't it?' said Ernest happily.

We were snowbound for the rest of that week, and the thaw came slowly, leaving piles of snow at the sides of the lanes and under the field hedges. The roads were filthy, churned up during daylight by farm transport and the occasional lorry or Land Rover. At night everything froze solid again. It was a bitter spell.

School re-opened on the last Monday morning of term, but a number of children still stayed away, some because travelling was impossible, others the victims of coughs and colds. Our usual Christmas party, for parents and friends, was postponed to sometime in the New Year.

Bob Willet, muffled to the eyebrows, was busy clearing the playground as I walked across. A few children were making their way to the school door, one kicking a snowball before him.

'Now then!' shouted Mr Willet sternly. 'Lay off that lark!'

I smiled my approval, wondering the while about the idiocy of some of our daily utterances. Why 'Now then'? And 'there, there' was pretty silly too, when analysed.

I pushed open the door into the lobby. Mrs Pringle, bucket in one hand and floor cloth in the other, stood there, looking grim.

Before I could make any greeting, she jerked her head towards the footprints I had made on the floor.

'I just done that,' she said flatly, and all at once I was transported back to my first encounter with Mrs Pringle one wet July afternoon all those years ago – when she greeted me in the self-same place and with the self-same words: 'I just done that.'

That last skirmish with Mrs Pringle happened an hour ago, and I shall not dwell on it. She has not changed over the years, and is not likely to now.

Outside the snow still falls. The playground, which Bob Willet cleared so recently, is white again, and the sky looks menacing. But here, in the school house, all is snug and quiet. The fire crackles,

Tibby purrs, and soon I shall make some tea. The Christmas holidays lie ahead, and what a comforting thought that is!

Meanwhile, I must stir myself to wrap up a box of chocolates, my annual present to Mrs Pringle.

After all, this is the season of peace and goodwill.